Lindsey Barron Series
Volume 7
Cross and Double-cross

Vic Broquard

Published by:
Broquard eBooks
http://Broquard-eBooks.com
author@Broquard-eBooks.com
103 Timberlane
East Peoria, IL 61611

For Morgan and L. Ron Hubbard

Table of Contents

Chapter 1—Resurrection

Thaddeus Black watched the news on his giant flat screen as it was unfolding. KMAG's own Hugo Whitefield could scarcely keep up with the rapidly unfolding drama, but he made sure that his ultra-white teeth shone through his smiling lips as he reported the capture of the evil wizard Dominus Malefic, all the while working hard to impress his many viewers, especially those of the fairer sex. The old wizard swore a curse and suddenly paid close attention. Thaddeus was sixty-five. Grey hairs predominated in his rapidly thinning hair, which had ages ago been black. Arthritis joints creaked as he rose to brew a pot of Columbian coffee.

Just now, Thaddeus needed a strong cup of coffee. He always did when he had a serious problem to solve. This one, he knew, would be enormous. Dominus had been captured again. "So close, darn it, so darned close," he grumbled. He'd spent his entire life trying to get wizards elevated into positions of power from which to run the world. After all, wizards were the power elite, not the darn norms, who couldn't do anything but pollute and destroy Mother Earth. Already global warming was having an impact. Yet the fools in Washington continued to deny any such thing. Of course, it didn't help that scientists couldn't agree on the specifics of the climate changes.

Thaddeus was an ardent Dominus supporter, having voted for him in the past presidential election. He'd cursed when Dominus lost the election to President Snow, but then he'd gotten behind the National Health Care Program, which had been well on its way to placing wizards in control of the entire United States, where they rightfully belonged according to his thinking. Just when that program was beginning to bear fruit, Dominus was stupid enough to get himself captured once again. Thaddeus was more than a little upset with this terrible situation.

Sipping his brew helped take his attention off his aching joints. Thaddeus began to think about just how he could possibly spring Dominus out of jail. The last time, his mentor had spent fourteen years cooped up in a jail cell. Well, if he had any say in it, Dominus wouldn't spend another decade locked up. If he could just spring him quickly, perhaps the Health Care Program could be continued to its logical conclusion, and wizards would become the power brokers of the world. Thaddeus had spent his whole life trying to bring this about, but had failed miserably.

His home was a modest one in the northern suburbs of St. Louis, Missouri, far from the possible prisons in which they would be caging his mentor. Continuing to monitor the news, Thaddeus hoped that someone would identify the prison in which Dominus was being held—alas, that information was not forthcoming. Instead, he learned that Dominus was going to be brought to the Denver courthouse for his first court appearance. Thaddeus made careful preparations and teleported to Denver.

Unobtrusively, he took up a position near the courthouse steps. He was invisible, of course, and fully prepared to stun the Security guards as they brought him up the steps. After that, with a simple Teleport he would be able to free Dominus from these bastard wizards. He waited patiently. As the group apparated before his eyes, Thaddeus got the shock of his life. Someone put a large caliber bullet through the head of Dominus! He had a ringside view of the small, round hole right between his mentor's eyes and the massive destruction of his brain at its exit point behind his head.

Thaddeus stood there completely shocked! His eyes took in the massive confusion that resulted. Finally realizing his own danger, he teleported back to his home in St. Louis. After angrily punching a hole in his front room wall, he calmed down, brewed another pot of coffee, and sat down to think about what to do next. Somehow, someway, he had to rescue Dominus. Then it came to him. He could retrieve some of his DNA and pay to have a Clone spell cast. While the new Dominus would not be precisely the same man, he would retain his memories and abilities and could thus return to his Golden Path.

The next morning, equipped with vials and collecting bags, he teleported back to Denver only to find that someone had thoroughly cleaned up the blood and brain matter that had covered the granite steps! Thaddeus cursed a blue streak before teleporting home, thwarted once again.

Back home, he lowered his aching body into his easy chair. Now he did have to think hard. As he pondered this new turn of events, he realized that he now needed to know how they would be disposing of his body. If they were smart, they would cremate it, leaving nothing behind, certainly no useable DNA. While Thaddeus had no idea how the Clone spell was cast, he had done some research before and knew that the caster would need about an ounce of uncontaminated DNA material. The texts were filled with Clone failures when foreign substances contaminated the DNA material. He remembered reading about one failure in which the newly cloned body was half man, half lion. It didn't survive, naturally.

Weeks went by before Thaddeus finally learned what they had done with the body of Dominus. He shrieked with laughter when he heard that they'd buried him at Denver Memorial Gardens. "The idiots didn't burn him!" He laughed until his joints ached too badly to continue laughing. Once more, he made his preparations. First stop: the funeral parlor that handled the body of Dominus.

Late at night, he broke into the place using a simple Unlock spell. An hour later, he'd found the records and cursed once again. He smashed the filing cabinet, putting a large dent in it, defusing some of his anger. They'd embalmed him and thus contaminated his DNA. As far as he knew, cloning was not possible any longer. Only one avenue remained for Thaddeus to resurrect his beloved mentor, the one man who had very nearly succeeded in getting wizards promoted to world leaders.

It took him another week to find the actual gravesite where they'd buried Dominus Malefic. Late that night, he stood over the grave of Dominus, pausing to pay his respects. Then, he cast his Dig spell and began working. A half hour later, he reached the pauper's coffin. Its weight was too much for his teleport spell, so he had no choice but to open the coffin. There lay his idol with the large caliber bullet hole between his eyes. Carefully, he cast a levitate spell, lifting the corpse out of the coffin, placing it on a nearby blanket. Then, he closed the coffin and recast his Dig spell, covering the grave once more. That done, he cast numerous additional spells, trying hard to restore the plot so that no one would have any idea that the body had been removed. Satisfied, he then held onto the blanket and teleported back to his home in St. Louis.

After pulling all the blinds, he lit numerous candles in his living room and prepared himself for this most critical spell casting. Unable to Clone Dominus, Thaddeus had to settle for the only remaining possibility to save Dominus from death. That wasn't entirely true. He could turn the corpse into many forms of undead creatures, such as a zombie or a ghoul, but that would be pointless. Such would merely be a mindless, undead monster.

Leaving nothing to chance, Thaddeus restudied his spell, making sure that he had both the wand motions and the wording down precisely. He had this one and only one chance to resurrect his mentor, and he dare not blow it. He took one last look at his mentor, dressed in a second-rate business suit, and sighed, such a total disrespect for the greatest wizard that had ever lived. Then without further words and with great care, Thaddius Black cast his spell, the reversal of Cause Death—Cause Life. After the long incantation with appropriate wand motions, sort of sweeping upward motions, his wand activated. Magical energies flashed rather brightly, leaving a sort of fog over the corpse of Dominus. Thaddeus waited patiently, though brushing the fog away with his hand, using a simple Grade 0 useful spell.

It worked. The dead corpse of Dominus Malefic was gone. In its place lay the body of a young woman, dressed in the black suit and white shirt that the corpse had been wearing. She was shorter and thinner than the corpse had been. The clothes were quite ill fitting. She breathed and slowly gained consciousness.

"Welcome back, my Dominus, to the land of the living!" Thaddeus spoke softly to the prone woman. "I am your faithful believer and follower, Wizard Thaddeus Black. You are safe in my home here in St. Louis. I've had to use the Cause Life necromancy spell to bring you back because what remained of your DNA was too contaminated to risk a Clone spell."

"Thank you. Your action will not go unrewarded," she replied softly in a mellow alto voice, while her hands felt her forehead. "My head is throbbing!" Suddenly, Dominus realized that the reincarnated body was female, and she shrieked quite loudly. "Oh my god! A woman's body! How could you?" she fumed. Had she a wand, she would have disintegrated Thaddeus instantly, but she didn't have one. Besides, her head throbbed fiercely.

"Easy does it, my Dominus. You were shot in the head, killed instantly. I saw it happen. I was there. Someone shot you just as I was about to rescue you. It was broadcast live on KMAG. At least, you are alive and so must be your Golden Path. I have been quietly backing your path for years. We wizards simply must be the world leaders, not those pathetic norms."

Dominus continued to massage her head, trying frantically to come to grips with what was happening to her. "Cause Life?" she whispered.

"Yes, that was the only avenue remaining for me to bring you back from the dead. I have no control over what the reincarnated body form will be with that spell, only that you will return and remember everything that you knew, as well as your spell casting abilities," Thaddeus explained.

"But, but I'm a pathetic woman now, Thaddeus!" she fumed.

"A powerful witch and with your former spell casting abilities and vast knowledge," Thaddeus explained softly.

She grimaced. "Help me up. I'm very weak," she asked, holding up a hand. Gently, Thaddeus lifted her to her feet, catching her as she wobbled on very unsteady legs, still holding her throbbing head. "Aspirin?"

"Here, sit in my chair. I'll fetch some and then rustle up some food," he replied, helping her to his sofa. He moved as quickly as his aching joints permitted, returning with the bottle and a glass of water. She took them from him, and he headed off to his kitchen to fix a very late night snack. She popped three Aspirins and laid down, her head throbbing with an intense pain right between her eyes and across the back of her head.

Slowly, the Aspirin took effect. Darn it! I got shot! She began to remember. They had me in chains, and we were going up the steps to the courthouse, and then came this sudden and unexpected excruciating pain followed by a complete blackness. Well, that is until now, she corrected herself. The blackness of memory gave way to looking up at the greying hair and wrinkled face of this old wizard. Cause Life, Cause Death. "Darn," she muttered and then again, as she heard her new alto voice speaking. "At least, I'm still alive," she whispered.

"Clone. Darn it! There's nothing left from my old body to clone!" She calmed down, realizing that if Thaddeus was right and they had embalmed the body, the DNA would have been compromised. Her face cringed at the thought of what might have resulted had he tried that spell. But a young female body? God, what could be worse, she thought? Heck, look at this suit! The sleeves were several inches too long and far too big around. Her pants were equally dismal, three inches too long, to say nothing of the loose fitting shoes. She cursed again. After another long pause, she realized that at least the Idiot Mind spell was now off her. That was something.

Rolling the sleeves and cuffs up and slipping off the over-sized shoes, she answered Thaddeus' call for a 3 a.m. meal. "Thanks, Thaddeus, for everything. Couldn't be helped. I'm alive again. That's the first step." Famished, she dove into the meal he'd whipped up. By the time she finished, she felt an overwhelming tiredness sweep over her. She wasn't aware that he carried her to his couch and covered her up before turning in himself.

Both roused late the next morning. Over breakfast, Thaddeus chatted, explaining just how much he had been behind the fundamental concept that Dominus had espoused. "Indeed, wizards are meant to be the rulers of the world, Dominus. Anyone with an ounce of brains can see that. That wizard Erin Saks very clearly demonstrated that fact, even though he was very misguided in his actions. Norms and their guns simply cannot stand up to even a handful of wizards. Why should we, the most powerful humans, be relegated to equal status as norms? Makes no sense whatsoever. Too bad that the wizarding community was so divided on this issue. Guess there are ignorant, stupid wizards, just as there are ignorant norms. Still, I can't believe that there were so many wizards who just could not see the tremendous benefits of your Golden Path."

Dominus replied, "Well, that plan is shot to heck!"

"Aye. Unfortunately, it is," Thaddeus replied with a big sigh.

"I best catch up on what's happened," Dominus suggested. For the next few days, she watched the news and used Thaddeus' computer to surf the Net in search of older vid-casts. By Friday, the actual state of affairs became quite clear to Dominus. The States Justice personnel had raided and confiscated every asset that Simon Mac Fluide had amassed. Dominus was broke, had no magical items, and no wand. She had no homes or businesses. Everything that he'd spent a lifetime amassing was gone. Worse, it was being divided up among those pathetic people whom he harmed one way or another. Pity.

True, many of his trusted Death Stalkers were in prisons. They could be rescued, but what was the point? They'd failed him, allowing him to be captured and then killed. Heck, no one even knew who had shot him—a professional hit man was the speculation. Worse, the Death Stalkers wouldn't take orders from a woman, even if it was still him! "Darn it!" he cursed again. "This darn female body has got to go!"

Dominus could see no other way than to use his Restricted Wish once more. "Thaddeus, let me borrow your wand." The old man handed it over, rather reluctantly. "Stand back," she growled. She focused and cast her Restricted Wish spell, fully intending to wish her female body into that of a male, a young virile and handsome male at that. As the spell detonated, a giant flash of magical energies blinded old Thaddeus for a moment. Unfortunately for Dominus, his concentration was slightly off. As he was casting the spell, his mind flashed briefly onto the many women that he'd created for his amusement, his toys.

After blinking several times to get his vision back, Thaddeus stared at Dominus, who shrieked once more! She had a twenty-one year old female body this time, but she looked precisely like one of her toys! Her upper arms thinned down to the one inch in diameter cones ending at her elbows. A very restrictive corset crushed her waist down to fourteen inches, while her breasts had enlarged to the size of her head. Worse, she wore the same extremely tall stilettos. Gasping for breath, she lost her balance, swinging her stubs around madly before falling to the floor, breaking Thaddeus' wand, which had fallen to the floor when her hands had vanished!

"Get me." She stopped to gasp for air. "out of this!" She screamed, this time in a soprano voice.

"Oh dear god! Dominus, what have you done to yourself? My wand!" Thaddeus exclaimed, totally shocked at what he was seeing. He knelt down and tried to undo the corset. His arthritis-stricken hands could just barely undo the lacing. With a good deal of effort, he managed to get the corset off her and then the six inch heels. He helped the naked woman back onto the sofa. Gone was the burial suit that she'd been wearing. He limped off to find a sheet to cover her body.

Now what do I do? Dominus thought while the old man was gone. She looked down at the cracked wand and cursed a blue streak. She was as helpless as her toys had been! Worse, she couldn't cast any spells to remedy the mess! Neither could Thaddeus for that matter. Swelling emotions that he'd never felt before swept over her body, confusing her even more. Helplessness came to the forefront.

Thaddeus returned with a bed sheet and covered her. Dominus could hear his joints creaking. Lines of pain streaked his face. Arthritis had certainly taken its toll on this man, she thought. "There, sir. At least you are covered. I have to get me another wand and get someone to help us. You stay put while I'm gone." She nodded, watching him pick up his walking cane and hobble to the door. Why couldn't my rescuer have been healthier, she wondered.

Alone in the strange house and completely helpless,

Dominus began to cry. Her body was flooded with strange emotions that she'd never felt before, and she simply couldn't control them, not even remotely. Everything was so foreign to him. Soon, it became even worse. She had to use the bathroom. At least, Dominus was able to do this much for herself, though covering herself back up with the sheet was nearly impossible afterwards. At least, those overwhelming emotions were gone now, and she sat there on the sofa pondering how she could possibly get out of this mess.

Several hours later, Thaddeus returned. Obviously, the physical exertion had taken its toll on him. He always used Teleport spells to get around, had done so since the onset of his severe arthritis some years back. He did have a new wand, and he brought an older woman with him. She was also in her late sixties, her grey hair done up in a bun. She had a stern countenance. Dominus immediately had the notion that she was an old maid, never married. Thaddeus spoke up, "I've brought my sister to help us. Mirabel, this is Dominus Malefic. Dominus, this is my sister, Mirabel Black. I believe that his Restricted Wish somehow failed. What are we going to do now?"

She had a stern voice. "Dominus? Is this really you?" she asked pointedly.

"Of course. Who else would it be?" he replied in his soprano voice, grimacing as he heard it again.

"Oh dear me, Thaddeus. This is quite a mess you've made. We can't use a Clone spell. We'd end up with another just like her. Dear me, dear me," she sighed, shaking her head nervously.

Dominus spoke again. "Look. There's only one darn thing that you can do for me. Cast Cause Death and kill this body. Then, immediately cast the reverse spell. With luck, I'll end up with a male body, like I'm supposed to have."

"What if something goes wrong?" Mirable asked worriedly. "You're—you're Dominus."

"Sis, we have to do something. He can't live like this," Thaddeus pointed out.

"Well, I suppose you are right, but still we are playing with his life, Thaddeus. That's not to be taken lightly. What if he doesn't come back? What if the Cause Life spell fizzles?" she countered.

"Look. Don't stand there arguing," Dominus growled. "Do something. I can't live like this! I'll take the gamble. Do it. Do it now."

"But Dominus, we could purchase potions to regrow your arms. That would be drastically safer," Mirabel countered.

"I haven't got time to lie around for that. Just do it, please," Dominus replied. He didn't add, because I can't live in a woman's body.

"Dear, you have to do it. I'm afraid my joints are aching so badly that I can't even make the wand motions," Thaddeus sighed.

"Well, all right then," she countered, "but I'm not going to be responsible for what happens. Is that clear?" Her voice sounded rather huffy. She took her position before the young woman and focused. She could not afford any mistake, however slight. Slowly, she chanted and then made the proper wand motions. "Cause Death!" she barked the final action words. Magic flashed, and Dominus died once more.

"So far so good, Mirabel," Thaddeus praised her.

Once more, she focused and performed her chant, barking with conviction, "Cause Life!" Magic flashed. When their eyes recovered from the energy flash, a new living body replaced the corpse. Both stared at the new Dominus.

"See, I told you we should have left well enough alone!" Mirabel declared, looking at the seventy year old woman sitting on the sofa. Dominus look at her new hands, highly wrinkled with age. Her hair draped down her front, nearly white in color. He was spared a mirror or he might have killed them both on the spot.

"Again!" Dominus spat, her voice cracking.

Mirabel swallowed hard. "Er, right. This will never do." She focused and cast Cause Death, killing Dominus once more, though another few years would also have seen her natural death. Then, she repeated the reversal cast, clearly barking the command words, "Cause Life!" Magic flashed, and the corpse changed once more, returning to a living, breathing body.

"Crap!" Dominus spat out in a young girl's voice. Her body now was that of a twelve year old girl!

Exhausted, Mirabel collapsed into Thaddeus' sofa. "Well," she said with a sigh, "I'm drained for now."

Thaddeus volunteered, "Dominus, this might be for the best. Think about it. Your body is perhaps twelve years old now. That means you can go to some magic school and have another opportunity to expand your power spells and become even more powerful than you were." He couldn't think of any other positive thing to say just now.

Dominus ached now. His head throbbed once more, and his body felt like someone was sticking pins in it all over. "Okay, enough for today. Let me think a spell. You have a point, Thaddeus. If I spend six years in a magic school, I could well learn more Grade 8 and Grade 9 spells. This time, I could use my Restricted Wish to be able to learn any of the power Grade 9 spells. Foolishly, I didn't the last time. Besides, I will have plenty of time to figure out how that blasted Barron kid and that Cross kid got me."

Thaddeus hastily added to Dominus' notions. "Yes, plus once you have the Wish spell down, you can use it to change your body back into a male once more and safely too."

"I agree. This is probably the best route to take now. I don't think I can handle getting killed again," Dominus replied. "I'm going to need a name and funds."

"And clothes too and a place to stay," Mirabel added. "We aren't exactly rich, but we can afford to get you into the St. Louis School of Magic. We couldn't possibly afford Bradbury's and with that Barron girl now running it, you would be in deep trouble there."

"Okay. Get me some clothes," he replied.

Mirabel rose and headed off to visit some stores. Meanwhile, Thaddeus suggested, "We could claim that you are our niece from out east. Last name ought to be Black to keep confusion and questions at a minimum. We can claim your school records were destroyed in the recent fighting."

Dominus chuckled. "All right then. I'll be Monica Nicole Black, meaning counsel and victor of the wizards. But I'm going to need a wand soon. I have work to do before getting into magic school again. God, I'll be with all those stupid little girls!"

"Er, true. Tomorrow, Monica, we'll take you to Nerissa's Wands and More. She's got the best selection of wands in the St. Louis area," Thaddeus promised. "You'll have to be rather careful not to show off too much at school. Remember to. . ."

"Yeh, I already thought of that. No problem. I want to spend hours in the library researching spells like mad. After six years of study, I had darn well better know many more spells. This time, I will not fail. That, Wizard Black, I promise you!" He didn't say that he didn't know how he could endure this wretched girl body for six long years. Perhaps, he thought, I might be able to pick up the Full Wish spell on my own my first year there.

Mirabel returned with jeans and a blouse, among other things, and at last Monica was properly dressed. On Monday, Uncle Thaddeus, as she now called him, took her to Nerissa's Wands. Monica asked to see a wand similar to the one that he had always used. However, Nerissa pointed out that it wasn't the right wand for her. "Please, try this one, Monica," she suggested. Growling inwardly, Monica tried the alternative wand and found that it was a perfect match for her. "You see, the witch must be matched with just the right wand," Nerissa pointed out. "It is an art, you see, to be able to match the wand with the wizard or witch." Monica decided that she should really look into that branch of magic. Dominus had never bothered to research it at all. She decided to make a list of "research projects" to keep her mind occupied while at magic school. She put this one on the list.

Next, Aunt Mirabel took her shopping for clothes. Monica cursed when she discovered that she would need to have several dresses for school. "Oh god! Now I'm going to have to wear dresses! How humiliating!"

"It's just for six years, Monica. After all, if you don't, everyone will be staring at you and laughing behind your back," Aunt Mirabel pointed out. While Monica detested the whole idea, she had no choice but to pick out some dresses for school.

After that, the three worked out their story. Monica's

parents were killed many years ago, and she had been staying with her aunt and uncle here in St. Louis. Both had been slowly teaching her some beginning spells. That would permit her to be able to get away with some spells while at school. Their stories straight, the three paid a visit to the St. Louis School of Magic.

Fifty year old Governor Chelsey Brownstone met with them in her plush office. She wore a professional looking black skirt, white blouse, black nylons, and patent leather pumps. Her red hair was fluffed and short, making her head look rather large. "Welcome Thaddeus, Mirabel. It's good to see former students again." Of course, she'd never seen the two before, but had looked up their school records ahead of the appointment. "Please, have a seat. And this must be your charming niece, Monica is it?" she asked politely, but firmly. She wore a good deal of makeup, hiding her aging features somewhat.

"Monica Nicole Black, Governor Brownstone," she replied formally.

They chatted a bit before Governor Chelsey handed Monica a form to fill out. "Just answer truthfully each question. If you can't figure one out, go with your intuition, please." While Monica began answering the hundred questions, the governor chatted pleasantly with the two adults, going over the yearly cost of Monica's education and such matters.

When Monica finished, the results were automatically tabulated. "Ah, another Red Hall student, I see," Governor Chelsey looked up from the results in her hand.

"But I wanted to be in Black Hall, just like my aunt and uncle," Monica protested. *Red Hall! Good god, no way! They are complete losers!*

"Yes, well, I presumed *that* when you walked in, Monica Nicole, but your answers indicate that you would be best served in Red Hall, not Black Hall. While you do display many Black Hall traits, Red Hall is dominating over those. I do *have* an opening in Red Hall for one more First Year student. What say you try it for this first year? Then, if it doesn't work out for you, we can transfer you to Black Hall next year. What say you to that, Monica Nicole?" She looked quite sternly at the young girl.

Monica knew not to press her too hard. If she used any kind of mental scrying, the game would be up before it even began. "Yes, Governor Brownstone, that is fine with me. Anything to get a real magic education." She added the last bit because it seemed what the governor wished to hear. She had not lost her gut feelings about what others *wished* to hear. As Dominus, she'd had plenty of experience doing just that. Manipulating people had been his specialty.

"Well done, Monica Nicole. Let me be the first to welcome you to the St. Louis School of Magic. Red Hall it is. School starts on September 1, but you will be picked up a week earlier for student orientation week. That way, you can become familiar with our campus before the big rush starts." She had the adults sign several forms, and they chatted about what she needed to bring with her. While her "missing" school records were somewhat of a problem, due to the massive destruction of the recent near Civil War, that detail was "swept under the rug." Achievement tests would be administered to see how Monica was doing, education-wise.

Once that cycle was finished, Uncle Thaddeus teleported them back home. Monica Nicole now had about four more weeks before school began. She needed money and magic items. *I absolutely have to have some kind of anti-scrying device. Otherwise, any of the professors will know far more about me than they need to. And that costs money.*

On Tuesday night, Monica Nicole teleported to LA's First Federal Savings and Loan. There, she used a dozen Disintegrate spells to get into the building and their vault, taking a substantial amount of cash, shrinking it into a small bag. The next day, with her uncle's help, she opened her own checking account, claiming she was depositing her parent's life insurance. From there, they visited several magic stores, purchasing a Pin of Anti-Scrying and a Ring of Spell Storing. She put Teleport, Magic Door, and Major Invulnerability into it. These would allow her to be able easily to escape any adverse situation that might arise while on the school grounds. Even with these major purchases, she still had over a hundred thousand dollars left. Monica resolved to invest that small nest egg wisely, adding that to her list of research projects.

In the remaining days before school began, Monica Nicole went through every bit of news reporting done during the last four months, determined to learn all that she could about what had happened and what changes were now occurring, as they were certainly big changes. The first of many subtle changes in her began now. There is power in knowledge and information about what is going on in the country, she concluded, an idea foreign to her before now. In addition, she took careful note of the Rodents who had captured her and the Death Stalkers, her methodical mind filing the data for the future. Part of her desperately wanted revenge, to eliminate these cursed Rodents, but she knew now was not the time for such considerations. Again, delaying was a foreign idea to her.

"Hello First Years. I'm Ginny Halls, your Red Hall Floor Monitor. Whenever you need anything, come to me." The yellow school bus had picked Monica Nicole up from her "uncle's" house a half hour before. Now she stood beside a small group of other twelve year olds, listening to Ginny, who was introducing them to their new school.

"First thing, we need to get your bags to your rooms. Let's see," the Fourth Year Red Hall girl said looking at her clipboard. She had curly, short blonde hair but her bright red lips stood in stark contrast to her rather pale complection. "When I call your name, step forward with your bags, and I'll Move them to your new rooms. This year, five will be rooming together. It's simplest if I do all five at one time. Monica Nicole Black, Misty Worth, Enya Homes, Ericka Van Nie, Crystal Holliday—you are all in Room 2." She promptly cast her Move Object spells, and their single backpacks vanished, appearing in their new dorm room.

Monica Nicole got a good look at her roommates and her likely constant companions, if the classes were conducted here as they had been at Bradbury's so long ago. All five girls were twelve years old, but Monica saw differences right away. Misty had wavy blonde hair, a pale complexion, and deep blue eyes. She was also short. Enya was nearly the same height, but had short, bobby brown hair and a rather plain face.

In contrast, Ericka was quite tall and thin, with very long, straight blonde hair, which bordered on platinum blonde, reaching the small of her back. In contrast, her sky blue eyes were quiet striking. Crystal was equally tall; both girls were six inches taller than the two shorter girls were. Crystal's rich, thick black hair was also long, but not nearly as long as Ericka's, and she had cute bangs over her forehead that caressed her eyebrows, giving her hazel eyes a rather mysterious look.

Monica Nicole was only an inch shorter than these two girls were. Her hair was also black, but slightly wavy, falling to the middle of her back. She'd followed her aunt's advice and not had it cut as she had intended to. Why? Having longer hair would secure her appearance as a girl, whereas the short cut that Monica had suggested would perhaps raise undo questions. Her cheekbones were high and her lips, thick. Combined with her vertical oval face, her appearance was quite appealing, bordering on those of teen fashion models.

As the five followed Ginny into the pentagram dorms, Crystal said somewhat accusatively, "I *see* that you already have your wand, Monica. We aren't *supposed* to get them until now, here at school. Why do you have yours ahead of time? Have you learned to cast any *spells* yet?"

"Oh! She has a wand? *Do* show it to us, please, Monica," Ericka turned to have a look at this precious object. Monica could sense her drooling over the idea of holding a magic wand.

"It's Monica Nicole, please. Yes, my aunt and uncle have been teaching me a little during the summers," she replied. "I don't know if we are allowed to cast any spells yet," she added, hoping that Ginny would come to her rescue. While Monica Nicole wanted to show them just how incredibly powerful she already was, that would only blow her cover wide open and probably bring the filthy Rodents pack down on her.

Ginny turned and explained, "It would be best *not* to cast any spells just yet, Monica Nicole. Wait until you get into your casting class next week, please. Girls, as soon as we get you settled in your rooms, I'll take you down to the bookstore where our wand master will give you your wands too. Now we are on the second floor." She began her lengthy introduction to the layout of the dorm proper.

Deja vou. The layout of the dorms was precisely the same as the old dorm at Bradbury's! Only there, Dominus had been in Black Hall, not Red Hall. Even the enormous dining room was identical. The only significant difference was that St. Louis had only five hundred total students, not the six hundred per each of the six grades that Bradbury's had. Why? There were more larger cities here in the mid-west and east than there were in the rangelands of the west. Hence, overall total population of students was spread out among the more numerous schools.

However, this campus lacked the fantastically shaped buildings that Bradbury's had. Here, they were modern glass, steel, and concrete buildings, easily constructed. Monica Nicole sensed that this school didn't have the aurora and atmosphere of Bradbury's, but was a purely functional magic school. Certainly, the yearly cost was half of that of Bradbury's—that she already knew, having paid her tuition for this year, of course, from the money she'd stolen from the LA bank.

Later, she got her new cell phone and inexpensive laptop computer, as did everyone else. Standing in line to get their books, she and her four roommates looked over their printed class schedules. As expected, they were all in the same classes together.

        8:00 Math
        9:00 Science
       10:00 English/Literature
       11:00 Physical Education
       12:00 lunch hour
        1:00 History of Magic
        2:00 Beginning Spell Casting—Grade 0 and
  I
        3:00 Conjuration-Summoning Theory I
        4:00 Enchantment-Charm Theory I
        5:00 Dinner

"Oh darn, no potion making this year," Enya complained. "I *so* want to be a potion maker and open my own potion making store when I graduate."

Ericka commented, "Well, that's a lucrative business, but isn't it awfully stinky? Really icky stuff goes into them or so mom says."

Monica Nicole dryly commented, "Potion Making I comes in your fourth year, Enya. There are usually three classes in it, but only if you *pass* the previous ones. My aunt told me." She added that last quickly, finding a reasonable way for her to have known that.

Their Floor Monitor, Ginny, spoke up, "She's right. Fourth Year. I have Potion Making I this year. Of course, even to get into it, you *have* to do really well in Chemistry in your third year, Enya."

Not to be outdone, Misty spoke up, "Well, I want to be a wand maker. Wizards and witches are always needing new wands. That's what I'm going to do when I graduate."

"I don't think that there's a class in that," Ginny countered. "So I expect you will have to do a lot of studying about them in your sixth year."

Next, Ericka and Crystal complained about math and science classes. Crystal added, "I've *heard* that they are really hard, that we have to take lots of math classes, and that physics is almost impossibly hard."

Monica Nicole commented, "You best become *expert* in math and physics, that is, if you want to command power spells." Hastily, she added, "At least, that's what I heard from my uncle."

Ericka declared, "Well, I aim to be a very powerful witch!"

"Me too," Crystal added.

Both girls' illusions crinkled after sitting through their morning math and science classes. "These are going to be awfully hard," Ericka commented as they headed to their PE class.

Monica Nicole took a liking to these two and said, "Don't worry. I'm good at math and some sciences. I'll help you out if you need it." That brought big smiles to the pair.

In PE class, all four of her roommates moaned when their professor said, "Okay girls, today we are running laps."

Misty complained, "Why? We're girls after all. We're supposed to look pretty and not run around like the boys do."

Monica Nicole whispered to her roommates, "Look, if you want to stay alive out there, you have to have fast reactions or you are going to be unable to dodge out of the way of a Disintegrate spell. Only the fittest survive in the real world. Get yourselves in shape if you want to live a long life. Come on; no pain, no gain. You heard her." Reluctantly, the four began jogging beside Monica.

In their afternoon History of Magic class, the professor began his usual discussion about the use of magical spells. After reciting the early history of magic, he explained, "The Wizard Board of Review then opened the New Age by casting down these four inviolate laws. You must have these memorized verbatim by Monday or spend next week in detention!"

He wrote these out on the board:

1. Thou shalt not use magic to injure or harm another unjustly.

2. Thou shalt not use magic to kill another unjustly.

3. Thou shalt not use magic to steal from another that, which is not yours.

4. Thou shalt not use magic to force another to do something against their will unjustly.

"Beginning wizards and witches, violate any one of these and the Department of Magical Misuse will arrest you and throw you into prison for a very long time. It is only our strict adherence to these laws that allows the norms to tolerate our open presence in society. After all, we possess extraordinary powers from their viewpoint. If we do not follow these laws to the letter, the norms will become terrified of us and seek our destruction, as was done all throughout the Old Age."

"We all know just how badly Dominus Malefic and his Death Stalkers disobeyed all these. Look where that got him? He and his men were either killed or captured and residing in jail for the rest of their lives. Why?" He threw open the floor for discussion.

One Black Hall boy spoke up, "Unjustly so! Wizards are the most powerful people in the world, and they should be in the commanding, leading positions. Dominus was right. Just look at the Battle of Virginia. A few wizards sure showed the norm's Army a thing or two! Wizards should hold the ruling power, not the weakly norms!" Monica Nicole smiled. Others still felt as he had. A very lively discussion followed!

A Yellow Hall boy countered, "While there's no argument amongst any of us that a wizard or witch is vastly more powerful than norms, Dominus went too far. He was like Adolf Hitler, creating the Master Race. It failed miserably. Norms aren't automatons. Look what happened in New York and D.C. They had to bring in hundreds of us just to keep any remote semblance of government and industry going. The poor automatons were not able to do anything more than menial labor. Civilization very nearly broke down. Even now, they are hanging on by a mere thread until they get the antidotes for their heroin-addictive pills. No way could Dominus have kept the entire US going as robots. There aren't enough wizards in the whole world to run the US, let alone the rest of the world. His plan was doomed to failure from the get-go."

Surprising Monica Nicole, Crystal raised her hand. "Look, Dominus made a second major blunder. We witches are just as powerful as you wizards are. Yet, he relegated women and witches to mere sex toys, play things. If you watched the news any, that was his downfall," she zinged back. "Most *all* the Rodents were witches, not wizards! Even Able and Bill were really witches, not wizards. We witches are *just* as powerful as you wizards are, maybe more so! Passions rule, not physical might. That ought to be very clear, unless you are blind and deaf or are ignoring all the news."

Monica Nicole flushed. The truth of her pronouncement struck home. *Could she have a valid point? Have I been blinded by dad and his ideas about women? Oh dear god, how could I have made such a gigantic blunder all these years?*

Just then, the determined Black Hall boy, Phil,

challenged Crystal. "Bah! Wizards are always more powerful than you silly witches! We'll show you! Just wait until we get to spell casting class! You're just a bunch of pretty wallflowers who know simple spells. Look pretty, Crystal, and some of us might take you to a dance."

Crystal glared back at him. So did Ericka, Monica Nicole noted and smiled covertly. However, she realized that Phil was displaying the same basic attitude that he had. *Crystal's right. I was brought down by a pack of witches. I sure as heck don't know how they did that, but they did. She's on to something, something extremely vital that I have always overlooked!*

Later on in their first spell casting class, Monica Nicole now had to exercise extreme caution. Why? Obviously, she could cast all these silly beginning Grade 0 spells and rapidly as well. Those spells that she didn't know began around Grade 7. Still, she sided with Crystal and Ericka, not the arrogant Phil. She found herself teamed up with Crystal as they began learning how to do these, the simplest of spells, beginning with Chill and Warm, followed by Clean.

Crystal, on the other hand, said, "Come on, Monica Nicole; we just *have* to learn these before those nasty Black Hall boys do! We *have* to show them that we are passionate about our spells." Monica Nicole grinned and was the first to cast successfully their initial three spells, naturally, allowing just enough time to make it seem reasonable to her professor.

"Good going, Monica Nicole! You sure showed that Phil!" Crystal exclaimed. Monica merely smiled and saw an avenue opening up for her. If she could somehow get her four new friends casting the spells faster than all the other kids, they would gain mountains of respect. Dominus had never remotely spent any time actually "helping" another student learn a spell when he was at Bradbury's. However, right now, her command of spell casting was comparatively huge. Hence, as Monica Nicole, she found it rather easy to coach her four new friends. Quickly, these five students became the first in their class to learn to cast every new spell.

Of course, a solid bond of real friendship quickly formed between these five twelve year old girls. In addition,

Monica Nicole soon began helping Misty and Enya with their math and science homework as well. Crystal also helped her out with English Literature, a subject that Monica Nicole could have cared less about. Quickly, the five girls became inseparable.

Then, in mid-December, the bonds became even more solid. When Monica Nicole got up that morning, she found her sheets were bloody as well as her panties. "Oh no! I'm bleeding! Something's horribly wrong with me. Clean! Clean!" Her four roommates came over to her bed at once to see what was wrong.

Ericka grinned. "Silly, there's nothing wrong with you. You are having your period. Haven't you ever?" From Monica's red face, she knew she hadn't known about this. "Oh my. Well, now you are officially a woman, Monica Nicole! Didn't your mother tell you about it?"

"Er, no. My parents are long dead," Monica muttered, grimacing. Here was something new that she hadn't expected.

"I'm so sorry, Monica Nicole. Here, you need one of my tampons," Ericka explained, showing her how to use it. "So you really don't know anything about being a woman, then do you?" Monica shook her head no. "Don't worry. I do. I'll teach you all that I know."

"Hey, how about us?" Enya suggested. "Misty and I haven't bled yet either. Mom won't let me wear makeup. No matter, I'm too homely to worry about it."

"No you're not, Enya," Ericka countered. "We all have some growing to do. I know many tricks. My mother showed me. That's about all that she's good for, really. She's a norm, well really an escort if the truth be told, but dad's a powerful wizard.

From that moment on, Monica Nicole's greatest fears, dealing with feminine issues, vanished. Ericka looked after all them, even to educating them on the best products to use. After that, Monica's long black hair never looked so good. In effect, the five each had things that they could share to help the others, solidifying their tight bonds of friendship.

Bit by bit, Monica Nicole's point of view began changing from what she had held as Dominus. More and more, she began to see that women and witches, in particular, were in fact the true source of power, not the male wizards, for whom brute power was all, at least as she had once believed. They ruled from behind the scenes, so to speak, at least from her current perspective.

Chapter 2—A New Kind of Power

As her school years progressed, Monica Nicole Black likewise moved forward. Being cooped up in the school for nine months of the year, she could hardly go around robbing and amassing another fortune. Instead, she recalled the long arguments that she'd had with her father so very long ago. His argument had been that the route to power was through economic means, while his had been to use brute force. At the break point, his father had given him half of his wealth along with the challenge to prove his power by force method would work. It hadn't. In fact, despite all his clever, methodical planning, Dominus had only gotten himself killed. Worse, in many circles, his name was synonymous with the devil. Now he'd been given a second chance or rather, she had, Monica reminded herself.

Thus, using the rest of the stolen hundred thousand dollars as seed money, she invested her funds via online trading. As she waited for the school bus to pick her up at the start of her fourth year at the St. Louis School of Magic, she had already returned all the money that she'd stolen from the bank in Los Angeles, anonymously of course. Her portfolio was currently worth ten million and climbing. Knowledge and money are power. Of that, she was now very much convinced.

Her "uncle" had died during the summer, and she'd inherited his estate, which included his small home, a few magic items, and most importantly another million dollars. He'd taken out a hefty life insurance policy three years back. fully intending to further his mentor's new rise to power. Officially, she was now staying with her "aunt," who had also taken out an identical insurance policy. "After all, dear, we want to do all that we can to help get you back into power," she'd explained to Monica Nicole.

Monica Nicole had not been idle these past three years. She spent as much time as she could in the school's library, scouring every book dealing with any aspect of magic that she was allowed to read. Of course, she wasn't permitted into the

Restricted Section, not yet anyway. Still, she literally doubled the knowledge of magic that she had as Dominus.

When the bus stopped to pick her up, she joined her four roommates, now called the Gang of Five around the school. All five had three years of straight A's in all their classes, rather unheard of at the school, especially for Red Hall. Each helped the others out, though Monica Nicole provided the most help, naturally. Even more importantly, these five always seemed to be the first in their class to get the new spells working for the first time, a fact not lost on the many in Black Hall. Heading into their fourth year, all their professors were quite aware of the stellar accomplishments of the Gang of Five.

The shy, short brown haired Enya Homes was animated. "Monica Nicole, I'm *so* excited! We finally get Potion Making class!" Monica knew from three years ago that Enya had her heart set on becoming a potion maker. "I don't know how to thank you for having gotten me through chemistry class last year. I just know I would have flunked if you hadn't helped me constantly."

Monica smiled, "Well, now you get to shine. I suspect that you are now going to have to help me a lot. I don't think I'm any good at potion making." She didn't add that she had hated it when she was Dominus; that's what chemists were for—making such things. He'd just hired those who did to manufacture his pills for the ill-fated National Health Care Program.

The blonde, conservative Misty Worth added, "But have you seen we now have trigonometry? I can't imagine a harder math class. I think that we are doomed this year. Besides, what does this have to do with making wands? Nothing, I say. I just got this new, terrific book. Able Jorgenson's <u>Treatise of Wand Construction</u>. I can't wait to read it."

Crystal Holliday had just had her bangs trimmed. Her long black, full-bodied hair shone in the sunlight. "Oh don't worry, Misty. I have you covered on trig. I studied up on it some over the summer. Don't look so shocked, Misty. You didn't think I spent my whole summer reading the Teen Fashion magazines, did you?" Crystal was the fashion geek of

Red Hall. Rightly so, she already had made the magazine's cover of the July issue, her first photo shoot. Misty gave her a questioning look, as if she had thought just that. Crystal grinned at her.

Not to be outdone, the long blonde haired Ericka Van Nie grinned. "Gang, wait until you see the September issue. I'm on its cover."

"What? You too?" exclaimed Crystal, rather surprised.

"Really?" put in Enya.

"Yes! Someone sent in some photos of me back in May. In July, I got interviewed and had the photo session in early August!" Ericka exclaimed excitedly.

"Wow! Way coolest!" Misty gushed, uncharacteristically excited. Then, she sobered up. "I wonder who sent them the photos?"

Monica Nicole, who had been quiet after greeting her four close friends, was grinning, especially when Misty looked at her. "You didn't, did you?" Misty asked.

"You?" Ericka asked, growing curious. All summer, she'd wondered who had sent in her photo to Teen Fashion, which had led to her big break.

"Hey, we stick together," Monica Nicole answered slyly. "Besides, I wanted Crystal to have a little competition." All five girls chuckled. Ericka mouthed a thank you. Monica then added, "Trig is vitally important to our spell casting, particularly from now on. The spells are much harder this year. We're going to have to work hard to master them. Don't worry. I've been studying up on them."

She'd added that last to relieve them somewhat. By now, the four knew that always Monica Nicole was the first in their entire class to cast any new spell, no matter what it was. Miss Hot Shot, the Black Hall boys teased her, though by now it had long ago lost its derogatory emphasis. The four heavily depended on Monica's help in learning the spells as rapidly as they did. They didn't realize that Monica Nicole had come across the Slow Motion spell that many teachers used to help find what was going wrong with a student's spell and had been using it to help her coach her friends.

Monica Nicole then added, "I'm going to need lots of

help in World Cultures and the foreign language class. I hate them." Indeed, as Dominus, he could have cared less about these two studies. Here was another outlet for her four friends to contribute back to her for all of her help with magical studies, math, and science. All five pulled out their Fourth Year schedules and compared them. They were identical, naturally.

```
 8:00 PE
 9:00 English
10:00 Trigonometry
11:00 Physics
 1:00 World Cultures and Foreign Language
 2:00 Alteration Theory II
 3:00 Potion Making I
 4:00 Spell Casting Grade 5
```

"Is physics really hard?" asked Enya? "I don't see what physics has to do with potion making."

"Vital to spell casting," Monica Nicole pointed out dryly. "Don't worry, gang, I've studied up on physics over the summer. After all, what else was there for me to do? My aunt is almost seventy now. You can only clean the house so many times." The four giggled.

"Don't worry about the foreign language, Monica Nicole," Ericka explained. "You see, my grandparents came from the Netherlands. So if we all choose Dutch as our foreign language, I can help all of you with it." She winked her long eyelashes at the four and grinned.

"Hey, look at what I just got," Monica Nicole changed the subject. "It just came out, <u>A Collection of Non-Grade Spells Found in Industry and the Home.</u> It's by Professor Pam Betts of Bradbury's. She's catalogued hundreds of other spells that wizards and witches have invented that are not in our formal spell books. Isn't this just an incredible time-saver?"

"Cool! We have to get a copy for each of us!" Crystal declared, drooling over Monica Nicole's great find. "I've heard that we get to scrounge the library for some of these in our last year. This will make that lot's easier."

"I thought so too," Monica Nicole grinned and proceeded to hand out a copy to each of her four roommates.

"I took the liberty," she teased them. The four thanked her, praised her, and gave her a hug.

"I don't know what we'd do without you helping us so much," Ericka declared quite truthfully.

"We're a team," Misty pronounced. Monica thought this one over. She'd never been part of a real team before. As Dominus, he controlled his followers, dictating their actions. Something new was happening with herself and these four friends. She couldn't quite grasp its significance just yet. The idea of a team was actually rather new to her. *This must be important, because the Rodents acted as a team. I couldn't stand up against seventeen of them. Power must be related to a team somehow. I need to think this one through.*

Later in their room, the five began unpacking their things. Misty broke her special news first. "I've got a boyfriend now. We've been on a bunch of dates this summer. He's pretty nice."

"Who is he? Come on, Misty. You have to tell us!" Ericka exclaimed, pausing her unpacking to stare at Misty, who flushed and then giggled.

"Yes, who? Out with it, Little Miss Conservative," Crystal put in, teasingly.

"Jasper Williams, Brown Hall. He's in our class, you know. He took me to the dances here last year. He wants to make wands too, that is, when he graduates. He's so cool," Misty explained.

"Well, Brad Scorsky has asked me to go steady with him, too," Enya broke in. "He's the Brown Hall fellow who danced with me lots last year. I know. He's not the handsomest fellow, but then I'm not a model as you two are. Besides, he's really into potion making. I do hope that he does well in it. I've promised to help him if he has troubles with it. He thinks we can open a potion shop together, once we graduate and all that."

After the others congratulated the pair, Ericka asked, "So Monica Nicole, have you got a boyfriend now too?"

"Gag me! I detest men! I'd rather vomit than go out with a man, let alone have—well you know what I mean. God, men are revolting to me," Monica Nicole replied. *Good god! I never thought about this detail before. God, kissing a man? I couldn't do it! Not ever!*

"We didn't know," Misty tried to smooth over this unexpected news. "Sorry. Really, Monica Nicole."

"That's okay. You two are welcome to your two boys. Just don't ever try to set me up with guys," Monica Nicole replied, trying to sound more respectful of her friends.

Ericka flirted towards Monica, "So are you into women then?"

Monica Nicole couldn't conceal her instant smile. "Of course." She kept it simple, flashing her and Crystal a smile.

"Like us?" Ericka wiggled her hips and moving up close to Monica as though she were about to seduce her.

Monica grinned back. "Yes dear. Best be careful around me. You too, Crystal. I'm rather fond of teen fashion models."

Both Ericka and Crystal laughed. "No, Monica Nicole. It's you who had best watch out for us," Ericka teased her and then gave her a loving hug. All five laughed. However, at their many school dances, Monica Nicole had always danced with Ericka and Crystal, for the most part. Now the two understood their roommate far better.

Later on, both Enya and Misty headed off to meet with their boyfriends before classes got underway and the workload became so heavy, leaving the other three in their dorm room. Crystal, always the one to take charge, said sweetly, "So Monica Nicole, you've got a crush on Ericka and me, eh?"

Monica flushed. "Well, who wouldn't? You both are very beautiful—models no less."

Flirting, Ericka asked, "So if you detest men, what do you like to see in your women? Long hair? Blondes? Or lush black haired beauties?" She slid up close to Monica. Not to be outdone, Crystal moved in close to the two of them.

"I do love your hair—both of you," Monica Nicole replied honestly.

"So what do you like in your women?" Crystal insisted on knowing.

"Well, big boobs. Really big boobs. And fancy satin gowns," Monica Nicole replied, omitting the other things that as Dominus she'd done to her play toys.

"So you'd like us to have big knockers, eh?" Ericka asked teasingly. "We could accommodate that one."

"You could? Oh, right, we know the spells," Monica Nicole asked, before realizing that they could do just that.

Crystal countered, "So you'd like us better with big knockers. Okay, but in return, we'd like something from you too, you know."

Monica grinned. "Like what?" This was almost too good to be true, she thought.

"I like my women with really long nails so you can put them to use on my body," Crystal replied.

Ericka put in, "And I like my women to wear fetish gowns and heels, tall ones. Have we got us a deal, Monica Nicole?" she said teasingly.

"We certainly do," she replied.

Crystal pointed out, "Well, we're somewhat limited here in school. The regulations don't permit us to have nails longer than an inch. Large boobs will also cause a big stir. Besides, we are still developing. How about we do the best that is allowed for now?" The three agreed. Monica Nicole attempted to seal the bargain by giving both a passionate kiss.

"Jeesh, Monica, I'm going to have to show you how to kiss properly," Ericka declared. She promptly began educating Monica Nicole in the art of lovemaking.

The following year, in PE, they had the option of learning martial arts. Admittedly, it was being taught as a self-defense class. Monica Nicole saw the immense value of this class and got her roommates to take it with her. "Look, if we take this class, we will be better able to defend ourselves, and can dodge spells far better." The other four accepted her explanation and took the nine-month long class with her, becoming quite skilled in the art of dodging both magical and physical attacks. Monica Nicole had added one more layer of protection and power to herself and her four dear friends.

In 2189, the five began their sixth and final year at the St. Louis School of Magic. The past summer, Monica's aunt had passed away, and she inherited a second home and another million dollars from her aunt's life insurance. This she invested in her growing portfolio. Being eighteen now, she no longer needed a "parent."

Already, Enya positively shone in potion making and was taking Potion Making III as her elective, though none of the others did, but her steady boyfriend, Brad, was with her. Misty was elated to be taking Wand Making as her elective and her boyfriend, Jasper, was taking it as well. Crystal, always fascinated with the truly occult, took Extra Planar Studies as her elective. She wanted to know all about demons, daemons, and devils, along with ways and means of protecting oneself from them. Of course, no one seriously believed that such things actually existed. On the other hand, Ericka found that she desired eventually to create magical items and took as her elective The Construction of Magical Items I. Of course, she hoped and prayed that she would be able to learn the Make Permanent Grade 8 spell. Secretly, Monica Nicole decided to cast her Restricted Wish on Ericka, should she not be able to learn it directly, thereby ensuring that her lover somehow succeeded.

For five years, Monica Nicole had looked forward to this year. Now she had the chance to research the truly powerful spells and have another opportunity to learn the many topmost spells that as Dominus she'd failed to learn. She wanted to learn every spell in Pam Betts' new book, though she already knew a quarter of them, such as Slice, Melt, Leather to Plastic, and Plastic to Steel, among others. Hence, for her elective, she took Casting the Industrial Spells. True, during their three-period spell casting class, the other students would have some time to learn a few of these, once they'd finished their attempts to learn the terrifically powerful spells. Monica wanted to use that time for other things, focusing on really learning the many power spells that she didn't know.

The sixth year proved successful for the many students. While several Black Hall boys and girls celebrated Phil having learned the Full Wish spell and Elaine learning to Stop Time, many others in the five halls were meeting with their own flavors of success. As Crystal pointed out, "Look ladies, we don't need a Full Wish spell. It ages you an entire year with each casting! We women have our beauty as one of our powers. We'll lose it soon enough anyway, so let's not go around prematurely aging." Monica Nicole hadn't thought about that aspect and gave it considerable thought.

Because Monica Nicole already knew a third of the Grade 7 spells, the fivesome were able to learn well over half of these spells quickly. However, none officially went for the Restricted Wish spell. Monica cleverly didn't report that she already knew that one. From there, they headed for the ultimate power spells of Grade 8 and 9. Again, since she already knew some of these, all five picked up the Antipathy spell that Dominus had cast on several of his "homes." They all were able to learn the Pounding Fist spell and the Many Symbols of Protection spells. Several didn't wish to try to learn a few others that Monica already knew, such as Blind.

However, Ericka quickly picked up the Make Permanent spell. Monica Nicole breathed a sigh of relief. She didn't have to cast her Restricted Wish on Ericka. Further, Ericka turned around and coached the other four into being able to cast it as well. At this point, Misty simply was unable to pick up more powerful spells. They seemed beyond her ability. Enya picked up only one more, the ability to Morph Any Object into whatever she desired, useful in potions, she thought. Ericka also learned this one with Enya's help.

Ericka also picked up several other Grade 8 spells, including the powerful Symbols and Wards, which she could work into the magical items that she intended to make later on, Force to Dance (a spell which made the victim have to stop and dance for quite some time and which she thought would make a good defensive spell), and the ability to Charm the Masses (a spell that Dominus had his "chemist" associate place into the many rings that he gave out during his presidential campaign).

Crystal picked up an Anti-Scrying Screen, Make One's Mind Totally Blank to Others, and Physical Binding of Demons and other such extra-planar creatures, a spell fitting with her newfound specialty of the occult. Monica also discovered that she could also learn some new Grade 8 spells. She also added the same mind-blanking spell as Crystal learned, along with two versions of Suspended Animation. The alternate form also embedded the person underground as well. She also learned the Clone spell, the very one that Dominus' father had used to create Dominus many years ago. Unfortunately, Monica Nicole had to register in the official database as being able to cast this spell.

When the almost unclassifiable Grade 9 and up spells came, only Ericka, Crystal, and Monica Nicole were able to learn some of them. As Dominus, she only knew Kill and the Crushing Hand spells. To her utter amazement, she learned how to cast two other top spells. The Have Foresight spell, the top divination spell, suddenly opened Monica's eyes to future possibilities! Via this spell, she now possessed some divination skills, which as Dominus she didn't have and which led to his downfall! She also learned the Suspend All Magic in an Area spell. Again, she thought that this would be a most useful spell in a tight pinch.

On the other hand, Crystal totally surprised her, learning four of these top spells. Mostly, they had to do with her occult studies. She could Travel in the Astral Plane. She could Stop Time Briefly. She could Open a Gate to other planes and Imprison Others, such as demons who came to ravage the world. Crystal was very impressed with these, but as an Open Gate caster, she too had to register with the authorities. Monica Nicole now saw Crystal as truly a take-charge type of person. There was no longer any question of that.

Ericka also surprised everyone by picking up two of these top spells, one of which would be highly useful in her line of work, making magical items. It was the Fabricate Object with Teleport to Safe-house. With it, she could create small objects and give them to her friends. If they got into serious trouble, they could simply break the object and be instantly teleported to Ericka's designated safe-house. Monica Nicole thought this was a particularly valuable spell that Ericka had learned. She also was able to Change Her Shape into anything that she desired. When she successfully cast it in class, she appeared to be a very blonde wolf with large fangs.

This opportunity to learn the ultimate power spells concluded, leaving them with another four months to study as they wished. A few of the other students tried to invent new spells. The five roommates didn't bother wasting precious time on that. Instead, they focused on learning as many of the "Industrial Spells" as they could, though thanks to her elective class, Monica Nicole already knew most of them and worked with her roommates much of the time. The remainder of their time was spent on trying to learn to cast spells sans wands and sans words.

This, Monica Nicole knew, was just what the world-famous Dispeller Lindsey Barron-Cross was doing—only in spades. Rumors had it that she could cast nearly every spell this way, frustrating Dominus and the Death Stalkers and ultimately leading to their downfall. While all five worked hard at casting sans wands, sans words, they were able to cast only a very few useful Grade 0 spells this way, leaving Monica Nicole more than a little frustrated.

The first of May, when the five were in their dorm room getting ready for bed, Monica Nicole decided that now was the time to formalize some plans. She saw that they were a team and wanted it to continue. There was true power in their team, something that she'd never experienced before.

"Okay, in a few weeks we are going to graduate. I have a proposal to make to all of you, my dearest friends. I want us to all stay together. Let's start our own business called Protections, Investigations, Wands, Items, and Potions or PIWIP for short. It's a palindrome. We can set up shop, and Misty and Jasper can make and sell their wands. Enya and Brad can make and sell their potions. Ericka can invent all kinds of magic items and sell them. Crystal and I can handle providing all manner of protections for sale and even handle some investigations."

Ericka enthusiastically exclaimed, "Wow! That's sounds fabulous to me. I've saved up some money from four years of modeling. I can donate some of it to help us get started."

"Way coolest!" Crystal relied. "I've saved up some too from my modeling."

"Wow! That would be just super. Only I'm afraid that we don't have the startup money," Enya added, downcast.

"Same here," Misty quickly added. "We aren't sure how much we are really going to need to get into the wand making business."

"Look everyone. I know that you two don't have funds. I also know that Ericka and Crystal don't really have all that much either," Monica Nicole explained. "On the other hand, I've been investing like mad these past six years. Right now, I've got close to a hundred million, but it keeps on growing every month. I will finance our new PIWIP business entirely. Together, we are the best! So let's only get the best stuff. Finest ingredients for your potions, wands, and Ericka's what-evers." Ericka giggled. She still didn't know just what magical items she was actually going to make. Until this moment, it was mostly her dream.

"I'll finance us all. What say you?" Monica Nicole ended. Four women hugged her tightly in answer. She added, "But first, we should get you two married." They all giggled as Monica Nicole suspected they would.

"But how are we to pay you back, Monica Nicole?" Crystal asked, once the excitement wore off.

"You don't ever have to pay me back. None of you. Look, I can't make potions worth a darn. Without Enya's help, I would have flunked Potion Making. I haven't any idea how wands are made. That's Misty's department. I surely don't know anything about the occult stuff that Crystal knows, and I'm not too interested in making many magical items as Ericka is. I'm more into investigations, making money, and getting us women into our rightful places of power in this world. We are a team now, and there is immense power in a team." She didn't add—I should know; a team of Rodents did in Dominus!

That settled, Enya and Misty rushed off to tell their fiancés this great news. "So Monica Nicole, are you still in love with us?" Ericka asked, flirting with her.

"Of course I am, but I don't see how we can be an official union of three, not legally," Monica Nicole replied, "though I sure wish we could."

"Silly, we can't, not legally. But we can be a threesome otherwise, in all ways," Ericka countered. "Only you must be willing to allow us our freedom too. One of us just might fall in love with some man later on, though as powerful as we are, it's going to take one hunk of a guy." Both she and Crystal laughed at that. The three quickly reached an agreement on becoming a threesome.

With all that settled, Monica Nicole began looking for the ideal quarters to house their new PIWIP company, preferably in an ideal location and with attached living spaces for everyone. It took her a week to find the perfect building. Hunting for real estate was easy; everything was up on the Net. On Riverview Drive, just north of I-270 cradled in the hills on a small, forested estate lay the former St. Anne's, once home to nuns. The construction consisted of re-enforced concrete shell with a red brick outer wall. A blacktop drive led up to the building, ending in a giant circle with a fountain and flower garden in its center. An ornate portico marked the main entrance squarely in the center of the long side of the building. A hallway went down the length. There were two large rooms to the left and two to the right of the entrance reception area. On the opposite side of the hall, there were four giant rooms.

At either end of the hall, stairs led to the basement, where an identical long hall ran the length of the basement. Towards the front, there was a giant kitchen and then a huge dining hall, with a smaller storage room beyond that. On the other side of the hall were four more large rooms, though a corner one was double the size of the other three, perfect for living quarters. Monica Nicole decided that they all had to check out this possible building.

Ericka's comments were pretty much what Monica Nicole had thought. "Look, it's heavily re-enforced. Good, solid stone. That makes for vastly better protection since stone takes our major spells far better than glass. The grounds are secluded and incredibly picturesque. We won't have to worry about someone coming in and messing up our spells in progress or potions that are brewing. But as far out as it is, we should have some cars, don't you think?"

"It would make a great place to get married at," Enya added. Misty agreed.

Monica Nicole purchased the building for cash, unwilling to have a mortgage and financial obligations. After they graduated, they moved into their new accommodations and began remaking it into their ideal spaces. She also gave each fifty thousand to spend on furnishings and supplies, but donated another fifty thousand to Misty and Enya so they could obtain their necessary supplies to setup their shops and another fifty thousand to Ericka and Crystal so that they could do the same with their beginning business ventures.

Two hectic weeks later, the wedding ceremonies were held here. Monica Nicole, Crystal, and Ericka acted as the bridesmaids for Enya and Misty. The four invited some of their relatives and outside friends; over two hundred were in attendance for the wedding. Both Ericka and Crystal took note that Monica Nicole had absolutely no one there. No family, no friends. Now they realized just how isolated their lover actually was.

That night, the two couples teleported off to Tahiti for their honeymoon—two weeks in a tropical paradise. Tahiti was a very frequent honeymoon location for wizards and witches, because of its climate and isolation.

Alone at last, the three women, who now shared the master bedroom in the basement corner, the largest of the bedroom suites, got down to their own private business. "Okay, Monica Nicole, we are ready to make our own union of three," Ericka said rather romantically. "Remember the deal?"

Monica Nicole grinned mischievously. "Of course I do. I can't wait to get you two into bed. I've longed for this for a very long time."

"Okay then. Crystal, get your wand ready. Just how big do you want our knockers to be, Monica dearest? Say when," Ericka teased. By mutual agreement, the two now had rather giant, but perky breasts. "Gosh, these are huge, at least a G cup. You sure you want us to have them this big?"

Monica grinned just broadly. "You bet. You both look fabulous."

"Well, they are darn big. We'll have to alter our whole wardrobe," Crystal complained.

"Dear, we haven't bought many clothes yet," Ericka countered.

"Okay, now you have to alter yourself to our desires,

dear Monica," Crystal hinted, a wry grin on her face. "Larger, larger. Okay." Monica's were now D cup sized. "Now your nails. We want them long so you can properly service our knockers. Longer, longer. Okay. How's that, Ericka?"

Monica sported three-inch long claws, and Ericka grinned, nodding her approval. Then she added, "Okay, tomorrow, I'll take you to get your new gowns and heels. Remember, no complaining about heels, Monica. Now come on, you two. I've been waiting forever to get you both into bed!"

The next day, the three hit the stores for new outfits. They each acquired a "professional woman's" outfit. That is, a white silk blouse with a dark grey skirt and black patent pumps. Ericka and Crystal's pumps sported pencil thin-five inch heels, while Monica's were six-inches. In fact, the two insisted that Monica wear nothing lower excepting for tennis shoes and fleece lined moccasins. They added several fancy satin gowns, rather form fitting styles.

"Here, put these gel-soles into your shoes, Monica. They'll be good for your feet," Ericka ordered. Indeed, that made all the difference for Monica's feet. "There now, you too look absolutely stunning in our eyes." Arm in arm, the three headed for home.

"We should usually wear our gowns and look fabulous most of the time," Ericka insisted. "Clients will be quite taken with our appearance."

"Distracted you mean," Crystal interrupted her.

Ericka grinned mischievously. "But of course. Woman power." All three chuckled.

A month later, PIWIP finally opened its doors for business. Their ad read: Protections, Investigations, Wands, Items, Potions—your one-stop magic store.

What of the Rodents and Dominus Malefic? In August six years ago, Governor Lindsey Barron-Cross received word that someone had stolen the corpse of Dominus. She summoned her Rodents for a private meeting. "Well, it had to happen! Dominus' body has been stolen, gang. Someone officially goofed up. His remains were supposed to have been cremated. That way, there would not be anyway for anyone to bring him back. However, his body was embalmed and buried."

Professor Pam spoke up, "Big mistake. Someone's in deep trouble now. Wait, if he was embalmed, then they can't clone another Dominus, can they?"

Lindsey answered, "No, I researched that as soon as I got word that his body was stolen. No, it's contaminated DNA. Cloning is not possible. We caught a break on that one."

"Right. But how else can they bring him back?" asked Jim Whitewater.

Pam bit her lip. "Well, there's always Cause Life. You know, the reverse of Cause Death. Of course, that's more like reincarnation."

"Dear god! Here we go again," Jim grumbled.

"Hey, don't worry," Deiter spoke up. "I can catch him just we did before. Only we need Ashley and Audrey to say when and where."

"Okay, I get the message. Don't bother me for a bit. I'll see what I can pick up on Dominus. Gosh, I thought we were done with that beast!" Ashley replied. She closed her eyes and focused.

A half hour later, she opened her eyes. Already, Deiter had his Staff of Power at hand, ready to go into action once more. Ashley said quietly, "Well, this is queer."

"What? Did you find him?" asked Lindsey.

"Nope. It's strange. For the briefest instant, I thought that I was connecting to Dominus, but it fizzled. It is almost as if he doesn't exist, but not quite. How do I explain this? You see, when I try to divine something about someone who is dead, I get a certain sense. This time, Dominus is supposed to be dead, but that sense is missing. And no, it's not because he's got his usual anti-scrying protections in place. Those are easy to sense, kind of like you get when you take a cold shower. This is wholly different. I honestly don't know what to make of it,'" Ashley replied.

Pam said didactically, "Then we know for sure that Dominus isn't dead. Thus, most likely, he's been reincarnated. Now how do we find him?"

"I don't know. I need much more information to go on," Ashley sighed.

"Well, I will keep alert for any unusual crimes and such," Pam declared.

With little else to go on, Lindsey dismissed her Rodents. "We'll keep a vigilant watch. Eventually, Dominus will be up to his old tricks. Some women's arms will be found or something. Stay sharp, everyone."

Chapter 3—Parry Oscar Tuttle, Private Investigator

About time I get the chance to tell my side of things. Don't like others telling stories about me. Never get things right, but then you probably already know that. Bad as newspaper reporters. And I can't stand anyone who twists and slants facts to fit their agenda. Guess that's what also keeps me in business and also poor. Parry Oscar Tuttle. That's my name, though on my business cards I put P. O. Tuttle, Private Investigations. It's a joke, by the way, though sometimes I just abbreviate it as POT. Another joke. My liaison officer at the St. Louis Division of the FBI, Oliver Easton, just doesn't appreciate the second one, but he does get a laugh over the first one. Seems we both share that in common, more than either of us would like, getting PO'ed at things we can't handle.

We get a lot of those kinds of cases. Strange deaths, strange happenings that seem inexplicable. Oliver's job is to solve them or sweep them under the rug with plausible deny-ability. Makes the bosses happy and lets the newspapers sell more papers. Oliver and I go way back. Grew up together until we were thirteen. That's when my parents were killed, and I got sent into the back boonies to live on my uncle's farm down in the rugged part of Missouri. As I said, we were good buddies way back then.

Got my office in downtown St. Louis, near Sal's Bar and Grill, the hangout for wizards and witches, though some nights he does get some of the overflow crowds from Bush Stadium. I'm a wizard. Okay, a wizard of sorts. No formal training, you see. Some of us can't afford the expensive magic schools and the snobs who run them. Long story short, my uncle saw my budding potential as a wizard and taught me just enough to be dangerous. The rest, I picked up on my own, reading all the spell books and such. He's dead too now. Fool had to go join up in the local militia and fight for Virginia against the US Army. Got himself killed on the first day of battle.

He did leave me with a Staff of Power, my ultimate weapon, a wand that I use for blasting away, and a few smaller protection items. Would have been far better if he'd left me some money. Same thing with my folks. After their estate was settled and their many bills paid up, I got a whopping hundred dollars and some change. At least, I got a small bit of change from the sale of my uncle's place, enough to set me up in my second-class office here in downtown St. Louis. I'm in the seedier section of town. I know. It used to be the hub of action, but suburbia sprawl hit here a century ago.

Here at the start, I was wondering where I was going to find November's rent. It was just the first of October, but I was worrying anyway. That's when Oliver paid me a visit. We're both twenty-two, but he looks like a suit. Always wears impeccable black suits and grey ties. Always. You can set your watch by him on that. He's built like a football player and stands six inches over me, and I'm big at six feet. I'm more of a runner. I have to be fast in order to stay alive when the spells fly. He just uses his 9mm automatic and fancy vest. Oh, and his fists as well. Remind me not to get in the way of his fists. They're deadly.

Anyway, I was sitting in my office wondering about how I was going to pay the rent when Oliver drops by. "PO! How are you?" he barked loudly. The door creaked and threatened to fall off its hinges as he entered. I knew better than to extend my hand too quickly. He had one of those overly enthusiastic handshakes, the kind that leaves your hand paralyzed for ten minutes. Much as I was pleased to see him, I didn't want my hand full of pins and needles just now. Still, if Oliver came to me, it had to be important and that meant money.

You see, Oliver and I have this thing going. Mutual help. Of course, he only comes to me with the weirdest cases imaginable. But then, that's why he comes to me—strange answers. Still, I can't gripe; I do get paid as a consultant for the FBI.

Seeing him coming to my office and looking like we hadn't seen each other in years, I knew that something was up, probably a particularly nasty one. Those are the ones I don't like. I tend to get clobbered and not in a good way. That last case we worked on, I very nearly got myself fried in a ball of fire. "Morning Oliver. What brings you to my humble office? It's not yet Halloween, is it? Or have I lost track of the days?" I rose and shook his hand. Enough time had just past so his attention was on what I'd said and not on crushing my hand.

"Got a case for you, if you need the money," Oliver said taking a seat in the only other chair in the room. I'm cheap. Only got the one chair for clients, but what the heck, when do I ever get more than one client at one time? He looked immaculate, every hair in place, just as he always did, but I could see the outline of his black 9mm in its holster. Oliver never went anywhere without it. Me, I prefer my old trusty 45 with its pearl handle.

"Okay, I don't seem to be busy at the moment. What 'ya got for me this time?"

"A kidnaping. Name's Jessica White. 20. Secretary for Holmes, Holmes, and Associates. Single. White. No record. Disappeared during her lunch hour. Went out to Lou's Grill and never returned. Reported missing later that afternoon. Her blue SUV is still in the company lot. Lives alone. One cat. No break-in there. No phone call asking for a ransom. Parents are in Chicago. Got a tap on their line just in case the call goes to them. Taken two days ago. Here's a recent photo." He handed me one of those cheap 3X5 photos like school kids often get. Average looking, but a bright secretary, I thought.

"So why me?" I asked.

"She's a witch, but not a particularly skilled one or so I'm told. If this was a normal kidnaping," Oliver pointed out, "we would have heard from her kidnapers before now. We've checked. Only has a small bank account balance. Charge cards are about half-filled. Firm has a policy of no negotiating, no ransom. Long standing policy. Frankly, Parry, we're baffled by this one. It's not following any of the usual scenarios. Have checked all the hospitals and morgues in the greater St. Louis area. Nada. Will you take the case? Usual consulting fee?"

"Yeh, sure. You know I've a soft spot for dames in trouble. Not much to go on is there," I replied.

Oliver actually sighed, something he rarely did, unless it was a case he pulled me into. "No, I'm afraid not. Figured they must have snatched her using magic. Good luck. I'll keep you in the loop if anything turns up. K?"

"Right. I'll get on it right away. Thank for the business, Oliver," I added. He rose rather solemnly and left. I waited until I heard the outer door shut before I snatched up my Cardinal's jacket, stuffed my wand in its sleeve, and headed out of the door. First stop, check Lou's Grill and the possible route that she must have traveled from the law offices to the diner.

A half hour later, I had hit the same dead end that Oliver and his associates had. Jessica was a regular. She'd ordered a Ruben and tea to go, charging it as usual. Five blocks. That's the distance between her office and the diner. Short by city standards and at lunchtime. The streets would be thronged with people. Kind of hard to abduct someone this way.

I re-walked the route, pretending that I was about to abduct a young woman, looking for the ideal location for the snatch and grab. I found it. She must have passed this one alleyway. I pivoted on my heels and headed down it, noticing the graffiti covered walls. Gang markers. Smelly dumpsters lined up its entire length, holders of the vast amount of waste we perpetually seem to generate. I tried to picture in my mind how it must have gone down.

She was walking back to her office, carrying the sack in one hand and the covered paper cup of hot tea in the other. As she passed the alley entrance, probably her kidnaper was standing here, Invisible most likely. Probably against that wall there, where he could see her coming. Of course, he had only seconds to react. I walked the short distance, pretending to be her, counting out the seconds. Three.

Okay, there is a whole lot you can do in three seconds, that is, if you have the spells ready. While I knew about all the spells that are taught in the magic schools, the vast majority I haven't yet learned to cast. I keep telling myself I need to take time off and learn some of these. Sometimes, I also wished that I listened to myself. This was one of those times.

I muttered to myself, "Probably cast a Silence spell around the entrance, so her cries would not be heard. Probably cast a Teleport on her. That's a fast one to cast if I remember right. So let's get the timing right." I pretended I just saw her coming along, lunch in hand; I stepped out quickly to touch her. "Excuse me, sir. Sorry." I nearly bumped into a man in a business suit. He glared at me and continued his walk.

Okay. Doable within the three-second window. I looked around the alleyway further. That's when I spotted conclusive proof. Behind the first dumpster, I spotted the torn bag with Lou's logo on it. Using a pencil, I moved part of the paper away and saw a partially eaten Ruben. Further, I spotted an empty cup, which also had Lou's logo on it. Now I was convinced that I'd found the crime scene. Obviously, Oliver's people hadn't, and I dug out my cell phone.

Five minutes later and with lots of flashing red lights, Oliver stepped out of his black SUV, along with another two men. "Forensics are on their way. What's ya have for me?"

"Crime scene. There's her dropped Ruben and tea," I pointed out.

"Looks like the rats got here first," Oliver replied.

"Yeh. For sure." I outlined my theory on how the abduction went down. "Might see if the perp left any trace on that wall there. He probably stood here quite some time waiting for her to pass by."

"Good work. Keep on it," Oliver replied. "I'll let you know if forensics comes up with anything. So she definitely has been kidnaped. Why? What's the motive?"

"Don't know yet. Mind if I have a look at her apartment?" I asked.

"Sure. Just flash your badge. The cop will let you in," Oliver answered. I nodded and left.

I headed to my own parking lot beside my office building, where I kept my beat up old Ford Fusion 2200. It had seen better days, but it still ran. The odometer had long ago ceased working. I have just not gotten around to having that detail fixed, partly because of my insurance. My St. Farm policy stated that I drove less than five thousand miles per year, giving me one of the lowest rates they had. This way, their periodic odometer checks couldn't disprove it. Besides, I liked the old heap. I couldn't survive without the GPS navigation system in it. I'd tweaked the voice to sound like a British woman. Cool accent. Sexy sounding. Without it, I'd never find my way around St. Louis. I hate maps. Too confusing, and you can't read them while trying to navigate the rush hour traffic or any traffic for that matter. Okay, I'll admit it. I can get lost with the best of them.

Jessie White lived in an apartment off Page and Hanley in Hanley Hills. Sputtering a bit of black smoke, I shut the Ford off. The cop on the scene gave me a dirty look. Thank goodness you can't get a ticket for that, because I was sure he would have given me one if there had been such a law. I flashed him my FBI Consultant's badge, and begrudgingly, he let me into her apartment. Cops always thoroughly search a victim's home. It's just done; don't ask me why. The victims get the third degree just because they are the victim. Gives the cops something to do, I expect. I'd rather catch the criminals, but that's just me.

So why was I here nosing around in some poor young woman's home? Clues. Like the FBI, I wanted to know more about her. Why would someone abduct a seemingly nobody, a lowly secretary? A CEO I could understand, but not a secretary. Ransom was out. They'd picked the wrong target if money was their motive. If rape was it, her body should've been found before now. A rapist is not known for keeping his victims around for going on three days now. Too dangerous. Besides, their fun would have been long gone by this time. No, I was looking for something deeper. A real why.

Of course, there was no escaping the idea that she was snatched at random. That was the most likely scenario at the moment. No diary. That would have been too easy. I checked her clothes closet. She had a couple of nice dresses, but mostly business attire. Nothing fancy. She lived within her means, I noted.

I looked around for pictures. Did she have a boyfriend? I'd discounted that theory when Oliver first came to my office with this case. If she had a boyfriend, Oliver would have been all over him in a flash. Domestic violence is a hot issue these days. Why? I surely don't know. I ruled out boyfriends, but did find one thing of note. She had several Sister Anne necklaces.

Those were only worn by virgins. So she was religious and wore hers with some pride. Good girl, I thought. You don't find too many of those types of young women these days.

So, they kidnaped a virgin. Now things began to look far darker from my point of view. In the occult world, virgins are often used in ritual sacrifices. I read all about that in some of my uncle's magic books. Was someone practicing the Dark Arts here in St. Louis? If so, the Feds would come down hard on them if they found out. The Department of Magical Misuse prosecuted those with a passion. Good reason. All manner of nasty things come from the Dark Arts. Inexplicable things. Things that go bump in the night and kill people. Things that defy traditional explanations. Hence, my job at the FBI.

I left her apartment, nodding to the cop on duty and headed back to my office to think. I couldn't call up Oliver and cry Dark Arts just yet. I had no proof, just a wild hunch based solely on the fact that Jessica might still be a virgin. Who knows if she still was? I didn't. She could answer that one, but if I could ask her, she wouldn't be kidnaped now would she? I was in an ill mood when I returned to my office. I hate the Dark Arts. Nasty business.

Much to my surprise, I found a young woman standing just outside my office door waiting for me! Now I like dames like any other fellow, but this one took my breath away. Six feet of golden angel! She had a copper hue to her smooth skin, suggesting a tanning salon. Her wavy long black hair smelled of lilacs, but perhaps that was just her perfume. I knew that I'd not forget her, not ever. Her face put all models to shame! She wore a touch of makeup. Her lips were quite red. A light blue eye shadow accentuated her eyes. She wore black nylons and tall black pumps, making her legs exquisite—legs to die for. I hoped that I didn't look too much like a slobbering dog as I walked up to unlock the door.

"Mr. P. O. Tuttle?" she said in a mellow alto voice. She had one of those voices that demand your full and undivided attention!

God, what a woman, I thought, and tried to speak, "Yes. Sorry, I was out working on a case." Darn it! That sounds lame! I bet she's heard that line a thousand times. "Come on in, please." I fumbled to get the old chair for her, wishing that I'd spent some funds on a better chair for my clients. I made a mental note to do just that, but it would be too late for this goddess. I took a moment to find my own chair, swallowing hard and calming my rising passions.

"Yes, sorry about that. How can I help you?" I asked trying to sound as business-like as possible. Our eyes finally met. God, she didn't let go. Her eyes penetrated me like no others ever had. For a moment, I felt utterly naked, like my soul was being laid bare before her gaze. Like I said, what a woman!

"I would like to hire your services, Mr. Tuttle," she began, but our eyes still had not disconnected.

"I'm yours. What is it that you need?" I somehow managed to mutter. Was my voice actually squeaking like that? Is my voice so utterly harsh sounding? Her voice sounded angelic.

"It is my niece, you see." I didn't see, but didn't say anything. "Miss Ari Glaston. Here, I have a picture of her." She produced another one of those 3X5 pictures from her purse. Now I noticed her nails, at least three inches long, painted to match her lips. Exquisitely. I barely glanced at the photo.

"She is a witch in her own right. She's twenty and engaged to be married in six months. She still lives with her parents, Herbert and Sandra Glaston. Their address is on the back of the photo, Mr. Tuttle."

"Parry, please, Miss. . ." Darn, I forgot even to ask her name! What an idiot I must seem!

"Miss Glasya Winterhaven. Okay then, Parry. I know she's in some kind of very big trouble. Nasty trouble. Her life is in grave danger, and I don't know who else to turn to," she batted her extremely long, thick, black eyelashes. I nearly melted in my seat!

"What—what kind of danger? How do you know? Have you been to the police?" I mumbled.

"The kind that results in death, Parry. It's my intuition. I've nothing concrete, just a horrible feeling. You can't take those to the police, now can you?" I must have shaken my head no because she continued. "I just know that she is in very bad trouble. She is precious to me, and I will do anything to protect her. I want you to follow her and find out what she is messed up with and protect her from any danger she might be in. Can you do that, Parry?"

"Of course," I think I said. I couldn't be sure of anything that I was saying.

"I could be all wrong and Ari is not in any trouble at all, but I'd rather be safe than sorry. I don't know if I could live with myself if I did nothing and she came to harm, Parry. You can understand that, can't you?"

"Absolutely, Glasya, absolutely!" I've a soft spot for women and children and don't ever want to see them come to any form of harm. Men, let them bash their brains out, but leave the women and children alone!

"So you will take my case, then?" she asked, smiling at me. That smile would have melted me if I had ever dared to say no!

"Of course, Glasya. I will take the case. I'll get right on it."

"Thank you. About your fee. Here's ten thousand in advance. Will that be sufficient to start with?"

Considering it was triple my usual fee, it would. I tried not to sound too shocked and surprised by the amount. She handed me an envelope with the cash in it. "Yes, it will more than cover my expenses. Here's my card. How do I contact you?" I didn't even bother to look at the money. For all I knew it could be an empty envelop, but I would still have accepted her case!

"I'll write it on the back of your card. I already have one of yours." I watched her pull out a pen from her purse, with immense grace and poise. I watched her fingers and nails as she wrote out her name and number on the back of the card I'd just handed her. Quit staring, I told myself, but that was utterly pointless.

As she handed me the card back, her nails touched my fingers, sending an electrifying feeling through them and down my spine! God, what a woman! She rose and I longed for her to stay, but could say nothing. "I will leave you to your work then, Parry. Good luck and do be careful." I watched her leaving my office, totally enthralled. I watched every wiggling motion of her beautifully well-defined hips as she teetered out on her tall spikes. Finally, I noticed her curve-fitting dress, a red satin that matched her lips and nails. Not sure how I could have not seen her dress before now. The last image I had of her was her black seamed nylons and heels as she disappeared when the door shut. I needed a cold, cold shower!

"Parry Oscar Tuttle, that was some woman!" I said to my walls. I sat there like a dumb log for several minutes, still smelling the lilac perfume that she'd worn. Finally, the scent gone, I looked inside the envelope. Ten grand. Next month's rent and then some. "Okay, best get to work on this one, Parry!"

I looked up the address on my well-worn city map. She was in Hazelwood, close to the Conservation area, just off the 270. While I could drive, if she was in some kind of trouble and since she was a witch, using a car to follow her would be pointless. No, I'd have to depend upon my trusty Staff of Power. I know—most schooled wizards know tons of spells, but I'm all self-taught. Okay, I don't know how to cast very many spells, but that's where the staff comes in. It has some fine spells that it can cast. In this case, I needed two of them, Invisibility and Fly. I'd planned to go invisible, fly to her home, stake it out, and then follow her as best I could. Of course, if she used a Teleport spell, I could be in big trouble trying to follow her.

That's were all my electronic gizmos come in handy. What I lack in spells, I make up for in fancy gadgets. I got out my electronic tracking bug and receiver. All I had to do was somehow put the bug on her. Then, if she teleported anywhere, I could follow her, using the GPS receiver. Of course, the range of the bug was only the greater St. Louis area, but then Glasya hadn't suggested that Ari was going out of the city. God, I hoped not!

Figuring that this might be a bad one, I took all of my protective devices, making sure that my blasting rod was in its side holster. I also strapped on my trusty 45, just in case of really serious trouble. Just as I was about to head out of the door, Oliver called. Darn, I'm now juggling two cases at the same time.

"Hi, Parry here. What's up Oliver?" I decided not to tell him about my recent client. Okay, I was a bit jealous of her.

"Found her. Jessica. Rather what's left of her. I need you to see this and tell me what you can." He sounded terribly grim, and I jotted down the address. It was on the Mississippi River bank, north of the rusting arch.

"On my way," I replied and hung up. This didn't sound at all promising. Since I was ready to Fly anyway, I decided to use my spell to get there. Besides, it always makes for an impressive show to Oliver and the other norms.

Yellow tape and a mass of cars surrounded the grassy bank along the river. This was a fairly deserted location. The medical examiner was already on the scene. I took one look at Jessica and made a hasty exit, vomiting up my lunch. Looking a bit pinkish and ignoring the other snide remarks from the cops, I returned to the scene. Oliver merely grimaced my way and said softly, "Really a bad one. Take a look."

Her body, rather what was left of it, looked like it had been through some kind of meat slicer. Giant slice marks raked her entire body. Some had cut open her belly and parts of her internal organs had the distinctive appearance of having been dined upon, raw. Evidently, the ME thought along the same lines. What was left of her clothes had been shredded, matching the vertical slices. "She was standing up or lying prone when the attack came," I said softly to Oliver, who dutifully wrote down what I was saying.

The ME looked up. "Animal?"

"Doubt it. What kind of animal could slice a person in five-foot sweeps? No animal on earth has that long a reach," I replied.

"Clean cuts, like a very sharp knife. Into bones. So extremely sharp. Lots of force. This rib has been cut clean in half on this stroke," the ME added, pointing to something that I didn't care to see. Heck, I never cared to see women or children cut up like this or harmed in any way. There was something sacrilegious in my book about harming the fairer sex and defenseless children.

The ME added, "Strange. Looks like a knife or dagger to

the heart too, out of place with the rest of her wounds. No defensive wounds either. Very strange. Prone is more likely from the blood pooling."

Oliver added, "Body dump. Hardly any blood around here." Well, that was plainly obvious, but I allowed Oliver to sound important. Heck, we all needed something to keep our sanity while looking at this horrific crime. I pitied the ME, though. He did this for a living. He asked, "Cause of death?"

"Can't tell for sure until I get her on my slab, but I would hazard that she was stabbed in her heart first. The slice and dice and devouring came post-mortem. Know more once I've finished the autopsy."

Oliver led me away from the others, out of hearing range. "Well?"

I knew that he wanted answers and answers fast! "Dark Arts. Ritual sacrifice. She was a virgin. Found some Sister Anne necklaces in her apartment."

"Ritual sacrifice? Virgins? What the heck is going on here, Parry?" he boomed, then lowered his voice.

"Someone has deliberately performed some Black Art ritual using her as a means to open a Gate to some other place. And not a good place, Oliver. Something came through that Gate too. It probably dined on the remains. I'll look into it today. Let you know what I come up with."

"So it's not a serial killer? Or can we expect more mutilated bodies?" Oliver asked what I sensed was uppermost in his mind. Would there be more? A few more like this one and the press would be all over it. He had to have some answers and soon.

"Probably," I replied, rather lamely. "I'll look into it right away." That satisfied him, but how could I look into it now? I remembered the gorgeous Glasya and my promise to protect her niece, Ari. If she was also a virgin, good god! She might well become victim number two. I had to act now. I activated my staff and flew off into the heart of St. Louis. I needed a beer or five, but stopped at Sal's, gulping down one beer to kill the acid remnants in my mouth. I needed a clear head on this one. I plunked down a buck and left without saying anything to old Sal. I know that's not like me, but my mind was on Ari. Okay, on Glasya.

I flew across the bustling city of millions, zeroing in on I-270, following it on out to Hazelwood. From the air, the Conservation area was pronounced. After some trouble, I finally found Ari's home. Now the question was: is she home or has she left? If Ari was gone, I could well be in big trouble. I dare not face her Aunt Glasya if something happened to Ari. I waited patiently. Okay, not so patiently.

Chapter 4—On the Trail

Around two in the afternoon, Ari stepped outside to feed their dog. I took the initiative. Invisible, I set down close to her and slipped my tracer bug into one of her pockets. Thank goodness, the dog was more interested in chowing down than barking over my presence. I took up a perch in a nearby tree, rather an uncomfortable position, and waited. I held my GPS receiver and watched the red light. If she left the house and if she still wore the same clothes, I was in luck. If not, well, I'd rather not go there.

Just after supper and at dusk, I was rewarded for my patience. I seem to have a lot of patience. The red light began blinking. She was on the move! I looked around and saw nothing, except lights were on in the house and in their basement. Stiff and sore from sitting in the tree, I again used my staff to cast my Fly spell and took off. It's a simple matter to follow the GPS location signal, accurate to within ten feet. While she probably simply Teleported to wherever she was going to, I took far longer, but flew quite accurately, as long as the bug was still on her person.

About an hour later, I finally arrived at her rough location, down south along the river in Marine Villa, just opposite Cahokia Mounds. For a moment, I wondered if there was any connection to that ancient Indian site, but quickly discarded that notion. No, something big and awful had torn Jessica to shreds and it wasn't a reincarnated Indian.

She was inside a rusted out, abandoned warehouse. Brown rust covered everything, making the site even more dismal. I landed and began looking around. I spotted lights coming from inside the structure and looked for a way inside. A door was ajar. Double-checking my invisibility and with my trusty staff in hand, I headed for the door.

As I neared it, I heard voices, both men and women. I hoped to heck that one of them wasn't Ari's! I held my breath. Don't know why. It's just something that happens when you stumble upon some clandestine activity that is likely to kill you. I pushed the door more open and looked inside. The warehouse was mostly empty, a rusting shell, long overdue to be torn down.

I spotted five older men and women wearing hooded robes standing in the center. I didn't put it together just then, but their bodies formed a pentagram. I saw a strange looking woman in the middle of the group. I didn't get much more observing done, though.

Invisibility is a good thing, but sometimes, it isn't good enough. This was one of those latter times! I also saw three monstrous winged creatures between me and the group—something like seven-foot tall flies, with insect-like four back legs and gigantic claws on hands at their fronts. Each had a foot-long, pointed beak, a gaping mouth, the ugliest, most gigantic fly-type eyes, and wings. Worse, they spotted me in spite of my best efforts to be completely invisible and silent! From their front claws, I knew at once, what had sliced and diced poor Jessica. Only now, I was about to join her, becoming supper for these demons!

Off to my right, I distinctly heard a woman's voice casting a spell. I did see the flash of magical energies, hoped, and prayed that it was Ari getting the heck out of here! Aunt Glaysa was more than right. Ari was in very big trouble! So was I just now.

The three fly-like demons flew towards me, making a hideous noise. From the corner of my eyes, I spotted the group of humans looking my way. Time for a hasty exit! I whirled, dashed for the door, and bolted outside.

Not soon enough. One of the demons caught my leg, and I went down hard onto the rough concrete. For a second, I saw stars, but I knew I had to act or Oliver and his ME would be looking down on what was left of me! I used one of the power spells in my staff, casting a giant ball of fire at the demons clawing at me, as I simultaneously wiggled free of its grip.

Hey, a ball of fire has never failed me before. Usually, things get incinerated quite nicely. Not this time. It had no effect except causing a bit of confusion. For a moment, the three demons lost track of me in the resulting smoke, giving me an instant to jump to my feet. I felt something wet along my lower right leg, but ignored it. You would too if you were facing three of these beasts.

Thank the stars! Two of the fly demons turned around and headed back inside. I guess after that ball of fire, they decided one of their kind was enough to finish me off. I didn't like the sound of that at all! I had no time to use my staff for another spell. The demon was almost on top of me. I wished that I was a quick draw.

You know, you've probably seen the ancient westerns where two gunfighters face each other. When the bell tolls noon, they draw and shoot. The fastest draw usually wins. Unfortunately, getting my trusty 45 out of its holster took too long. The demon pounded on me, all seven feet of it. God, it must have weighed a ton. For a second, I couldn't breathe. Then pain. I felt its front claws starting to slice and dice me. I was about to become another Jessica in short order!

Somehow, I got the pistol out. I didn't bother to aim it. Heck, with a giant seven-foot monster on top of you, eagerly slicing you to bits, you don't take time to aim. How can you miss? I fired. Actually, I emptied the gun faster than I'd ever fired it before. All six heavy slugs hit the beast.

It howled in pain. Good for it. I saw greenish ooze dripping onto the concrete, mixing with something red. My blood. Lying there, I finally spoke a command word and my staff activated, teleporting me to my office. My clothes were shredded. I was bleeding profusely from so many slices I couldn't count them. With a bloody hand, I grabbed my cell and punched speed dial 1, Oliver's number. I think I said, "Come quick. I'm dying." However, I don't really recall anything beyond punching the 1 button.

I came to in a hospital. A nurse was finishing wrapping bandages over me. An IV was pouring blood into me. Yes, there was Oliver standing patiently over me, waiting for his report.

Seeing me regaining consciousness, Oliver commented, "I take it that you found our culprits?"

"Is it that obvious?" I retorted. My body ached in more places than I knew even existed. But I had the good sense to say, "Thanks."

"Don't mention it. I had to save you so I can hear what you discovered, Parry," he grinned. "Seriously, you lost a lot of blood. Another fifteen minutes and you would have joined Jessica in the ME's office. So what happened to you? In case you are interested, we've had two more bodies appear, both men."

"How long have I been out?" I asked, trying to absorb what Oliver was saying.

"Four hours."

"Oh. Well, I found them. Warehouse. Abandoned. Down by Marine Villa, just across from Cahokia Mounds." I gave him a good description of the place. "Hey, if you go there, go armed to the teeth! I think I shot one of the nasty beasts."

"Okay. I'll check it out. You rest up. I'll want a full report when I get back," Oliver stated dryly. I knew that he would indeed want answers, but right now, I didn't have them. Not the full picture. Certainly, someone was using the Dark Arts and evil magic, but I wasn't too sure just what was going on, not yet. Did I dare tell him about Ari? Well, she did get out of there in time and was unharmed so far. I guess I did protect her after all. Hard way to earn my ten grand though. I need time to research what I'd seen, to make sense of what was going on, to identify just what type creatures we were up against. I had to get back to my place where my library is.

"Son, you aren't going anywhere just yet," the nurse gently pushed me back onto the bed. "You have to get the rest of this blood transfusion in you. Besides, you have two hundred stitches in you right now. Best not to move a muscle. That's a pain killer dispenser there. Press it, and it'll inject you with another dose."

Darn it. I was laid up and I knew it. Yet, if I was to be of any real use to Ari and to Oliver, I had to do some research and fast! I tried to sit up and found myself frantically pressing the button. Ah, relief. Whatever they were giving me for the pain was working. No, I was going to sleep! I remember thinking, not now, before I lost consciousness again.

I woke up around noon the next day. A nurse immediately began feeding me. I hurt too badly to do it myself, but at least they weren't giving me any more blood, and that pain killer device was gone. I guess they figured I didn't hurt any longer. Oliver came in just as the nurse finished. "Ah, awake at last. I had them call me when you woke," he said, pulling up a chair to sit close to my head.

"I'll go first," Oliver added, quite uncharacteristically. "We found the place. Took some samples of goo that we found out on the concrete. No body though or carcass. I was hoping that you would take a look at the site as soon as you can. The forensic boys left everything as they found it, though they had a field day taking samples. Don't have any reports back from them yet. The ME has confirmed that the two men were killed in a similar fashion as Jessica, except they weren't stabbed before slicing and dicing. They died from massive blood loss. That's about all I have. The warehouse has been abandoned for years. Are you ready to look at the site? Ready to give me your report? How did you find that place anyway? And what happened to you?"

"Help me up and get dressed. I'll go with you now. Have to see what's there before I make too many conclusions based on insufficient information, Oliver. You know me, got to be sure about these things." Did I dare tell him about Ari? How was she mixed up in all this? I decided not to mention her just yet. After all, she'd been there and seen what I had. At least, she had the good sense to get the heck out of there pronto. If she was smart, she'd stay well away from that place.

"I was following a tip. I snuck in there and saw a group of five hooded men and women. Another strange looking woman, I think, but I can't be sure yet, was standing in the middle of that group. There were three of these incredibly nasty demonic-like creatures there. They spotted me and came after me. I emptied my 45 into one and got away. Say, did you find my 45 there?"

"I see. Yes, we've recovered it. I have it in my car. So bullets harm these creatures?" he asked. I could tell that he was keenly interested in this fact. It meant that he and his boys and their big guns could take them out, if only they could find them again.

"I think so. I emptied my 45 into one. It reeled and was

58

definitely in pain. Otherwise, I'd be on the ME's slab with Jessica. I suggest you all carry really big guns when you go up against them. My 45 packs a wallop, but I think you're going to need an even bigger hit."

"But what the devil were those creatures? Where did they come from? Are they on the loose running around the city?" Oliver asked the key questions that he needed an immediate answer to, ones that I couldn't give him, as much as I would have liked to.

"Research. Not sure yet. If more bodies show up, then you know they are still around. If we are lucky, they have gone back to wherever they came from, at least for now. I suspect that they will be back though. Have to research. I'm not an encyclopedia, Oliver." He flashed me a smile and helped me get dressed.

My god, I had bandages everywhere! Well, except for one place that is. I ached all over. Even walking was painful, and Oliver kindly carried my heavy oak staff for me. An hour later, his SUV pulled up by the warehouse. I struggled to get out of the car, wishing it were lower to the ground. I used my staff to help me keep my balance as I ambled slowly into the warehouse.

By day, I could see how decrepit the place actually was. It should've been torn down ages ago. Once inside, I could see all manner of forensic markers littering the floor. Most, I ignored, heading to the center where the group had been standing. I cringed. My worst fears materialized. There on the floor was a pentagram incised within a circle. The Dark Arts! Someone had indeed opened a Gate here, summoning these vile creatures. But from where and why? Those questions were of paramount importance. "Well?" Oliver brought me out of my thoughts.

"Dark Arts. Someone performed the darkest of magic here and summoned those creatures here. No doubt about it, Oliver. I'm going to have to research this further to say more. We need to know the what and the why if we stand any chance of finding them. Besides, now that we've found this place, they won't be using it again. Not unless they're idiots. They can't be that and still have done all this. Sorry. I have to do some research."

"Okay. I'll drop you off at your home on the way back. Just do it fast. I don't want more bodies piling up. Three are two too many. Heck, one's too many," Oliver added. I could only agree with him.

A little while later, I limped into my basement apartment. I live in the basement because it is cheap and solid. Hence, my protection spells hold up better, what few I can cast. I live alone, a true bachelor's pad. Messes lay everywhere, but I headed to the fridge and got out a dark ale and popped the top. I had half of it downed before I headed to my sofa. I felt drained, exhausted, starved. Every bone in my body seemed to ache at the same time. Somewhere in my pocket, there was a prescription for a heavy-duty painkiller, which I didn't bother filling just yet. I needed a clear head to think. I was supposed to be protecting Ari. Just because she saw those creatures didn't mean that she would give up whatever she was doing. Was she somehow involved in this Dark Arts mess? God, I hoped not.

I had a notion to call up Aunt Glasya and tell her to take Ari out of the city immediately—heck, take her out of the state! Unfortunately, her card was back on my office desk, and I was in no state to go retrieve it. I just wanted to lie on my sofa for a time. I guess drinking a beer isn't such a good idea after you've suffered such massive injuries as I had. I fell asleep on my couch.

It was mid-morning when I woke, stiff, sore, and starving. Finally, my brain got the right idea: food! I somehow managed to get my body up and into the kitchen. Thank god for TV dinners. I popped one into the microwave and a few minutes later dove into it. Then, I cooked up a second one, before I finally felt full at last. A bit later, I smelled heaven: my coffee was brewing!

Careful not to spill my mug, I slowly navigated into my study, where I keep all my precious magic books. They filled one whole shelf. I still ached all over and was limping badly, but I managed not to spill my coffee. Sitting it on my table, I went to my books. Books contain knowledge, vitally so in this case. However, I wasn't certain what I was looking for, not precisely.

My head throbbed. I didn't feel like reading, so I decided to try to identify the creatures that had attacked me. I could look at sketches without eyestrain. I flipped through <u>The Creatures of the Dark Arts</u>, by Professor Tomlinson. It was my best bet on identifying them. I looked at one ugly creature after another, wondering how in the world anyone could dream up such terrible looking monsters. Well, people are certainly inventive. Just look at all the Grade D movies that have been made through the centuries.

An hour later, I found them. Chasma. They were minor demons from the Abyss! Nasty buggers. They were obviously evil, through and through, but wholly unpredictable. As I strained my eyes to read about them, I discovered what I had already had found out the hard way. They had a hefty resistance to magical spells. That explained why my ball of fire did nothing but obscure their vision of me for a few seconds. "Heck!" I said rather emphatically. This meant that I wasn't going to be able to kill them with my staff or spells. Even my trusty 45 barely slowed one down. It probably didn't even kill it, firing at point blank range. "I need a bigger gun!"

I read on and discovered that I was one mighty lucky wizard! The Chasma can make a sort of rasping noise with their voices. Had they done that, I would very likely have fallen into a comatose sleep. After which I'd become their dinner or, assuming they weren't hungry at the moment, merely sleep for a third of a day. The only positive thing was that their spell casting was rather limited. Cause Fear was their most offensive spell. Well I was scared of them when I just looked at them. They didn't need a spell for that!

Seriously, what's going to take one of them down? I need to know that to relay to Oliver. I made my best guess and speed dialed Oliver. "Hi. Yeh, doing some research. They have a name: Chasma. They are definitely demons from the Abyss. Very nasty flies. I think you're going to need to put about seven fifty-caliber shots into them to take one down. I said big guns and I meant it." I heard a curse on the other end of the connection. I know, those are big guns.

"Okay, okay. But what about who is behind this? And

why?" Oliver asked.

"Sorry, I haven't worked that out yet. Need more time. I hope to heck we have the time, though. I'll get on it, okay?"

"Yes, right. Thanks. You are earning your pay on this one," Oliver managed to tease me. I growled and hung up on him.

I headed to the bathroom. Slowly. I took off the hospital clothes that they'd sent me home wearing, as mine were shredded. Besides, Oliver sent them to the forensic boys. Bet they got a kick out of sampling my blood. I stared at what had been by body. I had bandages covering most of my legs, torso, and some on my arms as well. Luckily, they missed my chest or I probably would still be in the hospital. Still, I looked like crap and felt that way too. Carefully, I got dressed in my loosest fitting shirt and pants, scrounging for a new pair of sneakers that wouldn't hurt the bandages on my feet where the Chasma had grabbed me.

Back at my sofa, I sat down, nearly exhausted from the effort just to get dressed. I had to get to work. Ari was out there, and perhaps didn't fully realize the extreme danger she was in, and I was being paid to protect her. Somehow, I had to find out who was behind the pentagram, who was doing the summoning, and why. Somehow, I had to stop them. I was assuming that poor Jessica had been killed by one of these demons, but why? Someone was responsible for kidnaping her and getting her killed, probably as a sacrifice. I had work to do, but I could just barely move! Darn it!

Help. I knew that I needed help. I'm not too proud to admit that, at times, I need some assistance. This was one of them. I was in way over my head. You can't go out and buy fifty-caliber guns at your local store. Besides, they are heavy. I needed all my senses right now, but my body was barely functioning. I'd been hurt before and knew as bad as I was cut up, it would be weeks before I was back to battery. I didn't have weeks. Heck, there could be dozens of bodies piled up long before then. But physically, I was in no shape to do much of anything. I had to get some help. No doubt about that, yet who?

As I sat on my couch thinking this over, I recalled

having seen a recent ad. A new store had opened up fairly recently, catering to us magic users. What was it called? I couldn't remember. My mind wasn't firing on all cylinders at the moment. I rose and headed for my computer. A few minutes later, I found the ad and their website: Protections, Investigations, Wands, Items, and Potions. Well, I certainly could use some healing potions. I hated to part with some of the hard-earned ten grand, but I wasn't good for anything unless I did so. I just hoped they didn't charge a lot. I jotted down their address and headed out to find my trusty old Ford.

After transferring their address into my navigator, I decided to trust to the automation. I hurt too darn much to try actually driving the car. I pressed the automatic guidance system and hit activate. They were way up north of the city, and I sat back and relaxed. With the heavy traffic, it would easily take a half hour to get there.

Chapter 5—A Little Help

Around two in the afternoon, my Ford pulled into the circle before their store. It looked like an old convent or something. Still, it was picturesque. A large sign said PIWIP and below it was their full name: Protections, Investigations, Wands, Items, and Potions. I very gingerly got out of the car and walked up to the front door. Inside, I found a large waiting area with nice soft chairs.

I did notice that some spell activated when I entered, probably alerting the owners that they had a customer. I presumed correctly. Shortly, a very elegantly dressed woman wearing the tallest stilettos that I'd seen came slowly over to me. She was dressed in a red satin gown that fit her curves rather beautifully. She looked as though she was about to head out to some formal affair. Her black hair was rather long, reaching the small of her back. Her eyes were green and sparkling, though I admit I was drawn to her well-endowed bosom and very long fingernails, painted the same shade as her red lips. For a moment, I thought that she was Aunt Glasya, but no woman can compare to that beauty.

"Hello. Welcome to Protections, Investigations, Wands, Items, and Potions. I'm Monica Nicole Black. How can we help you?" she said in a very business-like tone.

"I need some help, but I don't know exactly how much I can afford. Do you have healing potions for sale, perhaps? That's my biggest problem at the moment."

"Absolutely. Come this way, Mr.?" she paused enough to indicate that I ought to introduce myself. She'd already done that for herself.

"Parry Oscar Tuttle, Private Investigator, Miss Black. Sorry if I'm keeping you from something important. You seem dressed for a formal affair. I can come back later, if you prefer." Heck, here I was keeping this well-dressed woman from some probably critical meeting.

"Oh, no. I always dress like this. Do you approve of my appearance, Mr. Tuttle?" she replied demurely.

"Well, sure. You look, well stunning," I answered, hoping I wasn't drooling again. She walked very slowly in those heels, but that was perfect for me. I was barely able to keep up with her. We passed by a shop that had some wands on display. To my right were two workrooms. From their signs, I could see this was where they made the wands and the potions. At the very end of the hall was the shop with the Potions sign.

Just as we entered the shop, a shy, relatively short young woman came dashing out of the potion making room and into her shop. "Hi there. Just making potions. I'm Enya. Oh! You're hurt." She suddenly noticed how I was moving. "Please have a seat." I took the first chair I spotted. It was nicely padded, just like those in the entranceway.

"Yes, I'm in need of some healing potions, but I don't know how much they cost or how many I need or can afford, for that matter."

"Well, you are in luck. We are just getting started with our new business. So we are not charging the going rates just yet. Monica Nicole thinks that we'll stimulate more business this way. Normally, one goes for around four hundred dollars, but for you, how does one hundred sound?" Enya asked politely. She had short brown hair and wore a simple dress, quite unlike Monica Nicole.

"Sounds great to me. I'll take at least one. Not sure how many I need though."

"We should have a look at your wounds," Monica Nicole suggested. "That way, we can best judge your needs." I think I flushed, because she added, "That bad. Well, don't be shy. Let's have a look, professionally."

"It's pretty bad." I very carefully took off my shirt and pants. I know, I felt funny undressing before the two. Perhaps it would not have been so bad if Monica hadn't been there looking all dolled up for a party or something. I could relate to Enya.

"Oh dear god! What happened to you?" Monica Nicole exclaimed.

"This is really a bad one," Enya gasped. "There are stitches everywhere!"

"Tell me about it. I had a run in with a demon. A Chasma to be exact, but I suspect you don't know what I'm talking about."

"No sir. I am afraid I don't. Let me see what I can do for you," Enya replied, walking over to her shelves.

"I'll leave you in her capable hands," Monica Nicole added, leaving hastily via a spell that created a magical door. I'd read about them in one of my magic books. I looked at the layout of Enya's store. She had hundreds of small vials, test tubes really, all lined up neatly on racks, rather like a bunch of wine bottles only drastically smaller. She returned with one.

"Here, drink this first." I did so. It had a sort of mint taste to it. "It should start working about now." I noticed that she had been counting down on her fingers. Suddenly, I felt good. Then the itching associated with healing began. In my case, half of the front side of my body itched all at the same time. "Try not to itch just yet." I grimaced and did so, but I'm not sure how I managed that.

After a few minutes, she said, "Okay, the stitches should come out now. Then, we can finish the healing process. Probably need another two. I can take them out for you, if you wish."

"Sure go ahead. Sorry to be this much trouble, Miss Enya."

"Mrs. I recently got married. My husband is also a potion maker. We're having a ball making all kinds of potions. Honestly, I can't think of anything better to do. Sit back. This is going to take some time. Golly, there are so many stitches."

"I know. At least, I was out when they stitched me up. Had to get a blood transfusion as well, but I barely remember that part. Nasty business." We chatted and I resisted the tickling sensations as best I could. It took her a half hour to get them all out. Then, I drank another two of the potions.

Another half hour later, I was amazed. Only if you looked really close could you see any scars. "Amazing, Enya. Thank you. That was three hundred well spent dollars." She giggled.

As if on cue, Monica Nicole returned just as I finished getting dressed. "Ah, Mr. Tuttle, if you will follow me, we can see about additional protections. I'm afraid that you're going to need them."

"Yes, but can I afford them? That's the real question," I countered somewhat seriously.

As we walked all the way back down the long hall on past the entrance area, I found myself having to work to keep from going faster than she could walk in those tall heels. I guess that comes from just being fully healed up. We entered what I would call a library. Two walls were filled from floor to ceiling with books. I recognized several. I had copies of the Grade Spells myself, though I'd only been able to learn a handful here and there.

Another young woman was present, and I did a double take. She wore an elegant blue satin gown, but what struck me at once was her bosom. While Monica Nicole was well-endowed, this woman was massively endowed! She had very long black hair with the cutest bangs over her forehead. Her hazel eyes missed nothing. However, she wore more sensible patent leather pumps, at least an inch shorter than those worn by Monica Nicole. She too looked dressed for some fancy party. "This is Crystal. Ericka will be joining us shortly."

I heard more high heel clicks and turned to see Ericka arriving. She was a knock-out blonde, just as massively well-endowed as Crystal. She wore similar heels and a sky blue satin gown. I swear these three were ready for a party or something. However, both Crystal and Ericka were extremely pretty and could be models, I thought. Further, all four women had to be in their late teens.

As if reading my thoughts, Monica Nicole said, "True, we five have recently graduated from the St. Louis School of Magic, but don't let our youth fool you. We know what we are doing, Mr. Tuttle. I presume that you went there too?"

I flushed. I was in the presence of three real witches. "Er, well no. I'm self-taught. I couldn't afford to go to school. My uncle taught me some spells and such while I was growing up. I've a Staff of Power that I depend on and a Blasting Rod."

"I see. How interesting," Crystal replied. "Please, have a seat Mr. Tuttle. We'd like to know more about what happened to you. Is this the demon creature that attacked you?" She had the same volume open that I had back at my place.

"Right. I identified it before I came here. There were three of them. I was invisible but they saw me anyway and right away too. I tried to slow them down with a ball of fire from my staff, but it had no effect on them. According to the book, they have some kind of resistance to magic. Hindsight is just perfect. So I shot one with my 45."

"How very interesting, Mr. Tuttle," Crystal said once more. The three took seats across from me. "Please, would you tell us what happened, in detail, I mean. It is not every day that we have demons from the Abyss wandering around St. Louis."

"Well, I can some. You see, I'm a private investigator," I handed them one of my cards. Parry Oscar Tuttle, Private Investigator. It had my phone and office location below that. Rather plain business cards, really, but cheap. A picture on them would have cost me more. One day I think I will add a picture too.

I told them about what had happened at the warehouse and how Oliver had come to my rescue. Purposely, I didn't say why I had gone there, nor did I mention Ari's involvement nor her aunt. They were still my clients. "So yes, I occasionally do some work for the FBI. My ID." I flashed them my consultant's badge, hoping to impress these teens. It didn't work though.

"You were very lucky, Mr. Tuttle," Crystal commented.

"True. But others haven't been. It's not on the news just yet, but there have been three other victims. I got into this case because of the first woman who was kidnaped." I went ahead and told them about Jessica and the two men that Oliver had found.

Ericka then said, "Well, you should've had more protections on yourself before you went in there. Skin of Stone would have prevented all of your injuries. Did you think of trying a Disintegrate beam? There is always some chance it will get through its resistance and kill it."

"Er, sorry. I don't know how to cast those spells. They aren't in my Staff of Power either." I sheepishly admitted my shortcomings. How could I not? These were rather beautiful teens across from me, and they were actually interested in me, not like some wizards that I've come across.

"Just what kind of a wand do you use?" asked a fourth woman who just entered. She was also short and had blonde hair, short but fluffed up. She wore an apron and was probably working on something before she stepped into join us. "Oh, I'm Misty. I heard what was going on. You are lucky to be alive, Mr. Tuttle."

"Please, ladies. Just Parry. I know I am. Lucky me. Only needed two hundred stitches. Seriously, I don't have a wand. I never could get the hang of all those fancy motions. Either I can just cast a spell or I use my Staff of Power or get down and dirty with my Blasting Rod. Say, do you have a way to recharge a Blasting Rod?" I had been meaning to research this detail a bit but just hadn't gotten around to it yet. Besides, it would likely cost money that I didn't have. I might have, if I wasn't spending my ten grand.

"Oh, you must be really lucky, Parry," Misty replied, taking a seat across from me.

Crystal then spoke up, "So have you and your FBI friend contacted the Department of Magical Misuse yet? Gating in demons from the Abyss and then allowing them to kill or harm others is a serious crime."

"Er no. Not yet. We don't know who is behind this or why they are doing it or even what they are trying to accomplish. It's probably premature. However, I assure you ladies, that as soon as we know for sure, we'll bring them in. Honestly, I vomited when I saw poor Jessica's body. It was just awful."

"Okay then, Parry. Could we possibly have a look at the crime scene? We'd like to verify the designs on the floor. It's important," Monica Nicole asked.

"Sure. I have my car out front. My ID badge will get us in there; only don't touch anything. Forensics may well want to do further analysis on the site."

"Good. By the way, Parry, do you know that giving out your full name can well get you into trouble? If someone knows your full name and how it's pronounced precisely, they can cast a Summons spell and force you to do their bidding," Crystal pointed out.

"I wasn't born yesterday, Crystal. I've a fourth name that I keep secret. I read all about that in some of my magic books. Mind you, I've no idea how those spells are cast, though."

"Excellent, Parry, excellent. You had me worried there for a moment. We too do not divulge all our names," Crystal added.

"But Monica Nicole Black. You must have a forth name like I do then."

She smiled, "Nope, I don't. Don't worry about me."

"Right. Let's take a quick trip to the crime scene, before we go any further with this," Crystal took charge again. "Lots of quacks draw pentagrams and circles. It could well be nothing at all. Come on. We'll teleport there and back, Parry. Just tell us the precise location, and we'll do the rest. Oh, Monica Nicole, let Enya know we are going for a bit and to watch the store."

I saw a bit of magic flash and figured that she'd sent a Message spell. I could do that spell, which is probably why I figured out what she'd just done. Anyway, I had them find me a city map and then pointed to the exact location of the abandoned warehouse.

"Okay, Parry. Have you ever teleported before?" Crystal asked.

"Er, well, yes. My Staff of Power does it for me, but not very often. I think it's kind of risky, isn't it?"

"Certainly, it can be, especially if you arrive too high and begin falling," Ericka replied.

"I don't worry too much about that. My staff allows me to fly."

She smiled and looked relieved. Strange. These women appeared to care about my welfare somewhat, wholly unlike most other wizards. Actually, as soon as other witches and wizards discovered that I was self-taught, they wanted nothing to do with me. Snobs.

I also must admit that taking a hold of their warm hands was a rather exciting experience. After all, two of them could well be models. Okay, later I learned that Crystal and Ericka had been teen fashion models. Monica Nicole did the actual casting, waving her wand in a very precise fashion. The next thing I knew we were all falling down to the ground, very gently, and from about twenty feet up. They must have cast another spell on me. One cop car was still present along with a mile of yellow "Do not cross" tape.

Arm in arm, we walked up to the bored policeman, who suddenly got very non-bored. I caught him staring at the three elegantly dressed women and their large endowments. I smiled and flashed my FBI badge. "We need to take a peek at the crime scene. Won't be a minute." Amazing what the right badge will get you. We all walked on inside, and I led them to the central area where the inscribed pentagram was still very visible on the concrete floor.

"Crummy place," Ericka commented.

I couldn't disagree with that. "Should have torn this place down years ago. There it is. So is it a real one or a fake?"

All four began casting several spells. I only recognized one, which I think was a See True spell or something like that. I will say this though: these four were very thorough in what they did. Monica Nicole finally spoke. "Yes, this was a working Gate to the Abyss. It's been used three times now. We've seen enough. We should get back to the shops now."

While they could have teleported us from the inside of the warehouse, I wanted to let the policeman know that we were leaving. Politeness counts in my line of work. If nothing else, he appreciated seeing these women again, if only briefly. A few minutes later, we were back in their library.

I was impressed with the sheer number of books on magic that they had. "Great collection. I've around fifty myself—all that I've been able to afford."

Monica Nicole smiled at me and said, "Knowledge is power, Parry." I couldn't disagree with her on that point.

Crystal took charge once more. "Okay. We know it is a working gate to the Abyss. Parry, let's continue looking at sketches and see if you can identify the other thing that was in the center of the five men and women—that is, the focus of their Gate spell."

"I'm sorry. I just haven't had time to look for her—at least it looked sort of like a woman."

71

Crystal began leafing through her thick volume, occasionally stopping to show me another sketch. A half hour passed before I spotted it. "There, that's what she looked like. Ah, a succubus! Nasty."

Crystal sighed, "That's what I was afraid of, Parry. This isn't any ordinary Gate that's been constructed. This one is calling forth very specific demons. I need to do some further research on this situation. Meantime, you need much better protection, Parry, if you are going to continue your investigation."

"True. But I really don't have much money. Kind of go month to month, just barely making it."

"Well, you've come to the right place," Ericka spoke up. "I've just the ring for you. It stores three spells, but I'll put in three uses of the Skin of Stone spell for you."

"Sorry, it probably costs more than I had." I dearly wanted just such a ring. Maybe the next time that I met these demons, I'd not be shredded, but the cost would be so far beyond my means that it wasn't funny.

"I know that, but we can't send you out fighting demons without some protections. Here's what I'll do for you. You put say a hundred dollars deposit down on the ring. Whenever it needs recharging bring it back to me. When you are finished with it, return it to me, and I'll give you your money back. How's that sound?"

"Well, I can't say that I don't need it, because I surely do. I don't want charity either. What say you keep the hundred when I return it? That way, you've made some money off of your ring."

Ericka flashed me one of those killer smiles. I would have melted if I was butter. "Deal, Parry. I'll go get it for you." I handed her another Ben Franklin. My rent money was rapidly vanishing, and I'd only just gotten it. Not every day I get a client who hands me ten grand.

A half hour later, I left with a new golden ring on my ring finger, but I was fully healed and more importantly, I was protected if I ran into more of those clawing demons. I was also starving again and dropped by the Golden Arches for a burger and fries. Worrying about cholesterol didn't match up with these demons and their claws. By the time that I got back to my apartment, it was getting dusk. Equal days and nights had come again. Fall was here, but the leaves hadn't started turning yet.

I made a quick call to Oliver to see if there had been any further developments. I didn't expect there to be, not in the daylight hours. These conjurers would certainly not be working this magic in the light of day. No, darkness hid all. That meant that Ari might well be in danger once more. I checked my bug. Its battery had died. Besides, she probably changed her dress. The question was: is Ari home or has she gone off in search of these Dark Arts wizards and witches? I honestly had no way of knowing.

Chapter 6—Round Two

Crystal had said that I had a whole lot of luck. That's not how I look at things. I have hunches. Gut feelings. I act on them. They've been phenomenally accurate. If you call that luck, then I am filled with luck. I used my Invisibility spell from my staff and flew on over to Ari's folks' home. I waited a little while before I had a strong hunch that she wasn't here.

Of course, she was an adult and twenty. She could have gone anywhere. To the grocery store, to the beauty parlor, bowling, a movie with her fiancé, anywhere. All those would have been vastly safer for her. Why did I think she wasn't off seeing the latest movie? Would you, if you'd seen Chasme demons from the Abyss? No, I figured that if she had a good reason to go spy on them the other night, then she'd have just as good a reason to go tonight. The question was where?

If these five were smart, they would have known that the FBI was all over their warehouse site. Their location had been completely compromised. Little did they count on me bringing the FBI down on them! So would they go back and reuse their circle and pentagram once more? Ignoring the cops and the yellow crime scene tape? Would Oliver have a flotilla of armed men there waiting in case they showed up? I certainly wouldn't go back there, but then I also wouldn't be opening up a Gate into the Abyss either.

Where was my client? That seemed to me the biggest question right now. What did she know about all this? In fact, how had she discovered these five hooded figures? What was her angle? If they moved their location, was Ari onto it? Was she perhaps there spying on them now? Getting herself sliced and diced? Darn it. I couldn't stop thinking of her Aunt Glasya.

Okay, I couldn't stop thinking of that woman, the most perfect example of womanhood that I'd ever seen. Aunt Glasya could well be the top super-model. She had the looks, no doubt of that! But what about Ari? Where was she?

I had no choice but to rely on my gut hunch. I only knew one location: the abandoned warehouse. Best go check it out. Just then, the dark thunderheads rumbled, and the sky began dumping water by the bucket-fulls. I put on my jacket and then a raincoat. After double-checking my 45, I picked up my staff and headed out into the fall storm.

Flying through a downpour with lightning streaking all around me was not the brightest idea that I'd ever had. I tried to stay as low to the ground as possible, hoping the building lightning rods would stand between me and the sky bolts. At times, I was so drenched that I couldn't see where I was flying and prayed that I wouldn't run smack into the side of a building.

Finally, I spotted the old warehouse and came in for a landing quite distant from it, back at the end of the parking lot. Between flashes of lightning, I could see the yellow crime scene tape was still in place. One squad car was parked there. I imagined the officer was sitting inside, sipping a hot cup of coffee, while I was shivering and soaking wet. I had half a notion to join him, but didn't. No, my job was to observe. Had the five returned? Was Ari here invisible and watching too?

I glanced around the lot, using the intermittent lightning bolts as my flashlight. Then, I spotted someone. Hey, invisibility isn't all that it's cracked up to be. I saw rainfall outlining a human shape not far from where I stood. My gut told me it was Ari. I took a chance and moved very slowly over to the form, keeping my eyes on the darkened warehouse and the obstructed rainfall. "Ari, I presume. Can we talk?" I whispered.

"Who's there?" a woman's voice whispered back.

"Me, Parry. We ran into each other here the other night, spying on the five hooded figures and the demons."

"So it's you again. I thought you were dead."

"Quite alive. Takes more than a pesky demon to take me down." Okay, so I boasted a little bit. Makes a good impression. I hoped so anyway.

"Honestly, I thought you were dead. I saw the demon cutting you up pretty badly. You all right?" she whispered back. I detected real concern in her tone. My gut told me that she was being sincere, but maybe that's what I wanted to think about my client.

"Hey, whoever these guys are, they aren't coming here tonight. The cops are watching it. I'm freezing. What say we go fly somewhere and grab a hot cup of coffee and talk a bit?" God, I hope she accepts. I'm shivering so hard I can't stand up!

"Okay. Starbucks? Fly? Can't you teleport?" she whispered music in my ears.

"No. Star-b-b-ucks it is." Darn, my teeth are chattering.

"Oh here. I'll teleport us." She sounded annoyed, but I felt her hand feeling for mine. I canceled my invisibility and the next thing I knew, we were standing outside a Starbucks. I opened the door for her, and we went inside. I was shivering so badly, that she had to place our orders.

I headed back to the warmest corner of the room, hogged the hot spot, and waited. Soon she came back my way, carrying two hot brews. She looked just like her photo, but had her poncho pulled back now. Her face was dripping water, but otherwise she was dry. I finally remembered one of my useful spells. Warm. Warm. Warm. I rather overdid it. Steam rose from my soaked pants, bringing a smile to her face as she sat the coffee in front of me. "Thanks."

"So what are you doing following me?" Ari got right to the point.

How do I answer that one? While I could concoct a story with the best of them, I decided to play it straight with her. "Ari, you are my client. I've promised to protect you. That's why I came to the warehouse that night."

Her face twisted up. Then, she said slowly, "Well, okay. I suppose I should thank you for that. The demons spotted me too, but I was too quick for them. My teleport. I assumed that you could teleport to safety too. Sorry. So why am I your client? Who are you anyway?"

I handed her a slightly soggy business card. "Parry Oscar Tuttle, Private Investigator. Your Aunt Glasya hired me to protect you. You've got a very concerned aunt."

Now her face really did twist. "I don't have any Aunt Glasya. You must be mistaken, Parry."

"No, she came to my office and paid me ten grand to make sure you are safe. Gave me this photo of you so that I'd recognize you. Gave me your parent's address on the back of it.

See?" I showed her the slightly damp picture. It was of her, a recent one I estimated from her appearance.

"Well, that's my graduation picture all right. But Parry, I don't have any such aunt. Did my dad hire you?"

"No. She claimed to be your aunt. She was incredibly beautiful. The super-model type, a real knock-out." I hastily described her to Ari.

"Sorry, Parry. I've never seen anyone like you are describing. My aunts are all quite old and don't get around much these days. They are in their late sixties, and their health is none too good. I wonder if dad hired someone to do this for him. Well, I'll ask him when I get back."

"Okay. Still, I took her money to protect you, so I aim to fulfill my obligation. So how did you know that these five hooded figures were in that warehouse anyway? What are you trying to do? Spy on them? What's your story?"

She bit her lip before replying. "Sorry, Parry. I can't tell you that. But yes, I was trying to see what they were up to. They were Gating in demons from the Abyss. That's what dad told me when I described what I saw that night. I don't dare tell you more than that."

"Well, if you go off spying on them again, can you let me know? I aim to protect you somehow."

She didn't agree or disagree with that, but merely sipped her coffee. I said, "Okay, you've got my card. I'll leave it up to you at least to give me a call before you try spying on them again. Those are five very nasty people who wouldn't hesitate to kill you, Ari. They are doing serious magic, the Dark Arts. Eventually, the Department of Magical Misuse will corral them and put them behind bars where they belong. Their work has already killed three innocent people." I hope putting a little fear into her mind might help persuade her to let me in on her next spy trip. It was worth a try. After all, Ari was barely twenty, had a fiancé, and her whole life to look forward to.

"Well, I best be getting back, Parry. Thanks for the coffee." I handed her a five to cover the cost. She did flash me a smile before she turned and vanished. Her wand made a sharp motion, and I heard her say "Teleport" but couldn't hear the rest. Magical energies flashed, and she was gone.

I finished my coffee and headed back out into the deluge, flying back home, hoping to avoid being struck by lightning. Once there, I took a long, very hot bath before turning in. I needed sleep badly. Plus, I had far too many unanswered questions now. What started out complex had become an incredible ball of complexities. I needed to think and find some answers and soon.

The next morning, I got another call from Oliver. This time, I remembered to bring along some pink stuff for my stomach and a bottle of water. Wise of me. See, I learn from my mistakes. I flew over to the St. Louis Zoo this time, wondering if his 'We got three more bodies' meant that the demons sliced and diced some elephants or lions. Perhaps, they had given the fly demons a taste of their own viciousness. No such luck, but at least I made my impressive arrival, swooping down like some giant pterodactyl. Er, okay a tiny one at least. Then, I promptly made a fool of myself.

I up chucked near the first body. A man, what was left of him, lay in numerous pieces scattered over a ten-foot area. The ME was already finishing his cursory examination of the body and his aides were placing the pieces in a black body bag. Quickly, I downed the pink stuff and opened my water bottle. See. I got wise. I ventured a question of the ME, who recognized me from the previous encounters. "So, was he stabbed in his heart, perhaps before this happened to him?"

He looked up at me over his half-glasses. "Nope." He moved on over to the next body, a woman. I saw that all three had been dumped on this grassy area, more or less at random spots, though I don't think that point was at all relevant. Even I could tell this was just a dump site. I did pay attention, but the ME didn't think that any of these had been sacrificed before being slaughtered.

Oliver took me aside. "Well? Any news?" I shook my head. "This settles it. One more of these and I have to call in the Department of Magical Misuse. This is getting way out of hand."

I could only agree, though I thought it was way out of hand back when we found poor Jessica. "I'm on it, boss. I will try to have more for you today." I know. He wanted to hear something like this, and I know that I had no idea how I was going to come up with something concrete, but I darn well was going to try. These three and the others deserved it. I also knew the heavy rains last night would have wiped out all potential forensics here at this spot.

Yet, I had one key piece of useless information this morning that I had not had last night. Namely, the five hooded figures had built and used another incised pentagram. Lord knows where it was located, but they hadn't used the one in the abandoned warehouse. I was darn certain of that. Still, on my way back to my apartment, I did stop and check the warehouse out. There were no signs that it had been reused. The site was undisturbed. I rightly concluded that they'd gone ahead and built another one. Somehow, someway, I had to find it today. I had a sick feeling this slaughter of innocent people wasn't going to stop.

I'd just gotten back to my apartment, when my cell vibrated. I'd forgotten to turn up the ringer after turning it down when I went out in the storm last night. I didn't recognize the number. "Hello, Parry here."

"Ah, Mr. Tuttle. Monica Nicole Brown here. Can you drop by our shop? Today. It's very important." Ah, I recognized her voice. After agreeing to head up to their place right now, I added her phone number to my contacts list; then fired up the old Ford. Traffic was lighter mid-morning, and I got there in twenty-five minutes. A gardener was cleaning out the driveway-encircled flowerbed as I pulled up. He didn't pay any attention to me, and I walked in.

Right on cue, Monica Nicole appeared ahead of me. I suspect they've some kind of alert spell on their long driveway entrance. In those heels, she needed some time to get to this front entrance. Still, she looked like she was ready to go to a very formal affair. Today, her satin gown was a lighter shade of red, which went well with her black hair, but there was something different about her appearance. Ah, the earrings. Who said that I'm not an observant fellow, only interested in one thing? Well, I am interested in that, mind you, but this was business.

Her earrings were huge and probably heavy, from the

way that her ear lobes were pulled down. Gold and large gems dangled down, touching the skin of her shoulders. "Striking earrings," I complimented her as I got to her side.

She smiled, showing me plenty of pure white teeth surrounded by her light red lips. "Magically enchanted. Ericka's latest. We all have them now. Extra protections. This way, Mr. Tuttle."

"Cool. Parry please."

"Parry, it is then. Since we last chatted, we have been doing some research of our own. But tell me, have there been any more of these demon attacks?" she asked pointedly.

I suspected she already knew the answer to that one, but I verified it for her. "Yes. Last night in the storm. Three more. Dropped off at the zoo. Grim. No sacrifices though, just murders." Me? I thought that must be significant somehow.

We joined Crystal and Ericka, who also wore similar large earrings. I related what I'd seen this morning. "They've got another incised pentagram somewhere. I was at the original site last night. Plus I checked it out just before you called me, Monica Nicole. Site is undisturbed."

Crystal sighed. "I suspected as much. They won't go near the old pentagram. It's been despoiled and would have to be rebuilt anyway, if it was to be reused."

"That's what I thought. What I find hopeful is that there haven't been any more virgin sacrifices since that first one, Jessica." I decided to pump them for a little more info. After all, I really did have to have something to report to Oliver. "Plus, if one more body turns up sliced and diced, the FBI will be calling in the Missouri Department of Magical Misuse."

"Well, they should," Crystal declared. "Yes, Parry. The virgin sacrifice is quite illuminating. We've been doing our homework too. We also don't want demons from the Abyss running around our city either. This virgin sacrifice is critical, I believe. According to the lore, only the sacrifice of a true virgin will allow an incised pentagram Gate spell to summon a Demon Lord or his messenger. Well, of course, using that lord's true name would also work, but knowing those names is rarer than an oak tree growing at the North Pole."

I swallowed hard. My voice squeaked, "A Demon Lord?"

None of the three smiled. Crystal replied grimly, "Right Parry. The question is: why would some wizards and witches wish to summon one of the ungodly powerful Demon Lords to St. Louis?"

"Dunno, but it can't be good." I know. I sounded terribly lame.

"No, it can't, Parry," Crystal continued quite seriously. "This is a very serious situation. We've not yet seen the real impact of it yet. We're sure of it."

"Well, it only is getting stranger." I decided now was the time to tell them about my client, Ari, and her aunt. It felt right. As I said before, I always go with my hunches, and it felt right. "You wanted to know how I found that original abandoned warehouse. Okay, I was hired to protect a young woman, Ari Glaston." I related the whole story beginning with the visit of her supposed Aunt Glasya, that is, Miss Glasya Winterhaven.

"So last night during the thunderstorm, I visited that abandoned warehouse and spotted Ari there too. We both got soaked, and we went to Starbucks for a coffee and a chat. I told her about her aunt hiring me. Guess what? She doesn't have an Aunt Glasya. I described the woman in detail, but Ari had never seen her. She thinks maybe her father hired some woman to hire me to protect her, but I seriously doubt that. Still, Ari is going to look into that and get back to me on it. So isn't this really a strange one?"

Crystal looked a bit pale when I finished up. Something unspoken passed between her and Monica Nicole. Crystal rose and headed to their library, while Monica Nicole spoke to me. "We've done a bit of investigation of our own, Parry. Something bad is likely to happen to you tonight. That's why I asked you to come here today. Ericka?"

Ericka of the mammoth breasts rose and moved over to me. I was sitting in one of their plush chairs. My head came face to face with those incredible knockers of hers. My god. What a sight! Worse, she leaned over me, placing a fancy pendant on a golden chain around my neck, but her bosom pressed hard into my face. I think I must have been quite red!

With a sly grin, Ericka backed off and explained

sweetly, "There you go, Parry. A bit more of my special protections. I've enchanted this pendant to help protect you from tonight's attack. If you get in serious trouble, you only need to touch the pendant and say clearly, "To Safety." Remember those words, Parry. Your life may well depend upon it."

"To Safety," I squeaked a couple of times, before my voice began to sound like myself.

"No charge. Just bring it back to me undamaged, if possible," she added sweetly, sashaying seductively back to her seat opposite me. Monica Nicole merely watched all this with a broad grin on her face. She was really enjoying this spectacle. Okay, I did too. Perhaps way too much. I swallowed and said thanks. Kind of lame. If someone just gives you an enchanted pendant that will save your life, a mere thanks seems wholly insignificant. Unfortunately, I couldn't think of anything else to say. The image of those knockers in my face was burned into my mind, indelibly.

Monica Nicole added, "Just be darn careful tonight, Parry. Something big is brewing, that much we do know. It is huge, whatever it is. Demon Lords are unbelievably powerful and are not to be trusted in the slightest, not ever. Ah, here comes Crystal."

I watched as the gorgeous super model's hips swayed as she walked back into the meeting room, carrying an old leather-bound book. She certainly knew how to walk! After she took her seat, from her extremely serious mien, I knew that she had found something major.

She opened the book to a specific page and then turned the book around, showing me the sketch. "Did this Aunt Glasya look something like this?" Her voice was incredibly stern for an eighteen year old young woman.

I swallowed hard. "Minus the wings and small horns, pretty good likeness." I think the temperature in the room must have dropped fifty degrees! I found myself staring across the table at three very shocked looking faces, their lips outlining slightly opened mouths. No one said a word for the longest time. Well, it seemed an eternity, but was probably a second or so. You know how time sort of stands still when something momentous occurs?

Crystal swallowed. "Okay then. That's another piece of the puzzle. This Aunt Glasya is Glasya, Princess of Hell and the Consort of the Arch-devil Mammon no less! Good god, Parry! You are messing around with Arch-devils and their consorts!" I admit it. I sat there completely stunned. I didn't know what to say.

"Well, it doesn't surprise me, Parry. She's reputed to have an ego the size of our Gateway Arch!" Crystal said decisively. Was there a hint of jealousy in her voice?

Ericka turned to Crystal and asked, "So could Glasya be bringing in these Abyss demons, these Chasma fly demons?"

Crystal turned her head to face Ericka. "Hardly. Devils and Demon Lords don't have anything to do with each other. They are archenemies or so the books all say."

Monica Nicole spoke up, "So the puzzle has just doubled in size, then. Now we have devils somehow involved. What is this Ari woman doing in cahoots with Arch-devils? Devils want souls, right Crystal?"

"Right. Devils play for your soul. That means you, the person, Parry. Demons play for tormenting bodies, bringing you along with it. You are your soul, but most religions have long lost the significance of that bit. They think you have this mysterious, unseen thing they call a soul somewhere around you. Ha. It's you. Devils want to trap you into their service in Hell, while the demons only want to torture your physical body endlessly. They get off on feeling your pain. Monica's right. What *is* going on here? If Demon Lords and Arch-devils are both here in St. Louis, whatever it is, it must be gigantic in scope. Positively enormous."

"But this Glasya wanted me to protect Ari Glaston from these demons," I countered.

Monica Nicole asked, "Has Ari sold her soul to Mammon? If so, then that would explain why Mammon's Princess and Consort hired you to protect her physical body."

Crystal nodded. "That could well explain it, Parry. If this theory is correct, then Ari is already lost, doomed to reside in Hell for all eternity. Grim."

Their theory seemed to ring true. If Ari had sold her

soul to this Arch-devil Mammon and if she were somehow in big trouble investigating the five hooded figures that were somehow working with the Demon Lords, then it would make sense for him to hire me to help protect his investment in Ari. Like I said, it sounded right.

But then, I've always got this problem with my gut intuition. And right now, my gut was telling me that there was no way that Ari was in league with the devil. She seemed pure, an innocent twenty-year old virgin, about to get married and start out her whole new life. It seemed incongruous to me. Why should she sell her soul? No, it just didn't feel right to me.

"I'd best go have a long talk with Ari," I declared.

"Yes, you had best do that, Parry. But please be extremely careful!" Monica Nicole advised me.

After thanking Ericka again for the protection pendant, I rose and headed out to my car. I had much to ponder, so I set the auto-guidance controls and allowed my trusty car to drive me home. By the time I got back, I'd not really thought of anything useful, other than I just had to talk with Ari.

I had a hunch that she was probably at work right now, so I took a gamble and just sent her a brief Message.

Have to talk. Urgent. When? P.

My magic flashed and I waited.

Lunch break in ten. Meet at same Starbucks. A.

Good. I had just enough time to get there, but only if I rushed. Holding my trusty staff, I cast my Fly spell and headed down south. By the time I got there, she already had our table and was eating her lunch. Not knowing how long she had and seeing the length of the ordering line, I headed to the table.

"Thanks for seeing me on such short notice, Ari. I have a lot to tell you. First, the woman who called herself your Aunt Glasya is really Glasya, Princess of Hell and Consort of the Arch-devil Mammon. What have you gotten yourself mixed up in, Ari? These beings play for keeps!" I know I must have sounded rather harsh, but my god, things were going from bad to worse in an awful rush.

She looked at me rather stunned. Turning pale, she stammered, "I, I, I learned about them in Magic School. Parry, I don't know what you mean? I know nothing about this

Glasya Princess. I've only read a little bit about such things years ago in school."

Again, reading her body language, seeing her pale face—all convinced me that my hunch that she was innocent was entirely correct. That could only mean that someone was using her. That was perhaps even worse to my way of thinking. After all, I believe that women and children should be protected and immune to such awful, terrible things. Sacred Femme and all that.

She was about to start crying. I've seen that in women before. Hastily, I said sincerely, "Ari, I believe you. I really do. But for some reason this Princess of Hell wants me to protect you. There has to be something behind all this. I don't know a whole lot about demons and devils, but I think that they have to have a very good reason to butt into the affairs of us humans. So think, Ari. Can you think of any reason whatever that this Glasya would want to hire me to protect you?"

I could tell that she was trying hard to keep from crying. It would ruin her mascara. "No Parry. I can't think of anything. I don't understand it either, really I don't." She was pleading with me.

I changed tactics. "Okay. Let's approach this from a different direction. Why were you spying on the five hooded people? How did you know where that warehouse was located?"

At that instant, I felt someone inside my head, looking out of my eyes and listening with my ears! Freaky! I'd never felt anything like that before. However, my gut did react, positively. A moment later, I had the thought, Monica Nicole Black.

"It's. . ." she started to tell me, but then something prevented her from saying another word. I got spooked.

A thought appeared in my mind. *Parry, she's under an Inhibition spell. She wants to tell you but the magic will not let her. Try this approach.* I went along with the voice in my mind. "That's okay, Ari. I understand fully. Just try not to think of the name."

Ari looked up at me, rather startled. Her eyes opened wide. I think at that moment, she too realized that she must be under the effect of some kind of spell preventing her from speaking. She flushed beet red. Then, she pulled a pen out of her pocket and wrote something on a grease-stained napkin. She rose and said, "Parry, I have to get back to work now. See you later on."

Involuntarily, I rose. Men are supposed to show that bit of respect for women when they get up to leave. I watched her pull out her wand and teleport back to work. I sat down, picked up the napkin, and stared at what she'd written down. It was a name. Wil Blackthornby. Now I did have a solid lead to pursue. I sent a thank you message to Monica Nicole Black and headed to my office and my small, handheld computer. Time for some investigation.

He lived in Lindenwood Park, just off I-44. The information suggested that he might be sixty-four and had graduated from the St. Louis School of Magic back in 2137. He was in Black Hall. Well, that much seemed to fit. Black Hall seemed to produce the most wizards who had tendencies to turn to the Dark Arts. Still, I had little to go on, except that Ari was somehow following this man, who was somehow involved with the gating of the demons.

Hitting another wall, I decided to make use of the resources that I had. Namely the FBI. I called Oliver. "Hi Oliver. I have some really bad news and some good news. Yes, it's about our situation." Hastily, I outlined the bad news, that Demon Lords and Arch-devils were involved. He laughed and said I was dreaming again, suggesting I hadn't recovered from my slice and dice. Well, I couldn't blame him. When was the last time you saw or heard of Demon Lords and Arch-devils, eh? He was a norm, after all. Then, I gave him the good news.

"I think Wil Blackthornby is behind the gating of these demons, these fly creatures that are killing innocent people." I told him the man's address and what little was available about him on the Net. "So, you should check into him. Find out what real estate holdings he has access to. Is there a connection between him and that abandoned warehouse? If he's the one behind these attacks, he's already built another incised pentagram at some other location. I think this is our best lead yet. Keep me posted." Oliver gave me one of his truly heartfelt thank you's. Finally, he had something to sink his teeth into, but in a different way than these Chasma demons did.

I headed back to my apartment to fix something to eat and think about my next move. I had perhaps another five hours before dark came, and the hooded figures would likely continue their evil works. Carefully, I prepared all my offensive and defensive things. My blasting rod was ready. I did need to recharge my staff so I cast several spells into it until it was three-quarters charges, just the way I liked it. I double-checked my 45. It was fully loaded and ready to go. Time flew by. As dusk approached, I fixed another TV dinner and quietly ate, while listening to some antique rock tunes from centuries ago. They were quite popular these days.

I was just about ready to head out when my Alarm spell detonated. You see, like any good wizard, I have the spell cast on my entrance, the only door into my basement apartment. That way, no one can barge in on me and take me by surprise. How else can a wizard get a good night's sleep, eh?

At the same instant that my door literally splintered into a hundred bits of wood, glass, and metal, my Alarm spell sounded. Kind of redundant in this case. Obviously, someone was breaking into my apartment in a rather big way. For a split second, my mind tried to imagine how strong the invader must be to splinter my door. Bits of flying wood and metal came towards me like last night's rain. At the last instant, I dove and hit the floor, allowing the flying debris to pass harmlessly over me. I do have fast reactions, though now that I think of it, I did have Ericka's Skin of Stone spell on my body so that the flying projectiles wouldn't have harmed me. My instincts told me to dive, and my body obeyed.

I looked up to see the largest creature I've ever seen, outside of the St. Louis Zoo, that is! It was bi-pedal. I first saw its feet, which looked like enormous pig's feet, cloven hooves. As my eyes swept up its huge, muscled form, I saw its absolutely massive arms, almost as big around as my chest! Its head was rather ape-like, but with enormous bat-like ears. And it had wings on its back, currently folded. It stood at least ten feet tall. It bent low to get though my doorway. As it forced its way into my apartment, its wide body literally tore the framing from my door away from the studs supporting it.

As it drew close to me, I finally got to my feet, summoning my staff to my hand. It took that long for me to realize that I'd dropped it when I dove for the floor. I saw it raise its mighty fist over my head. Then, darkness fell. I recognized the spell. It was one that I could cast, though I usually preferred its opposite, Light. Thank god for the Skin of Stone spell! His fist came down on me like a ton of bricks. I should have been utterly squashed into a pancake, but I was only knocked to the floor, the wind knocked out of me. I fought to get some air in my lungs. I wasn't thinking about how to fight it. I just wanted to stay alive somehow.

Then, it spoke. "Keep your nose out of our business or the next time we will kill you!"

I tried to say something smart, like "Whose business might that be?" Unfortunately, I couldn't get any air into my lungs. I was still trying to breathe.

Making matters worse, a Message suddenly appeared before my eyes.

Help! Demons are after me. I'm at Starbucks. A.

When it rains, it pours. Nice old saying, but quite true. At last, I sucked in some air, but I saw that his fist was about to come down on me hard once more, punctuating his declaration to me a moment ago. I was still holding my staff. I had one lung-full of air. I used it wisely. "Teleport: Starbucks!"

Magic flashed. I was lying on the concrete just outside Starbucks, gasping for air, my staff securely in my hand. I ached all over, but managed to get to my feet and staggered into the coffee shop. Thank god for small favors. Ari called out, "Parry! Over here." She was sitting in our usual place, and I somehow managed to get to her and sit down. She's an angel. She had a cup waiting for me. I took a sip and felt the warm rush from the inside outward.

Still gasping, I said, "Thanks." She looked horrible though. Terrified. Her mascara had seeped down her face like two black lines of some Gothic kid.

"What happened to you?" she asked.

"Oh nothing much. Just some ten-foot tall, gorilla-like demon splintered my apartment door and gave me a pounding that I should not ever forget. I think we now have their attention, Ari. You okay?"

Okay is not a very precise term, rather relative I think. I mean we were both alive. I expected to be aching for several days and that was from a single punch. He hadn't meant to kill me, I don't think; just warn me. Scare me off. Still. . .

Ari whispered, "I went to, well you know. I went there to try to follow them. Two monster creatures came after me, trying to kill me, I think. I very nearly got killed; teleported at the very last instant! Parry, I'm scared."

"Hey, I know, I know. This is something really to be scared of. They are very nasty beasts. Thanks for the coffee. It's what I need just about now. You're doing okay. See, you had the good sense to get out of there before they could harm you. Good going, Ari." I knew that she needed a big, big confidence boost about now. She was still shivering all over from her fright. She flashed me a smile. I was right. She began to calm down some.

Just then, my cell vibrated. It was Oliver. "Parry! Come quick. We're in a battle." He rattled off his location.

I checked. My 45 was still in its holster, and I had my staff and blasting rod tucked in my upper leg's holster. "Okay, Ari, there's a battle going on right now. I have to go help the FBI with it. You can't go back to your place. It's not safe. You can't go to my place. It's doorless at the moment. So you come with me. Stay back and cast all the protection spells that you know on yourself." I took her hand and used my staff again. "Teleport. . ."

We arrived at a scene out of one of those ancient dinosaurs versus Japan movies. Three of these enormous gorilla-like creatures were smashing up about a dozen police cars. I spotted six FBI black SUV's behind us. Police were shooting their shotguns at the ten-foot tall demons, while Oliver and his eight men were firing some rather high-powered rifles at them. Oliver nodded to me as I materialized close to him. The noise of the gunfire was rather loud, and I quickly emptied my 45 into the nearest one. I don't think it did a whole lot of good.

After that, I began using my staff, shooting spells their

way. Standing behind me, Ari finally joined us. She began shooting Disintegrate spells at one of the giant apes. She shot six at it, but the creature merely ignored her. The spells seemed simply to fizzle out when they reached its massive body. It continued to pulverize cars, moving closer to the line of cops who were firing everything they had at them, all the while backing up, staying out of their physical reach. Wise of them, considering I'd been the recipient of one of their fists a short while ago.

Everything changed when Ari cast her seventh Disintegrate spell. This time, it struck, boring a large hole through its belly. It let out an enormous bellow, rattling glass windows in the entire block. At once, total darkness covered the area where the demons were standing. Quickly, I cast my Light spell and then my Dispel Magic. The magical darkness was gone and so were the three demons. I guess they'd had enough bullets for one night. The street was littered with shell casings of all calibers. I figured the forensic boys would have a field day sorting this one out.

I turned to Ari and said, "Nice shot!"

"Is, is it dead? Are they gone?" her shaking voice asked timidly.

"Sweet heart, you drove them off. Well done." I figured she needed a little morale boost. Oliver didn't. He didn't bring big enough guns. I told him to bring really big guns. Perhaps next time he'd bring the fifty-caliber ones that I'd suggested.

"Thanks," she whispered.

Oliver turned to us and said, "Thanks Parry. I owe you one. I think we may have wounded them. Let's go take a look see." Indeed, there was some strange goo splattered about the street. More goodies for his forensic boys to play with, I thought. "You two can take off now. My people will take it from here. Magical Misuse people will be here tomorrow. Thanks again, Parry."

I nodded. Ari and I stepped back. Now what? "Ari, it's not safe for you to return home just now. Have you got any safe place you can go?"

"No," she stammered. "Nothing like this has ever happened to me before. Parry, I'm scared."

"Hey, that's normal, Ari. These were powerful and nasty creatures. I'd be really worried about you if you weren't plenty scared of them. I sure am. They've wrecked my place. We can't go there. We need to hold up somewhere that they don't know about. You can Message your folks and let them know that you are safe. Just don't tell them where you are at—to be on the safe side. If no one knows where we are at, we should be safe until morning comes. I've an idea. Oops. My staff is empty."

Ari kindly recharged it for me. She cast a couple of spells, and I had my staff suck up the magical energies. Then, we took a walk. "Where are we going?" she asked softly.

"To the nearest phone booth."

"To call someone?"

"No, to find us a motel. One picked totally at random. That way, only we two know where we are at." At the time, it sounded like a very good plan indeed. I'd overlooked the fact that we both had our cell phones turned on and could easily be located if someone had the right electronic equipment. I doubted that the demons had such skills. We took a room at the Red Roof Inn off I-270. While I wanted her to have her own room, she was too scared to be alone, so we doubled up.

While she took a long, hot shower, I cast a number of Clean spells on her clothes and then did mine as well. I had to admire young Ari. She hadn't given in to her fears, but had chosen to stay and fight back. Whoever her fiancé was, he ought to be quite proud of her. I sure was.

When she finished showering, I let her have the bed and took my own shower. After that, I curled up on the floor using the extra blankets that came with the room. Eventually, I heard her sleeping peacefully and relaxed. I realized that I was still no nearer to knowing what was going on than before. Only now, the stakes had grown significantly higher. Well, there is always tomorrow. That the Department of Magical Misuse was stepping in would certainly help us all. Still, there were two mysteries here to solve. What were the devils doing with Ari? What were the five hooded figures trying to do? What did the Demon Lords want? It was all so confusing, and I hate confusions. I think I fell asleep about then.

In the morning, Ari looked refreshed. The nightmare

was behind her. We ate a quick breakfast, and she teleported off to work, but I did get her promise to Message me when she was getting off of work. Nothing was likely to happen to her during the daytime. I headed to my apartment and called the landlord to get my door replaced. "This is coming out of your deposit," he growled.

I countered, "Someone broke into my apartment, and I have to pay for it? Get real." He conceded the point, particularly when the cops showed up to take my statement. I played dumb, saying that someone had obviously broken in, but had not taken anything. Heck, I didn't have anything here worth stealing. At least, this got me out of having to pay for the repairs. That's why the landlord should have insurance. If he didn't, that was his problem.

Just then, Oliver called. "We got a search warrant and went through Wil's home. We didn't find a darned thing, except one thing. It might not be important, but his desk calendar has a big notation on Saturday at six p.m. Not sure if it's relevant or not. There's no trace of Wil or his wife. We've put out a bolo on his car, but he's a wizard so I doubt that's going to prove fruitful. The Magical Misuse men are arriving. They'll probably want to see you, so head on down here soonest. Bye."

Saturday night. That's two days from now. If that was the critical date, then we only needed to survive one more night before then. That also meant that we only had two days to figure this whole mess out and find a way to stop it! It didn't look promising to me. I put on my best clothes and headed out to my trusty old Ford, punched in the coordinates for the FBI building, and activated the auto-guidance system. I spent the driving time wondering about these Magical Misuse fellows and how they would react to this mess.

Chapter 7—A Meeting of Minds

I arrived at the super-secure FBI headquarters in downtown St. Louis. I liked flashing my ID badge at the entrance station, allowing me—a non-suit—to enter, quite unlike all the black suited men and nearly similarly dressed women, though some wore black skirts and white blouses. Honestly, they all looked so darn serious all the time, which made me quite pleased that I somehow had not ended up in their bureau. I've a hard time with being serious twenty-four/seven.

I stopped at the reception desk, manned by a woman in skirt and blouse. She had her hair up and probably hadn't smiled in a decade. "Where's the Magical Misuse meeting at?" I asked. She wore thick black-framed glasses, and she peered down from her slightly elevated perch onto me, wearing a new pair a jeans and a fresh western, snap button shirt. Was that disdain I saw on her face? I smiled anyway.

"Room 202," she said briskly.

I thanked her and headed to the elevators. I restrained myself from laughing though, as other suits piled in beside me. They never failed to give me a look of disdain or contempt. I just smiled back at them all, hopefully confusing the heck out of them. Perhaps, they thought that I was being arrested by the Magical Misuse personnel or something.

I hadn't met the St. Louis director of the Department of Magical Misuse, let alone the Missouri State department head, but I was about to. I entered Room 202, more curious than anything else. Oliver was just welcoming the two visitors. He spotted me and motioned for me to join him. "Parry, I want you to meet the head of the St. Louis Department of Magical Misuse, Henry Wilkens, and the head of the Missouri Department of Magical Misuse, Mrs. Leslie Traub. This is my associate, an FBI Consultant, Mr. Parry Oscar Tuttle, Private Investigator."

"Very pleased to meet you," said to each in turn, shaking their hand. Leslie was probably forty. She could have been attractive had she let her hair down and worn something besides her black suit pants and smiled more. Her face was stern, a no nonsense woman, I gathered immediately and resolved to avoid making any jokes at this meeting. I also sensed that she really knew her business. Henry, on the other hand, wore a camel hair brown jacket and slacks, quite different from the other suits in the building. I wondered if that was keeping him from advancing in his department, but that's the sort of thing you don't ask someone when you first meet them. Perhaps, it would be wise never to mention such a thing.

"Please, everyone, have a seat. I've constructed a Power Point presentation that outlines what we have observed, documented, and learned. There is a time-line with this as well," Oliver explained. I'll give him this point—he sure knows how to organize things. In about thirty minutes, he'd accurately explained everything that had happened during the past five plus days. Even more interesting, someone had the presence of mind to snap photos of the gorilla monsters while they were attacking us, making me wish that I'd been able to do the same with the Chasma fly demons or even "Aunt Glasya," for that matter. Okay, I was just a little envious of Oliver and his team.

When he finished, you could hear a pin drop in this meeting room. Henry deferred to his boss, Leslie, who finally spoke. "Well, Oliver, it would seem that we do have a situation developing here. All right then, let's begin at the beginning, with the deceased Jessica White. What do we know about her background? Do we know conclusively that she was indeed a true virgin?"

Here, Oliver was on solid ground. He chatted a bit longer, confirming that she was. "As far as we can tell, Jessica had no connections to anything having to do with the Dark Arts."

"Okay then. This is a major detail. Your ME is positive that she was stabbed in her heart? That is the COD?" Leslie asked pointedly.

"Absolutely," Oliver declared.

"Well, then that is pretty conclusive evidence that a Major Summoning was undertaken by these unknown five hooded figures. The sacrifice of a virgin is about the only way that a Demon Lord or his direct representative can be gated to our world from the Abyss and not devour its summoner. Excepting, of course, if the summoner knew the true name of the demon," she added hastily, desiring to be precise in her declarations.

She continued, "So initially, either a Demon Lord of his direct representative arrived via a Gate spell. That much is clear at this point. The question is why did they do this? What was the bargain that the five were trying to make, a bargain so vital that they needed to call upon the powerhouses of the evil Abyss? Certainly, whatever their reasons, they must be extremely motivated to take such a gamble. One positively cannot trust any of the Demon Lords or any creature from the Abyss. So whatever they intended to get from the Demon Lord, it must be something that they could see no other way of obtaining, via magical means at hand."

Leslie went on, "I did some checking before I came. I couldn't find any political issues or economic ones that might be solved with such a summoning. At this point, I'm inclined to believe the 'what' is something quite personal to these five and of immense importance to them."

She then turned to me. "That brings us to the next event, Mr. Tuttle, your meeting with this supposed Aunt Glasya Winterhaven. You say that she was at your office door?"

"Yes." I began describing that encounter once more, trying hard not to leave out any detail. Both Leslie and Henry seemed particularly interested in everything that I had to say about her.

When I finished, Leslie said, "Parry, I'm going to cast a spell on you. I want you to bring back to mind your memories of this Aunt Glasya so that Henry here and I can see what she looked like for ourselves. Okay?" I nodded and her wand activated. I sensed both of them peering into my mind, as though looking at whatever I was seeing. I tried very hard to recall only Glasya and our chat. I was quite glad when the spell ended, though. Who knows what else they might have seen in my mind that I might not want them to know?

I looked over at Leslie. Her face seemed even grimmer

so I presumed this was indeed the Princess of Hell. Leslie spoke for Oliver's benefit. "Parry's correct. This Aunt Glasya Winterhaven is not what she pretended to be. I am quite certain that she is Glasya, Princess of Hell, and Consort of the Arch-devil Mammon. Parry, how did you figure this out? You didn't know that she was a devil princess when you first met."

"Er, well, I had some help. Once Ari confirmed that she didn't have any such aunt and had never seen a woman matching Glasya's description, I got a little help. A new magic store has recently opened here in St. Louis. Protections, Investigations, Wands, Items, and Potions or PIWIP for short. Five recently graduated witches have opened the store. Monica Nicole Black, Crystal Holliday, Ericka Van Nie, Misty Worth-Williams, and Enya Homes-Scorsky. Crystal helped me identify Glasya. She is very up on this lore. They've a great library at their store, and she showed me a sketch in one of them. It was Glasya all right."

"Okay, she paid you ten thousand dollars in hundred dollar bills. Do you still have some of them or have you put them into the bank?" Leslie asked.

"Er sorry. Banked them yesterday. Wait, I paid Enya some for her healing potions. They might still have them around their store." I really didn't want to get them in trouble. Did Leslie suspect the bills were fake or perhaps counterfeit? If so, I'd be behind the eight-ball, money-wise. I was so counting on them to pay November's rent.

"Henry, Message those proprietors. See if they still have those hundreds. In any case, ask them to come here in say an hour, please," Leslie ordered. "Now then, Parry." I squirmed a little.

"She wanted you to protect her 'niece' Ari. Correct?" I nodded. "And she gave you sufficient information so that you could find her?" Again, I nodded. "So how is it that you were able to follow her to that warehouse?"

"Er, I planted a bug in her pocket and used my GPS tracker to find where she'd teleported to—that warehouse." This was the precise truth.

Leslie commented, "Well, perhaps not so ethical, but a wise move to use norm's methods in this case. I've looked over your magical education or rather the lack of it. Frankly, I'm impressed that you manage as well as you do. Anyway, you've been protecting her ever since?"

"Absolutely. As far as I'm concerned, she is my client. I took Glasya's money, and I will do as I promised, even if the money turns out to be fake or something. My word is my honor in this business."

Leslie added, "And getting results, Parry." I grinned. Yes, that too. I'd been doing pretty well with Ari.

She went onto a different topic. "So we are now faced with both Arch-devils and Demon Lords somehow being involved here. Beyond nasty. Okay, back to the obvious escalation of hostilities, as witnessed by last night's events." We chatted about it for a while. I quickly realized that Leslie was waiting for the five women to arrive. I was right.

Before long, the five entered the room. I noticed both Oliver and Henry did a double take when Crystal and Ericka entered, followed by Monica Nicole. Enya and Misty brought up the rear. The two models wore matching blue satin, pencil-style gowns that brought out their most impressive curves. They wore black nylons and five-inch black pumps. Monica Nicole wore a light red gown, quite similar to the other two, but her heels were at least six inches high. In contrast, Enya and Misty wore professional women's outfit. That is, black skirt and white blouse, but they too wore black pumps, though only perhaps with three-inch heels.

This time, I did the introductions. After that, we all sat down. Monica Nicole brought out the four hundred dollar bills that I'd given them in payment. Of course, we all stared at her three-inch long nails, painted to match her lips and gown. She deftly slid them over to Leslie. She said, "We do believe that they are authentic."

God, I hoped so. I found myself holding my breath here. If they were bogus, I was in deep waters, financially! Leslie cast several spells on them, before handing them off to Henry, who fired up his laptop. I'm not sure what he did with them, but I'd guess he might have been checking serial numbers. At this point, he looked up and nodded. Leslie then said the three words that allowed me to breathe again. "They are authentic.

That means she had access to our country's money, somehow. This only gets stranger by the minute."

"So you are an official Gate spell caster, Crystal?" Leslie asked. Why did I suddenly feel like I was out of my league? Like I was on Mars? Like I wasn't a wizard?

Crystal replied rather formally, "Correct. That's why I so quickly recognized the actual use of the incised pentagram that Parry found. Couple that with the apparent virgin sacrifice and it's not hard to predict that someone executed a Major Summoning. What bothers me is that the demons arriving here in St. Louis are steadily growing in power. Chasma demons are not very powerful, comparatively. I believe the gorilla-like demons that Parry and Oliver faced last night were Class Four demons, substantially higher up in the demon hierarchy. I suspect that all this is a build up to some as yet unknown climax."

"I agree with you, Crystal," Leslie replied. "My conclusion precisely. Now then, what do you make of this Ari business and the involvement of the devils?"

Crystal explained, nearly quoting her textbooks, "Devils, unlike demons, have and follow rules and such. They go in search of a person's soul, their personality, the person themselves. That's their paymaster, new souls to torment for all eternity. The demons' paymaster is the pain that they can inflict upon bodies, sadists really. Big difference between the two, though for us, the difference hardly matters, I think. Anyway, if we assume that Glasya was here in St. Louis, someone's soul is the payment. It could well be Ari's. That would make sense if she hired Parry to protect her. However well that theory fits the observed facts, Parry here doesn't think that's the case."

I was about to interrupt her. I'd not told them about my feelings about Ari, my hunch, my gut feeling. I'd listened to her theory and could not dispute it. On the surface, it seemed a very rational conclusion. So how did Crystal know that I thought differently?

She glanced at me and added, "Parry has a tendency to follow his intuition. We've done a bit of research on him and his career as a private investigator. Unlike most men, he makes heavy use of his intuition, more like us women." She grinned, and even Leslie's stern face cracked the briefest of smiles. So while it would seem that Ari is the soul in question, perhaps Parry is right. Some other soul is at stake here. If so, we need to find the connection between the devil's appearance here in St. Louis and the demons. One thing that I am certain of is that these two are somehow related to each other."

Oliver chose this moment to interject, "What I'd like to know is that calendar date that we found in Wil Blackthornby's desk calendar somehow related to all of this? If it is, then we have now a day and a half to figure this thing out. Kind of a time crunch. If that date is irrelevant, then perhaps we have much more time."

"What calendar date?" Crystal asked. Quickly, Oliver explained what they'd uncovered during their search of Wil's home, but not before he received a nod from Leslie.

"Well, that does change things," Crystal replied when he finished.

"How so?" Leslie inquired, growing curious.

Now I saw what Leslie was doing. She was cleverly bringing everyone in on the situation so that she could get as many points of view as possible. Beats sitting back and brainstorming up multiple ideas and scenarios. No wonder she was the head of the entire Missouri department!

"Demons are an impatient lot, at least according to the texts. If that's right, then keeping them focused on a single plan for an entire week is pushing it. I'm surprised that some of them haven't already gotten other ideas than the one that brought them here in the first place," Crystal explained.

Monica Nicole spoke up. "Perhaps they have already done just that. Last night, with the rampaging gorilla-like demons. That's a total change in modus operandi. However, we must also consider the warning that the demon gave to Parry here last night."

Darn, I'd forgotten all about that detail. "Yes, I was warned to keep my nose out of this business," I added. It seemed a trivial addition to the conversation, though, and I shut up quickly.

She smiled at me before continuing. "Of course, he has

no intention of keeping his nose out of it." I think that I must have flushed, as all eyes quickly glanced my way. "So why do the demons want Parry to mind his own business? I think that is perhaps *the* most profitable question that we should be asking at this point."

"Why do you say that?" Leslie asked. Again, I saw her motive behind that question. She'd get an inside track on another key idea. Clever leader.

"Parry must be getting too darn close to what's really going on. Only neither he nor we know just what that might be," she answered. "So we should focus more on Parry and the actions that he has already taken. See where that leads us."

"Well, I did agree to protect Ari. I followed her to the incised pentagram and its summoning or gating. The Chasma fly demons spotted me before they did her, which allowed her to escape. So quite by accident, I stumbled upon their summoning pentagram. That probably forced them to have to make another one at some other location. Then, when the demons came after her, I got her to safety. I've been looking out for her."

"Precisely, Parry. You've somehow kept them from Ari. Conclusion, Ari must be playing an important role in all this. She is also a virgin, right?" Monica Nicole asked.

Oliver answered, "As far as we know, she is. So you think that she could be their next virgin sacrifice?"

Monica Nicole raised her eyebrows. Her gesture affirmed that she thought so. Oliver continued down this line of thinking, asking, "So Parry here has kept them from kidnaping Ari? But if these demons are so powerful, why haven't they easily captured her so far? She's been at work all during the daytime. Jessica was at work on her lunch hour when she was taken. Do these demons only work at night? I don't see it yet."

Leslie answered him. "Jessica was the first victim. Her sacrifice probably began this whole mess. It would have been humans who did the actual kidnaping of her, not demons. But you are right, it would be a relatively simple matter for a Demon Lord to kidnap Ari. Night or day. I don't think that bothers demons. They are able to change their physical forms

100

to some extent. They could pass, at least cursorily, as human beings. Yet, these are only in operation during the nighttime. I believe that is most significant in this case."

"Indeed. I believe you are right," Monica Nicole backed her up. "While the five hooded figures could perform their rituals in the daytime, why are they choosing to do it only at night? The answer I keep coming up with is that they are otherwise occupied during the daylight hours."

"Occupied with what?" Leslie probed.

Crystal answered this one. "From my own work in school, I can truthfully say that casting Gate spells and then keeping the summoned creature bound and preventing it from attacking you really burns up your energy rapidly. I suspect that part of the daytime, they are sleeping, recovering from the previous night's work. It's mentally exhausting work, and one tiny, minuscule slip up and the demon will use it to attack you. After all, they hate being Summoned and forced to do something. I know anyone would, not just demons. My guess is that they are sleeping for part of the day. Notice that the demon activity has not gone on into the wee hours of the morning either."

Monica Nicole added, "So they must be doing something vitally important in the afternoons. That's what we should be figuring out as well. What are they working on?"

Crystal continued, "Our only clue is that Parry here is somehow getting too darn close to what they are doing; only he doesn't know it. Hence, their severe warning to him last night. And Ari seems to be the key here. I think that it may be likely that they intend to sacrifice Ari when the time is right, just like they did with Jessica."

"But what's the right time?" Monica Nicole asked. "Is there some significance to Saturday or to that calendar date? If so, that would give us a bigger clue, perhaps. Or is there some significance to the period of seven days in demon lore? Sorry, this isn't my area of expertise." She looked at Crystal.

"Seven is. It's a prime number and a mystic number as well as playing a significant role in the occult world," Crystal answered. "You should remember that, Monica dear." I think that Monica Nicole flushed for a brief second. "But you have a valid point about the date. I'll need to research that one, 10-10-2190."

Leslie then stated flatly, "I believe for now we should regard Saturday night as being the focal point of this entire affair. Seven seems to be too significant to ignore. If tomorrow night passes without event, then we can readjust our thinking to longer time spans. Next area. We need to pool all resources into finding the whereabouts of this Wil Blackthornby. Who are his known close friends? Associates? Affiliations? We need the full scoop on this man. Oliver, this is your area, I believe."

He cleared his throat, "Well, ordinarily yes. However, the man is a wizard and has retired. There is no information past his retirement some six years ago now. All database information is very stale-dated. Apparently, he graduated from the St. Louis School of Magic, Black Hall, it seems, which, if I understand you wizards and witches, means that he must have had at least some interest in the Dark Arts. So that fits. He used to work at the airport, an air traffic controller. Beyond that, our data is limited. Perhaps, you have something more in your magical databases?"

I grinned. Oliver cleverly turned it around so that he would be getting key information that was only available to the Department of Magical Misuse. Clever Oliver. Remind me never to cross wits with him.

Leslie nodded to Henry who typed away on his laptop. Then he spoke up, "Well, it seems that Wil was an ardent supporter of Dominus Malefic when he was running for president. He did some campaigning for him, but nothing further. He didn't have a ring so he wasn't being controlled by Dominus later on. That's it, though. No complaints. No known offenses. No reprimands. No warnings. Nada. Not much here, I'm afraid."

"Darn," Leslie cursed. "So we have no idea who his friends might be, who he ran around with, or who he might confide in."

Ericka volunteered, "Say, you could perhaps check with some of the older professors at the St. Louis School of Magic. They might remember him. If so, they might know what other students he associated with. Just an idea. Probably take too long to find out. We don't have a whole lot of time."

Leslie turned and said, "Make a note of that, Henry. For your information, I've tried some other approaches to get in touch with Wil. I've sent him a Message, but it wasn't received. He's blocking all normal magical means to contact him. He likely has all manner of anti-scrying protections on himself. Has to, if he's dealing with Demon Lords. One stray thought could well be used against him."

She went on, "I'll be honest with all of you. If there is another round of demon attacks in the city tonight, and we are still nowhere in this investigation, then I have no choice but to request the services of the Rodents, our top guns, so to speak. We simply have to prevent whatever is going to happen on Saturday night, if indeed that's the target date. Anyway, here's what our plans for tonight will be." She hastily outlined what her department would be doing and that of the FBI. "Parry, you stick close to Ari."

"Of course," I grinned. I wasn't about to let anything bad happen to Ari, not if I could prevent it. I suggested, "Any chance that we could talk with her parents and see if they know anything about all this?"

"Okay, I'll see what can be done," Leslie answered and then dismissed us. She did ask me to stick around for a while. I headed down to their vending machines for a dark chocolate bar and a soda. I'm not worried about my weight, and I love chocolate, the dark kind. Letting it melt in my mouth, I thought about Ari. She was living with her parents and was able to Message them last night. Probably they were worried sick about her. Surely, Leslie would get something useful out of them. I knew that they'd probably not even talk to me or end the conversation the moment I mentioned devils. No, if they knew something about this mess, it would take a bigger gun to get it out of them. I'm a peanut in the world of wizards and witches. I was just thankful that Leslie thought enough of me to let me sit in on her big meeting, though I hardly said much at all.

Leslie Messaged me, and I rushed back into the room. "Well, this becomes more interesting, Parry. It seems that her parents have also gone into hiding. I can't reach them by any magical means. Can you have Ari see if she can Message them? If so, have her ask why they are in hiding and if they will agree to talk to me?"

"Interesting indeed. On it," I replied. I sent a long Message to Ari, hoping that it wasn't coming at an inopportune time for her. She sent a quick acknowledgment. I didn't have too long to wait, though.

Sorry. They are in hiding, fearing for their lives. Told me that they will speak to no one but me. I'm supposed to stay with you tonight. I'm getting really scared again. A.

I relayed what she told me to Leslie. "How interesting. Henry, look up all that we have on Herbert Glaston and his wife, Sandra, will you?" She looked at me and added for my benefit, "We are accessing Professor Pam Betts' famous database. She's got all known criminals in there along with all manner of data concerning the rough times when Dominus was around."

Henry soon spoke up. "Hey, this is really weird. There are no records anywhere of Herbert Glaston or his wife, Sandra. He doesn't exist."

"But he has to," Oliver spoke up. We obtained a search warrant for his place, but haven't gotten to the search yet. Let me try something. I've a hunch." I watched my boss carefully, wondering what his bright idea was. He wasn't a wizard, but a very bright norm, one who wasn't spooked by the unnatural things that we'd been facing. Guess that's why he was always getting the "strange cases." He typed determinedly. Then, I saw that familiar spark in his eyes and knew that he'd found something that these wizards had missed.

He looked up triumphantly. "Well, well. Isn't this interesting. Henry, try accessing Herbert Athos. It seems his entire family has been placed in the Federal Witness Protection Program, given new names, and relocated here to St. Louis. That's why nothing is coming up on Glaston."

It was Henry's turn to type furiously. He looked up and exclaimed, "Now this is interesting! He too was an outspoken supporter of Dominus' Golden Path and supported him for President. Coincidence? But there's a whole lot more. It seems that he has two daughters. Cherrie Athos was twenty-one when she was kidnaped by Dominus, mutilated, and kept as one of his play toys. Later on, some of the Rodents rescued her. She's one of the many recipients of States Justice Compensation. One million dollars to be exact. She and later her whole family were put into the protection program and moved to St. Louis from Florida. She quickly got married and went to college in Denver. She's a teacher now. Ari is his youngest daughter, ten years younger than Cherrie."

Leslie commented, "Well, this gets even more interesting. What's Herbert's angle in this? Is he still a Dominus supporter or is he out for revenge of some kind? Can't see the revenge angle. Dominus was assassinated eight years ago. This whole mess just gets more and more confusing. I'll let the five other witches know about this twist, Henry. Perhaps, I shouldn't have dismissed everyone so soon. Anyway Parry, you best get to work now." She dismissed me, but I thanked her for letting me know all this useful information.

As I drove home, I pondered this new tidbit. Both men were Dominus supporters. I bet they were pissed off when he was assassinated. Still, this was interesting. They supported the notion that wizards were somehow vastly more important than the norms and that they ought to be in positions of power and dominance over the average joe-blow. I know that sounds silly to me, but some people have a big ego and an oversized notion of self-importance. I sure don't. Can't afford it in my line of work. Besides, I barely know magic, compared to all those others at the meeting. I knew just how Oliver felt this afternoon.

But what about Ari? How had the awful torture of her older sister affected her? How had being uprooted and forced to move to a strange new life affected her? How much of all this did she know? She couldn't have been more than about eleven at that time. Well, at least the family hadn't needed to worry about Dominus coming after them again, not for over six years now. That was certainly positive. That fear had probably vanished long ago. I wondered if I dared talk to Ari about this. Perhaps it would just stir up unwanted bad memories.

Traffic was heavy, and I didn't get back home until

around four. Some workers were working on repairing my door. I ignored them and grabbed up everything that I thought could be useful in protecting Ari tonight. I had my staff in hand. My blasting rod was secure in my hip holster. I checked my 45 and stuffed another clip into my pocket. I verified I still wore Ericka's ring and pendent. I also grabbed a few other little protection pieces as well, stuffing them into my other pocket.

As I headed out, I told the workers, "Hey, if you get it done tonight, give the keys to the landlord. I'll get them from him. Thanks." I bet they have never seen a demon-destroyed door before. Then again, I hadn't either and don't wish to see another for that matter. I briefly thought of Ericka. I owed her my life. Her ring saved my butt, and I hoped that I wouldn't need it again. Something about hammering fists coming down on my head isn't too appealing to me.

As I stepped out, I sent a quick Message to Ari asking her to meet me at Starbucks as soon as she left work. I cast my Fly spell from my staff and headed there, hoping I'd get there before she did. I didn't dare risk another Teleport spell from the staff. First, it uses far more magical charges. Second, I'm not very confident in using that spell, even though the staff is actually executing it. I've a fear of arriving six feet under, if you take my meaning literally.

I got there just ahead of her. She came walking in, having teleported there. Ari looked quite stressed out. Who wouldn't be, if you had demons coming after you? I got us a snack and a pair of coffees. It was going to be a long night.

Chapter 8—Round Three

I decided the smart thing to do was do the unpredictable. After we got our snack and coffee, I had her teleport us to my favorite diners, Sal's Bar and Grill. I ordered us a pair of steak dinners, ignoring her plea for just a salad. "Look, you need a good, nourishing meal. You're probably burning up all your B vitamins like mad. We need to stay alert and healthy. So eat up, Ari." I didn't add that this might be your last meal. I'd seen that line on some old movies. That wouldn't cheer her up any or me either.

Ari ate, but reluctantly. She was scared. Her face was drawn, but she was determined, I'll give her that. And cute. I forced such thoughts out of my mind. Over our coffee kept warmed up by a few Warm spells, she finally opened up to me as much as she could.

"Parry, I know that I'm under the influence of some spells, really powerful ones. I tried to Dispel them while I was at work and no one was watching me. I can't do it. Every time I try to do it, I get this message in my mind that says if I do it, cancel the spells, then I will die at once. I'm really scared, Parry. I don't dare let anyone cancel them, but I don't know what they are forcing me to do? Well, that's not entirely true. I know that they are trying to force me to find this Wil Blackthornby wizard, but honestly, I can't find him. Whatever I did before isn't working now."

She went on, "It's kind of like a compulsion that I can satisfy. I keep trying, but I can find him. I know that I simply must find him, but I can't. It's driving me nuts when I think about it."

"So don't think about it, Ari. It's just some darn compulsion spell someone put on you. I wonder who did it? Maybe your father is under something similar," I suggested, moving her mind off herself.

She shrugged her shoulders. "Maybe. But why? Who is doing this to me, Parry?" She looked so vulnerable, so scared. Darn it. Whoever was doing this to this lovely young woman ought to be hanged or something. No one should ever do such things to the fairer sex or even children for that matter. Too bad I'm not a senator or something. I think I might try to pass such a law. But thinking of that, it reminded me of her sister and her family's flight into the witness protection program. I decided to inquire gently.

"Say, Ari, isn't your last name really Athos?"

That registered. She jerked her head up and stared directly at me, her lips parted slightly as though to say something. Then, her whole body slumped in an enormous sigh. "Yes, but it's supposed to be a secret. It was my big sister. We did it to protect her. I was only eleven then." She began telling me all about it, at least as much as she knew. Cherrie had been abducted by Dominus and mutilated. Ari didn't give specifics though. I couldn't blame her. That had to be rough on a kid who looked up to her older sister.

"I can't see any harm in telling you now. That evil man is long dead and his henchmen are still locked up. Cherrie did get a nice settlement from the States Justice Program. She's married and teaching in Kansas City and has two little boys. We get together at Christmas time for a couple of weeks."

Since she was being so open about it and had relaxed somewhat just by telling me this private information, I decided to probe just a little bit. Call me eternally curious if you will. "So how has your father taken all this? Was he supporting Dominus at one time?"

"Oh, he was devastated. We all were. Cherrie told him all about what Dominus did to her, but I've never been able to get them to tell me. Whatever he did to her, it must have been really bad. I know that dad and mom were supporting him in his failed presidential bid. After Cherrie, he didn't support Dominus anymore, but he still thinks wizards are the master race though, but me, I just don't know. I mean, we're just people like everyone else, only we can use magic and others can't. It's not so open and shut is it, Parry? I mean, you are kind of in the middle, sort of using a bit of magic, right?"

I flushed. "Well, yes. Couldn't afford magic school. Had to teach myself mostly, though my uncle did help a lot. So I see what you mean. I'm kind of half and half."

She smiled. God, that was so good to see her smile again, a true smile, an honest one. Ari said, "See. We are all people; that's what I think. I know dad thinks that we should be the ones in power. Mom does too, but not as much as dad does. At least, I don't think so. Cherrie always gets into arguments about this with mom and dad. She says people are people. She says there are good wizards and bad wizards, just like there are good and bad norms. I do feel better, Parry. So what do we do now?"

"We run! Get your wand out and teleport us to the bus station now!" From where I was sitting, I saw two of the Chasma demons landing just outside the diner's front windows. Those multi-faceted, giant clusters of eyes stared through the windows looking for us. I saw them focus on Ari and then me.

Startled, Ari rose, her terror returning in an instant. Unfortunately, she too saw the two demons, just as the front window glass shattered, raining shards down on a pair of very surprised older couple. Both instantly teleported away. I hoped that Ari would obey me and teleport us. Just in case she froze, and who wouldn't freeze seeing two hideous demons coming through the window after you, I squeezed my staff hard, ready to gamble on casting it myself. I didn't want to do that. Besides not having teleported another with me, I wasn't overly confident in using this spell. As I said, I've a big fear that I'll muck it up and wind up prematurely buried.

I have to give young Ari a whole lot of credit. While I could feel her hands shaking from the sudden rush of fear, she kept her cool. Her soft voice said, "Teleport: Bus Station!" Magic flashed. We stood just outside the bus station. "Parry! They are after us again!"

Tell me something I don't know. Okay, think fast, Parry. My job is to protect Ari. I don't know how they found us at the diner, but perhaps because that's a famous wizard diner. Lou's steaks are some of the best in St. Louis. I was glad that I had chosen that place. Innocent people would not get hurt by these demons. Most everyone there was a wizard or witch and likely teleported out of there in a hurry. Lou would have to get his window replaced, but there would not be any likely other harmful outcome. Now if we'd gone to the Golden Arches, my god, the sheer number of norms who might have been harmed was staggering, many kids too in those germ-infested playgrounds. No, I had made a good call on choosing Lou's.

"Okay, teleport us to the top of the FBI headquarters building. Do you know where it's at?"

"Er, not exactly, Parry," Ari sheepishly admitted.

"Okay, then teleport us onto the roof of some building that you do know about."

"Why?"

"Look, that's the last place they will think of looking for us. Also, there won't be any innocent bystanders who could get injured or killed."

"Oh! Okay. Good plan. I like that," Ari replied, once more bravely flashing me a smile. God, I love her smile. I wish that she would only smile forever and never feel such fear and terror ever again. Magic flashed, and we landed on top of a hospital.

My turn to smile. "Brilliant Ari. I get it." If anyone else were injured, they would be mere feet from the emergency room. She flashed me another smile, as we sat down on the gravel and tar roof. "Well, we're safe enough here for now. We best pick another spot to teleport to, just in case they find us up here, another place where innocent people can't get hurt."

"I got one."

"Good girl. Let's sit back to back. That way we can watch all directions at one time."

"You're good at this, aren't you Parry?"

I smiled. "I hope so, Ari. I sure as heck don't want anything to happen to you."

Ari chuckled. "Men. You are all so different. Take my ex-fiancé."

"What? I thought that you were going to get married soon?" Through our touching backs, I could sense her muscles tensing a little. Something had happened.

She sighed. "I told him about the demons that were coming after me. I turned to him first, before I Messaged you for help, Parry. Sorry, but he was, well, my fiancé, you have to understand."

Sure kid. "Of course."

"He, he fled. He said he didn't want anything to do with me and demons. I tossed his engagement ring after him. Don't care if he never finds it. So now, I'm not getting married, at least not to him. I can't marry a coward. How could I marry him if he's going to toss me to the wind when something bad happens?"

"He's a clod. You are a darn good kid," I backed her up. "He should've done everything in the world to protect you."

She giggled a little, sounding like a young teen. True, she was twenty now, but she did relax some and that's what mattered to me right now. "So tell me, where do you work?"

"It's sort of temporary. A receptionist at St. Mary's Children's Home. Why?"

"Just curious."

"I want to get my education degree so I can teach young kids someday. You think that's silly of me?"

"Not at all, Ari. The world needs good elementary school teachers."

"Thanks. So how did you get into the PI business, if you don't mind me asking?"

"Not good for much else. Sort of half-baked magic trained. No money for junior college. Not skilled in any trade. Folks died when I was young. Lived with my uncle on his rural farm in the Missouri back woods. I can slop the pigs with the best of them. Not much call for that here in St. Louis." She giggled. Plus one for Parry. "I always seem to have a knack for finding out things. So I decided to do what I do best, help people find things. Mostly, it's simple investigations. Cheating husbands and wives or lost items. Believe it or not, last Christmas, a wizard lost his car and hired me to find it."

"Did you? Find it?"

"Yeh, he left it at the airport. He partied a wee bit too much and got so drunk he forgot where he'd left it. Thank the stars he didn't try to drive it home."

She laughed. That was so good to hear. Then, she sobered. "You think they'll find us up here?"

"Don't know. I've thought about heading into the FBI building, but I'd rather not have the demons come smashing into their place. That would cause quite a stir among the suits and norms there."

"Okay. So are we just going to spend the night hopping from place to place?"

I hadn't thought that far ahead, but I didn't want to tell Ari that. She had enough worries on her plate. Besides, it's my responsibility to protect her. Crap! Just then, I spotted two more Chasma flying demons heading our way. So much for the hospital roof.

"Ari, time to teleport again. Got your spot. No, don't turn around. Just get up and keep holding my hand. You have time. Teleport us out of here." I kept my voice low and soft, trying hard to sound perfectly natural, as if nothing of any major importance was about to happen. I know, that's rather hard to do with a pair of those slice and dice demons flying directly towards you. I heard her voice bark determinedly, and again magic flashed.

I was a bit surprised at her choice. We were standing beneath the Arch, close to the river. I could smell the river muck. "Good spot. No one is around. No one else can get hurt here. Good choice. Okay, start thinking of another spot, just in case."

"Parry. They keep on finding us!" I detected her efforts at trying to keep her growing fears at bay. Brave woman.

"You are doing great, Ari. Not many women would be able to keep their heads in a crisis like this one. You are doing super." I felt her relax a bit. Good. I needed to think and think fast.

We've been located yet again. Surely, the demons would be flying here too. If they found us at the diner and then on the roof of the hospital, surely they'd eventually find us here as well. Darn, how were they homing in on us? Better ask how long can we keep on avoiding them? Eventually, Ari is going to tire and not be able to teleport us again. Everyone has limits to the amount of magical energies they can use. Besides, it was getting late. I pulled out my cell and checked the time. Ten. I decided to text Oliver and see what else was going on.

A short while later, my phone vibrated, and I read his text. I didn't share it with Ari though. He and the others were fighting three separate battles with demons but at three widely distant locations around the city! What was going on here?

Distractions! It suddenly came to me. The demons were distracting everyone, pulling their attention and forces off what really mattered. Was that us? Ari? Was she the key? Perhaps. It seemed like it to me. I was sworn to protect her, even if my promise was made to a Princess of Hell. That didn't matter to me. I gave another my word to protect and look after Ari, and by god, I would do that, if it killed me.

I knew that I needed a new plan of action. While the current one should have worked, it wasn't. Eventually, they'd have us cornered, probably when Ari tired. I needed something new, something clever, something that would keep Ari safe. Then it struck me. They were likely after Ari, not me. They'd only warned me to stay out of this. Ari had to be the key.

"Ari, do you know the spells that can morph someone into someone else?" I kind of forgot their names. I'd read about them in the spell books though and thought they were sort of cool spells. Complicated ones thought.

"Sure. Why?" Ari asked, slightly confused.

"Okay, kid. I want you to morph me into you and morph yourself into me."

She turned and gave me a very queer look.

"Hey, they are after you, Ari, not me. They only warned me to stay out of this mess. It's you they want. So you morph me into you and you into me. If they come after us again, we are about to throw a huge monkey wrench into their plans. I'll let them capture me, but they'll think it's you. You can make a clean get away."

"But Parry, they might kill you!"

"Hey, I've got some good protections on me now. Besides, if they do take me, then you can tell Leslie, Oliver, and the others, and maybe they will be able to track me and find where they are all hiding out. We might be able to put an end to this nasty affair in short order." I didn't mention the Saturday night deadline, though. No use scaring her any worse than she was already.

"I don't know. I don't want you hurt, Parry, not because

of me."

"I won't get hurt. You know me, Ari. I get out of nasty situations. Water off a duck. A slippery eel. Just do it now while no one is watching, before they come again. Will it hurt? The morphing, I mean?"

"No, it just feels really weird, that's all. Are you sure, Parry?"

"Absolutely. Do it, Ari."

She focused and cast her spell on herself first. I found myself staring back at myself. Now that's the strangest thing that I've ever experienced. "It worked."

I heard my own voice say, "Of course it worked. For all visible things, I'm you now. Of course, my mind is mine, as are my reactions and thoughts. I hope that doesn't give us away. Okay, here goes." She cast another spell. Magic flashed.

Now I did feel really, really strange! "Oh! I've got. . ." I was able to stop myself before I uttered boobs! I felt very strange indeed. I looked at Ari or rather myself. She too looked rather nervous. Then I saw the bulge in my pants, er her pants, and realized that she was growing just as embarrassed as I was. "Well done, er Parry. This is so strange. Going to take some getting used to. I see my staff has become my wand. Cool. Oh, your wand now looks like my staff."

I cleared my throat, er, rather she cleared her throat. "Of course, the spell changes our possessions to look like the other's things." She moved her arms and legs about some, testing the feelings of her new form. I followed her lead, trying hard to get rather used to the feel of her body, er, my body in its new form. Too late to be worrying about our sexes. I knew this had to be done. I had a hunch the demons would not stop until they got Ari.

"Okay. If the demons find us again, we'll shoot a couple of spells at them. I'll shoot my ball of fire, though I know that's not going to harm them. It didn't before, but that's my main damage spell from my staff. The other one I use is a bolt of electricity. So you best shoot that when I shoot the ball of fire. Then, when we see that it is not going to harm the demons, I'll pretend to fall down, while you teleport the heck out of here."

"But where will I go?" I, er Ari, asked.

"Do you know about that new magic store that opened up north, where they sell wands, potions, and other magical items? Five women have opened it recently."

"Yes, I visited it once. Rather a cool place."

"Good. Go there. They are friends of mine. They will look after you. Just tell them what we've done. They'll know what to do. This nasty business has to stop, so we are just going to have to make that happen. Don't worry about me, Ari. With the protections I've got on me, I should be all right."

"Okay, Pa- er, Ari, but I don't like it. If something bad happens to you because of me. . ."

"Hey, kid. It's not your fault. It's those darned demons, not yours. You're supposed to be able to live your life free from such terrors as these. All women should, children too. It's not right, and I aim to settle matters once and for all."

Parry, er, Ari leaned over and gave me a kiss, a passionate one! I felt my morphed body grow very hot and moist in a strange area of its anatomy. "Thanks," she whispered as our lips parted.

"Most welcome," I whispered back, not daring to say more.

Once more, we sat back to back, watching all directions. A half hour later, she or rather she as I, spotted three incoming flying demons. Darn, these creatures just don't give up! I realized that they must want Ari really badly to have put so much effort into finding her.

Fireworks are always going off at nearby Bush Stadium and here on the fourth. Well, Ari and I created a bit of ad-lib fireworks. I shot off a couple of brilliantly exploding fireballs, while she shot a pair of arcing lightning bolts. They did look impressive and brilliant. Didn't do squat to the Chasma flying demons though. Didn't expect that they would. However, for my plan to work, I needed to convince them that we were getting frantic and trying to stop them.

"Hold, hold. Just a bit longer. We need to make this look convincing." The creatures were now drawing very close and beginning their descent. Another few seconds and they'd land on top of us. At the last instant, I called out, "Now!" I dove to the ground some distance to Ari's left, while she cast her teleport spell. I thought that we'd choreographed this ploy extremely well, timed to the last second. Perfect! I felt a Chasma landing on top of me. I tried to struggle a bit to add to the game. Then I felt a hard knock on my head. With my protections on, I wasn't hurt, just knocked out. I saw stars and darkness came, though I was aware of being flown away. So far, my plan was working to perfection!

Chapter 9—Frantic Exercises

Oliver, Leslie, Harry, and their forces, along with Monica Nicole and her group, were kept busy Friday night from about seven o'clock until close to eleven. Someone reported two gorilla-demons charging down I-44 by the Botanical Gardens. A half hour later, another report came in from down by Benton Park. Two more were causing trouble there. Around eight, another sighting put two more creating havoc in St. Louis Hills. The demons were active in three widely separated areas around the city.

Oliver, his men, Leslie, and her crew tackled the two around the gardens. Then, Henry and his group intervened down in Benton Park. When the call came in from St. Louis Hills, Monica Nicole and her four companions headed there to see if they couldn't stop the carnage.

"This is ridiculous!" Monica Nicole exclaimed, exasperated beyond words. Two of the gorilla type demons were thundering down the street, smashing up the cars parked on its sides. Mostly, they were bent on destruction, not killing people. Several uniformed policemen were firing their various weapons at them, having formed up a crude defensive line but they were continually falling back. None wanted to get too close to these demons, whose fists were crushing the tops of cars and trucks like a trash compactor.

The five had arrived a few minutes ago and began shooting various killer spells at the demons. They had come prepared to do battle. All wore heavy jeans, tennis shoes, and black, leather jackets. However, their very long, heavy earrings looked rather out of place, but those Ericka-enchanted earrings provided them a good measure of protection.

"Hey, that's working a bit," Enya called out. "Use Push spells, to force them backwards. Maybe we can hold the line with them that way."

"On it," Misty yelled, casting another Push, temporarily halting a demon in its tracks, but otherwise leaving it unharmed.

"Yes, but we're not stopping them," Crystal yelled.

"Hey, I've an idea, cover me," Monica Nicole called out. She focused and cast her Magical Door. She stepped partway through it. Her friends saw her hand appear in space just above and behind the shoulders of one of the demons. Monica cast another spell and her friends saw her fingers touch the back of the gorilla demon. A giant flash of magical energies detonated. Monica reappeared beside her four friends. The creature groaned, frozen in place. The ground below its feet opened up, and it slowly sank into the ground.

"What the heck did you do to it, Monica?" Crystal yelled. She could hear the policemen cheering, though they still continued to pour round after round into the remaining demon, ignoring the simple fact that their bullets and shot gun pellets were having no effect whatsoever.

"Suspended Animation and Sink into the ground. It's imprisoned, though I don't know how long it will remain there," Monica Nicole answered. Enya and Misty continued to keep their Push spells concentrated on the remaining demon, keeping it from advancing. All five wished the police would stop firing their guns. The noise was deafening, and they had to yell just to communicate.

A few minutes later, the demon was totally buried below ground, though the street would need re-pavement work now. "I'm going to do the same thing to the other one. Keep it occupied," Monica Nicole yelled. Once more, she cast her Magical Door, having it appear just above and behind the remaining demon. After stepping partly into it, she cast her other two spells, reached out, and touched the back of the struggling demon. This time, her magic fizzled, and it swung its massive fist around, intending to flatten her. Just in time, she stepped back out of her door. Its swing hit empty air, and it lost its balance. Misty's next push knocked the off balance demon to the ground.

Crystal seized the moment. Suddenly, time seemed to stand still for everyone except her. She raced up to the demon, her feet trampling over spent casings and shells. Hastily, she cast another spell. Magic flashed and the demon vanished from sight. As fast as she could run, Crystal dashed back beyond the line of policemen with their many guns in the process of firing towards the now gone demon and herself. Then, she heard the loud noises again, as time began moving forward. She'd just barely made it. The firing ceased. "Where'd it go?" someone yelled. "Dunno!"

"Nice going, Crystal. You got it," Misty called out.

"Where'd it go?" Enya yelled, before realizing the gunshots had ended.

"It's imprisoned somewhere below the ground, and it's going to stay there forever as far as I'm concerned!" Crystal declared flatly. "Okay, come on. We're done here. Let's go see if Henry needs a hand." The five joined hands in a circle, and Monica Nicole cast her Teleport, arriving near Benton Park. Again, their ears were assaulted by the rapid firing of some very heavy weapons!

Henry spotted them and came over to them using a Magical Door. It was faster than running. "Ah, good to see you. Having a bit of trouble with these, so I called in the heavy weapons. 50-caliber, like Parry suggested. It's having some effect, though these demons sure can take a beating."

Holding her hands over hear ears, Crystal yelled, "Monica Nicole got one with a combination of Suspended Animation and Sink. I got the other with an Imprison spell. Don't know how long they will stay that way though. Loud enough for you?"

"What's that you're saying?" Henry yelled back and then grinned. Crystal's annoying look vanished, as she duplicated his tease. "I gave up after we hit them with twenty failing Disintegrate spells. Nasty apes."

Enya yelled, "Hey look! They got one!" Indeed, one of the demons had fallen to the ground. The other one was bleeding goo everywhere, and it promptly vanished from sight, probably teleporting away. At last, the deafening noise subsided. The sheer number of 50-cal shells littering the street made walking up to the dead demon extremely treacherous. Now the five could see a dozen national guardsmen manning the rather large guns. Gun smoke almost obscured the whole area. While they were trying to move up to the fallen demon and stay on their feet, the demon suddenly vanished. When they got to its location, the street was covered in masses of green goo.

One lone FBI man, who had been standing back the whole time, stepped forward, also trying to keep from losing his balance on the brass casings littering the street, and barked, "Okay, we'll take over from here. I'll get the forensic boys here pronto. What is that stuff anyway? Blood? Or what passes for blood in those things?"

Henry spoke up, "Yes, probably. Okay, I'll get the guards back to their barracks. Why don't you five go see if Oliver and Leslie need a hand? Quite an interesting night, don't you think? Can't wait to get my hands on those who did this Gating!"

Monica Nicole chuckled. "Indeed, Henry. Just don't kill him too quickly." All laughed. Then, Ericka teleported them up north to the vicinity of the Botanical Gardens. Here, things had turned rather ugly. Four Chasma demons had wreaked havoc on the interstate. Traffic was blocked up for miles in both directions. Many cars were wrecked. Injured lay everywhere, but the battle was over when the five arrived.

"Ah, you are just in time. Got a bit of a disaster going here," Leslie commented dryly. "Can you help teleport the injured to the various hospitals? The emergency vehicles are taking way too long to get through this mess."

"On it!" Misty answered. The five rushed out to see what they could do to help. Already six other wizards who had accompanied Leslie to the battle were making hospital trips. Oliver coordinated everything via his cell phone. "Take those two to St. Mary's. Thanks. Those three go to Proctor."

Around eleven, the combined group of wizards and witches, along with the many emergency responders had the injured taken to five different hospitals, the many disabled vehicles removed, and the interstate opened to traffic once more. A number of TV news crews were on hand filming everything both from the ground and from three helicopters in the air overhead.

Henry and his staff had already joined them, helping to transport the injured. "Well, this has been quite a night," Leslie said to the group. "You have my sincere thanks, everyone. Tomorrow, the Rodents will be coming to lend us a hand with this mess. Say, has anyone heard from Parry and Ari?" No one had, and the groups disbanded, heading for their homes or hotel rooms.

Ericka teleported her friends back to their place. While Jasper and Brad were still there protecting their shops and home, Ari had not known that. Instead, she had merely sat down before the front doors to wait. As she sat there all alone, tears trickled down. Parry had made the ultimate sacrifice for her, guaranteeing her safety, at least for tonight. No one had ever done that for her before, excepting her parents, but even they were now in hiding and not really helping her at all. Only Parry. Suddenly, magic flashed, and the five women arrived before their front doors.

"Oh! Parry. You're here. How did it go?" Crystal took charge.

"I'm not Parry. I'm Ari. He's me and was captured," she sobbed and quickly cancelled her morph spell.

"Oh my god! Okay, inside everyone before any prying eyes can see her!" Crystal ordered. A minute later, they had her inside and in their study. Enya and Misty dashed off to let their husbands know all went well, while the other three assisted Ari.

"Okay, Ari, start at the beginning of tonight and tell us everything that happened. How did Parry come to be you?" Crystal asked, rather gently.

"He, he did it for me, to protect me," Ari sobbed and then began telling the three all about their eventful evening. Slowly, she told them their story.

"Parry has a head on his shoulders," Monica Nicole exclaimed when Ari finished up. "Incredibly good thinking. He had you going to totally random locations and ones in which no innocent bystanders could get hurt—far cry from the I-44 disaster this evening! So he rightly worked out that the demons were indeed tracking you. That you are here now is concrete proof that they were after you, Ari, and not Parry."

"But why? Why me?" she wailed.

"The truth? You're not going to like it, but you deserve to know," Monica Nicole declared. "I, we believe that you are a virgin." She nodded. "And that they are intending to sacrifice you to complete their bargain with some Demon Lord."

"Oh god! No! Parry!" she looked up, her face suddenly extremely pale. "He'll be . . ." Her voice cracked, and she couldn't finish her thought. It was too horrible to say.

"We know. So Parry must have worked this out too and that's why he had you Morph him into you, Ari. The ultimate protection. Parry, you are one quick-thinking fellow!" Monica Nicole exclaimed, rather impressed with the half-trained wizard who had more guts than good sense. He was very likely to get himself killed when they discovered his deception. He was sure to piss them off rather royally, she thought, but didn't vocalize it.

Instead, she asked, "Crystal, let Leslie and Henry know what's happened. I have some spell work to do immediately. See that I'm not disturbed, please."

Crystal replied, "Got it. What's the best route to take now?"

"That's what I aim to find out," Monica Nicole answered, moving hastily out of the study.

Ericka said softly, "Come on Ari; let's get you a hot bath and cleaned up some." She escorted the young woman off to her room, leaving Crystal to send all the Messages.

Alone in her room, Monica Nicole sighed. "Well, at least this time around, I do have one powerful divination based spell that I can use. Best use it now." She sat down in her easy chair, focused for several minutes, blocking all thoughts from her mind, then cast her Grade 9 spell, looking, she hoped, into the future while focusing on Parry, disguised as Ari. For some time, she could sense nothing at all.

Then, she saw a number of the Rodents, the very ones who had captured her, or Dominus rather, and his band of fifty Death Stalkers, ending his grand plan, his Golden Path. They would be coming and be involved. She shivered some, an involuntary reaction, but she continued to attempt to glimpse what would likely happen and more importantly where. She had the very strong impression that someone or something was blocking her spell, rather significantly. Growing a bit frustrated, she decided to change her focus and tried to see how she might locate where Ari-Parry was being held. She got a glimpse of a warehouse, but more importantly, she saw Amanda using her Tracker skills to home in on a Message being sent to Ari-Parry. It was early evening when Amanda was doing this. At last, she had a clue and ended her spell.

Meanwhile, back at their hotel rooms, Leslie and Henry compared notes. He finally had some free time to continue his background checking. "Boss, here's something strange. I've been verifying the five teens that came to help us tonight. Thought I should know a bit about them. Seems that they all went to magic school together, rooming together all six years. Red Hall ladies. Bet you couldn't guess that one," he teased. She smiled.

"Anyway, they all check out just fine, setting scholastic achievement records for Red Hall students. Straight A's for all five of them for all six years. Pretty impressive," he commented.

"But? What's the but, Henry?" Leslie countered.

"Well, Monica Nicole Black. She doesn't checkout. There are no records whatsoever of any Monica Nicole Black, prior to her first year at the St. Louis School of Magic. Her entrance records state that she lost her parents when she was very young and was raised by her uncle and then later her aunt, all Black Hall graduates and strong Dominus supporters. Both are dead now, old age, but he had severe arthritis. How could they possibly have raised a small child? What is quite strange is that there are no other records predating this school entrance. Don't know what to make of it," Henry stated, rubbing his head.

Before Leslie could answer, both received a very long Message from Crystal, outlining what had happened to Ari and Parry. Further, Parry was now morphed into Ari and was in the hands of these demons! "Darn, darn, darn! It was all just a diversion!" Leslie cursed. "They got us all chasing all over the city, while they homed in on their prey, Ari."

"Darn it! We were had!" Henry exclaimed. "Poor boy, likely going to get himself killed for sure."

"Well, I'm contacting the Rodents now. I know it's midnight, but if that date is accurate, we have about eighteen hours to figure this thing out or we are in really deep trouble!" Leslie declared. "See that I'm not interrupted for a while." He nodded, and Leslie focused and began a very lengthy spell casting.

That done, they turned in for the night, quite exhausted. Leslie rose at dawn. She had much to do before eight a.m., when the Rodents agreed to arrive. After showering and dressing appropriately in her professional dress, she met with Oliver for breakfast. Henry soon joined them, looking a bit weary. Oliver said, "It's all over the newscasts. Even the west coast outlets are sending reporters here. They are having a field day with this hot potato. Good thing that they don't know what's really going on."

"Neither do we, not really," Leslie countered. She was in an ill humor as well. The situation had gotten wholly out of hand last night. The I-44 disaster would raise far more heat than she desired. Being in the national spotlight was not what she wanted for the Missouri Department of Magical Misuse. Worse, soon, they would know that she'd used her powers to call in the Rodents! Now that *would* make headline news.

"Come on. Hurry up and eat. We need to get the presentation room ready. They'll be here around eight," she explained.

When they got to the large meeting room, the five women were just arriving, walking slowly towards them—slowly, because three of the women were wearing their very tall heels. Again, they appeared dressed for a formal ball or gala event. Monica Nicole wore a dark red satin gown, while Crystal and Ericka wore gowns of a similar style done in light blue satin. Their black nylons and black patent leather pumps contrasted nicely with the three's gowns. In contrast, Enya and Misty wore simple day dresses and flats. Leslie could not help thinking that those two were the practical ones.

Leslie helped herself to a cup of coffee and took her seat at the head of the table. Henry followed suit, joining her at her side. The five entered and were about to sit when a small crowd came wandering into the room.

"Is this where we're supposed to meet?" a male voice called out. Deiter Cross led his pack of Rodents into the room, as Leslie rose and nodded his way. "Found it gang. Come on in. Hi everyone. I'm Eliminator Deiter Cross. The Rodents have arrived, well some of us anyway."

"Thanks for coming on such short notice. I'm Leslie Traub, head of the Missouri Department of Magical Misuse. Henry Wilkens, head of the St. Louis branch. Come on in, Deiter."

"I'll introduce those of us here now," Deiter began, taking charge. He was in a hurry to get to the action, as always. So the sooner the introductions were done, the sooner they could get into action. My wife, Governor Lindsey Barron-Cross, world class Dispeller. Professor-Sleuth Pam Betts-Ryker. Mrs Mrs. Amanda Whitewater-Orondarka, best Tracker ever. Mrs. Ashley Stokes-Compton-Whitewater, Diviner Supreme, and her husband, Jim. Mrs. Kathy Townsend-Lopez, potion maker. The other ten will be along later on, if needed. So what's all this about demons anyway?"

"First, these are five recent graduates of the St. Louis School of Magic and who have opened their own magic store here," Leslie refused his bait. "Crystal Holliday, Ericka Van Nie, Monica Nicole Black, Enya Homes-Scorsky, and Misty Worth-Williams. With them is Miss Ari Glaston or rather Athos. This is Oliver Easton, head of the FBI Special Investigations here in St. Louis. Okay, have a seat. Coffee if you wish."

Ashley spoke up, "Ericka Van Nie? Crystal Holliday? Wow! It's really you. I've seen your photos on the cover of Teen Fashion. Cool. I was on there too back when I was in school. You've filled out some since then, but you both look fabulous. Are we keeping you from a special occasion?"

Now that Deiter had the chance to look at the others, his eyes nearly popped out, as he got a good look at the two former models and their bosoms and outfits. Jim did a double take as well. Ericka laughed. "Hardly. We dress like this all the time, except when we have to fight the demons like last night."

Pam added, "Red Hall graduates?"

Ericka flashed a smile. "Is it that obvious?" Everyone chuckled and began taking their seats.

After sitting down, Pam spoke up again, "Ari, are you

any relation to Cherrie Athos?"

"My older sister. We were in the Witness Protection Program. Glaston, but now I can't see any reason not to use our real last name, Athos. Why?"

"Just putting two and two together. I helped rescue your sister. We all did. Last I heard she was off at college and married," Pam replied, confident that her Sleuthing skills were still as sharp as ever. She never forgot a name.

"Yes, she's a grade school teacher in Kansas City. Has two small boys," Ari replied, rather pleased that someone of this extreme importance and a professor to boot actually remembered her sister.

Deiter spoke up. "Can we get down to business? If we let them, Ashley will talk about photo shoots and modeling all day long. So what's up?"

Leslie grinned. "Okay, okay. A little lightness is needed after what we all went through last night. Let's begin at the beginning. We believe that we have about ten hours left to solve this thing before all hell breaks loose. No pun intended. Oliver, why don't you begin with Jessica's kidnaping? Fill in what you know about our missing man. We're short Parry Oscar Tuttle, Private Investigator. He's currently impersonating Ari here and is likely to die at dusk unless we can solve this mess. Oliver." She sat down and began sipping her coffee, but watched the Rodents' reactions like a hawk.

"Jessica White was a twenty year old young woman, a virgin. She was kidnaped as she carried her lunch back to the office where she worked. Parry found the location where the crime was committed." He began his rather lengthy outline of the events, but put a big time-line up on the overhead projector. He related how Parry had found their initial incised pentagram where they had initially summoned the demons. He added a new fact. His forensics team had positively identified a trace of Jessica's blood on the concrete floor. DNA match. He described Parry's encounter with the Chasma demons, allowing Ari to escape unharmed. He told of Aunt Glasya's hiring of Parry too, along with how the five teen witches had helped him get healed via Enya's potions.

Deiter interrupted him. "So let's just pound these

demons with our spells!"

"Sorry, Mr. Cross," Crystal interrupted him. "The demons and devils, for that matter, have some immunity to magical spells."

Oliver backed her up. "Precisely. I'm getting to that. Let's just say that last night Henry and his associates fired off twenty disintegrates at one of these demons and achieved nothing at all. I'll get to that, patience my boy." He then got back on track. It took him an hour to brief them fully on the complete details. He ended with, "So you see, Parry was right. We need really big guns. Thank goodness Henry was able to call up the National Guard last night."

Henry added, "Right. We put about a thousand rounds of 50-caliber shells into one demon before it died. Guess we'll need tanks next." Several chuckled at that.

Leslie then took charge again. "So we now have nine hours to solve this before Parry is sacrificed, if he is still alive."

Pam spoke up. "First, let me get the identifications clear. I'm sorry. The Rodents have never dealt with demons or devils before, just wizards and witches."

Crystal broke in, "I am well versed in these matters. I'm a registered user of the Gate spell and have had electives in these matters. Yes, the identification of Glasya, Princess of Hell, and Consort of Mammon is positively correct. Matches the sketches in our books. Likewise, we have exact matches with sketches of the Chasma demons and the gorilla types, Class Four demons to be technical about it. The identifications are not suspect. Further, the sacrifice of a virgin is what would be needed to summon a Demon Lord or his representative. Nothing less would get their attention, excepting their true names, of course. So we have a real mess here. The Glaston or Athos husband and wife have gone into hiding and have so many protective spells on them that we can't reach them or track them. We've no idea where Wil Blackthornby and his group are located or where they've created another incised pentagram. Essentially, we are in the dark, with eight and a half hours left before disaster strikes again, though it may not, since Parry isn't a virgin maiden. Say, does anyone know if he is a virgin? A male sacrifice might also work."

All heads turned to Oliver, his best friend. "Sorry, I don't know. He might well be, just don't know. Never seen him on a date. No known girlfriends, so it's possible. Darn it, Parry, what have you done this time?"

Leslie defended him, "Saving Ari's life. Keeping his word and promise."

"Darn, there isn't much time to research these demons and devils is there?" Pam said disgustedly.

"Couldn't be helped really. Until last night, we didn't fully realize what we were up against here," Leslie countered.

All this time, Monica Nicole was covertly eyeing Ashley. She was the Diviner who had been instrumental in getting Dominus and fifty Death Stalkers captured six plus years ago. She also eyed Deiter and Lindsey, recalling how the Rodents first entered that old warehouse in Montrose, all morphed into duplicates of Lindsey. She also recalled Lindsey's actions taking the Rod of the Apocalypse from him as well as the Crown of Moses. Monica Nicole felt a little ill at ease.

Amanda spoke up, "So let's get cracking. If someone will Message this Parry, I'll follow the magic streak and lead us to him."

Leslie sighed. "Sorry. Won't work. We've tried getting a Message to him or her. Fails completely. If you want to watch, I'll try it right now." Amanda insisted and she cast another Message spell. Amanda watched the streak of magic sail from her wand and then promptly returned to the ground, discharging its power into the building.

"Well, that's sure strange. Never seen magic streaks do that before," Amanda sighed. "These Demon Lords and devils must really be powerful."

"Of course they are," Leslie replied. "At this point, I am at a loss on how to proceed. We have pretty much worked out that last night's triple battle was a mere distraction that allowed them to capture what they thought was Ari. Parry's improvised plan worked, perhaps too well, but at least Ari is safe with us."

Governor Lindsey, who had been silent so far, finally spoke up. After all, she was still the leader of the Rodents. "Gang, our secret weapon is going to be useless, I'm afraid.

These demons are quite used to traveling to and from our universe. Since they are resistant to magic, the Idiot Mind is not going to work either."

Deiter looked perplexed. "Darn, if that's out and if they can take twenty Disintegrates, how the heck are we going to stop them? Pound them to death?" He looked very frustrated indeed.

"More importantly, Deiter," Pam spoke up rather didactically, "how do we find them? Don't put the cart before the horse."

Monica Nicole spoke up at last. "Excuse me, but I have something I can add that might help. After I heard about Parry last night, I cast my Have Foresight spell. It was rough going. He's under very strong blocking spells, but I did glimpse that we will be able to get a Message spell to get through to him around six tonight, and Amanda will be able to track it, and we can get to him that way. He's just got to stay alive until six."

"Excellent, Monica Nicole. Finally, something that's useful," Leslie praised her, greatly relieved. Already she was beginning to make plans for the assault that was sure to come.

"Hey, we could have Peaches give it a try as well as Ashley," Kathy suggested. "I'll Message Peaches now, if you like."

Ashley smiled, "Okay. I'm curious about how they have him blocked. Let Peaches know. So is there a quiet room around here where I can do it?"

Henry rose and led her and Jim, who refused to leave her side, into a side room, Oliver's office actually. He and Jim stood guard outside, while Ashley sat in his fancy leather chair and cast her identical spell. She figured that she was more than likely going to obtain more data than this Monica Nicole was. After all, she was the Class 4 Diviner.

When she was off working her spell, Oliver received a phone call and stepped out of the room to talk. He returned with a smile. "Good old shoe leather comes through." Everyone looked at him for a change. "That was one of my agents. I sent some out to interview the neighbors of both these two families. Now this is interesting. It seems that Herbert and Wil know each other and have gone on at least one fishing trip into the Ozarks together. Further, another neighbor often plays cards with Wil. One time, Herbert joined them and got into a heated discussion with the other players, insisting that there was nothing wrong with Dominus Malefic's Golden Path. Wait, there is more. Another agent checked the Magical Library downtown. Herbert has been reading Mallory's <u>A Guide to Bargaining with Devils</u>, among other occult volumes."

"Oliver, this is interesting," Leslie smiled. "Perhaps, Herbert Athos has been trying to make some use of it. Could Ari's own father be behind the devil's side in this fiasco?"

"But as yet, this Glasya Princess hasn't done anything but try to protect Ari," Deiter countered. "Couldn't the devils just take her soul right away or something? Why the long delay?"

"Her soul is herself, Deiter," Pam pointed out. "But you have a point. If Herbert sold his daughter to the devil—no wait. That doesn't make sense. Princess Glasya's actions don't fit. She should be absconding with Ari in tow back to Hell or wherever. Instead, she's gone out of her way to help protect Ari. Could Herbert have bargained for Hell's protection for Ari? Does Herbert know something that we don't know? This is so confusing without proper data!"

"Ripples in time," Leslie commented. "How interesting."

"What's that?" Oliver inquired.

"Oh just something you mentioned with that Golden Path of his. It's amazing how a person's actions ripple onwards through time long after they are gone. He's been dead what, over six years now, and still we have two Black Hall wizards arguing for that awful plan of his. It was riddled with big lies, very cleverly disguised. People can be so gullible, wizards and norms alike. Ripples. May they soon die out." She grinned.

Pam then said, "I should have a look at the holdings that Wil has. Perhaps I can get a clue on where they could be from that."

Oliver volunteered, "They are in my office. Come, I'll take you there, but I think Ashley's using it right now. Maybe she won't be long." The two left.

"So how do we pound these demons? Ideas?" asked Deiter.

"Well last night Monica Nicole was able to use a Magical Door to get herself up behind one of the demons. She cast her Suspended Animation spell by reaching out of her door and touching it on its back and then cast Sink into the Ground spell. That worked. Stopped it cold; buried it too," Crystal explained. "I took a hint from her and did something similar, opening my door behind the other one and casting my Imprisoning spell and touching it on its shoulders. That also worked. But Monica Nicole tried her same sequence on that one, but it didn't work. So we know that it is possible to take them by surprise, and it is possible for spells somehow to get through their innate resistance to magical spells. I can't explain Henry's twenty failed Disintegrate spells, though."

"I can," Governor Lindsey replied. "Assuming their innate resistance, a good percentage of spells simply will be reflected or nullified by that aspect. Those that get through they can then attempt to dodge or avoid them. For example, when we were trying to undo some of the nasty spells that Dominus had cast upon his play toys, those poor women, we must have cast the Dispel Magic spell thirty times before it finally worked. What I am saying is that if you hit them enough times with deadly spells, eventually one will connect."

"You mean I have to hit it with thirty Disintegrates, dear?" Deiter looked at her aghast.

"Yep. Good luck with that, dear," she grinned teasingly. Kathy chuckled.

He brightened up. "Hey, with all nineteen of us Rodents casting it at once, we should succeed on our second try. That's nearly forty of them. Bring 'em on!" Again, Deiter was ready for action.

Ashley returned to hear the end of the discussion and chuckled herself. Jim too. "So what did you discover?" Lindsey asked, as Ashley and Jim took their seats.

"Well, that was interesting indeed. These are some 'big boys' that we're playing with. No doubt about that. They have several layers of anti-scrying spells on themselves and Parry. Dislocation spells as well. I finally got through their

Dislocation spells though. I don't think they counted on a Class 4 Diviner. They most certainly are somewhere here in St. Louis, but I can't say where. Their minds are so foreign to me. However, Monica Nicole is right. Whatever they are planning to do, they will have to lower some of their protections to do it. She's right, sometime around six tonight, we will have our one and only one chance at this. I'm very certain that Saturday night is the key time for whatever they are planning. Unfortunately, I haven't any idea with that plan actually is. I need to make contact with either this Wil fellow or Herbert, but they are effectively blocking me. I wonder if Peaches will be able to add anything further? She'll be along later on with the rest of the pack."

"Well done, Ashley," Leslie complimented her. "That confirms it. Monica Nicole and Ashley both agree on the date, time, and means. What remains is for us to work out just how we are going to respond."

"Might we take a look at that original incised pentagram?" Lindsey asked. "Perhaps we can detect some after-traces of magic there that might give us a clue. Deiter, why don't you stick around and help work out a plan of attack? Amanda and I can check it out."

"Sure thing, dear. Don't worry. We will figure something out; we always do," Deiter replied confidently.

"I'll take you there," Monica Nicole offered. "Crystal and Ericka need to be in on the planning."

"Sure, but you aren't exactly dressed for rummaging around old warehouses," Lindsey replied.

"Oh, we dress like this all the time, except when fighting, of course. Keeps the fellows distracted, you see," Monica Nicole replied with a smile of her dark red lips.

Amanda chuckled. "Aye, that it does. Okay then, let's give this a shot. It's an outside chance at best. Too much time has elapsed." She and Lindsey each took a hold of one of Monica Nicole's hands while she cast her Teleport spell. She arrived quite gracefully, in spite of her six-inch heels.

"You've had a bit of practice in those heels," Amanda teased. "Like your really long nails. They look good on you."

"Absolutely and thanks. Crystal and Ericka love them

long. I'd rather they were a bit shorter. Okay, here we are. I see that they've taken the yellow crime scene tape down. Come on. It's just inside." She headed towards the door, her steel heel tips clicking on the concrete. Lindsey and Amanda, wands at the ready, followed after her, but rather wished Monica Nicole could move faster.

"It's over there, towards the center. Oliver's forensic team has been all over here, so expect things to be a bit messed up," Monica Nicole explained. "Crystal's our Gate and Summoning expert, not me."

"Okay. Let's let Amanda have a long look. Meanwhile, let me wander around here and get a feel for these people. You can tell a lot about people from their possessions," Lindsey explained.

Monica Nicole couldn't resist and asked, "So what about me? What can you tell about me?"

"Elegant, refined, brilliant, attention to detail, power tempered by strong passion, but there's something more. Can't put my finger on it yet," Lindsey replied and moved off to examine the old rusting warehouse.

Meanwhile, Monica Nicole kept her eyes on Amanda, but simply couldn't see what the Tracker was observing. She even got down on all fours and sniffed the circle a bit, before getting back up and dusting her hands off. She paced around the circle several times. Finally, she said, "Pam needs to see this site. I'll Message her, but can you go get her for us?"

"Sure. On my way," Monica Nicole replied. With a firm wave of her wand, she vanished. "Real power in that woman, eh, Lindsey?"

"Very much so. I think it's tempered though. Find anything?"

"Yeh, quite a bit, but I want Pam's analysis before I commit."

Just then, Monica Nicole returned, bringing Pam with her. The professor looked annoyed. "I was just in the middle of my analysis. This had better be good, Amanda."

"I think so. Cast your spells on this circle and its center. I've detected some pretty strange things here. See what you see, please Pam," Amanda asked.

"Okay, okay." Pam's irritation vanished. She focused and cast another spell that Monica Nicole didn't know, but made a note to research and try to learn. After a few minutes, Pam's spell ended. She looked a bit pale, Monica Nicole noted, and listened carefully.

"You see the sacrifice?" Amanda asked. "I saw traces of the energy released."

"Yes, pretty darn brutal. Single stab into her heart. She didn't stand a chance."

"Okay. That action sealed the Gate and bound the summoned demon," Amanda pronounced.

Pam added, "I think it was a female demon of some kind that got summoned. Guess I'll have to look at some books to identify it," Pam said flatly.

"What did she look like?" Monica Nicole asked, very curious about what the two had seen. Here was power that she didn't know existed.

"Well, she looked sort of like a female. Had breasts, but she was huge, just barely fitting inside this pentagram. She had flames surrounding her body. They caused the scorch marks there on the floor where her feet stood. Her hair was short and wild, kind of like the Goth look. She had horns, small ones, on her head, and carried a sword and a whip," Pam answered.

"Ah, bet it was one of the powerful Class Six demons then. I've been looking at Crystal's books the last few days," Monica Nicole explained. "I'll see if Crystal can produce a sketch of one so you can identify it."

"Yeh, what's really sick is that once this thing materialized, the first thing that she did was drink poor Jessica's blood, but not until she kissed the corpse. How revolting," Pam added.

"Has to be a Six'er then. That's what they do to their victims, according to Crystal's books, that is. Sick is right!" Monica Nicole replied.

"Well, I'll be getting back to my research now. I hope to find some possible locations to search long before six," Pam stated and cast her teleport spell, leaving the three alone in the warehouse.

"I'm done here too," Amanda said.

"Yes, I guess I am too," Lindsey replied. "I think that we are dealing with an old man, close to the end of his life. He's not in good health, kind of rotting away like this warehouse. Possessions should be in similar disrepair. Probably he is focused on one final single thing, which has totally taken over his entire thoughts. Something that he feels he simply must do before he dies."

"You get all of that just from looking this place over?" Amanda asked. Monica Nicole grinned and agreed fully with Amanda, but was glad that Amanda had asked instead of herself.

"Yep. Ripples. This place is in disrepair and nearly 'dead.' Yet, Wil hasn't gotten rid of it and has used it for his recent action, which, you will have to admit, is extremely dangerous and powerful. So whatever it is all about, it has consumed his every thought, beyond his own frail health. It's literally driving him."

"Well, I should have seen all that," Monica Nicole admitted. "When you point that out, it sounds perfectly logical. Duh. I can see that I need to hone up my powers of observation some. I've been too dependent upon magic. Got to use my eyes, eh Lindsey?"

Lindsey smiled. "Yep. Come on; let's get back, and see what hair-brained schemes Deiter has dreamed up." Amanda chuckled, but Monica Nicole had no idea what the inside joke was all about.

When they returned, Crystal had popped home and back, bringing one of her book of sketches with her. Monica Nicole had alerted her to what they'd found. After their brief report, Pam glanced at the sketch and pronounced that the original summoned creature was a Class Six demon.

"I kind of thought so from your description. Monica Nicole relayed it to me. Now I've some research to do," Crystal replied. "I think this might just be a really important clue about which Demon Lord was actually summoned, at least initially. Monica, come lend me a hand." The two moved to the back of the room and began paging through several books that Crystal had brought from their library.

While the two were off doing that, Leslie continued making their plans, but brought Lindsey and Amanda up to date. "Look, based on what happened last night and before that, we suspect that they are sending out a number of demons to force us to put our attention elsewhere but on them. We were all so tied up dealing with the three separate incidents last night that we failed to monitor Parry and Ari, which were their real target. It's my guess that they will attempt to do the same thing tonight. Launch several demon incursions into the city, raising havoc to distract us while they carry out their original plans."

She went on, "Worse, they must know we simply can't ignore the rampaging demons. We're obligated to protect the citizens of St. Louis and will have to send an effective response team to each group of demons."

Lindsey grimaced. This wasn't good. Splitting up forces never was, particularly so since these demons were so darn hard to handle. Leslie explained further, "So Henry is off arranging a coordinated effort with the National Guard. He's going to have at least three platoons with heavy weapons on standby, ready to deal with any threat. Hopefully, there won't be more than three separate ones. Just in case, Henry is alerting the base commander to field more as needed. That will free Henry and me up to assist with the real situation. Our subordinates will coordinate and assist with the guard platoons."

"Of course, the real question is how do we stop them when we don't know what they are doing or why," she added. They discussed the situation until lunchtime. Oliver conveniently had lunch brought in for the large group.

Over lunch, Crystal decided to voice her fledgling opinion of the root cause. "Monica Nicole and I have been pouring over the few written books on the Abyss and its history. I am basing my search on the premise that Wil's sacrifice of a virgin was of paramount importance, at least initially. That said, the reason for it would be to summon a Demon Lord or his trusted servant, binding them, thus preventing them from harming the summoner, and coaxing them to listen to his proposal. Nothing less than that could

136

guarantee any success at all. So I asked myself if a Demon Lord didn't appear himself and sent his trusted servant, then which lord has a Class Six demon princess as his closest associate?"

She went on, noticing that everyone was listening closely, though stuffing their mouths with the burgers and fries. "That's what Monica Nicole and I have been looking for. We think we have one or two possibilities. The most likely one is not a Demon Lord, but a prince called Graz'zt. The books say that he has a Class Six'er as his mate, one Anastasia. The history book said that he was in some kind of Abyss war with Demon Lords when some wizard here on Earth summoned him from his battlefield, costing him the war. Of course, he supposedly killed the summoner, but that was over three thousand years ago. I doubt that he holds a grudge that long."

"The other is less likely. The Prince of Deception, Lord Fraz-Urb'luu. Apparently, he was also summoned to Earth many millennia ago and even imprisoned here for a time. Not too sure if his close associate is a Class Six'er though. We'll keep on looking after lunch."

Pam then outlined what little she'd learned. "I just wish I had more time. I'm certain that I can lead us to the right location. Wil Blackthornby has quite a few real estate holdings in this area. The trouble is that he's been recently selling them off and the transactions haven't been posted yet. I have to check on each one manually with real people via phone calls. That's burning up precious time."

In the early afternoon, the remainder of the Rodents arrived, including Peaches Colt, Audrey Lemon, Fern Whitewater, Orenda Orondarka, Tom Ryker, Emilio Lopez, Ahana Orondarka, Andy Rains, and of course Eliminator Bill West and Tracker Able Monument. Lindsey had kept them up to date on what she'd learned here this morning, so Leslie didn't have to backtrack, just handle the many introductions.

Around one in the afternoon, Pam announced, "Okay gang. I have it down to three possible locations around St. Louis. I haven't been able to get a hold of anyone by phone at these locations. Some may have been sold. Why don't we divide and go check these places out. Get a head start before the six o'clock doom comes."

"But we aren't familiar with St. Louis," Deiter grumbled.

Leslie took charge. "Look, we are facing some really powerful people and demons here. You are my responsibility now. So we're not going to split up. We will all go enforce to each of these places and check them out. If we are lucky and find them, we'll need our entire combined firepower, I expect."

She went on, "So everyone cast your protection spells, and let's get an organized teleport set up. Pam, what's the first one?"

The large group arrived at an abandoned warehouse off South Broadway way south of the heart of the city and along the Mississippi River. The place was also rusting and a sold sign was on its outer fence. Nevertheless, the group spent over an hour searching this place and did find another incised pentagram here. Amanda and Pam guessed that it hadn't been used for several days. Some rodents had left their marks on the outlines of the symbols on the concrete floor. Still, everyone's hopes were raised. They were definitely on the trail now.

Around three, they searched another warehouse way west, out by Unger Park. Here, they were taken by complete surprise with what they found. In the concrete floor, a very expensive and permanent summoning circle had been very carefully constructed. The outer circle was made from pure silver, while the pentagram outline was done in gold. Both had been carefully set into grooves etched into the concrete. This one was not easily destroyed.

Leslie had to make a decision. "Okay, let's take the time to destroy this one. If we don't, it can easily be used, perhaps even tonight. I hate to waste the time, but I've an obligation to destroy this vile thing."

"Okay, we're heading home to change into something more appropriate for a battle," Crystal said. "We'll be back soon. What are we going to do about supper, assuming we don't find them sooner?"

"I'll have Oliver order us something around five if we strike out. How's that?" Leslie suggested. It was accepted, and the five left for home to change and prepare for the coming battle.

"Darn, it's resisting my flames!" Deiter growled. He's just tried to heat up the soft metals so that they could be removed from the etched lines.

"They are radiating magic. Probably a Make Permanent spell," Lindsey explained after a closer study. "We're going to have to physically demolish the concrete. Stone to Mud isn't going to work because of the spells on the symbols."

It was nearly five o'clock before they had the entire pentagram and enclosing circle obliterated, leaving a large hole in the floor of the warehouse. The five had already returned, this time wearing jeans, sneakers, and black leather jackets. Three had their long hair up in a tight bun, out of the way. Right on time, Oliver pulled up in his black SUV, bringing a mountain of food, Chinese cuisine in white cartons. This hit the spot.

"Okay, it's getting dark. So we best go check out this third one," Leslie suggested.

Just then, Oliver's phone rang. "Shit!" he yelled. "The demons are back. Massive pile up on I-44 again. I best get going. Henry, you are with me!"

"Come on then. Let's try having Amanda trace a Message spell to Parry," Monica Nicole suggested.

"Well, it's close enough to six. Why not? If it doesn't work, then we go quickly and check out Pam's last site," Leslie ordered. "Ready Amanda, Able, when you are."

Amanda and Able focused their attention and nodded. Monica Nicole watched them very carefully. She was intensely curious to see just how Trackers actually were able to do what they did. Leslie cast her Message spell to Parry. A small bit of magical energy flashed.

"Got it!" Amanda called out.

"Ditto. We have a solid bearing. That way!" Able added. Twenty-four wizards and witches, including Ari, cast Fly spells and took off, with Amanda and Able leading the way. Leslie alerted her staff of ten others who would answer her summons just as soon as they found the right place. The race was on, but would they be in time to save Parry? None still had the slightest idea what was really going on or why. Never had

Lindsey felt so insecure. What was she leading her dearest friends into this time? Pam was right. They needed far more time to prepare for this adventure!

Chapter 10—The Final Round

"Oh crap! It's all my fault!" cried Pam, as the huge group landed at an desolate hangar at Lambert Airport. "This was the last location we were to search! We should have come here first! It's all my fault!"

"Cool it, dear!" Tom whispered to his wife. "You had no way of knowing. Be thankful that you had found it. Come on; the game's a foot, as they say in the movies." He, like the other Rodents, was rather excited.

After the Chasma landed on me knocking me out, everything went black. Strangely, I don't recall having any thoughts or dreams. Is that what it's like being dead? Was I dead already? No, I was coming around. At least, I think so. Then I remembered Ari's parting kiss! What a woman. No, I'm her now. Hey, I'm thinking again. Must not be dead yet. Where the heck am I? Why can't I move a muscle? My nose itches. Ah heck, I can't scratch my nose. Why should that bother me? Parry, get your act together.

I couldn't move a muscle, but my eye lids were open a tiny crack. I could see light. I felt for my body. I still had arms and legs. I got the sense that I was lying down, spread eagle. No, just my arms were stretched out perpendicular to my body. My feet were tightly together. I figured I must look like a human cross.

I'm not a religious man, but that thought struck a nerve in me. A cross. I was about to be killed cross-like. I felt a bit spooked by that revelation. Still, I wasn't dead yet. The nice thing about being a human being is that we have more than one sense. I had four others. Since I couldn't move, I decided to see what those told me about my predicament. Smell. I detected the faint odor of gasoline. No, it smelled more like jet fuel. And oil, yes for sure oil. Nothing else.

Sound? Ah, I hear airplanes—no make that jets taking off or perhaps landing. No way to tell that detail. Couldn't touch anything. Had a bad taste in my mouth, which I didn't recognize. I rather wished I could have one of Lou's dark ales about now. That would have been quite pleasant and calmed my nerves some. Are the condemned supposed to have a last meal of their choice? I wondered if my captors would let me have one. I was starving to death and quite thirsty.

Think man. Oh yea. I must be out near the airport. Lambert Field, if those are jets. Must be in a hangar. That would make sense. God whatever I'm lying on is freezing. Must be concrete. It's harder than bricks. Well, that's good for my back. Crap! Focus Parry, focus. Okay, okay. I'm in a hangar on the concrete floor out by Lambert Field. Oh crap! That means I am probably inside another one of those nasty pentagram things, as I saw before. Crap.

No, wait. They think I'm Ari. So they don't know that they have the wrong person yet. Cool. You really pulled this one off big time, Parry! You sure showed them a thing or two. Yes, but they are about to plunge a knife into your heart so stop wasting time. Got to get out of this mess. Think.

Okay, okay. I can't move. I'm lying on the concrete, probably inside one of those pentagrams in a hangar at Lambert. What does that get me? Likely dead. Crap. I have to think of something else!

What else can I hear? Listen man. Are others around? Nope. No footsteps. No breathing. No sounds besides the jets. Still can't move. Wish I could cast some spells, anything. Nope, no way. It would help if I could move though. Stop your wishful thinking and figure a way out of this mess, Parry Oscar Tuttle!

Yes, I was in a jam this time. I honestly couldn't see any way out of it, not unless I could move some. So I did the only thing that I could think of doing: day dreaming. If I was going to die in a while, I might as well enjoy myself first, as best I can. Dreaming of what? Then, the stimulating memory of Ari's passionate kiss came back into my mind. It was at that point that I realized that I was highly attracted to her. I wanted to do far more with her than a simple kiss! Is this what love is all about?

I spent some time thinking about my life and total lack of any love life. Not even one girl friend. I'd never had time for the fairer sex. First, I was cooped up on my uncle's farm, a zillion miles from nowhere in southern Missouri not far from a town called Trail. Then, I came to St. Louis, but had to work my bottom off just to make enough to survive somehow. Besides, I never met others my own age or nearly so.

So what had Ari's kiss meant to her? I know what it meant to me. I promised myself that if I somehow survived this mess that I would find out, even if I got severely embarrassed by it. Okay, that's settled. Now what do I think about or dream about? This is driving me nuts. Isn't your whole life supposed to flash by you when you are dying or about to? It always does in the movies.

I know. I'll just daydream whatever comes. Well, that didn't work out so well. All I could do was dream of Ari kissing me again and again. What's weird about this whole experience was that I was a duplicate of her body and what I was experiencing were her sexual responses, wholly different from my own, which I was expecting to experience. When I realized that, my mind was rather blown. Now I really did have to have a long talk with Ari, embarrassed or not.

Finally, I did get a good idea. Count sheep. I'd heard that if you have a hard time going to sleep, one way was to count sheep. One. Two. Three. It worked. I lost count and fell asleep, quite different from whatever I was before I woke up back there a bit ago.

Voices speaking in low volume roused me from my restful sleep. I strained my ears to hear what they were saying. I got snatches, but enough to realize there were three men and two women present. They were doing something, just not sure what. However, my disguise was holding up. They kept referring to Ari and something about payday was at hand. I rather wished that they would give me a hefty amount of pay. November's rent was due in a few more weeks. Besides, I wanted to have enough funds to buy candy to hand out to the many trick-or-treaters who came by every Halloween.

Chanting. I came alert. The five were chanting in unison. From their voices, I could also tell that they were walking around me, probably in a circle. This must be it, I decided.

143

Then, I felt something changing. My eyelids fluttered. I could move them again. No, I could move my whole body. No, it was still tied up. I was on the ground, staring up at the steel tresses supporting the roof far overhead. I rolled my head around. Now I could see my predicament well.

My arms were chained to a pair of spikes shot into the concrete and held taught, spread eagle like. My feet were similarly chained to another spike. I twisted and turned, relieving some of my cramped muscles. I saw five hooded figures moving slowly around a circle centered on me. In the background were a rather large number of candles. Quite why they were using candles eluded me. They were ignoring me wholly, focused on their chanting, which was picking up in both tempo and volume.

"Hey, what is the meaning of this? Cut me loose. Are you a bunch of wackos?" I yelled as loudly as I could, hoping to distract them from their chant and break their concentration. They ignored my soprano cries. So I just yelled all the louder. What else could I do to bust up their attention? Struggling physically was useless, so I just yelled, wishing that I could cast some spell without my staff, wishing that I could reach my blasting rod, wherever it had gone to.

That reminded me of my own protections. My Skin of Stone spell was still active, thanks to the ring of Ericka's. My protection pendant was still around my neck, resting between my breasts. Good god, I'd forgotten that I now had breasts. I calmed my nerves. I was still protected, and they had not yet discovered my sneaky move. There was hope yet, just not much I'll admit. I had a fanciful idea of some rat coming up to me, pulling my blasting rod out and bringing it to my hand. Then I could give them a taste of their own medicine. Didn't see any rats though. Think, man, think!

Why is it when you don't need to think of anything, you have all kinds of thoughts, but when you desperately need to think of something, your mind goes entirely blank? Rats. I was drawing a total blank this time, but I wasn't about to give up just yet. Something will come to me, I told myself. Not sure that I truly believed that, but I did feel a bit better.

Now the five's voices were quite loud indeed, and then I

began to grasp their final words of their ritual. A man's voice cried out, "Oh great Graz'zt, Prince of Demons, all is finally prepared. All awaits you as agreed upon. Fulfill my wish as I fulfill thy wishes. Come now to the mortal plane. Thy virgin sacrifice is at hand. Taste the delicious blood of life as it pours forth upon thee!"

I didn't like the sound of that, but those thoughts were soon wiped from my mind. A flash of magical energies the likes of which I'd never seen before illuminated the room in such a white brilliance that I was temporarily blinded and blinked like mad. Then I saw this enormous demon, quite black, quite handsome in a strange way, with huge pointed ears like Spock on steroids, standing over me. He must have been at least eight feet tall. His arm was thicker than my legs. Er Parry's legs, not Ari's. His hair was strange too, short and brushed back, but it grew out in half-arcs from a point just between his eyes. Taken together, it gave him an incredibly stern, threatening demeanor.

I looked up at him and said, "Well, I suppose if you are a demon prince, you ought to look the part." He looked down at me and stared, but licked his lips. Just then, one of the hooded men came up on my other side, carrying an ugly looking dagger. I called out, "Careful you don't cut yourself with that."

"My Demon Prince, accept your virgin sacrifice now!" For a second, I thought, shit, this is it. The end. He plunged the dagger at my heart. When the tip struck my skin, the blade shattered into several shards. I was uninjured, but quite jarred from the force of his deathblow. He screeched, taken by total surprise and total shock.

"Told you to be careful," I called out.

Just at that instant, a whole lot more magical energies blinded us all, even the Demon Prince himself. I blinked and saw a whole lot more arrivals! Some I recognized; some I didn't. I had the good sense to shut up.

Off to my left, I saw another tall man, a very strange man, about a foot shorter than the Demon Prince still standing over me. One of his feet was cloven, like a pig or horse perhaps. He wore a crimson robe, highlighted in black, probably velvet. He was completely bald and had a pair of small horns prominently on his upper forehead. He carried a wicked looking staff in his left hand and some kind of blasting rod in his right. Standing beside him was another elderly human man, with nearly white hair, a wand in his right hand. An older woman stood beside him. Some ten feet to his right and a little behind him stood Aunt Glasya, rather Glasya, Princess of Hell, and Consort of Mammon. She looked every bit as gorgeous as she had when we first met. She winked at me.

I couldn't help myself. I called out, "Hi Glasya. Good to see you again." The man in the red robe merely smiled. Then, I saw all the others, which I later learned were the Rodents, Leslie, the head of the entire Missouri Department of Magical Misuse, Ari, and my five new friends who owned PIWIP. I did notice that Ericka, Crystal, and Monica Nicole were wearing jeans. I think I liked them better all dolled up. Crazy thoughts, all things considered.

Then I noticed that somehow most of them were more or less standing there frozen in place and wondered why. I twisted my head some and saw the five hooded figures who had summoned this giant of a black demon. With all these people present, I figured today wasn't my day to die. I was about to say something when the black giant spoke in the deepest bass voice that I'd ever heard. Darn, he sounded incredibly beautiful. I had the thought that he ought to be in someone's choir, but then he probably wasn't into singing.

"Dispater! What are you doing here? Why are you interfering in my business? Who the heck are all these people?"

"Graz'zt, what's going on? We have a deal. Fulfill our bargain," one of the grey hooded men cried out, his voice shaking. He still held the shattered hilt of the dagger that he'd tried to plunge into my heart.

Graz'zt turned to the man, glared, and commanded, "Silence!" The man shut up.

"That's telling him," I barked. Graz'zt's gaze passed over me, totally ignoring me. Don't know about you, but I hate being ignored, even if these were demons and devils. Perhaps it all had something to do with the relief I was feeling about not being killed immediately. Or maybe it was just the adrenaline rush that surged through me when the dagger plunge had come. I decided I wanted to hear this Dispater fellow out and was silent.

The red robed Arch-devil took a step forward and spoke, "It seems that we have similar goals here, Graz'zt. I believe that host of humans there have come to try to stop you and your fellow demons. Don't worry. I'm keeping them motionless for the moment. I believe that you and I both have business to attend to first. I'm not here to interfere in your business, but I am most curious about what you are doing on my fertile hunting grounds. Nevertheless, you were here first. So please, conduct your business. I'll not interfere in that. Then I'll conduct mine. Oh, I've no idea why Mammon sent his princess here. You'll have to ask Glasya yourself, unless you prefer that I ask her."

Graz'zt glared at Dispater. "I don't give a rat's ass about some Princess of Hell. She's your problem. Your word on this?"

"My word," Dispater replied with a wry grin. I think he must really be enjoying himself. Why? Darned if I had any clue, but the red-robed devil added, "You probably already know that she isn't what she appears to be."

Now Graz'zt looked down at me and glared, before he looked very hard at the grey hooded wizard who had summoned him. For once, I was quite glad that he didn't look that way at me! I swear that the man was actually physically shaking. He had nerve though. He threw back his hood, and I could finally see his face. He was an elderly man, thinning white hair, gaunt, and somewhat emaciated. He didn't look any too healthy to me, but then I'm not a medical man.

Then I realized something. Graz'zt had been standing close to my prone body, fully within the inscribed pentagram. Somehow, I could see magical energies shimmering around the five sides, apparently holding him captive within its boundaries. At that instant, the magical energies suddenly vanished, and he stepped out of the giant symbol on the concrete floor of this hangar. The summoning spell and Gate were shattered, but I didn't know why. I didn't have time to ponder that though. The old man backed up two steps, terrified. His mouth opened and shut, sort of waggling-like. His four other hooded companions also stepped way back. This can't be good for them, I thought.

Then, the other older man standing beside Dispater cried out, "Wil! You were going to sacrifice my daughter Ari? Good god, Wil! What are you thinking? She's my daughter!"

That rather brought Wil out of his shaking fit. "Had to Herbert! You know that. I had no choice. You know how hard it is to find a virgin these days? You know as well as I do that nothing less than a virgin is required. Think of our goal, before it's too late! We have to succeed. We just have to, Herbert!"

"Wil! Not my daughter! The Golden Path—yes, of course. But not that fiend. Not my youngest daughter Wil," Herbert screamed angrily. "Not my daughter." He rather slumped as he finished.

Apparently un-bothered by Herbert's outburst, Wil screamed, "Graz'zt! I hold you to your bargain. I've lived up to my part. Now do your part. Bring Dominus Malefic back to life now. I command you. There lies your ultimate sacrifice, the virgin Ari Athos. Take her and give me my Dominus. I order you to do it now!"

I was rather surprised at Wil's sudden change. His terror had given way to a vehement anger that I'd seldom seen. Almost a rage. Perhaps, he'd seen his ultimate failure and was making a last ditch attempt to pull this off. Heck, even I would have tried something, if I were in his shoes. Utter doom was about to land on his head. Best at least to try something, anything. I had to agree with his approach. I'd of done the same thing, I think.

However, Graz'zt then turned his gaze downward onto me. Oh heck! I yelled, "Hey big one. I'm not Ari. Ari, if you can, cancel your spell now! I'm Parry, not Ari." Magic flashed. I saw Ari from the corner of my eye. She'd done as I asked. I was me again. Thank god. "See, fooled you all. Sorry, no sacrifice today. Some other time, perhaps. Will someone undo these chains? My back is rather frozen. Besides, everything looks too weird from down here."

148

Lindsey, though her body was being magically held immobile, was nevertheless still able to use her magic. She cast a Dispel Magic followed by Unlock. Suddenly, the three chains binding my arms and legs released! Awkwardly, I struggled to my feet. I was quite wobbly and staggered a bit, trying to get my legs working again, to say nothing of my balance. My back felt like it was frozen solid. "Thanks," I said to the room at large, not knowing who had released me. I moved as fast as my shaking legs could carry me over to Ari, positioning my body in front of hers. No matter what else transpired here, I wasn't about to let them harm Ari. My contract wasn't over yet. I honor my contracts.

Now Graz'zt spoke up. "Wil Blackthornby, thy contract with me is not fulfilled in total. However, thanks to you, I now have what I wanted out of this bargain."

"Oh, pray tell us what that might be?" Dispater suddenly spoke up. He'd been silent until now, allowing Graz'zt to handle his deal. "Sorry. I'm just too curious, Graz'zt. Humor me?" If that wasn't a jab, a tease, I don't know what is!

Graz'zt took the bait. For all his giant size, his smarts were not proportional. He answered. "I have been waiting for this opportunity to return to this pathetic world and wreak my vengeance upon it! I was in a mighty battle in the Abyss and just about to overthrow the very ruling lords themselves when some pathetic human wizard had the audacity to summon me here to this realm. Can you imagine what happens when the battlefield commander is jerked away right at the most critical moment when victory is almost at hand? When I got back, my army had lost its mighty victory and was crushed. So yes, I'm very pissed off about that. I swore to get my revenge on this world!"

Crystal, who had been completely silent, though neither she nor Ericka, Monica Nicole, and Ari were being held motionless like the others in the Rodents and Leslie, gushed out in total surprise, "But that was three thousand plus years ago!"

Graz'zt turned and stared at Crystal. "Puny human. That's a mere blink of my eye. Well, okay, I see your point, two blinks. Still, I've returned now. Thanks to Wil Blackthornby.

He got my attention with his petty wish and summoning. While I sent a few minions to do his dirty work, my real servants also came through his Gate and have been quite successful at building the necessary permanent Gates so that my army can swarm over this measly world. I will have my vengeance now. So I do have Wil Blackthornby to thank for these Gates, which can only be constructed on this side, not from the Abyss, but you already know that, virgin woman." He smiled evilly at Crystal.

"But our bargain," Wil countered desperately. "If you have what you wanted, then you must honor my wish. Give me back Dominus Malefic! I demand you do as we agreed!"

I have to admit the man had balls! Even though the situation had totally reversed itself, and the demon prince was no longer bound by the summoning and could easily kill Wil, the man continued to press his case. Since Graz'zt had gotten what he desired, it was therefore legally binding that the demon prince fulfills his part. Crystal later explained that detail to me.

Dispater chuckled. "He's got a point, Graz'zt."

I didn't think that demon princes could smile, but Graz'zt actually did. His shiny, black face cracked a very big grin, a demonic grin at that! He bellowed officially, "Wil Blackthornby, thy wish has been granted. Dominus Malefic, step forward!"

Shock. I think that pretty well summarized the mental reactions of everyone present, save for one—and probably those from the other planes of existence. Monica Nicole Black slowly walked towards the incised pentagram from where she had been standing with the mass of Rodents and others. She took a deep breath and said, "Yes and no. I was but now am not Dominus Malefic."

Graz'zt declared, "I've kept my bargain, Wil Blackthornby. Here is your precious Dominus Malefic."

"You lie! You lie! She's not Dominus! She's a woman, a witch, not a man, a wizard. I explicitly said that I wanted Dominus Malefic, not some woman. You cheat!" Wil screamed, his voice cracking from the sheer volume he put in it.

"Silence!" Graz'zt commanded. Wil's voice was stopped instantly. Sometimes I wish that I could have that kind of command presence. Pretty impressive. Could use it in arguments. "Let Monica Nicole Black speak. Woman, tell the truth to this pathetic man. I so command it."

"You don't need to use that tone on me, Graz'zt," Monica Nicole countered rather sharply. She had spunk. I'll give her that. "I fully intended to anyway. I was called Dominus Malefic, but I was assassinated over six years ago. I remember walking up the steps to a courthouse in Denver, I think. Then I felt a massive pain in my head and darkness came. Nothing but darkness. Then, I was alive again, staring up at a stranger. Thaddeus Black had dug up my corpse and cast Cause Life on it. Reincarnation some say. Well, this is the body that resulted—a twelve year old girl back then. It's grown up some since then."

"But, but you can't be Dominus Malefic. The Golden Path? We must have the Golden Path," Wil stammered.

"You can't have it, Wil Blackthornby. It is nothing but a lie. Yes, I made a mistake, a very big mistake I have learned. I'm truly sorry for having misled you, Wil," Monica Nicole said softly, but clearly. "I was blinded by hate. Sorry."

Nice speech. Holy cow. Monica was Dominus? Oh, there was going to be hell to pay now, I thought. Here were the very wizards and witches that had captured Dominus back then. These people were world famous, and they once more had Dominus surrounded. But wait, Monica Nicole hadn't been doing anything evil that I had seen. She'd been helping me keep my word and protect Ari. I felt confused. Look, if I was confused, I would bet anything the Rodents were just as confused as I was. I looked at Dispater and then Glasya and realized this was far, far from over!

Graz'zt spoke forcefully. "Wil Blackthornby, our business is finished. Come!" With that, the body of Wil scooted over the concrete, pulled by some invisible force. The giant grabbed his hand. Before anyone could react, another giant flash of magic illuminated the hangar, temporarily blinding us all. I blinked several times and saw both had vanished. I didn't care to speculate where they had gone, but I felt a small pang for what Wil had gotten himself into. It couldn't be pleasant. Remind me never to bargain with demon princes or lords!

"What of our bargain?" Herbert spoke up, looking at Dispater. His voice sounded somewhat weak in comparison to Wil's.

Darn it! I'd forgotten about him. He was Ari's father no less. What bargain had he struck? I hate all these mysteries. I remembered Crystal telling me that the devils went after people's souls, that is, the person themselves. At this moment, I didn't know the difference. Graz'zt had just taken Wil off to who knows where, probably the Abyss, wherever that was. Was Dispater about to abscond with Ari? Not if I could help it!

"Wait. You can't have Ari or her soul! I won't let you," I barked sharply, rather amazed at how forceful and determined my voice was.

To my amazement, Monica Nicole also spoke up. "No, you cannot have Ari's soul. Nor can you have Herbert's, Dispater. This has to end sometime. If a soul is required, then take mine, but I assure you that I will fight you until my last breath!" She stood there with a totally determined look on her face. Remind me never ever to cross Monica! I would probably die a horrible death!

I rather expected an angry outburst from him, if Graz'zt was any comparison. I don't know if it is proper to compare demons and devils, though. Perhaps not. Dispater merely laughed. Still chuckling, he said, "Hardly necessary, Dominus or Monica Nicole, but I will consider your offer in the future. No, souls were not part of our bargain. Not at all."

I saw Glasya give him a rather surprised look. Now I was in mystery. If he didn't want a soul, what was he doing here? What was this other bargain? My head hurt from all the possibilities that sprang forth in that instant. Funny how a single look can generate a thousand thoughts.

He continued, "Herbert Albert Athos, alias Glaston, our bargain is complete. I have what I wanted from you."

Her hands on her hips, quite defiantly, Princess Glasya barked seductively, "And what, pray tell, is that, noble Dispater?" Oh how her voice cut. I didn't ever want to be the recipient of such a slice! And from such a gorgeous woman at that. Oops, she wasn't a woman or was she? Rather hard to really pin down, now that I think of it. Women don't usually have horns and small wings on their back. Still, she was beautiful. Probably more deadly than I could possibly imagine. However, I began to relax a little. If a soul wasn't part of this, then perhaps Ari was finally safe, and at this moment that was all that mattered to me.

"Spying for Mammon again, are we, Glasya dearest?" Dispater smirked.

"Obviously," she shot back.

"While I could leave you in mystery, I suppose that's hardly fair, since you took it upon yourself to watch over Ari, saving me the trouble. I heard rumors that Graz'zt was trying to get back to Earth. This is *our* hunting ground, not his. I needed to find out what he was up to. Thanks to Herbert and his wife, we now know that our hunting grounds have been invaded. You can tell your lover all about it. I doubt that he will be *pleased* by this news."

Princess Glasya relaxed. "Accepted. I will relay the news. I agree, this is not good news. Mammon will probably be fuming, if I know the old boy. Get on with your bargain. I won't interfere."

Dispater laughed. "As if you could interfere, Princess!" I glanced at her. Was that a flush on her smooth golden skin? I think I need a crash course in all this. He said, "Herbert, would you like to tell them what you desired of me?"

Herbert took a step towards Monica Nicole. His face turned red with long pent up hostility. "Dominus. I wanted your Golden Path. I supported you, convinced others of its merits. And what did you do for me? You mutilated and tortured my eldest daughter, Cherrie! I still believe fully in the Golden Path. Wizards should be the rulers of the world, not the sheep norms, but I want revenge for what you did to my Cherrie! I want you to suffer as she suffered. I want justice! Not money. Oh Cherrie is content with your money, but not Sandra and me! You must suffer like she did, you betraying piece of trash!" He fairly spat out that last. For a second, I thought he was about to kill Monica Nicole or something.

Dispater intervened. "Monica Nicole or Dominus,

would you like to say something to Herbert and Sandra here?"

Monica Nicole sighed. "Yes, yes I would. You don't want to do this. Revenge isn't the answer. I learned that the hard way. I was wrong, and I apologize. Revenge will eat away at you. Rise above it. Prove that you are better than I was."

I wondered what that was all about! Certainly, there had to have been some serious history between these three, but what? What revenge was Dominus or Monica Nicole talking about? I couldn't recall ever reading anything about all that. I did remember something about several sets of women having been rescued by the Rodents. Obviously, Ari's older sister had been one of them. I was just thankful that I didn't have any enemy upon whom I wished revenge. I've led a simple life, at least up until now that is. I watched, very interested in how this would all work out.

I guess Monica's plea fell on deaf ears. Either that or the hatred and desire for revenge were far too strong in them. Herbert answered, "Dispater, fulfill our bargain. I insist on it! He, she must know what our Cherrie had to endure. Only that will give me justice!"

Surprising me, Ari yelled out, "Dad! Don't do this. Monica Nicole has been helping keeping me alive! She's been helping Parry. Dad, you don't want to do this, please. Cherrie doesn't want it."

"You're just a child. You don't know what torture and betrayal is. Your mother and I do. Do it, Dispater, do it now. Fulfill our bargain!" Herbert barked, ignoring his daughter's pleas. "It's already half-done; he's a she."

"As you have commanded, so it shall be done. She is a witch and you have not requested that be denied her." Magic flashed, covering Monica Nicole. When I could finally see again, I gasped. Her body had been altered. Her lower arms were missing and her upper arms now tapered down to small rounded cones where her elbows had been. She was dressed in one of her fancy red satin gowns, but her breasts were enormous, dwarfing the giant knockers that Crystal and Ericka sported. She was still wearing her six-inch stiletto pumps. I think that her hair was somewhat longer, but I wasn't too sure about that aspect. She was gasping for air, and my eyes finally moved down from those knockers and saw that her waist was extremely tiny.

"As you requested, she wears the same corset as Cherrie did, melted into her body as you so stated. Her legs are altered so that she can only wear heels of this height. Her wand. . ." My eyes drifted to the cement floor. Her wand had been dropped in the transformation process. He continued, "will now be part of her upper arms so that she can continue to cast her spells via her upper arm stumps." My eyes saw her wand changing into two wands, identical wands. Or was it that he duplicated her original wand? How can one tell that detail? I made a note to ask the wand expert, Misty, later on. As I watched, the wands rose up and seemed to fuse into her upper arms.

"There, it is done. Our bargain, Herbert is concluded. Now, if you will all excuse me, I have urgent business elsewhere. Glasya," he actually bowed slightly to her. To the throng of others still being held motionless, he added, "I leave this mess in your hands." With another flash of magic combined with a bit of smoke, he vanished.

At the same instant, the Hold spell on everyone else vanished. At that instant, two things happened nearly simultaneously. I think that the others had a very long time to work out just what they were going to do the instant the devil left them. Deiter cast his spell. I heard him say, "Disarm those four!" The wands of the four grey hooded compatriots of Wil Blackthornby suddenly went flying across the concrete floor of this hangar, rather startling the four. Six other men from the Department of Magical Misuse suddenly appeared. Leslie cried out, "Arrest those four grey hooded individuals!"

After that, many began talking at once, but I felt Ari's arm slipping around my waist, holding me tightly. Princess Glasya ignored all them and the mad dashing of wizards across the space intent upon arresting the four. She walked up to me and Ari. "Well, we meet again, Parry Oscar Tuttle, Private Investigator. A job well done. I believe this will cover the remainder of your expenses on this assignment." She handed me another envelop, which I mechanically took. She winked at Ari and whispered, "You have quite a man here. Don't lose him. Bye-bye for now." She departed in with a small flurry of magical energies, though I could still smell the scent of her body for a moment. Yes, she was quite impressive. I wondered if anyone had sold their soul to her? I suspected that it might be terribly hard to refuse her!

Just then, more magical energies flashed. The six men teleported the four other participants off to jail, I presumed. They'd certainly abused their magical talents.

As Ari and I watched, Crystal, Ericka, Enya, and Misty hurried over to the still gasping Monica Nicole. Crystal and Ericka put their arms around her, steadying her. Leslie barked out her orders, "Everyone. Oliver's office. Now. Make sure those two come along. Arrest them if you have to." She pointed to Ari's parents. "You bring Monica Nicole Black with you," she pointed to the five. Crystal nodded. Magical energies flashed left and right. I heard the word Teleport said by many voices. Ari took me. Next thing I knew, we were walking into the FBI headquarters, following behind the others. So many were talking at once that I couldn't follow any thread. Probably just as well. My back was still freezing, and I ached.

Chapter 11—Now What?

The place was crawling with suits! Leslie must have alerted the whole department! They made darn sure that Herbert and Sandra weren't going anywhere soon. We marched like penguins up to Oliver's spacious meeting room. I felt a little sorry for Monica Nicole. She was having a terrible time just breathing.

Ari was clinging to me for dear life. Well, I have to admit, she had to be terribly worried. After all, it was her own folks that had been deeply involved in this whole mess, and now they too were highly likely to be thrown in jail or wherever they stow wizards and witches who misuse their magical gifts. It didn't look too good for them, as far as I could see. I just made sure that I still had a good hold on Ari's waist, supporting her silently.

We all entered the room and took seats. Because so many were talking at once, I still couldn't follow any of it, excepting Monica's occasional gasp for air. I pulled out a chair for Ari and helped her sit. As I sat down myself, I saw Crystal doing the same for Monica Nicole and flashed them both a quick smile.

Leslie walked to the front. "Okay. The National Guard has taken care of the other demon attacks tonight. Quite a mess to have to clean up, but that's not the important thing right now. First of all, the four others who participated in the summoning of the demon prince and the death of Jessica White will be swiftly prosecuted. They'll not likely ever see the light of day again. However, we are left with the Athos situation here. It would appear that until this evening, neither Herbert nor Sandra had a direct role in the summoning of the demons. Still, we must have the complete and utter truth from them. Oliver, if you would be so kind as to arrange the Lie Detection System so we can interrogate them?" He nodded and left the room briefly.

"Since many of you are not familiar with our methods, we will be having video cameras trained on those two. Highly skilled men and women will be studying their micro-expressions and can detect any lie to a 99% accuracy. Governor Lindsey, if you will be so kind as to remove all magical spells that they may have upon their persons and all magical items, we will begin."

Lindsey smiled. I didn't see her do anything at all. Impressive. I did see a number of magical discharges on each of her parents, so she was doing something, probably dispelling magic. Well, she was supposed to be the world's best Dispeller. After that, she apparently cast another spell, because she went over to them and removed several small articles, rings, pins, and a brooch. "Okay, Leslie, they are both clean as a norm." She returned to her seat beside Deiter, who gave her a big smile and a peck on her cheek, which reminded me that I wanted to do that and more to Ari, but now wasn't the time for that.

Leslie then began grilling the two, firing question after question at them. "Did either of you know of Wil's bargain with the demons? Did either of you have any advanced knowledge that he was planning this fiasco?" She asked many similar questions.

"He and I go way back," Herbert explained. "Yes, we both wanted to see wizards taking their rightful place in ruling the world. Heck, it would be so much better with we wizards running things! But no, I had no idea what he was planning, not until Dispater contacted me."

"So you claim he contacted you first? You didn't summon him?" Leslie fired back.

"Not exactly. I may have wished and prayed to anyone who would listen to me. But that's in the arena of religion, prayer, not magical summoning. You can't try me for that," he defended himself.

"So what precisely was your bargain with Dispater?" she challenged him.

"He wanted me to find out what Wil and his group were up to. He said that demons were involved somehow and wanted me to find out where they were doing the Summoning and Gating. He didn't care how I found that out. In return, I asked him for what I got: revenge on Dominus for what he did

158

to my Cherrie! Only I expected that he would be raising him from the dead and then doing it. I didn't know Dominus was back. I hope you suffer long and hard for what you did to my Cherrie and all the others!"

Monica Nicole replied, "I am sure." She gasped. "That I will." She was having difficulty breathing properly.

Herbert had a most satisfied look on his face. Leslie asked, "So how did Ari get involved in all this?" His face grimaced.

Sandra spoke up. "We're getting too old to do the spying that was needed. Herbert can barely get around these days. I know that we shouldn't have, but he asked Ari to do it for him. He put a Compulsion spell on her and all sorts of protections and a Do Not Divulge spell on her as well. We figured that she would be safe. We had no idea that Wil was going to sacrifice her! We would never have allowed that."

Leslie countered, "It seems that he would have sacrificed her despite your intentions had not Princess Glasya intervened on her behalf. I guess she wanted to know what Dispater was up to and figured she'd find out if she kept close tabs on Ari here. Anyway, you both are completely disgusting. Sending your own daughter off to do your dirty work! I don't have any choice but to hold you for trial. It's not my place to assuage your guilt at this time. I can say this, taking revenge into your own hands is not allowed. That's why we have the Departments of Law and Magical Misuse. I will be turning you over to the Department of Law. Your misuse of magic, as much as I hate to admit it, is relatively minor, forcing your own child to do your work for you. Those issues will be taken up once the Department of Law is finished with you. Even though you had Dispater wreak your vengeance for you, that does not absolve your own guilt. If everyone went around obtaining their own brand of justice, we'd have nothing but anarchy."

Herbert spat out, "Fine justice system we have here. I'm happy that Dominus got what he deserved! He mutilated and tortured so many women, including my Cherrie, and now he gets a taste of his own mutilations. Enjoy them, Dominus!" he spat out his hatred.

"Take them away. I'm sorry Ari," Leslie ordered and

said to Ari.

Ari fumbled, trying hard to keep from crying before everyone, "I—I didn't know. After meeting Parry, I began to think that I was under some kind of spell. You have to believe me; I didn't want this to happen to Monica Nicole or Dominus. Cherrie doesn't either. She's put it behind her and is very happy with her States-Justice settlement, really she is."

"I know, Ari. You're not to blame at all. You were under a Compulsion spell. Overall, I'm amazed that you did so well. Don't worry. You are facing no charges at all," Leslie explained. I squeezed Ari's hand and felt her return it.

"Now then, the larger issue. Good grief. I don't think that I've ever encountered one this complex or twisted before. Dominus-Monica. Officially as the head of the Missouri Department of Magical Misuse, I can state without reservation that Monica Nicole Black has not performed anything over which I have any jurisdiction. There has been no magical misuse on her part. Those responsible for the misuse of magic, namely Thaddeus Black and his sister are now dead. We don't prosecute those who are deceased, obviously."

"Yet, there remains the larger issue. As Dominus, my god, the lists of known crimes that you've committed are astounding. Professor Pam Betts has compiled the definitive list of all those, and it fills many pages just with their titles! Had you not been assassinated, I assure you that you would have been put away for the rest of your life. I believe that you have set the record as the world's greatest criminal in all history. But be that as it may, here you are again. What do we do with you? I think the Rodents and I would just as soon lock you up and throw away the key!"

Professor Pam raised her hand. "Might I have a word or two?"

"It's not a classroom," Kathy whispered to her.

"Certainly," Leslie replied.

Pam began, "The problem that we have here is one of reincarnation via the Cause Life spell. Our legal system does not prosecute anyone who has died, since they cannot defend themselves. We can and do confiscate their possessions, as we have done with Dominus Malefic. Similarly, we don't group prosecute clones. We consider each clone to be its own person and try them only for the crimes that clone has committed. We cannot hold all clones of a person guilty of crimes that only one of them has committed."

Lindsey recognized immediately what she was referring to. Namely, the being that had been called Dominus Malefic was in fact a clone of Simon. Simon had been living in France and had covertly been working to help undo the damage that Dominus had inflicted on the world with his ill-fated Health Care Program. She also knew that Dominus never new or suspected that he was a clone and not the real man!

"Likewise, in this case, we are facing reincarnation. Right or wrong, good or bad, we cannot prosecute the reincarnation of a person, for they are not the same. Exactly how, no one really knows. I don't think anyone wants to get themselves killed and then reincarnated just to study the actual effects on themselves. So legally, Leslie, we cannot arrest Monica Nicole Black for the crimes that he or she committed during her previous lifetime as Dominus Malefic."

Several Rodents groaned. This wasn't what they wanted to hear, not remotely. Undaunted, Professor Pam continued, "What we can do is keep a very sharp eye on her and make darn sure that she doesn't commit crimes this time around." That seemed to appease many in the room.

"That said, I'd like to ask her a question or two if I may."

"Go ahead, Professor," Leslie replied. I could tell she was quite curious about what Pam would ask.

"Monica Nicole, earlier you said that your Golden Path was wrong. Can you elaborate for us please?" Pam said flatly.

Monica Nicole knew that she was still in the hot seat. That she was fighting for each breath didn't help matters. She had to gasp for breath every couple of words. "Can't speak well yet. Power lies in ... knowledge, information, ... passion, and dear friends. ... Women are ... as powerful as ... men. Magic doesn't ... matter so much."

Pam replied, "Well, you heard her, gang. That's a far better life philosophy, don't you think?" She sat back as if she'd just won her oral presentation in a law court.

Deiter remained unconvinced. "Maybe she's just saying that to save her skin. She's had over six years to prepare her story. I don't trust her."

Lindsey spoke up, "But Pam has made quite valid points, Deiter. We will keep an eye on her, nothing more. If she does commit more crimes, then we will act. I know you are disappointed that your number one criminal isn't a criminal just now." Several Rodents chuckled. She added, "As you are well aware, Deiter, people can change." He seemed satisfied and didn't say anything more.

Pam added, "Besides, Monica Nicole has been quite helpful in this entire mess and at obviously a great personal risk. I think that we owe her and her four friends a thank you for helping with the demon situation."

Heck, I couldn't agree more. So I clapped for Monica Nicole. I don't care what Dominus did. I only knew Monica Nicole, and I liked very much what she and her friends had done. Heck, I'd be dead if it wasn't for them. I clapped loudly and noticed that Monica smiled back at me in spite of her intense discomfort and humiliation.

Leslie took control of her meeting once more. "All right then. I must have everyone's word that you will not divulge that Monica Nicole Black is the reincarnated Dominus Malefic. Good lord, if that became public knowledge, she'd be besieged with those wanting her to continue the Golden Path and those who want her dead again! I will see that the others we've arrested are placed under an Inhibition spell so that they can't go around spreading the word."

After everyone did so, Monica Nicole said simply, "Thank you."

"Now then, we have far more serious business to tackle. This Demon Prince Graz'zt did say that his assistants have already laid the groundwork so that his forces could invade our world. This cannot be allowed to happen. This information is going to have to be widely disseminated. I wish you all would research just what this groundwork must have been and how we can undo it. I know that there is another one of those gold and silver incised pentagrams in the hangar we just left. My men are destroying it as we speak. Are there more? What else must we be alert for? What kind of demon forces can we expect? Their numbers? Their objectives? And most importantly, how do we kill them? We have been very lucky so far, but we need better knowledge. As Monica Nicole pointed out, power lies in knowledge and information. So I charge you all with doing your homework. I will coordinate all data for the near future. I'm worried that Wil has opened up an enormous can of worms that we are going to have to handle. Men!" she said with some disgust.

"Okay, that's all for now. You all have other duties and it's late. Keep me posted. Thank you all for your fast response. I truly wish this was the end of it, but I seriously doubt it. Thanks everyone," Leslie said warmly.

Rapidly, the Rodents teleported from the room. Likewise, the five women did so, with Crystal helping Monica Nicole. Meanwhile, Leslie gathered up all of Ari's parents' magical items and wands and put them into a small sack, giving it to her. "Keep them safe, Ari. I'm truly sorry about your parents. Will you be all right?"

"I think so. I'll have to let Cherrie know. They are really old, but I didn't know mom and dad still had so much hatred in them," Ari answered quietly.

I slipped my arm around her waist and we walked slowly and solemnly out of the FBI building. I know I looked a bit strange carrying my tall oak staff. Once on the dark street, the cool October winds hit us. "I don't think I can stay at my home, not now, not just yet," Ari whispered.

"Hey, you are welcome at my place, even though it's a bit messy."

"Thanks. I'd like that. Can we drop by my place so I can get some things?" A minute later, via her teleport, we stood in her own bedroom. I watched as she gathered up some clothes and things, putting them in a bag. At last, she turned and faced me.

"Parry, I want to thank you for saving me," she gave me another passionate kiss. Then, she whispered, "Don't you think that we should do it now so that we aren't virgins? Just in case the demons return for us?"

"I'd love to, Ari, but not for that reason. I, I love you. I want to do it for that reason," I whispered back, hoping this was the right thing to say. I surely didn't want to do it just to get some demons off our backs. That didn't feel right to me.

She answered with yet another passionate kiss. As our lips broke away, she whispered, "I love you too, Parry Oscar Tuttle! That's a whole lot better reason. Right there, she began peeling off my clothes. Around midnight, she and I finally entered my messy basement apartment, arm in arm. At that moment, nothing in the world mattered to us, except to be together, always. I admit it, I was head over heels in love with my Ari.

Only then when we were storing our things did I open the envelope that Glasya had handed me. I was very pleased to see another ten grand in hundred dollar bills inside. Yes, that more than covered my expenses. November's rent was paid and then some!

Monica Nicole allowed Crystal to take her home, but was silent. She was too embarrassed to say anything. Her dark secret had been laid bare. That she was in dire physical straights didn't help matters, as she focused on trying to breathe and fight the intense, crushing pressure of her torso that threatened to pop off her head. Had this been what his women had endured? She dared not think about that, not now.

Once inside, they all headed to their suites in the basement. Moving significantly slower than the rest because of her heels, Monica Nicole fell quickly behind the others, especially since Enya and Misty dashed down the stairs to tell their husbands all that had happened and to let them see that they really were okay. When she reached the stairs, she found herself alone. She looked down to the steps but could not see over her bosom! She twisted her head in all directions trying to see where to put her foot, but saw only the satin covering her protruding chest!

The handrail, which she always used when negotiating the stairs in her heels, was now useless to her, though she tried to reach out to it with her right upper arm, missing it by several inches. Oh dear god! She thought, nearly panicking. Eventually, she very carefully felt for the step with her foot and found it. She went down one step, pausing to catch her breath. A scary eternity later, she finally reached the floor and calmed down. Just then Crystal came back for her. "You okay?"

"Can't see my feet," she gasped. "Can't reach the rail."

"Come on. Let's get you into our room and see what the devil has done to you," Crystal again took charge.

A few minutes later, they three discovered that Monica Nicole's leg muscles had adapted to a person who constantly wore such tall heels. Namely, her muscles wouldn't stretch enough to allow her to put her foot flat on the floor. She had to tiptoe around now or wear the heels. Ericka removed her outer fancy corset and then slipped her satin, pencil style gown off her, and then her slip, and garter belt. Finally naked, the three looked at her waist and bosom.

"My god, that looks like a corset there underneath your skin!" Crystal declared, totally shocked.

Ericka then grinned, "So now, dear Monica Nicole, we know why you wanted us to have these big ones. Glad we don't have them as big as yours."

Crystal finally put it all together. Teasingly, she said, "So this is how you wanted your women to look like!"

Monica Nicole's face turned beet red. She slumped onto the bed. For some reason, she couldn't keep from crying. "I know, I was ... awful to them. ... I'm sorry, truly... sorry. I didn't ... know how bad ... it was, not really. I can't ... even cry properly! ...Now I am helpless too!" She cried and gasped for air at the same time. "I don't know ... why I am crying. ... I feel so embarrassed. ... I never felt ... this way before."

Crystal declared, "Well, our bargain is shot to heck now. Since you can't have long claws, we don't have to have these monsters weighing us down. Ericka, time to reduce ours to what we prefer. I think I would like to have mine the size that Monica had hers." Both women cast some spells and reduced their endowment considerably. "That's much better. Honestly, Monica Nicole, you are going to have to wear that corset just to get enough back support to carry the sheer weight of yours."

That didn't help much; she continued to sob. "I never cried ... like this before!"

Ericka commented, "Well, I think that we women are

more sensitive to such things than men. They're rather crass and insensitive most of the time." Monica Nicole nodded her agreement.

"I'm sorry. I should've told you about me long ago," Monica Nicole blubbered. "I'll move out tomorrow." She was still gasping every few words.

"You'll do no such thing, Monica Nicole Black!" Crystal declared, putting her hands on her shapely hips. "We both love you. You're not going anywhere. But yes, it would have been nice if you had told us about your past. Don't know if it would have made any difference. Say, when we were in school, did you already know all the spells? All the math and science? Were you secretly helping us learn them so quickly?"

Monica Nicole nodded. "I wanted to help you all."

"Well, you certainly did that! We all got straight A's and set new records for Red Hall. Impressed everyone. Now, so much makes sense! Ericka, it all makes perfect sense," Crystal gushed.

"Gosh, we really do owe Monica Nicole big time, don't we?" she replied. "Well, don't worry, dear. We are here for you. Probably going to have to make a lot of changes though."

Monica Nicole continued to cry. "You don't have to. I put those women through utter hell. I deserve to suffer like they did." She continued to gasp and cry, quite a strange combination.

Ericka commented, "Well no doubt about that, you are going to have to deal with all this, suffer it I mean, but we're here to lend a hand. Come on; let's get your streaked makeup off. Time for bed, I think. Only tonight, we're doing you, Miss Monster Boobs," she teased Monica Nicole, who finally got a handle on her wild emotions.

"I don't understand why I am so emotional," Monica Nicole whined.

"We women are just this way," Crystal declared, seeing this as a way to make her calm down and relax.

"I never knew that."

"Well, you do now, dear. Come on—into bed with you."

"But I can't even reach my own. . ." Monica suddenly realized the depths of her loss of arms and hands. Unable even remotely to bend enough because of the metal stays of the "melted" corset, she couldn't even wipe her own butt. She broke down and cried again.

Later on, the three finished loving each other, and finally Monica fell asleep. The next day, she was still fighting the awful compression of her torso, but her breathing was a little more controlled. As the day dawned, one after another, she discovered routine activities of life that she could no longer accomplish on her own. That first full day consisted of one continuous embarrassment, beginning with having to have help going to the bathroom, followed by getting dressed, and then being fed her breakfast. At least, she didn't eat much at all.

While the others then headed to their library to begin researching as Leslie had asked them to, Monica Nicole attempted to see if she could actually cast any spells. While Dispater hadn't lied, with the limited motions that she could make with only her upper arms, to her dismay, she could only cast a very few spells. When lunchtime came, she again had to let her friends feed her, but reported, "I can cast ten spells out of all those that I know. I guess I should be thankful for even those."

"No, that's just spells, Monica Nicole. Rather be thankful that you have four friends who love you like a sister," shy Enya spoke her mind. Crystal and Ericka stared at her, as though she lost her mind. "Really. Friends, sisters, who are there for you means more than anything else, excepting your husband and children. Brad and I are going to have a baby," She announced, patting her belly lovingly. "We create new life. Men can't."

Monica Nicole was struck by the utter simplicity of Enya's statements. "She's right. You four mean more to me than all my magic, really you do. I can't imagine living life without you four in it with me. I've been thinking a lot about life this morning while failing dismally to cast my power spells. Last time, I had no love in my life. My father despised me, beat me, and showed me that the only relationship worth having with a woman was to torture her, turn her into a helpless dependent. I never knew anything else, so naturally I thought ultimate power was everything."

She continued, "Good god, that's only one tiny, minuscule part of life, just yourself. Like Enya says, there's your loving family and creating and bringing new life into the world. There are you, my dearest friends, the ones who support you through good times, and the bad ones, like you are all doing for me now. There's all mankind out there that deserves a better life. Plants, animals—we can't live without them. Our possessions, the universe. Where would we be without our wands and pizzas? And as I personally know from having been raised from the dead by Taddeus and the Create Life resurrection spell, there's me, a soul, or whatever you want to call me. I'm not this body, thank goodness for that. I'd be in an awful shape if this body was all that I was. Enya is right, true power must also encompass all these things, not just one's own self. I do love you all."

At that exact instant, a giant flash of magic engulfed Monica Nicole. When the energy dissolved, she was standing there dressed in her jeans and sneakers, just as she had been when Dispater cast his magic on her last night, only she was now whole. Her arms were restored; the melted corset, gone; her wand was in her hand; her massive bosom was back to her usual large size.

Enya shrieked in shock. Misty squealed. Ericka merely held her hands over her mouth, too shocked to say anything. Crystal blinked several times and then tried to Dispel Magic, believing this was another illusion of some kind. "What just happened?" Monica Nicole squeaked, while touching one hand on the other in complete disbelief.

Crystal commented, "Well, this isn't some kind of illusion. It's real. I bet I know what happened. When Dispater granted Herbert's wish, there was no mention of any time limit or duration on how long Monica Nicole would have to endure it. I guess it was short lived. Wishes can be tricky things to state right."

Monica Nicole touched her face with her hands and then brushed tears of joy from the sides of her face. She whispered, "No, I think it has everything to do with me realizing that. Enya, thank you. You've saved me. I do love you all, truly." All five rushed together and hugged each other.

Crystal then said, "Now I suppose that you want us to renew our bargain and have those big boobs again."

"No, dear. I love you all just the way that you are. You look just the way that you want to look, and I will love you for that. I have no right to tell you how to appear. Be true to your own desires and passions, and I will admire and respect you all the more," Monica Nicole replied rather humbly.

"Agreed. I still want to dress up fancy. I like the power over men that it gives me," Crystal declared.

"Me too," Ericka added.

"Well, I liked wearing the fancy gowns and tall heels. I felt sexy and turned on, so I guess I will continue," Monica Nicole said with a grin. "Come on; we have research to do. I hope the demons don't come back tonight. We need to figure out how to handle them better. Did you see all the fire power the guards unleashed on just one of them in order to kill it?"

As they walked back to the library, Ericka commented, "Well, if you want to continue wearing those six-inch style heels, I've an idea that you want to hear. I've been doing some research, and I think I can enchant them, but I have to have a high quality pair of heels in order to do that. Stilettos of Speed. How's that sound?" The five chucked.

"Don't make me a pair," Enya chuckled. "I hate heels. Besides, I'm going to get really big soon."

"Have you and Bart picked out names yet?" Misty asked.

Later that evening, Monica Nicole wrote out a lengthy letter, outlining her revelations and sent Governor Lindsey Barron-Cross a copy asking her to forward it to all the others in the Rodents and copies to Leslie Traub and Henry Wilkens. She said to herself, "I don't know if they will believe any of it or not, but I have sent it and that's what matters. I'm finished with this Dominus business. May the world forget he existed."

After that, she ceased having others call her Monica Nicole. No longer did she like the meaning of counsel and victor of the wizards. Now she just became Monica. However, her name mostly stuck.

Chapter 12—Research Days

Crystal and Monica Nicole spent several days culling through Crystal's leather bound volumes of arcane lore, piecing together any data relating to the Abyss and its demons. Meanwhile, Ericka was kept busy in her lab working on additional magical items that the three thought might be needed in battles against demons. Specifically, if a number of wizards and witches banded together to go up against them, as they had been, the three thought that protection devices were essential, as witnessed by Parry's very close calls.

Ericka wanted to be able to provide their forces with items that supplied Skin of Stone spells and an In Case of Severe Bodily Injury Teleport to a Place of Safety. She also added her major protection spell that nullified all Grade 4 spells and below, figuring that they wouldn't necessarily have a Dispeller with them. Thanks to the financial support of Monica Nicole, a new batch of enchantable gemstones had just arrived, promising her at least two weeks of solid work to get this batch ready.

Crystal and Monica Nicole made copies of the sketches of the various demons that they found, particularly those that had already been faced. To each, they then jotted down specific details that they uncovered, most notably its weaknesses and some guess as to the level of resistance that demon had to magical energies or spells. Some of the older volumes referred to fighting them with enchanted swords, the lore being handed down through many generations. No one really had such swords these days. Big guns were more likely, but killing one by this means had been difficult. One died only after taking hundreds of rounds of 50-caliber shells! Would they stand up to RPGs for example? No one knew that answer yet, though Henry was ready to find out. He'd requisitioned a dozen such devices and was just waiting for another round of demon attacks to test them out.

A week of complete quiet followed the arrest of Wil and his four associates. Even so, the Department of Magical

Misuse was kept on high alert each early evening, since that had always been the time of the demon attacks. None came.

Leslie had also been busy, though taking a very different approach. She reached out and contacted every person that she could find who had any knowledge in the arcane lore, occult lore, Gating, or demons. A week after the capture of Wil Blackthornby, she had just the men for the jobs she had in mind. The day before their arrival, she paid a visit to the PIWIP (PI-wip) store as it was commonly called.

Monica Nicole met her at the door, since it was her turn to deal with customers. "Oh, hi Leslie. Come on it," she said politely.

"Hello Monica Nicole. You are looking well. We all were very pleased to hear that Dispater's curse was short lived, but do you always go around ready for a fashion party? Those heels of yours must be killers."

Monica Nicole laughed. "We like to wear elegant, sexy clothes. And no, I'm quite used to them. Actually, Ericka has magically enchanted this pair. I can nearly fly in them if I have to move quickly. So what can we do for you? Sure glad the demons have been quiet."

"Well, it has to do with the demons and the threat made by Graz'zt. I've located some out-of-town experts and was hoping that I could arrange to have them stay here at your estate and store. They are under my protection, and this place is vastly more defensible that a motel room or one of those econo-apartments. I'll cover their costs, naturally."

"Cool. How many?"

"Four, but one is quite old, and one will only be here for a few days at most."

"Okay, I'll see that we get our guest rooms ready for them."

"Thank you all very much. I take their safety seriously. The elderly man will be accompanied by his youngest son, who looks after him. Touch of dementia, I'm told, un-curable. One works for our department out of Kansas City, making magical items for our personnel. I've asked him to come and work with Ericka, in hopes that she can share some of her ideas. If this turns out to be an invasion, we're going to need many magical assists. The other is a specialist in reading psychic events. I'm hoping he can get further readings on the incised pentagrams that we've found. Oh, by the way, we forced two of Wil's associates to spill more of their work and have located two more that they built in old warehouses they owned. Got them all under twenty-four hour surveillance now. I'll bring the people by tomorrow around ten. Will that be okay with you?"

"You bet. I'll tell the others. Thanks."

The next day, the five were waiting to see these new arrivals and to greet them. Right on time, Leslie and six of her assistants arrived, bringing the four with her. The assistants, wands at the ready, spread out, taking flanking positions, as though they expected an attack at any moment. Leslie led them inside the Protections, Investigations, Wands, Items, and Potions complex. "Ah, waiting for us, I see," she grinned.

"This is Enya Holmes-Scorsky, potion maker. Misty Worth-Williams, wand maker. Crystal Holliday who can cast Gate and is quite knowledgeable in this area. Ericka Van Nie who makes all their magical items. Monica Nicole Black." As usual, Ericka and Crystal both wore their light blue, satin gowns, black nylons, and black patent pumps with their five-inch heels. Monica wore her bright red satin gown and her new magical six-inch pumps. The three younger men were rather dazzled by the women's appearance.

She continued, "This is Professor Kyle Mac Pheerson. He's originally from Scotland and his son, Gregor. Kyle was seventy-six with thin, white hair and a very wrinkled hair. Having lived for so long in the States, he'd lost much of his thick accent. "The professor and Gregor have brought along a number of ancient volumes that will aid us in our research." His son was twenty-one with reddish brown hair. Both he and his father wore brown camelhair jackets and corduroy pants that matched. Both had reddish freckles.

"This is Tyler Green, from our Kansas City office. He's been making protection magical items for the department for the last three years. Ericka, I would like you to get him up to speed on the items that you've made that have worked well for us." Tyler was twenty with black hair and dark hazel eyes. He was working on growing a moustache, but was quite shy.

"And finally, this is Rob Finch from Denver, a specialist and who hopes to be able to give us more clues about what came through those gates. He was twenty-one, rather blonde and had light blue eyes. He wore jeans and a Colorado Rockies baseball jacket and cap.

Tyler commented, "Gosh, we must be keeping you from some fancy event. Red Hall graduates?"

Ericka laughed, "No and yes. How can you tell that we're all Red Halls? Crystal, Monica, and I always dress this way. Crystal and I were models for three years—Teen Fashion, but then you probably haven't see those mags."

"Pretty amazing for Red Hall. Yellow Hall or Black Hall. That's what I rather expected to see, not passionate Red Hall women. You must be extremely intelligent women too," Tyler replied.

Crystal commented, "Naturally. We broke all school records for Red Hall. Monica, why don't you give them a tour while I make us all some coffee?"

Monica smiled and said, "Follow me. This is a very defensible building. Brick overlaying concrete and steel. Good buy too. Our stores and workshops are on this floor. On your right is Misty's Wand shop and her workshop and husband, Jasper, is on your left. Here at the end is Enya's Potions shop and her workshop and husband, Brad, is on your right. The stairs at this end leads to the basement and our living quarters."

"Wow, Enya, you sure do have a state of the art lab. So do you, Misty. I've not seen some of this equipment outside major labs," Tyler commented, very much impressed with their setup. Both women were quite pleased that he was so observant.

Enya replied, "Yes, Monica Nicole here provides us with whatever we could possibly need. It makes the job a whole lot easier. Right now, we're working up a large batch of healing potions, just in case the demons come back again."

Monica Nicole led them back down the hall past the large reception entry room. On your right is Ericka's workroom and on your left is her magic item shop. Here at the end is our library on your right and one of the guest rooms where two of you can stay. Let's go down the stairs now." She finished showing them the facilities.

After the four took their rooms, with Gregor and his father taking the guest room on the first floor so the older man didn't have to negociate the stairs, they divided. Tyler joined Ericka in her workshop, while Gregor took his father into Crystal's library, where he Unshrunk their precious books. The three began a heavy discussion about the demons.

Meanwhile, Leslie explained, "Monica Nicole, I'm taking Rob to visit each of the known incised pentagrams and see if he can glean any more information about what came through the gates. Care to come along and document any of his findings for Crystal and the professor's use?"

"Sure thing. Let me grab my coat." She donned her fake sable fur jacket and joined them.

Rob commented, "You sure you don't want to change or something?"

"Nope. I look perfect. Don't worry. With Ericka's new enchantments on my heels, I can keep up. Let's go. Say, where's your wand?"

"Don't have one. Don't need it for my spells."

Monica Nicole's eyebrows rose. Another Lindsey? She thought as they walked out and joined the six security men. As soon as Leslie told them that they were going to the rusted out warehouse opposite Cahokia Mounds, many Teleport spells flashed. The group arrived back at the first site where Parry and Ari had discovered the gate and demons, and Leslie's six guards quickly secured the area.

"This way," Monica Nicole said, leading Rob and Leslie into the abandoned warehouse. "Should have been torn down ages ago. Sure is rusted out. The incised pentagram is there, in the center. Pretty crude one, Crystal says." Her steel tipped heels clicked noisily on the concrete, breaking the complete stillness.

"Okay, I see it. Please stand back and give me some time to see what I can sense and perceive," Rob asked softly.

Monica Nicole and Leslie stood back and watched him. The young man took a deep breath and slowly exhaled it. Then, he began moving slowly around the circle, being careful not to touch the remains. Here and there, the lines had been broken and samples taken by Oliver's forensics team. It had been walked across and scuffed up, all of which destroyed its ability to Gate and Summon.

After some ten minutes, he looked up. "I got all that I can from this one. Pretty evil goings on. First, they sacrificed a young woman to power their Summoning and subsequent Gating." He outlined pretty much what Leslie already had learned from Parry, Ari, and the others. He added, "What's curious, is that the next day—it was light here—four invisible beings arrived here and left. Two returned and went back through the Gate a few hours later. Curious. The next night, the fly demons came through. Oh, and four more invisible beings came through as well."

"But this time, they canceled their Invisibility spells and were met by four others here. They morphed into what the other four looked like, ordinary men and women. Strange. I will have to talk with the professor to work out just what kind of demons these are. Let's see the next pentagram, please," Rob said quietly.

"How can you tell all that?" Monica asked, growing quite curious. She'd not seen him doing anything. No spells, no casting. Nothing but walking around the pentagram several times, quite slowly.

Rob let out a small chuckle and grinned, "Didn't see any magic wand waving eh? All you wizards and witches are so dependent upon them aren't you? Well, your magic is powered by your wands funneling in the energy needed by the spells you cast. Me, I don't use wands. I power the spells myself. Think of me as kind of like that Energizer bunny on the TV commercials years ago. I provide the power behind the spells, but I will admit, I'm more limited than you all are. You can keep casting seemingly endlessly, but I run down and have to eat and sleep to recharge. I think the world famous Dispeller, that governor, she does it my way too."

She didn't get a chance to respond. Leslie and her group teleported them to the next site. It was way past lunchtime before Rob finished up with the last two sites, which Monica hadn't seen yet. Leslie and Henry's security personnel closely guarded these two recently disclosed locations. As they prepared to head back, Rob asked, "Hey, I'm starving. Have to recharge some. Can we possibly visit that Sal's Bar and Grill? I've heard he has the greatest steaks in St. Louis. I could use one or two about now."

"Sure, I know the place," Monica replied, looking at Leslie, who nodded her agreement. They appeared next just outside the doorway. The lunchtime magical crowd was nearly gone. Only three witches were still inside, sipping their coffee. Like all the small diners here in the downtown area, his outer wall was all windows, albeit heavy ones and enchanted with a number of protection spells. Sal's was a common meeting ground for all kinds of witches and wizards and of all persuasions. Sal's was neutral, an unspoken neutrality. Sal was a big man, six-six and all muscle, probably from all the steaks that he had eaten over his fifty year lifetime. That he also had a large shotgun behind his bar and wasn't afraid to use it or his Staff of Power, combined with his tough guy appearance, kept that neutrality.

This didn't mean he wasn't friendly; he just didn't talk much. He nodded and allowed the party to sit before moving over to them to take their orders. "I'll have your steak special and one of your best ales. The Department here is paying for it," Rob teased Leslie, who did grin and gave her okay to it. Considering the price of the special, everyone ordered it as well, but Monica also asked for a doggie bag with her order.

Leslie gave her a curious look. She replied with a big grin of her red lips, "No, I don't have a dog. The proportions are Sal-sized. You'll see." Indeed, the steak nearly filled the plate, leaving barely enough room for the mashed potatoes, gravy, and peas that rounded out the meal. Rob dove into his, polishing it away in short order. Monica Nicole gave him a teasing grin.

He chuckled, burped a little, and replied, "Like I said. I burn up energy working my magic. Have to recharge the old batteries. Eat up. That's the best steak I've ever had. Sal's reputation is not unfounded."

A half hour later, the group returned to the shop and estate, where Rob then sat down with Professor Mac Pheerson.

He described the other demon creatures that he'd seen gating in from the Abyss on the sly.

"Oh my. Oh dear, this is bad, then, isn't it?" the elderly man said, pulling on his chin. "Gregor, find me the pages on the succubus and the Cambion will you. We did bring those didn't we? I can't remember. Is it Sunday already?"

"No dad. It's Monday. We're in St. Louis, helping. Yes, we brought them. I'll get them for you," Gregor replied, sympathetically. Shortly, he brought in two very old leather-bound volumes, placing them before his father.

The old man touched them lovingly, before opening them. He went right to the correct pages. "Yes, that's what three looked like," Rob said, before the old man even looked up to ask Rob if this is what he'd seen.

"Oh my!" the professor exclaimed, turning to the second volume. Once more, Rob pointed out that most of the "secret arrivals" were of this additional type, the Cambion. "Oh dear me. This is really bad, really quite bloody bad, Gregor."

"You better explain them to everyone, dad," Gregor whispered softly.

"Yes, I had better do that, hadn't I?" He launched into a description of what the two were. The succubus was an exceptionally intelligent, female demon, highly resistant to magical spells, on the tall side, and with an extremely attractive, human form. Well, that is except for their spiked horns on the top of their foreheads and their large wings on their backs, which gave them away. They preferred to use charm-based spells, getting others to do their dirty work. Because of their beauty, cunning, and intelligence, they were often quite close to the demon princes and lords, working for them. Further, if they were hard-pressed, instead of fighting, they would Gate in the extremely powerful demons, including their bosses, the princes and lords!

"Strategic planning," Professor Mac Pheerson explained. "That's probably what they are here for, that and to scout out the world for its strengths and weaknesses. Not good at all. Never, ever let one of them kiss you! After a few of her kisses, you will be quite dead. Even one kiss will rob you of much of your life and powers. Very nasty demons, very."

"Now the Cambion are very likely this Demon Prince Graz'zt's soldiers. They are bred by himself. He uses captured human women, personally breeding them to create these hideous sons who look much like himself. Of course, with all children, you get a wide variety of personalities, intelligence, and sizes. Some are almost as tall as their father is, over seven feet. None is ever short. The weaker ones have only a small resistance to magical spells, while the stronger ones have about twice as much as their weaker siblings. All are quite strong, getting that from their father. They are bred as fighters, though the smarter ones do know quite a few spells, but rarely more than about our Grade 4 spells. No, these are fighters. These are likely Graz'zt's generals and majors and foot soldiers. This is not good, not good at all."

"Darn it!" Leslie exclaimed. "So what do you think that their objective is right now, professor?"

"Hard to say. Graz'zt was last here over three thousand years ago. Back then, the world was primitive. Swords, spears, bows, and arrows. Now we have bombs and guns. My guess is that he has them scouting our world, observing the changes, and preparing the means for his assault on our world."

Crystal spoke up. "If we shut down all these incised pentagrams, won't that prevent them from reporting back?"

He sighed, "No, my charming young woman. You see, he has no way independently to open a Gate from the Abyss to our world. However, that wizard and his group were able to open a Gate from Earth to the Abyss, allowing him and his minions to come here. Once here, they can, of course, Gate home at any time. Worse, now that they are here, they too can open a Gate from here to the Abyss, bringing in more forces. On the positive side, only the succubus and the top generals can do that. Pity that the wizard didn't see them making use of the Gate that he opened."

"You can bet your bloody tartans that the three succubuses have already fanned out and created their own incised pentagrams. They've had what—two weeks—to do just that. Could be anywhere in our world now, even in Edinburgh, I'm afraid to say. This is incredibly bad, bloody well bad."

"Well, the one thing that we have going for us is that

there has been enormous changes during the last three thousand years. That ought to make them slow down and study us for quite some time," Leslie suggested.

"Quite true. I would not expect Graz'zt to act in haste. While, as you say, he said it was but two blinks for him, three thousand years of human evolution has brought us quite a long way in technology," the old professor commented. "I wonder if all that has been wise? Do we really need video games?"

"Hey, dad. They are fun," Gregor defended them.

"Son, bring me a stout from our fridge, will you?"

Gregor replied softly, "Dad, remember, we're not at home now. We're visiting the good folks in St. Louis."

"Oh we are? How nice. You don't suppose they have a stout in their fridge do you?"

"I'll get you one dad," he promised, "just as soon as the meeting is over. You want to be as helpful as you can to these people. Remember all the demons?"

"Oh yes, yes, the demons. We are in trouble, son, aren't we?" he muttered, having forgotten just what he'd said earlier.

"True dad." Gregor looked up at the others. "He's slipped again. Best get him some rest. Until he recovers some, you won't get anything useful out of him." He pointed to his head, and they got the message. Dementia. Gently, Gregor helped his dad rise and walked him across the hall to their bedroom. "No dad, a stout isn't good for you right now. You need to take a nap. Then you can have your stout."

When Gregor returned, he heard Leslie summarizing, "So then there is no way to know just how many of these demons are on our world right now. They will be disguised as normal people and are probably casing our world in preparation for the demon prince's assault."

Crystal added, "And there is no way to know just how many more Gating circles they have already built or intend to build or even where they are building them. Doesn't sound good to me."

Leslie nodded. "So we have to find ways to locate these new circles and to find and destroy the demons already here. The only thing we have going for us right now is the massive changes that have occurred since this demon prince was last here. Perhaps, that will slow them down considerably or give it up entirely. We can always hope so. I best be off and let the higher-ups know all this. Grim indeed. Carry on your good works." She nodded to everyone, rose, and left, taking her six men with her as she walked out the shop's front doors.

Rob patted his full stomach. "If you will excuse me, I'm taking a nap. I rather used up a lot of my energies this morning." He rose and headed to his room. Tyler and Ericka headed back to her workshop, leaving Crystal and Monica to continue their work, assembling all known data. Now they added this newfound information to their every-growing compilation. Before long, Gregor rejoined them.

"Dad's sleeping now. He has a few good hours each day, but that's about all. Pretty awful, but I'll take care of him until the end."

"You are doing a good job of it. What happened to your mother?" Crystal asked.

"Oh, she passed away a few years ago. Dad's second wife. Spry old dude. Married her when he was in his fifties, after his first wife died. I have really older brothers and sisters, but they have their own families and jobs. I'm all that he really has. Besides, they just wanted to put him into some nursing home and forget about him. I can't do that. He's my dad, after all. Come on. I'll lend you a hand adding dad's new data to your documents. I think I can help fill in some gaps." The three set to work.

Nearby in her lab, Ericka was working on another set of protection pendants. Tyler said shyly, "I can give you a tip, if you like."

Ericka didn't know if she wanted some fellow to be telling her how to work her magic, but decided at least to let him speak. She nodded to him.

"Well, I find that it's more efficient to attempt to first install the most powerful spell that you want a new item to hold. That way, if it doesn't take, you haven't wasted all the time and effort of installing the lesser spells only to have a fizzle from what you wanted to make," he said softly.

"Hey, that is a good idea. If it doesn't take, I can then

rethink that whole item. Maybe come up with an alternative powerful spell to try to install in it. You're right. I've wasted quite a bit of time when one of them can't take the big power spell that I'd intended to put in it. Cool. Guess you really do know your stuff."

"Yeh, been doing it lots longer than you have. Give yourself time, Ericka, and you'll catch on to many tricks. There's not too many of us who can actually make magical items. Make Permanent is a Grade 8 spell. I have to admit that I didn't expect to ever see a Red Hall witch knowing this spell."

"Why? Because Red Hall witches are so into fashions and passions?"

"Yeh, that. At my school, they were mostly interested in making themselves look really beautiful and sexy. Don't know why though."

Ericka giggled. "To attract boys. You know the right boys. Wealth and power, that sort of thing."

"We called them air heads. No offense, Ericka."

She laughed. "Yes, that's a pretty good description of a lot of Red Hall girls. But some of us put our passions into magic."

"And looking really good," Tyler added shyly. She flashed him a smile with her quite red lips, causing him to flush slightly.

"Hey, your idea really works. This pendant didn't take the big spell. Cool, Tyler. Any more hot tips for a budding inventor?" she asked. He really does know what he's doing, she thought.

"Well, I do have some tricks that I've found useful, but you might not," he said rather reservedly.

That evening, Parry and Ari dropped by to see Ericka. "Hi, here, I wanted to return the protection pendant. Looks like the demons are finished here."

"Oh, thanks, Parry," Ericka said, "but why don't you keep it a while longer. The demons are barely getting started! Come on. I'll fill you both in."

"Okay. Thanks!"

"I'm staying with Parry now. I've quit my job and am going to work for Henry in a few weeks," Ari proudly announced. "Plus, I'm teaching Parry here how to cast lots more spells."

"Yes, she's a really good teacher. I'm up to Grade 1 spells now. Really cool! But what's with the demons? I thought we knocked them back to the Abyss."

"It's far, far worse, Parry. Sit down. This is grim," she said. Ericka proceeded to tell them all that they'd learned today.

"Thanks, Ericka. I do believe that I'll keep your pendant and ring a whole lot longer, at least until I can cast that stone skin thing. Saved my butt, you know," Parry replied. After that, the two left.

Outside the shop, Parry thought rapidly. "You know, Ari, if this Graz'zt fellow takes human women to use to breed his army of these Cambion thugs, then where's he been getting all his humans from? Especially if he's not been here for three thousand years."

"Don't know," Ari replied, grateful for not being a virgin any longer. Perhaps, the demon prince wouldn't be coming after her now.

"If he has had a long drought of no new women, I bet anything that some of these new agents of his have been kidnaping women, taking them to the Abyss for him!" Parry declared.

"So you think some of the demons are still around St. Louis?" Ari asked growing worried once more.

"Don't know, Ari dear, but I'm going to check with Oliver and see if there's been an abnormal number of either missing women or kidnaped women these past few weeks." He didn't have to explain further. Ari understood and shivered, as she teleported them to his apartment.

The next morning, Rob left for his home in Denver. On Wednesday, Crystal exclaimed, "Wow! I found it!"

"Found what?" Monica asked, curiously. They'd been going over ancient records of past civilizations, looking for clues.

"It wasn't three thousand years ago that Graz'zt was imprisoned by wizards here on Earth, but rather, and dig this

Monica; it was three thousand three hundred thirty-three years ago! See, 3+3 plus 3+3. Numerology wins. That's when he was here, the year 1197 BC! Rather, that is when he busted out and wreaked havoc before splitting back to his home. He assassinated King Tikulti-Ninurta of Assyria, causing the downfall the Assyrian empire back then! Isn't that just fascinating?"

The professor who had been sort of dozing at the table opened his eyes and spoke up. "Oh yes, there are depictions of some demons in Wizard Salazar's journal of those years and some crude sketches. Writing is tough to translate. Later, in the middle ages, they used some of these images as the models for the gargoyles found on all the major Gothic cathedrals of the thirteenth century or so. Fascinating reading." He promptly slumped over, resting his head on his hands, dozing off once more.

Gregor spoke up, "There must be an English translation around. I'll see what I can dig up. Could provide some additional information. Probably horribly dated, though."

Crystal put her long nails against her cheeks, thinking hard. She looked up. "You know, I think we haven't been asking the right questions here."

"How's that?" asked Gregor, suddenly rather interested in what this gorgeous Red Hall graduate had to say. He had been mostly trying to ignore her rather obvious sex appeal, focusing on what she was truly about. She had a brilliant mind, he had written in his diary. He kept a listing of every person he had met, jotting down tidbits of useful data about them. In his line of investigations, knowing the right person to ask the right question of was the key to success or so his father had drilled into his head.

"Who and how did a wizard back then actually manage to summon Prince Graz'zt from the Abyss there to Assyria and then imprison him? That's what we ought to be asking. How and why? If we know that, perhaps we can reproduce it and capture this beastly demon, putting an end to his threats to harm our world today. Come on. Let's hit the books harder!"

"Brilliant, Crystal, positively brilliant!" Gregor exclaimed. He knew that he was going to have to revise his notes on Crystal in his diary tonight. "When dad gets back again, we'll see if he knows anything more about it."

Seeing the two of them diving into the books again, Monica decided to leave them to it. She needed a break to think about everything that was happening. As she walked by Ericka's lab, she saw those two working well together and didn't disturb them. Instead, she headed to the reception area where she had a great view of their picturesque grounds, at least the front portion of it.

As she stood there looking out at the few remaining marigolds in the circular garden that their drive encircled, she heard a voice in her head. "Dominus Malefic alias Monica Nicole Black. I hereby Summon you." A giant flash of magic blinded her, engulfing her. When the energies died down a second later, only her heels remained on the floor near the main doors.

Hearing the sound of the magical energies, Ericka and Tyler stopped what they were doing and headed out to see what was going on. "Good god! What happened to Monica? Those are her heels! Where is she?" Hearing her crying out, everyone else, except the dozing professor came running to the reception area only to stop short, staring at Monica's heels.

"We just heard this loud pop of magical energies, and we found only her heels left," Ericka exclaimed, growing very frightened for her dear friend. "Something awful has happened to her! I just know it!" Crystal's face was very pale, and she swallowed hard, unable to think of what to do.

"Don't touch them," levelheaded Enya said. "That way we don't contaminate the magical trace energies. Someone Message Leslie and Henry."

With his wand at the ready, Gregor cast a number of detection spells, but found nothing. He then attempted to send Monica Nicole a Message. The spell failed to detonate, though he tried it three times. Then, he sent a Message to Rob Finch.

Leslie and six of her men arrived within a minute. "That's all that's left of her?" she asked incredulously. Enya nodded. She ordered her men to do a thorough search of the extensive grounds, looking for perhaps the body of Monica Nicole Black.

At this point, everyone began talking at once. The four women were terrified that someone had somehow snatched Monica Nicole in spite of all their protection spells. "We must put up even better spells," Ericka said determinedly, biting her lips.

Acting on a hunch, Leslie sent a Message and scarcely a minute later, Rob arrived, teleporting in from Denver. "What's happened?" he asked, walking in the reception area.

Rapidly, Ericka explained what little they heard or knew. "That's all that's left of her, just her heels!"

"No one's touched anything. I mean we haven't disturbed her heels," Crystal hastily added. "Please, can you sense anything? What happened to her? Is she. . ." She couldn't make herself finish the sentence; she just couldn't.

"Okay, don't bother me for a while," Rob said softly. He took a deep breath and let it out slowly. Mechanically, Crystal realized that he was temporarily increasing his metabolic rate and wondered if that had anything to do with his special skills. Slowly, he paced a small circle around the tall stilettos, magically enchanted by Ericka. One moment, she'd been standing there in them, and the next she was gone, but her heels were just as she had been in them that previous moment. Then he saw what he was looking for.

Rob said, "She was Gated, Summoned to be precise. I'd like to share something with all of you. If you can cast your spells to see what I am seeing, I can show you something." He need not suggest it twice! Quickly, her four friends and Leslie cast the same spell and were now seeing whatever it was that Rob was seeing. More precisely, they were picking up his thoughts as though he were speaking to each one of them directly.

"As I walk around the shoes, look at what is totally surrounding them. Can you see it? The magical trace remnants of the spell used to capture Monica Nicole," Rob said to each one directly from mind to mind.

"My god! That's an incised pentagram!" Crystal exclaimed in her thoughts.

"Yes, it is the residue left over from the spell that was cast. Someone knew her full name and used it to Summon her.

She will arrive there inside their pentagram and has no choice but to do whatever the summoner wishes." Rob broke his concentration and the image faded. The five took that as a sign to cancel their spells.

"So someone used a Summon and Gate spell on her?" Crystal asked. Rob nodded. "So, every time someone uses a Gate spell, the spell leaves this kind of energy residue?"

"Yes. All spells leave some energy traces for a time. The more powerful the spell, the longer and more intense the residue," Rob answered.

Crystal bit her lip, deep in thought. "So it is a real energy trace?" He nodded. "So if it's real, I wonder if it can be picked up by any kind of electronic detector? Excuse me. I have some research to do. Please, find Monica Nicole. I know that I don't know how. Please. She is very dear to us all."

"Don't worry, Crystal. I will be making the full resources of the Missouri Department of Magical Misuse available on this case. Top priority," Leslie stated decisively. Crystal had no doubt that she would do just that. Armed with a brilliant new idea, she took Tyler and Ericka back to their lab.

When Leslie and Rob were finally alone and the others had returned to their own work, she asked him, "So is there anything else that you can tell me about this abduction? I need a few more clues, if you have any."

"I didn't show you everything. I recognized the voice of the summoner. I didn't want to freak out her close friends, Leslie."

"It was that demon prince, wasn't it?" Leslie dared to whisper her own dreaded thought. Rob merely nodded. "Heck, she's probably not even on Earth any longer." Rob nodded again.

"Keep searching, Leslie. I will do what I can for her. These demons have to be stopped somehow or life is going to go all to hell, pun intended," Rob said rather quietly.

"Thank you, Rob. I owe you big time," Leslie whispered back. He smiled, nodded, and vanished. She suspected that he'd just teleported again. In a way, she thought, he and Governor Lindsey Barron-Cross were rather similar, casting spells sans wands, sans words. However, she had no idea just how vastly different the two's approaches to magic actually were.

"I don't care how much the electronic equipment costs, Ericka. Just get them. We are on to something very big here. And yes, I know it isn't going to help Monica right now, but we have got to think of the rest of the world," Crystal explained.

At this same time, back in downtown St. Louis at the FBI headquarters, Ari and Parry were going over the records of crimes during the past three weeks. Oliver was looking over their shoulders, trying to follow their rapid searches. "Just what are you looking for anyway?"

"Missing women," Ari explained. "You see, that demon prince fellow captures human women, and he breeds them himself. They only have sons, which are these Cambion demons that Rob has said have been gating in from the Abyss. They are the demon prince's army soldiers. Crystal pointed out that he's not been here for over three thousand years, so we figured one of his first targets will be young women to kidnap and take back to the Abyss so he can breed more of his soldier demons."

Parry butted in, "She's right. Only we're not seeing them in your crime statistics at all."

"Well I could have told you that, Parry. I've been keeping an eye on them since the kidnaping of Jessica White," Oliver said.

"Oh," Parry flushed. "Guess I should have asked. Still, it makes logical sense that he needs more human women. It's been three thousand years. Unless he gets them from other sources. Say, what's this strange report?"

"Oh, someone filed a missing persons report on Lilly Jones. Only when the police went to her apartment to check on her, they found that she'd sold it and moved out. Rather sudden move. Nothing more. Nothing suspicious there," Oliver said. Parry had a hunch and wrote down the name and address.

"Okay boss. Sorry for the time. Ari and I have something we want to check out. Thanks," he said hastily. Before Oliver could protest or reply, Parry whipped Ari around and dashed out of his office, leaving the agent just shaking his head.

Once out of the building, Ari asked, "What *are* we doing? I thought we were trying to get some clues?"

"We just did. I want to check this one out. According to that report, Lilly Jones was single, twenty years old, and a native of St. Louis. So why would she suddenly pack up and move, leaving no forwarding address? Doesn't make sense."

"Well, maybe she had a sick aunt who needed her or her parents got deadly ill," Ari came up with a reasonable explanation. They were walking down the sidewalk, hand in hand. After she said this, Parry stopped, pulling her backwards.

"See, Ari, you are doing just what the average person does. Give them a strange situation like this, one that lacks all the key details, and they are very eager to supply hypothetical reasons why it happened. Right out of thin air. Makes it all quite understandable now. Yes, her aunt got sick and needed her to move in with her on a day's notice. Perfectly reasonable. So that explains the big mystery; let's move on and forget about it. All tidied up in a nice believable package," Parry explained.

"So come on, Ari. We have some Private Investigating to do. We may or may not have a client in this Lilly Jones." They found Parry's old Ford, and he drove, while Ari punched in the location of the woman's old apartment.

It was on Delmar, out by I-170. A half hour later, they pulled into the parking lot behind the building. The two got out and headed into the main entrance. After checking apartment numbers on the array of mailboxes, Parry pointed out, "Still has her name on it. #12. Come on; it must be upstairs."

The hallway was quite. A red carpet ran down the long hall. #12 was at the back end of the hall. The two walked silently down the hall and stood before the door. Parry put his ear to the door, but heard no sounds. He knocked lightly. Then twice. After waiting enough time for someone to get off the toilet and answer the knock, he tried the doorknob. It was locked.

"Now what do we do?" Ari whispered.

"Keep watch. Sleuthing." He took out his lock picks and quickly unlocked the door. After glancing around, he opened it and stepped inside with Ari on his heels.

"Isn't this illegal?" she whispered.

"I thought I heard someone crying out for help. Didn't you?" Parry winked at her. She broke into a smile. "Look around and see what you can. Don't touch anything, though."

After two minutes, she whispered, "She didn't take her clothes. The police report said a single man now lived here. What's he doing with all this women's clothing? I don't see any men's clothing either."

"See if you can find a hair brush. Something that has Lilly's DNA on it," Parry suggested, while he continued his search. A few minutes later, she joined him, a hairbrush in a zip lock bag.

"Time to go," Parry whispered. After peeking at the empty hall, the two stepped out, locking the door behind them. Only when they were safely inside his Ford did Ari finally breathe deeply.

"Now what?" she asked.

"We go back to Oliver with the hair brush and this document I found in there! Here, read it yourself! I told you we were on to something!"

Ari read it.

Lilly Jones!

Congratulations! Your name has just been drawn as the Grand Prize Winner in the 2138 Clearinghouse Sweepstakes! You have won $25,000,000.00!

All taxes have been paid. Yes, the full amount is yours! Please sign here to authenticate your acceptance of our Grand Prize and a representative of ours will meet with you immediately to discuss the terms of the receipt of this prize: lump sum, annual installments, monthly installments, etc.

Acceptance   Signature: _Lilly Jones_____

❂

"Wow! No wait! There is a faint incised pentagram just below the signature," Ari called out. "She signed it and then received the terms. I bet she didn't like the terms. I've never heard of this sweepstakes. There's a Publisher's Clearinghouse Sweepstakes."

"Right. I'm going to have Oliver check on this outfit right now. I don't think it exists."

"But who wouldn't sign it? I mean for that much money. Tax free?" Ari gushed. "That's diabolical."

An hour later, Oliver fumed! There was no such company. It was a fraudulent contract. Further, Lilly Jones is a normal woman, not a witch. Against demons from the Abyss with their magic spells, Lilly was defenseless! Oliver barked to his agents, "Get on this immediately. Find out how many other unsuspecting, single women have been kidnaped with this hoax! Put out a citywide alert on the news. Better yet, send it out nationally! Get me headquarters in Washington, D.C. now! Parry, let Leslie know about this. Ah, excuse me. My secretary has Washington on the line now." Parry and Ari stepped out of his office, but heard him barking into the phone. Both sent a flurry of Message spells.

Chapter 13—Breeding Grounds

Monica was looking out of their reception windows at the late October landscape. The trees were at their height of splendor. The reds, yellows, browns, and oranges created a comforting sight and yet perhaps not so. Winter was near at hand. This demon problem seemed unsolvable to her. *What I did as Dominus pales compared to this demonic threat. We could all be killed or turned into slaves,* she thought to herself.

Then the Gating Summons came. She heard her precise name being spoken and recognized that voice, the Demon Prince Graz'zt! Monica didn't have time to react to her sudden realization of the voice. Magical energies blinded her for an instant. Her body felt as though it was falling, twisting, turning, like some wild jet cascading from the skies on its irrevocable, but brief journey to the ground. *If this is what it's like to be Gated, I hate it.* But that was all the time she had to think before she arrived.

She appeared on a raised stone platform, standing on a pentagram at least ten feet on a side and made from pure gold with a pure silver circle outlining it. The landscape was rolling, a dismal grey, devoid of all color. The odors that impinged on her first inhale were putrid, like rotting flesh. Trees, if that's what they were, looked more like twisted sticks, angling in all directions in search of sunlight that appeared absent. Yet a greyish gloom illuminated the awful landscape. The shimmering cylinder of magical energies of the Summons spell was just barely visible surrounding her. From her education, she knew she was currently trapped inside the incised pentagram with no escape possible. That her shoes were absent struck her as somehow funny.

The giant black-skinned demon prince took a step towards her on the platform, grinning wickedly. "Paralyze!" he barked. Monica felt her body go rigid. She'd been paralyzed many times before by her classmates when they were learning their spells. Had she been free to move, she knew she could have avoided or dodged it. Not this way, though. She was immobile in the pentagram.

Monica Nicole couldn't quite hear what he cast next. She didn't understand the language that he spoke. Had she been able to draw her wand and cast her own spell, she could have comprehended what he was saying. Suddenly, she felt an excruciating pain in her arms! From the corners of her eyes, she could see her arms smoking, burning, turning into charred cinders, but from the inside out! Pain! Such unendurable pain! She wanted to scream—to do anything to make that intense pain end, but was frozen in place, unable even to gasp, only watch as her arms turned into a ghastly brown, then black, and finally to grey ashes, falling in small cascades onto the gold pentagram on which she was standing. Now she could just barely see her shoulders, but somehow they were intact, undamaged by the internal fires that had consumed her arms. Her mind could not grasp what had happened to her, only the pain, pain, pain.

She saw Graz'zt watching her. Seldom had she seen anyone so utterly happy, so incredibly pleased. This demon relished in her pain. He thrived on feeling her pain! "Ah, that was exquisitely delicious, Monica Nicole Black, superb beyond measure. In fact, that was so fabulous that I've a mind to redo it again and again! But no, I've work to do."

Monica Nicole wanted to do many things, but remained paralyzed, frozen to the spot. Graz'zt again cast his spells, two she thought afterwards. All of her clothing vanished, save her long earrings, which she hoped would still provide her some small measure of protection, once she got out of this prison. She next felt her body somehow rising up, such a queer feeling. It was as if she were rising to a ballet en pointe position. Once more, she felt intense pain, this time in her feet. Unlike her arms, this pain was short-lived. Still trying to grasp what was happening to her body, she felt shoes, no boots, suddenly encasing her feet, bringing warmth to them. Only then did she realize how cold her feet had been while standing on the golden surface of the platform that rose about six inches from the ugly grey ground.

He spoke another command word, and the imprisoning energies vanished at last. She was free from his Summoning spell. Prince Graz'zt took another step towards her. "Welcome to my Cambion Production Center, Miss Monica Nicole Black. So good of you to volunteer to assist me here in the Abyss. I know you've been anxious to visit me, so I have accommodated your desires. Oh, yes, the boots are a necessity. Without them, your feet would slowly dissolve as you walk over the ground here. I believe your word for it is toxic acids, but here, it is lovelier than your smelly grass, which always needs cutting or so I'm told. Please step down from my gate platform. Do be careful and not take a tumble. Walking on your toes is a bit challenging, but you will have the hang of it in no time. They all do. Can't have you running around on my world, getting into mischief. Oh no. Here, so many demons would love to torture you. As long as you stay in my center, you will be very safe. Come on; step down please."

Monica Nicole fought to keep from screaming in terror and panic. She was still reeling from the intense pain from her now gone arms and could barely wiggle and wobble to keep her balance on her toes. Somehow, she wasn't going to give this beast any more pleasure watching her suffer. "See, I've made it easier for you. I've fused your feet into this position, though I suspect that you'd rather have cloven feet. They work so much better down here on my grounds, but as I said, I can't have you wandering around, teasing my demon staff. This way." He slipped his arm around her waist, but was careful to slip it under her long black hair, and then gently guiding her along, providing some support, as she took her first steps in these awful boots, which had eight-inch metal spikes for a heel.

"This is but one of my Cambion Production Centers that you see before you." They were on a low rise, and she could see a domed structure ahead of them, roughly shaped like a leaf with four prongs. They were heading towards the stem, which held its main entrance.

"Inside, you will be joining a number of other women, my breeding women. You see, it works this way. When I breed with human females, sons are always the result, my army of Cambions. However, your gestation period of nine months is wholly intolerable. My wonderful Doctor Menninger has worked out a far more satisfactory method for all concerned. He has a formula that I'll soon be feeding you, which will permit your body to create a egg each day. He will painlessly, unfortunately," he sighed as though this was just horrible, and then continued his explanation, "extract said egg from you, and then in the adjoining lab, fertilize it with my robust sperm. Once fertilized, the egg is then inserted into one of my female dretch hosts, and she will carry it to term in about six weeks."

"I've got more dretch than I know what to do with, so this gives them a real purpose here in the Abyss—to bear my offspring. Once born, they are then raised and trained to be my soldiers. Now then, don't worry. It is a painless process. You give up an egg each day, and I'll see that you are properly fed, housed, and protected. Fair trade. After you have adjusted and are producing your eggs, then Dr. Menninger will be extracting some of your blood. Later on, when your body has matured and is no longer producing eggs, it will be painfully killed, much as your arms were burned. From your blood, Dr. Menninger will clone a new you, complete with all your memories and the process of egg creation will continue."

"It is so good of you to come to me, Monica Nicole, along with several other newly acquired women from your world. You see, I've been reusing the human females that I brought back here some three thousand years ago. Thanks to you and several other young women, I finally have some fresh breeding stock, and hopefully, you will help me generate even more powerful Cambion soldiers, which I will used to take over your puny world. With all those women in my production centers, I'll have a large enough army to take over your world and the entire Abyss! I will reign supreme! Good plan, is it not, Monica Nicole? Can you see the vital role that you and the other recently acquired women are playing in it? Marvelous, devious, diabolical. Using their own women to defeat them. Brilliant, eh? And such a role I'm allowing you to play in it. Think of it, Monica Nicole Black, your sons will be taking total control of your world, something you were unable to do before. Brilliant, eh?"

Monica Nicole listened to his every word. While she fought to keep from vomiting or even opening her mouth in reply, she decided not to give him any satisfaction. Instead, she focused on taking the next step without falling down, and the next, and the next. This was a nightmare without end!

"Now don't go getting any ideas about running off. If your skin touches the ground of the Abyss, it will burn you, much as your arms did. Also, there is a form of time suspension going inside the Center. I've had to install that because of the sheer number of times some of the older women have been cloned. After three thousand years of cloning, if some of the older women try to leave, once they get outside where we are now, their bodies will instantly burn to dust. See, foolproof. And you can see why I do so need much new human blood. Here, let me get the door for you, since you will now have such a hard time with doors." He covertly grinned at her, taunting and teasing her, all the while relishing in her unspoken, wild emotions. He'd not had such pleasures in far too long a time. Why had he not gone after Earth long ago?

The floor of the stem of the leaf-shaped center, as though mocking the stick trees outside, was something akin to concrete or perhaps a grey stone. The transparent dome arched overhead, some twenty feet above her head, plenty of headroom for the giant prince. "On your left is the egg reclamation room, where once each day, Dr. Menninger removes an egg from each human woman in this Center, Number Five. Ahead is your general living area with plenty of comfortable sofas on which to lounge. On beyond that are your bedrooms. Finally, to your right is the dining room, where you will receive three healthy, balanced meals each day for as long as you live or produce eggs to be more precise."

"Three of the women in this center have been here a very long time. Well, that's not entirely correct. Each woman only has a relatively brief number of fertile years, as you know. These three are clones of their original selves, the one hundred twentieth clone to be precise. I know. I've been bored with the same women over and over and over. But I know that you don't mind being a clone in say another twenty-five years or so, since you were a clone when you were Dominus. Besides, you get to keep on living your life forever and ever. Such a gift

I don't offer many—a chance for real immortality, defeating death."

"Ah, my beautiful ladies, I've brought another charming young woman who will be joining you. I hope you will show her the ropes and how things are done around here." Monica Nicole saw eight women were sitting on two couches. Three had rather darkish skins and from their voices, she knew they were speaking some unknown language, but there was some kind of permanent understand languages spell translating for the women. These older three welcomed her first.

"Hello. I'm Zeta of Ur. My friends, Melani of neighboring Arbela, and Nasara-Sin of nearby Harran. We are pleased that you're joining us."

"Hello. I'm Martha Ann Lodge. Please, do you know if they found the man who shot our President? I was at the theater and heard the gunshot and panic. Did they find him?"

Monica Nicole looked at Martha strangely and asked, "What was the President's name?"

"Why, President Lincoln. What a silly question."

"Why yes they did. He's paid for his crime."

Zeta spoke up, "Thank you ever so much. She keeps asking everyone that question but I'm afraid that we don't know him." Monica Nicole began to think that these women may well be under the influence of an Idiot Mind spell.

She looked at the other four women. They looked much as she did, young and in their twenties. All had red eyes from crying, but one bravely spoke up next. "I am Lilly Jones. I won the sweepstakes, fifteen million dollars, but I don't know when they are going to give me my first check. Do you?" Monica Nicole could only shake her head no.

"Kind sir, do you know when?" she asked Prince Graz'zt.

"I'm sure it will be soon now. Why don't you introduce your three friends? They are from St. Louis as well," he replied. His face had a covert grin on it.

"Oh. They are waiting for their money too. We all won. She's Patricia Whitestone. She's Gracie Stalls, and she's Janet Bridgewater. Please sir, can you check and see when we will get our money? How much longer will it be?"

While Monica Nicole waited to hear his answer, he cast Idiot Mind on her, when she was least expecting it. She then said, "Oh my. You have all won so much money. That is super. What are you going to do with it?" *What am I saying?* Monica Nicole tried to fight off the spell's effects, but the demon prince broke her concentration.

"Now ladies, why don't you show Monica around your beautiful estate? Besides, it is almost suppertime, and she doesn't know where the dining room is located or even where her new fancy bed is."

"Oh yes. We must," Zeta gushed. With that, the prince turned and left Monica Nicole standing precariously on her toes. All eight of the other women were also naked and wearing similar boots that came up to their ankles. Only the tips of their toes touched the ground on a very tiny sole and with a tall, metal spiked heel at least eight inches tall. Four of the women's hair fell nearly to their ankles in varying shades of blacks and browns. The four new arrivals had blonde to light brown hair, some short, and some shoulder length.

"We don't walk very well yet," Lilly explained, "but Zeta, Melani, and Nasara-Sin walk really well. So you should watch them, not us. We almost fall down."

"It's horrible, I think, but I'm not too sure," Gracie put in.

"I don't think we are quite all right," Patricia added.

"Oh sure, you are perfectly fine. You are just like us. And we are fine," Zeta declared.

Melani looked a bit confused. "I think that you just need more of something. It's a big word. Just do it more. Walk around more. That's it."

"She's got lovely long hair," Nasara-Sin said. "So do we. So you should see how we toss ours around so we don't step on it or sit on it. Watch us, Monica."

"See how we get up," Zeta explained, sort of lunging to her toes, wiggling a bit to get her balance. "See. Nothing to it, really. Must do it a lot, we think. Come on. Let's show Monica the dining room." Monica saw that the four older women did indeed walk gracefully and without much of a problem, though they went slowly and watched each step that they took.

She couldn't help herself from saying, "You do walk really well. So graceful. Like a ballerina." Of course, the four didn't know what that big word was, and Monica found it too difficult to explain. "You just walk really nicely."

"See, ladies," Zeta pirouetted to face the five newcomers. "You just must do much walking. Then, you be good as us. Tomorrow we all walk." She pirouetted back, and they entered the dining room. Ten chairs and a very long table comprised the dining room. Of course, the walls and ceiling were transparent.

"The trees look bad. When does spring come?" Monica Nicole again couldn't help herself from asking.

"One day. Perhaps soon. Not sure." Zeta seemed a bit confused about that detail. "See. Push chair out. Just so. Monica must shake head like us. See." She tossed her head this way and that to get her very long black hair either off to one side so that she could sit down without sitting on it.

Of course, Melani, Nasara-Sin, and Martha also just had to show Monica Nicole this as well. "Come, you try it, Monica," Zeta insisted. "Toss hair. Sit. Soon supper comes. Toss hair. Sit."

"Okay," Monica Nicole said against her better wishes. She nearly lost her balance swinging her head about, but managed to get it off to her left, and she sat down a bit hard. One by one, the other women took their seats as well.

Before long, a very pretty young woman entered. She had with shoulder length black hair and two small horns protruding from the top of her forehead and with a pair of small bat-like wings attached to her upper back. She pushed a cart ahead of her. She wore a grey blouse, a black skirt, and flats. "Hello. Monica Nicole, is it? I am Nisha. I bring your meals for you."

She went around the table asking what they would like for dinner, beginning with Zeta, the eldest at perhaps forty. Zeta replied that she wanted lamb, and Nisha set a flat plate of food before her. "There you go, Zeta. Lamb it is." She asked each woman what she desired, and then sat an identical plate before them, telling them it was just what they asked for. Monica asked for a steak and got it. Somewhere in the back of her mind, she believed that all nine of them got the same food, if food it was. It looked absolutely horrid. If she were in her right mind, never in a million years would she even taste it. However, she thought that she was being given a steak dinner.

Once everyone was served, she sat a hot cup of liquid close to each woman, inserting a straw in it so that they could drink. "There you all go. I will be back later for the dishes. Happy supper everyone. Eat up. Produce many fine eggs to make fine little boys."

"Oh we always do," Zeta replied, encouragingly.

"How do we eat?" Monica Nicole asked after the pretty woman left them alone.

"Oh, like this." She leaned over and began eating much like a dog. Again, in the back of Monica's mind, she tried to revolt, but found herself starving and leaned over, biting at the morsels with her mouth. "Keep hair out of food," Zeta added.

In spite of herself, Monica, like the others, finally used her tongue to lick the plate clean. Then she saw how the others were using a straw to drink and emulated them, believing that she was sipping coffee. However, it was far from that!

When they finished, Zeta suggested that they all take a shower to wash off their mouths. Wiggling wildly, Monica got to her feet and followed the others out of the dining room, across the spacious living room and into another leaf wing, where there were both showers and toilets or what seemed to be those things.

"Go potty first before bathe. In case have accident," Zeta advised. Again, Monica nearly fell down trying to get her long hair out of the way so she could sit down on what appeared to be a toilet. In fact, it was a caged small demon, whose mouth was chained open. After she went, it licked her privates clean. "See, it wipes us clean."

Again, in the back of her mind, Monica wanted to scream wildly, but merely found herself smiling. "Cool. All clean now."

The shower controls could be operated by pressing one's knee onto a lever that adjusted the water flow. It was always a comfortable warm temperature. Once showered, they stood before a blow dryer—again, another demon that blew out warm, dry air, but it appeared to the St. Louis women as a modern blow dryer found in all restrooms, only larger.

"Now we go sleep. Soon sun goes down. Very dark. Can't see. Hard to walk. You come bed now," Zeta explained. The nine women walked out of the restroom, through the living room, and into the remaining large leaf of the Center. "This is your bed, Monica," she leaned slightly towards one bed.

"Watch Zeta. Show how." She leaned over and used her teeth to pull down her covers. After crawling into bed very awkwardly, mostly a falling motion, she used her teeth to pull them up.

"Zeta! You forgot pleasure part!" Melani exclaimed.

Zeta's face reddened slightly. "Oops."

Nasara-Sin said, "I will show Monica how to do it. Tomorrow, Zeta can have Monica."

"Okay," Zeta replied.

Before she knew what was going on, the dark skinned woman pushed into her, forcing her onto her new bed. After Monica laid down, mostly by falling, Nasara-Sin joined her, but in the opposite direction. The woman's head was near her privates. "Oh!" Monica Nicole exclaimed. Pleasuring was something that she loved. In the back of her mind, images of Crystal and Ericka doing her and she, they, came into her mind. "More. Oh, yes, yes," she exclaimed, becoming very excited.

A half hour later, all the women were very much satisfied and in their own beds. Suddenly, the entire Center became dark, taking Monica by surprise. She squealed. Zeta called out, "Sun went down. Time for sleep, Monica."

"Oh. Okay." Monica Nicole lay in the dark beneath a warm blanket. Now she had time to think and to reflect on what had happened to her today. Something just wasn't right about all this. In the back of her mind, she was terrified, more afraid than she'd ever been. Yet in the front of her mind, everything seemed perfectly fine, perfect. She was being fed, protected, and had no worries at all.

She heard whimpering and listened. Yes, it was the four other women from St. Louis. *They're crying softly to themselves, but they shouldn't be. They've won fifteen million dollars. They're to get it soon. They said so. They should be very happy. Yet, they are crying.* The back of her mind kicked into high gear, blowing the effects of the Idiot Mind spell.

She sat up like a rocket! *Oh my god! I've been taken prisoner! I'm mutilated! I can't escape. I'm in the Abyss! Oh dear god no!* Her mind registered the full impact and re-experienced the excruciating pain of having her arms incinerated from within her arms themselves. Gritting her teeth to avoid shrieking and likely bringing more doom down upon her, she endured the flashback of pain and realized that was what was powering her unprecedented neutralization of the Idiot Mind spell.

Concluding that things magical must play out differently here in the Abyss, she whispered to Lilly, Patricia, Gracie, and Janet. "Are you feeling the pain of having your arms burned to a crisp? I did and it woke me up."

"They hurt, I think, but I am supposed to be perfectly fine," Lilly whispered back.

"Me too," Gracie added, followed by the other two.

"Okay. Focus on that pain, but whatever you do, don't cry out loudly. They'll hurt us some more," she whispered back. She listened carefully, trying to sense what was happening to the four other women. She could hear them writhing on their beds, probably a reaction to the re-experienced pain from the incineration of their arms. It was a likely possibility, Monica Nicole thought.

After some time passed, Lilly whispered, "Where are we? We're being tortured, right?"

"Yes, we are, Lilly."

"I remember now. A man came to my door with this official document that said I won fifteen million dollars. If I would just sign the document, they would discuss how I wanted my payments. I did it and then something terrible happened. I wasn't in my apartment anymore, but standing naked on some platform. I couldn't move and my arms—they just burned up! The pain was so bad that I wanted to pass out, but I couldn't move or do anything. Monica! I'm terrified. How do we get out of here? I want to go home, but now we're totally helpless, and we can barely even walk."

"I know. We are all in the same boat. I'll think of something, Lilly," Monica Nicole whispered. She knew well that these four normal women needed some thread, no matter how small, to hang onto or their nightmare situation would devour them.

Within a half hour, the other three broke free of their Idiot Mind spells as well. Monica then said, "Okay. We best get some sleep. Remember, tomorrow play along with whatever happens. Don't let on that you are aware of everything or we'll be clobbered again. Give me time to think of a way to escape."

"Okay Monica. You are a million times braver than I am. I will try my best," Lilly whispered back.

Somehow, Monica finally fell into a fitful sleep. The next thing she knew, someone had turned on the "sun." It was daylight again, but that's being generous with the term. Rather say it was a light grey outside, enough to see by anyway. One by one, the older women rose and headed for the bathroom.

Without her arms, Monica felt acute panic returning, as she tried to get up and onto her toes in these strange boots. She saw the panic-stricken faces of her four new friends as well, facing their first day of their capture fully aware of what was around them and their horrific limitations. Somehow, each managed to get to the restroom and saw Zeta finishing up. Lilly looked aghast at the open mouth of the demon that Zeta had just sat upon while relieving herself.

Zeta said, "Fine bed pans. We don't have any finer ones back in Ur. Go ahead use it. Breakfast will come soon."

The four looked at Monica for help. "I guess we just pretend that these are toilets," she whispered, struggling to sit down on the demon, but mostly fell onto it. She felt quite sick, but nature had to be handled. Shortly after that, all five were very glad to be wiggling and wobbling across their prison to the dining room.

After struggling to get seated before the table, Monica whispered, "One thing I know for sure is that we have to learn to walk in these boots as well as Zeta or else we have no chance to escape."

Before long, the pretty woman called Nisha entered

pushing her cart. Monica recalled seeing a sketch in one of Crystal's books and recognized Nisha as an alu-demon, the child of a human man and a succubus demon. Children of those unions were always female. While Nisha politely explained the various dishes as being chicken and dumplings, the five could see that all the plates held an awful looking grey mush, with unspeakable lumps in it. Their morning coffee was some pale liquid, but it must have had some caffeine in it. Monica felt the familiar kick after sipping it.

That done, Monica asked Zeta to help them learn to walk better. She explained, "Take normal steps. Like walking. Not your baby steps. See how I walk? Watch me. You learn soon."

The five spent the morning walking around and observing their prison cell. Late morning, a man entered and called the four older women, one by one, into the medical leaf, where he had them lie down and spread their legs so he could harvest another egg from each of them. He told Monica that it would be a few weeks before she was laying an egg a day. Monica Nicole wanted to yell at him that she wasn't a chicken, but bit her lip instead.

Monica Nicole saw the gating-summoning platform some distance from the entrance of this Cambion Production Center. However, she also knew that it wouldn't work to get them back to Earth. Someone back home would have to Gate them back, but there was no way to let anyone know where she was being held prisoner. The only other way was to know the name of someone and to cast a Gate spell from here, pulling them down to the Abyss, just as Graz'zt had done to her. Besides, she didn't have her wand any longer. Just as well, I can't hold it or cast with it anyway. Now I really am completely helpless, she thought.

Then, she realized that as Dominus, she had been doing similar things to many women, making them helpless sex toys, just as Graz'zt had more or less done to her. Men, she thought, are we all evil beasts? My only hope is that my friends can somehow figure out where I am and come rescue me. Heck, then what? I'll be a helpless person after that, as bad off as these four normal women are. Hey, I just called them normal, not norms. Peculiar, but we five are in similar straights. My magic isn't going to help us one iota because I can't do any, not without my arms, even if I could find my wand. Best practice walking, as the other four are doing. She lunged up onto her feet again, wobbling and wiggling to get her precarious balance. Then, she joined them walking around their rather large prison cell.

After a few days of mostly walking, the five had become rather skilled at it, just as Zeta had promised they would. Still, everything was a living nightmare without end and probably would be for the rest of their lives, but all five wanted to escape somehow. One lunchtime, when Nisha brought their lunch, Monica decided to see if she could learn anything useful from her. Would she chat with them?

"Hi Nisha. We walk good now. Can we go for walk outside sometime? See pretty sights," Monica Nicole pretended to be an idiot.

"Oh, I suppose that would be all right. I can't take all nine of you at one time. Maybe one of you each day. Would you like to go for a walk?" Nisha asked politely.

"Yes I would. Oh thank you, thank you, thank you," Monica Nicole poured it on a bit thick. Nisha smiled and agreed to do it when she returned for the empty plates.

Later, after opening the door for Monica, Nisha led her outside. "We must stay on the paths. It will be harder walking for you, Monica, because the ground is not smooth like inside your house."

"Okay. I be careful. So nice out here. What are those?" she asked innocently. She saw that off to their left were another four identical, leaf-shaped, domed structures or five Cambion Production Centers. Nisha explained that they were just that.

Then she saw that there was a narrow hall connecting the medical leaf of their quarters with a large rectangular building, completely opaque. "That is the maternity ward, where your eggs are fertilized, and your sons are born to surrogate mothers. Do you understand me?"

"Yes. Good mothers. Raise fine sons," Monica played her role. "What is that one?" There was another even larger rectangular building some distance from the maternity ward.

"Ah, that is the nursery and children's home, where your sons are raised. We will soon walk by their playground, and you can see some of your sons."

"But I no have egg yet."

"Oh right. I should say Zeta's sons. You are walking well, Monica. Good for you."

"Yes, walk well. See pretty world and sons. But others. They worry."

"What about?" Nisha asked, probing for more data about the women in her care.

"Lilly wants to see her money. She won lots. Wants to see it. So does Patricia. So does Gracie. So does Janet. No think they will get money. Worry lots."

Nisha laughed. "I see. Okay, I will see what I can do about that. We can't have you egg producers worrying about something as simple as that. We best head back. You don't want to overdo it on your first walk."

"What's overdo? I pay my bills."

"I mean get too tired. I don't want to have to carry you back."

"No carry Monica. I fine. Walk back. You see." Nisha smiled. While her feet ached by the time that she returned, she knew that her leg muscles were strengthening and that they really did need to practice walking a whole lot more.

The next day, Nisha had a pleasant surprise for the four women who had "won the sweepstakes." "Look. Here are your millions. The dollars have been exchanged for these very valuable gemstones. It is a better investment." She had a sack for each of the four and laid them out on the dining room table in front of the seats that each usually took when they were dining. "See, these are yours. Now you can look at them. Feel better now?"

"Oh yes, yes. See. We rich women now," Lilly pretended to be a simpleton, having been forewarned by Monica that something like this might happen. Later on after Nisha left, she whispered, "If these are real, they are lots better than trying to carry around a huge stack of bills. Besides, gems are always going up in value. Any idea how we can escape yet? Or how we can get the gems back into the bags? If so, we can carry them between our teeth. Monica realized that the four didn't want to leave without their money. Besides, they would need it to pay someone to care for their every need once they got home.

Dutifully, the five women continued to walk around the complex during the daylight hours. Each day, Nisha took one of them outside for a longer stroll and soon all five realized that it was much more difficult to walk on the uneven ground and vowed to walk as much as possible. Lilly pointed out, "My legs are getting much stronger now. So that's hopeful, isn't it?"

"Yes, we must be very strong if we are to escape," Monica whispered back.

The next day during her outside walk with Nisha, the pretty, but short alu-demon, said, "We need to talk, Monica. I've been keeping your secret. I know you are planning to escape. I want to escape to your world with you."

"What?" Monica Nicole said, so surprised that she nearly stumbled and had to wiggle about just to keep on her feet.

"Something happened to you days ago and to the four others. I don't know how you five were able to throw off his Idiot Mind spell, but you did. I suspected that the four are planning to take their winnings with them. That's why I talked Graz'zt into letting them at least see the gems. He thinks it's harmless. And I want to get free of this awful place. I want to be free. I can't take all the wicked things that go on in this place. That's why I volunteered to help care for these women. It isn't right, what he's doing to you and the many others. He has to be stopped somehow. Please, when you escape, take me with you, please."

"Well, if you come with us, others are going to think that you are just another wicked and evil demon," Monica Nicole tried to think of some counter argument.

"I will show them that I want to do right things, not bad things. I will help take care of the four others too. Please you must take me; I can't live like this any longer. This area here is the nicest part of the whole world, Monica. Out there, it's just too horrible to speak of. My father came from your world. I want to see his world," Nisha begged.

Monica had little choice but to agree to help Nisha get free as well. Nisha then replied, "Thank you. But you must be careful. Graz'zt—he knows your true name. That's how he was able to Summon you. If you escape, he will just Summon you back. Perhaps, there is no escape for you."

"Darn it! What about the other women. Does he know their true names? Yours?"

"He does not know their true names. He tricked them into signing a magical document that opened the Gate, bringing them here. No one knows my true name, just call me Nisha," she explained.

"Good. These other women will be safe if I can get them back home," she decided. As they continued walking along, from the corner of her eye, Monica Nicole saw a shimmering effect, a slight distortion in the foreground. Instantly, she knew that someone was there watching them under an Invisibility spell. "Hush. Someone is Invisible over by that tree, if those really are supposed to be trees.

Just then, a Message scrolled by her eyes.

Monica, Rob here. I've come to rescue you. R.

"Come on; let's walk closer to that Invisible person. He's come to help us, Nisha," Monica Nicole whispered, suddenly growing excited. Her mind raced with millions of questions, but in the back of her thoughts was the truth that her friends had not deserted her. There was power in having many good friends. Perhaps even male friends.

As she got close to Rob, she began explaining what had happened to her and the other women, along with what was going on here at this Cambion Production Center and Graz'zt's ultimate plans. "Whatever you do, you have to get all this information back home before you rescue us. They have to know what he is planning. We have to stop him." She received another message.

Got it. So be ready to go tomorrow. R

When they returned from their walk, Monica Nicole had Nisha pack all the women's many gems back into their bags. When Lilly whispered why, Monica whispered, "Be ready to go tomorrow."

That night, as she drifted into sleep, Monica Nicole imagined what must have happened back home. Her friends thought enough of her and against all odds to figure out a way not only to find her, but also to rescue her. *Alone, I am but one; together with my friends, we're far more powerful. What a complete idiot I used to be, thinking Dominus could singlehandedly conquer the world, another Alexander, the Great. Ha. Together, we are powerful, just as the Rodents are. Interesting.*

Chapter 14—Rescue

Monica Nicole ate the slop that was breakfast, knowing that she needed her strength soon. Today, she was being rescued. Exactly how, she had no idea. While Nisha was clearing away the plates and cups, another message scrolled before her eyes.

Monica, get the four women and Nisha out onto the golden pentagram now. R.

"Okay, Nisha. It's time to go," she whispered. "You are to get these four and yourself onto the golden pentagram right away."

Cleverly, Nisha said, "Come on; time for a walk. Lilly, Patricia, Gracie, Janet, you four can come along with us today." She lowered her voice and whispered, "I'll bring your bags."

Lilly almost gave the escape away to Zeta. She was so excited that she forgot to pretend to be an idiot. Thankfully, Zeta wasn't able to work out why Lilly was so excited or why all five were going on a walk. Before, Nisha had taken only one at a time. Carefully, all five women followed Nisha, who opened the door for the group.

Once outside, Monica whispered, "Okay. You and Nisha are to go over to that platform and stand on the golden pentagram. Hurry up and be as quiet as you can." She looked there herself and saw another shimmering patch and knew someone was there, but Invisible. At first, she thought it was Rob.

Monica Nicole nearly jumped when she heard Rob's voice whispering from her right side. "Rob here. Have to stay Invisible a bit longer. That's Crystal on the pentagram. I brought her here, and she's going to use her Gate spell to take them all back."

"What about me, us?" she whispered, extremely pleased that Crystal was putting her power spell to fantastic use.

"We are the safety line. Graz'zt may well sense what Crystal is doing before she can get that lengthy spell cast. If so, we have to delay him and anyone else that tries to interfere. Besides, he knows your true name now. If we just take you back, he'll be so angry that he'll Summon you right back here. So I have a plan that I hope will work, at least temporarily," he whispered to her.

Monica Nicole had dozens of questions going through her mind, but decided that she'd best help keep watch. So many things could go wrong. She watched the poor women struggling to get up onto the platform. Just as Nisha finally stepped up, her arms encircling the four women, she heard Crystal's voice beginning her lengthy and complex chant. If she only had time to complete it, Monica Nicole thought.

Just then, she saw two forms coming their way, far down the path, walking here from Center 1. "Over there. Big trouble. That's Dr. Menninger, and the tall one is General Falnor." Rob looked and saw what appeared to be a normal human standing beside a giant of a demon, at least twelve feet tall, positively huge in all dimensions. The general carried a giant sword that could cut a man's head off on one swing and a long whip. His wings were more like a giant parasail!

The general bellowed something. So loud and deep was his voice that the ground shook beneath Monica's feet! She didn't understand his language, but didn't need to. Both were staring straight ahead at the circle of women and the alu-demon standing on the gating platform. The secret escape was no longer a secret!

Rob became visible. No use in hiding now, besides, he sensed the demon had already seen him as well. "Darn, that one has immense mental powers, possibly stronger than me," he whispered, though Monica Nicole didn't know why he was still doing that. The game was up. She almost broke down because she felt completely helpless. She wanted more than anything to fire off as many of her spells as she could to protect Crystal and the others, giving them a chance to get home. Soon, the demon would be attacking them, and hobbled up as she was, she couldn't even dodge a spell. She was a sitting duck, a helpless one at that.

"Delay. Monica, all we have to do is delay them. Come on; go as fast as you can up the trail away from the platform. I don't dare try to attack the demon. He's too strong. Instead, we delay them. Run, Monica, run." She saw a giant grey fog engulf the approaching demon and man. Must be Rob's spell, she thought. Run? How? She walked as fast as she could, hoping and praying the she didn't fall down. If she did, it would take forever to get back up on her feet, if she even could. She cursed her helplessness and moved as quickly as she could, wiggling and wobbling about to keep her precarious balance, but moving more like a moderate walk than a brisk walk, let alone a run.

"Doing fine, Monica. We've split the demon's attention. He's casting something," Rob called out. She felt waves of fear flooding her body and nearly stumbled. Rob's hand caught her just in time. Fear spell. Shake it off Monica, she told herself and kept on moving as fast as she could.

Just then, she heard Crystal's spell energize! While she couldn't see the brilliant flash of magical energies, greatly amplified by the silver and gold of the gate, she sensed it and saw a slight brightening of the dim grey illumination of this terrible place. She hazarded a quick backwards glance. The demon was doing a flying jump. He was going to land on top of her and Rob! Now she did stumble!

As she began falling, she felt Rob's warm hand around her waist and braced herself for the crushing landing of the monstrous demon who was sure to drop directly down on top of them, squashing both her and Rob. The demon probably weighted a half a ton!

Confused, Monica Nicole found herself not being crushed or even falling! No, she was walking along a featureless grey plain, utterly flat. Rob's arm was around her waist still, leading her onward! She looked around and saw absolutely nothing, no landmarks, no objects, nothing but grey in all directions. Yet, she continued to put one foot in front of the other. She seemed to be walking, though effortlessly. Could I even fall? Where is this place? What is this place? Where is up? Where is down? Am I walking on nothingness? Monica Nicole's mind struggled to grasp what was happening.

Then, a brownish zone appeared ahead of them. Rob seemed to be steering them towards it. She blinked and now they were on a grassy plain. The air felt pure and clean. The sun, warm. In the distance, she saw hairy buffalo grazing. Off to the left and right, small stands of forest appeared. The air now had a faint trace of burning pine. A fire? The sky was pure blue, but a few billowing white clouds floated effortlessly overhead. A teepee appeared. Several of them. Her feet were definitely walking on solid ground, but it was hard to walk and keep her balance. Without Rob's steadying arm, she knew that she would have fallen several times already.

They reached the trio of teepee dwellings, and Rob called out in a strange language that she didn't understand. *Darn it! I can't even cast that simple Understand Languages spell; now I really am worthless, far beyond worthless.* A deep voice answered Rob, coming from inside the nearest teepee. Rob held the flap up, and she ducked her head, stumbled inside, and blinked several times, though Rob came up to her side, his steadying arm around her again.

She saw what appeared to be an Indian, if the ancient videos and photographs were accurate. He was tall and thin, dark skinned, with long black hair. He wore leather fashioned into a simple shirt and pants. A pair of moccasins covered his feet. His headband was red, cotton perhaps, with a single feather dangling from one side of it. Apparently, this man was also a wizard because she began to understand what he was saying; he must have cast Understand Languages for her sake, she guessed.

"Welcome again, He Who Walks with the Winds. You have come as you said you would."

"We seek your sanctuary Running Eagle, at least for a few days. This is she of whom I spoke last time. Monica Nicole Black. This is Running Eagle, a friend of mine. His wife is Pale Moonbeam."

"Welcome to my humble lodge, Monica Nicole Black. Pale Moonbeam is out on a mission of her own just now. Sanctuary is granted, conditionally. Allow me to examine her, He Who Walks with the Winds."

"Thank you, Running Eagle. I would be so honored if you would. As I said, I just rescued her from the Abyss, Level Sixty-six, Prince Graz'zt's kingdom," Rob said formally.

Monica Nicole didn't know what to make of this exchange, but if this man was a friend of Rob's, then she decided to trust him. Yet, what did he mean by examine me, she wondered. Although she was still standing and naked except for the strange boots, Monica Nicole wasn't shy or embarrassed to be on public display. She hadn't been educated to be so. The Indian closed his eyes, and she felt some kind of energy, a tingling sensation, fleetingly though, across her entire skin.

He opened his eyes. "She has been contaminated by the Abyss, He Who Walks with the Winds. I must ask her to go to the bathroom only in this copper basin until whatever comes out no longer fumes. I can't have my lands contaminated by the foulness of the Abyss. She must have eaten the filth that they call food in that realm."

"Well, yes, I have. I've been captive for quite some time, though I don't know if their days correspond to yours or ours," Monica Nicole ventured to explain a little.

"So it would seem," Running Eagle replied. "Your arms have been burned off by the hellish fires of the Abyss. At least he was wise enough to provide insulating boots or your feet would have combusted as well. Leather is a good insulator, as I told He Who Walks with the Winds here. Strange boots. Feet fused. Nasty business down in the Abyss. He probably relished and savored your pain when he did this to you, but then I also see that you too have done similar things to others in your past."

Monica Nicole nodded. "Please, can I sit down somewhere?" A chair appeared, and she sat down quickly. "Yes, in the past, I knew no better. I was once an evil, self-centered man, but I have learned my lessons, well I hope. People can change. I have to believe that or I'm worthless. Well, I'm pretty much worthless now anyway, but that's not what I mean."

"Then I shall name thee She Who Has Seen the Light. Come. I'm being a terrible host. You need to eat and drink so that your system can flush the filth of the Abyss out of it. Just remember to use this copper basin," Running Eagle replied.

Rob smiled, "I like that name, She Who Has Seen the

Light. Pretty cool, Running Eagle."

He looked up and returned his smile. "Of course. It is appropriate for her." Suddenly, the Indian looked distracted. His voice said, "Ah, no, Graz'zt, Demon Prince, you cannot have her just now." He looked at Monica and explained, "Sorry, he was trying to Summon you back to his domain. Perhaps I should have been more abrupt with him. How do you say it, 'Get lost' or is it 'Cool it?' I have a hard time with these new idioms. Folks should take the time to say what they really mean; don't you think so, She Who Has Seen the Light?"

"I agree. Things are simpler that way. You don't have to try to read between the lines to figure out what the person really means," she agreed with him. "So Rob is right. He's trying to Summon me back there, to his Abyss?"

"Aye, She Who Has Seen the Light. He Who Walks with the Winds was wise to bring you here. Graz'zt has no power in my domain. You should eat, drink, and rest up. It is most important to flush the filthy Abyss from your body as soon as you can. There is food and drink, He Who Walks with the Winds. I will leave you two alone for a time." He rose and left the teepee.

Rob set to work, pouring a cup of some type of juice and then scooping up a wooden plate from a stew pot. He sat before her. "Guess I get to feed you for now. Open wide," he teased her a little.

"Where are we? Who is that Indian? How come Graz'zt can't Summon me from here? He knows my true name, so he ought to be able to Summon me anytime he desires. How did you find me? How did you get to the Abyss? Why does he call you He Who Walks with the Winds?"

"Open wide. That's a lot of questions."

Speaking with her mouth full, Monica Nicole mumbled, "I have more when you are ready."

Rob grinned. "That's the spirit. Okay, we are in a different domain, Running Eagle's. It is part of the Seven Heavens. He's like one of the gods of the Cherokee Indians, I think. I ran into him two years ago when I was exploring the other planes. He's really a great fellow, very friendly, but he is many times more powerful that Graz'zt, probably on par with the Demon Lords of the Abyss, but he will never say so. After I found you, I came here asking him if I could bring you here for a time. We have to work out this name thing. As long as Graz'zt knows your true name, you are not safe on Earth. He understands." He fed her another mouth full.

"As to how I found you, that's a long story. I suppose I'll have to reveal a little more about myself than I normally do or you'll never understand. It's complicated. The average human only uses a small fraction of their mental powers. The brain is more like a switchboard that acts as a go-between the mind and the body. My gift is the ability to use so much more of my mind, focusing and controlling the magical energies that you witches depend upon your wands to do for you."

"Leslie sent for me right after you were Summoned. I saw the Gate spell residual energies and showed them to the others. It took several days, but I finally homed in on you, Monica Nicole. Every person gives off a little energy at their own unique wavelength. That's what I homed in on. However, there are so darn many levels to the Abyss, that it took quite a lot of hunting until I found the right one."

"I travel between realms or planes of existence with my special gift of Planar Travel. While my skills are different from yours, I'm severely limited in how much energy I can use in one day before I need to eat and sleep. I'm shot for today, so we stay here for now."

Monica Nicole thought for a moment. "So Crystal, she knows what to do for the four women? I mean with the Abyss stuff in their systems? Will they be all right? None of them is a witch. They were just normal young, single women. Now their lives are ruined, but I did manage to get their supposed winnings out of Graz'zt."

Rob looked puzzled. "I know their Summoning letters claimed that they won fifteen million dollars, but they didn't really get it, did they?"

"Well, no. That was just Graz'zt's lure to get them to sign and activate his Gate spell. They were under the Idiot Mind spell and kept wanting to know about their winnings. With Nisha's help, we got him to lay out a pile of gems worth that much before each of them. I know, they couldn't even pick them up, but they could see them. I had Nisha bring them along with them when Crystal Gated them. I figured that with the gems, they would have some way to pay someone to care for their needs. We're almost totally helpless, if you hadn't noticed. In fact, I'm worse off now than when Dispater changed me. At least then, I could cast a handful of spells. Now I'm just a useless, helpless woman."

Rob validate her, "Excellent thinking on getting the four some descent compensation. Well done. Say, how did you and the four overcome the Idiot Mind spell?"

"I don't know. Perhaps magic works a little differently in the Abyss. Honestly, you can't imagine how much pain we felt when our arms burned up and from the inside out. It was as if my bones caught fire, burning up my muscles and skin last. We were all paralyzed when he did it. I couldn't even scream, pass out, or move. All I could do was stand there feeling that awful pain. I think that's what allowed us to nullify the Idiot Mind spell a bit later on. Graz'zt just stood there watching my arms burn. He got off on my pain in a major way. Sadist."

"Well, that's what the Abyss is all about, physical suffering for all eternity—death, decay, rotting—a grim place. Well, now that you are full, why don't you lie down and take a nap? Let your body recover and begin flushing out the putrefaction of the Abyss," Rob suggested.

"I am so tired. Okay. Cover me please." She mostly fell onto the bedding blankets, and he covered her up.

Rob stepped out of the teepee. Soon, Running Eagle appeared, and the two began to chat. Rob said, "Thanks for giving us sanctuary for a time while we figure things out."

"It is as it should be, He Who Walks with the Winds. What are you going to do with She Who Has Seen the Light? You know that there is great power in her, great potential as yet untapped. And yet the Abyss has left its indelible mark upon her physical body."

"I'm not sure, Running Eagle. Yes, the marks are obvious. I was hoping that there was some cure for her."

"Alas, the Abyss incineration cannot be undone with your normal re-growth potions and magics. Her bones have been destroyed. Have you seen her feet? All the bones in her feet have been fused into a single bone with the toes pointed downward. Re-growth cannot undo that, but she's done something similar to other women in the past. Perhaps, it is karma returning to her."

Monica Nicole was not quite asleep. Something in the food that she'd eaten was causing her to feel very drowsy. Still she overhead what the two men were saying about her, and she decided to listen in until she drifted into sleep. She thought calmly. *I didn't think a re-grow potion would work on my arms, but I was hoping they would for my feet. Karma? Well, it serves me right. I did this to Lindsey and Ashley. I can accept this. It's only fair that I do.*

"Well, I don't know about karma, and I don't know about her physical condition. You say your potions will flush out the vile stuff that they fed her? No lingering stuff in her body?" Rob asked.

"Aye, that it will do. Probably in twenty-four of your hours, she will be physically cleansed completely, but what about her mental state? Her mind? That is a different story, He Who Walks with the Winds. For some who have been to the Abyss, the mental scars never heal."

"Well, I'm more worried about her true name. As long as Graz'zt knows it, he's going to keep Summoning her back into his filthy realm. It seems that has to be our number one priority."

"Aye, He Who Walks with the Winds. Names have power, especially in the wrong hands. Yet, names can be changed. She Who Has Seen the Light will need to be re-christened properly."

"Can you do something like that?"

"Yes and no. Better ask, He Who Walks with the Winds, just how far are you willing to go with She Who Has Seen the Light. Answer that first, the rest will follow."

Rob chuckled. "Never do give a straight answer do you?"

"On some things, but not on the important ones," he chuckled back. "Come. We smoke the pipe of peace and friendship."

Whether they left the vicinity of the teepee or whether she fell into a deep sleep, Monica Nicole couldn't be sure. She was at peace for the first time in what seemed days, if the concept of a day in the Abyss was remotely comparable to a day on Earth.

She awoke but it was dusk. No one was around, and she desperately needed to go to the bathroom. Remembering the copper basin, she wiggled, lunged, and struggled to get to her toes and over to the basin. Squatting, she ejected a surprisingly large volume. Some kind of disintegration smoke rose as her excrements hit the basin. When she finished, the basin was entirely empty. She grinned, thinking that was a very useful spell indeed. She heard the crackling of a log fire and pushed her way out of the teepee. Only a hide flap marked the door. She saw Rob cooking by the fire and very carefully walked over to him.

"Hi. Sleep well? Got supper cooking. Not too cold?" he asked.

"No, it's perfectly comfortable. Kind of strange that it should be so."

"I know. Running Eagle has kept the temperature around you rather warm since you are naked. Come sit by the fire, and I'll feed you supper. After that, we should talk some," Rob said.

A half hour later, the rosy twilight had given way to a brilliant field of stars. Both quite full, they returned to the teepee and its bedding blankets. He helped her sit down on the blankets and took a deep breath. "We've got to do something about your true name so that no one can Summon you against your will ever again."

"I know. But what?"

"I've been thinking about that all afternoon, Monica Nicole. I really like you so I am going to take a gamble. Will you marry me? If you do, then your last name will officially be different," Rob finally said what was on his mind most of the afternoon. "I know that we hardly know one another. If it doesn't work out, we can always get a divorce. No matter how it goes, your true name will have changed. What do you think? Heck, I haven't even got a ring for you."

Monica Nicole laughed, further embarrassing Rob. "No, I'm not laughing at you, silly. It's a brilliant idea, one that should work. No, I'm laughing because I don't have any fingers for a wedding ring. I'm pleased that you would do this for me, Rob. I accept your proposal. Thank you."

"Er, there's a catch. It won't be sanctified until we consummate the marriage. Only then will the true name change go into effect. I know that you used to be a man and still think of yourself that way."

Monica Nicole laughed. "I knew there had to be a catch. It was too simple. Yes, I'm well aware of that *little* problem. That's why I've been so *close* to Crystal and Ericka. They understand me, and we do well together, in bed I mean. Well, we'll just have to do it somehow. I'll never ever be safe from Graz'zt if I don't do this. No matter what happens, Rob, I really do respect you, and I like you. I don't want to do anything to hurt you. I will do my best."

"I respect you too, Monica Nicole. You do have a very attractive body, and you yourself are, well let's just say you are immensely powerful. I have admired how much you have changed—for the better, I mean. I suppose that we ought to have Running Eagle perform the ceremony. After all, he is a god or near enough to one to sanctify our union."

"Okay. The sooner the better, Rob. Thank you."

A bit later, Rob returned with Running Eagle and his wife, Pale Moonbeam. Finally, she got to meet his wife. She wore a long leather dress and moccasins. Her black hair was even longer than Monica's, nearly reaching her ankles and perfectly straight. Her face was a shade lighter than his, hence the "pale" adjective. Her face radiated kindness and love, much like the moon. As she entered the teepee, Monica Nicole felt a sudden calm and tranquility emanating from her, encompassing everyone.

She helped Monica Nicole rise. "If you men will give us a minute to prepare the lovely bride," she teased the two, who quickly stepped outside the teepee. "I know that Running Eagle still wants you to remain naked for another day so that the putrid Abyss matter can readily be collected in the copper basin of his. Still, let's brush your hair and perhaps wash."

She waved her hands, and Monica Nicole felt as though she was getting a shower! Indeed, water rained down upon her, but all was collected in the copper basin at her side. When it finished, she finally felt clean again, but she was dry almost as soon as the rain ended. "Clever bit of magic," she commented.

Pale Moonbeam grinned. "Indeed, a gift from the moon for this occasion." She then brushed out her long, black hair, which had grown some, reaching the small of her back. "I do so love very long hair. So does Running Eagle. I'm glad that you do too. And such magical and beautiful earrings."

"I know. I love it too. My dear friend Ericka made these protective earrings for me. Thank you, Pale Moonbeam. I finally feel clean again. It was so hideous there in the Abyss! I've no words even to begin to describe it, rancid, vile, and filthy. None come close to it."

"I know, She Who Has Seen the Light. You have been exceptionally brave and survived that experience."

"Say, why do you both call me She Who Has Seen the Light and not Monica Nicole?"

Pale Moonbeam laughed. "We see the true person behind the mask of the physical body. Running Eagle saw what is truly you and so named you, just like quite some time ago, he saw the true nature of your companion, He Who Walks with the Winds. Me, I am akin to the moon, and he, my husband, runs with the eagles when they fly. That is what he was doing when I first met him, running along the ground while the eagle was soaring in the blue sky. Both are free, but in different ways. There, you look positively radiant.

As if on cue, the two men entered the teepee. Pale Moonbeam stood at Monica's left, her hand gently supporting her as she stood on her toes. Running Eagle stood beside Rob and performed a brief ceremony, keeping it brief, unlike normal Indian ceremonies. Finally, he said, I now pronounce you man and wife for all time. You may kiss and seal your vows. Choose your names, but tell no one." With that, he and Pale Moonbeam quietly walked out of the teepee, leaving the two still embracing each other.

Rob laid her gently down on their pile of bedding

blankets. Both knew that choosing names would mean nothing unless their marriage could be consummated. This, Monica Nicole was dreading, but swore somehow to do it.

On the other hand, Rob had given this very careful thought. If they had any chance to make this work, he would have to overcome her viewpoint, that of being a man. He also knew that she always slept with Crystal and Ericka and had a very good idea what the trio must have done to and for each other. He began to put his plan to work. He had her laying on her side so that they could kiss, and he put everything he had into his kisses. Slowly and gently, he moved his hands over her body, touching all the right spots, as she later told him. He was using his special talent to go into rapport with another so that he could sense what she was feeling and desiring.

Before long, she was craving him. She threw her leg over him, and he sensed that she had to be in control, which is what he expected all along. Holding her up by her shoulders so she could lean down and kiss him, he allowed her to do the work. Later, he cradled her head on his shoulders. "I can't believe that! Rob, it worked. That was perfect. I was in. . ."

"Control," he finished her sentence for her. "I know. I don't think it would have worked out any other way."

"I know. It was like you were with me, in my mind, knowing just what I needed next."

"I was. Have to show you how to do that later on." He gave her another gentle kiss. "Now we can pick a new true name for you, one that no one but us knows."

"Monica Nicole She Who Has Seen the Light Black-Finch. How's that?" she replied demurely. "No one will ever guess that."

"Mine is Rob Ellison Finch, He Who Walks with the Winds. Running Eagle so christened me years ago when we first met."

"Very perfect, Rob. Brilliant even. Of course, I really don't know what you want with a totally helpless wife though, but I thank you. Now I am free from further Summons from Graz'zt and anyone else for that matter."

"We will just have to see about that helpless bit, but it can wait until tomorrow. We should sleep now. I'm exhausted." She kissed him and fell asleep still in his arms, feeling more secure and tranquil than she had ever known.

In the morning, first she relieved herself into the copper basin. This time, nothing smoked, and the basin was definitely not empty. "Looks good. You must be free of all the Abyss contamination. Come. Do you want to do it again?" He didn't have to ask twice. A half hour later, Monica lay back panting slightly from her exertion.

"God, Rob. That was just as good, maybe even better because I could see you this time. I hope you don't mind me being on top and in control. I don't think I could do it the other way around."

"Fine with me, love. I'm famished, and we have a lot to do today." After eating, though she saw no one actually cooking, they said their farewells and profound thank you's to both Running Eagle and Pale Moonbeam.

"Home now?" she asked.

"Sort of. You have a great gift that you don't realize that you have. I'm going to see if I can get your gift fully materialized. We're going to my place in Denver. I've a small house on the edge of the huge city and a cabin up in the Rockies."

"But I can't go like this, naked, can I?"

"I know. I've taken the liberty of having Crystal send along some of your clothes to my place in Denver. Come on. We've lots to do today." He put his arm around her, and they began walking.

"So we aren't teleporting?" she asked.

"No, we are walking. Planar Travel. See, we've already left the Seven Heavens behind us. We are now moving through the astral medium, and there comes our world, good old Earth. Home soon."

He was right. Earth grew rapidly larger and a few steps later, she saw the Rocky Mountains and Denver. Then, they walked into a front room, rather a messy one, but cozy. "Home. Ignore the clutter. I had to leave in a big hurry to rescue someone we both know. Have a seat while I see if Crystal's package has arrived yet." It had and he came back in his front door carrying a small package. She'd obviously cast

Shrink Objects on her clothing.

He then took her on a quick tour of his small place. One bedroom had been converted into a study and library. There was a very small kitchen and dining room combo, and the master bedroom. Then, in the bedroom, he opened the box, and the many objects un-shrunk themselves. Monica exclaimed, "That's clever of her. In Case the Box Is Opened, Un-shrink Object. Clever of her, since I can't cast anything anymore.

Rob looked at all the articles and flushed. "Oh my, love. I've no idea what goes on where or how."

She laughed. "I guess I will have to talk you through this or I'll have to go around naked all the time." He chuckled. After having her sit down, he undid her boots. The two of them examined her feet. They were fused just as Running Eagle had said.

"Okay, there are all kinds of clothes in the box. I see you as always being elegant. So the red satin gown?" Rob asked. Rob got a speedy education, from slipping on her garter belt, aligning the back seams of her black nylons, slip, and so on. A half hour later, Monica was now properly attired, except for the shoes. At the bottom of the box were a note and another box of boots.

The two read it together.

It seems that this style of boots is called ballet boots and is designed for mostly sexy bedroom encounters. I found these extra-well-made pair for you. Black patent goes with most everything. Enjoy. Crystal.

He put them on over her nylons and then laced them securely. They were a perfect fit. "Now, brush out my hair, dear," she said charmingly. Again, she had to tell him how to do it. Finally, she lunged up onto her toes and wobbled a bit before she walked over to his lone mirror. "I do look smashing, even if I am helpless."

"Indeed. Only one small problem, love."

"What's that?" she replied, doing a small pirouette to face him.

"You are so hot that I want to do it again!"

Monica laughed. "Silly, that's the point. Look great, feel

great, confidence. Tackle anything."

"Right. So let's tackle your untapped potentials. Remember, Running Eagle said that you had immense untapped potential. I think that you are going to be even stronger than I am. Let's go out to the living room and begin."

She walked as elegantly as possible, feeling human again, albeit a completely helpless one. Still, he had been kind and patient enough to get her dolled up properly. That was something. She had no idea what he meant by the rest.

"I use my mind to make the magical connections. In your case, you have always used a wand and can cast perhaps ten times more spells than I can cast. What are important are the words and the intention behind them along with your certainty that it will work. What we are going to do is work on using the words and your intention and certainty, but power the magical connection via your mind. I've given this some thought. I want you to imagine that your mind is your wand, if you please. It might help if you also imagine the wand motions that you are used to making. We'll begin with the Clean spell."

She tried it a few times, before she explained, "I usually bark the command words out."

"Okay. So do it just like you would if you were using your wand," Rob suggested.

"Clean!" Magical energies flashed, and the small pile of dirt from his vacuum cleaner vanished. "My god! It worked! Rob, it actually worked! Sans wand!" Monica was elated and cast it several more times, before Rob stopped her and gave her a loving kiss.

"Well done. See, I told you. I have copies of the Grade Spell books in my library. Sit tight, while I get them. We've a lot of work to do now, that's for sure!"

They spent the rest of the day going through the many useful Grade 0 spells. One by one, Monica relearned how to cast them, with Rob's constant encouragement and support. That night after devouring a Domino's pizza, Rob changed his sheets, and they turned in. She then gave him the ride of his life as a way to thank him properly.

The next two days were spent on the Grade 1 spells. However, Rob soon saw that she was really going to need not only a safe environment in which to practice some of them but also a better coach. He sent a lengthy Message to Governor Lindsey. When he received her reply, he smiled and told Monica, "Dear, tomorrow I have a better location for you to practice at and a better coach. We're going to Bradbury's and Governor Lindsey will be helping you."

"What? Lindsey? Bradbury's? I can't believe this. She's going to help me?" Monica hastily sat down before her legs gave out.

The next morning, Rob teleported them to the gates of Bradbury's School of Magic, where Governor Lindsey, dressed warmly, was there to greet them. A light snow covered the ground, making it nearly impossible for Monica to walk, considering the only traction that she had was about a square inch of toe soles on the ground. Rob had to support her constantly, as she slipped and slid through the gates. Once Governor Lindsey had re-secured the gates, she opened a Magical Door and helped the two through it, arriving in her office.

"Deja vou. I never thought that I would ever set foot in this magnificent school again. Thank you for agreeing to help me, Lindsey. I'm almost completely helpless like this, but I'm trying hard to learn alternate ways to cast, thanks to Rob here. We got married too, did you know that?"

Lindsey smiled, "We heard. Congratulations. By the way, the four women and that alu-demon are doing well. Thanks for all that you've done for them and for bringing us all back such critical information on the demon prince's plans. Anyway, Rob says you have gotten through all the Grade 0 and 1 spells?"

"Yes, I still need to bark the command words, just like I would if I was waving my wand, which I obviously can't ever do again. So far, it's working," Monica said rather proud of her achievement.

"That's really incredible, Monica. So few wizards and witches can cast many spells sans wands. Well, we best get started. You can help, Rob. I'll need a gopher from time to time."

He chuckled. "Ah, reduced to a gopher already, and

we've only been married a couple of days!" The two women laughed loudly.

They spent an entire week at it. At first, the process was slow, but once Monica reached the Grade 5 spells, suddenly, she picked up speed. Lindsey said that was because she was now very certain that she could cast spells sans wand. Whatever the reason, they flew through the spells that Monica knew. By the time that they reached the Grade 8 spells, she was casting them on her first try. Once they finished the last spell book, Monica asked if they could do the ones from Professor Pam's new book. "I learned to cast most of them too."

Lindsey grinned. "Even the teacher spells?"

"Yes, how do you think I coached Crystal, Ericka, Enya, and Misty through a Red Hall record number of spells learned?" Lindsey chuckled.

"You sure have changed, Monica, and for the better. Okay, let's do those too. Only now, you have to realize that you aren't helpless any longer. Besides, a while back, we graduated another young woman who was forced to always wear similar ballet boots. She did well in those boots, so in time, you can too. I know you once told me quote 'Practice, practice, practice.'"

"Yes, I remember. Not my finest hour, Lindsey. Can you ever forgive me for putting you and Ashley through that torture?"

"I did that long ago, Monica or I wouldn't have asked you here to practice. Come on. There's a lot of spells in here."

Finally, on November 5, they finished up, and Rob teleported them back to his home in Denver. After they arrived, Monica gave Rob a very passionate kiss. "I owe you my life, Rob. While I have to use spells for most everything, I'm hardly a helpless wife now, just slow. Always give me time to see if I can find a way to do something via a spell before you lend me a hand. How's that?"

"Perfect, my love. Now we should talk about living arrangements. You probably want to go back to your place now. I've already received permission to carry on my work from St. Louis, so I can go with you. We can keep this small home as our get-away place, but let's wait until spring to visit my mountain cabin. You and snow don't mix too well."

"Thank you, Rob. Thank you. I was prepared to abandon my place in St. Louis just to be with you. Funny. A month ago, I never would have dreamed that I would be married and wanting to move just to be with a man, but then you are not an ordinary man, are you?"

He laughed, "No, I'm the loving husband of one fabulous young Red Hall woman who is unimaginably sexy!" Both laughed and packed their things. An hour later, they arrived just outside their front door. Using a spell, Monica opened the doors and walked in, Rob following, carrying their shrunk baggage.

"I'm back," she called out.

Two Magical Doors opened and Crystal and Ericka stepped out into the reception area. Both wore their usual blue satin gowns and tall heels, dressed as elegantly as Monica. They were so excited to see her that they'd used magical means to get here faster. Enya and Misty jogged up a few seconds later, dressed in sneakers and jeans, as usual, though Enya was definitely showing her pregnancy now. All five women squealed and hugged, nearly knocking Monica off her precarious balance.

"I've got great news!" Monica said when the hugs ended. "Two things actually. One, thanks to Rob and Lindsey, I can cast all the spells that I know again. Yes, sans wands." All four cheered, and it was a minute before she could relate her second bit of news. "Two, Rob and I are married. We don't have to worry about Graz'zt Summoning me ever again." More squeals echoed in the reception area.

"Tell us all about it!" Crystal exclaimed, while Rob turned a shade of pink. She chatted about it while they all headed downstairs, where Jasper and Brad added their congratulations to the mix, shaking Rob's hand rather hard.

"Well, we have a little surprise, Monica," Crystal announced. "Gregor and I are dating."

Ericka added, "Tyler and I are dating too."

"Great news, both of you!" I guess we need our separate rooms now," Monica teased and the women chuckled. Rob's face remained pinkish.

"You two get settled in and then let's hold a conference. A lot has happened since you were abducted," Crystal suggested.

Chapter 15—Countermoves

Monica saw that already her two girlfriends had moved all their things into their own bedroom, presumably so they could spend time with their new boyfriends. "Looks like we have this room all to ourselves," she said.

"That's good, because I want you all to myself," Rob teased. Then he added seriously, "Honestly, we have lots more work to do with your training. We've only dealt with what you already knew how to do. There is a whole lot more that you may be able to do."

Monica looked at him a bit surprised. "Like that Planar Travel thing?"

"Yes and lots more, most sexy woman," he teased her.

"But of course. Glad that you recognize this major detail," she replied, and both laughed. As they continued unpacking, she added, "Well, at least I can do some things for myself now with my spells. It must really be awful for Lilly and the others. I wonder how they are doing."

Rob looked serious. "I don't know, but I think that we should look in on them as soon as we can. Now that they are back, they are probably suffering both mentally as well as physically." In the back of her mind, Monica just had an idea of how she might help them a little and resolved at least to try.

Later, the ten men and women met together over tea in their dining room to discuss everything. Naturally, her friends wanted Monica to tell them all about what had happened to her, and she spent a goodly amount of time describing it as best she could. Eventually, they cast spells so that they could see her memories of just what the Abyss actually looked like.

"One thing I noticed is that our magic is somehow reduced down there. My protection earrings failed to work, but they resumed as soon as I was out of there. Plus, there is the unusual way in which I and then the other four were able to undo the Idiot Mind spell. The hideous, overwhelming pain memories shot completely through that spell. Yet, the four normal women were also able to throw off the effects of that spell. None of us should have been able to do that on our own," she explained.

Gregor spoke up, "In the Abyss and in the Hells, our magic is greatly reduced. Lesser magical items cease to be magic at all while they are in those places. That's a recorded fact others have made. It's in one of dad's books, but this business of the Idiot Mind spell, now that is interesting. I will ask dad about it whenever he is alert again."

Monica thanked him. However, as she relived her experience, describing it fully, one small remark that Graz'zt had made to her she did not reveal. He's said that she had been a clone. No, he'd said, "But I know that you don't mind being a clone in another twenty-five years or so, since you were a clone when you were Dominus." *When he said this, I was so overwhelmed with the pain and shock of the Abyss, that I missed it. Does he know something about me that even I don't know? I have to find out!*

She didn't tell them about Running Eagle and their visit there. She and Rob wanted to keep that a secret for now, helping to ensure that Graz'zt wouldn't be able to find out her new true name. While he might find out that she'd gotten married and could make likely assumptions on her new last name, he'd never guess how the Indian had so christened her. Instead, she focused on telling them how Rob had coached her into being able to cast her spells sans wand, and then how Governor Lindsey had asked her to come to Bradbury's, where she drilled her on all of her higher grade spells.

Monica concluded by saying, "So now, gang, I have to use my spells as a substitute for my arms and hands. Tricky, but it's mostly working. Now you have to tell me all about what's been going on here while I was gone."

Crystal giggled. "Well, I hope that you don't mind that we spent another two hundred thousand of your dollars."

Monica faked a shocked expression, but Rob gasped. "I've only got fifty grand saved."

"For a good cause," Crystal continued, explaining how Rob had shown them what he was seeing, the lingering energy traces from the Gate and Summoning spells. "It is really a unique trace that the Gate spell leaves behind. So I figured that if it is an energy trace, it should be visible at some wavelength, since Rob was able to perceive it."

"Right," Ericka broke in, unable to sit quietly. This was so exciting and such a momentous discovery. "So she had me buy sensitive detection devices that went into the Infrared as well as Ultraviolet portions of the spectrum. We had them shipped overnight delivery. Then, once I had them set up, she cast her usual Gate spell, contacting our little testing demon, Fluffy, who was pleased to have another slice of pizza again. Anyway, I found that trace energy visible in the Infrared! It is visible, if you observe at the proper wavelength! Pretty amazing."

"Right," Crystal took control of her report back from Ericka. "So the next step was to get time on one of the government satellites. Oliver and Leslie handled that for us, and we received a mountain of images taken of St. Louis over the past week, all in the IR portion of the spectrum. Guess what we found?"

"I can't," Monica grinned.

"Oh, getting ahead of myself. Parry and Ari discovered that Lilly had been kidnaped and taken to the Abyss by Graz'zt. He's a great PI, that's for sure. Anyway, we knew about her, and so we scanned through the IR images, and guess what? We were able actually to see the Gate spell's signature residual energies around her apartment from when she was taken!"

"Wow!"

"No kidding. Oliver and Parry worked their bottoms off and came up with five more kidnaping situations, and we matched them to the IR images as well. Leslie claimed this was the breakthrough of monumental proportions. She took this on up to the Department of Law and to the worldwide Board of Regents. They've had a team going over all IR images for the last month all over the world. I can't imagine how much work that is! But they've found another two dozen similar Gate spells. Already, they've been tracking some of them down to other wizards or witches doing their own work and such, but they've also located ten more kidnaped women, taken like Lilly was."

Ericka broke in, "Plus, they've found five more of those incised pentagrams that the demons constructed! Those places have been raided and the gates destroyed! Graz'zt's advance team is being shut down now almost at once!"

Crystal retook control. "Once they use a new incised pentagram, it is located and destroyed. They've become one-use pentagrams. That has to put a huge monkey wrench into Graz'zt's plans! The world and its technology are vastly better than when he was last here three thousand years ago. Isn't this the greatest news?"

"Way to go you two! Indeed. I was really worried that his plans were unstoppable. It sure sounded like that coming from him," Monica validated her friends.

"Well, not totally, but it sure puts a crimp in his plans. We've not yet figured out how to find the Cambion soldiers of his scouting party or at least three of his succubuses who are building the Gates. Still," Crystal declared proudly, "it is a good start. Honestly, we have to stop him from doing these awful things to innocent young women. Should we try to rescue all the others who are probably being held in the other Cambion Production Centers, like you were?"

"I don't think that we can easily pull it off again. He's now probably fuming and has them heavily guarded," Rob said quietly and soberly.

Enya took over now. "The four rescued women were taken to St. Anne's, and I got to help with their needed potions. It took us almost a week to get all that putrid slime out of their bodies. You've never smelled anything so rancid as that stuff that we got out of them. They were moved to a private apartment in the rehab wing of the hospital. Nisha has been with them the whole time, except when Leslie and Henry were questioning her. She's been providing a wealth of information on Graz'zt and his plans and even the Abyss as well. Her reports have validated what you reported and added even more details."

"The five are still being kept in quarantine at the rehab wing. Their parents and next of kin have not yet been notified. The doctors are still working on their recovery. They anticipate massive psychic shock to set in soon. They are still mostly just numb to the world," Enya explained. "Of course, they couldn't have normals visiting them while they were being detoxified. And now, with the anticipated psychic shocks about to spring, they fear they might go completely insane before it's all over."

"We best go see them soon," Monica declared.

"Right after lunch," Rob suggested.

"Oh Monica," Ericka put in, "I'm working on some magical enhancements for some boots for you. Have them ready in a few days. Honestly, we all don't know how you can even walk in those. They are supposed to be sexy bedroom shoes only. We all tried standing and walking in them—when Crystal found them and got some in for you. It has to be really hard to walk in them."

"Thanks, Ericka. I need all the help I can get just now. Stairs are scary now. I keep trying to hold on to the railings, but can't, obviously. My knees are taking a beating," Monica replied. "If they work out, maybe we can make some for the other four women."

"On it!" Ericka declared. After that, they chatted and soon dispersed going back to their various works in progress, leaving Rob and Monica still in the dining room.

Rob commented, "Say, if their having spent a couple hundred thousand of your dollars is hurting, I can pitch in my paltry fifty grand, if that will help any."

"No need, Rob. Thanks for the offer. I don't need money. Which reminds me, I best check on my finances. Summon: Laptop," she commanded. Magical energies flashed, and her laptop appeared before her, having flown from her desk in her bedroom to her. "Move Object: lift lid." Her laptop opened up. "Honestly, Rob, this is so darned difficult, but I am doing it. How about typing in my password for me? Passion5." He did so.

A dozen email notices popped up. "What's all those?" he asked.

"Financial tips and offers that came in while I was gone. Okay, let's see where my portfolio stands today." One by one, keys depressed, as she focused intently on each tiny motion her magic spell provided via moving objects around. It was slow work, but she did get her bank accounts brought up. "Ah, it's gone up some while I was gone. Not as much as it would have if I had been here to deal with the tips that I received."

"My god, Monica! Is, is that amount real?" Rob said completely flabbergasted.

"Two hundred ten million and change?" Monica asked. "Yes, that's the current balance. Crystal's expenses are hardly noticed. I started out with about a hundred thousand when I entered magic school. I inherited two million from my uncle and aunt when they died. Life insurance policies. I know how to properly invest, you see."

Rob squeaked, "I had no idea."

"I know. Few do. I use it to help everyone, not like last time when I used to further my own ends. Want me to see what I can do with your fifty grand? We ought to be able to double it by summer, maybe more."

Rob swallowed. "Yeh, sure. Incredible, Monica. I had no idea. You're a millionaire and a super sexy one too."

She grinned. "Why of course, silly. Glad you noticed." Both laughed, and she began setting up an investment portfolio for him.

After lunch, they headed over to St. Anne's Physical Rehabilitation Center to visit the four women. As they navigated their way through the hospital, Rob kept a steadying arm around her waist, which she appreciated, allowing her to focus on simply walking and not losing her balance dodging the many hallway obstructions and people who walked faster than they did.

When they got to the women's suite, six armed guards with wands and guns stood outside, providing protection for the women. After checking the two's identity, they were allowed inside. "Hello everyone," Monica said as she entered the room.

She found the four women sitting on a couch. They wore simple hospital gowns, but their eyes were red from crying. Nisha had morphed herself a little, removing her horns and wings, but otherwise, she looked much as she had; only now she wore a simple cotton day dress that someone had given her. In turn, they saw Monica dressed in her red satin pencil style gown, with black nylons and black patent boots.

She looked very elegantly dressed indeed.

"Wow, you look very pretty, Monica," Nisha commented, very much impressed with her appearance. "They have gotten the contamination out of their bodies with some potions," she began to report quite seriously, "but now they are, well I don't know how to say it, they are having very bad reactions. I think that they were mostly in complete shock while they were in the Cambion Production Center, and now that they are back and their bodies have been cleansed, the horror of it all is overwhelming them."

"I guessed as much. I've come to help them. I've just the spells to use, but I need you to keep any loud noises that they might make silenced. I don't want to be interrupted," Monica explained.

"Yes, I can do that," Nisha replied.

"On it dear," Rob added.

Monica walked up to Lilly first. "I'm going to cast a spell on you, Lilly, that will erase the pain and emotional trauma that you've experienced along with the rest of us. For a time, you will seem to be reliving it, but when the spell is done, all of that will be erased and have no more force upon you, though you will be able to remember it all. Will that be okay with you?"

"Why don't you just kill me now, Monica? I can't live like this! The pain, the nightmares—I'm going insane, I just know it!" The other three agreed with her.

"I know. I know, just have a tiny bit more faith in me," Monica asked. Tears trickling down her face, Lilly nodded, and Monica cast her spell. While she had intended it only to affect Lilly, somehow it got all four of them at the same time. Patricia, Gracie, and Janet all began to re-experience everything! The noise of their screams as they re-experienced their arms incinerating from their bones outward was deafening, but Nisha and Rob kept their silence spells working overtime. Outside, the guards heard nothing.

An hour later, the last bits erased, and Monica ended her spell. "It's a miracle! The nightmares are gone. I feel light as a feather. But Monica, I still can't live like this," Lilly pointed out.

Monica grinned, "But I'm not done yet. I'm going to cast another spell on each of you. We call it a Morph spell. I'm going to alter your bodies to what they were just before you were abducted. As long as you don't resist it, it will remain in force. Of course, you have to avoid any Dispel Magic spell, as those they have at the airports for passenger screening. That will undo it. I'll give each of you a card with my number on it so if the spell accidentally is cancelled, just call me, and I'll come by and recast it for you. Okay?"

"Will I still be me? The same?" Lilly asked.

"Absolutely. You will age and grow just as though this never happened. But if you run into a Dispel Magic spell, then it will be cancelled, and you'll be as you are now, only however much older you are at that time. Okay?" It was, and she focused and cast her Morph Others spell four times.

"Look at me! I'm okay again," Lilly waved her arms and hands wildly in the air.

"Remember, it is just a magic spell. Your bodies are still as they were, so make sure you don't run into any Dispel Magic spells. I'll see if I can't get you all released from the hospital really soon. Here's my card. Remember; keep it with you at all time, just in case the spell gets undone. It will only take me a minute to get it redone if that happens. Okay?"

They gushed out their thank you's. Then Monica said, "Now I have a little favor to ask of you. Nisha here is completely lost in our world. Will you look after her and help her learn about our world, starting with getting her and yourselves some nice clothes? And a place to stay? She knows nothing about our world."

"Absolutely, Monica!" Lilly exclaimed. "She's been our guardian angel all this time, so it's the least that we can do for her. She can live in my apartment with me. Don't worry, Nisha. I'll teach you everything. Besides, we now have money."

Monica left Nisha crying tears of happiness as well. She and Rob then visited the doctors in charge of the women, outlining what she'd just done for them.

Dr. Abel commented, "Well done. Excellent ideas. We were about to summon someone to cast that spell to eradicate their trauma. Saves us the trouble." He glanced at his team of doctors and then added, "The Morph spell is a good idea. We've conducted very extensive tests of their physical bodies. I'm afraid that their arms and yours too cannot be re-grown. The incineration removed all traces of them, so that there is nothing upon which the potions can work. As far as their feet are concerned, x-rays show that all the bones in their feet have been completely fused together into one solid bone. We've never seen anything like it before. It is our professional opinion that potions will be unable to undo that fusion. We've run some sample tests while we were detoxifying them. I'm afraid that nothing short of a pair of Full Wish spells will be able to restore them or yourself, Monica. Terrible price to pay, but as I understand it, they received substantial monetary compensation, so perhaps they will be able to get by."

"I certainly hope so. Will you be able to release them soon then? I know some are desperate to let their folks know that they are alive and safe now," she asked.

"Yes, we'll see to the notifications today. Thank you," Dr. Abel replied.

With that handled, she and Rob headed out of the hospital and teleported back to her place. As they arrived, Rob said, "That was a truly wonderful thing that you did for them, you know that dear?"

"I know. It had to be done. They are normal women, and it was magic that mutilated and tortured them, so it had to be magic that helps them back on their feet, at least partially. I don't think that I can get my hands on ten Full Wish spells, though. While I've the money for it, no wizard is going to age ten years just to get us restored. Besides, I wouldn't accept such an action. No one should have to prematurely age. We can somehow get by, dear; at least I sure hope so, even though it's a bitch for me. At least as long as they don't run into too many Dispel Magic spells, they ought to have normal lives now. Not me. I run into so darn many of those spells that it's pointless even to bother with a Morph Self spell."

Rob sighed. "I know. I thought about that many days ago and came to the same conclusion. I like your attitude towards unnatural aging though. Impressive, my sexy young woman. You continually keep on impressing me." He gave her a passionate kiss.

That afternoon, after things quieted down, Rob took her into their bedroom to explore her mental potentials further. "You have more powers available to you than you are aware of. I can see a tiny mental block that is preventing you from seeing it and making use of it, like I make use of mine. I'm going to remove that block and then we can see what you truly possess, okay?"

"Okay. I think you are just dreaming, Rob. Will it hurt?"

"I don't think so, but I've never done this before. Here goes." She saw him concentrating, but nothing more.

Suddenly, she had a terrible thought: *I don't dare look at this! It might kill me!* Then, she felt Rob's super gentle touch and her resistance to it dissolved, just as her resistance to intercourse with a man had. Before her, she felt what she later described as a vast source of power, of energy, untapped, there within her, something she'd never realized was there. She stared at Rob, wide-eyed and mostly collapsed onto her bed, sitting on her hair.

Rob spoke, though it seemed as if his voice was coming from some distant location. "We don't have a name for it, but I call it psi power. It is part of you, Monica. It is your untapped true power as a spiritual being, I think. Initially as you begin to tap into your powers, they will tend to focus on one or two Primary Zones and perhaps three Secondary Zones. Again, we don't have any real nomenclature for all this. There are only a very few of us in the whole world."

Monica's voice also sounded distant to herself. "What do I do now?"

"I'am going to rattle off some skills, and you let me know when you think one of these is a hot one. That is, one that you sort of feel or have a hunch you could do, with some training of course."

"Okay. Intuition, eh?"

"Right. Women are supposed to be big on intuition." Monica found herself involuntarily giggling a little.

Rob called off some actions, but when he said, "Planar Travel," Monica got a flash of energy. "There, something happened. I saw something on that one. That's what you do, right?"

"Yes, I thought that you would be able to do it with me. I'm writing that one down. Okay, let's see what other possible Primary Zones indicate with you." He continued rattling off actions. Once more, when he said, "Heal Self Fully," she reacted, seeing another flash of energy. He wrote that one down and continued with his list. A bit later, he added, "Awareness of Psychic Residue." "Hey, that's another one that I use all the time. Cool." She smiled.

"Well, that's all the Primary Zones. You have three to start with. Darn impressive. Now let's see the Secondary Zones," he explained. It was a rather extensive list of minor actions. When he finished, she'd seen five more energy flashes. He wrote each down including Heal Body Cells, Maintain Balance, Adapt Body to Hostile Environments, Send Thoughts, Physical Rapport and Empathy.

"That's it. I must say, I rather expected some of these, considering what you've been through. Healing self and others, keeping your balance on your toes, adapting your body to nasty environments, even rapport like we've been doing at bedtime—they all seem just like you, dear."

She grinned. "I guess I'm somewhat predictable. I really want to be able to help others in need and somehow survive myself. So what do we do now?"

"Now we train you in how to do these things one at a time. Of course, there is an Achilles heel to all this. Others out there like to prey on us with our mental powers. If you remember when we were in the Abyss and that giant general came attacking us, I told you that he was far stronger than I was and that I dare not attack him. If he'd realized that I had these psi powers, he would have attacked me and probably fired my brain, killing me. So we also have to work on getting your mental defenses going so you can withstand these kinds of attacks."

"Heck, I didn't know there was going to be danger to having these powers," she commented. "Well, we best get started before anything else happens. You know, I think that we might have been made for each other." Rob smiled, thinking much the same thing.

A few of her new abilities were very easy to handle. Sliding into Rapport and Empathy with Rob was almost second nature to her after her first try. *My god, Rob! This is so utterly intimate!*

I know, my love, I know.

Likewise, Sending Thoughts was as easy as her Message spell. Next, they worked on her balance skills, something that she truly needed. Lacking arms for balance, walking only on her toes was more than a little challenging. Rough ground and stairs were killers for her. Each time she faced one of them, she felt a rise of nervousness bordering on panic. Hence, they spent the rest of the day dealing with this. By suppertime, Rob was able to give her a push while she was trying to go down the stairs, and she was able to activate her balance skill, preventing herself from taking a bad fall. As they walked towards the dining room, she commented, "Well, I can prevent taking a tumble, but Rob, I still get scared when I encounter stairs. I guess I can live with that. Right now, my knees are killing me. I think we overdid it a bit."

"No pain, no gain," Rob said teasingly. Both laughed, joining the others.

"So does this mean that you are no longer going to be taking your turn cooking our group suppers?" Ericka asked while the ten dined, eleven if one counted the aged professor who sometimes remained in his room where Gregor would later feed him. His condition continued to worsen.

"Crap. I've not thought about that. I need to pull my own weight around here," Monica replied, discovering another new inability that she now had. How can I possibly cook? She asked herself. I have to try. "Okay, I'll give it a try tomorrow night."

"Well, I don't see how you can," Enya said sympathetically. "Honest, Monica, it's all right with me if you can't."

"I have to try, Enya. I just have to. Maybe with many spells I can manage it. We'll see," Monica replied, but she wasn't very confident that she could. She missed her arms far more than she dared to let on. Then, images of Ashley Stokes came into her mind. She had lost hers in an accident when she was two, and yet there she was a third year magic student, budding Diviner, and even a track and soccer player. She used her feet as hands, she recalled. Heck, I can't even use my feet as she was able to do. I dare not dwell on my loss. I must not, she told herself. She felt tears trying to form and fought against them.

After dinner, she used magic spells to help with the dishes, something that she'd always done in the past. Then, she joined Rob in their bedroom. Just now, she wanted him badly. Casting more spells, she carefully, but painstakingly slowly undressed herself, leaving her garter belt, hose, and boots on. Without her boots, she would have to resort to moving about on her knees.

She then began using her spells to undress Rob, much to his surprise. "What are you doing to me?" he said playfully. "It's kind of strange having my clothes coming off of their own accord." She said nothing, but continued focusing, controlling her spells.

When he was stripped, she moved forward, pressing her body into his. Again, she suppressed her awful feeling of not having arms to hold and squeeze him, but moved her body against his. She felt his instant arousal and smiled. Before long, they were both in an intimate rapport with each other and in bed. As always, she was on top, controlling their mutual actions, but now sensing his needs as well as her own.

Later, both exhausted, she lay on his shoulder, her hair draped wildly over them both. "That was indescribably fantastic, Rob. I do so love you," she whispered.

"I love you too, Monica," he whispered back, and she fell into a deep, relaxing sleep, perhaps the best night's sleep that she'd ever had. However, in the back of her mind, she still acutely felt the awful loss of her arms and hands. She knew that she would never get used to their loss, not ever. While she had her magic and powers to make do somehow, it wasn't the same. Still, she had Rob now and that meant the world to her.

Across town in a hotel room, four morphed people met. Three were succubus demons, and one was a Cambion demon. Yet they all appeared human, three very attractive women, one handsome man.

Donatella Ratini said, "This world is so vastly complex. So many strange inventions. It's hard to know what is going on here."

"Duh, tell me about it!" Bella Zaronetti complained bitterly. "This was supposed to be a super simple operation. Gate in while invisible, build several permanent Gates, snatch up some young human women, and prepare for the onslaught."

"No kidding. Simple, this isn't," Gisella Harmoni barked her displeasure. "Everything's so vastly different here. Not at all what our Prince led us to believe. All this electronic stuff."

General Franco Porti added his bass voice to that of the three sopranos, "Indeed. They are able to locate our new Gates after we use them only once! How can that be? Have they invented vastly more powerful magical spells?"

"No, it is fancy electronics, I think," Donatella replied. "Something is way up there in the sky, invisible to our eyes. These humans pose far more of a threat than we ever imagined. Prince Graz'zt needs to know what we are up against."

"Oh, he is very upset that the bitch Monica Nicole Black escaped the breeding center, the Cambion Production Center, and took four others with her and that stupid alu-demon too. I sure am glad we're here and not back home," Bella commented.

"You can say that again," the general added. "But we have to do something quick or he's going to Summon us back and execute us. I don't know about you ladies, but I value my head just now."

"You are right about that, General Franco. If we don't do something fast, he will have our heads or worse. Believe me, he can think of worse things than cutting off our heads," Gisella replied, spitting on the floor.

"We have to change our plans," Donatella broke in. "We need to operate differently. Since our Gates are only usable once, we can make them throw-away-able. That is, we don't have to pick good locations—anywhere will do for a one time use. Second, we need to round up a bunch of women to send back. The heck with trying subterfuge. They are on to us anyway. So we find the women, kidnap them around the same time, and deliver them to the Prince on the one-shot use of the Gate. Third, we should have the Prince send through as many of his soldiers as he wants during that onetime use of the Gate."

Gisella added, "Fourth, we ought to spread out to other large human cities. They have the humans in this city on high alert, especially fertile, unmarried, young women. There are lots of large cities now, not just a few like Graz'zt told us."

"Hey, we need to discover what new weapons the humans have invented," General Franco added. "I've not seen a single sword anywhere. So they must have very different weapons now. Garg actually had his body killed here by those explosive flying metal particles, though it took an awful lot of them hitting him to do that. We need to learn about these humans and their new weapons."

"True, true, but who is going to tell the Prince all this, eh?" Gisella asked. "He'll be furious."

"It sure as heck isn't going to be me!" General Franco declared. "You bitches are in charge. You tell him."

"He's right. Donatella, you do it," Gisella spat out.

"All right, but let's round up another ten human women to send along with our reports and new plans. Gisella, you write up the report. Make darned sure you tell him what we are really facing here. General, you get your men ready to snatch the women. Bella and I will identify them and prepare a crude, throwaway Gate."

She went on, "Once we do this, I'm heading to that city called Los An-ge-le-s."

"Oh, I think they just call it LA, Donatella," Bella countered. "I'm all for the warmer weather. This Mi-am-i sounds like a great place. Many women to snatch there. Gisella, you have to stay here until the reply Gate opens. In the report, tell him to prepare a bunch to come through in say a week after we send him this batch and report. After you bring in the new arrivals, you can pick your own city, but do send us some of that new help."

"Why do I have to stick around here?" Gisella asked.

"Because you have to write the report and deal with the Prince's answer. Besides, I told you so," Donatella barked.

"Crap. Say, should I ask him if he wants us to find that traitorous alu-demon and kill her?" Gisella asked.

"Nah. If he wants her dead, he'll want to torture her first. Leave her to him," Donatella replied.

"Okay, but how long is it going to take us to learn all these things?" Gisella asked.

"How the heck should I know?" Donatella barked. "As long as it takes to ensure the Prince's victory here. I wouldn't want to be in your skin if we act too hasty and lose. He loves to inflict pain more than I do and that's saying something!"

"Ah, you are just jealous that he's got more ability and skills to inflict pain than you do, Donatella," Bella remarked. Donatella glared back at her, but said nothing.

Gisella commented, "Well, I wish I knew how to incinerate their arms like he does. It would simplify dealing with these human women."

"That's why he's the Prince and you aren't!" General Franco barked, thankful to be able to get in at least one dig with these succubuses. "Let's get moving. We have a lot to do. I for one will be glad to get to this LA place. Here, the ground has this stupid, cold white stuff over it. I slipped on it. Nasty stuff. Maybe I should go to this Mi-am-i place with you. It's warmer."

The group chatted a bit longer on specifics and agreed to wrap up their St. Louis operations in three days, sending the report and ten more women back to Graz'zt. Once that was done, they'd head for better climates, except for Gisella who grumbled about having to stick around for eight days.

Leslie and Henry met officially with Monica Nicole and Rob the next morning. The two teleported to the FBI headquarters and met in an office near Oliver's. Both wanted to discuss more precisely what the actual environment there in the Abyss at these Cambion Production Centers was like. "We've been discussing putting together a raid on them, rescuing the women who might be in those Centers," Leslie began the discussion. "We know that some magical protection devices will be inert, just not precisely what ones. We were hoping that you might shed a little light on this as well as what kind of resistance we might anticipate. Failing that, would a nuclear bomb function there? The President doesn't want to risk an invasion of demons in this country. We can't blame him for that. Will guns be effective? We could send a SWAT team along with us."

"Well, my fancy magical earrings failed to function at all down there. Beyond that, I've no idea. I wasn't able to cast any spells then, not as I can now. You'll probably have to carry the women out of there. We were able to walk the short distance to the Gate platform only because Nisha was kind enough to violate the rules and take us on long walks outside of the Center. Walking on rough ground is quite difficult in these boots," Monica explained.

"As far as resistance goes, Nisha would be better able to answer that one. I only saw a general, who was a giant of a demon, and that Dr. Menninger fellow. Who knows about the bomb? Crystal and Gregor might have some idea. Guns? They weren't too effective on the street battles here, so I don't suppose they'd be much better down there. I know that magical spells are going to be somewhat limited because of their innate resistance to magic, though the amount varies from demon to demon."

She continued, "I did hear Gregor explaining that he found an ancient record that states the demons are susceptible to both corrosive acids and to iron. If we could find a way to dump a gallon of sulfuric acid on a demon, that would make an interesting test. Do they make bullets out of iron?"

"Copper slugs," Henry answered her. "I will see about having some rounds specially made from pure iron. I like the acid idea, except you're right. How do we deliver it?"

Just then, there was a commotion at the door. A man's voice bellowed, "I demand to Mrs. Leslie Traub, head of the Missouri Department of Magical Misuse! Immediately! I'm Senator Lew Parsons. I was told that she is here, so out of my way, lackey!" He barged his way on inside the room, followed by two of her guards, who looked apologetically at her.

"It's all right. Senator, I'm Leslie. What is it that you

wish of me? We are holding a meeting here," she replied briskly and sternly.

"It's my daughter, Jill Anne. She's been missing for over a week now. I'm sure that she's been taken by your darned demons, that's what," he fumed. He was quite overweight, and his roundish face was somewhat red with anger.

"Have you filed a missing person's report with the police or the FBI?" she asked.

"Of course, but all they did was give me the runaround. I don't know what this Abyss thing is or what you are calling demons, but I want you to drop everything and find my daughter. Immediately. That's an order," he bellowed.

"I'm sorry, Senator Parsons. You must miss her very much. Were you able to give them a recent photo of her? Along with details? Where she lived? How old is she? When did you first know that she was missing? I presume there hasn't been any ransom note," Leslie replied, seeing no easy way to dismiss the man.

"Are you an imbecile too? I gave all that information to the FBI man, but there has been no word on her. Nothing. This is intolerable. Women go missing and you do nothing at all!"

"Look, senator, I promise that I will look into it as soon as this meeting is finished," she tried again to get rid of him. She sensed that he was a normal man, not a wizard. Hence, she did not attempt to explain the magical abductions or the Abyss. He would have no grasp of any of that.

"All right then. I'll give you three days to find her. After that, I'll take it over your head. Someone will listen to me, I assure you!" He pivoted and stormed out of the room.

"What a rude man," Rob commented.

"He's hiding something," Monica added. "He's way overreacting. I don't trust him."

"Well, sorry about that. I will look into it and see what we have on file for her."

"While you deal with that, we'll have a chat with Nisha and see if she can answer some of your questions. That'll save you some time," Monica suggested. Besides, she wanted to see the short alu-demon again and make sure that she was adapting to this strange world reasonably well, particularly since her four charges were likely to be returning to their previous lives. She felt responsible for the five-foot tall woman.

She sent Nisha a Message and received a reply. She was staying with Lilly now. A few minutes later, she and Rob arrived there and met with the two. "See my new dress? It is similar to yours. I do so like the bright red. It goes well with my black hair, don't you think?" Nisha bubbled with pride.

"You look stunning," Rob praised her, and a big smile appeared.

Rob and Monica chatted with her about Leslie's questions. She had no idea about some of them, such as a nuclear bomb, but she had a wealth of information about the forces that were near the Cambion Production Centers. "You see, other demon princes sometimes attempt raids on his facilities, trying to steal some of his young Cambions for their own armies. So he has an entire garrison of two hundred stationed nearby. Plus, there are dozens of very powerful demons always around the complex. They are there to train all the younger Cambions. He has all sorts of Alert spells in place, so if you landed a bunch of people to raid the Centers, by the time that you got inside them, they'd be swarming down on you. We were able to escape because we only had to walk that short way to the pad and Gate. Another couple of minutes and there would have been hundreds of demons charging us. Not so good, I think."

They chatted a bit longer before Monica changed the topic and began asking how it was going for her. Nisha's reply was simply, "Peachy. Lilly taught me that expression. She's taking me everywhere. I'm learning fast. It is so much nicer here in your world, heaven actually." Once Monica was satisfied that Nisha was being well treated, she and Rob returned to the FBI office.

Leslie looked a bit glum when they joined her. "Well, here's a photo of Jill Anne Parsons. She's twenty, blonde, and works for her father as his campaign finance officer, while going to the university. I've been going over her case file, but there's not much in it. In all likelihood, she may well have been taken to the Abyss. She matches the profile of the women who have been abducted. However, I've sent off for her medical records just to be thorough. Of course, now what do I tell this raging senator? Want my job?"

Monica laughed. "No way!" They all chuckled, and then she and Rob reported what they'd learned from Nisha.

"Well, that's pretty much what I expected to hear. This prince has to guard his production facilities. He'd be stupid if he didn't," Leslie sighed. "Still, I have to meet with the other state leaders and our boss and see what they want to do."

"So are you going to recommend a raid?" Rob asked.

She sighed again. "As much as I'd love to, I simply can't. It is too risky a venture and for a zillion reasons. Never fight a battle on the enemy's homeland when you don't have good Intel on it. We'd likely be walking into a nice pile of traps. I'll keep in touch. Thanks for coming by."

Since they were obviously done, Rob slipped his arm around her waist, and the two strolled on out of the office. Once on the street, the air was quite chilly. Snow was in the forecast, but only a light one. Rob teleported them home, and the two decided to spend the rest of the day working on her new psi skills.

Late afternoon, Monica had an urge to take her car out for a drive, something completely different for a change. "You have a car?" Rob asked.

"Sure do. Come on. It's in the garage. I haven't taken it out for a spin in many months! Oh!" She stopped short.

"What?"

"Here's another thing that I can't ever do again: drive my fancy car. Crap!" Monica exclaimed. Emotions swept over her, but she fought against allowing them to surface. She couldn't wipe her own tears if she broke down. Worse, if she did, her mascara, which she'd spent thirty painstaking minutes trying to apply using her spells, would streak, and she couldn't do anything about that either. Instead, she tried to add another reason, "Besides, my feet wouldn't be able to operate the pedals on the floor. Grab the keys there by the door. You are driving, Rob."

"Which ones?" he asked, seeing five sets.

"The one with the Cardinal's key ring," she replied.

While he did that, she used her spells to get the side door opened. Their garage held five cars, parked close together. She sighed. "Guess which one is mine?" Again, she tried to cover up her intense feelings by distraction.

Rob looked them over. "Must be the red one."

"How did you guess?"

"You are partial to red. Crystal and Ericka like blue. The other two cars are quite practical ones, so that one has to be yours. What kind is it? I've never seen one like it," Rob asked, impressed.

"A Ferrari 4000. Hottest car on four wheels. Great acceleration. Sleek, low, bursting with power and every feature I could get on it," she declared proudly.

"Wow! Hot car for the hottest girl," Rob teased her, bringing a flash of a smile to her face.

It quickly dissolved. Standing there beside the passenger-side door, she realized that as low to the ground as it was, she wouldn't be able to get herself into its leather bucket seat easily, not without arms and in these boots. "I think that you are going to have to lift me into the seat. I doubt that I can work enough spells to get me into it."

Rob sensed just how much this was hurting her, especially to have to say this aloud. "I understand, dear. Still, we can go for a ride, can't we? Soon, you won't want to take it out in the snow and slush mixed with salt that covers the roads, will you?"

"True, true. It's spotless, but you can see that. Thanks." She allowed Rob to lift her up and put her into her seat. While he went around to the other side, she experimented a little with her en pointe boots and saw that she really wasn't going to be able to get herself into the seat unless she had arms and hands to maneuver her body around. My life truly is becoming a nightmare without end, she thought, but managed to keep her eyes from watering by sniffing through her nose just before he got in, hiding it from him as best she could.

After a few instructions, she discovered that he had no idea how to drive a stick shift vehicle. "Okay, punch in Bush Stadium in the navigator. Good. Now press start. The car will drive itself. I don't want you stripping the gears on this baby," she teased him back.

When they returned an hour later, both felt invigorated. Just getting out among all the normals going about their sometimes hectic lives felt good for a change. They were back just in time for supper.

Two days later, around ten, Crystal received a hot call from Leslie and quickly relayed the word to everyone. "Gang! Great news. A new Gate has just opened up to the Abyss! Thanks to our IR detection devices and a hundred people monitoring the satellite images in real time, they've just spotted one opening up ten minutes ago. Come on, everyone. Cast your defensive spells, and let's teleport to the action. It's in Hazelwood, just north of the airport."

Two minutes later, Crystal, Ericka, Gregor, Tyler, Monica, and Rob were ready, and Crystal teleported them to the location, a simple brick home that was for sale. When they arrived, Leslie, Henry, Oliver, and two dozen other wizards, witches, and SWAT team members were already there, preparing to charge into the house. The new arrivals were forced to remain behind the strike force. One man smashed in the door, and the large group charged inside.

Crystal had her group watching the outer perimeter. "Look for invisible demons," she barked her orders.

Monica grinned. That's precisely what she would have ordered, but also realized that Crystal had rather usurped her position as leader of their band of five women and now their husbands and boyfriends. Well, I really don't mind her taking charge; she's more than earned it, Monica thought and began casting her spells, looking around for any invisible demons that might be trying to flee.

"There goes one!" she yelled, but was unable to point to it! Again, she fought hard to keep from breaking down, as her friends had to find the fleeing invisible man themselves. She couldn't point to him. Instead, she shot a ball of fire, centered over the fleeing form. She was in luck this time. His magic resistance failed him, probably because he was fleeing. The demon screamed, but kept on running. A large volley of magical missiles rained down on the demon, who suddenly turned around and charged the group!

Even with magical resistance, to charge a group of ten wizards and witches was pure folly, chaotic yes, but a folly nonetheless. So many spells hit him that he was dead before he got to within ten feet of the bunched group. "A Cambion fighter," Crystal pointed out the obvious. "Good going, Monica. Everyone, keep alert. There could be more! Plus one for the good guys!"

While they now paid close attention to the surrounding area, no more were sighted, and shortly, Leslie summoned them all inside. "We're too late. At least, you got one. There's the incised pentagram. Pretty crude at that. But we've got one casualty. She's in a bad way, but I think it's the senator's daughter. Monica, can you see if you can do anything for her before we teleport her to St. Anne's? Rob, if you would check out that Gate please?"

Monica walked on inside and found the victim sitting on an old sofa, totally naked, armless, and wearing the same ballet style boots that she'd worn when she was there in the Abyss in Graz'zt's Cambion Production Center. She had very tangled, long blonde tresses, now filled with unspeakable filth from the Abyss. Her body was covered in the slime, and Monica guessed the woman had likely fallen onto the disgusting ground of the Abyss. The woman was in total shock, staring into space; her eyes, vacant. She knew right away that there was nothing that she could do for her right now, but she swore to the woman that she would stay with her.

She heard Rob relaying what he sensed with the Gate. "This one is remarkably hot with psychic residue and energies. Ten young women, unconscious, were taken through the Gate, while one was brought back and dumped on the couch. Then, thirty more demons came through. Two succubuses, four of the Class Four demons—their guards I think, and then twenty-four Cambions. They all went invisible right after they arrived, and they fled the house. Actually, they arrived running. They must be on to the fact that you are able to pinpoint the Gate when they open it and are countering it by moving very rapidly once it is opened. Leslie, they are quick learners. We've now got twenty-nine more demons roaming the streets of St. Louis!"

She cursed and then took charge, ordering a forensics team to scour the place for any possible clues. It was at this point that the EMT's from St. Anne's arrived to take the victim to the hospital. They wore plastic suits so they would not be contaminated by the Abyss slime that covered the poor woman. They lifted her onto a collapsing transport cart and teleported her to the hospital.

"Okay if we go with them?" Monica asked.

A harried Leslie replied, "Please!" She sounded greatly relieved.

Chapter 16—One Life at a Time

Rob and Monica arrived a few minutes after they got Jill Anne Parsons into the decontamination room. Two doctors, wearing protective suits, had already entered to examine their new patient. Hence, the two took seats just outside the room and began a long wait.

"She's a normal woman, so why did they send her back?" Monica asked.

"Don't know. Maybe there's something wrong with her," Rob suggested.

Monica focused her mind, using her newest skill, the ability to work on a person's cellular level to heal. From her seat outside the decontamination room, she began to probe the woman's body. She didn't see Enya and Brad arriving, handing a bag of potions to the nurse. They took a seat beside their two friends, not disturbing Monica. Ten minutes later, Monica opened her eyes, surprised to see Enya and Brad sitting with them. "Oh. Hi. Didn't see you coming in."

"Brought the needed potions for her. It looked like you were focusing so we didn't bother you," Enya replied. "Is she going to survive? Why did they bring her back?"

"She's pretty much in total shock right now, but I think I know why they rejected her. She had a blockage in her reproductive system. I think that Dr. Menninger discovered that he'd get no eggs from her and so sent her back instead of simply killing her. Probably sent her back as a threat to us—trying to create fear in us," Monica theorized.

She went on, "But I used my new gift, Rob. I removed that blockage. She can have children now, if she wants them. That's something. I think it will be best if we stay with her. She has no others with her. No company to share her misery and no Nisha either for moral support."

"I agree," Rob said softly. "Well done on your gift." She flashed him a smile.

An hour later, the two doctors came out of the room, discarding their suits. "Well?" Monica inquired.

"She's resting now. Deep in shock. Will know more if she makes it through the night. She was covered in that filthy Abyss slime. Her system is full of it, just like the other four were. Enya's potions are going to work, assuming she lives."

Enya spoke up, "It's a revised potion, based upon what we learned from handling the other four women. If we did it right, she should be detoxified in three days."

"Excellent, excellent. We will continue to relay how the process unfolds, Enya. I'd hoped that we'd seen the last of these poor victims. But obviously not. Well, we've other patients to handle. Are you sticking around?"

"Yes, we will," Monica replied and the two doctors left. After that, Enya and Brad also left, and Rob headed down to the cafeteria to find them some lunch.

Around suppertime, Jill began vomiting up Abyss slime, and the doctors hastily donned their suits and went to assist her. Through the window, Monica watched them bathe her again and helped her to sit up on a sofa chair. She was more alert now, which everyone thought was a very good sign.

The next mid-morning, Senator Lew Parsons came charging into the waiting room, his loud bass voice demanding to see his daughter. "Look, her body is contaminated. You can't go in there until she's decontaminated, unless you want to spend days getting decontaminated yourself!" the nurse bellowed back at him. "You can talk to her. That speaker there. Push the button and talk. She can hear you and reply. You can hear her over the speaker."

"My god! There's nothing left of her. Pathetic! Worthless child. Jill Anne, you hear me? Jill Anne!" Monica's ire rose. It was all that she could do to keep from lashing out at this insensitive fat man. "Where's the campaign finance logs? That's all that I need from you. Where's the darn log? Jill Anne, you answer me now!"

Jill was still pretty much in shock, but she recognized his voice, turned her head mechanically towards the speaker, and saw his face through the window. She whispered, "On my laptop. Password: mom's name."

He yelled back, "Your computer? Mom. Okay, got it. What have you been mixed up in this time? Heck, you're worthless now. There's hardly anything left of you anyway. I disown you. Go live with your trashy friends. You are no daughter of mine!" He turned and stomped out of the waiting area. Only Rob's gentle hand on Monica's waist kept her from teaching the senator a lesson that he'd never forget.

"Men! They can be such beasts!" she spat out.

"Yes, we've beastly men here on Earth, just like beastly men down in the Abyss," Rob countered.

Monica looked through the window to see how Jill took her father's diatribe. It hadn't fazed her much. She still had a mostly vacant stare, and Monica realized that she'd mostly mechanically answered her father's question without even thinking about it. Monica calmed down and took her seat again.

Enya's potions worked just as she and Brad had designed them. In three days' time, all the contamination from the Abyss had been flushed from her system. Finally, Monica and Rob were allowed to go inside and be with her up close. It was tragic. Jill Anne merely sat there sobbing continuously, all the while her body was shaking in terror, a strange mixture of emotions. Monica took a deep breath and cast her spell, designed to allow Jill to re-experience her horrid trauma and thereby erase it, turning the awful mental images of pain and unconsciousness into mere harmless memories. She also had to cast a silence spell to keep Jill's incredible screams from terrorizing the entire hospital wing! Jill had lungs, that was certain.

An hour later, Jill finally had erased the trauma and hideous pains that she'd endured, and now they no longer had any affect on her mental state. However, her physical body condition captured her full attention, a very real grief, a bitter hopelessness, and helplessness. She was also aware that her father had disowned her, leaving her alone in her abject misery. "They should just kill me. Put me to sleep, Monica. I can't live like this. I'm helpless. I can't walk or do anything but sit here. Please, have pity on me; put me down. Tell the doctors to do it. Please, I beg you," Jill wailed and pleaded.

"How come you got sent back?" Monica asked sympathetically, hoping to turn the conversation down a different path. It worked, but only temporarily.

"They, they found out that I can't have babies. They said the mere sight of me would strike fear in everyone's minds. Please, have them kill me. I can't live like this, and I don't want to strike fear in everyone who sees me like this," Jill wailed again.

"Well, Jill. I'm a witch, and I've removed your ovarian blockage so that now you can have all the babies that you wish. That's something isn't it?"

She cried all the louder. "No it doesn't. Nobody is going to want me, not like this. I can't take care of a baby, let alone do anything for myself. Dad doesn't want me around. That's clear enough. I tried so hard to please him, after mom died, but nothing I do is ever good enough for him. Now I can't do anything at all. Please, have someone put me out of my misery, please," she begged again, her face drenched with tears.

Monica decided to try another approach. "Look a week or so ago, we rescued four other women who have been through what you've endured. I cast a spell on them that morphed their bodies into what they looked like just days before they were abducted and mutilated. As long as that magic spell isn't dispelled, they can live quite normal lives. They have hands, arms, and proper feet. If the spell ever is cancelled, they only have to call me, and I'll recast it, fixing them up again. I know, it is only a sort of fix, but as long as it isn't dispelled, it works. I would like to try that on you. Would that be all right with you?"

"I wouldn't be me, then, would I? I suppose so, but if it doesn't work, can you please kill me? Well you can't. You're just like me, so have your husband there do it. Please," Jill answered.

Monica focused and cast her spell. It worked and was cast. However, while the magical energies formed over Jill's body, nothing happened. Nothing at all! "Now this is strange. I've never seen anything like this!" Monica commented in a hushed tone.

"It isn't working is it?"

"I'll try again." She did, but again nothing happened, though Jill's body received the magical energies. "Let me bring

Rob in on this one, please! I'm baffled." She stepped out of the room, using her Open Door spell.

"Rob! The strangest things are happening here," Monica whispered, quickly explaining what she was trying to do and that the spell failed twice. "Can you cast it?"

"No, but I'll ask Crystal to come and try it while I watch. How's that?" Rob replied. She nodded. Five minutes later, dressed in her light blue satin gown, Crystal appeared in the waiting room, having teleported over. Quickly, Monica related what she had tried and that nothing had happened. All three stepped into Jill's room.

"Jill, this is my very good friend, Crystal. She's going to try it, and Rob's going to watch and see what we are possibly doing wrong. Okay?" Monica explained.

"Okay, but please, one of you kill me if it doesn't work," Jill wailed again.

Crystal focused, waved her wand in the precise motions, and barked, "Morph Jill Anne Parsons into Jill Anne Parsons a Month Ago!" Magic flashed. The energy covered Jill, but nothing happened. Frustrated, Crystal tired it again, barking, "Morph Jill Anne Parsons into Jill Anne Parsons as a Baby!" Again, nothing. "Morph Jill Anne Parsons into Crystal!" Nothing at all, though magical energies flew about the room.

"Well, I've never seen anything like this before!" Crystal said, quite exasperated, as though her last attempt hadn't illustrated it.

"Hold on there," Rob cautioned. "Something very strange is going on here. We need to think, not act."

"Now will you please kill me? I can't live like this," Jill wailed. They ignored her pleadings.

"Okay, Jill. Have you ever had magical training?" Rob asked.

"No, never. So go ahead, kill me. It can't hurt as much as my burning arms."

"Jill, I'm going to examine you a bit. It won't hurt at all," Rob said gently. He focused, and slowly paced the floor around the stuffed chair that she was sitting on. She wasn't being shy about being naked with three strangers around her, he noticed, rather her attention was on her mutilated body and utter helplessness.

Monica wondered just what Rob was doing or sensing. As the minutes ticked by, she grew more and more impatient. Just why was her spell failing? Even Crystal's? This wasn't right. Just when she thought she couldn't stand to wait a second longer, Rob broke his concentration and looked up.

"Well, this is intriguing. There are some faint traces of magical energies in small locations on her body. Ladies, use your spells and join with me and see what I'm seeing," Rob suggested. Magic flashed and both Monica and Crystal were right there in Rob's mind seeing what he was seeing. Not even the slightest hesitation. He laughed, focused and showed the pair of inquisitive witches what he'd seen.

A pair of identical streaks of a magical energy trace lay vertically just at the edges of her shoulder blades on her upper back. Each was about three inches long. Another pair of energy traces in the shape of small circles was on her upper forehead, just at her hairline.

"How very strange!" Monica commented after cancelling the spell. "What are those?"

"That, my good witch, is the sixty-four thousand dollar question," Rob replied. "I've never seen something like that before. If I might make a suggestion?"

"Please do," Monica replied.

"Jill's ready to be discharged from the hospital here. She obviously can't go to her home."

Jill piped up, "I don't want to ever go to dad's place ever again! So just please kill me and put me out of my misery!"

Rob ignored her outburst. "So why don't we take her home with us. We all can look after her and see if we can figure this out."

"I should have thought of that myself. Of course," Monica gushed, pirouetting to Jill, she added, "Jill, you are coming to our place. There are ten of us, and we will look after you until we can get this all sorted out. Rob, go see that she's properly checked out, and we'll teleport her home."

A few minutes later, the four arrived at their reception area, though Rob was carrying Jill. "Bring her to my room, and let's get her some proper clothes," Monica ordered.

A bit later, Jill sat on Monica's bed, while Rob rummaged through Monica's clothes, following Monica's instructions. To Jill, she said, "I'm way too slow doing these things, so Rob's is being my hands right now. See, there's nothing wrong with letting someone else help us." She added that last in an attempt to cheer Jill up a bit, but Monica Nicole didn't believe a word of what she'd just said!

Neither did Jill. "Don't patronize me! We are both helpless, and you know it." Monica tried not to react outwardly, but inwardly flinched in a major way. Jill struck a very raw nerve.

Monica changed the topic. "So would you like to be dressed up in a really fancy gown like me, like Crystal?"

A tiny spark of life flashed on her face, the first she'd seen. "Really? Yeh, sure."

"Well, I hope you like red, because that's about all the Monica here likes to wear," Rob teased both women.

"Don't worry, Jill, tomorrow we can go shopping and get you better colors," Monica hastily added, after seeing the slight frown on Jill's face.

"I prefer blues. They go better with my really light blonde hair and blue eyes," Jill added. "But why are you bothering? Just kill me, and we will all be done with this."

"Sorry, I'm still getting the hang of dressing Monica," Rob apologized as he began dressing Jill. "Honestly, you women have so many garments, it's a wonder you even know which goes where." Both women cracked a smile.

A few minutes later, Rob had her dressed up in one of Monica's outfits, magically altering each garment slightly to fit Jill who was a tad smaller than his wife was. "There you go, Jill. Let's get you up on your toes so you can see how you look in my mirror," Monica suggested. Rob helped her up and kept a steadying arm around her waist.

"Wow! I always wanted a gorgeous gown—to be dressed up for a fancy ball." Jill stared at the woman looking back at her from the mirror. Then, her demeanor changed again. "But I am still totally helpless, only now I look stunningly, gorgeously helpless. When you kill me, you can bury me in this gown, okay?"

"Hold still. I'm going to do your hair a little," Monica suggested. Using her spells, she levitated her hairbrush and began working slowly on Jill's blonde tresses. Shortly, Jill began telling her how she usually arranged it. Her hair was wavy and draped about three inches below her shoulders.

"Okay, Jill. You look good. Time for something to eat. Rob, will you escort our charming Jill to the dining room, while I see to the food?" Monica asked, though he already was doing just that, recalling how much Monica appreciated his steadying hand around her waist. When Monica got to the kitchen, Crystal had already whipped up a hot soup-based lunch for everyone, and Monica merely had to use her spells to help levitate and push the tableware over to the table. She whispered her thanks to Crystal, who smiled. Once more, Monica realized just how much passionate power there was between her and her four witches. Crystal knew just what was needed and had gone ahead and done it without even being asked.

By the time that Rob and Jill made their "grand entrance" into the dining room, everyone else was already there. "Wow, Jill, you look smashing!" Crystal complimented her.

"Stunning is more like it, Crystal," Ericka added.

"Well, she does look great," Enya commented, "but don't you think that she'd be more comfortable in a simple day dress like I've got on or maybe Misty's? Unless you are planning to take her to a ball after lunch. Did someone forget to tell me about a ball?"

Several laughed at Enya's tease. Jill managed the tiniest of smiles. "I can hardly walk. I'm helpless. I don't know why you are making me eat. Just go ahead and kill me and put me out of my misery."

"Not until we solve this big mystery, Jill," Monica countered. "After all, we are all wizards and witches here, and we don't like it when our spells don't work. We just have to know why they don't. So you're just going to have to stick around a while yet, until we figure this out. Rob, will you assist Miss Mysterious Jill here with her lunch?"

"Of course, Miss Gorgeous," Rob teased her back,

already planning on it.

Monica's coffee mug had a straw in it so she could easily manage it without spells. Likewise, Jill's tea mug had a straw for her to use, and Rob kept it within Jill's easy reach. She ate ravenously, quite unexpectedly, though now that Monica thought about it, her hunger should have been predictable, considering she was just out of detox.

After lunch, Monica began by asking Jill to tell them about herself and her life, prior to her kidnaping. "Well, I'm twenty now. I have my CPA. I love figures and have the credentials of a top accountant. I'm also kind of an organizational nut. You know, I organize absolutely everything, from clothes in their proper places, to well, everything. I'm so good at organizing and keeping very precise financial records, that dad made me work exclusively for him, running his senatorial campaigns, until now that is. Now I'm totally helpless and completely useless. Dad could see that at once, which is why he's disowned me. Rightly so. I'm worthless now, to him and to everyone, particularly myself."

"So what's your IQ?" Rob asked curiously.

Jill laughed coyly. "Wouldn't you like to know? Ha. I'm a genius, 150. Top of my CPA class. Valedictorian too." Her coy demeanor vanished in a flash. "So what does all that do me now? My IQ can't get me dressed, feed me, or anything. I'm a helpless, useless cripple. There's no point to my life anymore."

Rob ignored that last. "Well, I figured you were a bright one. You sure don't take after you father, the senator, excepting your blue eyes and blonde hair."

She gave a haughty laugh. "Obviously! Dad's an idiot. He can't organize his way out of a paper bag given a blowtorch! He is one of you, a wizard, but a poor one at best. If it wasn't for me, he would never have been elected a second time. Got lucky on his first try, while mom was still alive."

"Got it. Tell me about your mother, Jill," Rob asked gently.

"She died when I was ten. Car accident, I was told. I never saw her body. Her casket was covered. He said that was because her face was so badly damaged. Dad was never the same after that. So I took over running his campaigns, handling all his financial dealings. If I hadn't of done that, he would have been broke in a year or so, the idiot."

"I'm sorry. You were close with your mother?" he inquired.

"She was pretty, smart, always told dad what he needed to do, but no, she was mostly cold and distant to me. But I loved her, and she must have loved me too, more than dad ever did. I'm sure of that."

"Makes sense. A mother's bond is a strong one. So did they ever test you for magical ability? I ask because your father is a wizard, you said," he probed a bit.

"Yes, but nothing ever came of it. I don't have a magical bone in my body. That's what dad always said. For once, I think he was right about that. Are we done talking? I'm ready to be killed now."

Monica spoke up, "Not yet, Jill. We haven't solved the big mystery."

"What mystery? I don't know why your spells failed. That's your problem. Maybe you goofed them or something. Can you goof up spells?" Jill retorted.

"You most definitely can mess them up, Jill, but I assure you that neither Crystal nor I did so. We are both quite powerful witches. So is Ericka, Misty, Enya, and the men as well," Monica replied.

"Well, I don't see how you can be one. You are like me, a helpless cripple. You can't even hold your wand like Crystal and the others do. So your spells probably aren't even real."

"Oh, I don't need to use a wand any longer. Yes, I used to have to use a wand, but not since I lost my arms like you did. Graz'zt got me too, but Rob here and Crystal helped me escape along with four others."

Jill yawned. "I feel so tired."

Rob took the hint. After all she'd been through, she was probably way beyond exhausted. He helped her up and walked her to their spare bedroom. He laid her gently on the bed. By the time that he got a soft blanket over her, she was sound asleep. He then hurried to join the others.

"We've got to unravel this mystery," he declared.

"Of course we do," Monica replied.

"I'm going to hit the computer and see what I can learn about her mother and the car accident," Ericka suggested.

"I'll see what I can find out about her mother and father. Perhaps, I can learn something about her schooling," Crystal suggested.

"I'll call her old high school and see what they can tell me about her," Monica suggested some action that she could easily do.

"Well, I've got a bit of her DNA now," Enya commented.

Brad added, "So we're going to do a quick DNA analysis using our new machine."

While Jill slept, the gang "hit the books," researching the past of Jill Anne Parsons. Finally, around three that afternoon, they met to compare notes. Things began to look even more mysterious.

Monica talked first. "Well, I talked with her high school guidance counselor. She's lying about her IQ. The last time it was taken was just before she graduated and along with all the college testing. She had an IQ of around 175! According to her, Jill had a phenomenal ability with math and accounting, along with incredible organizational skills. She was rather obsessed with having her world completely organized and took a lot of ribbing about her compulsion during her four years there. Plus, she spent most of her free time running her father's political campaigns. She's not lying about that."

Ericka explained, "Well, I found out that the car accident sounds a bit fishy. Her car was totaled, but her body wasn't found there. Rather, it was found in the funeral parlor, so badly damaged that it was hardly recognizable. Senator Lew identified the body as his wife's, but based on the mortician's report, that's hardly possible. I believe he used his political powers to squash any real investigation of the accident, if it was even an accident. Frankly, I'd like to see what is buried in that coffin. We could dig it up, run a quick DNA comparison, and see if it really is her mother."

"Well, she's definitely a bright woman," Crystal took up the reporting next. "She has been masterminding every one of his reelection campaigns. Brilliant strategist, handles people extremely masterfully. Her business sense is acute, and she's been filing all his tax returns since she was ten years old. Without her behind the scenes, I don't think he's got a prayer of a chance at reelection this coming summer."

"Well, you can't guess what Brad and I found from her DNA!" Enya gushed, quite uncharacteristically.

"Not in a million years," Brad added, just as enthusiastically.

"Well, what?" Monica replied, taking their bait.

"Not entirely human, that's what!" Brad declared.

"What?" echoed nearly everyone else in unison.

"Right. Well partly she is human," Enya tried to explain, "but she's got some really, really strange genes that are definitely not human. Of course, we have absolutely no idea what that other part comes from though. Sorry about that detail. Still, it's got to be a clue!"

"This just gets weirder by the minute!" Crystal declared. "I wasn't quite finished. I found the senator's birth records and Jill's, but not for his wife. In fact, gang, there are no records whatsoever of his wife prior to their wedding some twenty-one years ago. None. Nada. It's as though she didn't exist before then."

"Well then, we need to take a look at her mother's corpse and see if we can get some usable DNA from it," Enya declared. "Does anyone know how we could get the senator's DNA for comparison with Jill's?"

"Well, I guess we become grave robbers tonight," Monica suggested. "We simply have to have more data, but I don't think we can get permission to dig up her mother's grave, what with her being a senator's wife."

"We can be discrete about it," Enya suggested.

"I'll locate the grave for you," Crystal suggested. She, Brad, and Enya headed off to do just that and make their preparations for the midnight grave robbing adventure.

"It's my turn to try to make supper," Monica said. "I best get on it now or it will be terribly late. Don't worry. If I can't do this, Rob, I'll order out."

"Okay dear. Holler if you need something. I'll keep an eye on Jill. If she wakes, I'll see if I can get her to practice walking some," Rob advised.

Alone in the spacious kitchen, Monica faced cooking supper for the whole group for the first time. Every tiny action required her to find a way to utilize a spell to make it happen. It went pitifully slowly, so much so that she finally broke down. Tears streamed down her cheeks. "Who am I fooling? Jill's so right. We are so helpless, so useless, so dependent on others. I'm kidding myself. Make supper for everyone?"

She poured out her long suppressed grief. Followed by a dozen Dry spells, she finally resumed her pitifully slow dinner preparations. By the time that everyone congregated for supper, she had everything ready, but she herself was exhausted, having cast more spells in those two hours than she had ever cast in her life! That the others complimented her on how good it was didn't register in her mind. She only wanted to eat, get to bed. and forget her life just now. She did just that, excusing herself from the table.

"I think Monica really tired herself out making supper for us. She's sound asleep," Rob pointed out a few minutes later, having helped her undress and tucked her into bed.

"Well, the plan is about to be executed," Crystal whispered. "You keep Jill occupied."

After supper, Rob insisted that Jill walk all over the complex. "Look, it's time that you had a complete tour of this place. It's amazing. You don't often have five stores under one roof."

"But I can't walk," Jill protested.

"What do you call it then?" Rob retorted playfully.

"Sort of stumping along," she replied arrogantly.

"Then, stump along, Miss Jill. Time to see the whole layout of this place." He insisted. She couldn't do much of anything else, since when he gently nudged her forward, it was either take a step or fall down. The latter, she didn't want to do. She had no arms and hands to catch her fall, and she was terrified of falling, but didn't dare tell him that. They spent two hours walking over every inch of the complex. He did notice the magic stores fascinated her. Further, by the time they were finished walking, she was doing much better at it, but he also knew what she was hiding. It was the same thing that Monica hid: a terror of falling and being unable to do anything to prevent it. Wisely, he decided that she'd done enough for one day and helped her into bed. Her knees were throbbing, and he gave them a massage, though she fell asleep at once.

Around midnight, the trio returned, but without any sample. "This only gets weirder and weirder!" Enya exclaimed to the eager listeners, though Monica was sound asleep. "There is no body in that casket! It's an empty casket. No signs of any corpse ever having been in it!"

"I have more research to do in the morning, that's for sure," Crystal added.

"How very strange," Ericka added. She and Tyler headed for their bedroom, quite sleepy and having no idea what this all meant.

Over breakfast the next morning, Monica decided to let Jill in on the big mysteries surrounding the young woman, particularly so when Enya told her what they had found last night.

"Jill, you are one enormous mystery woman. First, your DNA isn't entirely human."

"Of course it is. I'm obviously human, only a helpless, useless cripple now," she retorted. "DNA doesn't lie. You've obviously made some gross error!"

"Let me show you what I found," Enya defended her and Brad's work.

Ten minutes later, Jill said, "Well, this is really strange, isn't it?" Her attitude had subtly changed. She too was now curious.

Crystal explained, "Look, there is absolutely no record of your mother's existence prior to her marriage to Lew. None at all. You can search the Net and databases yourself if you don't believe me."

"Obviously, I can't do that, unless you are blind!" Jill retorted, then softened, "None at all? How can that be?"

"Don't know yet. It gets stranger. Ericka researched your mother's car accident," Crystal explained and had Ericka relate what she'd found. Then, she added, "So last night, we dug up your mother's coffin. Guess what we found inside? Nothing. It was empty. There wasn't the slightest trace of any corpse ever having been in it. Your father buried an empty coffin!"

"This doesn't make any sense at all!" Jill exclaimed. "Why would he do that?" Then, she gasped and answered her own question, "Cause mom's not really dead. Why would he fake her death? Did she run away and abandon me and dad?"

"We can only theorize, Jill," Monica explained, "but it is likely that she left him or went away for some unknown reason. Since your father really did mourn her loss and, as you said, wasn't the same afterwards, she either just up and left or had to leave for some reason. Whatever it was, your father didn't want anyone in the world to know that she was gone. Permanently gone, what with the faked death."

"You think dad killed her and got rid of her body?" Jill asked in horror.

"I highly doubt that, Jill. From everything that you've told us and from what we have learned from the records, your father depended heavily on her, probably loved her deeply. So no, we don't think that he murdered her, nothing like that at all. Rather, we think that she must have run away for some reason. However, even that doesn't make a whole lot of sense, since she was doing very well as his wife and your mother, even if she was somewhat cold to you. I'm inclined to think that someone else forced her to leave your lives forever. Why? We don't have a clue."

"This is so confusing, you know," Jill commented, thinking about all these revelations.

Monica continued, "And then there are those really strange residual magical energies on your back and forehead." She described them to Jill. She immediately wanted to see them for herself. Ericka held up a mirror, but her forehead looked perfectly normal. "Rob, show her, if you can." He did so.

"Weird. What does it mean?" Jill asked, growing even more curious.

"We don't know yet," Rob explained. "You see, every magical spell leaves behind faint traces of the magical energies. The weaker the spell, the fainter and shorter lived are the traces. In this case, the traces are faint, but still there. Hence, it is my opinion that only the strongest of magical spells were involved, whatever those were, because you are twenty years old. This is an exceedingly long time for a magical trace to still be visible."

Monica asked, "You don't remember having any operations, surgery, magical spells cast on you, do you? Perhaps in the last few years? Maybe as a little girl?"

"No, I've been in perfect health. I almost never get a cold even. I'm sure that I would remember someone casting a spell on me. God! I'll never ever forget him burning my arms off or even mutilating my feet!"

"That's really evil, bad magic," Monica hastily added.

"Well, I have an idea that I want to explore," Enya spoke up. "See you all later on. Come on, Brad. We have work to do." She refused to say anything further.

"Well, Jill. We ought to get you practicing your walking some more. We all need to think about all this, don't you agree?" Rob hinted.

"Yeh, sure. Think. This is all so very unreal. Mom's not dead. Why did she leave us? Did dad drive her away?" Jill asked rhetorically and allowed Rob to help her up and get her walking again. For once, her mind was preoccupied.

At noon, while everyone was dining, Enya and Brad finally surfaced from their potion lab. Enya had a very strange look on her face, when the two joined the large group. "Well out with it," Monica exclaimed, curious and impatient with the two. This was wholly out of character for Enya, the shy potion maker.

"Brad and I have identified the foreign DNA in Jill's DNA. In fact, it is a perfect match. Well, not that perfect, I mean, they don't have the same parents and all that, but the species is a match," Enya explained.

Crystal barked, "Enya, if you don't tell us what you found, we're all going to box your ears for a week!"

Enya flushed. "Well, I had a hunch, and we compared Jill's DNA to Nisha's. They match to a ninety percent agreement."

"What? Nisha's?" exclaimed Monica. Crystal dropped her spoon. Ericka's mouth opened, but said nothing.

"Who is Nisha?" Jill asked. All eyes turned towards Jill.

"What?"

Monica cleared her throat. "Ah, there's no easy way to tell you this, Jill, but Nisha is an alu-demon from the Abyss. Her mother was a demon, called a succubus, and her father was a normal human, a wizard. The children of the mating of a succubus and a human are always an alu-demon, sort of half and half. Nisha helped us rescue the four women and stole about sixty million dollars in gems from Graz'zt for the women to use as recompense for what he did to them. She's living with one of the rescued women now."

"I, I'm not human?" Jill asked astounded. Her eyes were wide open, almost in disbelief.

"Half human."

"But I look like everyone else, well I used to. I've always looked like everyone else," Jill protested. "What does a demon look like anyway?"

Crystal summoned one of her volumes and hastily showed Jill a sketch of an alu-demon. Jill stared at the sketch and declared, "Look, it has horns and wings, small ones, on its back. I never had any wings, and I sure don't have any horns like that. Never did. I've got all my school pictures to prove it, excepting I'm never going back to dad's house to get them."

"We believe you, Jill," Rob said gently. "In light of these revelations, I'd like to examine you again, if you don't mind. It won't hurt."

"Yeh sure. This can't be right. I feel normal, like everyone else. I don't have any horns or wings," Jill continued to protest.

Rob focused again and made use of one of his special gifts. Pretending that Jill was a mere object, he zeroed in on her psychic history, particularly highly emotional or painful past events. He skipped over her recent trip to the Abyss and watched as time rushed backwards. Then, he saw something and zeroed in on it. Now he understood. Without breaking his concentration, he sent Monica a message. Within moments, everyone, including Jill, was seeing just what he was seeing.

There lay Jill, a tiny baby girl, in her bassinet. Tiny horns were unmistakable as were the carefully folded, tiny wings. Her mother was looking down at her, frowning. Her father was reading a scroll over her. Magical energies flashed. When the bright light faded, there lay Jill in her bassinet, but her horns and wings were gone. Her mother was crying, though. Rob ended his concentration and returned to the present.

Jill began crying. Monica exclaimed, "Oh my god! He used a Wish spell on her to hide them!" She wanted to put her arms comfortingly around Jill, but couldn't. Crystal did so instead. "Your father loved you so much that he spent a fortune to have you look like a normal human being."

"So why did he do that? A demon no less? Why has he abandoned me now? The bastard," Jill's grief began to rise to anger. "So this makes me one of those despicable demons." Her hostility was plainly obvious. "So now you really do have to kill me and not just to put me out of my misery. Do it. I don't care anymore. I'm some kind of hideous freak and a helpless one at that!"

They all knew better than to try to reason with someone who was in anger or worse. Wisely, they allowed her to vent. "Well, I am a freak, aren't I? A helpless, useless freak! But I've never done bad things in my life! I've tried to help everyone I've met. This isn't fair! Darn it, this isn't fair! I've been a good person, mostly. I'm not an evil monster, even though I am by birth I suppose. Maybe that's why that demon prince rejected me because I'm not evil like he is. My babies might be good babies. I'll show him! I'll show dad! Heck, I'll show everyone! I'm not some evil, wicked, hateful demon, even if I am one. You can't make me evil. No way. So there, mom, dad, and demons everywhere—you're never going to make me evil, not ever. Okay, Monica. Now I am ready for you all to slay me, since I am a demon, and demons have to be slain. Just know that I'm not evil. Never have been; never will be. Put that on my headstone, will you? Demon born, but never ever was evil. Right, here lies Jill Anne Parsons, demon born, but never evil. That's a good epitaph, don't you think?"

Monica answered, "Yes, Jill, that is a good one. We'll see that it's done, but not until you have grown old and shown the world your goodness. Not every demon is wicked, cruel, and evil. Nisha certainly isn't that. So you have company. You aren't alone, and you owe it to yourself to show everyone your goodness. We'll back you all the way."

"Really? You'll back me up? You see that I'm really a good person, not a wicked demon? Nisha is like me?" Jill asked, finally becoming curious.

"You bet. She still has her horns and wings, but she is forced to keep them hidden while she's here in our world. Nisha is a very loving, caring young woman. I think you will like her. However, she's never been to our world, and she's still learning about nearly everything."

"Okay. I'll go along with this, but only under one condition," Jill said determinedly.

"What's that?" Monica asked.

"That if I ever do some evil, wicked thing, that you will kill me right away."

"That I can agree with, Jill. Promise."

Rob spoke up next, "You know, Jill, with your incredible intelligence and your unique body, you really ought to be able to learn a number of magic spells. Nisha does her spells without a wand. In fact, she's never held a wand in her life. So you should be able to cast some too."

"Really? Is that possible?"

"I believe so. I give you my word that Monica and I will work with you all the way and see if we can't get you fully trained to the maximum of your potential. How's that?" Rob offered.

"That would be fabulous, if it's possible. But I just love organizing things and handling finances, accounting, doing taxes, that sort of thing," Jill added.

Monica made a suggestion. "Jill, we need someone to do all that for our new businesses here. What say we hire you to do all our organization, financial accounting, and yearly taxes, and even be our receptionist? That way, you would also be earning your keep around here, doing the things that we just hate to do and keep on messing up. Will you lend us your assistance?"

"Sure. It's what I love to do, Monica. Wait, I'm still helpless. How can I do any of these things?"

"We will find a way. There is always voice activated

programs for the computer," Monica suggested.

"Right! All those records are on the computer anyway. That will work," Jill replied, smiling broadly for the first time. "But wait a minute. I still can't do anything else for myself."

"Don't worry about that. We will figure something out," Monica replied. "We have for me, but we will just have to see. Can't promise you anything, but we will all do our very best. All we ask is for you to do your best. Okay?"

"Sure, okay. I really do want to do more accounting things and organization. A messy place is a disorganized place, and sometimes the disorganized can't even find something in their mess," Jill explained.

"Great. Tomorrow, we'll get you your own powerful computer and all the software you are going to need, but you'll have to tell us what programs you want, beside the voice activation one. We've only been open for business a few months and have kept all the receipts. I'm afraid it is a mountain of confusion right now," Monica explained.

Jill chuckled. "I expect so. Very few people are really organized, financially I mean. Well, I will get you all squared away, but I can't say how soon. I really am helpless, but you can see that. Anyway, at least I know what to do."

Enya broke in, "Hey, welcome aboard, Jill. It is going to be great having a receptionist out there. We all keep being interrupted from our work when we have to stop and go see who's there and all that. That's bad news when we are brewing another batch of potions."

"Same with our wand making, Jill. We lose our focus when we have to stop and see who has come and what they want. Having a receptionist out front is going to be fabulous. Thanks," Misty added her approval as well.

Ericka suggested, "Monica, we should install some kind of intercom system so Jill here can call us when she needs us or we have a customer. Indeed, we should have hired someone months ago. I hate being interrupted too."

Crystal spoke up, "Jill, tomorrow we are going to have to get you a whole new wardrobe. You see, Ericka, Monica, and I always want to look our very best, elegant, refined. . ."

"Impressive," Enya interrupted her.

"Darn sexy," Misty joked.

"Well, yes. Being elegantly dressed only adds to our powers, our charms, and our mystique," Crystal tried to pick up her original thought. "Yes, we three almost always dress like we are now, unless we are off to a battle or something. Now Enya and Misty are always working in their labs so they wear something more appropriate."

"We only dress up when the occasion is right," Enya corrected her, grinning. "Besides, we've already snatched our men."

"Oh low blow!" Ericka teased the shorter woman. "Tyler and I are doing just fine." They all laughed.

"That reminds me, Jill. Do you have a boyfriend or anyone else that we should let know where you are now staying and working?" Monica asked.

"Hardly. No, I've been focused on dad's reelection campaign. No time for such things. It's just me, but now it is always going to be just me. What man would even date me like this?" She could only shrug her empty shoulders, and Monica knew precisely what she meant.

Rob interjected, "Look ladies, if she's going to be your receptionist, we had best get her far more nimble on her feet. So I'm confiscating Jill for a while. Up you go, practice, practice, practice."

"But it's so hard, so scary," she whispered.

He whispered back, "I know. I've been through all this with Monica too. Trust me. I won't let you fall and with enough practice, you will be walking as well as Monica. She's still terrified of stairs."

"Oh! She is too? I am too, very terrified. I keep trying to use my arms, and they aren't there."

"I know. Even that will pass in time. You just have to get used to how you are now, and you'll do just fine. Come on. Let's walk some. Your legs will quickly get stronger. Monica's did."

"Really? Okay, but it's still terrifying, Rob. I've never been helpless in my life before and I hate it! I hate being completely helpless like this, unable to do anything for myself."

"That's a good sign, Jill. No one should have to just sit around doing nothing and letting others do everything for them. It's not mentally healthy."

"Well, that demon prince fellow certainly knew how to make a woman completely helpless and totally dependent. I never realized how much I depended on my hands and arms before, let alone my feet. Maybe if I can learn a bit of magic, that will help. Do you think so?"

"It has helped Monica a good deal, but just between you and me, she's not out of the woods yet. I think she needs a good cry and to get over her fear of stairs. That's just my opinion."

"How come you married her? I mean since she's helpless like me."

"I married a brilliant woman, and I wasn't looking at her physical limitations. She's a powerhouse."

"She is very attractive. Say, would a Full Wish spell like dad used on me be able to give me my arms back and fix up my feet?"

Rob sighed. "To be honest with you, none of us know the answer to that one. What Prince Graz'zt did to your bodies was extremely powerful magic. Certainly, the usual regrow potions won't. However, what other powerful magical spells and such might work, we just don't know yet. Full Wish spells cost a fortune. Plus the caster ages a year with each Full Wish. Since we don't know if that will even work properly, given what the demon prince did to your bodies, Monica isn't about just to try it and cause someone to age a year without knowing that it will work correctly, especially if we can find some other way to do it. We just need time to figure it all out. Such magic is extremely powerful, known only to a few."

"Okay. Then, I best adapt, hadn't I?"

Rob smiled, "That would be a wise move, Jill."

"But what if I can't do things for myself with magic like Monica does? What if I am still as helpless as I am now?" she asked.

"Well, I wouldn't worry about that, Jill. There are ten of us who can take turns helping you with what you need, though I don't expect you want us fellows helping you in the bathroom."

She giggled. "Well not really. Still, Rob, I am terrified of living like this. I'm going to have to have someone always around to help me, like a permanent babysitter. What if I have to open a door and no one is around? What if I have to use the bathroom and no one is here? What if I have to go during the night? I can't even walk without these weird boots. Really, Rob, I'm petrified of living like this."

Sighing, Rob answered, "I know. All of you victims are in the same boat. I know Monica has similar fears, but I've not yet been able to get her to admit them. She puts up a brave face, but I know that she's hurting inside. It's perfectly all right to feel terrified and petrified of having to live like this. The important thing is that you are alive and otherwise healthy. We all want to make this work out for you and for Monica. Just keep doing your best and things will take care of themselves. We all just need time."

Jill changed the topic. "So these alu-demons—they are sort of immune to magical spells?"

"Yes. Just how much we aren't quite sure. Tomorrow, Nisha is coming over at suppertime to visit you and us. We can find out more then, but we want you dressed nice. Monica won't settle for anything less than the best outfits for you. Don't worry about money. She's loaded."

"My legs are really getting sore and tired, especially my knees."

"We'll stop for now. You are doing great, Jill. You are one brave young woman."

"But it looks as if I'm not a woman, am I? I'm a demon or a half-demon anyway."

"Hey, you are every inch a woman. No one can tell you apart from any other human, so don't even think such thoughts, Jill."

"Okay. I always thought of myself as a woman, but. . ."

"No but's about it. I think that's why your dad bought that Full Wish spell so that you would be a normal human woman."

"But I'm not, not really, am I?"

"In every way that counts, you are, Jill. In every way."

She flushed, picking up what he meant.

The next morning, Monica, assisted by Ericka who also was quite blonde with blue eyes, helped Jill pick out a dozen, appropriate, new outfits, all but two of which were elegant enough to wear to any fancy ball or party. She also had a jeans outfit and a simple day dress. Once their large order was completed, Ericka volunteered to go pick them up. Again, Monica felt badly that she no longer could do this simple thing either, but she bit her lip and didn't say anything.

While they were waiting for the new clothes and boots to arrive, Rob again took Jill for a long walk. Meanwhile, Monica used her spells to run her computer, picking out a new and powerful one for Jill, along with the voice-activated software. Then, she carefully found and ordered the six special accounting programs that Jill had said that she would need. She requested overnight delivery on these. As she prepared to hunt down a fancy phone-intercom system for their entire complex along with a fancy receptionists desk, Ericka arrived. Once more, Monica felt horrible. All this time, she'd only gotten a small part of her work done. Pathetic. But she didn't say anything and joined Ericka who absconded with Jill into Jill's new bedroom, their guest room. Monica made a note to order a new guest bedroom suite.

An hour later, Ericka assisted Jill in standing up gracefully and had her look at herself in the full-length mirror. "My god! I look like a fashion model or something! I've never had such expensive clothes. I do look good, don't I?"

"Like a sexy goddess, Jill," Ericka pointed out. "The blues match your eyes really well. You are a knock-out."

"Well, I'm not as pretty as you or Crystal. After all, you said you were both models for Teen Fashion a while back. But still, I do look good, don't I? If only. . ." She didn't finish her sentence.

"I know, dear, I know. We all wish that too," Ericka sympathized with her. "Still, you look smashing and that's what counts around here. See, now there are four of us who always look smashing. Maybe we can get Enya and Misty to start dressing in style too." The three chuckled.

Rob came to check on them. "Wow, Jill. You look

fabulous!" She blushed a little. "Okay, if you two are done with her, I need to get her walking. Remember what I always told you and Monica, no pain, no gain." With his steadying arm around Jill's waist, he ushered her out for another long walk, strengthening her muscles and getting her more comfortable with her situation. Monica returned to her computer to figure out the rest of her orders.

As supper approached, Rob pointed out to Jill that she'd walked twice as far today as yesterday. That brought a smile to her face. She was still petrified and scared, but doing better. Right on time, Lilly and Nisha arrived for dinner and to spend the evening with Jill and the others.

"Oh Jill, I'm so pleased to meet you! Now there are two of us here. I don't feel so alone! I hope we can become good friends. I've been looking after Lilly here and the others like you and Monica, only now thanks to Monica, they really don't need my help anymore. I'd love to help you, if you need me," Nisha bubbled with excitement.

Suddenly, Monica realized the situation that Nisha was facing. She was wholly alone, an alien if the truth be told, in an unfamiliar world. Now suddenly, here was another of her kind, the only other alu-demon that anyone knew of, and one who desperately needed the assistance that she'd been giving tirelessly to the other four women. The loneliness, the emptiness that Nisha must be feeling struck her hard. Monica said, "Nisha, we certainly could use your help around here, Jill and I. Would you be very much opposed to coming and living with us, that is, if Lilly is okay with that?"

Lilly spoke up, "I'm perfectly fine with that. I'm doing perfectly well. No problems at all, but I do keep your card on me at all times, just in case I run into one of those spells that undoes the magic. What do you think, Nisha?"

"Oh yes, very much so, Monica. Indeed, I would. I can help Jill lots. Well, you know that already. Lilly really doesn't need me anymore, thanks to your magic. Neither do the other three. They've all gone back to their own homes—I mean apartments. I hope I have the right words. It's all still pretty strange to me. Lilly has shown me around quite a lot. We visited the zoo today or we'd have come sooner," Nisha replied.

"Excellent, Nisha. We'll work out the details after supper. Enya has dinner ready for us. Come, this way," Monica indicated. Once in the dining room, Nisha insisted on sitting beside Jill and feeding her, just as she'd done for the other four and Monica. Monica noted that Nisha was very observant and correctly judged when Jill needed anything, a perfect solution for now, she thought.

After the dinner was finished, Jill, Nisha, Monica, and Rob met in private, while the others entertained Lilly, showing her around their stores and workshops. Monica began by explaining what they had learned about Jill's past, along with how they had discovered the truth of it all.

"So this is what you actually look like?" Nisha asked. "It must be so good for you not to have to always go around putting up an illusion for everyone to see."

"I'm not sure what you mean, Nisha," Jill replied.

"I don't really look like what all of you are seeing as me right now. It is an illusion, a change of our body's shape, one that I have to remember to keep up always. Here, I'll show you." Nisha dropped her illusion, and Jill stared at her, seeing an alu-demon for the first time, other than a sketch.

"You look the same except for . . ."

"I know—the horns and little wings. It's easier to keep up the illusion if I'm only changing it a little bit," Nisha explained. "It must be so wonderful for you not ever to have to worry about hiding them. But don't you know how to make illusions?"

"No, not at all. I don't know any magic. None at all."

"Oh! But," Nisha looked confused, "all we alu-demons can do a few magic spells. Changing our shape a little is one. We can charm a person or give them a suggestion, even hear their thoughts, if we want to."

Jill chuckled, "I've been doing that all my life, only it wasn't magic, I don't think."

"You ought to be able to use a Magical Door too," Nisha added. "Now if one of us is really smart, really intelligent, we can learn to cast many spells, though nowhere near as many as Monica can. Unfortunately, I'm not that bright. I only learned

278

a few other spells, like sending a Message."

Monica spoke up. "Jill is really very intelligent, so I hope that she will be able to learn some magic spells that she can use to help her do things for herself, like I can. I've promised to help her learn them. Nisha, if you don't mind talking about it, Jill and I really do need to know what other special abilities she is supposed to have. We're totally ignorant of her abilities and potential weaknesses."

"Oh I don't mind. Jill really should know them. The one thing that makes me feel safe here in your world is that I, and you too, Jill—we can't really be harmed by your weapons, not unless they are magically enchanted. Have you noticed, Jill, that you can't even cut your finger with a kitchen knife?"

Jill's face lit up. "Yes! I've noticed that. I always thought that was because I had tough skin or something, maybe a dull knife. So that's why I never really worried about running into trouble."

Nisha smiled, "Right. I don't think that they can harm us if they hit us over our heads with one of their hammer things that they use to pound nails into a wall." She then lowered her voice, "But there is one thing that we can do that I think is evil, so I've never done it before."

"What's that? I don't want to accidentally do it," Jill asked, growing concerned.

"If we get hurt, we can heal ourselves by touching another human and trading some of our injuries with them. We get cured a bit, and they get wounded a bit. I've never, ever done that. Don't want to. I think that's really not a good thing to do," Nisha explained.

Jill shuddered. "I should think not. I promise never to do that either! I hope there isn't any more that I have to worry about."

"Nope, that's all."

"What about your resistance to magical spells?" Monica asked.

"Oh, that varies from person to person," Nisha answered. "I think I'm about average, but the really smart alu-demons often have a very high resistance to them. I once knew one who almost rivaled Prince Graz'zt in her ability to resist magical spells. Of course, he didn't like that and killed her. Anyway, even if we are affected by magic, if it is a spell that is freezing, noxious gas, fire, or even electrical based, it doesn't harm us half as much as it should hurt us. Of course, if it's a magical missile or poison or acid, then we get hurt just as bad."

"Well, this is really good to know," Monica replied. "I won't have to worry about Jill getting hurt easily."

"Oh wow! I almost forgot some spells!" Nisha added. "Thinking of spells, I forgot what all demons of nearly every kind can do. We can teleport. We can make it dark and so hide. We can see the infrared heat of warm bodies. Also, we can Gate in others, but I don't want to bring evil demons from the Abyss here, though, nor do I ever want to go back there. It's wholly evil! And so ugly too,"

"But I can't do any of those things," Jill protested. "I must be the dumbest alu-demon ever. I hope I'm not disgracing you, Nisha, with my complete ignorance."

"Heavens no, Jill. You only found out what you are. How could you know these things, if your mother didn't tell you and help you to learn to do them? She must not have been very good to you if she didn't do these things for you."

Jill bit her lip. "Maybe dad wouldn't let her, especially if he wanted me to pass as a human."

Nisha nodded her head. "That would make good sense, Jill. If you did these things, someone might figure it out. You have been safer not knowing, I think, but now maybe Monica can teach you what you should already know."

"I promise I will do my best for her, Nisha," Monica said again. "Say, we do need a cook around here, to fix our breakfasts, lunches, and dinners. Have you learned how to cook our food yet?"

"Only a little. Lilly got me a recipe book. If I follow it, she says I can't go wrong. I remember all those dishes that the women were asking for when we were in the Cambion Production Center. Now I know what some of them are. I can learn."

"Superb, Nisha. You can be our cook and Jill's aide when she needs something. This is going to work out very well for all of us," Monica declared. They chatted a bit more and then joined the others.

That night after Rob fell asleep, Monica was still awake. She couldn't get over how blind she'd been about Nisha's situation and how she'd managed to salvage two lives. However, she also realized that she was also taking the easy way out with the cooking. Tears trickled down her face as she recognized what she'd done. *I can't really cook much at all anymore. I'm just too darn helpless in the kitchen. In spite of everything, I really am pretty much helpless—better off than Jill is right now, but not by very much. I've been kidding myself. I really am quite helpless.* Crying herself to sleep didn't help matters. Nothing would. That was her last thought before she fell into an ill sleep.

Chapter 17—Wintertime

The next week was rather hectic around the PIWIP complex. Movers brought the heavier furniture, and rooms had to be rearranged. A receptionist area was setup in their foyer, along with a fancy intercom system that Jill could activate by voice commands. Her new computer was positioned here as well, and it took some time to get it all setup and working properly. Monica again found herself useless at doing it, though she successfully kept from crying about it. Rob was a godsend with the computer and intercom system, for which she was grateful.

All that week, the five women took turns teaching Nisha how to use their kitchen appliances and how to cook various dishes that they frequently ate. Plus, Ericka insisted that Nisha also have many elegant gowns and outfits, similar to those of herself and Jill. Even with the hectic days, someone always took the time to walk Jill around for hours it seemed. By the end of the week, her legs and knees had definitely become stronger. More importantly, Jill felt a bit more confident in getting around on her own, though she was still terrified of the stairs. Even Monica toyed with the idea of putting in an elevator system, but decided not to—that would be too much like giving in to her and Jill's physical limitations. She wasn't ready to give up and be a victim totally. Not yet anyway.

After that first chaotic week, things settled down into a semblance of normalcy. In the mornings, Monica worked with Jill on her spell casting. In the afternoon, Jill began organizing their company financial records and handling their accounting. In the evenings, both Monica and Jill spent walking around the complex, building up the strength in their legs and especially their knees, along with their sense of balance.

Spell casting was Monica's highlight of the day. Magic was the love of her life, as it had always been, though she really enjoyed helping others learn, which she had done for her four friends during their six years of magic school. With Jill, she found that it was just as Nisha had suggested. Because of Jill's high IQ and intelligence, she began picking up the beginning spells rather rapidly, after she finally got the hang of it on the useful, helpful Grade 0 spells. She was able to learn most all the Grade 1 and 2 spells, over half of the Grade 3 spells. Beginning with Grade 4 spells, her batting average began dropping. Monica discovered that Jill had reached her peak skills at Grade 6, of which she learned to cast only five, one of which was Disintegrate. All Grade 7 spells and above were beyond her grasp, and she refused to even try to learn the power Gate spell. This process occupied their mornings until nearly springtime.

Almost from the first afternoon session, Monica saw the Jill was going to be an invaluable asset. The woman began by organizing their financial accounting records. Using a host of spells, Monica gathered up everyone's monster pile of receipts and sales and brought them to Jill's new desk in reception. What should have been a couple minute's chore frustrated her immensely. She had to levitate and move each one, collecting them into a box for each sub-business. Worse, they'd all just made piles of these in whatever room they happened to be in when they'd dealt with that bill or sales receipt. Hence, she had to bring all five boxes to each room in the complex. Plus, she had to go up and down the stairs numerous times. That she and her friends kept remembering where they'd put some other ones, making her have to return to a room to find them, didn't help.

By the end of the day, she was an emotional wreck, but kept it nicely suppressed, putting on a brave face. She felt she had to, because there was Jill sitting at her new computer on her reception desk trying to organize and enter the data on all these papers. The immense frustration emanating from Jill as she struggled somehow to do this, which she used to be able to do extremely rapidly, was acutely felt by Monica. She'd already given up trying to use spells and was leaning over, grabbing them with her mouth, placing them where she could read them, and then vocally entering the data. Once done, she repeated the process on that one, placing it into specifically designated piles, but that meant standing up and walking over to the pile, before dropping it into the box.

In spite of all the physical difficulties, Monica could already see just how valuable the computerized records were going to be in a few months, come income tax time. Certainly, this job was critically needed, if their businesses were going to be efficiently run. By the end of the year, Jill had all the accounting finished. All their records were perfectly organized. Jill could rapidly locate any item. Further, Jill had established new financial policies that everyone now had to follow. She gave each a pair of wire baskets for their various rooms. Whenever they received or paid a bill, it was put in the bottom basket. Whenever they made a sale, the company's copy was placed in the top basket. Once each day, Jill visited over twenty of these boxes, collecting the documents, taking them to her desk. After she entered the data, she then stored them in their appropriate location.

By January, Monica had replaced all the boxes with some fancy metal filing drawers. However, because Jill would be the one accessing them, she had the various filing cabinets sitting on a shelf raised about two feet from the floor. That way, Jill could open them, lean over and retrieve or place a document into its proper folder. In fact, when the filing cabinets first arrived and as Jill began the lengthy process of setting them up and moving the boxes of records into their proper folders, she complained, "Monica, this whole process shouldn't take me but one afternoon at the very most. Now it's going to take me days and days! It's so horrible trying to live like this. Sometimes, I just can't take it anymore." Tears trickled down Jill's cheeks. So Monica dove in and spent several afternoons helping her do the filing. She also felt the same up welling of grief over how hard this was to do, and it was such an idiotically simple thing to do.

Yet, Jill's organizational skills paid off. She had their taxes and sales taxes done and sent in way early. And after that, the financial record keeping of their various enterprises ran like a well-oiled clock. Jill was worth every penny of her very nice salary. So much so, that after Monica struggled to get her own personal taxes done, she gave up and brought Jill into her own rather enormous financial portfolio, allowing her to "bring order" to it as well.

"Incredible, Monica! I had no idea that you have so much. This will take some work, but sure, I can do it. Look, this figure here ought to be over there on Line 14a. That will save you a bundle in taxes."

"Thanks. I'm good at making the right acquisition at the right time for the right price, just not on dealing with these impossible forms," Monica chuckled. Inwardly, she again realized that part of her problem with it was her physical limitations. It took forever to accomplish some little task, and she'd been simply not doing them because of that. Now she had shuffled that very same task over to Jill, who faced the same limitations. She felt rather guilty about doing that.

During the early evenings, she and Jill did their walking exercises together. As long as they were not in any hurry, they could navigate the long hallways with relative ease. Even though both women could also cast Gentle Fall in a hurry when they began to take a tumble, that didn't ease their fears when it came to the stairs. "I keep reaching out with my arms and hands!" Jill confessed. "My stomach keeps knotting every time I do that. A reminder, I think."

"Hey, me too. I still am terrified of stairs. I know it's irrational. We both can Gentle Fall if we tumble, but it's such a terrible feeling, losing your balance and falling. Embarrassing even," Monica admitted to Jill.

"I didn't know. I thought that you had it all down. I guess I don't feel so badly about being so scared of the stairs now," Jill said greatly relieved.

"No, it's not just you. I'm the same way. It's worse trying to walk on rough ground or gravel. Walking on the slippery snow is quite bad. A slight misstep and down you go before you even know it. But we're going to have to face it now. It's snowing outside, and as cold as it is, it's not going to melt soon."

At that same time, Enya popped her head around the corner, "Hey Monica, Jill. It's snowing out. We're all going outside to mess around in it. Join us. It'll be fun. Nisha has never seen snow before."

"We'll get out cloaks on and be out in a bit," Monica said bravely. She suddenly remembered all the times that the five of them had gone outside in the new fallen snow and had some winter fun, even a snowball fight once with some Black Hall boys. Newly felt pangs of loss swept over her, but she headed for her room to don her heavy winter cloak. Both she and Jill now had easy to fasten cloaks instead of coats whose arms caused no end of troubles for them.

By the time the two reached the front doors, everyone else had been playing around in the snow for half an hour. "I don't think I can do this," Jill whispered nervously as she tried to take her first few steps onto the snow covering the driveway. As if in answer, both women suddenly slipped and went down with a thud. Neither even had time to cast their Gentle Fall spell. Humiliated again, Monica cast Levitate on herself and then on Jill, who was fighting to keep from crying again.

"Sorry. We forgot about you two," Rob said, coming up to the two and putting an arm around each of them, holding them securely, as they continued to slip around some as they walked over the rough, snow-covered ground to the others who were working on making a tall snowman. As long as he didn't let go of them, they were able to navigate the trampled path and enjoyed watching the antics of the others who were letting off steam and having fun. That she could no longer join them felt like an enormously heavy weight on her shoulders now, one that she could never lift off. Biting her lip, that night, Monica decided to do some more research into possible cures for herself and Jill.

Before long, the Christmas holidays were upon them. Jill had always liked to decorate for the occasion. Hence, Monica donated some funds for her to spend to fancy up the reception area for the holidays. Using her voice-activated computer, Jill ordered a small tree, decorations galore, and many lights. She spent some of her afternoons decorating the area. When she was finished and having cast hundreds of spells to get the job done to her perfectionist point of view, she received accolades from everyone else.

"Absolutely splendid job, Jill. It's beautiful!" exclaimed Ericka when she saw the final look. "We should decorate for every holiday." The praises she received meant a lot to Jill, who had to struggle to accomplish what ordinarily would have been a simple job. In the end, this was one of the happier Christmas holidays that the large group had experienced to date. Further, Enya and Misty were definitely showing their pregnancies now. Enya was due in June, while Misty wasn't due until July.

Based on her dismal mental state during November and December, Monica decided to do some rather desperate research experiments to find a cure for herself and Jill. She knew the Clone spell and decided to risk giving it a try in her own private workshop. It helped that Rob was now off on official business in both LA and in Miami, giving her more private time than before.

She carefully extracted some of her DNA and then spent two long afternoons making her extensive preparations. On the third afternoon, she cast a Hold spell on the door to her workshop and a Silence spell so that she couldn't be overheard or interrupted during the extensive casting. Then, she took a deep breath, calmed her nerves, and began the very long chant, just as she had learned in her sixth year at the St. Louis School of Magic. When she finished, magical energies flashed. There on the carefully prepared cot lay the slowly evolving duplicate of her. While the new body would take about two months to develop fully, she could see at once that this was going to be a fruitless exercise. Hastily, she cast another spell that moved the body just above the sun, where it was instantly destroyed. A few Clean spells later and the experiment was finished. Using more spells and painstakingly slowly, she jotted relevant notes in her logbook and cancelled the spells on her workshop door. With a heavy heart, she headed down to the kitchen to have a cup of hot tea.

As slow and clumsy as she now was, Monica graciously allowed Nisha to fix it for her. Soon a steaming mug of Earl Grey was sitting in front of her with her usual straw pointing up at her. Wisely, Nisha allowed her the private time. Once more, Monica fought back tears. Not even a Clone spell would salvage her life or Jill's for that matter.

There remained two further avenues for her to explore. She refused to go down the road of finding and using a Full Wish spell. No way would she force another to age an entire year at her or Jill's expense. As Dominus, she'd been there, done that. No, that road lead to disaster. He'd been forty when he was assassinated, but his body was over fifty and no longer truly dexterous or fit. No, that she would never again inflict on anyone.

Rather, there was a very obscure necromancy based potential cure, albeit extraordinarily expensive. A ring of regeneration. Surfing MAG-Google, she found only one such ring for sale. The seller wanted forty million dollars for it. However, before wiping out nearly half of her net worth, Monica needed to be certain that the ring would work, assuming it could somehow be forced onto one of her fused toes.

After more research into the necromancy magic that lay behind the construction of such a ring, she did discover that the ring would expand or contract to fit the finger or toe on which it was being placed. That solved one problem, but would it actually restore their feet and arms? Monica needed answers and found almost no data available on the Net, save one small tidbit. In Prague, a Professor Kazimir Jakub was reputedly the leading expert on such magic. Hastily, she fired off a MAG-email to the professor, asking if she could visit him and discuss the necromancy regeneration magic. His address was on Slovenska, one block north of Fransouska. She looked it up on the Net and saw that it was an old apartment building. Now she waited for his reply, noting the significant time difference between there and St. Louis.

The next day, she had her invitation to visit him. Rob was still off in LA, so she decided to make the trip herself, even though it would be challenging for her. She told Crystal where she was going and refused her offer to tag along. "Are you sure, love?" Crystal asked.

"Yes. I have to be independent sometime. See you in a while." Monica tried to sound confident, but she was far from it. She'd never been to Prague, and now she was going there alone and darn near helpless. Besides, it was winter, and they likely had snow too. Nevertheless, she dressed warmly and wore her fancy red satin gown. She'd go looking her very best.

She focused and cast her Teleport spell, arriving

precisely at the correct address. She immediately cast her Understand Languages spell and carefully made her way to the entrance door. Snow and packed snow covered the sidewalks and streets, and she was thankful that she didn't have to attempt to navigate beyond the few feet to the door. The building was old, grey stone with old-world, wooden doors. Picturesque, quaint, but not extremely modern. After casting an Open spell, she stepped inside and looked for directions.

His apartment was in the basement. More stairs, she thought, pushing down a sudden rise in panic. Very carefully, she descended the many steps to the basement hall. Here, her nose was greeted with strange odors, one of which was that of musty books. The other odors—she decided that she didn't want to recognize them. Finding the door was easy. She used another spell to push their doorbell and waited, anticipation rising.

A young man with blonde hair, bowl cut, and sky blue eyes opened the door. He had the start of a beard. Either that or he hadn't shaved in a few days. His face was roundish. A playful smile announced his attitude towards life. "Ah, she's here. Come on in. You must be the Monica Nicole that dad told us about. Come in; take off your cloak. Haven't seen many cloaks around, but then that must be the fashion in the States. Oh, I'm Milos, Milos Jakub."

As she took a step inside, an identical young man popped into view. "I say, Milos, you are blocking our guest from the States. Hi, I'm Jiri Jakub. Come on it. Let me take your cloak for you. Where's your manners, Milos. Dad's in his study, where he always is. You know the studious types. Oh god!" He'd just taken off her cloak and saw her physical form. Both brother's eyes moved upwards from her boots to her empty shoulders, but taking in her black patent knee high ballet boots, traces of her black nylons, her bright red satin, form fitting gown with a wide walking slit, and her very long black hair that she'd just jiggled back into place down her back after he'd removed her cloak.

Both young men were staring at her. "Well, boys, do I look sexy enough for you?" Monica decided to go with a joking tease to help hide her own embarrassment.

Milos swallowed. "You look, well incredible. What happened to you? Aren't those boots impossible to walk in?"

"Come on. We best get you to dad quick so you can sit down. We didn't know," Jiri hastily said.

"Lead on, boys," Monica replied, flashing them a wink and grin.

"You need a supporting hand or something?" Jiri asked, suddenly very sympathetically. "Sorry about sort of joking around there."

"No, I'm fine. I enjoyed your jesting, but I do need to see the professor," she replied. They led her through their living room, filled with old sofa chairs and couches that had seen a good deal of use. Some were rather threadbare. However, she could tell that this was definitely a bachelor's pad. No woman would have allowed the incredible messes that lay scattered about the room: old newspapers, soda cans, and even a couple of pizza boxes, complete with crumbs.

"Dad, she's here," Milos called out to his father in the study. As she entered, the odor of old books assaulted her nose, in a rather comforting way, reminding her of Crystal. Three of the walls were lined with bookshelves, all overflowing with books of all possible shapes and sizes, many with ancient leather bindings. These were the ones giving off the distinctive odor, she noted.

Professor Kazimir Jakub was in his sixties, with thinning blonde hair in dire need of a trim. He had the same light blue eyes as his boys. He was rather thin and his back seemed to have a permanent bend in it, probably from having spent a lifetime bent over his books. He wore wire-rimmed glasses with octagonal shaped lenses perched on his lower nose. He looked up over them at Monica and then did a double take. "Please, have a seat. Boys, help her please."

"No need," Monica replied, hastily casting a Move Object spell and seating herself.

The boys pulled up chairs too, fully intent upon hearing what she wanted to discuss with the professor. He in turn looked at Monica and asked, "Did you want to meet in private with me?" He gave his boys a stare.

"I expect that they will find a way to listen in if we expel them," Monica teased the two lads. "I sure would if I were in their shoes. It probably isn't every day that you get someone like me dropping by for a visit. Fellows, I'm married, so forget any other ideas you might be having." She knew that she'd hit the mark. Both flushed slightly.

"We'll stay, if that's okay with you. You might need a hand with something," Jiri replied.

"So you wanted to see me about a Ring of Regeneration, if I remember your email," Professor Kazimir began. "I can now see why you are so interested in them."

"Let me explain what happened to me and to a number of other women that I and my associates have rescued from the Abyss," Monica began. She spent a half hour outlining what had happened with the demons and Graz'zt, including the two alu-demons. After all, she also wanted to know if these rings would work on Jill as well. She left nothing major out. After all, if the professor was the world's expert on this dark magic, she wanted him to have the full data at hand. She couldn't afford any goofs.

When she finished up, the professor began. "This is very critical information that you've told us. It is aligning with some recent happenings here in Prague as well. Pieces are, as you say, falling into place. But that's not why you are here. Rings of Regeneration. Perhaps they are the most powerful of all necromancy magic. Such knowledge and skill is known only to a very, very few practitioners down through the ages. The reason that they are so expensive today is that there is no one alive who now possesses the knowledge of how to cast that spell, let alone infuse it into a ring."

"There hasn't been one for quite some time. Centuries ago, the Druids possessed such skills and most of the currently existing Rings of Regeneration were made by them. The last known maker of such rings here on Earth was Merlin. You know, of Arthurian legends, that Merlin. He was known to have made one for each knight of Arthur's roundtable and for Arthur as well."

"I see, so such magic is impossibly rare in today's world," she concluded.

"Precisely so. Such rings are carefully hoarded by their

possessors, often kept in total secrecy. Understandably so. They are extraordinarily valuable. We are dealing with nearly godlike power here. Now, let's be specific. Obviously, you wish to find one so that you can restore your arms and feet."

"And those of my alu-demon friend along with four other normal women. Perhaps others, if a way can be found to rescue them from the clutches of Graz'zt in the Abyss," Monica added.

Professor Kazimir sighed. The excited looks on his boys' faces dropped. "Alas, in this particular case, your arms were destroyed by a very special spell. I can point you to the spell that was used. The important point is that the demon prince used an Incinerate spell on them. No currently existing Ring of Regeneration can restore lost appendages that have been so destroyed by the fires of Incinerate. I am so sorry to have to tell you this. Obviously, it is very bad news for you and your friends, Monica."

He continued, "As far as the restoration of your fused feet, these rings will also be of no use, but there is the possibility that if you cut your feet off and then used the ring, it might regenerate normal feet. However, if you cut off your feet, then there will be no finger or toe on which to place the ring. Hence, failure. Again, I'm most sorry to have to tell you this."

Monica sighed. "Well, I had to try this approach. The only other option is to use a Full Wish spell, and I refuse to do that. I will not be responsible for having the person who is helping me age an entire year just so I can get them restored, let alone six years to help us all. No way. So there isn't any other options?"

The professor sat back and rubbed his chin. "Milos, fetch me Abelard's tomb, will you? There is possibly another approach that could be used. I'm not at all certain that it will be practical, though." Milos hopped up and rummaged through the mountain of old books. It took him several minutes to find it and lay it before his father. "Thanks. Now, let me see. Where did I read that?"

He rummaged through a number of pages and then brightened up. "Here we are. Yes, there is indeed a very remote possibility. It was a demon prince, a ruler of an outer plane of existence who did this to you. It is possible for someone of equal or greater power to undo what's been done, but it will take a godlike being that is known to possess the necromancy Regeneration spell. I've gone to the actual source of the original Druids who were able to command this most powerful spell. There are in fact two such godlike beings. They are known only today in ancient Celtic mythology, but I assure you that they were very real back then and are still likely to be alive today. The best possibility is the Celtic Physician of the Gods, known to us as Diancecht. He was known to heal both enemies and foes alike. Of course, the legends say that he always demanded that the person he cured turnabout and cure others for some time. As I say, this is your best possibility."

"The other one is the Celtic God of the Dead, Lord Arawn, also known as the Dark One. He too is a supposed master of this incredible spell, and many powerful Druids worked with him to seal this spell into the rings. There is still some debate over whether Merlin got this power from Arawn or Diancecht. Lord Arawn works with those who have saved or restored to life one of his close followers. So I'm not so sure how easy he will be to work with. Besides, he is known for his evil actions. My suggestion is to try Diancecht first, saving Lord Arawn as a last resort."

"So how do I contact this Physician of the Gods?" Monica asked. The task seemed way beyond her.

"Well, I didn't say this would be easy, Monica. Some two thousand plus years ago, the Druids and the Celts were quite active in Britain. Back then, if you prayed well enough you probably could reach him. At least, the records suggest that was the case. But as you know, the Druids and the Celts are long gone, ancient history. So the only way that you can reach him is to go to his homeland."

"Fascinating. Just where is this land?" Monica asked, wishing she could somehow take notes.

"I will write down very specific information for you," Professor Kazimir replied, in obvious deference to her physical limitations. "It lies in the outer plane called Concordant Opposition. The Celtic super-beings reside there in Dagda the

Dozen King's realm called Mag Mell, the Field of Happiness. Somewhere in that realm, Diancecht is reputed to have his own estate. You will have to go there and search for his realm. I would suggest finding a specialist in the arcane study of these outer realms. I've no idea how one gets there or anything else about them. Such is way out of my specialty." He finished writing all this down for her and tried to hand it to her, before flushing at his mistake.

"Just lay it on the desk. I'll retrieve it by magic. I've no other choice but to use magic for just about everything now. Thank you enormously, professor. You've given me some hope that I may find a cure for us all." She focused and the paper floated over to her and then into a small pocket in her gown.

"I am so glad that I was able to be of some minor assistance to you, Monica. There is something that you could do for me. Let me explain. It is about this demon invasion. The Board of Regents has put us all on high alert over this demon situation. I myself am a consultant for our Department of Magical Misuse—a bit too old for an active agent role," he grinned.

"Anyway, we've had a few disturbing encounters with some Abyss demons here in Prague during the last couple of months. I would like to send my boys back with you and have them learn and study all your methods of dealing with this threat. They are accomplished wizards, mind you, but a bit too fun loving. In this battle, that can be fatal. I would like them to meet with these alu-demons personally and find out firsthand more about the Abyss and how we may be able to defend ourselves from them. Would this be possible, in the spirit of international cooperation?"

"Certainly. I'd be delighted to host them and introduce them to our Department of Magical Misuse leaders. It's quite a fight that we have on our hands, well those of us who have hands," she added playfully. Both boys cracked a smile.

"See, pop. She isn't so serious either," Milos declared.

He glared at his son. "It has been a pleasure meeting with you. Please let me know how it works out. We may well have some young women being kidnaped here in Prague. If they were taken as you were, we may well be needing your help with them. Sons, go pack your things and look after Monica. She's bearing a heavy load. Monica, don't put up with their sometimes silly antics. They've not grown up yet. As you know, this is a deadly serious business at hand, far worse than the old Dominus scare over in the States."

"I will and thank you again, professor," Monica replied. She sort of lunged up onto her feet and walked back out into the living room, the boys hot on her heels.

"Have a seat, Monica. We won't be too long," Milos explained.

"Say, it's almost suppertime here. Want to share a pizza with us before we go?" Jiri asked.

"Sure. We have it all the time back home. Just don't ask me to go for a walk in the snow. I can't stand up well on the slick stuff," she replied. "Perhaps a coke with a straw?"

"Coming up!" Jiri acknowledged and dashed off, presumably for their kitchen.

A few minutes later, he brought the familiar red and white can to her with a straw inserted. He sat it on an end table for her. "Thanks." He dashed off to pack.

While she moved over to the drink, she began to ponder what she'd learned and thanked the stars for not having gone ahead and blindly spent half of her fortune buying that ring only to find out it wasn't going to work. The professor had written down a reference to the spell that Graz'zt had used on her and the other women, and she wished she was at her computer so she could study up on it. Maybe there would be another clue in its casting that might help.

Thirty minutes later, the pizza arrived, just as the twins finished their frantic packing. "Do we feed you? Sorry, we've never been around anyone like you," Jiri asked apologetically.

Monica put on a brave face. "Ah. No, I'll just help myself, if you don't mind. Levitate." A piece rose up and then she used Move Object. While it hovered in the air before her mouth, she began eating it.

"Now that's clever, Monica!" Milos exclaimed, much impressed. "So you cast sans wands?"

"I had to learn how. Didn't before I was summoned to the Abyss. When Rob rescued me, it was learn how to do it this way or forsake my magic career. No way am I going to do that," she replied and took another bite.

"So how many power spells do you know? We didn't fare so well on the Grade 9 ones. Only learned one, how to change our shapes. Not a whole lot of use for that one," Milos asked.

"A whole bunch of Grade 9 spells and most of the Grade 8 ones too," Monica answered between bites.

"Wow. So you can cast everything sans wands, just like the world famous Dispeller, Governor Lindsey Barron-Cross?" asked Milos, rather impressed with her.

"Yes, once I got the beginning spells down with Rob's help, she coached me through all the others." She was surprised to know that Lindsey was known even here in Prague! Well, Lindsey was probably the most powerful Dispeller in the history of the world, she thought.

"Wow." Milos repeated himself. "So you are like a super powerful witch."

Monica chuckled, "Not so powerful. No arms, no hands, and I can just barely walk on level ground. Not so powerful, fellows."

"Well, I don't know how you can manage anything at all," Jiri sympathized with her. "Honestly, if I was in your shoes, I know I couldn't do it. I'd just let my body die. Give up. No way could I possibly manage it. And on top of it, you are dressed for a fancy party. Did you just come from one?"

She laughed again. "No, I always dress like this. Keeps you men in your places."

The lads laughed. Miros added, "No, it keeps us hot! Your Rob had better watch out." The three laughed again.

With the pizza soon gone, the three joined. Monica had each young man put an arm around her, and then she teleported them to the entrance of their estate, right in front of their sign PIWIP, which she had to then explain stood for their business: Protections, Information, Wands, Items, and Potions.

Jiri opened the door, and the three entered the large reception area. Jill looked up. "Oh hi boss. Back already? Looks like you have some company."

"Fellows, this is Jill Anne Parsons. Jill, this is Milos and Jiri Jakub from Prague. They will be staying with us a while, learning all they can about the demons. Seems they are finding them in Prague now. Don't ask me which is which. Identical twins."

Jill had lunged a bit to her feet and stood welcoming their new guests. She was also dressed very elegantly, wearing her newest light blue satin gown. She looked very much like Monica to the two young men. Monica added, "I've told them about you and they wish to talk with you and Nisha about the Abyss. I told them that you know virtually nothing about it, so it will have to be Nisha who can satisfy their questions. I hope you don't mind."

Jill had flushed as she heard that they knew she wasn't human, but managed to smile anyway. She also knew that if Monica had told them about her, there must have been a very good reason. Beside, thanks to Crystal, everyone knew that Monica had gone to Prague in hopes of finding a cure for them all. Perhaps this was related. She replied, "Hi fellows. I have never been there and know nothing about it, except when I was captured and taken there for a week. And all I know about alu-demons has come from Nisha telling me. Sorry."

She then spoke clearly, "Intercom: All. Please come to reception. Monica is back and has brought two guests with her. Intercom: Off." The two fellows looked at her and she blushed, "I'm the receptionist. Monica has a voice-activated intercom system for me to use along with a voice-activated computer. Without them, I would be totally useless in this job. Everyone's coming up, Monica," she added, though Monica already knew that would be happening.

Within a minute, the entire gang except Rob, who was still in LA, arrived. Once more, the two men were quite surprised to see Crystal, Ericka, and Nisha all wearing similar really elegant gowns and heels. One by one, Monica introduced the two young men to the group.

Crystal spoke up, "Darn it. So there are demons in Prague now. Bad news. I've got to let Leslie know about this development. Hello fellows. I'm our resident arcane lore expert along with my boyfriend here, Gregor Mac Pheerson.

His father is teaching us quite a lot as well."

"Professor Kyle Mac Pheerson?" Milos inquired.

Gregor replied, "Yes, that's my dad. He's here, but, well, dementia is giving him trouble. He still has some good moments each day."

"Incredible, we've studied all his publications, Gregor. Could we possibly meet him—when he is having a good moment that is?" Milos begged.

Gregor smiled and nodded. Monica then asked, "Since the fellows wanted to meet you two, Nisha and Jill, why don't you take them on a guided tour of our place, while I report in to the others?"

"Love to," Jill replied. "This way, but I can't tell which of you is which."

They laughed and Jiri explained, "My hair is a tad lighter than his. I'm Jiri, Jill. Do you need a steadying arm?" He offered her his.

"Sure. It really does help me a lot. Even though I'm able to cast Gentle Fall, I'm still terrified of handling the stairs. This is my area, reception. I also handle all their accounting and organization stuff. So you are from Prague? You speak English very well."

"Thanks, we've practiced some, but we're still using a spell to help out. You are incredibly attractive, Jill, but I bet all the guys have told you that," Jiri flirted with her a little.

Nisha laughed, "Okay Milos. Don't you go calling me attractive. I'm much too short even in these cool new heels that I've got. Come on. I'm usually in the kitchen. I'm actually learning to be a very good cook. I like helping the others who are really in need. Did Monica tell you what I was doing when we first met?"

The two couples wandered off, and Crystal put her arm around Monica's waist and cast her Magical Door, stepping them into her library. Ericka, Enya, and Misty were right behind them. No sooner had Monica gotten seated when, with her hands on her hips, Crystal asked, "Okay, so what did you find out? Any reasonable cures? Tell us all about it!"

"Okay. In my dress pocket—there are some notes. Can you. . ." Monica didn't finish. Crystal quickly retrieved it.

"Please, there should be something there about an Incinerate spell. Can you see if you can find that data? It's the most important detail right now," Monica asked.

"Great. He has written down a URL for it. One second," Crystal replied, bringing up her laptop and entering the address. A moment later, she showed the page to everyone. All five tried to read it over each other's shoulders. The spell originated over two hundred years ago down in Brazil as a clever way to burn out tree stumps, part of their unwise move to deforest the Amazon, turning some into farmland.

"So that's how he was able to burn out your arms, from the inside out. We'd never have figured that one out," Crystal declared. "We should see if we can learn that one and add it to our list of spells."

"My thinking too. I'll use it on Graz'zt if I ever get the chance!" Monica declared. "Anyway, that spell is key. It incinerated our arms by fire. Normal Rings of Regeneration will not restore appendages removed by fire this way. So I'm glad I didn't go ahead and spend the forty million dollars on the single ring being offered for sale."

"But what's all the rest of this?" Ericka asked, looking eagerly over Crystal's shoulder.

"Druids," Monica began explaining what she'd learned about the creators of these rings, which held such an immensely godlike power. A bit later she pointed out, "So the only possible chance we have is to contact one of the godlike beings who bestow such spells on their Druid worshipers. The Physician of the Gods, this Diancecht fellow is our best possibility. He resides on one of the Outer Planes that Rob and I visited. I've no idea where this realm is, so that's what I have to research next. If I can speak with him, perhaps he will help us with this regeneration problem, but I'll probably have to make some sacrifice for him. No idea what. Guess I'll find out if and when I can talk to him."

"Wow, Monica. This seems to be a wild idea. No other way besides a Full Wish spell?" Crystal asked, but she already knew the answer.

"Nope. I refuse to use Full Wish spells. So this is really my last hope for us." They chatted a bit more, and the others headed back to their workshops and to chat with the new arrivals when Nisha and Jill brought them by their shops.

Because of the nearly twelve-hour time difference between the two cities, Monica felt quite tired and retired for the night. Again, she had to cast numerous spells just to get undressed, her hair brushed out, and into bed. All the while, she continued to fight back tears of grief over her pathetic situation, refusing to give in to it, not just now. She had Jill to consider.

She missed Rob and his loving, kind, gentle ways, perhaps tonight more so. Her hopes for an easy cure had been dashed, and she felt her acute loss painfully. At long last, alone in her bed between her blue satin sheets, Monica finally stopped fighting her loss. She cried, cried volumes of tears, letting it all out. *We really are darn near helpless this way, just as Jill says,* she thought. After crying quietly to herself for an hour, she felt drained. *Well, if this is the way that I must live from now on, then that is the way it is. I have to stop holding out for a cure, a way back to being normal again. Lord knows when or even if I can find and speak with this godlike being or even if he has any hope to give me. I simply will not use a Full Wish spell no matter what. Accept yourself for what you now are, Monica, a helpless witch. Find some way to go on and forget about it all. But how? Not even cloning is going to work.*

As she thought about cloning again, she suddenly remembered that Graz'zt had alluded to the fact that she had been a clone. *Dominus? Was I a clone? Was that whole lifetime a clone's life? Somehow, I have to figure that out, but how? Is it important now, Monica? Compared to everything else? No, one day I'll see if I can figure that one out.* With that, she finally fell asleep.

The next morning, she was late to breakfast. Once more, she had to use many spells to get herself dressed and her hair done. At the last minute, she decided to put on her makeup. "I'll be darned if I'm going to let my helplessness keep me from looking the way that I want to look!" It took her many more spells and nearly an hour to be satisfied with her makeup. Lunging to her feet and wobbling a little to catch her balance, she headed off to breakfast.

She found Jiri was feeding Jill, who was enjoying his constant attention. Milos was chatting with Nisha. Something about how to make a Czech dish. She found Nisha had already set her place. All she had to do was sit and feed herself, using another volley of spells. Long before she finished, the others had already left. Jiri walked Jill to her desk, promising to chat with her as she did her work. Milos and Nisha headed off into the kitchen, still discussing recipes. Alone, she finished her breakfast and headed to her lab to think. An idea was forming. She sent a Message to Parry and Ari, smiling when she received their reply.

Chapter 18—Unraveling the Past

"Hi Parry, Ari. Glad that you could come," Monica welcomed them to her lab. Jill had used the intercom to let her know they'd arrived and sent them on down. She did hear Jill giggling about something that Jiri whispered to her. Imaging Jill smiling in spite of everything brought a smile to Monica's face.

'Bout time I get to continue my part of this tale. Been boring. Find my lost dog. Find my lost ring. Is my husband having an affair? Business hasn't been very exciting since the demons stopped kidnaping young women. But I will say, Ari has been beyond wonderful! She's been teaching me to cast magic spells, at least those that I'm able to learn. I can now actually safely teleport and that's saying something! I know I've a long way to go. Ari keeps telling me I can't cram six years of magical training into three months, but I keep trying. Honestly, once you get a taste for casting spells, it's so darn addictive. Okay, Monica is giving me the evil eye. Best pay attention here.

"Parry. Off in dreamland? Ari tells me you are doing great at learning to cast spells. You are on Grade 2 spells now?" Monica asked me.

"You bet. She's a goddess. Well, we skipped around a little, owing to the demon attacks. I can teleport now. That's going to be useful. So okay, you wanted to see me in my professional capacity? I've my PI cap on, only it's mostly invisible."

Ari giggled. "He's teasing you. Honestly, business has been slow, which is fine. Learning magic takes a lot of time, but you know that. Okay, two PI's are here. What's the assignment, madam client?"

"Strictest of confidences. I must swear you to utter secrecy on this one. Not a word about this investigation to anyone but me and never ever to anyone else. Will you so swear?" Monica said very sternly.

"We so swear. What's with all the secrecy? Must be very important?" I asked. Heck, it had to be for Monica to make us swear. But then, I don't make it a practice to go around blabbing my client's secrets. Very bad for business and right now, I do need the business. I have some idea that she is very wealthy, and I can really use the money. Have to support Ari too.

"Okay then. This has to do with my last lifetime, when I was Dominus Malefic. Do you recall what was said to me?" Parry shook his head no. "He told me that I ought to know about clones, since I was a clone last lifetime. I never ever knew that I was a clone. Dominus never had any remote inkling that he was in fact a clone."

Ari spoke up. "If I understand the theory of that spell, if Dominus, er you that is, would have known that he or you were a clone and that the real Dominus was out there somewhere, he would have dropped everything, sought him out, and killed him. Right?"

"Right, Ari. If I had known I was a clone and the original man was still living somewhere, I would have put everything else on hold and gone after him. But I didn't know. I never even suspected it. When he told me that, it was news to me."

"Got it boss. So what do you want us to do?" I asked.

"Find the original body that was cloned to make Dominus Malefic. There is ten thousand dollars there on the table as your retainer. Let me know when you need more funds. "I have very little to go on. I know that I had a father and that he divided his fortune with me, fifty-fifty. We had a challenge going or a wager. He claimed that the way to power was through building up an enormous economic base. Power through money. I claimed it was power through magical powers. My might wins all, not his silly financial empire building. I know I had a mother and a sister. Both died when I was in my sixth year at Bradbury's. I think they died over Christmas vacation. Beyond that, I know nothing else. I've no idea what happened to dad. He was an angry man anyway, and I hated him, so I never contacted him after I returned to magic school when that vacation was done."

Monica told me the names of Dominus' father, mother, and sister. Darn little to go on, though. But hey, I've worked with less. "One detail, Monica. Supposing I do find this man. Do I have your sworn word that you intend him no harm? I can't accept this assignment if it means harm might come to the man. That's not how I operate. Goes against my principles."

Monica answered, "I swear to you both that I intend no harm to him. I would like to meet him, if possible. I think I need to ask him some key questions, but no. I don't want to hurt him at all. I've no grudge with him, Parry. It has to do more with me. I think that I do need to know something from him. Okay?"

"Thanks, boss. Yes. Ari and I will take the assignment, though you do realize that there is very little to go on in this case, and it is very stale-dated. Something like a quarter century late. We might not be able to find him." Heck, for all I know, the man might be dead. Maybe he had an incurable disease and cloned himself to live on. Some idiots think that's a good way to go. Not me. When I kick the bucket, I want to be done with it. Well, maybe not now. There's Ari to think of." Dames. They always seem to complicate matters.

"Yes, I know that it's very little to work with, but just do your best."

"Might I ask why you are not doing this yourself? Or is that prying?" I asked. After all, part of the PIWIP stores is Information, which is precisely what she was hiring us to do. Call me curious, if you like, but I like to know the whole story.

"You may. Do you realize how many spells that I had to cast this morning from the time I got up to sitting down in this room?" Monica didn't wait for the pair to ask. "Five hundred and six. Darn it, Parry. I'm almost completely helpless like this. I know, spells make me somewhat independent, but not much. Yes, I could do the research myself, but it's going to take me years to do what you both could do in short order. Besides, I have to research possible cures for us women, and I don't think you'd be of any real assistance in this arena."

I nodded and smiled. "Thanks for telling me that. It must be god-awful hard for you and for Jill too. I can't imagine what you are going through every hour of every day. And you are right. I've no ideas about cures. I will admit, Monica, I did look up the Clone spell, thinking it might help you and Jill out some, but the fine print didn't add up. Remember, if you really do need some help, you only have to ask us."

"I know, Parry, Ari. But you have to see my position. I'm humiliated if I have to ask for help with something that I used to be easily able to do. Now if it were something that I couldn't do easily before all this, then I wouldn't hesitate, but now, it is really humiliating, Parry. I can hardly bear it. Neither can Jill, but she's doing a bit better about it than I am."

Ari spoke up. "Monica, I know how you must be feeling. My heart aches so to see you struggling so, but I keep quiet because I know how utterly embarrassing and humiliating it is for you and for Jill. Still, when you do need something, please, please just let us know. We want to help in any way that we can."

"I know you do and so do all the others. It's just my own humiliation that keeps me from doing it. I keep thinking of all those other women who are right now down there in the Abyss in those awful Cambion Production Centers and without the slightest trace of hope. I have to make this work somehow," Monica admitted.

Heck, I think at that moment, she really did level with us both. My opinion of Monica rose even higher after that. "Okay. We best get on to our new assignment. We will keep you posted, boss."

"Thanks, Parry, Ari. I'm counting on you to find him, somehow, someway. I really do need to have a frank talk with him. I think that it's really important to my own well-being now."

Ari and I left, but not before we each gave her a hug. I must admit, I love to hug a hot dame. And hot Monica was, even if she didn't think so in her current state. Heck, I've known plenty of women who would have traded places with her just to look as dolled up as she always did. Ari teleported us back to our office. Did I tell you? Ari is now my partner. I got her her very own desk and computer too. Even changed the sign on my door. Parry and Ari, Private Investigations. That really pleased her.

"So where do we even start?" I asked, firing up my laptop.

"We best search out all the info we can find on his parents and sister. Probably some of that information has never been computerized, but we will see. The game's a foot," Ari teased me with an old Sherlock Homes line. I liked it and flashed her a big grin.

"We start with the only piece of information Monica gave us, that Dominus Malefic was really Simon Mac Fluide and his father was Ross, his mother was Jacqueline and his sister was called Michelle. Funny how the Rat Pack did the same thing with their real names, juggling the letters around," I said.

Ari teased me back. "I can't do much juggling with just Ari." We both laughed and set to work. I figured that this Ross Mac Fluide fellow must have owned a huge fortune, if the vast estates that Dominus had that got confiscated and sold off to compensate his many victims was only half of it, as Monica suggested. While Ari worked on the genealogy aspect, I tackled the money trail. I do love following money—having it too. The ten grand would be quite handy as Ari and I were soon to be married. God what a woman. Oops, back to business.

I followed the money trail. Unfortunately, that was very short-lived. Shortly after he died, he and his half of the funds totally vanished. His home in Colorado was sold. Old Ross just vanished. Well, I know enough to see a covert deal when I see one. This was one of those. Probably a shell game. Ross didn't want to ever be associated in the future with whatever Simon did. Hey, I have to hand it to old Ross. That was a darn smart move on his part. The States Justice folks might have confiscated all of his holdings as well when they grabbed Dominus'.

I was able to discover that Ross apparently gave the other half of his estate to another person called R. B. Folquet. After that document of dissolution, Ross vanished without a trace. In my lingo, that meant he probably changed his name and moved some place far away from where Dominus was going to be working. Since Dominus attempted to conquer the whole United States, to my way of thinking, if I wanted to get out of the picture, I'd go overseas. Europe probably. England would be too close for comfort, since they speak nearly the same language as us. I couldn't see a middle aged American moving to the Far East or even Down Under. Even South America was a tad too close. Possibly to some remote South Pacific Island. No, not there. This Ross was a businessman. He would want to stay connected to his still vast economic empire, especially since he believed that true power came through economic means, according to what Monica told us about his father and their argument.

So who was this Folquet person anyway? In my mind, I equated him with Ross Mac himself. It would be the kind of subterfuge that I might dream up if I had billions and wanted to "disappear."

Ari spoke up. "Hey, I found their death certificates and the birth certificates for Simon and Michelle. If Simon is still alive, he would be around fifty-one and his sister, Michelle, would have been around forty-one or so. Plus, look at this, Parry! I found Ross' marriage license from 2135! Ross Bernard Mac Fluide and Jacqueline Blanche Folquet united on May 25, 2135, in Marseille, France."

I let out a war hoop! "Ari, you are a genius investigator! Brilliant, brilliant. Old Ross didn't give away his half of his business empire. Didn't figure he was that stupid. He adopted his wife's maiden name! So this R. B. Folquet was in fact old Ross himself! I wonder something. Hold on a second, love." I hastily brought up the International Magic Ledger. Anyone who is able to cast certain high-powered spells is forced to register with this group. I clicked on the Clone spell and scrolled through the pile of alphabetically listed names.

"Bingo, Ari. Guess who is a registered Clone spell user? Ross himself! So I'll bet anything that Ross cloned his own son, gave the clone half of his empire, changed his own name, and fled the country."

"Right, Parry. That makes perfect sense. Question is: where did he move to? What about his wife's hometown, Marseille, France?" Ari suggested.

"Dunno. Let's see if there is anything on the Folquet empire listed in Marseille." I typed away, knowing that I was hot on the trail of old Ross. He and I thought alike, at least in some ways. Or maybe I am just able to put myself in his shoes, at least financially. We hit the proverbial jackpot. "Ari dear, type this URL in." I relayed the site I'd found.

"Wow, this is something else! This is the enterprise, which created all those cures for the millions that were addicted to that awful Heath Care fiasco—heroin pill really. This corporation did all that for free! What are we onto here anyway? Who is Simone? Could it be the Simon? His son, the one that he cloned?" Ari asked rapid-fire questions.

"Hey, it must be. Look. There are photos of all the CEO's of the many affiliated companies, but absolute nothing at all on the headman, Simone Folquet. Hey, if I was in hiding, I sure wouldn't want my mug shot on the Web, especially since anyone looking at it would recognize me as Dominus Malefic and thousands might well come gunning for me."

"Spelling for me, you mean," Ari teased me.

"Yeh, either way, my goose would be cooked. Makes sense. What have we here? See that lone reference that says 'To reach Mr. Simone Folquet, please contact his attorney, Mrs. Isabella Folquet at the law offices of Folquet et Associés at 4520 Rue Jean de Bernardy.' That appears to be the sole way to reach him. Lawyers!" I hate them. They get rich off other's troubles. Sure, we'll settle with you. You get half of the money and your attorney takes the other half. Robbers and lawyers are synonymous in my book. Maybe if the States Justice people finally get done rewriting all the laws, ordinary folks like me can figure out what's legal and what isn't. I'm not holding my breath. They are still at it.

"Well, do we call her and try to see him ourselves or do we let Monica take this next step?" Ari asked.

"Well dear, we are darn sure that this Simone fellow is the Simon. I can't think of any other angle. Unless we can find out anything more on him. Best we see if we can dig up anything more first. I don't want to send her off to Marseille, not as vulnerable as she is." Especially since Rob is still gone. He shouldn't have left her alone for so long, but then these darn demons shouldn't have invaded our world. Stay in their own cursed Abyss.

"Well, I got lucky with the genealogy angle once. Let's see if I can dig up anything else," Ari suggested. "I wonder what the background of this attorney Isabella Folquet is. Same last name. Maybe a sister of Ross' wife or a cousin." She typed away. She added, "I like this kind of PI work. No danger, just fun."

I chuckled. This was turning out to be the easiest ten grand I ever made. Last time I got ten grand for a case, it was a devil beauty queen, Glasya, and her case nearly got me killed. Ah, I can't complain. It netted me my dear Ari.

"Bingo, Parry. Come look at what I found. Ta da! Ari's magic fingers. Got her marriage license and that led to two birth certificates. Guess who Isabella is married to?"

"Not Simone?" I asked somewhat taken aback.

"You bet. They have two children now. Rolande is five and Chantal is three," Ari pronounced with authority. "We've got it all solved, don't we?"

"Yes, as long as this Simone turns out to be the Simon. Can't hide from public records," I joked. "Okay, how long did this investigation take us, dear?" I asked.

"Ten minutes," she grinned back at me.

"Hey, we're good. That's a thousand dollars a minute. Pretty steep rates," I jested, and we both laughed. I figured that I'd give most of it back to Monica. That rate would vastly exceed even the greediest of lawyers. We took five more minutes to print out a hard copy for Monica of the key web pages with their information. That done, I Messaged her, and we teleported to her place.

"Back so soon?" Monica grinned, flashing her white teeth outlined in crimson. She did look good today, well as good as she could, considering. Okay, darn good considering.

"Solved it," I said quietly.

"What? I just gave you the assignment! What, not even a half hour ago?" Monica grinned, but looked very surprised.

"Yep. You did hire the hottest PIs in St. Louis," I teased her. "Okay, here we go." I began by laying out the printouts on her table, explaining our reasoning as I went along. After showing her the nicely printed out ad:

To reach Mr. Simone Folquet, please contact his attorney, Mrs. Isabella Folquet at the law offices of Folquet et Associés at 4520 Rue Jean de Bernardy, Marseille, France.

I laid out the final pieces, her marriage record, and the two birth certificates. I continued, "We are nearly certain that this Simone is in fact the Simon Mac Fluide, whose body Ross cloned to make Dominus Malefic. Everything fits. However, there is only one way to be a hundred percent certain and that is to go there and via Isabella, get in to see Simone. We figured that you would probably want to do this yourself. Just remember that you swore you would not harm him or his family." I reminded her. I doubted that she had any such intentions, but I sure as heck didn't want to be used in some kind of revenge plot. Not my style. I've ethics, you know. So does Ari.

"I've given you my word on that, Parry. I just want to talk to him, that's all. This is simply amazing work, you two. I did hire the best, didn't I? Okay then, if this Simone does turn out to be Simon or he can lead me to him, I'll pay you the rest of your fee," Monica explained.

"Whoa there Miss Terribly Pretty. You've already overpaid us. I can't charge you a grand a minute. I figured I'd give you back most of what you already paid me," I countered. I know, I really do need the money, but then a grand a minute is beyond highway robbery.

"No, you keep it all, Parry. I can't begin to tell you how much this means to me, personally. I planned to pay you another ten grand when I find Simon. To me, it isn't about how much per hour, though I know that's how you charge. It is about the result, Parry. Twenty grand to have a chance to talk to him is well worth it. I absolutely insist that you keep every penny, Parry. This is really important to me," Monica explained.

Seeing how she was determined to pay me this exorbitant amount, I decided to accept it. I'd done what was honest and offered to return most of it. That she felt we deserved it, well, that's her choice. "So do you want us to make contact with the attorney or do you want to do it yourself? If you are going to Marseille, want us to tag along? Just in case?"

"No, I'll contact her. If she'll see me, then I should go alone, Parry. If it is Simon, he's been going to extremes to remain obscure. If I go there with a bunch of others, he's liable to get spooked and not see me. Best if I do this myself. Thank you Parry, Ari, for offering. Thank you for a terrific job of finding him. I'd hug you both, but I can't. Sorry."

I hugged her instead. So did Ari, and Monica melted both of us with her smile. After that, we left, our hard copy printouts still on her desk. Of course, I really would have given anything to overhear her conversation with this Simone fellow, but then it was meant to be private. To be honest with you, I had no inkling what Monica, alias Dominus, could possibly want with the man from which he was cloned. We left in mystery and teleported back to our office with our rent paid up until at least spring. That was a relief.

Monica had butterflies in her stomach as she looked at the contact information. If this were Simon, would he even agree to see her? Would he agree to talk about what she desperately wanted to discuss? It was likely to be as painful for him to tell as for her to hear. "Well, I can't go forward until I've closed the past. Not really. It keeps coming back to haunt me. Monica, you've got to do this, somehow."

She stared at the page. Here it was—the connection to her dark past. How to proceed? Should she just make a phone call to Isabella? Send an email? Visit her in person? Her intuition kicked in. If she just showed up at Isabella's office, she could well panic the woman, who would likely be quite hostile and not allow her to find Simone. A phone call was too impersonal. Isabella would be trying to second-guess her every word. Besides, she could just hang up on her. Best to send an email. While far less personal, it allowed Isabella the opportunity to retain her distance from Monica. Far less threatening.

A hundred spells later, Monica began to think that she should get the voice-activated software on her computer too. She had not done so, feeling that she'd be too humiliated if she had to resort to that. Still, a hundred spells just to get the email done perfectly. . . It read:

Dear Mrs. Isabella Folquet,

Per your web page, I am contacting you in hopes that you can arrange a discrete, private meeting with Mr. Simone Folquet for me. It is about a very personal matter that I wish to discuss with him. It is very important to me to meet with him for a short while. Thank you.

Sincerely,

Mrs. Monica Nicole Black-Finch

Proprietress, Protections, Investigations, Wands, Items, and Potions

St. Louis, Mo, USA

She looked it over for the tenth time, said a brief prayer of hope, and hit the Send button. Now all she could do was wait for the attorney's reply. She knew that there was a large difference in time zones between here and Marseille, and she didn't expect an answer soon.

The next morning, she checked her laptop and found a very brief reply.

Dear Monica,

Are you the woman who helped rescue the kidnaped women from the Abyss?

Sincerely,

Mrs. Isabella Folquet, Attorney at Law

"Well, that's not what I expected for a reply," she stated flatly. "Does the whole world know about what Rob and I did? Ah well, maybe it will help get me in to see Simone." She sent a brief reply stating that she was.

The next morning she had another reply.

Dear Monica,

If you wish to meet with Simone, then be at my law office shortly before five p.m. tomorrow evening.

Sincerely,

Mrs. Isabella Folquet, Attorney at Law

She fired off a quick reply saying that she would be there! Considering the time difference, she rose early the next morning and dressed in her finest outfit, a cherry red satin gown. After brushing out her hair and spending countless spells to get her makeup done to her satisfaction, she looked herself over in her full-length mirror. Satisfied that she looked as good a possible, she checked her magical protections. Her earrings went well with her gown, and her new neck pendant with Ericka's special enchantments rested perfectly above her pronounced cleavage. Satisfied, she Messaged Crystal and cast her teleport spell, handling the seven hour time zone difference by leaving at ten in the morning.

Monica arrived just outside the law office building in downtown Marseille, France, at 4520 Rue Jean de Bernardy. It was warm and balmy. Her sense of smell was assaulted by the strong odor of the Mediterranean Sea. Before her stood a quaint old building with three floors. A sign proclaimed Folquet et Associés. Monica cast Understand Languages first and then another spell to open the door for herself. Carefully watching her step, she entered and walked up to a secretary-receptionist desk. "Est-ce que je peux vous aider?" the blonde young woman asked.

Monica answered in French, "Yes, I would like to see Isabella Folquet, please."

"Oui, chambre nombre cinq," she said, indicating a long hallway. However, the receptionist stared at her as she walked carefully down the hallway whose woodwork was done in mahogany, carefully polished. The faint odor of the lemon polish filled the air. A lush carpet muffled her footsteps but made walking more difficult for her. Keeping her balance was very challenging and several times, she had to wobble a bit to keep it. Part way down the hall, a door on her left had a sign that read, Isabella Folquet No. 5. She paused before it, cast another spell to open the door, and entered.

A secretary with long black hair sat at a beautiful old desk. "Est-ce que je peux vous aider?" she asked pleasantly.

Monica's translation spell was working perfectly and she replied. "Yes, I have just come from America and am supposed to meet with attorney Isabella Folquet at five p.m., please. Mrs. Monica Nicole Black-Finch."

"Oh, oui, American. I speak English, little. Un moment." She pushed an intercom button and relayed her arrival.

She rose and motioned for Monica to follow her. Monica noticed that she wore a smart business suit with hose and low heels and knew that she had dressed properly for this formal visit. She opened the door and motioned for her to enter. Before Monica was a stately attorney's office, complete with beautiful mahogany walls. A woman with long, wavy black hair rose and motioned for her to have a seat. The attorney was definitely very surprised at how Monica looked, her deformity, not her dress. Monica saw a gorgeous middle aged woman, perhaps in her late forties. Her makeup was subdued, but perfectly done. She had blue eyes and a kind smile.

"Bonjour. I be Isabella Folquet. I am very pleased to meet you, but I did not know about your physical condition. Pardon me. I speak some English." she replied in a mellow alto voice.

"I am very pleased to meet you as well. Yes, I too was kidnaped by the demon prince, and he did this to me, along with all the other women that he'd kidnaped. But with my husband's help, we were able to escape and bring four other kidnaped women with us. I hope that I'm on time."

"We. It is nearly five now. Simone and I are very pleased to meet with you, Monica. He wishes you to come dine with us now. Talk then. Only a short way," she explained. "Are you able to walk some? Do you need me to help you? I did not know about this."

"No, I'm fine. Still getting used to walking on my toes though. Thanks."

Isabella picked up her purse and motioned for Monica to join her. Together, they left her office. She wore four-inch black pumps and very nice black nylons as well, which went perfectly with her professional dress. Isabella's pace was surprisingly perfectly matched to Monica's, she noted as they headed out onto the street. "Is this first time in Marseille?" she asked, making pleasant conversation as they walked along the busy street at rush hour.

"Only short way now," she said as she turned onto the side street, Impasse de Montbard. "That be our home there," she pointed out. Monica saw a walled and fenced complex that occupied half of the block. Two stories tall, the building looked as if it were centuries old, fitting perfectly the decor of Marseille. At the main gate, she paused and pushed some numbers on their security lock. At least, Simone had some good security around his complex.

The gate opened automatically, and Isabella headed inside. "This way." She led Monica inside the first of several buildings within this complex. Once inside, she paused a moment. Just then, a middle aged man, also immaculately dressed, came hastily into the room, French doors wagging open and shut behind him. He was tall and thin, but wore a full, very bushy beard. His eyes caught Monica by surprise! Those were the very eyes of Dominus Malefic or herself last lifetime! Monica had no doubts whatsoever that she had at last met the real man whose body was cloned and that she'd had last lifetime.

Simone first hugged his wife, and took her purse off her shoulders, hanging it on the hallway hook. With his arm around her, he turned to face his Monica. "I'm Simone Folquet, at your service. So glad that you could take this time to dine with my family. I must admit you look quite attractive, but, well, we didn't know about your physical condition."

"I'm Mrs. Monica Nicole Black-Finch. I'm very honored to meet you, Simone. I can explain my mutilations, if you like. It does tend to shock people."

"Please, we would love to hear about it. But come on in; dinner is prepared. I hope that you enjoy roast duck with almonds. We certainly do. We can chat over dinner." Monica followed the pair into the next room, where her eyes saw a magnificent old style formal dining room, whose antique decorations alone must have cost a fortune.

He noticed Monica noticing the room and said, "Isabella's work. She is not only the world's best attorney, but has a real eye for interior decoration." Isabella smiled at the compliment. If you will take a seat on that side please. I should ask, do I need to feed you or assist you in any way? I will have a straw for the drinks."

"A straw will be perfect. No, I use my spells to eat. Thanks," Monica answered, but he graciously pulled out her chair for her and adjusted it as she sat down, rather elegantly, of course. She sat across the table from the pair and watched as a servant brought in the meal on stainless steel covered plates.

Simone watched her carefully to make sure that she really could manage herself, though he graciously filled her plate for her. After she'd convinced them both that she could manage, Simone said, "Well, we have heard all manner of wild tales about the demons and the Abyss and a role that you have played in rescuing some kidnaped women. However, as you probably know, hearing it fourth or fifth-hand, the truth often is wildly wrong. If you don't mind, Isabella and I would dearly love to hear about it, if it is all right with you. You don't have to reveal anything that we should not hear, mind you. We are just very curious."

"Oh I don't mind. Honestly, it was beyond horrific, almost beyond imagination," Monica began. When she finished her tale, they had all finished their dinner. Both Simone and Isabella had listened to her every word, intently even. Monica had a hunch that this was what was going to be needed when she finally broached what she'd come here to discuss. Little did she know that her hunch was dead-on!

Only when she finished did she have the time to notice that a fourth place had been set, but that no one had yet joined them. However, at that moment, the front door opened and another young woman with long black hair, wearing jeans and a tee shirt came walking in. Her left hand carried a wand, but her right arm was wrapped in a white cloth that had turned mostly red. Blood oozed down her arm. Small drops pinged onto the floor.

She, however, was jubilant. "Hi Simone, Isabella. We kicked those demons' butts this time! Killed them both. But I think I need to go to the hospital, Simone."

Monica stared at the woman, probably in her early forties. Even though she was wearing jeans, she had the tiniest waist that Monica had seen, and then she spotted the rigid, extremely tight corset the woman was wearing. Her eyes did a double take as she noticed the woman's boots. They were ballet boots just like her own! She was walking on her toes like herself. "Oh! I'm sorry. Didn't see you had company," she hastily apologized.

"Michelle! You're wounded! Simone, do something," Isabella gasped.

"Let's see how bad it is, sis," Simone exclaimed, rising and going over to her. He gently moved her over to the table and had her sit so he could examine her arm.

Monica saw the long gash and knew that it would need many stitches. Then, she remembered her newest skills and spoke up, "I can heal it up with no scaring, if you like."

"What? You can heal? That's some magic I've not got," Simone said, turning to look hard at Monica.

"That would be great, if you can. I hope it doesn't hurt," Michelle said.

"Nope. Not a bit. Just don't anyone interrupt me until I get done," Monica asked and focused. She felt her awareness expanding outward and onto Michelle and her wounded arm. Particle by particle, Monica began moving them into place. Shortly, the bleeding ceased. With the critical part over, she continued to help the cells modify and renew themselves. Finally, she could do no more and opened her eyes. She'd forgotten that she'd closed them.

"Wow! Look at my arm! You can't tell I didn't get out of the way of one of the demons in time. Thank you. Thank you," Michelle bubbled. "I'm Michelle, by the way."

"Monica Nicole Black-Finch."

"Oh, right. You've come to see Simone. Cool. I suppose that you've already told them all about your adventures in the Abyss and I missed it."

Monica smiled. "Yes, sorry. Perhaps I can tell you about it after I finish talking with Simone. But what happened to you?"

"Cool. Okay, Simone, Isabella, we kicked butt! Oh, I'm a member of the Marseille Defense Force. We go into action whenever demons appear, you see. Two of them just appeared down by the docks and started hurting people and smashing things, but we got them. Both are dead now, but their bodies sort of vanished, leaving piles of ugly gooey stuff on the road. I wasn't able to get out of the way once and got hit by one of the demon's claws."

She rattled on, "You see, my feet can only wear these ballet style boots, so I really can't run or dodge very well. Hardly at all, really. I've worn them almost all my life, so I do well with them, but just not fast things. You probably know what I mean. You have to watch each step that you take. It's so easy to stumble, but you know that. Other than running, dancing, and dodging, I do everything else okay in them."

Monica laughed. "I think I need to have you give me some lessons in them." Michelle grinned.

"Sis, why don't you eat your dinner now and let me talk with Monica some. It's already cold," Simone broke in.

"I'll heat it up for you, and then after you eat, your niece and nephew are going to want to hear all about your battle, Michelle. They're in the playroom right now," Isabella volunteered. "Simone, why don't you and Monica talk in your study? I'll see that you aren't interrupted."

Simone agreed, rose, assisted Monica, and then led the way towards his study. "I really must thank you for healing my sister. She is very proud to be helping defend Marseille with her magic. She's a very recent graduate of Bradbury's School of Magic in Colorado. Perhaps, you've heard of it?"

"Oh yes. Governor Lindsey helped me perfect my sans wand casting when I got back from the Abyss and found myself darn near helpless. What an elegant study."

After they both took seats in very expensive, plush leather chairs, Monica decided it was now or never. She took a deep breath and plunged right in. "Simone, I know that you were Ross Mac Fluide's son and that he cloned you. After that, he vanished from the States. Obviously, he must have brought you and Michelle, who obviously isn't dead, here. I really do need to know why he cloned you and what or why Ross so mistreated his wife, who was a normal woman, if I have my facts straight."

"So few people know about this. If I speak, Monica, I must ask you to swear to keep all this a total secret. I think you must know why," he looked her squarely in her eyes.

"Oh I do, I really, really do, Simone. I haven't told anyone yet and don't plan ever to tell anyone. It is just between you and me. There are some things that I simply must know about Ross and what was going on back then, at the time of the cloning."

"Accepted then. But might I ask why this is so important to you? You are such a young woman, and you have such a heavy load to bear. You have certainly impressed me with your skills. Healing. Honestly, I don't know of another witch who can do what you just did for Michelle. Usually, it's healing potions that are required."

"I will tell you if you make me the same promise not to reveal what I tell you," Monica replied, feeling this was a two-way street.

"Of course. I promise."

"I was that clone. Dominus. I was shot in my head while going up the steps to a courthouse. Months later, an ardent follower in St. Louis dug up my grave and cast Cause Life on me. It kind of was messed up. After a few tries, I ended up with a twelve year old girl's body and kept it. I went to St. Louis School of Magic, but I retained all of my memories and casting skills. I was put in Red Hall, if you can believe that. I've changed—I hope for the better. I really enjoyed helping my four roommates, who are now my dearest friends, with their casting. We all got straight A's those six years. I helped them open up the shops of their dreams. Enya is a hot potion maker. Misty loves to make magic wands. Ericka is big into making all kinds of magical items. Crystal is rapidly becoming an expert on these demons from the Abyss."

"So, yes, I know that I was darn near insane last lifetime, but I hope that I've come to my senses this time and am trying to always help others and do the right things. But I really do need to know about Ross and why he cloned you to make me. It bothers me that I just cannot pinpoint the real reason that I was about the most self-centered, sadistic, evil man in history. Somehow, I must know why that happened, Simone."

"Incredible. You were Dominus?"

"Yes, and thank you for cleaning up that horrific mess I made in the eastern states. I can't believe I got millions hooked on heroin. Yes, I was a real bastard. I'm trying to do the right things this time."

"Okay then. It all began as one of those silly kid things. My dad, Ross, was a Black Hall graduate and a real bigoted idiot and sadist. As I grew up, he drilled into my head that wizards ought to control the world, that normals were somehow very defective cattle, to be used and discarded as one would a cow. Stupid me, I believed it, and all through my childhood, I made grandiose plans about how I could bring about a new Golden Age for the wizarding world. I argued continually with my dad about how I ought to be supreme ruler and how I could easily take over total control of the entire world. You know how kids are. They get silly ideas in their young minds, and it sort of take them over. Well, that happened to me."

"Nearly every day, I hit my dad up with more of my ideas to conquer the world. I had it all worked out, all planned out. Dad, on the other hand, argued that to control the world, you needed to control all the major businesses, the major corporations, the world's finances—that was the route to total world power, not by force of arms and deception as I was espousing. Oh the late night arguments that we had. It got so bad, that he began to try to beat some sense into me. Then mom got sick. I begged dad to heal her, but he wouldn't. 'She's a pathetic normal. She doesn't deserve to get cured.' Those were his words. Right there, I decided that I had to conquer the world, so I could stop my dad and those like him. Mom, she went to the norm hospital, but to save her, they had to remove her arms and feet. Diabetes can be awful, if untreated."

Monica interrupted him, recalling something. "You say he referred to her as a pathetic normal?"

"Yes, his words. Dad finally relented a little and allowed her to wear prosthetic feet so she could move around some. I always helped her into them each morning, until I went away to Bradbury's. Because dad and I were so at odds with each other and so that other kids would not pick on me because my dad was a billionaire, I changed my name to Dominus Malefic, thinking that name really described the power that I wanted. Scares people, Malefic. Anyway, Michelle took care of mom when I went away to school."

"I want you to know that until Isabella here came into my life, there are only two women who I love with every fiber of my being. Mom and Michelle. I doted on my little sister. I promised her that she could come to Bradbury's too, when she was twelve. I remember even telling some of the teachers there to expect her and not to give her a hard time." He paused for a moment, reflecting, and then continued.

"I was in my sixth year. It was Christmas vacation time, and I came home. Yes, I was always homesick there at the school. I missed mom and Michelle so badly, but a Black Hall student must be strong and powerful or so everyone says. I kept it bottled inside and never told a soul. I came home, and mom was in a diabetic coma! Dad kept refusing to help her. Finally, I cursed him and took her to the emergency room myself. Too late. She died before the Insulin could revive her. I came home and very nearly killed dad. It would have been a godsend had I been able to do that. Hindsight is always perfect."

"But dad seemed remorseful, as befitting mom's death, so I just could not do it. After we buried her, dad took me into the study and locked the door. He said, 'So do you still think that you can conquer the world by force and deception magic?' I was angry, I was foolish, I was stupid, I was morning my mother, so I said yes. I wish I could take that back now. I was thinking only of myself. I'd give anything to be able to turn back time!"

Again he paused before continuing, "Dad was always big on making bargains. That's how he amassed his fortunes, bargain, bargain, bargain! He said, 'Simon, I will make an ironclad bargain with you right now. I want to prove to you that your way is foolish and will never, ever wind you up as the controller of the world.' I said, oh yeh, wanna bet, stupid old man?"

"We argued some more, but then he proposed his bargain. 'Son, I will give you half of my entire fortune, no strings attached, to do with as you see fit. Yet, even with all the financial backing you could want, you and your grandiose plans will fail. However, when you fail—oh, I do not want you to fail, son. I love you too much for that. So here's the bargain. He talked about the details for hours, but I was sick. I just wanted to mourn my mother's passing. We had just buried her an hour before all this, you see."

"What was that bargain? He refused to allow me to execute my plan and get myself killed. That he flatly refused to do. He wanted me around to gloat over, once he had proven that I had failed utterly. In short, he cast a Clone spell, making a precise duplicate of me at that hour. I gave him a bit of my blood, and he cast the spell. The clone became me, Dominus Malefic, and dad divided his entire holdings into two halves, giving my clone one half. However, he told the clone me that this was where we parted company. He had Dominus, or me— it was so confusing at that time—sign legally binding papers that said if Dominus, the clone, ever had any contact with him ever again for any reason whatsoever, what remained of the fortune he had given Dominus was forfeited and would be returned to dad."

Monica whispered, "Yes, I remember that part, the signing of the papers. I was then through with him forever. I remember thinking that."

Simone said, "Then, you know that dad told me that he told you that you—this is so confusing. You should follow my plans to conquer the world, but that you were never, ever to contact dad again. So you returned to Bradbury's later in January, as me. I never did finish magic school. And no, I do not know those advanced spells that Dominus or you learned during those last four months. I rue the day that I didn't somehow learn that Restricted Wish spell because maybe I could have stopped him or you."

"As this was happening, the rest of the bargain went like this. I had to disappear and change my name. Obviously, I could never be stateside again or ever cross paths with Dominus, my clone, er you. God, there would be hell to pay if that ever happened. From what I have heard about this spell, you would have stopped everything just to wipe me out. So it was imperative that Dominus or you never knew that he or you was a clone. He or you had all of my memories, skills, and knowledge that I had up to the point where dad drew my blood."

"Part of the bargain was that I had to work for dad, learning how he believed one could conquer the world, by economic means. If I did that, stayed with him and out of sight, then when he died, I would get the rest of his fortune. Greedy me, I agreed to his terms, which he once more had set down on legal documents. It was truly binding. If I broke that agreement, I was disinherited, totally."

"In hindsight, I think that he had been planning this for quite some time. He had secretly purchased this estate here in Marseille, and after drawing my blood and getting my signatures on all the legal documents, I was ordered to come here and await him. One of the documents I signed was to change my last name to that of my mother, Folquet. So Simone Folquet I became back in 2156."

"When I got here, I found servants had much of the place ready for occupation. There are three separate buildings on this large estate. One was given to me; one held the servants; one was reserved for dad. I also signed papers stating that I would never go into dad's house unless asked, and then never leave the first floor. His study in the basement and his upstairs bedrooms were off limits to me. If I violated that rule, I was again disinherited. Heck, I wanted to be rid of him, so I never went into his buildings back then. God, now I wish I had more guts and done so, but I'm getting ahead of myself."

"So I arrived and I waited in my new home. I mourned for my mother for what seemed days, before dad finally came. Then, I received the worst shock of my life. I asked where was Michelle, the only other person I truly loved. Dad told me there was an accident, and she was killed. He said the Children's Hospital in Chicago had been unable to save her life. He said he then buried her beside her mother! I was crushed utterly! Everyone I loved was gone. All I had left was the distant promise of unlimited fortune."

"I didn't come out of my room for six months! When I did, I made a sneak trip to that hospital in Chicago and donated a new wing in memory of Michelle. Finally, dad got me to follow some of the news of Dominus attempting to conquer the US. I began to follow his criminal career, but I also began to see just how stupidly foolish I had been, childish notions. Slowly, dad began to get me to start taking an interest in the proper way to control things, via the business world. I worked only half-heartedly at it, back then."

"Then came the news that the world famous Dispeller Sam Rabbor and the Rat Pack had finally captured Dominus. He was sent to jail. That night I went out of the complex here for the first time since I came here and celebrated like mad. I got good and drunk. At last, I could put an end to the stupid game that my dad had set in motion. I approached him about it the next day, but he laughed at me. 'Game isn't over until the clone is dead, proving to you once and forever that your methods are folly and that mine is the only true way to ultimate power.' Well, I was pissed as you might guess. Still I had hopes that he would die in prison. With this beard, I looked nothing like the images of my clone did on TV, so I finally was allowed to go out of the complex freely."

"By then, I was my dad's right hand man in the enterprise corporation. As such, I found that I needed some corporate legal advice, and I sought out the best lawyer in Marseille. That was the luckiest day of my entire life. I met Isabella here. She proved to be a super lawyer as well, and we fell madly in love. However, as you have probably noticed, she is a normal, not a witch."

"We dated for a couple years before I proposed. Well, that was a fiasco. I should have never told my dad about that! He became extremely angry when he found out that she was a normal and not a witch. I thought he was going to kill me on the spot or worse, kill Isabella! I was scared out of my wits. Yet, the next morning, he was calm as a cucumber. 'Son, you want to marry this creature. I won't stand in your way, but I will make you and Isabella a bargain to show you that she is not worthy of you, son. I will give my consent and release you from that part of the overall bargain, if she and you both agree to my bargain.'"

"You see, I had also signed away my right to marry whom I chose. Dad wanted me to marry for financial gain, not love, and certainly never under any circumstances a normal. If I went ahead and married Isabella without his consent, again I was totally disinherited forever. So he had me bring Isabella to his house, and he laid out the bargain, withholding nothing. He would give his consent only if Isabella agreed to have her arms removed at her elbows. He then gave her some options. If she agreed to do this and then marry me, he would at once transfer ten million dollars into her private account. If she later wanted out, finding the situation untenable, he would give her another ten million dollars and see to it that her arms were regrown."

"I screamed and argued and protested, but he said that we needed to give this some serious thought. He gave her the legal documents so that she could ascertain their veracity and that they were indeed ironclad, which she most certainly did verify. I think we talked about this for nearly a month. I was not about to have her do this, but Isabella finally made me agree to do it, but it took a whole month of persuasion on her part. Her argument was that with the ten million, we would have a giant nest egg on which to build our own *independent* fortune and so at last be able to get out from under dad's thumb."

"We signed the papers, and dad cast his spells on her. Then, we got married. All was going along fairly well. We both had to make many adjustments to our lives. I promised her that the day that dad died, I would get her arms regrown. I signed a legal paper so stating, setting aside a secret account to pay for it the moment we are allowed legally to do so. When we heard that Dominus had broken out of jail, Dad called me into his office and said that the game was afoot once more!"

"It was back into hiding for me. I dare not show my face around Marseille, for fear of someone thinking I was Dominus or for accidentally running into him. He was once around here, I heard. Then, we got a stroke of luck on our side. Dad contracted Alzheimer's disease, irreversible and incurable. Per the legal contract, I was obligated to look after his needs until he died. So finally, I got the run of his house. I began to notice that a servant carried dinner platters down into his basement. I thought this rather strange. One night, I followed the servant, discretely of course. Good god! There locked in a basement complex was Michelle! I found out that the servant was under similar legally binding documents to keep her presence here a secret."

"Anyway, I found Michelle. Dad had cut off her arms, blinded her, forced her to wear a binding corset. Her waist is very tiny as you have seen. Worse than that, she had been forced to wear those ballet shoes all these years. She was locked away in the cellar room with only a servant coming to tend to her needs when she would walk over to the door and press an alarm button. The only outside contact she ever had was a small radio that was locked onto a music station. I bawled like a baby when I found her. She thought I was dead too. The first thing that I did was to Dispel the Blindness spell so she could see. Then, I rummaged through dad's copies of his legal papers and found that if anyone re-grew her arms or tried to get rid of those shoes and corset, again both she and I would be disinherited. Upon his death, she would receive twenty million dollars to look after her care. Okay, I admit it. I cheated and cured her blindness, giving her a good deal of life back."

"Isabella went over the documents carefully, but dad goofed and forgot to mention her blindness so we were safe. I got Michelle out of that basement and brought her here to live with Isabella and me. We quickly discovered that she was still mentally a very young teenager. So I have spent every waking hour with her, being her teacher. Eventually, she was able to pass her GED. Dad soon died. Around that time, Lindsey and her friends discovered my secret. That Professor Pam Betts figured it out, and they visited me. I told them all this as well. I also agreed secretly to use all my extensive resources to find a cure for that hideous heroin pills that were being pawned off in the Health Care Program. I donated the cure to the States at no charge. Took us many years to get everyone off those pills. Also the day that dad died, I got Isabella's arms regrown and Michelle's too."

"Then, when Dominus was killed and Lindsey was made Governor of Bradbury's, she accepted Michelle into my old school, where she finally got to learn magic. Now we are so proud of her. She's so good at it that she's on the Marseille Defense Force, fighting these demons who have invaded our port town. However, she has such a weak back that she has no choice but to continuously wear that awfully tight and rigid corset. Her feet are fused and cannot be repaired. Lindsey did a very thorough examination of them. I refuse to use a Full Wish spell. I can't bear to have anyone age a year just to repair her feet. She does very well in them, except she has greatly reduced mobility, but you know that. There, that's the whole story. Does this help you?"

Monica sighed. "Very much so. You know, you and I are alike in many ways now. I too totally refuse to use a Full Wish spell to repair what the demon prince did to me and to the others. Same reason. I can't have someone losing a year of their life just to make my life more bearable. Thank you, Simone, for telling me all this. So much has begun to make some sense. As Dominus, I was actually being an awful lot like Ross, especially in my treatment of women and viewpoints of both women and normal people. I'm certainly not like that any longer. I'm devoted to helping others now, but I guess that's rather obvious."

Monica continued, "Now I understand something key. Ross cloned you and made me at your most vulnerable time, a time when he was certain to get a clone that would do what I as Dominus tried to do. Deep down, as Dominus, I was terrified of the grief and loss that you were feeling and unable to truly express, so I had no choice really but to take on the winning persona, that of Ross. And that was doomed to fail from the beginning. On the one hand, I was trying to make a giant financial empire, and on the other hand, trying to take over control of the States by my own power. The two were always at war with each other. So while I was trying to conquer the world, at the same time I was doing all that I could to get stopped in my tracks. In a very large way, I made the very people who were able finally to put a halt to my rampaging evil, the Rodents. Finally, it makes sense to me. Simone, I feel like a very heavy weight has been lifted from my shoulders. Thank you. Now I can press on quietly making amends to the world this lifetime."

Monica added, "I swear to you that I will not stop until I have rid our world of these demons, once and for all."

Simone grinned. "Well, I never thought that we would ever see eye to eye, but you have somehow miraculously changed. Perhaps, it is karma paying you back—I mean your physical handicaps now."

Monica flushed. "Payback can be a bitch," she jested, bringing a smile to his face. "I've taken up enough of your time. I suppose I should chat a little with Michelle, since she's helping fight the demons."

"Would you? I know it will mean a lot to her. Your story has been on the news, and she's been following your story as much as it has been covered anyway," Simone replied. The two headed back out to find Michelle and take tea. Simone and Isabella then entertained their two young children, though Monica saw that he was still keeping an eye on her and Michelle, ever the protective big brother she concluded.

She gave Michelle a brief accounting of what had happened in the Abyss and got her to tell her all about her battle with the two demons this evening. To her surprise, Michelle did ask some key questions. She was definitely not an amateur any longer. Monica also gave her a tip on how she and Crystal had taken out two of the giant demons, using a Magical Door to get themselves up as high as their shoulders and come at them from behind, taking them by surprise.

Michelle then gave her some encouraging advice. "Look, just keep walking a whole lot each day. The more, the better. Your legs and knees will get stronger and stronger. Pretty soon, you won't think much about walking in them, once you've toughened up enough. Still, you have to pay attention where you place each step. When I don't, I often stumble a bit."

She then asked, "If you get any more tips on how to fight these demons, can you let me know? I'll pass them on to the others in our unit." Monica promised to do so. And with that, she said farewell to the three, thanking Simone and Michelle again. After he saw her to his door, Monica quickly teleported back to her reception area. Now, she had much to ponder, but so many things now made sense. She wasn't insane, but had been effectively "being Ross" all those years, doing to others what Ross had done, particularly to women and normals.

Chapter 19—Made to Order

General Franco Porti and Gisella Harmoni did not leave St. Louis for warmer climates as did Bella Zaronetti and Donatella Ratini and the other two dozen who came thorough that last planned Gate. New orders arrived, based only in part on the human's technology that allowed them to detect the Gates to the Abyss opening up. Rather, these new orders were designed to take advantage of what the general had already found, not only in this city but prevalent in all major human cities: slums filled with drugs, prostitution, and all manner of crime.

In 2190, St. Louis was no different from any other big city. The Project, that ward of the city from Old North St. Louis down to King Drive, was the hotbed of criminal activities all kinds. The major drug lords, as they called themselves, worked out of this ward, as did dozens of pimps, extortionists, and many other "bosses," who filtered their "wares" out beyond this rundown zone. Few policemen ventured into this ward, and when they did, they remained in their protective squad cars. Here, laws were made and laws were enforced by the "bosses," those with the most money, thugs, and guns.

Gisella and General Franco cased out the Project during the last two months of 2139, following Prince Graz'zt's new orders. Following orders was antipathetic to all demon-kind, who preferred to follow their own orders. However, so strong was the power of Graz'zt and so vitriolic his malice, that those of his most trusted lieutenants dared not disobey his orders. Underlings did and quite often paid the price, though that seldom stopped them later on from doing what they desired to do. If one was killed while here on Earth, his body reformed immediately back in the Abyss. Within a few minutes, the demon was ready for action once more, but would be unable to return to Earth for a number of years. Such were the magical forces that connected the planes of existence.

In fact, suddenly released upon Earth, many of the lesser demons charged off in wild abandon, wreaking the havoc that Monica, Leslie, and the others had fought against back in October. These two trusted lieutenants of Graz'zt knew better and attempted to follow their new orders. Both rather enjoyed being on Earth, a vastly better environment than the Abyss. Besides, they had a wonderful freedom of movement and action. Never had they seen such "spoils" ready to be plucked—a virtual paradise. Hence, they were not going to blow this incredible opportunity. After hanging around for a couple of months as invisible spies, the pair had seen enough and finally acted.

Operating out of a rundown apartment complex in the heart of the Project, Black-eyed Bo ran one of the largest drug distribution operations in St. Louis. His suite on the fourteenth floor was a virtual penthouse, with every conceivable luxury money could buy. Surrounded by dozens of scantily clad, highly attractive women who were addicted to coke, Black-eyed Bo ran his vast operation with an iron hand. Double cross him or his army of dealers would get you a pair of slugs, one in each eye, hence his nickname. He had a deformity from birth, a skin discoloration around each eye, giving him the appearance of having a pair of black eyes, which he or his thugs emulated when they shot someone, the slugs in each eye.

His personal protection squad consisted of two dozen young men, armed with automatic weapons, 9mm semiautomatic guns with silencers, and even some grenades. In addition to these men and women, he had two highly skilled Cleaners, a man and a woman. These two delivered his answers to those who stood in his way or who double-crossed him: a bullet into each eye. The two were in a competition with each other. Cross, a twenty-three year old man, had thirty-three executions to his credit, while Anti-cross, a twenty-four year old woman, had thirty-four. She'd just penetrated a competitor's fortified suite by repelling down from the rooftop, cutting a hole in the glass window, entering there, delivering the twin shots from her silenced 9mm gun, and exiting the way she'd come—all done around three in the morning.

Black-eyed Bo was holding a New Year's Eve party in his suite. His trusted guards were present, along with a cadre of hired women, dressed in bikinis and tall heels. These were in addition to the dozen who always seemed to surround Black-eyed Bo, as he reclined in his ultra-expensive leather sofa chair. Two were feeding him sips of wine, while the other ten were undulating provocatively before him in time to the bounding, jarring beat of the dance-hall sized home theater.

It was eleven o'clock. Booze and coke trails lay scattered around the giant living room. Off to one side, a big screen was carrying the festivities taking place at Times Square in New York City along with other locations around the country and world. Amidst this chaotic celebration, the two demons cancelled their Invisibility spells, suddenly standing before the drug lord himself.

"What the heck?" Black-eyed Bo exclaimed, shoving two of his women aside so hard that they were unable to keep their balance on their tottering high heels. Both fell over sideways, knocking over two end tables, spilling six glasses of wine and a number of half-filled beer cans. Someone flicked off the home theater. Women screamed, and two dozen sets of guns flashed out of their holsters, though Gisella and General Franco completely ignored them.

"Who are you? How did you get in here? What do you want? Boys, watch them closely. If they try anythen' at all, kill'em!" he barked. "Ah heck! Kill'em anyway 4 Messen' up mo' party!" Guns blazed! Bullets bounced off of the pair, flying in all directions, wounding several of the women and three of his guards, before he screeched, "Stop!" while diving for cover behind his expensive sofa chair! The big screen had three holes in it and had stopped working. Bits of broken glass littered the floor. The ambiance of the party had vanished in just those few seconds.

"Come out from your hid-e-hole, Black-eyed Bo. We want to talk. If we wanted to kill you, why, you'd already be dead," Gisella barked. The drug lord did as asked, carefully though, staring at this rather beautiful, but naked woman standing prominently before his chair. The greyish-skinned man was dressed like some military man, but he didn't hold any weapons, visible ones that is.

"What the heck just happened?" he finally found his voice.

"Is this any way to welcome a naked woman to your party?" she toyed with him, sucking up all his delicious fear.

"The bullets," he tried to formulate a coherent thought, trying to align what he'd just seen with reality, but couldn't.

"Can't harm us," Gisella finished his thought. "Now then, if you will dismiss all these pathetic underlings, you and I need to talk before we celebrate the coming New Year."

Black-eyed Bo hadn't gotten to his position by being dumb or slow. "Talk? All right. You heard her, beat it. All of you, you too, he motioned to his dozen women, three of whom were sobbing, blood streaming down their arms from ricochets. Hastily, the guards and the women did as asked, filing out, but some taking the wounded to the floor below where they kept a doctor on hand for just such "accidents." "Okay, what's ya pitch?"

"Simple. We're now going to be your new drug supplier. We'll provide you with any kind of drug that you wish to order and in any quantity. Your cost will be zero," Gisella replied, getting right to the point.

"Hey, y'all think I's born yes'ta day ore sum'thn?" he countered. "None gets sum'thn 4 n'thn. Wat's the angle? Wat's ya wan'tin from me?" he asked.

"Simple. You get what you want, free, best quality. Quadruple your profits. What do we get? Simple. We are taking over this whole top floor and the whole basement. Your goons protect the two floors. No one, but no one is ever allowed up here or into the basement. Ask no questions about what goes on here. From time to time, we will ask you to provide us some young women for our use. No questions asked. Don't care where or how you get the women, as long as they are young and pretty. Oh, and you can take all of your things from this suite. We will be, as you say, redecorating the place."

Black-eyed Bo rubbed his hands across his face. This was too good to be true. There had to be a catch here somewhere. "Got'a see the quality merchandise first."

"What would you like to see?" Gisella asked, sensing she had him. Such a puny mind, she thought, so easily manipulated. Plus, he radiated such an exquisite fear that she rather wished that he would need more "persuasion."

"Kilo of high grade coke."

Magic flashed. A plastic wrapped bag appeared in her hands which she laid on an end table that magically up-righted itself. He produced a long knife from his pants and inspected the coke. "Got'a have it tested first," he stalled. This had to be some trick. She allowed him to send for his "chemist." While he waited for the results, he asked, "So you's just want this place here, but I gets to keep my stuff? Basement's trashed."

"That's right. We're moving in here and will fix it up according to our needs. In a few days, we will ask for a number of pretty, young women to be delivered to us. You comply. You get all the drugs you wish at no cost to you."

"Pure, boss," his chemist reported and hastily left, taking the kilo with him.

"You got a deal. Need twenty kilos coke and thirty kilos of weed in two days."

"Got that general?" Gisella asked.

"Yes. No problem. I'll have it delivered to the floor below this one in two days," General Franco replied without any emotion in his voice.

"Wa'cha want with the women?"

"None of your business. You bring them to us, that's all you need to know. We won't be giving them back, if that's what you were worried about," Gisella added.

"Mysterious, eh?" She nodded. He barked, "Okay. Deal."

"Cool. Let's party and celebrate the coming New Year," Gisella suggested.

The next day, the penthouse suite was vacated. He moved his entourage down a floor, making his men remodel it in a new style. "Time t'a change decor," he ordered.

As soon as the top floor was vacated, General Franco had his men bring in their voluminous shrunk packages that had been sent from the Abyss in response to the extensive report that Gisella had sent. Besides all the equipment, Graz'zt sent along Dr. Menninger, a dozen nurses, and his second in command, Gar-Tar, a very powerful Cambion and his wife, Benedetta. She was a powerful witch in her own right and gifted with many of the spells that her prince had taught her.

"You've done well, General Franco, Gisella," Gar-Tar complimented the pair as he, his wife, and Dr. Menninger paced the giant room.

"This will do just fine," Dr. Menninger declared, "as long as we cover the windows. Can't have outsiders looking in."

"Already worked that out. These humans have something called paint. With your permission, my men will paint the windows black," the general pointed out. The doctor nodded. While the soldiers did just that, the doctor and his staff began preparing the room and setting up his various pieces of equipment.

A day later, all was ready for operations. Next, Benedetta opened up a permanent Magical Doorway to the basement. With that done, the general took his men down there and began reworking that filthy space. After cleaning up one area, they canceled a shrink spell on a massive roll of copper-lead mix. Carefully, they attached the huge sheet to the roof of the basement. While they were doing that, Gisella very carefully constructed a new incised pentagram beneath the overhead shielding. Later that night, Benedetta joined them and set up an extensive set of protective spells on the only entrance to the basement. Any human trying to get in to see what was going on down here would be killed by her magical wards.

The next day, the nurses headed out to lay in a large supply of human foods, while the soldiers looted a Rent to Own facility, stealing a kitchen, sofas, tables, chairs, and other furniture, including quite a number of beds. And so it went. A week later, a large living complex and medical laboratory was fully setup. Benedetta hadn't been idle either. She'd cast a very large number of Silence spells into the floor, ceiling, and walls of the suite, also making them permanent, along with adequate protection spells to keep pesky humans from entering uninvited.

With all in readiness, Gisella headed down a floor to speak with Black-eyed Bo. "I take it the drugs have met with your approval?" She found him lying on a new couch, surrounded by nearly naked young women, fawning over him, rather high on the new drugs.

"Aye. Best deal ever," he answered. "Making a kill'en on 'em."

"Good. Good. Now it is time for you to live up to your bargain. We need a dozen young women today and another twenty, a few each day. Make sure that they are pretty and young. Don't care where you get them or how, just get them," Gisella barked with full intention.

"Ah, her 'u go. Take 'u're pick 'o these. Got 'em all doped up 4 u," he replied.

As Gisella picked out the best twelve, a nurse escorted the bikini-clad women in their stilettos out of the room, up the stairs, to where Benedetta was waiting for them. Each demon nurse cast a Charm spell on her woman, ensuring their full cooperation and so that they would offer no resistance.

Gisella picked the last woman and then ordered, "Okay, bring us two new women tomorrow. We require another twenty women, two per day. Your next drug shipment will be when you deliver the last of the twenty women. Enjoy." She turned and walked out, amazed that the drug lord hadn't even asked what she wanted with so many women. Fool, she thought.

As each drugged and charmed woman was brought before Benedetta, she cast a very precise series of spells. First, she cast a Paralyze spell. Once she verified the woman was "frozen" on her feet, she cast Incinerate: Arms, followed by a Clean spell to remove the foul vapors. She nodded to the woman's nurse, who then sat the paralyzed woman on a chair and removed her bikini and heels. "Fuse: Feet Vertical," Benedetta barked next, followed by "Idiot Mind," followed with another nod to the nurse, who promptly put the hardened ballet boots on the women. "Shrink To Fit," she barked, finishing the sequence and canceling the paralyze spell.

The drugged woman could no longer grasp reality. All this had seemed like a very bad trip, especially when the helpful nurse got her up and made her walk. "Please! Don't let go of me. I can't walk like this!"

In a soothing tone, the nurse replied, "Sure you can.

Practice makes perfect." She led her into the living quarters, where there were a large number of beds, an open bathroom, sofas, and a dining room table with an equal number of chairs. She led the woman over to the table and helped her sit down. She slid a plate of food in front of the woman and told her to eat. While the confused woman attempted to obey, she filled up a cup with coffee and inserted a straw for her, placing it with the woman's reach. That done, she left her alone.

Two hours later, the dozen new women were all sipping their coffee and trying to figure out why they were having such similar nightmare hallucinations. Their extremely limited intelligence simply could not work it out, but they knew that they were extremely helpless in this bad dream and hoped they would wake up soon. Of course, they didn't.

After General Franco and Gisella personally inspected the dozen new women and their living arrangements, Gar-Tar ordered them to begin work on Phase II of the new operations. With broad grins, the two left, picked up the rest of the general's men and headed out of the building. Some twelve blocks further west, they repeated the same action on the second largest crime lord, second only to Black-eye Bo. He called himself, the Reaper, because he specialized in killings for hire among other nefarious dealings.

At this second location, they established a maternity ward on the top floor. It took them a month to get it fully equipped to handle and care for twenty pregnant women at one time. Gisella commented to her general, "This is a brilliant plan by our illustrious prince. Why bother taking all these human females to the Abyss? Just set up the Egg Production Center right here where they reside."

He replied, "What I like is that he's not putting all his eggs in one basket." Both laughed at his pun. Twenty women would be kept here at the maternity ward while their baby Cambions gestated. Once they'd given birth, they would be re-impregnated and the process repeated until their bodies stopped working, at which point they would be replaced by one of the other egg-producing women. However, the vast majority of the fertilized eggs would be kept in stasis and then periodically shipped back to the usual hosts in the Abyss.

Either way, Prince Graz'zt was guaranteed a large supply of new Cambions for his massive army being grown, all his own offspring.

Between mid-January and late March, this same scenario was played out in LA and in Miami, compliments of Donatella and Bella. When the last one became operational and at capacity, sixty women were producing an egg per day, which the good Dr. Menninger fertilized. Another thirty-six women were staying in the maternity wards, but a dozen of them were nearly three months pregnant. Once per week, a demon used his own ability to open a temporary Gate to the Abyss, sending along the canister of accumulated fertilized eggs and receiving back some additional supplies. These native-cast Gate spells were not detectible by the IR satellites, since they didn't involve the incised pentagrams. Further, the locations from where the spells were cast varied all over the city, done at night, and with Invisibility spells in force. A perfect plan indeed.

However, this was only the secret part of Graz'zt plan. In other cities of the world, he periodically had some of his demons put in an appearance. Wreak some havoc. Kill a few humans. Attract the attention of the humans and their annoying wizards, and then vanish, only to make another random appearance a few weeks later. For this batch of demons, this was utopia. They had free reign to wreak all the death and destruction their hearts desired, and unfortunately, they were quite often unable to wait that long between attacks. Many were themselves killed and were forced back into the Abyss, unable to return to Earth for many subsequent years, much to Graz'zt's displeasure. Still, it accomplished his objectives, keeping the humans preoccupied and away from his new Breeding Centers, as he now called them.

Further, Prince Graz'zt had also sent along another six succubuses with sufficient garrison forces. Their task was to visit major cities of the world, abduct ten young women, and then use a temporary Gate spell to send the batch to the Abyss. Once sent, they were to move immediately to some other major world city and repeat the process at two-week intervals.

This would ensure a steady supply of egg producers for his planned massive army of his offspring. Nothing could go wrong this time.

Chapter 20—The Visit

"Man, is LA ever gang infested!" Rob declared to Monica and Crystal. It was mid-January, and he'd just returned from LA. "There are whole sections of that gigantic city that are totally controlled by criminal gangs. So when you respond to a demon attack, you may well also find yourself fighting the gang thugs as well. Just unreal. But I was useful to them. Graz'zt's forces have changed tactics. They know that we can detect their permanent incised pentagram Gates, so they've adapted. Now they kidnap the women, hold them until they have around a dozen of them, and then the succubus casts a Gate spell, sending the prisoners through to the Abyss. Sometimes, a few more demons come through on the spell as well."

He went on, "So I'm one of the very few people who can actually sense what transpired during one of these Gate spells. Without my observations, they wouldn't know that Graz'zt is still abducting young women, taking them to the Abyss. What scares me more is that we are only finding out about these after the fact, and that more and more of these demons are walking among us, morphed into human forms. Where's this heading?"

"To a disaster, that's where!" Crystal replied. "And I just thought that things were quieting down. We think it's been quiet here in St. Louis anyway, but now I'm not so sure. Darn these demons anyway. I thought we had them stopped with the IR observations."

"Hey, you and the Board of Regents too," Rob added. "They are now heavily involved, since the demons seem to be moving all over the country. They are worried about the demons expanding across the whole world."

"Hey, there have been some in Marseille, France, and Prague," Monica pointed out. "I think that they already are worldwide. So what do we do now?"

Rob answered, "Form up City Defense Units. Henry is doing that for St. Louis. I hope you all don't mind, but I put our names in with Henry. Whenever a demon pops up around here, you will be Messaged, and we go off to counter them. Otherwise, we wait until the Board of Regents figures out a better strategy. Say, I'm tired, and I really missed you, Monica. What say we get me tucked into bed?"

As the two walked slowly to their bedroom suite, she whispered, "I've really missed you too. Keep on rubbing your hands over my backside. Feels good." By the time that they got to their suite, they were both rather frantic, passions exploding. This time, Rob got them undressed rapidly, not waiting for her to use her clumsy spells. A passionate half hour later, she lay on his shoulder while he drifted into a deep sleep.

I've missed him more than I can say, she thought, and enjoyed just lying beside him, though it was only just after lunchtime. Eventually, she quietly rose without disturbing him. Using spells, she got herself dressed again and headed to her study. She had much to ponder.

Monica Nicole had never paid any attention to formal religions and certainly wasn't a religious person, never having been to any church nor had she as Dominus. With so many mentioning this thing called karma, she thought she should at least find out what it was. She looked up karma and reincarnation on the Net. Cause and effect. What goes around comes around. Many views, in many religions, she read, tended to believe that what one sews, one will reap. There were some differences on just what physical form the reincarnated soul would take, though. The bottom line, she began to believe, was that if one did evil in one lifetime, they would somehow become the effect of that evil in the next.

Well as Dominus, the evil that I did was positively gargantuan. So am I supposed to be helpless this lifetime like those that I made helpless last lifetime? To atone for my wickedness? Or to make amends for what I've done? It seems to me that I should make amends somehow. Maybe it's both. I am to suffer this lifetime the way that I made other women suffer, while making amends. That must be it. Monica finally concluded.

Her thoughts then drifted to making amends and the possibility that the Physician of the Gods, this Diancecht, might be the answer that she sought. That decided, she knew what she had to do: seek out this godlike being wherever he was in the Concordant Opposition plane of existence. She'd have to tell Rob and get him to teach her how to use her gift of Planar Travel, but she also knew that she alone would have to face this godlike person. She couldn't have Rob actually beside her, as much as she desired to have his firm hands supporting her. She had to do this alone; she just had to.

He awoke smelling supper and was pleased to dine on Nisha's fancy new dishes that she'd been learning how to prepare. "You've become a real chef, Nisha," he complimented her. Of course, he had to tell everyone about his adventures in LA, but they were grim ones, leaving them somewhat depressed afterwards. All this time, they'd been thinking the demons were mostly inactive.

After dinner, Monica took Rob back to her suite and told him about her discoveries concerning the Rings of Regeneration and the Incinerate spell that Graz'zt had used. "So the rings simply can't be used. They will not regenerate appendages lost by the Incinerate spell or by acid dissolution. However," she continued, explaining about the Physician of the Gods, this Diancecht, a Celtic deity, and the possibility that he had the power to regenerate even limbs lost to the Incinerate spells. "So, I have to find Diancecht and see if I can't get this from him. So many innocent women are having their lives ruined by this. I have to try. I need you to teach me how to use my Planar Travel ability. Then, I need to find this Concordant Opposition plane and find the realm called Mag Mell, the Field of Happiness. From there, perhaps someone can direct me to where he lives."

"Brilliant love. Brilliant. If you can get something from him to restore all the women, we have a chance of salvaging their lives, once we find ways to get them back from the Abyss. I'll go with you," he replied.

"Partway. I have to meet him alone, I think. This is my need, my situation. I have to face him alone. So when do we start? I'm not tired," Monica explained, hoping that he would just accept this and not pry into her reasoning behind why she felt that she had to do it alone.

"Why not now?" Rob suggested, and her heart raced a

little with anticipation. He grabbed a piece of paper and drew a central circle with sixteen spokes radiating out from it. He placed a square at the other end of each spoke. Finally, he drew another square some distance from the connected collection. "Okay. This isolated square represents our universe, specifically Earth. Some call the intervening space the Astral Plane. It connects us with the Outer Planes, this other large collection. Some call it the ether. Your Concordant Opposition is this central circle. It has a super-vortex at its center, perhaps a super-worm hole. Who knows? It's like a tornado when you see it."

"Now our mutual good Indian friends are here," he pointed to the northwest square, "the Seven Heavens. The Abyss is exactly opposite, down here in the southeast square. It's not to size, since there are six hundred sixty six levels to the Abyss. Got it?"

"Right. So how do we get there?" Monica asked.

"Well, there are three ways. In the past, there have been permanent conduits or Gates as we now call them. Usually, they were permanent Gates erected here on Earth at a powerful temple or church dedicated to that specific deity or god-like person, with the other end connected to that god's corresponding location. One just steps into the Gate and arrives at the other end."

He went on, "Since he was a Celtic deity type, there's not much chance of us finding any permanent Gates. They'd been gone for over two thousand years now. There are also random color pools that will take you there, sometimes. They are a bit chaotic in that sometimes you don't end up where you wanted to go. Besides, we could spend years looking for one here on Earth, if they even exist any longer. So we use the third way, our special gift."

"You start walking and intend to reach the Astral Plane, a kind of featureless grey void. Just keep on walking while holding your destination plane firmly in your mind. Shortly, you will see it appearing in the distance. Just keep walking towards it. Our speed of travel is dependent entirely upon our intelligence. The higher our intelligence, the faster we travel and vice versa. Once you take a step into that destination plane, focus your mind on the destination realm, and keep on walking. Shortly, you will reach the solid ground of that realm. That's all there is to it."

Rob then cautioned her, "However, there is a catch. All manner of people, monsters, and creatures either are also passing through or live there in the voids. We have to be careful and be prepared to fight, if nasty creatures decide to attack us en route. Also, our spells work differently there too. All magic is a little twisted in the Outer Planes. It is said that as you approach the vortex at the center of the Concordant Opposition and all the Outer Planes, even Grade 9 spells cease to function. So dear, there is always some risk when traveling this way."

"Okay. I'm ready. Shall we begin?" Monica said, steeling her determination to see this through.

"Sure dear. Best cast all our protective spells on ourselves first." Both did so, but Monica also placed a number of defensive spells on him, those that he didn't know how to cast. Finally ready, he put his hands around her waist, steadying her, and they began to walk. "Okay, focus on walking into the grey void. . ." He didn't finish his sentence. She did so, and they found themselves walking across the void. She found at once that communication was via thoughts, not speech here.

"Oh. This is so cool and easy to do."

"Right. Now let's not stick around here for long. It's too dangerous. Focus on the Concordant Opposition, the big circle with the tornado at its center. Right, like that."

"I see them! The Outer Planes. There they are!" She saw what looked remarkably like his crude sketch, though the sixteen squares were much larger and more complex than he'd drawn them.

Rob looked around. "Hurry up. I think that we are being followed. I don't what to get into a fight, if we can avoid it."

"Okay. Focusing on Concordant Opposition now." She did so and continued walking. While I say walking, it was very strange. She appeared to be taking steady strides, but her feet were touching nothing but the void of the plane. Rather, it was her intention, her focus that gave the apparency of moving by walking. Soon a swirling disk of a multitude of colors appeared, growing larger and larger. "Do I focus on Mag Mell now?"

"Right," Rob replied. Monica did so, focusing her will on that single name, the Field of Happiness. As she did so, she felt that there must also be a large number of other realms also located here on this strange disk. Some were trying to attract her attention to themselves, but she re-enforced her will to Mag Mell only and saw a set of rolling hills appearing before her.

Suddenly, her feet touched solid ground, and she nearly stumbled so sudden came the change. Rob caught her just in time. "We're here," he said, looking around. Monica saw rolling grasslands and hills dotted with dense oak forests. The sky was crystal blue and clear; the air, fresh as though just after a cleansing rain. She breathed deeply.

"I like this place," she said.

"You had better like this place," a deep bass voice startled both of them, coming from behind them. They turned, Monica doing a pirouette on her toes. There stood a man wearing a grey, homespun hooded cloak that hid most of his body. They could see the crude leather sandals on his feet just below the bottom of his cloak. A black bearded face peered out at them from beneath the hood.

He gave them a moment to observe him and then spoke. "I am Bran Cadman, Door Warden of Mag Mell. Please state the reason and purpose of this visit."

Monica spoke up. "I am seeking Diancecht. I want to discuss something with him. Please, sir, can you direct us to where he lives, that I may speak with him."

"You do not lie. Follow me," Bran replied. Monica realized that Bran was speaking in what was probably an ancient Celtic language, but that she'd understood his every word. Fascinating, she thought. "It is not far," the man added. As they followed him, she appreciated Rob's steadying arm. Keeping her balance on the relatively uneven ground was nearly impossible. She knew that alone, she would have not been able to keep her balance at all.

As they moved along, she noticed that they actually

traveled at a fantastic speed, probably akin to what they had just been doing with their Planar Travel! Great forests sped past them in a blur, but she focused only on following the hooded man and not falling down. Bran felt like talking. As they walked, he said, "It is my duty to greet all those arriving from the planes and ascertain their business here in Mag Mell. If hostile parties come, I summon a counter-force, and we expel them. I also deal with those who lie, harshly, I'm told. Ah, your destination lies there." He pointed to a rustic looking village. Monica had a hunch this looked much like ancient Celtic homesteads, with their unique wood and mud dwellings, simple, yet functional.

"You will find him sitting on his throne awaiting you. I bid you good day," Bran replied. He turned and simply vanished, leaving the pair standing at the edge of the village. A number of men were working around the village. Some were making swords, she noted. Women were tending flocks, drawing water from one of two wells, while some were carrying fruit, vegetables, and loaves of bread. Several children were running about playing on the dirt streets of the small village. All wore traditional Celtic garb that Monica had once seen in her history books at magic school.

"Okay, Rob. You wait here for me. I will walk this last way myself. I have to do this alone, dear," Monica said, hoping that he would understand and not make an issue of it. She didn't want to explain why she felt as she did. Not yet. Not now. She was too uncertain of it all herself. Karma? Perhaps, she thought.

"I will be here for you," Rob replied and let go of her waist.

As she began taking very careful steps down the uneven dirt street, she thought, "Why did I have him let go of me? I'm so vulnerable. What if I fall? What if I need help? They are all staring at me! Well, I'm quite a sight." She was wearing her bright red satin gown as she always did when going to an important meeting. Look the best I can was her guiding principle, as it had been for many years now.

Somehow, she kept her balance, though not too gracefully at times and reached the heart of the small hamlet.

346

There couldn't have been more than a dozen of these dwellings here. At the center stood an enormous oak tree with massive roots. There sitting on one of the roots was a young man, also dressed like the other men in traditional Celtic garb from some two thousand years ago, if the history books were accurate in their representations. His face was roundish, but he had a short black, full beard, and kindly blue eyes. He looked like any other normal man, except perhaps he was far more attractive.

He spoke. His voice was as soft as a gentle summer's rain, but there was an immense sense of power in it as well. "Come. You wish to speak with me. Sit beside me. I believe this root is tall enough for you. Such tall heels I have not seen before. Come. Sit." He gestured to another root that stood as tall as a bar stool, which she often preferred. It made getting up easier than lunching to her feet from the lower chairs, sofas, and couches. Careful not to stumble and make an utter fool of herself, Monica had to wiggle and wobble about to keep her balance over the very uneven ground by the roots. She was very relieved to sit down beside him. "What is it that you wish to speak to me about? Long has it been since I spoke with you humans."

"The Earth has been invaded by Prince Graz'zt and his demons," she began. She began at the beginning with her own abduction and what she discovered there in the Abyss. She outlined how she and Rob had rescued Nisha and four other women, and later Jill. Monica explained that an Incinerate spell and a Fuse spell had been used to make the women helpless pawns in his monstrous breeding program. Further, she added the more recent news that Rob had uncovered, that unknown to them, many more women had been kidnaped and taken to the Abyss to be similarly used.

Monica then got to the reason for this trip. "While my Morph spell has sort of helped the four women somehow live a semi-normal life, I simply must find a permanent way to heal Jill and all these other women, who somehow I will rescue from their torment. A Ring of Regeneration would have been the answer, and no matter its cost, I would have gotten one to use on each of these poor victims, but alas, they will not work when the appendages were removed by this Incinerate spell nor will it restore their Fused feet."

She took a deep breath and came out with it. "I have learned that you possess the kind of healing powers that could be used to restore these women's lost arms and destroyed feet. I have come to ask you to make it possible for me to do this for all these women. Perhaps you have a special ring that will work or some other magic. I will do or pay anything to obtain it so I can help restore these women's destroyed lives. As I said, I've been able to remove the pain and trauma of their mutilations, but I must also give them their lives back. They cannot live as I am now, since most of them are just normal women and cannot cast any spells at all. Please, Diancecht, help me."

"Ah, terrible, just terrible," he spoke at last. "Have you not tried a Full Wish spell? I'm sure that would undo Graz'zt's magic."

"Yes, it probably would, Diancecht, but with hundreds of women or even for myself, I simply will not be part of making someone age unnaturally one year just for me to regain my arms and feet, let alone hundreds of years for all the other women. I can't do it, sir. I just can't ask another to age like that, not even for myself. I've—I've done that in my last lifetime. I swear I will never be party to that again, not ever."

"Ah, yes, your past is as clear to me as is my village to you. You have walked an evil path, but that was in the past. Now you are walking a different path, are you not?"

"Yes, I swear it. I'm not as I was. I was psychotic, but I did unspeakable things—things that I wish with all my heart I could undo, but cannot. I've not done any of that now. I'm trying to help others, particularly other innocent women victims," Monica replied honestly.

"Indeed, it is so. I will give you just such a ring, but it will only answer to you. Only you will be able to see it. Only you will be able to put it upon the toe of those you seek to heal. I charge you to heal ninety-nine others, be they friend or foe, be they deserving of such healing in your eyes or not. Ninety-nine. Only on the hundredth use can you place it upon your toe to heal yourself and only on the hundredth use will it heal you. Once all the victims have been healed, you must return the ring to me. Is this clear, Monica Nicole Black-Finch?"

"Yes sir. I will do as you ask. I cannot begin to thank you enough. You are salvaging the lives of many women with your kindness."

"That is as it should be. I am the Physician of the Gods. Go now. The ring lies on a chain around your neck. Use it wisely."

She looked down and saw a plain golden ring hanging from a golden chain around her neck. Thanking him again, she got to her feet, and with some wiggling and wobbling to keep her balance on the rough ground, she finally reached the more level dirt street. She turned around for one last look at the man, but he wasn't there nor was his tree! She pirouette again and headed back towards Rob, who was playing games with some of the children. He looked up and smiled. "Just having some fun with the kids. All done?"

"Yes. Time to go home and to work. I've got a way to heal the women! I really do!" she said very excited. Monica was vert glad to feel his steadying arm around her waist once more. This time, she allowed him to walk them home. She had much to ponder now, vowing to start on Jill tomorrow morning. As they made the return trip, once more they both felt as though someone or something was following them, but they didn't catch sight of him or her or it and arrived safely home.

Once there, Monica gathered everyone and told them her great news. Naturally, everyone wanted to see this most precious and extraordinarily powerful magical ring. Monica used a spell to lift it up on its chain so they all could see it, but they all saw nothing at all.

"We can't see it, Monica, but we believe you," Crystal pronounced.

"Will it really restore my arms?" asked Jill, almost in tears.

"It is supposed to do that and fix up your feet too. We will try it first thing in the morning," Monica declared. "I'm really exhausted at the moment. Oh! Rob, you're right. It does use up an enormous amount of my energies to do all that."

"Told you so. Come on; let's get you to bed, my love." She didn't need any further encouragement.

Right after breakfast the next morning, and another hundred spells just to feed herself, Monica took Jill to her bedroom. After Jiri took off her clothes and shoes for her and getting her into a nightgown, he left Monica to work her magic. Again, using several spells, Monica got the ring off the necklace and over to a fused toe of Jill's. As she pushed it towards her little toe, the ring began expanding until it slipped easily onto her toe.

"There. It's on your toe."

"I can feel it. It's rather cold. Oh!" She felt magical energies flooding over her body. "Something's happening!"

Monica saw Jill's body outlined in a sort of yellowish glow and a few minutes later, the glow settled on her feet and where her arms would have been. She saw ghostly outlines of Jill's arms and hands appearing. Monica then had the strangest notion or hunch that she needed to sit with Jill until the ring came off of its own accord. She Messaged Rob, telling him that.

With little else to do, the two women just chatted about ordinary things. Neither had any idea how long the process would take. Monica sat or slept with Jill for two days before the ring slipped off her toe. Again, Monica cast several spells and got the ring securely fastened to her necklace and then examined Jill.

"Well, I think it's done. Can you move your fingers? Wiggle your toes?"

Jill began bawling. "Yes, oh yes, yes! They work just as they always did. See?" She made all manner of crazy motions with her hands and arms, even moving her feet about as well. "Monica, thank you! You've given me back my life! How can I ever thank you enough?" She sat up and hugged Monica tightly. Even Monica's eyes swelled up with tears of joy. Hastily, Jill got herself dressed, going barefoot for now. She dashed off to show everyone the holy miracle that had happened. Monica was left far behind, but she didn't care in the slightest. Rather, she was already planning to visit each of the other four women and heal them.

During the next eight days, Monica did just that, restoring the other four women's arms and feet. By then, word had spread on up the lines from Henry to Leslie and to the Board of Regents that Monica Nicole Black-Finch had a way to heal the victims of Graz'zt's evil work. Many people finally breathed a huge sigh of relief. The ultimate weapon was no longer such an awful, permanent weapon.

Chapter 21—A New Client

Ari and I were between cases. It's rather nice to sit back, put your feet up on your desk, and just relax, if only for a day or two. The demon threat seemed to have gone away to other cities, least that's what the newscasters kept saying. Of course, I never believe half of that those folks say. Still, things were quiet. We had deposited Monica's cash, and for once had a comfortable margin, money wise that is.

Just after noon, a pretty brunette came knocking on our door. As I said before, I'd already changed the sign to read Parry and Ari Tuttle Private Investigations. She wore black pumps with at least three-inch heels, black hose, and a black skirt. Okay, so I notice a person from the bottom up. Great legs, by the way. When my eyes reached her face, I recognized her at once. She worked as a bank teller where I do my business.

"Hello, you're from the bank," I welcomed her, wondering if there had been some awful mix-up and our funds ended up in Washington or somewhere.

Her round face, nicely done makeup, wavy dark brown hair that just touched her shoulders, all spoke of a respectable young woman, but one who is very frightened. I could tell that much from her eyes. I think Ari got even more than that from her quick observations.

"Hello. I'm Christina Gregory. Yes, I know you from your visits to the bank. That's why I came by. I do hope I'm not intruding or anything. I've never done anything like this before," she said hesitantly, very unsure of just what she was actually doing in my office.

"Have a seat, Christina. I'm Ari. How can we help you?" Hey, my gal is quick on the uptake.

"I—I think that someone is following me. I'm scared. All these demons around and all the kidnaping scares—well, I'm on edge. I'm probably just being paranoid, but. . ." Christina tried to explain.

"Hey, it's all right to be scared. These demons are very

evil beasts and have been preying upon young women like ourselves. You've a right to be worried," Ari declared with some emphasis.

"So where have you sensed that you were being followed," I asked a more relevant question.

"I live not too far from here," she explained. Right, her apartment complex was about a mile from the bank. Nice commute, I thought. She went on, "When I left my door to walk down the hall and out to my car, it felt as if someone was watching me. I kept looking back over my shoulder, but I didn't see anything. Still, it was creepy. Then, when I was walking from the bank employee's lot into the bank, I felt it again. This has been going on for the past two days now. It happened again when I came into work this morning, so now that it's my lunch hour, I thought I should perhaps do something. I remembered you are always coming by the bank, and so I thought maybe you could do something. I'm probably just imagining the whole thing. Certainly, I can't go to the police with this. I've not actually seen anything."

"Right. The police would tell you to wait until you were kidnaped before calling them," I joked with her, bringing a slight, brief smile to her face. I like to see women smiling, not scared for their lives. "Okay, you say you only detect someone is watching you while you are going to your car from the bank and while going from your car to and from your apartment?"

"Yes. Those are the only times I get this weird feeling, Mr. Tuttle. What does it mean?"

It sounded like someone was casing the woman, planning to do something not so nice to her. Probably being invisible. Possibly a wizard or even a demon. Too soon to tell, but not someone that Christina would want to meet. "Well, we aren't sure either, but you've a right to be very concerned. We'll take your case, Christina."

"But I haven't paid you anything yet. I don't know how expensive this is going to be," she said very reservedly. I suspected that she didn't have much money either. Bank tellers are hardly the top paying positions at banks.

"Hey, we won't charge you anything to keep an eye on you. If someone tries anything, we'll do what we can to stop them. We can worry about a small fee if we actually do something to help you. If nothing comes from this, consider it a goodwill gesture between us. How's that?"

The relief on her face told the full story. I'd just homered. Ari smiled too, pleased that we would be helping Christina and probably not charging her anything. Besides, right now, we didn't need the money, for once. "Thank you, Mr. Tuttle."

"Parry please. And Ari. So we need some details. What time are you off work? What model car do you have? Where's your apartment? That sort of thing. We will be watching, but discretely. You won't be seeing us, but we will be there, just in case."

"Thank you, thank you, Parry, Ari," Christina gushed. She rattled off the details and Ari took them down, saving me from having to do that. Beside, Ari's handwriting is a hundred times better than mine is. Come to think of it, most women's handwriting is superior to men's. I wonder why that is?

"Great. Here's our card. If you are going to change your schedule in any way, call us ahead of time. One more thing, at night have you felt that you've been watched? I mean while you are inside your apartment?"

"No. Just when I leave and am in transit. Should I be worried about someone breaking in?" she asked, growing worried again.

"Probably not, but keep the doors and windows locked at all times," I advised.

She chuckled, "I already do that, Parry. I'm a single woman living on my own. Actually, I'm taking night classes at the university. One day, I hope to be able to be one of those CSI technicians and do fancy lab testing to help capture criminals. That's several years away. I can only afford to take one class a semester."

We chatted a bit before she had to return to work. To be on the safe side, we walked her back and ducked behind the bank to spot her car, before returning to our office. Ari and I chatted about Christina and then prepared ourselves for the case.

We were there a half hour before she got off work,

invisible, and from a vantage point where we could see the whole lot. Okay, we were up on top of the neighboring building's roof. Both Ari and I kept a sharp eye out for other Invisible men or demons. Right on time, Christina came out of the bank, along with several other employees. She glanced around, but didn't see us. If she had the sensation that she was being followed, she was supposed to raise her left arm up just once, as though stretching. That would signal us to really bear down hard and try to spot who or what was following her. Nothing this time. No arm went up. Using Fly spells, we followed her back to her apartment. Still nothing. However, as she began the walk up to her hallway, her arm did go up!

Instantly, Ari and I began scouring the entire area, looking for the stalker. We spotted a dozen people in the area, but none of those seemed remotely like her unseen stalker. They were visible, for one thing. Just as she ducked into her hallway, keys at the ready, we spotted something dark at the far corner of the parking lot. Neither of us got a good look at whoever or whatever it was, because it used a magic spell to depart, probably a Teleport spell or a Magical Door. Something or someone was definitely watching her, probably getting familiar with her routine. I had half a notion to call her up and insist that she totally alter her routine, but thought better of it. She had to be at the bank at specific times. It wouldn't do to be standing around the bank for an hour before it opened or after it closed.

We watched her in the morning, but it was Friday evening March 10 that it happened. While we were watching her get out of her car, returning home from work, two hooded men jumped out of a panel truck as she walked by. One held a rag over her nose while the other picked her up. They tossed her into the truck and peeled out of the lot before either Ari or I could react. In all fairness, we expected something more sophisticated, not a simple snatch and grab! The suddenness of the attack took us both by surprise. By the time that we were ready to act, the rundown truck was already moving down the street, mingling with the other heavy rush hour traffic.

We cast our Fly spells and followed along after the truck, hoping to snatch her back once they stopped. I considered zapping the truck, stalling it, but in this traffic, Christina or others could well be hurt if I caused an accident. No, our best bet was to take them when they stopped. As we followed them, I began to get worried. They were heading into the Project, the gang infested part of town, where not even the police dared to set foot out of their cars! This was turning out to be a very bad situation. Why were hoods kidnaping Christina? It made no sense at all.

Finally, they stopped the truck outside a tall apartment complex. We thought better of taking them just then. Why? A dozen men armed with machine guns and grenades stepped out of the building along with two pairs of wizards and witches, wands at the ready, providing cover for the two men who quickly carried the unconscious Christina inside the building!

"What do we do?" Ari whispered to Parry as they hovered in the air watching them.

"We can't take on this bunch of thugs ourselves. I'll stand watch here, while you go get help. But who? The police won't go near this place. They would need a SWAT team to get in there. We need a bunch of wizards and witches. Okay, you go find Oliver and get him briefed. I'm going to visit Monica and her group. There are a lot of wizards and witches in one spot. Maybe we can get back here fast enough," Parry suggested.

"On it!" Ari declared, suddenly teleporting away. With a heavy heart, I did likewise.

"Hi Parry," Jill greeted me, as I arrived in the reception area.

"You look great with your new arms, Jill. Say, this is kind of an emergency. Can you signal everyone for me?" I replied.

By the time that everyone had assembled, Ari and Oliver arrived. He looked rather grim, I thought. "We've got a kidnaping situation," I began explaining, telling them about Christina Gregory, ending with the forces that we'd seen outside that apartment building.

That's when Oliver took over. "Listen, Parry. We need to use extreme caution here. Do you know whose apartment complex that is?" I shook my head no. "Only the most vicious drug lord in St. Louis! He has an armed encampment in there. Ground forces won't get within a block of there without being brutally ambushed! Lord knows what he has inside that complex or why he's kidnaping women. Extreme caution, fellows, extreme caution."

"But his men have taken Christina. We have to do something to rescue her," I protested.

Monica spoke up, "Parry, we will. Just give us time. We'll all need Skin of Stone spells on us so their guns won't work. However, if you are sprayed with machine gun fire, the spell won't last for long. Besides, there should be all sorts of protection spells up, since there are at least four wizards and witches there as well. Could well be more inside, if it's really fourteen stories high."

"She's right, Parry. We need to case the place before we charge in there," Crystal agreed with her. Well, she would; she's her best friend.

"But we can't wait forever. Someone should be watching to see if they take her somewhere else. While you all figure out the how, I'm going back there and keep an eye on them. I don't want them carrying her off somewhere else."

"I'll stay here and help them coordinate things," Ari insisted. I gave her a kiss, cast my Invisibility spell, and then teleported back to my observation point across the street from the building. I cast Fly and got myself up and out of the way. The beat-up panel truck was still there. I figured she was still inside, since I had only been gone a few minutes.

I could see lights on in several windows and decided to check them out. If I was lucky, I might spot where they had Christina. It took me a good while to look into every one of the windows. No luck. Saw many things I'd rather not have seen, though. Nasty things. What got my attention was the top floor, presumably where this Black-eyed Bo lived. All the windows were painted black. How utterly queer!

To me, that meant someone was hiding something, but what? Did the drug lord live up there? That was Oliver's most recent intelligence. I guess he wanted his privacy, but why? If I were the lord, I'd want the view out of there. Shoot, he could see the arch and even Bush Stadium, most likely. So why did he cover up his windows with paint no less? Wouldn't simple blinds work even better? You could see out when you wanted and block the view at other times. This just didn't make sense to me.

I'm one of those fellows to which things have to make sense. There is always a reason for things, even if the reason is as slim as the "person's insane." This just didn't add up, not with this being the top drug lord in St. Louis. As I flew around the top floor, I couldn't see any way in there, short of the main entrance. They didn't even have proper fire escapes either, but then no city code enforcer would ever set foot in the Projects, not unless he was trying to commit suicide. As far as I could tell, there was only one way in. But that works both ways; only one way for those inside to get out. I resolved to shoot a bunch of balls of fire at them, if they came out the doors. No way was I allowing them to transport poor Christina somewhere else! I gave her my word.

Shortly, I was joined by the others, all hovering around me, Invisible, and with Fly spells in operation. We landed across the street, being careful not to bump into one another. "So what's the plan?" I asked. "Only the one entrance there. What's weird is that all the windows on the top floor are painted black. I've seen some crazy things, but never that."

Monica whispered, "We're going to check out what kind of traps they might have around the door and protection spells. Hang in there a bit longer."

"Hey, everyone. If you are on the ground around here, watch your step. There are mountains of hypodermic needles all over, broken glass, nails, and all sorts of trash," I pointed out. I felt I owed my friends this alert. I'd been on the ground casing the place, but had to case my own feet. How could people let their environment around their home get in such a deplorable condition? Druggies. I guess they don't care about anything but feeding their habit. Still, if someone fell down, they could well get themselves in a whole lot of trouble. I landed about twenty feet in front of the door. My Fly spell had timed out. Besides, with so many others flying about and invisible as well, I didn't want to collide with one of my friends. That's the downside to the Invisibility spell—not so good when you have a group of us trying to do coordinated actions. We can't see each other either.

About ten minutes or so later on, I got a Message from Monica to meet across the street on the crumbling sidewalk. I picked my way carefully over there, crunching on several unspeakable things that made a crunching, breaking sound as my weight came down upon them. It was night now, and I couldn't see well. Besides, I didn't want to know what I was stepping on, not really.

When I got there, everyone was counting off, so I added, "Parry here." After Ari added her voice to the mix, Monica said that we were all present.

"We've got a really bad situation here. There are innumerable traps and protection spells all over this place, kind of like they've a gold mine inside there," Crystal explained. "Worse, thanks to Nisha and Jill, we know that we've got real trouble here. There's a half dozen demons on the top floor along with over thirty women. . ." Her voice faltered. "Mutilated, like Monica was," she finally managed to get the despised words out in a polite fashion. "Oliver's taken off to round up a SWAT team and alert St. Anne's. He's going to bring in Henry and the rest of the St. Louis Defense Team. Somehow, we have to kill the demons without harming the women."

"I thought this was the drug lord's place," I finally blurted out. I admit it. This news took me by total surprise. My simple rescue of Christina had really gone south. "Demons?" I muttered.

Monica whispered, "So they haven't been leaving St. Louis alone. They've been underground."

"It gets worse," Crystal added, "Nisha and Jill count close to a hundred or so humans inside, probably the drug lord, his goons, and their women. Probably all armed to the teeth. They are on all the floors except the top floor. We've got to fight our way through them to get to the women victims."

"Won't machine guns cut through our Skin of Stone spells really quickly?" Ari asked, growing concerned.

"No kidding," someone said. I didn't catch who though.

My mind was racing to digest this unexpected situation. There just had to be a way to get inside and not by gunning our way through a hundred trigger happy, doped up thugs. That's not my kind of party. Plus, I was worried about Ari getting hurt in all this. Bullets flying like rain isn't good for your health.

I had an idea. "Hey, do the stairs go all the way up here on this end where the entrance is at?" I asked, hoping it was so.

Jill replied, "I think so. I saw the heat signatures of two people climbing the stairs."

"Okay then, I have a plan. We Disintegrate a hole in the side of the stairs near the top floor. Then, we go in with Fly spells and leave the thugs below to the SWAT team," I whispered rapidly. All right, I also kept my fingers crossed while I said it. "Six demons can't kill thirty women before we get to them."

"Unless they have some powerful wards and protections on their door to the stairs," Crystal pointed out. "What's with all the others that we keep seeing going in and coming out?" she asked innocently.

"Drug buyers. Looking for their next high," I grumbled. "Filth. Don't worry about them. It's Christina that I'm after, not these scum!" I didn't add that I thought they'd be better off dead than living the pathetic lives that they were supposedly living. Menace to society and good folks everywhere.

"If no one has any better ideas, then we'll go with Parry's," Crystal ordered. "Jill, you and Monica stay here and coordinate with Oliver and the SWAT units. We don't want them shooting at us. As soon as those blue vans drive up, we will lose surprise, so let's time our Disintegration spells with their arrival. Monica, you Message me the second you see them. Has everyone gotten their protection spells on them? This could be a bad fight." Various acknowledgments echoed around me from my unseen friends.

"Way cool, Milos; we get to fight some demons!" Jiri whispered.

"Way cooler than cool! Glad we came. You all set, Nisha? I don't want anything to happen to my pretty cook." Milos whispered.

"Yes, but I think you are in more danger than I am, Milos," she answered from near his side. That's when I had a hunch that our two Czech fellows had more interests in sticking around than finding out more about demons.

Jiri was torn between his desire to fight demons and his strong desire to help protect Jill, who was staying back with Monica. I heard them whispering to each other, but couldn't quite make it out, except for her insistence that he go fight the demons. After that, we took flight again, hovering in an unseen line along the side of the complex, facing the concrete wall behind which the stairs climbed ever upwards to the top floor. Crystal, whispering constantly, got us into our invisible line, Ari at my side, naturally.

"Now!" barked Crystal aloud. She'd just received Monica's Message. Six blue SWAT vans pulled up on the street close to the sidewalk that led up to the fourteen-story apartment complex in the heart of the drug lord's kingdom. God help the druggies tonight, I thought. There was going to be dead bodies everywhere, and I hoped none of them would be us.

Disintegration beams shot at the concrete wall—at least ten of them, blasting gaping holes in the wall, enough that we could get inside. That canceled our Invisibility spells, and all of us headed inside. Not me, though. I figured they'd all be shooting those spells, so I held back, didn't cast it, and charged in first. As I landed on the landing, I saw a double steel door that led into the top floor's suite. I didn't need magic to see the numerous glowing spells warding the doors and protecting those inside. I'm not much on finesse or patience. Right now, the demons were being alerted to the assault, and I wanted inside immediately before they could cause Christina any further harm. As the others began landing behind me, I shot my Disintegrate at the side of the right door, figuring they might have some kind of re-enforcing spells on the doors proper.

I'm not stupid. If I was going to protect the doors, that's what I'd do. So I attacked the concrete in which the hinges were embedded. As the dust cleared, the right door creaked and fell inward, crashing onto the concrete floor. The loud bang definitely announced our arrival. However, a dozen other protective spell detonated. Well, let's get all those out of the way before we go charging in. Great balls of fire exploded around us. Several screamed. However, I knew that we all had our protection spells on, and these Grade 3 spells wouldn't harm us, just confuse us momentarily. Well, I was right, but we were rather a confused lot for a time.

I think I heard Crystal cursing me. I grinned as I cleared my head from the noise of the concussions the explosions had made. I also picked up more distant sounds of gunfire and many guns blazing from below me. Shattering glass too. I charged on inside, leading the way. I think I shouted, "Christina, I'm coming to free you!" But in all the confusion, maybe I was just thinking that I should say that, for her sake at least. Later on, Crystal said that I must have detonated a dozen Wards and protective spells all at once. Well, none of us got hurt by it. The demons certainly knew that we were coming after them.

Christina locked her car and began walking towards her apartment entryway, but had that feeling again. Per Parry's suggestion, she raised her left arm, hoping that he'd see it. Is there really someone out to get me, she wondered for the hundredth time? Just then from the corner of her eye, she spotted a man stepping out of the panel truck she'd just past. A grubby hand came around her face. A rag, awful smelling, covered her nose and mouth. She gasped and tried to scream, to wiggle free. Other hands, stronger than hers, held her waist. She fell, but was held up by those arms. Parry! She tried to scream and then everything went black, completely black. No thoughts, no motion, nothing at all. She'd passed out from the chloroform and didn't see them toss her into that panel truck and drive away.

She came to in a strange place. Christina tried to scream, tried to move, but her body refused all her commands. She saw a strange woman standing before her, chanting perhaps. *What's happening to me? Why can't I move? Someone, help me. Why can't I think?* A spell detonated. *Silly me. I can't move. I wonder if I ever could move. I feel funny.*

362

She's rather pretty. I wonder if I am pretty? What's she doing? Oh, my arms are up and out. Am I a bird? Do I have wings? I can't flap them. Can I fly now? Where would I fly? Another spell detonated. Her arms began burning from the bones outward. Pain! Unbearable pain! She tried to involuntarily scream, but still couldn't move, and she passed out, mercifully. Christina didn't see the ashes that had once been her arms settle to the floor nor did she see what happened next.

A woman stripped her of all her clothes and sat the paralyzed woman in a chair. Another spell detonated. The same woman put the steel re-enforced ballet ankle boots on her feet. Yet another spell detonated, and they shrank, tightly fitting her fused feet. A final spell detonated.

Christina woke up. Her body ached, but that awful pain was gone. So were her arms and clothes. "What's happened to me?" she asked, startled to hear her own voice.

The pretty woman now spoke to her. "You are very pretty, Christina. You want to look your best always, don't you?"

"Why, yes, yes I do. I want to look my best. Do I look my best?" she said innocently.

"You certainly do. Just look at how pretty you look," the woman said, holding a mirror up so she could see her new look.

"I do look good. My arms aren't there. Something must be wrong with your mirror."

"Oh no, Christina. You don't really need any arms my dear, do you? You look so pretty without them."

"Oh? I do? I do look pretty. No, I don't need them, if you say so. But aren't I supposed to have them?"

"Yes, but since you don't need them, I got rid of them for you, so now you look just perfect. Don't you think so?"

"Oh yes. Very much so. I look perfect without them. Thank you so much. But my feet feel funny. Why are my toes pointing down?" Christina asked, noticing them for the first time.

"You have the very sexiest boots ever. Why, you look ravishing in them, don't you think so? Don't you want to look really sexy, really beautiful?"

"Why yes, yes, I do. Of course. I do look sexy, don't you think?"

"Yes you certainly do, Christina, very sexy. You want to look your best, always, don't you?"

"Certainly. I want to look my best. Always. Now I do, don't I?"

"Absolutely, Christina. You look stunningly perfect in all ways."

"Oh thank you. I do look very good now. I think I want to go home. I think I am hungry. I think it is suppertime."

"Of course it is suppertime. But this is now your new home. It is far safer for you here. We will always look after you here. No one will ever harm you while you are here. Don't you want to be safe?"

"Oh yes, yes. Safe. I want to be safe. You will keep me safe?"

"Absolutely, Christina dear. As long as you are here, you will be totally safe. Now let's get you up and show you to the dinner table. There are many other perfect young women staying here too. They will help you to find where things are at."

"But I don't have any clothes. I think I should be wearing some. I don't know where mine went, though. What if a man sees me?"

"You don't need any clothes to hide your perfect body from others, do you? Besides, there are no men here, only you beautiful women."

"Oh. Yes, I don't need clothes. No men. That's good. How can I walk? I can't stand up!"

A nurse pushed her onto her toes; she wobbled wildly. "See, you are up and standing nicely. Come; this way to the others. I'm sure that they want to say hello to you, Christina."

"Oh, they do? That's good." She wiggled and wobbled wildly, but the nurse kept her arms around her waist, steadying her as she took her insecure steps after the woman who led the way. She saw a long dining room table with too many women for her to count sitting around it.

As she approached the only empty chair, Gisella said,

"Ladies, I want you to meet Christina. She's joining you now. I do hope that you will show her how to dine properly and where everything is located. Help her get settled in, will you?"

A chorus of voices spoke up, assuring her that they would. "Oh thank you, Gisella, for finding another perfect woman to join us. Hello. I am Kathy. You can sit by me. We are just about to have supper. It's stew tonight. See, they've put the plate in front of you."

Christina mostly fell onto the chair. She saw the plate in front of her. "But how do we eat? Don't we have to have a spoon or something?" she asked, her mind reeling with confusions. Forks, knives, spoons. Weren't they supposed to be here too?

Kathy laughed. "We don't need such things. Here, eat like this." She leaned over and began licking and picking up bits between her teeth.

"Oh. Like a cat. I get it." Christina leaned over and began to eat as well.

Gisella left them and went over to Jenny. "Jenny, you have been so wonderful here that you are being promoted."

"Oh that's wonderful. Thank you!" the brunette gushed.

"Yes, later tonight, we will move you to your new and even fancier home. There you will have a marvelous view outside."

"Oh that is so wonderful. We can't see out here. No windows. I can't wait. I am so excited," Jenny gushed once more.

Gieslla added, "Christina can have your old bed now. You will have an even better bed later tonight."

"Oh thank you, thank you, Gisella. You are so wonderful."

Gisella smiled and left them eating their suppers. She conferred with General Franco about tonight's dispatch to the Abyss. "Well, we've another ten women to send back. Are we all set to receive the new arrivals?"

"Yes, all set. But I am concerned about these thugs. They are kidnaping the women rather crudely. I've been monitoring them. I think it hasn't been wise allowing them to find us the women. Eventually, the humans will figure out what's been going on. I'd rather my men obtain the women we need. Black-eyes Bo's men are just too sloppy," he explained.

"I know. They are pathetic, but still we can use them when the time comes. Graz'zt is always looking for new recruits. This place here is just teeming with likely candidates. In fact, I've never see so darn many humans in one place that we can so easily recruit. It's almost like the humans have tailor-made these slums for us, a perfect recruiting ground," Gisella pointed out.

The general laughed. "Aye, perfect. But my men and I have come across something that bears watching."

"What's that? I miss something?" Gisella asked. It wasn't like her to miss anything, but then she had not been out among the humans anywhere near as much as her general and his men.

"We have detected some of Dispater's promised humans around the Project as well," he said cautiously. "We should tread lightly. Lord help us if we accidentally take one of his promised."

"You are certain of this?" she asked. Stealing a devil's promised soul would likely bring considerable wrath down upon them, something they didn't care to do. It would interfere with the Grand Plan.

"Yes. Very. After all, this Project is filled with the worst of the humans in this area. Most fit our criteria, but some want to follow 'rules,' and those are likely candidates for the devils. We should exercise a bit more caution. That's all I'm suggesting. I think everyone here in this building are not devil-promised. We're safe for the moment. Just use a bit of caution," he pointed out.

"Agreed. I have to admit that this new plan of our illustrious prince is working out ten times better than the old plan," she suggested.

He grinned. "That's an understatement, Gisella, if I ever heard one. Still, I don't trust these human thugs. I'm keeping everything ready for an evacuation, just in case the fools should ever lead the humans here."

"Always a wise precaution, general, but I hardly think that they are that stupid. No, then again, they well could be that stupid! Keep alert. The Guards and Wards ought to give us enough time to evacuate if worse comes to worse. I've already got several other locations prepped if we have to evacuate this one."

"Excellent, Gisella, excellent." He bowed and took the Magical Door to the basement, where he and his men stayed while not out scouring the city, disguised as human men.

Sometime later, they heard a very loud explosion outside of their top floor suite. Shortly after that, all the protection spells and wards detonated. That they were being besieged was obvious some ten times over. Grock, a giant of a demon, powerful and muscular, was the door warden. His instant reaction was to Gate in some supporting demons. Magic flashed and two vrock demons stood beside him. He bellowed, "Get them! Tear them to pieces!" He'd brought two large demons that were about two feet shorter than his eleven-foot frame, but they had very deadly claws and a vicious beak that could rip flesh from bones. The two charged into the charging Parry, knocking the human over like a bowling pin! They pressed on into the swarm of wizards and witches, as spells began flying right and left. Grock moved up and began stomping on the prone Parry, pounding him senseless, while wondering just how this human could possibly not have been crushed into mush already.

"Evacuate!" Gisella screamed to her nurses and attendants. The half dozen demon caretakers streamed through the Magical Door into the basement, where the incised pentagram was already being activated by an angry General Franco. The nurses grabbed the sealed containers containing the fertilized eggs of the many women, the very cylinders that were scheduled to be delivered this evening. Carefully, they placed them on the opened Gate and watched them vanishing into the Abyss. That done, they teleported away, arriving at the Maternity Ward, where a dozen human women were being carefully tended, three months pregnant with their Cambion sons.

Meanwhile, one of the general's men stepped through the Gate to advise those on the receiving end that this Center was under heavy attack. A dozen more demons then came through from the Abyss. Upon arrival, the general ordered four of them to join the defense on the top floor. They stepped through the Magical Door, arriving on the top floor, and rushed to join the battle.

"Recruitment time," Gisella barked her orders. She and several of the general's men teleported to the thirteenth floor, where Black-eyed Bo and his personal guards were firing their automatic weapons out of the windows, raining deadly showers on the SWAT team assaulting the building.

"Well, Bo, I give you a choice. You and your people can stay here and get yourselves killed or you can come with us and receive a body impervious to such puny things as those bullets you're all shooting. You can have immense powers to go along with your invulnerability. Choose now. No time to ponder your choice," Gisella barked.

"Really? Bullets can't hurt us? Power?" Black-eyed Bo asked. He glanced at the sheer number of men below, bullets ricocheting around the suite, and said, "Come on. Let's do this!" A dozen of his trusted guards and an equal number of their women stopped firing. While ducking low, they backed up to join the two at the backside of the suite. Gisella's men took hold of them and transported them to the basement. Gisella followed along last.

"Okay, just step on that pentagram and receive your new invulnerable body with immense powers to go along with it," she ordered. "Move! There isn't much time."

The others were followers; Bo knew this. Hesitantly, he stepped onto the pentagram and promptly vanished from sight. One by one, the others, hastened along by Gisella, followed him.

Black-eyed Bo arrived in the Abyss, where his body was instantly killed, and Prince Graz'zt moved him over into a waiting vrock body. The prince was kept busy for several minutes, killing the human men as they arrived, forcing them into the waiting vrock bodies. The dozen women he merely paralyzed and shoved out of the way. He'd deal with them later. Finally, after a Cambion came through with the report that this was the last of the new recruits, Graz'zt spoke to the stunned new recruits. "Welcome to the Abyss. Your new bodies are impervious to all those puny human weapons. Bullets will bounce off you. They can't even cut your skin with swords. Magical spells are equally likely not to affect you at all, about fifty-fifty, and you have the ability to cast some spells yourselves. If you will follow Grog here, he will take you to your barracks and see that you are trained to be able to use your new gifts. That will be all." Dazed and not comprehending what had happened to them, some forty new vrock demons ambled off awkward on their feet, following the giant demons.

Graz'zt then handled the dozen women, turning them into valuable egg producers. He already had places prepared for them, since the promised ten new women would not be arriving tonight. In spite of the minor setback, he'd gotten his new egg producers and many new beings to become his companion demons. All told, it was a good evening.

Back in the basement, with the recruits gone, Gisella, General Franco, and his men teleported to the maternity ward, bringing along with them the various supplies and equipment that were stored in the basement, leaving mostly crude sleeping quarters and the pentagram behind, along with the forty women. They could easily get more of them, once they'd established a new Breeding Center elsewhere in St. Louis.

"Darn you!" Parry screeched, rolling frantically into the suite trying to get out from underneath the stomping feet of the demon. He finally made it as his Skin of Stone vanished. He rolled more and got to his feet. Using his staff, he joined the attack on the three demons. Fighting demons on the small stairs and landing of the steps along with two dozen companions is not an optimum way to attack! The clawing pair quickly latched onto Crystal and Jiri, but their Skin of Stone spells prevented them from injury, though they were being knocked silly.

In such close quarters, offensive spells were somewhat limited. Magical missiles, missiles of acid, Disintegration beams, and similar spells rained down on the three demons. In the chaos and confusion, the demons had no choice but to depend upon their innate magical resistance to protect them.

They couldn't dodge the Disintegration beams. Besides there was no dodging the magical missile type spells, which always struck the specified targets.

The vrocks gave up trying to claw and peck their two humans and simply tossed them out of the gaping hole in the sidewall of the stairs and turned to grab another pair. Jiri and Crystal barely managed to get their Gentle Fall spells cast before landing hard on the ground. Both jumped up, cast more spells, and headed back into the fight.

I finally got to my feet, though my head was rather fuzzy from all the pounding the giant demon had dished out to me. I shook my head and focused, shooting a Disintegrate spell at the back of the demon's head. Finally, I got lucky. It penetrated his innate magical resistance. He didn't see his death coming. My spell bored a very nice hole clear through his monstrous head! I yelled, "The larger you are the harder you fall!" Unfortunately, the giant fell down on top of Ari! "Shit! Levitate: Demon!" I rushed to Ari, dragging her inside the suite. The air was just knocked out of her. After getting her to her feet and seeing my floating, dead demon, she cast a Push spell, sending it out the gaping hole in the wall. I cancelled my Levitate spell, and we both yelled, "Bomb's away!" We both liked that ancient movie.

Now more demons came rushing up behind us! Ah, these were Cambions and far less dangerous. I raised my Staff of Power, trying to figure out how best to slow down the four demons. Ari beat me to it. She threw up a Wall of Force between them and us. Wham! The demons ran smack into it, jarring them silly for a moment, giving us a breather.

Well, it didn't last long. Didn't count on their strength! They pushed her wall over like it was paper or something. Okay, we just didn't really hook it into any kind of support, like an I-beam. A couple of them shot balls of fire at us, but our defensive spells still held, and the flames only singed the curtains and carpet around us. Apparently, the decorators chose flame-resistant materials that were up to fire codes. Probably purchased by accident. I didn't figure these low lives would think about such things as fire safety. Hell, the entire building wasn't up to codes. There was only this single stairway.

One came at me baring its ugly fangs and swinging a wicked looking cross between a dagger and a sword at me. I did the best move I had. I swung my staff low, connected with his feet, sending him careening to the floor. I stuck one end of the staff into his neck and shot a Disintegrate spell at him. I guess his magical resistance was low. His severed head rolled back across the floor—just a bit more than I intended to have happen. I turned to see how Ari was doing. Wrong move.

As I did that, another Cambion came at me from my blind side and brought his wicked looking sword down squarely on top of my head! Once more, I was alive only because I'd recast the Skin of Stone spell. However, I saw stars! And a huge rain of magical missiles flying by me, hitting the Cambion fighter.

My head throbbed, but at least the stars stopped acting like comets flying around my head. The battle was over, our part anyway. We still heard sporadic weapons fire coming from lower floors. As I watched, the demon bodies turned partially into some unspeakable goo and vanished leaving only the goo behind. As I understand Crystal, with their deaths here on Earth, they were forced back into the Abyss where they took over new bodies, but were not able to return here for a goodly number of years. Good riddance, I say.

As I looked around at our motley crew, we all had torn clothes and likely some nasty bruises, but we were otherwise unhurt, thanks to all the protection spells we'd cast on ourselves. Any lesser number and we'd probably not still be standing. That's when I remembered Christina and called out, "Christina! Come on!" I charged past this entrance area and around an inside barrier wall, only to come up short! I saw a large number of beds against one wall, a whole lot of toilets against the wall I'd just passed, and a long table with thirty women sitting there peacefully sipping their evening coffee through straws. Thirty naked women without any arms and wearing boots like Monica always wore. As my eyes took in the horror of the situation, I quickly found Christina sitting at the end of the table and ran over to her.

"Christina. I'm sorry that we couldn't prevent this from

happening to you. We're here now," I blurted out.

"Oh. I think I know you. Parry? Oh, I'm perfect now. I'm with all these pretty women. We are all so perfect now. Don't you think so?" Her face then flushed a little. "Men. I thought Gisella said there were no men here."

A woman beside her spoke up. "I don't think that you are supposed to be here. Gisella, there is a man here!"

"But we're here to rescue you, Christina. Don't you remember?" I blurted out.

"I'm perfectly fine. I'm now very beautiful. We all are. Aren't we?" Christina said innocently.

Around her, several other women agreed with her fully. One said, "We are all just perfect. We are all quite safe. We are producing eggs for our sons. We have lots of sons. Isn't that grand?"

Okay, I groaned, realizing they were under the influence of an Idiot Mind spell. Thankfully, the others now joined me. Crystal spoke up, "Parry, go join the other men watching the door. We don't want men with machine guns or other demons coming up here." Mechanically, I obeyed her. I knew I was out of my league with this mess. A woman shouldn't ever be mistreated, unless of course she deserved it. These poor women had their lives pretty much destroyed.

As I walked back to the entrance doors, I heard Crystal explaining, "Ladies, there is a big hole in the wall. It's getting quite cold in here. Why don't we take you somewhere that's warm?" He heard many agreeing with her.

Ari sent me a message.

Parry. I'm taking Christina with me to St. Anne's. Don't worry. I have her. A.

I relaxed a bit as I joined the others. With nothing to battle, I began rubbing my aching head and body. I figured that I'd have quite a lot of bruises from all the stomping that I'd taken. I wasn't disappointed. Half of my body was very black and blue by the next day.

About a half hour later, Oliver poked his head into the entrance, stepping over the crushed steel door. "All secure up here?"

"Aye, sir," I called out. Rescued thirty women.

Mutilated like the others. St. Anne's. Killed us some demons."

"Okay, some of Henry's men are searching the building now," Oliver reported. "SWAT team took a few hits, nothing too serious though. Glad these thugs are such lousy shots."

"Bullet proof vests help," I added, and Oliver smiled.

"That too. Killed at least a hundred thugs, arrested around another hundred. Probably drug addicts, but we'll see," Oliver stated, but was distracted by a Message. "Oh, Henry says we should come to the basement right away."

Gregor said, "One of us should stay here, just in case someone tries to slip in here and hurt the women further." He stayed behind, while the rest of us headed for the basement. There Henry pointed out the incised pentagram and the copper-lead shielding fastened to the rafters above it, hiding it from the IR satellites. We also saw crude living accommodations for probably a dozen men, Cambions and demons I guessed from the various sizes. They'd been here for quite some time.

"Henry," I spoke up, "it looks like they haven't been quiet this past winter like we all thought and hoped."

"Understatement, Parry. Leslie has been informed. We obviously have a far bigger problem than we ever realized. Probably have to have a big meeting to discuss what we do now. Nasty business," Henry replied, somewhat disillusioned.

A few days later, Oliver reported that they'd incidentally discovered and confiscated the largest haul of illegal street drugs in nearly a century. I didn't doubt that, since Black-eyed Bo was the king of the drug trafficking trade in the Project.

But that wasn't what was bothering me. No, that image of those thirty totally helpless women was burned into my mind. I swore I would never rest until I could prove that there weren't any more such centers around our city. Hunting down these despicable centers became my obsession after that night's raid.

A few blocks away, Gisella and General Franco met with Dr. Menninger, Benedetta, and Gar-Tar. She reported, "Graz'zt is pleased with the new recruits and will be issuing some new orders about them later on the next delivery. Meanwhile, our

Breeding Center was compromised by the idiot drug addicts, who kidnaped Christina and led the enemy right to our doorstep. We need to plan to vacate this facility as well, before they get wind of it. Yet, this Project is filled with marvelous recruits for Graz'zt. Suggestions?"

"I've one," Dr. Menninger spoke up. "No, two. First, from now on, we should have our own forces handle the acquisition of new women. No more relying on the incompetent humans. Second, we should get us a new place that is much nicer than these slum dwellings, and one which no one will suspect. In my spare time, I've been casing this city, looking over their medical facilities. I believe I have just the place for us. It is in the western suburbs, an upscale neighborhood. Westwood Assisted Living. We should covertly take it over and consolidate all of our operations there. I will be better able to serve our breeding program from there. Their facilities are just magnificent."

"All right. I like those ideas, doctor. I'll see to it in the morning," Gisella replied. The next morning accompanied by General Franco and Witch Benedetta, she paid a visit to the facility. "This place has real class!" she remarked to the others, while waiting to meet with the owner, Jason Biggs.

"We want to purchase this facility," Gisella began, once they were seated in his fancy office.

He gave a nervous laugh. "I've no intention of selling. This is a very profitable organization." Gisella smiled at the man, while General Franco strangled him. Benedetta then cast her spell, which deposited his corpse just above the sun, where it was instantly vaporized. Meanwhile, General Franco changed his form into that of Jason Biggs. With a wry smile, he set about the process of transferring all their thirty patients to other facilities, insisting that he was closing the place down so he could move to LA. A week later, he dismissed the last of the dozen workers, giving them a healthy severance pay from the company's accounts so as not to arouse any suspicions.

That done, he brought in all their Cambion staff and reorganized the layout of the facilities, following the recommendations of Dr. Menninger. By mid-April, the facility was ready to serve as their new combined production facilities.

However, it was too late to salvage the dozen pregnant women in their other Maternity Ward in the Project.

Why? I got to them first! While Monica and the others were dealing with the thirty rescued women, I put my oath to work. With an Invisibility spell on me, I began systematically flying through the Project looking for more of these demon habitation sites. I figured if there was one, there were many more. While I certainly didn't know precisely what I was looking for, when I found another high rise whose top floor windows were all painted black, blocking all view, I guessed this must be another one of their joints. Oliver confirmed that it was occupied by the Number Two drug lord, second only to Black-eyed Bo, who no one had seen since the assault on his complex.

None of us really worried that we didn't find him or his select band of close associates. Probably it should have, but we missed that detail. As soon as I found this place and Oliver confirmed who lived there, our team swung into action again. I must really thank Nisha and Jill for their invaluable assistance. I don't know how they do it, but they can see heat images, rather like our IR satellites. Both reported seeing demons and women inside.

As you might expect, we conducted another raid, coordinating with Oliver's SWAT teams and Henry's Defense Force. Unlike the last battle, this one was routine. True, most of the combat was between the thugs and the SWAT men. For our part, once we smashed our way inside, the demons simply vanished.

Trouble is that I thought I'd seen the worst with the thirty women, but guess again. We found twelve women who were physically mutilated just like Christina and the others had been, but these were impregnated with the fertilized eggs and nearly five months pregnant! They were supposed to give birth to a dozen Cambion demons in four months! This nightmare invasion of the demons had gone to new, unspeakable heights! Especially so, when I later heard that if they'd gone full term, they would have died giving birth to their demon spawn! All I can say is that the doctors at St. Anne's were brilliant in removing these foul fetuses, saving them.

After that, I continued searching high and low for more of these disguised, disgusting places. Unfortunately, the demons learn from their mistakes. I didn't find any more of them. However, I continued to fear that they were still in business and decided to try other approaches.

Chapter 22—Recoveries

"But I'm just fine. I'm perfect. I don't need any help," Christina complained. She and the other women were placed in the isolation wing of St. Anne's where they could get the care they needed, and Monica could work on their cures. "No, I don't want any clothes on. I can't go pee with them on me. Just put the plate so I can eat. Can't you see that I am perfect? Where's all my friends? They're perfect too."

The Idiot Mind spells were definitely making life miserable for the nurses. Monica had come early the next morning to begin their recoveries. The doctors of the night shift had given all thirty a full checkup, despite the women's constant complaining that they were just fine, perfect women. The day nurses were now going around trying to get the women into hospital gowns and feed them their breakfasts, but the women were uniformly having nothing to do with this. Monica watched the antics of Christina and sighed. At last, the frustrated nurse did as Christina asked, placing the tray close to her and allowing her to feed herself as best she could. "Come on, Monica. The doctor wants to see you about them." Monica followed her to a side room.

"Ah, here you are. We certainly have a mess on our hands. All are healthy, but are under an Idiot Mind spell. I'm going to have to remove that first," he explained.

Monica bit her lip for a moment. "Doctor, it might be wiser of you to delay on that. The moment they regain their senses, they're all going to freak out something awful. They've endured excruciating pain and body mutilations. All that will come back to them the moment they are freed from this spell. It's going to take me close to two months to get them restored. Right now, they are trying hard to be as independent as they can. If we undo the Idiot Mind spells, they will become completely helpless and dependent on your staff. It might be wise to only undo them from the spell when I get to them to restore their bodies and erase their physical and emotional traumas."

"I see. What about undoing the spell and having you erase their traumas first and then individually over the two months restoring their bodies?" he asked.

"Well, that's possible too, but consider their states. Even with that done, they are still going to feel helpless and vulnerable. They'll likely fall into grief again, but if they know that I'm going to heal them as soon as I can, that might help keep them manageable."

"I'd like to try that, Monica. After all, you are doing well yourself. These Idiot Mind spells cause victims to do crazy things. One woman has already tried to walk out of here, trying to walk to her home. If we don't get rid of the Idiot Mind spells, I'm going to have to place a twenty-four hour guards on each of them."

"I see your point. Okay then, let's undo the spell, but allow me to use my spells on them right after they come out of it so the buried pain, unconsciousness, and severe emotional trauma can be erased," Monica replied.

"Good. How long does that take?"

"Several hours per woman, if past history is accurate. I've only done five so far," she replied.

"Okay, then we will stagger the administration of the cure by say three hours per patient. Starting with Christina?"

"Yes, with her. She was the most recent victim. Besides Ari will have a fit if we don't get to her first," Monica smiled.

The next morning, Monica was at the hospital sitting beside Christina's bed when the young woman finally woke up. The potion had done its work. The twenty year old's first reaction upon waking was to let out a blood curling scream at the top of her lungs! Who wouldn't?

Monica was prepared for this and had already cast a number of Silence spells around the room, ensuring that her screams would not be heard beyond the room. Monica wished that she had hands to cover her ears! "It's okay, Christina. You are safe in the hospital. I'm Monica. I'm here to heal you fully, but first, let's get rid of your awful trauma."

Christina simply continued to scream, so Monica went ahead and cast her spell anyway. After all, Christina was reliving what had happened to her, so she might as well work on erasing it, on running it out of her mind, turning the reactiveness into mere memories. Two hours later and nearly deaf, Monica finally achieved the result that she and Christina desired. The pain and trauma had been erased.

"But now I'm truly helpless, Monica. I'm like you and can't do anything for myself, can I?" Christina said rather calmly, all things considered.

"You are a brave woman, Christina. I'm going to help get all the others cleared up to this point. Once that's done in a day or two, I'll then see about healing your body fully. A few weeks from now, you'll be back to normal, just as you were before you were abducted and tortured. Okay?"

"Really? I'll have arms and hands again? My feet will work properly?" she asked.

"You bet. Good as new, but I need time. There are thirty of you to handle."

"Okay. Please work your magic on them. Somehow, I can get by. After all, if you can, so can I. Somehow," Christina said bravely, though she felt anything but brave at this point.

At least, she allowed the nurse to dress her and then to feed her, while Monica moved down one room to deal with the next woman. She was able to handle six women each day and estimated that she'd need four more days before she could start in on the true healing process, which would likely take some sixty days to complete. However, she now wore earplugs to help dampen the screams from the women.

When Monica returned on the seventh day to regrow Christina's arms and repair her feet, she was taken completely by surprise. This, she never anticipated.

Christina was dressed in her typical white blouse and black skirt which came down to just below her knees, her usual dress for her job at the bank. She was sitting on her bed waiting for Monica. "Look. I've discovered something extremely important. My bank has a terrific workmen's compensation policy. I'm fully covered, since I wasn't yet home from work when they took me. The policy will pay me twelve million dollars for the loss of each arm plus another ten million for the loss of function of my feet. All told, they are going to pay me thirty-four million dollars, Monica! Of course, if I let you restore them, I get nothing and have to go back to work. Honestly, even if I eventually get my CSI technician's certificate and get employed with the CSIs, I'll never earn that much money in my whole life, not a fraction of that amount."

"What are you suggesting?" Monica asked.

"If I take that insurance settlement, I could buy my own place and hire an assistant to help me with all the things I can't do, and I would still have all the money that I could ever spend. I could do all sorts of beneficial things. I could be a real philanthropist, helping so many others that—well, I can only imagine how many other lives I could help with survival donations. Food banks for the hungry, safe houses for battered women—honestly, Monica, the list could be just huge—the number of lives that I could help just by donating what is most often needed, money. Of course, I would have to research carefully each one, because there are many con artists out there who might try to extort money from me. Still, just think of all the good that I could do with that money! The number of lives that I could help make better—it's mind blowing, Monica."

"All I have to do is to accept the settlement and not get my arms, hands, and feet restored. Look, you have been getting by very well. I know, you are a powerful witch with all sorts of helpful, useful spells to assist you. I'd have to pay an assistant to help me, but I think I can do this. I have to try. I have to think of all the others out there who could really use the help that I could give them. It would be completely selfish of me to think of only myself, not with this one time fabulous opportunity I've been handed: injured on the job."

"I've talked with the other thirty-nine women. Two of them were also kidnaped while officially working, but their companies don't have any worker's compensation insurance policies. So they are out of luck. I am incredibly lucky and very fortunate, Monica. I simply have to do this."

Monica listened to Christina, utterly amazed with her and the line of reasoning. "You really do care about other people, don't you? More than your own self."

"Well, I care about myself too, Monica. That's why I would only hire someone who can really be trusted to help me with my many needs. It's just that there are so many others in our world that need help, the kind of help that my funding could help by providing food stuffs, housing—you know what I mean."

"This is incredibly generous of you, Christina. I am really impressed! I almost can't believe I'm hearing this. Without my magic, I'm virtually helpless. Well, not exactly. I've learned that with an awful lot of practice, walking in these boots becomes almost as easy as it was before, though I admit I haven't gotten that good in them yet. Okay, Christina. I'll fully support your decision. Further, if you need some help later on, just call me. If you don't mind, I would like to drop by and chat with you periodically, just to make sure things are working out for you. Say, I can also show you how to invest your funds properly so that they can grow. That way you'll have even more to donate to worthy causes."

Christina's eyes lit up. "You would? That would be great! I've some knowledge from my few years working at the bank, but I can see that proper investing is going to play a critical role. If some of the currently unused funds could be invested and grow, I'd be in an even better position to help even more."

"Also, I talked to my boyfriend about all this too. At first, he kept insisting that I get healed, but I thought that might be because he wouldn't want me, not if I was helpless like this." She shrugged her shoulders. "But I kept at him and that wasn't it. He felt really badly that I was so badly harmed, and he wanted me to get well. I think he loves me no matter what I choose to do. I guess time will tell. Your husband doesn't mind that you are like you are, does he?"

Monica flushed. "Er no. We have a very deep bond of love between us. All right then, I will let the doctor know to release you. Again, you keep in touch with me. Call me at least once a week. I must know how you are doing, especially if you feel down or depressed. I get that way sometimes too. And practice walking as many hours each day as you can."

"Cool! I'm so glad you approve of what I'm doing. I'll walk lots and call you every Friday. And you can call me when you feel down and out too, you know. We're going to be very much alike. I suppose I can now afford to get some elegant dresses like you and Crystal and Ericka always wear. I should look as good as I can, all things considered."

"Okay. I'll have Ericka get in touch with you and help you choose some great fashions. She's a pro at that, not me. I just wear what she picks out. I only choose the colors. I'll also call you when I feel down too. Bargain?"

"Bargain!" Christina gave her a melting smile. Monica noted that her eyes were bright and full of life. It wasn't some lingering part of the reactive nature of the trauma that she'd endured or a bit of the Idiot Mind that hadn't been cured. She was speaking from her heart and fondest desires. In fact, after hearing Christina talk about all the good uses that she could put her newfound fortune to, Monica began to think about her own situation. She'd accumulated a rather vast fortune already but wasn't actually putting it to any good use, beyond the smaller amounts that she used to help her four friends open their stores. Monica vowed to herself to monitor what Christina actually did with her money and the results that she obtained. Perhaps she could learn from this young woman and emulate her as well.

Then, she got a bright idea. "Christina. Why don't you move in with me, with us? We have many things automated so that Jill could do more things independently. She doesn't need them now that I've been able to heal her. That way, you and I could be close together, sharing our ideas and helping to support each other. I have wanted to enlarge the place anyway, and this would be a fabulous reason to hurry up and do it. Please, I'd be really honored if you would."

"Really? Well, I'd love to. You are right. We could be our own support group, but I insist on paying my way. I could use some help in finding the right assistant to help me with things. I'll talk to my boyfriend when he gets off work tonight and see what he has to say, but I think he will approve of it. This is working out even better than I imagined it would. Thank you, thank you."

Monica sent a Message to Crystal and her friend teleported over to St. Anne's. This was too important and too lengthy to try to put into a Message format. The two chatted for a half hour before Crystal left to work on the arrangements.

Crystal hired a "magical" construction contractor and via the use of magical spells, the new addition was completed in two months' time, adding another twenty suites onto the southern side of their basement, with an entrance way cut through the wall of one of the spare guest bedrooms. The construction was finished by the time that Monica finished the last healing in mid-June.

Further, Crystal really did research the "proper" assistant for Christina. She hired an English-born, young woman who was a trained Lady's Maid. She knew precisely how to assist an aristocratic woman. That she was offered double her present salary convinced her that this would be her dream assignment. Combined with Ericka's incredible sense of fashion, by June, Christina looked almost as though she was royalty.

Meanwhile, Monica moved on to the next women, slipping the precious ring around the woman's little toe. She then sat back and chatted with Kathy for the next two days before the ring fell off her toe. Her arms had regenerated and her feet were now normal. Kathy hugged, praised, and thanked Monica repeatedly, until Monica finally hinted that she needed to go on to the next victim.

By mid-April, Monica had fully healed fifteen of the remaining thirty-nine women, when Parry and her friends rescued the very pregnant women. "Oh dear god!" she whispered, when she first saw the condition of these dozen new women. In fact, while the doctors were conducting their exhaustive tests on the twelve, the other fourteen women, who were now able to do some walking on their own, came by to see the new arrivals. All fourteen absolutely insisted that Monica heal these women before themselves. All she could say to them was "Thank you!" Monica just knew that she had to heal them as soon as possible!

After studying the dozen women for two days, the team of doctors concluded that they had to terminate the pregnancies. Worse, these particular women had been long-term drug users. Several had the arm marks to prove it, though those were long gone with their arms. If anyone didn't deserve

Monica's healing, it was this batch, who had thrown so much of their lives away to date. However, Monica insisted that she would heal them anyway.

The doctors then explained the fetuses were far larger than normal humans were. Further, they decided the only safe way was surgically to remove them. Two days after those operations were finished, Monica used her Vanish spell to destroy these awful looking demon bodies. Then she set to work, following the same procedure as before. The doctors timed the curing of their Idiot Mind spells so that Monica would have time to use her special spells to erase their incredible traumas, compounded by their many months of pregnancy. That done, she then set about using her ring to regenerate their much-damaged bodies, especially their reproductive systems, which had taken an awful lot of damage trying to develop a demon.

In the process of all this, she accumulated a wealth of information about the operations of this evil Dr. Menninger. She swore to one day bring him to justice, though just now she had no idea how she might be able to do that. After she finished work on the first of these dozen women, the team of doctors re-examined her in depth. They were amazed to find that the young woman was now in perfect health. All the severe damage to her body had been fully repaired.

Greatly inspired, Monica continued her tireless work. For over two months, she didn't get out of the hospital, but was constantly sitting with her next patient. She listened to the life stories, hopes, and dreams of fifty-one young women, all of whom were only a year or three older than she. Monica learned a whole lot about other women, which more than paid her back for all of her hours with them.

On June 15, she finally was able to return to her own home and bed. She nearly tackled Rob when she arrived, pushing and shoving him into their bedroom and then onto the bed. Later, she met the new assistant, Ruth Anne Hogsworth, and checked on how Christina was faring. She was impressed with the woman's progress. She had been practicing her walking dutifully for hours each day, and then for another several hours at night when her boyfriend came by and walked with her. Perhaps, Monica thought, Christina may be very right about what she's doing.

Just the week before, Enya gave birth to a son, Tom. And on July 1, Misty gave birth to a daughter, Martha. With two new babies, a new dimension opened up around the estate. Even Monica began to spend time cooing over the two infants and their proud parents.

Chapter 23—Crystal Makes a Discovery

While Monica was tied up at St. Anne's healing the fifty-one women, her friends were not inactive. Neither were Henry or Leslie or Parry and Ari. Each had their own agenda to follow. With the discovery that the demons had merely gone underground and were continuing to be quite active and coupled with Rob's assessment that periodically many more demons were arriving in St. Louis via the secret Gates, Leslie was very concerned that this was not a local phenomenon, not when most other large cities in the world were seeing random demon destructive attacks. Her theory was that like in St. Louis, these random attacks were an attempt to conceal the demons' real purpose, the kidnaping and breeding of young women. Hence, she worked on a statewide program to pursue this angle and even got it going nationally. The Board of Regents then took it worldwide.

Henry focused on the St. Louis area, trying to track where the demons had moved their operations. He met with little luck, though he kept at it. Oliver began keeping very accurate watch on all missing persons reports, as well as kidnappings, trying to sort out runaways and normal kidnapings from those being done by demons. He had marginal success in separating the two types, however. Actual data on any given situation was very slow in developing, unfortunately.

Parry and Ari scoured the Project for any signs of demon activities, for any other rooms whose windows were painted over, but found nothing at all. Still determined, perhaps more so than ever, they began widening their search, fully intent on viewing every building in the greater St. Louis area! By June, they'd lost count of how many Fly spells they had cast just to fly up and down every street in the city, a Herculean task at best. They turned up nothing at all.

Conclusion: the demons had once again altered their

tactics, their modus operandi. This left a very bitter taste in everyone's mind. Surely, the demons were continuing to kidnap young women and mutilate their bodies. It was that they had no idea where the demons were now located.

By early June, Henry Wilkens had received permission from his boss, Leslie Traub, to attack the problem from a different angle, one that needed her written permission. He intended to violate one of the rules that their Department of Magical Misuse strictly enforced: unauthorized spying on private citizens. Specifically, he requested permission to use the spells See What Another Is Seeing and Hear What Another Is Hearing on those women who were on Oliver's extensive list of possible demon-abducted women. Ordinarily, spying on others was a misdemeanor offense unless information so obtained was subsequently used to commit a crime, in which case it became a criminal offense.

For example, one could use these spells to watch a bank manager enter the combination to their vault and thus subsequently be able to rob the bank. Hence, unauthorized use of these spells was monitored by the Department of Magical Misuse. Leslie gave her permission, and on June 2, Henry and his team tackled the fifty-nine women on the FBI's list of potential abduction victims. Some would likely turn out to be simply runaways, but he hoped that this would yield clues.

By the end of the week, Henry's team produced results. While some were merely runaways, he helped solve two real kidnapings. Oliver's agents handled those. Three cases ended up being turned over to police detectives; the women were dead. Some turned out to be simple misunderstandings between the parties. However, a dozen women most definitely had been abducted by the demons, subsequently mutilated, and were now being used in their evil Cambion production center. Another ten simply could not be contacted at all. These, Henry suspected, were no longer on Earth!

Leslie relayed Henry's findings on up the chain of command and was pleased to hear back that many other jurisdictions were now implementing this procedure in their cities. By mid-June, she heard back that a dozen other cities throughout the world had proof that women were being held by demon groups in their cities as well.

On June 18, worldwide results were sent to every major head of the Department of Magical Misuse, along with a very startling result, namely the day before, suddenly the See What Another Is Seeing spells failed. They could only see blackness. The obvious conclusion was that the demons had figured out what they were doing and had now used a Blind spell on the women! Along with the results document, the Board of Regents issued an order to avoid doing anything else that might make the lives of these poor women any worse.

Once Henry discovered they were able to get visuals on the environment of the kidnaped women, he pulled Parry and Ari into his office. Why? Henry's group had not been able to use what they were seeing to pinpoint where the women were being held. However, Parry and Ari had just completed a massive search of all St. Louis, looking for blackened out windows. Henry used a spell to replay the memories that he and his staff had for Parry and Ari to see. Specifically, the two saw the memories that Henry and his staff had of what they'd seen the abducted women were seeing. He hoped Parry and Ari might recognize something that they'd seen during their searches.

Parry's comment, while it didn't solve the problem, did point out a new and unexpected detail. "Hey, those are giant Joshua trees out beyond the window. We don't have those in St. Louis." Given Parry's astute observation, Henry and his group re-examined all their memories of what they'd seen and concluded that the St. Louis women were being held in a facility somewhere in the southwestern part of the United States! Not only were the women now blinded, but also they were being taken to other cities. There was no hope at all of finding the egg producing facility in their city. The women being held here came from some other city entirely. Grim.

Crystal had not been idle during the late winter and spring months. Frustrated that the demons had circumvented her brilliant discovery that their incised pentagrams could be located by sensing in the infrared the residual magical energies left by the Gate spells, she had focused her attention on other methods of detection. She correctly reasoned that the demons were abducting women from the larger cities because one missing young woman in a small town would be instantly noticed by the entire town. Thus, the demons would most likely keep their facilities to house these women in the larger cities, where such a place could be better hidden. An assisted living complex in a smaller town would be well known by all locals and its takeover by demons would be noticed right away, as well as the sudden appearance there of two dozen strangers—morphed demons disguised as humans.

Focused then only on the larger cities, Crystal was facing examination of most of the world's population, rather daunting. Her idea was to discover some way of identifying demons from the Abyss from normal humans. Based upon the previous success using the IR imaging satellites, she wanted somehow to use that system to do the analysis. Crystal's research thus focused on the critical notion that there must be some physical differences between humans and demons, something that would uniquely identify a creature from the Abyss.

That there were substantial chemical differences was acutely obvious. When the five women had been rescued from the Abyss, their bodies had been contaminated, and they'd undergone an extensive detoxification program, aided by Enya's potions. Crystal had kept some samples of this foreign matter that had been ejected from their bodies while they were being treated at St. Anne's.

During April, she and Gregor conducted extensive chemical tests on this matter from the Abyss, based upon Gregor's suspicion that there had to be some very significant difference that polluted human systems when fed Abyss food. Crystal made the startling discovery that Abyss material had an abnormally high alpha particle concentration in it. Further, she discovered that these decaying particles impacted the calcium in the body, causing an abnormally high excitation level, resulting in an emission line at 7326.2 Angstroms, in the infrared portion of the spectrum, not normally visible to our eyes.

Armed with this startling discovery, she again visited Leslie Traub. "Look, I need your help again. I think that I have come up with a way to locate demon bodies using our IR satellites."

"What?" Leslie's mouth indicated her complete surprise. "You can detect the demons from space? How?"

"From an abnormally high intensity of a spectral emission line of calcium. You see, the Abyss material composition is different from ours here on Earth. That material emits an abnormally high level of alpha particles, which are weirdly exciting the calcium atoms in bodies. Let me show you what I've discovered." Crystal went over her findings in detail.

"So I want to get time on the IR satellite over St. Louis and have it scan for this precise wavelength. Capture a days' worth of images and then let me study them. I think I should be able to spot demon bodies this way. Won't know for sure until I try it. Please," Crystal begged.

Two days later, she received a huge download of images. She and Gregor began studying them. "These are mostly all blank or sort of hazy," Gregor declared looking at the first few images."

"Duh. No kidding. Maybe this isn't going to work," Crystal sighed, looking at another pair of blank images. A hundred images later, she was about to call this idea a wash when she spotted a telltale bright line. "Wait! I got something here. Look at this, Gregor!" They saw the bright streak of the spectral line. Both continued their examinations. After going through nearly a thousand images, they had ten that showed the specific bright line. Next, based on the data coordinates, she pulled up a satellite image of St. Louis, superimposing the image of the spectral line on the map. Bingo, she had the location of the demon. He was on a downtown street! Of course, this didn't help much, just knowing that a demon had walked down Market Street yesterday around one p.m.

She Messaged Leslie, who arrived within a minute! "Look at this. It worked! There is a demon walking down Market Street around one yesterday afternoon! This will work, Leslie. We have a way to spot all the demons on Earth now! Well, at least until all the alpha particles in their bodies fully decay."

"Crystal, this is just incredible! I'll get us time on the satellite tomorrow, real time. Let's see if we can find out where they are keeping the women victims. Very well done indeed! I've got to let the others know about this immediately and get you your satellite feed!" Leslie was extremely pleased with this unexpected result and left at once, highly animated.

"Okay, Gregor, we've got a lot of work to do before tomorrow's live feed comes in," Crystal declared. However, that was delayed a short while. Everyone else knew about Leslie's sudden appearance, thanks to Jill in reception. The entire gang including Monica dropped by to find out what this was all about. Naturally, Crystal just had to show everyone the IR images and what tomorrow promised. Spirits finally rose.

The next day, Leslie arrived with the access codes, and she brought along a guest, Miss Christy Millbrook, the US member of the Board of Regents, one of the twelve members who oversaw all things magical worldwide. She'd been elected to replace Thomas White, who had been under the control of Dominus, via one of his diamond rings. To say that this group was impressed with the appearance of Christy would be a gross understatement! Christy said politely, "I'm here just to observe, Crystal. If this works, well, I don't have to tell you what this means for the entire world. Please, let's get started. I'll just watch."

For the first time in her life, Crystal was nervous, really nervous! Having one of the twelve members of the Board of Regents looking over your shoulders does that to you. The power that this woman wielded was enormous. All the other magical departments of the United States reported to her. Gregor sensed her nervousness and actually made most of the computer connections for her.

The others brought in chairs and over a dozen sat behind her looking over her shoulders. "Okay, I've brought up a wide angle view of St. Louis. Now overlaying the satellite IR images. There, we are in synch with the satellite. Right now, we don't see anything. We are looking for red lines appearing. The lines have been color enhanced so we can spot them more readily, since their true color is in the infrared. Without this map overlay, you would be looking at a mostly black screen, until a demon appears. Now we wait. I do hope the demons are out. Could be a long wait," Crystal explained. She took a deep breath and crossed her fingers, staring at the computer monitor.

Slowly the satellite began panning over the greater St. Louis area. Its angle of view wasn't sufficiently large to take in the entire sprawling city in one shot. It began centered on the riverfront and the arch. Nothing appeared. The satellite was programmed today to cut systematic north-south slices across the whole area, with each path showing approximately a dozen city blocks in width. The idea was to have sufficient scale that the precise location could be determined if they spotted a demon.

An hour passed before they got their first hit. One demon was on North Grand Boulevard just north of the university. That detection roused everyone's keen interest. However, another hour passed before they reached the western suburbs. Suddenly, a dozen red lines appeared, all closely spaced together!

"Oh my god! There's a whole bunch of them!" Gregor exclaimed, suddenly very excited indeed.

"Gotcha!" Crystal exclaimed, and began zooming in on the location. She brought up the FBI database and announced, "Hey, that's the Westwood Assisted Living complex. That must be where they are also holding all their kidnaped women! Yahoo, this really does work!"

"Hey, we can let Henry know and go raid that place today!" Leslie added. "We can rescue those women and put these demons out of business again. Crystal, you are a genius!"

"Hold on!" Christy Millbrook barked authoritatively. All eyes turned to the regent. "Yes, no doubt this is the very breakthrough that we've all greatly needed. However, we also know that these demons are smart and have changed their methods of operation to counter our moves. There is more at stake here than just your small group of women victims. There are likely many more in other cities. Here's what is going to happen."

You could hear a pin drop in Crystal's laboratory. "The Board of Regents will take charge. We will use this new technique to identify positively all these concentrations of demons. Once we are sure that we know the precise locations of them all, we will execute a coordinated raid on all them at precisely the same instant, rescuing all the abducted women and eliminating all the demons that we can. A simultaneous worldwide raid. I need your promise not to do anything to alert these demons at this Westwood Assisted Living complex. Just make your full-scale preparations for the raid. Leslie will let you know the precise time that we set for the raid. In one coordinated series of attacks, we may well be able to rid our world of this demon infestation, once and for all!"

She continued, "In the meantime, keep on with your observations for today. Make sure that this is their only location here in St. Louis. Tomorrow, the satellite will use your procedure to begin surveying all the major cities in the world. Demons, we have you at last! Very well done, Crystal, Gregor. I must be off. Much to be done in a hurry," Christy declared and promptly teleported away.

Meanwhile, Leslie Messaged Henry and Oliver, who quickly joined them, and she quickly briefed them on the fantastic results that Crystal had achieved. Everyone stared at the red lines on the screen. They weren't moving, another sign that this was the location of their main base and where the women were likely being held. Both men began working out their assault strategies. This promised to be their biggest breakthrough ever!

Monica, like the others, hated waiting for days before they could act on this new information. She had no other choice, however. Still, the days seemed to stretch on forever! Then the word came down. Attack at nine in the morning of July 1! They had less than a day to prepare. The notification came around three the previous day.

Oliver mobilized every SWAT team in St. Louis. Based upon Gregor's suggestion, they created special 50-caliber ammunition, replacing the projectiles with iron tips. Henry's crew consisted of a dozen wizards and witches. He decided to call in some favors and doubled his forces for this one raid. Monica and her group also joined him, bringing another dozen to the fight.

Monica double-checked all of her protection spells and her special earrings. Then, she had everyone else recheck theirs as well. She was nervous. This was the big one, she thought, a chance to end the demon plague. She wanted everyone to survive and the victims rescued. However, she issued one specific order to her group. "If anyone spots this Dr. Menninger fellow, do what you have to do to get him. Without their doctor, they are out of business!" She received eleven acknowledgments.

Parry added, "No doc, no abductions!" Shortly before nine, the SWAT teams began rolling. Their large vehicles would take some time to reach the destination. However, Oliver was in constant communication with them and his agents. Timing was critical. Only Enya and Misty were not involved in this attack. As new mothers, they remained home with their newborns.

The Westwood Assisted Living complex was laid out like a 'V' with a long administration wing along the bottom of the two wings of suites. Most likely, the captive women were being held in one or more of the wings, while the resident demons would be in the long bar at the entrance. A well-tended garden lined the front of the glass-surfaced front section where large glass doors welcomed visitors. An entrance desk was just inside. Steel doors blocked entrance into the two wings of the 'V' portion, and the long halls to either side of the reception area were quite open, with windows facing the gardens and office doors on the opposite sides. Anyone inside would have a very clear view of anyone approaching.

As the invisible host of wizards and witches landed on the driveway, Monica could see that this place offered little in the way of solid foundations for magical protection spells. Glass was easily shattered and didn't hold spells at all well. Probably they would at least have alarm spells on the doors. Certainly, wards could be on the metal doors leading to the two wings of the 'V'. Since Leslie was off coordinating raids in several other cities, Henry was in charge. At precisely nine, he issued the command to assault the complex. Right on time, ten blue and white SWAT trucks pulled into the driveway, and the wizards and witches struck, blasting the outer windows into a rain of crumbling glass bits. Monica noted that an Alarm spell detonated. The battle was underway.

This time, the demons were taken by complete surprise. They had no idea that their facility was known to the humans. Nevertheless, the demons were always ready for a fight. In fact, keeping them from fighting had been the hardest part of this whole operation for Gisella and General Franco. Three of their giant demons came rushing out of the right wing, itching for a good old brawl! From the left wing, a dozen Cambion fighters rushed the attackers. Gisella and General Franco peered out of their office at the back end of the left side of this administration wing. Their cook and nurses were currently in the 'V' wings handling breakfast for the dozen women, along with Dr. Menninger, who was preparing to retrieve and fertilize their day's eggs.

"Darn it! Not again! How the heck did they find us here?" Gisella barked.

"Don't know, but we're vastly outnumbered. We should Gate in some help from some of the other facilities," General Franco suggested.

"I'll do it. Let Gar-Tar and Benedetta know that we're under attack again. Darn it!" Gisella barked her orders. The general sent the messages, while she contacted some other bases.

A moment later, he looked at her, ready to report that those two were preparing to evacuate, when he saw her face turn white and then flashed to crimson. He was about to say, "What?" when she barked. "They're attacking all our other facilities right now! All over the world! How is this possible? We've nowhere to evacuate to! Quick, inside. Join Benedetta," Gisella ordered. The two vanished, appearing inside the one of the wings.

"What's going on?" asked Dr. Menninger, who was rapidly gathering the sealed cylinders of fertilized eggs ready to be sent to the Abyss on the next shipment. He intended to salvage what he could for his prince. Gisella looked positively furious, he thought.

"They are assaulting every one of our facilities around the world. A coordinated attack everywhere. We've got no place to evacuate to, that's what's happening!"

"Shit! I've got to save these eggs," the doctor barked.

"This whole operation has been nothing but one disaster after another. Prince Graz'zt has to be notified. Benedetta, let's go now!" Gar-Tar, his second in command fairly screamed. While she wanted to go kick some human ass, she reluctantly took his offered hand. Magic flashed and they Gated home to the Abyss.

"Double shit!" Gisella barked angrily. "If we go back, he'll hang our asses out to dry. Come on, general. I've an idea."

"This is not a good day to die," he replied calmly. "Now if I had my entire division, I could kick some butt here. Okay. Lead on." He took her hand and she barked, "Teleport: Fargo, North Dakota." The two vanished, leaving only the doctor and the six nurses and cook who had finally joined him, abandoning their patients and kitchen duties.

Just then, the sealed double metal doors burst open, ripped off their hinges by the combined power of several magic spells. They saw a host of wizards and witches coming at them. Two of the nurses and the cook promptly Gated back to the Abyss, just as three Disintegrate beams passed through the space where they had just been standing. The other four ducked out of the way. One beam wiped out one of the precious cylinders that Dr. Menninger was holding. He dropped to the floor, grabbed a hold of one of the nurses, and barked, "Teleport: Fargo, North Dakota." Hearing this, the other three nurses also cast their Teleport spells and vanished.

"What the heck are we doing here?" General Franco swore as they arrived in the far northern town amid vast wheat fields. A moment later, Dr. Menninger and a nurse appeared beside them, followed shortly by the other three nurses. All looked confused.

"So what now?" Dr. Menninger asked. "What's here? Wheat fields?"

"They won't be looking for us here," Gisella replied. "We don't dare go back to the prince, not right now. When he hears what's just happened, his wrath will be terrible. I value my skin. Guess you all do too, since you followed us. No, we hide out in tiny towns and wait until he cools down some, then make contact again. We'll need an entirely new plan. What we need to discover is just how did these humans find every one of our new facilities. That was a coordinated, worldwide attack or my name isn't Gisella."

General Franco smirked, "Well, that isn't you name, not wholly." She cracked a smile.

"Okay, anyone know the name of some tiny, remote town somewhere in this country?" Gisella asked. None had.

"I believe that they have maps at the fueling stations," General Franco suggested. "I see one with the yellow seashell logo a few blocks that way. I shall retrieve one."

"Excellent. We'll pick a random location and hide out there," Gisella replied. While he was gone, Donatella and Bella Messaged her and shortly joined Gisella. Both had several wounds; they'd done a bit of battling to try to save their fancy facilities. Neither wanted to face the wrath of Prince Graz'zt just now and had wisely abandoned their facilities.

Gisella commented, "I take it the weather is a trifle too hot for you two down in Miami and LA?" The two succubuses glared at her.

The battle was short-lived. With so many gunning for the relatively few demons, they were wiped out within a few minutes, in spite of their resistance to the magical spells. Even if they had a fifty percent chance that a spell wouldn't affect them, when bombarded with ten spells, odds are that half would. That the iron tipped bullets from the heavy weapons of the SWAT teams proved equally effective this time only tipped the odds in the favor of the attackers.

As Monica watched her friends blow apart the wards protecting the steel doors, knocking them completely off their hinges, she saw the evil Dr. Menninger assembling a number of the cryo-cylinders. "That's him! Kill him!" she barked and cast her own Disintegrate spell at him. At the last second, he raised the cylinder that he was working with up, using it as a shield. Her beam wiped out the cylinder. He dropped to the floor, hidden behind the stack of metal cylinders.

When they reached his position, he was gone, as well as the demon nurses. "That man has as many lives as a cat!"

Monica declared, very much annoyed that they had missed killing this beast of a man.

Rob spoke up, "Hey you all keep on hunting anyone that's left. I'm going to see if I can figure out where they all went." Monica decided to stand guard over him. He would need to focus all his attention on his spell and could therefore easily be taken by surprise. The others moved on down the long hall of this wing, calling out the occasional, "Clear!"

Five minutes later, her gang and Henry joined them. Crystal reported, "We've got a dozen blinded women here."

Henry declared, "Place is secure. The other wing held sleeping quarters for this bunch. We wiped out a dozen demons at least. Good going. Will contact Leslie and coordinate the rescues."

Rob finally broke his concentration. "Well, our doctor didn't Gate. He and three others teleported along with the two leaders. These other nurses gated, probably back to the Abyss. So Dr. Menninger is still around somewhere. We will get him next time, dear."

Somehow, Monica wasn't quite so convinced. Henry took charge again. "Okay, let's get the women over to St. Anne's. A team of doctors is waiting for them. Monica, will you come with me? They'll need your assessment and advice."

"Okay. Crystal, well done. Thanks to you, they are out of business big time," Monica praised her dear friend. Once more, Monica was struck with just how much power her group of friends actually wielded, so much more than just one lone man against everyone else. Even his Death Stalkers hadn't worked well together. True power lies in your friends, she thought once more, and joined Henry, as they teleported over to the hospital.

Within just a few minutes, the women were brought there as well. Blinded and under the Idiot Mind spell, these women were very confused. Monica quickly learned that they'd only recently been blinded. Their nurses had been insisting that perfect women didn't need eyes to see. They'd not been entirely convinced of this at first, but had grown slightly comfortable dealing with their confined room. They knew where their toilet was located and their small dining table and sofa. Now they were in unfamiliar surroundings, wholly lost, and completely confused. Hence, Monica and the doctors agreed that they should immediately restore their sight.

"Well, that is better. I think I need to see. I am still perfect, aren't I?" the first woman asked Monica immediately after she'd removed the woman's blindness spell.

"Yes, you are beautiful and perfect. So where did you live before you became perfect?" Monica asked.

"Los Angeles. Are we still there?"

"No, you are now in St. Louis. This will be your new room for a while. The doctors want to make sure that you are healthy and just perfect."

"Oh. Where's St. Louis? Is it near LA? Yes, I want to be perfect," she replied moronically. Monica didn't answer that one, allowing the doctors to begin their physical examination of her.

She'd just finished up with the twelfth woman when Leslie arrived. "Ah, good. I found you. We need to talk now," Leslie said quite seriously. "Twelve rescued here?" Monica nodded, indicating that was the correct number.

"Okay then, that makes a grand total of one hundred six women rescued today. The others didn't make it, killed in the crossfire of spells, I'm sorry to say. I've been asked to meet with you to determine just where to take all the women. Right now, they are at various hospitals around the world being checked out. I take it that Blindness must be cancelled right away?"

"Yes, they are totally disoriented otherwise," Monica replied quickly.

Leslie paused and sent a flurry of Messages, presumably to the other hospitals. "Now then, what do you think about where we should take the women? I really don't want you traveling all over the world to heal them. It's far too dangerous for you, since you are the only person who can heal them."

"Bring them here. There aren't many other options. I hope St. Anne's can handle that many," Monica answered.

"You realize that you are saving their lives, don't you?" Leslie asked, making sure that Monica knew that she really did know the magnitude of what she was doing for these women, now over a hundred more. "I am bringing in ten other specialists who can help you erase their traumas; that way you can focus right away on the healing process."

"Say, that would really help, if I didn't have to also deal with their trauma. Thanks, Leslie," Monica replied, a bit relieved. This would shave nearly two months off of the work ahead of her. Leslie left to make the arrangements, while Monica began removing the pain and emotional trauma the first of the dozen women had endured. By the time that she finished the woman, the others had been brought here. For a time, there was chaos in this wing of the hospital, as the staff worked rapidly to accommodate nearly a hundred more patients, ninety-four to be precise. Additionally, a dozen other witches showed up, volunteering to cast the requisite spells to help them erase the mental anguish.

On the other hand, Monica calculated that she would be at the healing process until near the end January, more than half a year! She groaned when she realized this detail, but braced herself for an extended stay here in the hospital. These women desperately needed what only she could give them— their lives back. While some of these women were also drug addicts, per the doctor's examinations, and at least two had been criminals, Monica decided to do them all. People can change, she thought. I'm giving them a clean slate, a chance to start over.

The hospital administration, now aware of Christina's worker's compensation settlement, visited with each of the women, once the Idiot Minds had been removed and their mental states handled. Ten of the women actually did qualify for this insurance settlement, and the administration staff very carefully explained this to the ten. The amounts varied a little from around thirty million to forty-four million. After very careful considerations, five of the ten decided to accept the enormous settlements. Monica and Christina then doubly verified that this was what the women really did wish.

Satisfied that the five were sincere, Monica suggested that they move into her place, joining Christina. There, they could experience what their lives were going to be like if they took the settlements. They didn't actually have to sign the papers one way or the other for ninety days. "Look, this will give you time to see if you can really do it," Monica explained. "If you change your mind, I'll get you back into the pool of women to be healed. After all, I'm going to be doing this until the end of January. You don't have to commit to it until the end of September. You've got all summer to see if it is going to work out for you."

The five agreed, and on July 4, Kathy Johanson, twenty-one and from LA, moved into the newly built addition at the estate, along with Jenny Carthage, twenty from Chicago, Becky Willis, twenty from Atlanta, Janis Breams, twenty-one from St. Louis, and Lea Ann Mc Carthey, twenty from Denver. Ericka also worked with them to get them elegantly attired and a personal assistant to help them. She left the walking practice sessions up to Christina.

Monica then dove into the huge task of healing a hundred and one women. On August 15, Monica had a huge decision to make. As she checked off the last woman fully healed, she saw that her healed count was now at ninety-nine. She recalled what Diancecht had told her, that she could only use her ring on herself when the count was at one hundred. She looked at the many women waiting as patiently as they could for her cure and sighed. Did she take a timeout and do herself or keep on going? *I can't stop now. They are desperate for this healing. This isn't the time to be selfish and think of myself, not when they are so desperate.* She plunged ahead, casting her spells to slip the ring on her hundredth patient, watching it expand and slip onto the woman's little toe, followed by the magic once meant for herself to activate. She sighed and began to chat with the woman about what her life had been before she'd been abducted from her home in Chicago. Now, she knew there was no turning back. This had to be done; it simply had to be.

As usual, Rob dropped by to bring her supper and to visit with her and whatever patient she was healing at the time. He whispered, "Isn't this one the hundredth?"

Monica felt a surge of emotions, but kept her eyes from watering. "They need it far, far more than I do, Rob."

"I understand," he whispered, leaned over, and kissed

her forehead. "Brought you both some pizza tonight," he spoke normally. "Figured you were getting tired of hospital food." That brought a smile to the patient's face, and he held up a piece for each to eat.

Rob also insisted that she take Sunday nights off and come home for a bath and some real bed time. Soon, she discovered she really did need these breaks from the long hours at the hospital. Time crawled along.

However, she did have one thing to ponder. A week after the assault, Monica heard some of the results. A dozen different facilities were raided that morning. Ten Dr. Menningers were reported killed. The obvious conclusion was that the doctor was being cloned as well! Monica also knew that somehow Graz'zt was keeping the knowledge of each Dr. Menninger a secret from each other. If not, the clones would probably cease everything else, search out, and kill off their clones. That was the side effect of that Clone spell: intense antipathy towards copies of themselves. Monica now knew that there were at least two Dr. Menningers somewhere around the world.

She also suspected that this man was the key to Graz'zt's big plans. The demon prince probably didn't have the knowledge or skills to be pulling off this diabolical creation of his Cambion army. *If only I hadn't missed him, there would be one less of him around here. Well, there will be another time to get him and him.*

Monica truly began to enjoy her Sunday evenings at home, away from the hospital. In a way, she felt like she was rather a mother hen to the six young women now staying with her group. She enjoyed the upbeat attitude of Christina and her English Lady's Maid Ruth Anne's dry humor and British accent. It was quite a change from the deadly seriousness that she faced with the other women at the hospital, that is, until her healing was finished on a patient. However, those women quickly left, heading for their homes, ready to resume their lives, thanks to her.

"Hi Christina, Ruth Anne," Monica greeted the pair early one Sunday evening. "All gone well this week?" She always asked this first, fully expecting to hear that it wasn't and that she too wanted to have her arms regenerated too.

"Oh hi Monica! Come on in. Just going over how my investments have progressed this week. Want to see if I have made any blunders?" Christina asked eagerly.

"Of course," Monica replied with a grin, taking a seat near her and her voice-activated laptop.

Ruth Anne commented dryly, "Is it likely that investments have progressed on their own? Surely, you had something to do with that. Oh, I forgot. We're in America where stocks magically grow." The two women giggled.

Monica retorted, "Yes, I'm afraid that in England, the stocks only hold prisoners for a time. So barbaric." They all laughed again. She looked over Christina's work. "Perfect, dear. I couldn't have done better. You now have a little excess beyond what would have to be repaid, should you decide this isn't for you. You could make your first donation using the excess."

"Really? I so hoped that you would say so," Christina replied, very excited about the prospect of making her first real contribution. "I've given it serious thought. I want to flow some support to the various food banks that help feed those in need, especially come the holidays, though I know those are still several months away. And next, I plan to donate to the Children's Charity so they can help purchase Christmas presents for children who might not get any present at all this year."

"Admirable, Christina. So you are doing well?" Monica asked.

"Oh yes. As you predicted, the more I walk, the easier it gets for me, though I'm still quiet terrified of stairs, going down them in particular. I keep reaching for the handrails with my hands, you know. Do you think that I will ever get over that?" Christina asked.

"I don't know. I still do that too," Monica admitted.

Ruth Anne commented, "Well, I should think that one would never get over reaching for handrails. After all, that's what they are there for. Just seeing them will be a reminder for you both. Me, I just couldn't imagine going through life like you both are or the other five, but then no one is offering me thirty million dollars either. I think it all depends on what you want to do with the money."

"What do you mean?" Monica asked, becoming curious about her line of thinking. She was British after all.

"If one only wanted to spend it on yourself, I suspect your life would end up being quite a rotten one. Christina and the others need assistance with most everything. If they kept buying possessions for themselves, it would be a constant reminder that they couldn't actually use or do anything much with them. What good is a car if you can't drive it? On the other hand, bringing hope and help to others in need, now that leaves you with a tangible result worth having," Ruth Anne declared, and then added, "Of course, that puts you in a league almost devoid of other wealthy people."

"Ah, we should start a league for ourselves," Christina joked. "Not the National League or American League, but the Women's League of Philanthropists or WLOP. Get it? Wallop?" They laughed again.

Ruth Anne commented, "Ah, is that something you Americans often like to do, wallop the oil billionaires of the Gulf States? Put them to shame?" Again, the three chuckled.

Christina then got serious, "Honestly, Ruth Anne, before this happened to me, I was always focused only on myself and trying to make ends meet each month. What little extra I earned, I spent on my CSI classes at the university. It was certainly not fun. Now I wake up each day and try to envision how much good I can do in our world for others. I really enjoy waking up each day now. No treadmill."

"Ah, perhaps that's what Christina should invest in next, a treadmill. Then, she wouldn't have to stroll endlessly around this complex," Ruth Anne teased her.

"Ah, but I simply must stroll around, Ruth Anne, if only so you get your proper exercise," Christina teased her back. Monica then rose and left the two to go check on how the other five had faired during the week. They were also doing as well as could be expected and planning for the future. Her duty to the six done for tonight, she headed off to find Rob, get a warm bath, and then some passion in bed.

Later on, as the ninety-day period in which to reach a

final decision to accept or reject the worker's compensation insurance money approached, Monica again met with each of the five women. With each woman, she just had to make doubly certain that a life like this was what they really wanted to have. Once they accepted the money, there was no going back, unless they somehow managed to pay back the money they'd accepted and with interest. This change in the worker's compensation laws had to be passed when magical cures became widely available.

That is, if a worker were injured on the job, the insurance would pay them in one of two ways. First, their medical cures could be paid in full. Or second, they could get the large settlement, such as these six were getting. However, if after they settled for the large amount, if they subsequently got their disability cured by magic, they were obligated to repay that large amount, less the cost of the medical cure, plus interest. This law was needed to prevent injured from taking advantage of the system by accepting the large settlement, and then turning around and getting healed or cured, pocketing a vast sum in profits.

Monica was again very much surprised that the five were not changing their minds, not in the least. They were working hard to adapt to their severe physical limitations and making excellent use of voice-activated devices. Slowly, Monica began to see these six as inspirational. None of them had any magic to help them, not as she did, and yet they were content with their new lives, as much as was possible.

In fact, what had started out as a joke, the Women's League of Philanthropists or WLOP became a reality, once the five were allowed to sign for their settlements and received their large monetary awards. Initially, the six formed the WLOP as a way to make their donations more effective by combining them into one larger endowment. Even Monica began to join in on some of their philanthropic endowments, adding some of her funds to theirs. As a result, the six made Monica a member too.

By early November, the five women had now had their settlements for some time and decided to move back to their respective cities. Ericka made very certain that each had a proper personal assistant to help them, kind and trustworthy women. Plus, they were now part of the WLOP, and as such stayed in touch with each other daily. With their voice-activated laptops and phones, this they could readily do.

Christina and her boyfriend Leonard Celli, and Ruth Anne, chose to continue to live with Monica and the others, having become good friends with these witches and wizards. She ran the WLOP from here. At Thanksgiving, Leonard proposed to Christina. Amid the gaiety, Monica insisted that they sign pre-nuptials that guaranteed that no matter what happened, Leonard wouldn't get access to Christina's funds. While she liked Leonard, she didn't want to have him rip off Christina, leaving her with nothing but a shattered life. The young woman fully realized Monica's concerns and agreed to it.

They were married on New Year's Day in a gay celebration at the PIWIP with some fifty relatives and guests in attendance. She wore a strapless, white gown and looked positively radiant. He wore a blue tuxedo and swore he was the luckiest man alive. Monica stood up as her maid of honor, while the others were her bridesmaids. Rob was his best man and the other fellows, his grooms. As they were all toasting the bride and groom at the reception, Leonard rose and said, "We chose this day so that neither of us would ever forget our wedding anniversary!" That brought many laughs from the older generation relatives.

Later after the celebration ended, Gregor proposed to Crystal, Tyler proposed to Ericka, Jiri proposed to Jill, and Milos proposed to Nisha. The four couples decided on a combined wedding to take place on Valentine's Day. When they announced this, everyone had to agree that this was a very romantic date to be married. Tyler jested, "This way, we fellows can't forget our anniversaries either. Christina and Leonard laughed loudly.

On January 18, 2141, Monica finally finished healing her one hundred fifty-eighth woman. Janice was very pleased finally to have it done. She'd been stuck here in St. Anne's since early July! However, her joy was no less spectacular when she finally had her arms and hands back, along with her feet. Though she had endured many months, she could finally get back to her own life again and thanked Monica profusely.

Monica returned home for good that night. She had a very satisfied feeling about what she'd accomplished. So many women had their lives returned to them, all thanks to her own initiative and action. However, she was also just a bit afraid. Per Diancecht's agreement with her, she was to have used the ring on herself on the hundredth use, but she hadn't. Now she'd gone way beyond that limit, but was very thankful that the ring still worked on the women beyond one hundred.

Further, she knew that there must be many more women suffering horribly down in the Abyss. If somehow they could be rescued, she would just have to heal them as well. Hence, she dared not use the ring for herself, not yet. Not until she could guarantee that there were no more victims to salvage. But that meant she had to continue to endure her own helplessness and that still scared her, though she didn't speak of it to anyone. She was just too afraid to do that, knowing that she'd probably break down and sob again. Perhaps, this karma thing was all that she could ever expect. Deep down in some recess of her mind, she knew that she deserved it, that the scales were not yet balanced and probably never would be.

Chapter 24—Graz'zt Makes a Move

"Is Peoria random enough?" Bella Zaronetti bickered to Gisella Harmoni. They'd just taken six adjacent rooms at the Motel 66 off I-74 west of the city. Donatella Ratini and General Franco Porti were with them in the large room. Dr. Menninger was next door with three nurses. The remaining Cambions, that is, the general's staff, were in the additional rooms. All had just teleported from Fargo, North Dakota to this random town, hoping to elude the dragnet that had just wiped out their breeding facilities, wrecking Prince Graz'zt's current plans for the takeover of Earth.

"It will do," Gisella barked, adding "for now. Turn on the MAG news." After this disaster, the other two succubuses begrudgingly allowed Gisella to run things. None of these demons dared Gate back home. Prince Graz'zt's anger would be monumental. Each had a strong drive to stay alive.

"Why?" growled Donatella, who was used to giving orders, not following them.

"Because these human fools will believe that they have just won the game and will be telling us what we need to know," Gisella answered, giving her a stare that said how can you be this stupid?

"Yes, I'd like to know how they found all the facilities?" General Franco dared to speak up among the three succubuses, anyone of whom outranked him, though he was partial to Gisella. "I know that my men took every precaution during and after the abductions. We didn't leave any clues whatsoever."

"Well, you must have," Bella barked, sneeringly. "How else could they have found us?"

"Quiet. It's obvious. They have invented a new way to detect the centers. Are you women complete fools?" Gisella countered. "Now shut up, and let's let the humans tell us how they did it."

By supper, Gisella and the others knew. Witch Crystal Holiday invented a way to detect anything that came from the

Abyss. While they didn't understand the underlying physics behind it, knowing that there were satellites in orbit above the planet that could spot their bodies at anytime, anywhere gave them all quite a fright! That the escaped egg breeder, Monica Nicole Black, was now healing the women's Incinerated arms also bothered Gisella. Such a thing should not be possible, as far as she knew.

Now armed with what really happened, Gisella had a counter-plan. "Look, they are looking for us in the large cities. If we hide out in small towns, they aren't likely to find us. However, Graz'zt needs to know what we've learned so he can plan his revenge. That means one of us is going to have to go back and tell him." She looked at the other three. "It's not going to be me. I got us this far." She looked at Bella and then Donatella.

"Oh all right. I'll go," Donatella gave in, after weighing her options. Staying here was now fraught with risk, possibly more than Graz'zt's wrath. Besides, he had time to calm down, and she would be giving him valuable information. That night, she Gated home, while the group teleported to another small mid-western town.

Graz'zt had already slain the returning Dr. Menninger, taking his sudden wrath out on him. Besides, he didn't dare let this version of the clone discover the other duplicates that were running his two separate breeding centers. He was very adept at keeping the two complexes quite isolated from each other. In fact, in his rage, he'd killed four others who had returned.

By the time that Donatella returned, he had calmed down and was most appreciative to hear how this disaster had come about. "How is it possible that this escapee Monica Nicole Black can regrow the breeder's arms? I used Incinerate on them just so it could *not* be undone!" Gat-Tar shrugged his shoulders. Such powerful magic was not his forte, pounding was. However his wife, Benedetta, did.

Benedetta bit her lip and then advised, "My prince, regeneration of limbs that have been Incinerated is just not possible, by all the rules of that spell. I find this is inexplicable and should investigate further."

"Agreed. However, twice now, this darn Crystal Holiday companion of Monica Nicole Black has destroyed my grand plans. I cannot allow her to do it a third time! I need them both here under my thumb. I want to parade this Monica Nicole Black around my realm. No, even better, I want her humiliated beyond all humiliations! I shall have her serve me as my horse. She can pull me in my royal cart around my realm so that all can see that she is totally under my control. As far as this Crystal is concerned, she must be brought here as well. I shall teach her to meddle in my affairs! She's cost me dearly, and now it is time that she paid the demon!"

"Donatella, Benedetta, put your heads together. Give me a plan to capture both of those interfering women. Mind you, I want them alive!" he barked, turned on his heels, and marched out of his throne room. He had other things to think about, primarily how he could conquer this meddling Earth.

Pacing his private room, he thought, I need these human women to breed a sufficiently large army of Cambion soldiers so I can take on Demogorgon and Orcus. So I simply have to subdue this world, period. I've been patient and sneaky for far too long. I need to take direct action this time. Just then, Gar-Tar came by, interrupting him. "Boss, can I have a moment?" his second in command asked.

"Aye. I do hope you have some ideas," he grumbled.

"Perhaps I do. I have been reviewing the various actions taken on this Earth world, combining them with my own observations of the human population there. In the larger cities, there are hundreds of thousands that we could easily acquire. They are already seeped in wicked, evil actions. Dealing and doing all manner of drugs, prostitution, extortion, assassinations—the list of their beautiful actions is nearly endless—prime recruits. I know we've done just that with some from St. Louis already. What about launching a giant recruiting operation? The other humans will be quite glad to be rid of those that we recruit, perhaps even thanking us for removing them from their world."

"There is that many? Indeed, they have worked out well so far. How many are we talking about getting?" Graz'zt inquired. Perhaps this was the answer that he was looking for.

"Millions, My Prince. There for the taking. Primed. Ripe. Plush. And ready to be plucked," Gar-Tar answered. "Offer them riches and power, and they are yours. Could this be the army that you've been desiring?"

"Hum, I like this. I had no idea there were so many humans that had fallen from grace. Millions, you say? I ought to have listened more to Gisella. She told me as much. Okay. Prepare a plan of action. Let's do this. We can get them some basic training and send them forth to conquer the rest of this annoying world. Once it is mine, I can establish an entire world dedicated to breeding our finest soldiers. Nothing in the Abyss could then stand in our way, Gar-Tar. Nothing!"

Later he met with Donatella and Benedetta, who had come up with their plan. Benedetta was the most powerful witch in his employ, and he trusted her advice. "We are dealing with a collection of most powerful witches," she explained, "as likely as powerful as I am. Taking those two will be challenging, but there are two ways to do it. One is riskier and one is foolproof, but expensive."

"Let's have the expensive one first," Graz'zt suggested, wondering just how much.

"Use a Full Wish spell, My Prince."

He chuckled. "Aye, nothing can stop that, but then the cost will be trivial compared to the riches that lie before us. The other one?" he asked.

"We can pay a visit to their magic store and meet with the two women, while we are disguised as humans. Once the two are together, I Stop Time long enough for Donatella and me to Stun both women and Gate them here, where you take over. Of course, the danger, the risk lies in the fact that they share their domicile with close to a dozen other wizards and witches. Chances are, one or more of them will accompany the two to meet us and offer significant resistance, forcing us to bring along other strong demons to hold these others off while we take the two women. Riskier. Things can go wrong, especially since we are dealing with powerful witches. One other detail, we will have to wait a while before we can get the two women together at their residence. I believe that Monica Nicole Black will be spending most of her time away, healing the many rescued breeding women."

"I see. I like them both, but I'm a patient man. I can wait a while. We have other actions that must be taken soon. I do still have that one Full Wish scroll available that I've been hoarding. We will try the riskier one first, Benedetta. Keep me apprised of when you can execute your plan," he said with some finality. The two females turned and left him. Both would be waiting to return to Earth when Gisella next made contact. However, Benedetta paid a quick trip to a semi-friend of hers, Jonellith, hoping to convince her to join them when they snatched the two women. That there would likely be one or more brave warriors for her to slay finally got her to agree to be Gated to Earth when Benedetta summoned her. A few days later, Gisella opened the Gate from a tiny village in eastern Colorado, bringing the three back to Earth along with their new orders.

During the fall and winter of 2140, the Board of Regents had the IR imaging satellites watching for more buildups of demons within the larger cities of the world. However, none was discovered. Only an occasional red line appeared here and there and only for several hours. The conclusion reached was that most of the demons had been eliminated, though there were still a few roaming around. Since no overt attacks occurred anywhere, by the start of the new year of 2141, the conclusion was that the demon problem had pretty well been eliminated. Everyone began to relax their vigils.

At the FBI headquarters in St. Louis, the first week in January, Oliver looked over the latest summary crime figures for the third and fourth quarters of 2140. Naturally, he first examined the number of missing persons and kidnaping reports. They were almost non-existent. In the current environment, anyone thinking about kidnaping a young woman thought better of it, knowing that half the world was on the lookout for these and would come swooping down on them, believing demons were behind it. So these results only confirmed the prevailing consensus that the demon abductions had been ended with the big summer raids.

What surprised Oliver was that the numbers in the

other crime categories were also dramatically down from a year ago. While he definitely liked what he was seeing, he just didn't see the demon raids as having any major effect on the criminal elements of his city. Yet something had caused an enormous drop in all the categories. A few weeks later, he received the national reports and compared them to his. What he found made no sense to him. In the major cities throughout the country, the crime rates all showed rather dramatic drops. However, in the towns with a population of a million or less, the rates were pretty much what they had been last year—a most confusing set of data. The only thing he could think of that might be playing a role in the dropping crime rates of the big cities was all of the demon hunting activities of the past year.

The Board of Regents was also active during the fall and winter. They first agreed that Prince Graz'zt's realm had to be raided, and the abducted women somehow freed and brought back home. No one disagreed on this point. Rather the how remained the sticky point. Here on Earth, only a few demons were faced in any one conflict and were pitted against a large number of wizards and witches, along with heavy arms fire from SWAT teams. Even so, more than half of the demons always managed to escape.

If they Gated into the Abyss, they would be on the demon's home ground, possibly thousands of them would join the fray, to say nothing of the harmful effects that environment might have on humans. Certainly, the rules of magical spells would be somewhat different there. There was very little hard data about such things upon which to know accurately what they would actually be facing. Hence, many talked, but few ideas of doable rescue scenarios were actually presented. Desires took a backseat to the reality of the situation.

In March of 2141, after the weddings were over and things had gotten back to normal around the Protections, Information, Wands, Items, and Potions estate, Monica looked over the response that she'd received from Leslie Traub, the head of the Missouri Department of Magical Misuse. She cursed, and at supper, she voiced her growing anger.

"Gang, guess what our illustrious leaders are going to do to rescue all our women who have been abducted and taken to the Abyss and tortured? Nothing. Nada. It's too risky. No one has any viable plan. It's official. Our wonderful leaders have just written these women off, like they were worthless or something!"

Crystal spoke up, "I know it's really harsh, Monica, but you have to look at it realistically. Even if a hundred of us Gated there, we might be able to rescue any woman still in the one complex that you know about, but we're likely to meet very stiff resistance, and besides we have no idea where all the other centers are located. We've no idea of what his realm is like. No maps or such things. It truly is rather a hopeless task."

"Justifications. These are women's lives that we are talking about," Monica declared, a little annoyed that Crystal was also supporting the government's policy.

"I know, Monica. It is really a harsh condemnation. I've been working on trying to figure out ways that we could do it. I think we could manage one sneak raid to that same center where you were held, but what if they've moved the women to other centers? Where are these other centers? We just don't have enough information. Not even Nisha knows where they are at," Crystal tried to soften the blow.

She then added, "Monica, I'm not giving up, not yet. I'll keep working on it." That satisfied Monica, at least a little.

Later in their bedroom, Monica asked Rob, "Couldn't we go there and scout out Graz'zt's realm? I know I can Planar Walk there."

"We could, but I don't know how long it would take us to find anything there. Even invisible, the demons can smell us and likely see us. Our magic works differently there. I don't think it's quite as powerful as it is here on Earth. While I was out in Denver, I spent some time discussing this with some of the Rodents. Deiter told me that their special techniques simply wouldn't work in the Abyss. In fact, you and I know more about the Abyss than all the Rodents combined," Rob explained.

"Really? We know more than they do?" Monica asked in disbelief. Until now, she thought that the Rodents must be the most knowledgeable wizards and witches on the planet. That she might know more than they did shocked her, even if it was about something as evil as the Abyss.

"Yep, we do. In my opinion, what little we do know realistically isn't enough to go on. However, dear, if nothing else happens in a reasonable time, I think we should at least try to rescue the women that might still be at the center where you were held. We might be able at least to do that much," Rob proposed. For now, That was enough to satisfy Monica.

Chapter 25—Disaster Strikes

Around ten on March 10, Jill saw three women appearing at the entrance to the store's reception area. Already the first green shoots of the daffodils were several inches tall in the oval garden just behind the three women. They entered, and Jill spoke up, "Welcome to Protections, Information, Wands, Items, and Potions. How may I direct you?"

"We would like to visit with Monica and Crystal, if we may. We have some information about the Abyss that we would like to share with them," Donatella spoke politely.

"You are in luck. Both are here today. Who should I say is calling?" Jill asked, reaching for the intercom button.

"Donatella," she replied, smiling pleasantly.

"Crystal, Monica, a Donatella and two other women are here to see you. They have some information about the Abyss to share with you," Jill spoke into the intercom. She looked up at the three women and added, "They'll be right with you. Monica moves a little slowly compared to us."

A Magical Door opened up in the reception area and Rob, Monica, and Crystal stepped out, followed by Gregor as well. Since Monica didn't have any hands to greet anyone properly, Crystal took charge, extending her hand, "I'm Crystal. This is Monica, her husband Rob, and my husband, Gregor. How can we help you today?"

Suddenly, Jill shrieked, "It's a trap!" Her vision in the infrared kicked in, and she saw demonic forms standing there. One even looked partially like a giant snake!

The warning came a split second too late. Benedetta had just finished casting her spell that stopped time. As fast as she could, she cast a pair of Stun spells on both women, barely finishing before time resumed its usual pace. Rob blinked! The taller woman changed into the most hideous demon he'd ever seen before! She was a naked woman above her waist, with a rather pretty face, but with six arms extending from her torso! Each held wicked looking swords of various kinds. Below her waist, she was a giant constrictor snake, both huge and many feet long!

He recognized the other demon standing to the right of the female spell caster: a succubus! Worse, she was casting! Jill dove for cover beneath her desk, frantically sounding the alarm that would bring everyone else in the complex to reception in a flash! Rob had almost no time to react. The many-armed demon was on him, and she was incredibly fast! However, his Skin of Stone spell was active, and her swords did nothing but jar him from the sudden impacts. Instantly, she changed tactics, quite aware of the spell that he must be using. Her tail whipped around him, before he could even dodge away. Her coils were lightning fast—three times around his chest in a flash, and then the coils began crushing him to death! His face turned red. He tried to push the coils of the snake off him, but it was futile! He was as good as dead and he knew it.

To his left, Bernedetta snapped her fingers and barked, "Stun!" Gregor had raised his wand about ready to cast a spell at the trio. Her spell activated a split second before his. He stood still as a statue. His partially completed spell did nothing as he joined Monica and Crystal who stood erect and motionless, stunned.

From the corner of her eyes, Monica saw the snake's coils around Rob, saw them squeezing the life out of him! His face was as crimson as her gown! Yet, she was utterly helpless to come to his aid! Her last sight was of her lover, her husband, her Rob was him dying while she stood there unable to do anything at all to save him. The next instant, Donatella's magical Gate activated and strong arms lifted the pair of women, tossing them like two sacks of potatoes into the opened Gate. Only later on, did Monica learn that the trio also vanished from their reception area seconds after they had and just seconds before all the others came dashing to their rescue.

With the horrific sight of the death of her husband burning in her mind, Monica found herself back in the Abyss standing on the very gold-plated Gate platform that she'd originally been on before. Graz'zt sneered. "Ah, back at last, Monica. You miss me? I've missed you. So good of you to return. I want you to watch me prepare your Crystal friend here." He moved her slightly so that she could see Crystal. The two motionless women were then paralyzed, frozen in place, their eyes staring at each other, but unable to move.

Monica was forced to watch as Crystal's arms Incinerated. She knew the horrific pain that Crystal was experiencing. It was visible in her eyes. Focus on the pain, Crystal, focus on the pain so the Idiot Mind doesn't work right, Monica thought as hard as she could, wishing that she had telepathic abilities to let Crystal know this crucial datum. Once the ashes of her arms had floated down to the rotten, grey ground, a nurse stepped up and hastily removed both women's clothing. Then, she sat Crystal in a crude chair and slipped the special ballet ankle boots onto Crystal's feet. That done, Graz'zt Shrank them to fit tightly and cast his Fuse: Feet spell. Watching the whole ordeal, Monica hoped that he would stop with this.

He didn't. He cast the Idiot Mind spell, but once more Monica fairly screamed in her mind for Crystal to focus on the pain so that the spell wouldn't have much of a hold on her. Finally, he cast his Blind spell on her before releasing her and going through his entire introductory speech again, basically telling her that now she was absolutely a perfect woman and so on.

Then, he turned his attention onto Monica. "You have been a thorn in my side for far too long, woman. It is time that you take your rightful place here in my realm. I can't have you casting spells. While I originally thought that I'd just cut your tongue out, I've been advised that you would find eating terribly difficult, and I certainly don't want you starving to death. No, you are to be here for the rest of your life, and I do want that to be as long as possible. I've decided that you will be my beast of burden, my horse. Since you are going to be my horse and pull my cart for me, I've made this special bridle for you." He forced her mouth open and inserted a steel bit, much like that used on recalcitrant horses. The harness was securely fastened by tight leather straps in several places around her head. Even if she had hands, she would have had a tough time removing them all to get the steel bit out of her mouth. With it in her mouth, she couldn't talk intelligibly, though Monica did try. Unable to speak, she couldn't cast any spells.

He then said, "But you are a clever pony. Ponies can sometimes get out of their harnesses. So I'm going to cut your tongue out anyway. We will force feed you if we have to!" With the cold bit in her mouth, she couldn't close it to resist him. She felt her tongue being pulled and stretched out. She saw the sharp, black dagger coming up to her face and tried to pull away, but strong arms kept her from moving. Monica then felt the shape pain and saw him drop most of her tongue onto the ground, where unspeakable worm-like creatures rose up out of the grey rotting ground eagerly devouring it. At least he commanded, "Heal!" Gagging on the blood in her mouth and with no way to clear it out, she was grateful that he cast several Clean spells removing the gagging blood.

That done, Monica was forced to watch as the nurse made Crystal stand up and begin walking. She could see her frantically wiggling and wobbling. The terror in her greyed-out eyes emanated like light rays in the night sky! That was in spite of her babbling about how perfect she now was and that she ought to be able to walk, sort of, maybe. "Focus on the pain," Monica tried to tell her dearest friend, but even she couldn't understand a word that she said. Her words sounded like pure gibberish. Now she could never cast another spell ever!

Next, Prince Graz'zt ordered some assistants to hook the pony harness onto Monica. They did so, strapping bits of leather around her waist and then forcing her to walk over to a pony cart, where they attached the two long arms to her waist harness. Monica now realized what Graz'zt intended for her to do. She was going to have to pull his cart around. She was being reduced to being a pony or horse! He then lifted the wildly wobbling, blind Crystal up, placing her onto the cart and then climbed up himself.

"Gather around everyone. Here we have my new pony, Monica, who dared to steal my egg-producing women from me. And here beside me is the woman who has twice destroyed our new facilities on Earth. Now, she has joined us here to be our newest egg producer. She will begat many fine new soldiers for me. Okay, Pony Monica, giddy-up! Pull us. In case you don't know, I have the reigns, and I'll direct you. We're going on a tour. I want everyone here to see how well you respond to being reduced to a beast of burden and how well Crystal will be as our newest egg producer. This is what happens to those who dare to cross me, Prince Graz'zt, Prince of the Abyss! Now pull us!" He cracked a whip, stinging Monica's bare butt.

Monica flinched, but attached to the cart, she couldn't move much to avoid the cracks of his whip. Standing only on her toes, she had very little capacity to exert any real pull. She leaned forward and forced her feet to pull the heavy weight. After slipping several times and enduring more cracks across her rear, she finally was able to get the cart moving by leaning forward at nearly a forty-five degree angle to the ground. She heard loud laughing and sneering coming from all sides, and saw that hundreds of demons of all shapes and sizes rapidly gathering to watch this spectacle. With the image of Rob's death and the mutilation of Crystal burning in her mind, Monica's humiliation was complete. The constant raucous laughter, sneering, and belittling comments from hundreds of demons watching her struggle to pull the heavy weight only added to her total humiliation, just as Graz'zt had planned.

"Oh, this is just *so* perfect!" he roared from his seat, giving her another sharp crack across her butt just for the fun of it. Monica didn't realize it, but her eyes were flowing tears like streams of water. She had lost Rob, lost Crystal, lost her tongue, and lost all of her ability to work magical spells. She was indeed reduced to being nothing more than a simple pony at the very best.

Numb beyond belief, Monica continued to place one foot in front of the other, though she was leaning heavily forward just to be able to get enough leverage from her toes to pull the cart along, albeit very slowly. Even the constant hooting, hollering, jeering, and taunting were turned out of her consciousness. She no longer even heard them, though it continued, seemingly endlessly. Graz'zt continued to repeat his little speech as they encountered other demons along the way that had come out to watch this grand display and see their glorious ruler in his splendid victory.

A tiny thought appeared in the back of her mind. *I'm seeing more of his realm.* She squashed that by thinking, so what? Then, she saw another complex similar to the one in which she had been held prisoner. *Here's another one. Now I know where two of them are.* Dr. Menninger stepped out from one of the buildings, adding his sneering and jeering to the cacophony of the many other demons around them.

When they drew close to the complex, Graz'zt pulled back hard on the reigns, nearly knocking Monica off her feet and breaking her neck. She stopped mechanically. Graz'zt dismounted amid lots of shouting and cheering. Evidently, he wanted to discuss something with Dr. Menninger, this version of the mad doctor, anyway. Catching her breath, Monica had another thought. *I can still use my mental powers. I can Planar Walk.* She turned her head and saw a partially sobbing Crystal still sitting helplessly on the cart. No one was close to them. After all, they were helpless and couldn't do anything, much less get away. Any one of the demons could easily walk faster than she could.

Still, that she could still use her Planar Walk filled her with some hope. She had to get Crystal out of here before they did more awful things to her. This might be her only chance. As rapidly as she could manage, Monica began to walk again, pulling the cart and Crystal along with her. Focusing, she moved out into the grey fog of the astral plane. She didn't see the sudden commotions behind her; hundreds of demons tried to stop her, as she and the cart simply vanished from sight. She didn't see Graz'zt explode in an angry, violent outburst or see him kill three other demons in his rage. Nor did she see his various magic users trying desperately to figure out where she'd gone or how.

Monica simply focused on taking the next step, concentrating on Earth. Still almost completely numb, she finally saw the bluish globe appearing amid the grey void and made for it. As it grew larger and larger, she turned her focus onto her home and the circular driveway around the flower garden bed just outside their front door. Just as she finally thought that she could not take another step, she felt the hard surface of the blacktop beneath her toes. She smelled the fresh, clean air, and the chill of late winter. She collapsed onto the pavement, her mind numb beyond anything that she'd ever known.

Crystal was still sitting on the cart, completely mystified. The Idiot Mind spell continued to work, and she was very confused. There's a world of difference between just being disoriented and in being very confused. She was in the Abyss being a perfect woman, and now somehow she was here back at her home, but she shouldn't be here. She should be with all the other perfect women. That she was completely blind only added to her reeling mind, which was trying to sort out the smells. She was sure this place smelled like home and was therefore the wrong place to be. "I'm supposed to walk by myself. I don't really need to see, do I? But I don't think I can walk. But I'm supposed to be perfect. So I should be able to walk. Is anyone here now?"

Inside the reception area, Jill looked up and saw Monica and Crystal arriving, but they were naked. Monica was pulling some kind of very strange cart. After double blinking, Jill used the intercom to get everyone out there immediately.

Monica woke up, confused as well. She was in a hospital. She could see out the window. It was dark out, but she vaguely remembered that it was light when she had collapsed. Her mouth felt funny. She couldn't open it. Had they removed that too? She panicked and tried to sit up. A gentle hand kept her down. She turned her head to see who it was and received the shock of her life. It was Rob! Dead Rob, returned from the dead, smiling kindly down at her, rubbing his hand gently across her forehead. Again, she tried to speak, but couldn't open her mouth.

"Sh. They have your mouth taped shut for a few days. They are regrowing your tongue. The doctors said that there was more than enough of it left that they can easily regrow it. Relax. They are feeding you intravenously. You and Crystal gave us all a big scare. We still don't know what happened or how you got back here, but that can wait," Rob said kindly.

He continued, "I'm in the next room, but they've moved me in here. I got several cracked ribs from the snake-like demon. I'm supposed to be out of here in another day, but I'll stay here with you until they release you, dear. Don't worry about Crystal yet. We got her blindness spell dispelled, and they are curing her of the Idiot Mind spell—probably already have that done. Someone's going to use their spells to help her erase her pain and trauma, just as you always do for the others. She'll be all right. Once you get healthy again, you can use your ring on her to fix her up too. So just lie back, dear, and try to get some sleep. I'll be right here with you."

Monica tried to process all this. Rob wasn't dead? Her tongue was growing back? Crystal was going to be okay? Suddenly, she began crying. This was all just too much emotion for her to process. Rob talked soothingly to her, wiping her cheeks several times. When she finally finished crying, she relaxed a little and drifted into a deep sleep. She hadn't seen the doctor enter and release a sedative into her tubes.

She awoke again to find the sun shining into her room. She rolled her head to one side and breathed a sigh of relief! Rob was here. She hadn't been dreaming! As she stirred, he looked up and came over to her. Oh, how Monica wanted to reach up and hug him, to squeeze him, to hold on to him for dear life, but again she was frustrated that she'd never ever be able to do that. Rob whispered, "Hug?" She nodded vigorously, and he did the best he could what with all the tubes injected into her legs. He gave her a long, soft kiss on her forehead and then rubbed her head gently. "Only a few more days, the doctors say, and I can take you home."

Two days later, the doctors removed the tape from her mouth and examined her tongue. "Good as new, Monica," he pronounced. "Before we release you, I'm having someone erase the pain and trauma that you'd suffered, just like we did for Crystal. Then, Rob here will be taking you home. Okay?"

"Thank you! God, I never thought I'd be able to speak again or cast spells!" Monica exclaimed and then wiggled her tongue about, testing it to see that it really did work like her old tongue. Two hours later and a lot of screaming, Monica had also erased the pain and emotional trauma that she'd endured, much to her own relief.

Rob quickly got her dressed and teleported her home as

fast as he could. He knew how badly she wanted out of the hospital and to see Crystal. Besides, everyone wanted to know what had happened. Crystal had been too wiped out to tell them much at all that made any kind of sense.

When Rob and Monica appeared in their reception area, the entire group was already there and spontaneously began cheering and clapping, causing Monica to blush. Gregor was holding onto Crystal, who was wearing her favorite sky blue satin gown, but looked rather terrible, Monica thought.

She walked up to Crystal. "God, I'm so sorry for you. I'll get you healed up today!"

Crystal managed a smile. "Monica, talk about walking a mile in your shoes—I can't do it! I'm terrified of even standing up on my own! Gregor has to support me constantly! I'm so utterly helpless, but then you and Christina already know what I mean. I don't know how you both can stand it. Please heal me, Monica, please."

"Of course, right away."

"No, let's go into the dining room and sit down," Rob countered Monica. "We all need to know just what happened, in case they come back after you both again. Ericka's placed some other protective spells on the reception area. Hopefully, they will alert us to the presence of demons, if they try again." Rob gently pushed Monica forward, knowing that she had little choice but to take a step or fall down.

Monica sighed and obeyed, so glad to be safe and home that she didn't object. Over tea and the intense interest of everyone, she related what she'd seen, heard, and done. "I now know where a second facility is located. I think I can find it again, so we've got two centers of women that we can rescue." She outlined how in utter desperation, she had seized upon the only thing that she could possibly have done to get her and Crystal out of the Abyss and a lifetime of eternal torment.

Rob's comment when she finished was, "Brilliant, love, positively brilliant. You sure showed Graz'zt! I wish we could have seen his face when he saw you taking off with Crystal, escaping from his clutches! I bet that was something else."

"Yes, but now he's going to be madder than ever with Monica and Crystal," Ericka pointed out. "We're going to have to have even more and better protections or they will snatch them again. Oh, Monica, Crystal has identified that weird snake demon. She's really a very powerful and nasty demon, very hard to kill too. Nearly got Rob."

Ericka added, "Tomorrow, I will have two broaches for you and Crystal to wear all the time now. They have an In Case I Am Stunned, Teleport Me to St. Anne's. I figured that would be the last place the demons would think that you've escaped to. I want you to both wear them for the foreseeable future. I should have thought of this one lots sooner."

"Thanks. You are right. We've really ticked that demon prince off big time," Monica stated flatly, wondering if she'd ever be rid of him. He was so huge and powerful that she didn't even know how she could kill him. Magic rolled off him like water.

They chatted a bit longer, but Monica was insistent that she get started right away on Crystal, who was extremely vulnerable right now, unable to walk much without Gregor holding her. He led her to their bedroom suite, while Monica went to her room. There was her precious ring right where she kept it on her dresser. Casting some spells, she levitated it up and got the chain around her head before canceling that spell, feeling it drop securely to her chest. She pirouetted and headed to Crystal's room. Gregor had her lying on her bed and had removed her boots and nylons, ready for the process. He kindly pulled up a chair for Monica and helped her get into a good position. Quietly, he kissed Crystal and left them alone.

Again, casting a number of spells, Monica finally was able to slip the ring onto Crystal's fused toe. Magic flashed and Monica finally relaxed, breathing a huge sigh of relief. The ring still functioned. She didn't know what she would have done had the ring failed to operate!

Crystal felt like chatting. "Thank you for having a level head and rescuing me. I was so wiped out by that pain and the stupid spell that I was useless. Honestly, I have never been so utterly and completely helpless in my whole life!"

Monica chuckled, "Dear, you were probably even more helpless when you were an infant."

Crystal cracked a chuckle. "Well that doesn't count.

Besides, I can't remember that far back. I don't know how Christina can possibly manage or why she wants to live like this!"

"Cause she knows that she can do so much more good for others by using her fortune wisely to help them than she could if she got healed and continued to work at her bank or even became a CSI technician. She really wants somehow to make a difference in other people's lives, dear. That's why she is willing to live like this. As long as she is happy and successful, I'm backing her up. For a while back there, I thought my life was over too—that I'd lost Rob, you, and even my magic skills. I couldn't live without this tongue of mine." Both women giggled. The disparity between the two's losses was enormous, but not in magnitude to each woman.

Two days later, the ring slipped off Crystal's toe. While Monica retrieved it and put in back on her chain using a number of spells to do so, Crystal rose, checked out her arms, hands and feet, before giving Monica a long, loving hug. "Thank you, love. I really owe you for this."

Chapter 26—An Invitation from the Devil

The next morning, Ericka's new alarm system in their reception area triggered, but Jill, who had just taken her seat behind her desk, simply froze, staring at the stranger. He wore a crimson robe, plush, with black trim. One foot was really a cloven hoof. His bald head didn't remotely disguise the two horns protruding from it, but he had a neatly trimmed, pointed beard, dropping perhaps two inches down from his chin. His right hand held onto a staff that was as tall as he was and with a carved dragon-like figure at its top. His left hand clutched some kind of rod. His eyes, intense. He waited patiently as Magical Doors appeared, and in groups, everyone at the estate charged out into the reception area, expecting a fight, everyone that is, excepting Christina who had no way to fight.

"Oh. It's you. Dispater? Right?" Monica asked, rather taken by surprise. This was not whom she expected. Rather, they all had thought the demons had come to try to retake Monica and Crystal again.

He smiled and bowed his head, just perceptibly. However, at that instant, more magic flashed, and Glasya suddenly appeared. Her hair was tussled, and it appeared that she had just dropped everything to get here so quickly. Dispater turned his head. "Might have known you'd show up," he said to her in a coy, sneering voice.

"Mammon doesn't trust you, obviously," she retorted, fussing with her disheveled hair. "Can't you give a girl a bit more time to prepare?" she shot back at him. His lips pursed in a slight smile.

Turning to Monica, he said quite politely, "Is there someplace we can sit down and have a civilized discussion?"

"Yes. Of course. The dining room. It's this way," she turned reasonably gracefully and began leading the way. He followed, and Glasya, flirting with the various men in turn, followed discretely behind him.

When she dropped back to Rob's side, she raked one of her long red nails across his cheek and whispered, "Is she any good in bed? Like she is, that is?" He flushed and refused to answer her. She teased him, "Ah, so I see that she is. Of course, I'm better. You should ask me sometime." He continued to ignore her.

After sitting down around their large table with Rob rushing to assist Monica so that she didn't have to use any spells or awkwardly try to push the chair out so she could sit down, Monica asked, "Would you care for some tea or something?"

Dispater smiled. "I believe that would be wise. We have much to discuss." Nisha took that as her cue and dashed off to heat some water. Everyone waited for her to return, though the silence was rather awkward. The Arch-devil didn't seem to mind it in the slightest, but Glasya continued to try to organize her hair and straighten out her fancy dress, clearly annoyed that she'd been ordered to come on such short notice.

After the tea was served and Nisha quietly put a straw in Monica's cup for her, Dispater took a polite sip and then began. "We have a very serious situation here on your world, this Earth."

"We know, demons. Graz'zt is trying to attack us," Rob pointed out the obvious.

"Precisely, but it is far more complicated than a few demons running amok," he continued. "You see, we devils also recruit here as well. In fact, it is one of our better, shall I say, hunting grounds. Always has been. However, Graz'zt has gone too far. Do you realize that his minions have been stealing away several million of your people?"

"What? No. Millions?" Crystal blurted out. "I thought that we mostly put them out of business when we raided their facilities."

"Ah that. Gave them a minor inconvenience. I see that you aren't aware of what they have been doing here for the last six months or so. Of course, you might feel that he's doing you a service by stealing these people. They come from the slums of your cities. You call them your criminal elements—your drug dealers and addicts, your prostitutes, your thieves and assassins, your extortionists. You are shocked. I see that this is news to you. I thought as much. Yes, they've been picking up these unwanted souls and sending them to the Abyss, where their bodies are slain, and they are forced into new demon bodies of various kinds."

"Well, isn't that sort of a good thing?" Milos asked, thinking this was one way to get rid of the undesirables of society.

Monica spoke up, "No, not really. People can change. If they are killed and taken to the Abyss, then they have no chance ever to change and redeem themselves."

Dispater smiled and replied, "Spoken from one who knows." Monica flushed. He continued, "However, in their indiscriminate theft of your people, they have taken some who have pledged themselves to me."

"Their souls?" Gregor asked.

"Precisely."

Not to be left out, Glasya put in, "And to Mammon. He's very upset about the theft of his promised souls. I have seldom seen him so angry."

Dispater went on, "So we find ourselves facing a key crisis here. I cannot allow this upstart prince of the Abyss to interfere with my work. I have given some my sworn word, my bargain, and now I find that they have been stolen from me and against their own wishes too."

"Same with Mammon," Glasya hastened to add.

"Do you know what he plans to do with his newly acquired millions of demons?" he asked. Without waiting to hear, he continued. "First, he will soon send them all here to Earth and attack everywhere at once. Within days, his minions will take over this whole world. Already you know what he intends to do after that. All fertile women will be impregnated to create a mighty army of Cambions warriors. He will use these to assault the Demon Lords, Demogorgon and Orcus, wrestling control of much of the Abyss from them and setting himself up as the new Demon Lord of the Abyss."

"I must admit that even the Hells would then feel quite threatened by his chaotic whims. With an army of hundreds of millions of Cambion warriors, he may well succeed in taking over the Hells as well as the Abyss. If he does that, in all likelihood, nothing could stop him from becoming Lord of all the Universes. Can't let that happen."

Glasya hastily added, "Mammon can't let that happen either. That's why I've been tagging along. We can't let Graz'zt succeed with his plans." However, if she had a remedy for it, she didn't say, but just as quickly became silent.

Monica took the brief silence as a subtle hint. "So what did you want us to do? Fight them in the Abyss?"

Dispater laughed. "Hardly. As powerful as you believe you are, I'm afraid that you wouldn't stand a chance against the demons that live there. No, you need an even more powerful ally. Me."

"Hey, and me, I mean Mammon," Glasya added, but she obviously had no idea where Dispater was leading the conversation.

He continued, "The root cause behind this whole mess is Doctor Menninger, who invented this whole egg production concept, including the many cloned women that he's been using for millennia. That man must die or more precisely all his clones must die along with his stored DNA so that new clones of him can't be created. All these egg production centers and the nurseries must be destroyed. If that's done, then his dreams of universe domination will be at an end. Even if he should take over the Earth, he would be unable to suddenly field an army of billions like he plans to do."

Monica spoke up, "Doctor Menninger is a human, isn't he? Some kind of mad scientist."

"Yes, almost two hundred years ago, he worked founded a hospital of horrors and worked heavily in the area of supposed demonic possession. He fooled nearly everyone back then and was working for Graz'zt, who obviously kept DNA samples of the doctor. He's had nearly two centuries to perfect his despicable 'science' of human-demon interbreeding. If we don't get rid of him and his DNA, I'm afraid Graz'zt's plans may well pan out."

Monica declared, "So far, I would totally agree with you. The man must be stopped. The horrific evil that he is wreaking on young women is intolerable. But if we can't raid his realm in the Abyss, how can we get this man or rather his clones? I know where two of the breeding complexes are located."

"I know where they all are located. I've come today to offer you a deal. I would like you and your people to conduct three separate raids, one on each of these centers. Rescue those that you like. There were five of them, but he's consolidated them down to three. I know that you have a tender heart for the victims so do what you desire with them. However, before you deal with the victims, search out and kill the Dr. Menninger clone who runs that facility. There should be three of them to kill," Dispater explained.

"We'd like nothing more than to rescue the women there, but we aren't strong enough to fight all the demons protecting the places and the swarms that will respond to us once we're detected," Monica pointed out.

Dispater smiled. "I'm not finished. I will see that all of Graz'zt's forces are very heavily occupied and will have no thought to rushing back to these breeding facilities. In fact, I suspect there will be very little resistance there. However, the window of opportunity will be short, I suspect, so do not waste too much time on any one of the three. If you fail to get the three doctors, I'm afraid the problem will only return some years in the future."

Glasya spoke up, "So what do you want Mammon to do in all this? Are you planning to leave him out? He's got sworn promises that he must live up to as well."

"I will let Demogorgon and Orcus know the precise details of Prince Graz'zt's grand plan. Those Demon Lords are not fools! They will almost certainly launch an all-out attack on Graz'zt's realm, especially since I'll promise to send in garrisons of devils to help with the fight. Of course, their mission will be something else entirely: the total destruction of the DNA storage facilities and the breeding centers, once you've cleared them out. Naturally, they will also be having a field day killing demons. We devils thoroughly hate all demons. Yet, in this situation, for our own survival, we will appear to fight along with the two Demon Lords."

Glasya broke in, "So what role does Mammon play?"

"Have him send in some of his forces. He and I can each take two of these critical sites to destroy, but my forces will hit the DNA storage facility and one of the centers. His forces can have the other two centers. So humans, do we have a deal?" Dispater asked.

Monica thought a moment, but couldn't see any loopholes. As if reading her thoughts, he added, "No, there are no strings attached. No souls being sold in this deal. I need the focus of you humans to hunt down and eliminate the three doctor clones. In the absolute chaos of war, not even my devils can be counted upon to stick to that task, whereas I know that you humans, especially you and your group, have a vested interest in ending the abnormal lives of these evil clones." He cleverly ignored the fact that he was also evil.

"Well, we certainly do have a vested interest in ending the horrible crimes that these clones have committed on our young women," Monica said. "Okay. Count us in. How do we coordinate all this? When does it happen?"

"To evacuate your women, use the provided permanent gates, the golden incised pentagrams on the platforms close to the centers," the Arch-devil explained. "As to when. Now that is a huge difference between us devils and the demons. With demons, you cannot count on anything, whereas if I give you a date and time, that will be quite precise. In this case, we will be dealing with utter chaos incarnate. I will try to give you as much lead time as possible, but just be ready to go on a moment's notice around that date. Let us plan this to go down on April 1, but again, no predicting the Demon Lords, so be prepared several days before that. I will let you know more precisely when to act. If Mammon is wise, he should send Glasya here along with you as an added insurance policy."

"Why, Dispater! I shall take that as a compliment!" she batted her long eyelashes at him, flirting with the Arch-devil.

Dispater ignored her flirtatious actions. "Just remember, get in, kill him, get the women out, but fast. I will have no control over when the devil brigades arrive at any center ready to destroy it. I'm afraid that if you are still there, they will just go ahead and destroy it anyway. They will be ignoring you, your people, and anyone else still there. Also, I will see that you know the precise location of the three centers beforehand. So do we have a deal or not?"

Monica looked at her friends for a moment and then took the plunge. "We have a deal. Thank you, Dispater. Glasya, thank Mammon for us as well."

"See Monica, it is very easy to do business with us devils. We are quite the understanding individuals. Am I not correct, Glasya?" he smiled her way.

She flashed her disarming smile back. "Of course. Always!"

He looked at Monica and added, "You know that I could do something about your missing arms, don't you?"

Monica roared with laughter. "Of course, but I'm afraid that your price is too high for me."

"Ah, but you haven't asked me what it would be," he countered teasingly. "Ah well. I've much nasty work to do today. Until we meet again." He rose and vanished leaving behind a faint cloud of sulfur.

"He likes to make grand entrances and exits," Glasya explained. "Now I prefer more subtle ones." Her magic flashed, and they detected the odor of exotic flowers in the air.

While everyone began discussing what they'd just heard, Crystal fired off some Messages to Leslie, Henry, and Oliver. Monica sat deep in thought. She was working out the mechanics. If there were three of these centers and if each held five of the leaf-shaped domed structures, then that gave a total of fifteen buildings to handle. He'd said to do it fast. If there were ten or so women in each one as there had been when she was held captive there, then that amounted to a hundred fifty women to handle.

The problem with that were the Idiot Mind spells that the women were under and their inability to move quickly. Each would have to walk quite some distance to the incised pentagrams on the raised platforms or else be carried. She knew that they could not waste time trying to reason with the women whose very limited reasoning capacity would likely delay them as well. Her only conclusion was that she needed more help than just her group and Parry and Ari.

Monica also knew that she could not just take any

wizard or witch with her to the Abyss. The risks were enormous. Plus, the very environment there was beyond putrid; magic didn't work quite the same way; and whoever went had to be battle-hardened. She thought of the various members of Henry's St. Louis Defense Squat who had volunteered to fight the demons on the streets of the city. While they were used to fighting here, if those people came with her, they would be fighting in that hostile, evil environment. In her mind, Monica believed that they would be wholly at risk. No, she needed wizards and witches that could stand up to this terrible situation and had already proved that they could. She only knew one group that met her criteria.

"So what are you thinking, Monica? You've been entirely too silent," Ericka broke into her friend's thoughts.

"Oh. Sorry. Been thinking this through. We will likely have a hundred fifty women to rescue quickly. We're going to need help, people who will not be freaked out by what they see in the Abyss. I've some ideas. I need to make a short trip, everyone. Keep on working out our plans," Monica answered. "I will be back in a while with some help, I hope." She slid her chair back, lunged to her feet, got her balance, and slowly walked out of the dining room.

When she got to her own workshop, she again sat down, rather clumsily she thought, and sent a Message to the one person she thought might have the answer that she needed. Would they help her, knowing that she had been their archenemy? Shortly, a Message scrolled before her eyes. She would see her now. Monica cast several more spells just to get her heavy winter cloak on her and securely fastened. Then, she teleported away. If she had fingers, she would have kept them crossed for quite some time, but she hadn't and could only hope and pray. When she landed in a parking lot, deep snow still covered the landscape, and she slipped. With only her toes on the ground and the tiny spiked heel, Monica would have fallen had she not hastily cast her Gentle Fall and then Levitate on herself. The gates opened just as she had gotten herself upright again, rather embarrassed at her true helplessness.

"Welcome to Bradbury's again, Monica," the soft voice of Governor Lindsey Barron-Cross reached her ears before her eyes saw Lindsey. "Would you like a hand getting inside? The parking lot here can be a bit slippery. It's still winter here."

"Please, if you don't mind. I hate to ask you, but I've already fallen just arriving," Monica had no choice but to accept her steadying arms around her. They walked carefully across the snow packed pavement until they were inside the gates. Here, Lindsey paused, closing the gates and raising the security protections, all without saying a word. Monica was still impressed with her uncanny ability to cast spells sans words even. A Magical Door appeared, and after taking another step, Monica arrived in the governor's warm office. A crackling pine log fire added ambiance and a refreshing odor to the plush room.

"May I take your cloak? Tea perhaps? With a straw? I remembered," Lindsey said with a smile.

"Please. Saves me from having to cast a bunch of spells. Tea would be nice. I've got quite a lot to tell you," Monica replied. While Lindsey took her cloak over to the coat rack, Monica moved over to a soft chair in front of her desk and sat down, tossing her head a bit to get the fall of her long black hair adjusted. She was rather unwilling to use magical spells just now.

After tea and biscuits were served, Lindsey said, "Okay. I admit, Monica, you have my curiosity level peaked. What's happening?"

Monica smiled. "I've come to ask a huge favor from you and the other Rodents. I really don't have any right even to ask you to help me, us, in this, but considering the circumstances that I am about to tell you, please forgive me if I'm in any way overstepping my welcome here. You see, I've just made a deal with the Arch-devil Dispater." Lindsey gasped and slumped back in her seat, but kept her eyes glued to this woman in red.

"It has to do with the current demon situation here on Earth and in the Abyss," Monica began to explain. For the next hour, she recited in detail all that the Arch-devil told her along with her and Crystal's most recent abduction as well.

"So I've agreed to do those two things that he asked: to kill the three Dr. Menninger clones that have been doing all this vile breeding and cloning and to rescue all the women

435

currently being held in these awful centers. Once we get them back, I'll do my best to heal them fully, of course, but my small group isn't going to be able to handle a hundred fifty of these helpless women in time, let alone make sure the three doctor clones are destroyed. So I've come to ask you to consider bringing the Rodents along on this mission. I simply can't ask the usual wizards and witches in St. Louis. While they mean well and have done an admirable job of fighting the demons rampaging around our city, they will be wholly out of their league in the terribly hostile environment of the Abyss. Our magic doesn't work quite the same there as it does here either, but we don't really know the full story on that detail."

Monica ended with, "So forgive me if I've overstepped my welcome here. If you and the Rodents don't wish to help me or us with this, I understand. The risks are just awful. Look what's been done to the women and Crystal. Besides, if I understand this right, we will be entering a very violent, chaotic war zone as well."

Lindsey hadn't spoken a word all this time. She refreshed her tea, but Monica shook her head no. "I've been following what you've been doing with the women who have been rescued from these demonic facilities. You've fully healed quite a number of them."

"Yes. One hundred fifty-nine to date," Monica admitted.

"And you haven't healed yourself? Your magic doesn't work on yourself?" she asked, curiously.

"It should have. I mean I was supposed to heal myself as the one hundredth cure, but there were almost fifty more very desperate women just waiting in line to have their lives salvaged. I just couldn't do it to myself then. I believe that my chance has come and gone. I just hope the magic keeps on working until I get these other women still being held in the Abyss healed."

"I see. Interesting. Well, I will talk with the Rodents today, Monica, but I believe that they will all agree with me. Count us in on this rescue. After all, we are these women's only hope of survival. If you can subsequently restore their bodies, a hundred fifty lives will have been saved. That is always something that we Rodents must do, help others in need and trouble. What troubles me is that we will have very limited time to reach and handle three separate facilities—with a war going on all around us. Perhaps, it would be wise for us to join our forces together and divide into three groups, each one taking on one of these centers. If we act at the same time, we cut the total time that we need by two-thirds, increasing our chances for success."

Monica replied, "I like that idea. It also limits any one person's exposure. They would only have to fight and secure one facility, not three of them. This is sounding more feasible by the minute. I can't tell you how much I appreciate your and the Rodent's help with this. Rescuing these women means everything to me."

"I can sense that. Glad to be able to help. Coordination appears to be the major hurdle. Timing will be at the very last minute. We should all probably be together and work out three teams and perhaps drill together some before the mission," Lindsey suggested.

"You are all welcome to come to our estate. We have plenty of guest rooms and workshops. It would be very wise for us to make our teams up and to drill just what we must do beforehand. Honestly, this is going to be a very dangerous mission. These demons are so darn hard to slay! One of our SWAT teams put about a thousand rounds of 50-caliber ammo into one large demon before it finally succumbed. Mind-blowing. I doubt that Prince Graz'zt could even be killed by us. But can I ask you something else?"

Lindsey nodded and Monica asked hesitantly, "Did I do the right thing by making this deal with the Arch-devil? I can't see anyway that he gains my soul or anyone else's in this."

Lindsey leaned back and laughed. "Well Monica, you have me on this one. None of us Rodents have ever had anything to do with demons and devils before. In fact, until all this started, we didn't even know they existed. So to be honest with you, I have no idea. On the surface, I can see nothing that you did wrong. My guess is that he is doing this for his own good and not yours, but he also wants these doctor clones eliminated, since if they aren't, then the problem will simply reappear in future years. I think that he's using you and now us to get to these three clones, which will very likely be residing behind the battle lines where his minions will be fighting. Thus, his minions might not be able to break through and get to the three doctors. So he's using us. That's my gut feeling. Anyway, I'll let you know later today, and we can make plans. We don't have an awful lot of time to get ready, do we?"

"No. Thank you, thank you. Please thank the Rodents for me, even if they don't wish to participate. This is an awful lot to ask of anyone. I best be going," Monica replied. Once more, Lindsey helped her with her cloak, saving her from the embarrassment of having to use many spells to get it on and fastened. She even walked her out to the parking lot, making sure that she didn't slip on the snow-packed ground. Only after Monica vanished and she re-locked the gates did she summon all the Rodents for a lengthy talk.

An hour after Monica returned, Lindsey sent her what she had hoped to hear. The Rodents would be joining her, all seventeen of them. They would arrive later this evening. "Yahoo!" exclaimed an exuberant Rob when he heard the good news. Everyone chimed in as well, before hustling to prepare the many guest rooms. Even Christina and Ruth Anne wanted to help, though Christina was very frustrated because she was mostly useless. Monica did find her something that she could do: be their messenger. Gladly she dashed around, relatively speaking of course, delivering their messages to each other, oblivious to the fact that they could have just as easily used their Message spells.

Meanwhile, Monica sat down to draw up a map of what the single transparent domed, leaf-shaped center that she had been held in looked like. Nisha came by and saw what she was trying to do. She saw that Monica was using countless spells just trying crudely to draw out the center and broke in, "Say, why don't I draw up a whole map of that complex for you? I know every inch of that place."

"Oh would you, Nisha? I would like each of the three groups to have a copy. I know it is only the layout of one of these complexes, but maybe the other two won't be terribly different. Thank you, Nisha," Monica replied, very grateful for Nisha's help. She didn't add that once more she felt so helpless just trying to do this simple thing.

That evening after supper, seventeen others arrived in their reception area. There followed a large round of introductions. Once that was done, the very large group went to the dining room for tea and coffee. There, Monica thanked everyone for coming and once more described all that Dispater had told her. Deiter asked her to tell them about Crystal and her most recent abduction, and she did so. In spite of the fact of the humiliation that she'd endured, Monica told them all about it.

Monica then said, "I've given this considerable thought, based on Lindsey's suggestion. We will divide into three teams with each one assigned to handle one of these facilities only. That way, we stand the best chance of getting in and out without too much fighting. All the rescued women will be Gated back here to our large reception area. I'm going to have Enya and Misty be there to help these women who will be in very poor physical shape and under the Idiot Mind spell. The St. Louis Defense Unit will then transport the women to St. Anne's Hospital where they are preparing to receive up to a hundred fifty women. I've asked Enya and Misty to stay behind for two reasons. They both have recently given birth, and they don't know any of the top power spells. This mission is fraught with danger, and I want everyone who goes to the Abyss to have the best chance of getting back alive. Christina and her assistant Ruth Anne will also be here to help with the terrified women, along with Jill and Nisha."

"I think that Orenda and I should perhaps stay here and help with the women too," Kathy spoke up. "She and I also have given birth. I sure don't wish to get contamination in my body. I'm still breast feeding my son."

"Excellent. You will have your hands full with these women. They will be very confused and quite helpless. Thanks, Kathy, Orenda," Monica agreed. "I've also decided that I should be with one team and Rob here with another. He and I can get us out of the Abyss and back home if the Gates should somehow become damaged. We can do it even if our usual magic fails us. I'm having Crystal go with the third group, since she can cast a Gate spell to get everyone back if all else fails. Ericka will go on Rob's team. We three, Crystal, Ericka, and I can cast quite a few Grade 9 spells, so I want to rather balance out the power of my group."

She went on, "I think the first thing that we should do is form up our teams now. Honestly, we have no idea just when we will get the word to go do this. He did suggest that it might be on short notice. Lindsey, I'll form up my friends into the proposed groups, and then you can use your discretion to assign your people."

After some discussion, switching around, and juggling, the three teams were finalized. Monica had with her Deiter, Pam, Ashley, Amanda, Ahana, Brad, and Jasper. Rob's team had Lindsey, Ericka, Tyler, Audrey, Bill West, that is, Wilma Weltsi, Able Monument or rather Monane Tumble, Fern, and Jiri. Crystal's team had Gregor, Peaches, Tom Ryker, Andy Rains, Emilio, Jim Whitewater, and Milos. With the teams settled, the seventeen were shown to their rooms.

The next day, Ericka took them all on a short tour of their estate and workshops. She received numerous compliments on their extremely well equipped potion making laboratory, their wand making workshop, and her own magical items workshop, which pleased her. This day, the three women chose to wear their jeans instead of their usual fancy gowns because they wanted to be ready when the time came.

After that, the three teams broke up to exchange ideas and drill working together. However, Nisha did provide one valuable idea. "Look, you need to get to the doctor clone right away before you start evacuating the women. I've an idea how you can do that." She explained what she had in mind fully, and it was quickly accepted.

"Brilliant, Nisha, positively brilliant," Deiter praised the little alu-demon. She was very pleased that she could contribute a little to the mission.

When they were drilling, Deiter asked, "So Monica, how do you do this magical thing to travel to and from the Abyss? I'm sure that I don't know that spell. It could be a very useful one. We didn't know that you could cast spells sans words too, like when you escaped pulling Crystal with you on that pony cart."

"I can't, sans words, Deiter. It isn't really a magical spell like we all cast. I'm not sure just what it is. Rob knows all about it. I'm just a raw beginner. He calls it Planar Travel, but I call it Planar Walking, since we just walk. I think it is something that I do with my own mental powers. Rob says it also as to do with one's intelligence, but you should ask him about it. Until I met him, I didn't even know that I had this gift," she replied.

"Thanks, I'll do that when I get a chance. I'm your Eliminator, so just line me up, and I'll take out this evil Dr. Menninger clone!" Deiter boasted a little.

Pam giggled. "Sure you will, Deiter. What if your Disintegrate spell doesn't work down there?"

"Oh, I'll think of something. If necessary, I'll do another Deiter." Both laughed, but Pam had to explain what "doing a Deiter" meant, namely goofing a spell and having it apply to everyone or everything present, such as by accident Disarming everyone around him. Monica then smiled, recalling that must have been what happened when the Rodents captured her or Dominus and his fifty Death Stalkers. More and more small, unanswered questions were finally being answered for her.

Just after supper that evening, their alarm system triggered again. This time a very large number responded with staves of power and wands at the ready, swarming into the reception area. "Wow! What a wonderful reception party and just for little old me," Glasya teased the group with her gorgeously disarming smile. She wore an elegant but skimpy gown. This time, her long hair was nicely arranged. Her long red nails glistened from a recent polishing, matching her red lips. That she had an extremely attractive female body was not missed by anyone. Deiter even let out a whistle.

"Glad that you approve of my looks, handsome fellow," Glasya teased Deiter, who promptly flushed. She also picked up his thoughts and tossed them back at him, "Yes, I know, I am even more attractive than Miss America and the Playboy models. Naturally I am that and *so* much more." He flushed even more, and Pam and Lindsey began laughing.

Glasya then said more seriously, "Dispater sent me this time. I have the location of the third facility, and I am to accompany you there."

"Okay then. You will be part of our third team," Monica suggested. "We've divided up into three teams. We will strike each facility simultaneously."

"Excellent thinking. I like the plan. Far less exposure. This plan of his just may work and save both our worlds," Glasya added. Then she became very serious, "I should warn you, this mission is likely to be a very dangerous one. Demons are never predictable. It could get pretty wild, since major battles will be going on while we do our raids."

"Oh yes. I am supposed to tell you that the date of the raid is likely being moved up some days. It seems that Demogorgon and Orcus have gone rather berserk after finding out what Prince Graz'zt was really up to. As I said, there is no predicting demons, unlike us devils. So stay alert. We could get the word to go at any time. Dispater is going to try to send us in at the most opportune time for us to be successful. A whole lot is at stake besides your few victimized women. Honestly, the balance of power in the Abyss and Hells has not had such a serious threat in millennia! In fact, Mammon himself would have charged into the Abyss and gone after Prince Graz'zt himself if Orcus and Demogorgon would have allowed it. Of course, the Demon Lords totally refused him. It would have set a precedent to have a devil in the Abyss. Ah well, I'd have loved to see that battle."

"Okay then we'll need to find you a room for the night," Monica spoke up. "We were about to head to bed. Come with me. I'll show you to the only remaining guest room, Glasya."

Glasya gracefully sauntered after her, swinging her hips back and forth very seductively. "Any of you handsome fellows care to join me in my room for the night?" she cooed. Deiter swallowed hard. That was his thought, but only if she had not been a devil and thoroughly evil in nature.

A bit later, Monica showed her into her private room. "I hope this will meet your needs, Glasya. I'm also glad that you are coming with us. Thanks."

"You are most welcome. Say, isn't it terribly difficult for you to be like this? You know that I can give you back your arms and hands anytime that you wish and your feet as well."

"I'm managing, Glasya. I don't think I even want to hear your price. I value my soul, myself. Sorry."

"I know Monica. I just had to let you know that. I do like you, as a person, you know. You, Crystal, Ericka, and I do have something in common. We like to look gorgeous. There is power in that, you know, looking absolutely, stunningly beautiful. Men think that they control the worlds, but it is actually us women who do, but in more subtle ways," Glasya explained quite seriously.

"Here, sit with me a while, Monica," she patted the freshly made bed. Monica pirouetted, tossed her hair to one side, and sat down beside her.

"You and I are alike in many ways. We each want to look our best. Women's power comes in part from looking highly attractive to men, as I see it. A woman must be entirely comfortable with her appearance so that she can focus on what is truly important to her. Yes, I know with some that merely means getting sex, but not with many of us. Not with you or me, for example. We want to look great just for our own sakes. Looking good, we are filled with confidence and are more able to work towards our own goals, am I not right in this?"

Monica replied rather hesitantly, "Well, I suppose so. When I look good, I feel more confident. That much I've found true. Crystal and Ericka look fabulous and claim that distracts men so that they can more readily get what they wish from them. Of course, what they wish are not evil things, bad things, you know what I mean."

"Yes, I certainly do know what you mean. No, they are not evil. In fact, I doubt it very much that I or even Dispater could ever tempt those two women. They are very strong willed, independent women, who love magic. Devoted to it, just as you are, Monica."

Monica sighed. "Well, that's a relief to hear. I admit that I'm very worried about your joining us. Ulterior motives and all that. I couldn't live with myself if you took this opportunity to do whatever it is you and Dispater do to one of us, take their souls, their selves."

"That is not how we devils operate, Monica. Always, such things are highly personal. We'd never use something like this situation to make our unique bargains with one of your people. Demons, now they certainly would just as soon betray you as help you. Not so with us devils. You can relax. You have my sworn word that none of us devils would dare even approach one of you on this mission. If we did, there would be hell to pay. Pun intended. Mammon would likely ban me for a millennia if I violated our laws and seduced one of your group. I assure you that I would not want that to happen, not ever."

"Thanks for telling me all this. I do feel more comfortable," Monica admitted.

"Good. You know, I do really like and admire you, Monica. I see a lot of my better qualities in you. When this is all finished, I'd like to share some beauty tips with you. I think that you could look smashingly better than you do, but let's save that chat until we finish this messy task. I feel deeply for those women too, you know. None of us should ever be subjected to such torment and torture. Men, that's another story, but not we women. They are perverting our gift of bringing new life into the universes. In my mind, there is no greater crime than perverting that precious gift that only women have. I just hope that Graz'zt makes an appearance. I would love to have the opportunity to teach that demon a lesson he'd never forget!"

"You think he will catch on to what we are doing and come after us?" Monica asked, suddenly growing rather worried. She knew that she had not the power to kill him or even subdue that demon.

"Oh, I suspect that he will sense it, but his attention will be elsewhere. If he loses this battle, he will be in a very bad way. A sure way for him to be destroyed would be to forsake the battlefield and try to intervene with these centers. No, I'm sure I'll not get my desire to battle him fulfilled, not this time anyway. But the day of reckoning will come, and I'll be ready for him. No one perverts women's precious gift and gets away with it."

Monica smiled. "I sure hope that I will still be able to heal them all and salvage their lives."

"Oh, I'm sure that you will, dear. I'd better let you get some sleep. The word could come at any time now. No predicting these Demon Lords, especially when they are mad as hell. Oops, no pun intended, dear. Night."

"Good night. Thanks for helping us rescue these women," Monica replied politely. She lunged a little to get to her toes, wobbling a little getting her balance once more, tossed her head back to get her hair behind her, and walked slowly out of the guest room. She had even more to ponder now.

The next morning as everyone was having their breakfast, Glasya commented, "Nisha, you are a really superb chef. My compliments, dear."

The little alu-demon smiled. "Thanks. I am still learning. It is so much fun to cook for everyone. I do my best."

Just then, everyone saw a Message scrolling before Glasya's eyes and watched her closely. A moment later, Glasya's smile vanished. "Okay. I just got word. The battle has begun. We should prepare. Dispater will let me know when he believes the best window of opportunity has come. Get yourselves prepared."

Chapter 27—War in the Abyss

Everyone dashed out of the dining room, heading to their quarters to prepare themselves and their companions. Following Monica and Lindsey's suggestion, every conceivable protection spell was cast upon every member of the three teams, since not every wizard or witch knew each of these spells. They assembled in the reception area, staves and wands in hand, forming up into their respective teams.

Monica explained, "Okay, everyone. I'm sorry that I don't have any arms and hands to hang onto, so two of you will have to put yours securely around my waist. Don't let go. The rest of you, hang onto these two. I will take us to our facility. Remember to cast Invisibility just as we are ready to go. Let Deiter and me go inside one of the facilities first. Give us a little room. Our job is to flush out the mad doctor."

Apart from her group, Rob was telling his group nearly the same thing, only he had hands to securely hold onto two of his group. Glasya took over for Crystal in the third group. She said, "Crystal, no need for you to use your Gate spell. I will take all of you directly there. Just join hands as though we were teleporting."

"I hate all this waiting around," Deiter grumbled, though he held onto Monica's waist securely.

"I know how you feel, Deiter," Monica replied, "but we must have patience. Timing will be critical. The Abyss is filled with monstrous demons. They are darn hard to slay. Trust me on this point."

"Yes, you should listen to her, Deiter," Pam countered. She was holding onto Monica from the other side. "Patience is important."

"Yeh, I know, but still, I prefer action. Always have; you know that, Pam," he grumbled a little.

At ten that morning, Glasya received another Message. "Okay everyone. Now is the time to strike. Let's do this. Good hunting everyone!"

Enya, Misty, Orenda, Kathy, Christina, and Ruth Anne

watched the three groups, as they simply appeared to be taking one forward step, but in fact vanished from sight. "I hope no one gets badly hurt or worse," Enya whispered to Misty.

"I know. I'm letting Henry know that the raid is on and to be ready for the first batch of women. I wonder how long it will be before the first arrive here?" Misty asked.

"It's pretty hard dealing with someone under the awful influence of the Idiot Mind spell," Kathy declared, having had some experience with that in the past.

"It's really bad because they are also so completely helpless," Enya explained. They chatted about it, with Christina telling them about her own experience with it.

Monica set everyone down on the slightly raised platform with its golden pentagram and surrounding circle of silver. This way, everyone knew just where to bring the women. All were invisible and used whispers to make sure they had the location of the others in mind. "My god! This place is horrid!" Deiter whispered.

This realm was a putrid emulation of the real world, he thought. True, the land consisted of low rolling hills. Instead of grass, ugly grey plants grew sporadically. In the distance, he could see what must be their trees—grotesquely warped branches, bare of all foliage, a grim parody of real trees. Ahead, he saw the five transparent domed structures and the more distant grey building that housed the maternity ward and further on down, the nursery where the babies lived and were eventually trained as killers. As he took his first step on the grey ground, he stumbled and kicked up some of the putrid grey soil. A mass of wiggling, hideous looking worms swarmed up, and he nearly vomited up his breakfast. "Don't look down," Monica whispered, though of course, she had to or she'd fall down. In her ballet boots, she had to very carefully place each step or stumble.

That they were in a war zone was more than obvious, but thankfully, the combats were some distance from here. In the grey sky, they saw enormous flashes of light. Gigantic explosions occasionally shook the very ground on which they were gingerly stepping. Deiter even saw a demon flying wildly out of control through the air, having likely been forcibly flung from the battlefield by monstrously powerful arms. As they approached the entrance tunnel at the stem of the leaf, the ground shook wildly from another explosion! Monica would have fallen had Deiter not sensed her misstep and put both his hands around her waist to steady her, though he had to feel a bit to find her.

At the door, he realized that he needed to open it for her and did so. They stepped inside and walked down the long tunnel. They found ten women sitting on several couches in their central living room. All were staring up at the sporadic lights in the sky. "Such pretty lights," one woman said. "I hope we can see more," another added. "I wonder what they are?" said a third. Deiter recognized the Idiot Mind spell at work.

Monica whispered, "We need to find their alu-demon caretaker. I've an idea." She canceled her invisibility spell and cast an illusion on herself. She walked up to the group of ten women, appearing as naked as they were. "Excuse me. Where is our caretaker?"

She received ten different replies, but one suggested that she was in their bedrooms. Monica headed directly across the living room to the bedrooms, where she spotted the alu-demon making up the bed. "Excuse me. But can you call the doctor? She's fallen. Her leg. It isn't perfect now. She can't stand up. She's crying. That's not perfect. Is it?" She did her best to imitate one under the Idiot Mind spell. That she also looked like one of the ten women helped.

"Oh dear. Yes of course. I'll send for him now. You go back to your couch and sit," she added. "I'm coming in a second."

"What's a second?" Monica asked, keeping up the illusion, frustrating the alu-demon slightly, who ignored her. She made her way back to the living room. Get ready, she mouthed hoping Deiter would see her signal.

Shortly, the alu-demon came rushing in to help the fallen women. "Stun!" barked Deiter. His wand flashed. The alu-demon looked up at him with a strange look on her face. "Darn it!" he gushed and simply knocked her out with his fist. Shaking his throbbing fist, he commented, "She wasn't even affected!"

"Like I said, they have a goodly resistance to magical spells. If we had hit her with a dozen at once, probably a few would have affected her. She sent for the doctor. Everyone get ready," Monica called out to the invisible others.

One of the ten women looked up. "You hit her. Why did you hit her? That's not nice. She helps us. She looks after us."

"We are helping her. She needs to rest a spell," Monica explained in simple terms.

"Oh! Yes, we must rest too." She was satisfied with that explanation. Deiter vanished from sight again, taking up a new position from which he could attack the doctor when he entered the leaf stem tunnel. Meanwhile, more explosions occurred, violently shaking the ground once more.

As she stood there waiting, Ashley sent her a Message. Ashley had used her powerful premonition spell and figured out that to be successful they'd have to remove some of his protective spells first.

Monica, use Dispel Magic on the doctor before attacking him. A.

The fighting seemed to be getting closer to them now. The light flashes and concussions that resulted were twice as bright as before. The ten women were growing more excited about the pretty lights. Just then, the door opened, and Dr. Menninger entered. Monica began casting Dispel Magic spells on him just as he entered the edge of the living room, taking him by surprise. She didn't know how many it would take and so kept casting them. Ashley and Pam also became visible as they cast them too.

Dr. Menninger was taken by surprise and failed to react at once, allowing several of the spells to detonate on his person. Finally, Monica saw a flash of magic and knew that at least one of his spells had gone down. He reacted and shot a bolt of lightning at her, whirled and shot a half dozen magical missiles at each other two other women who were standing against the back side of the dome some distance from him. None of his spells had any effect on the three, who continued shooting their Dispel Magic spells at him. Monica noticed that she was almost twice as fast getting hers off than those two were. She didn't have to coordinate wand motions with the verbal commands. Another magical flash indicated another of his spells had gone down.

At this point, Deiter, Brad, and Jasper became visible as they shot their deadly spells at Dr. Menninger. He was hit with a dozen Magical Missiles and a Disintegrate spell from Deiter. While the missiles definitely hurt him, he wasn't a fool. He dove to the floor, dodging the killer spell, which cut a hole in the transparent dome. He then realized that he was grossly outnumbered, rushed to his feet, and ran back down the long entrance stem hallway. Ahana became visible, standing at the door, as he fired off a powerful bolt of lightning at him. The mad doctor flew backwards through the air, smashing into the side of the room.

Deiter raced over to him and stomped down hard on his neck. Monica heard the sounds of snapping bones. "He's dead now! I'll burn him up. Leave no DNA," he called out.

"What have you done to our doctor?" "He helps us." "He takes our eggs." "He gives us sons." "You are bad people." A chorus of women talked all at one time, unable to comprehend what was happening.

Monica took charge. "Okay, get these women out of here and onto the Gate. It should activate and get them to safety. Then, go on to the next one."

The women refused to get up or cooperate with the others. Finally completely exasperated with them, Pam simply picked up one woman and physically carried her out of the building. The others followed her example, ignoring the wild protests of the women and their constant pathetic attempts to wiggle free. Pam reached the Gate first and laid her woman down on it. Magic flashed and the woman vanished. "Cool!" she commented.

As she turned around, she saw Ashley carrying another protesting woman out of the door. The second that the woman was outside of the chamber, the woman's body turned into ashes! Ashley now carried nothing. Monica also saw this and realized something that she'd been told when she was first here.

"Hey everyone, the women who have been held here for millennia will disintegrate like that when we rescue them. At least, we will be ending their lifetime of suffering," she called out and watched as another three women's bodies turned into ashes. Those women who had been taken several millennia ago had been clones of clones of clones so many times that their bodies were but barely alive anyway. Only the vile food of the Abyss and the mostly sealed living quarters kept their bodies alive. Six women from the Earth were rescued though, and the group headed to the second center of the five. Monica stuck around a bit longer ensuring Deiter's safety while he used his spells to incinerate the remains of the mad doctor. Then, the two joined the others, who were already carrying the women out of the second center.

Pam, carrying a wiggling, protesting woman, said, "I told the alu-demon nurse to flee for her life. The battle is coming this way."

"And it is!" Ashley yelled to them, while trying to manage her wiggling woman.

Deiter and Monica headed onto the third center. When they entered, the alu-demon, having seen them carrying the women away, asked, "What's going on here? You shouldn't be here. I've summoned the guards."

"Look, the war is about to land on top of you. Flee for your life, unless you have a death wish," Deiter explained. "Now get running."

She looked at Monica and then Deiter, and chose to run out of the tunnel, vanishing once clear of the door. The two headed on inside. Again, Monica felt helpless. She couldn't carry one of the women and decided that she ought to stand outside watching for guards or other trouble.

Minutes later, the last of the protesting, wiggling women left this one, and Monica moved on down to the next one. At this point, the light flashes and concussion noise grew even louder. It sounded as if it might be coming from just over the nearby hills. She knew that they had to hurry up. Most likely, Dispater's devils were on their way here to destroy these complexes.

Their luck still held. They raced into the last of the five centers. The caretaker there merely ran past them, fully intent upon saving herself. Once more, Monica stood guard while the others brought the women out. Four turned to ashes, and the carriers turned around and headed back for another woman. At this point, they were as far from the platform and Gate as they could be in this complex. She and Deiter were bringing up the rear, watching for any demon attacks. They did spot a large number of Cambions flooding out of a barracks some distance away.

As they neared the first of the evacuated centers, a giant explosion very close to them detonated in a brilliant flash of light, knocking Monica to the ground. As Deiter helped her up, Monica yelled to the other six ahead of her and who were carrying the last of the women, "Go ahead and Gate yourselves out of here as soon as you get to the platform. Deiter and I will be right behind you! Run! Run!"

She and Deiter saw at least twenty Cambion demons closing on them rapidly. Deiter wanted to turn and fight, but Monica kept him moving forward, though he did shoot several balls of fire from over his shoulder, claiming that might slow them down. One by one, they saw their six companions still holding the protesting women across their shoulders reach the platform, step onto the golden pentagram and vanish from sight. Then, their luck failed.

A monstrous flash detonated behind them. The shockwave sent both of them flying into the transparent dome of the first center. However, its glass-like nature had already shattered, raining shards down onto the floor. The pair went sailing into the building. Monica was facing their rear and saw the Cambions also being blown into the centers around them. She also saw the gating platform being disintegrated into a pile of rubble. Deiter crashed into the dining room table, stunning himself, while a glass shard sliced deeply into his arm. Close beside him, the falling glass had also stabbed the sill unconscious alu-demon that Deiter had knocked out.

Monica shook off her momentary stun and levitated herself back onto her feet. Looking down, she saw that she had two emergencies facing her. If she did nothing, both would die. The alu-demon was bleeding profusely. Deiter wasn't. "I have to help her." Ignoring the chaos of war going on all around her, she focused and began healing the alu-demon, while also using a levitate spell on the glass shard, pulling it out of her. Finally, she got the worst of the stab wound healed, just as the alu-demon roused.

"Quick. I've healed you as best I can. If you want to live, get up, and flee now!" Monica advised her. On her knees, she moved over to Deiter, who was moaning, and began to work on him, levitating the glass from his wound. Again, she focused and began moving tiny blood cells about, forcing the ruptured arteries and veins to close themselves.

She was kneeling over him. He was lying on his back and was able to see their certain deaths coming. A giant of a demon had come marching up to the center, spotted them, and was stomping his way towards them, as another explosion rocked the very ground. Nearby, the farthest center vanished from sight.

Deiter yelled, "Demon behind you!"

Monica knew that she couldn't run from it, nor could she effectively fight it, even if the demon allowed her enough time to get to her toes. She had only one thought. She yelled loudly above the din going on around them, "Deiter, put your arms around me now, hold on hard, and don't let go!" She felt his arms latching on to her, nearly crushing the breath out of her. She focused once more and began crawling forward on her knees, hoping against all hope that this would be enough "walking" to allow her to get out of the way of the demon.

Just as she took her first tiny movement with her right knee, the giant of a demon's fist came down. Unfortunately for it, his fist merely smashed a round hole in the floor. Monica, with Deiter hanging onto her, slipped into the astral plane. Monica heard a familiar voice inside her mind. "Thank you for saving her." She knew who it was and why. She'd cured one of the enemy, though the alu-demon was more like an ally than a real enemy. Still, she'd done it, and he knew that she had. She continued crawling along, unable to think of anything else to do.

"Oh, here comes the first of the women!" Kathy called out as a woman suddenly appeared on the floor of the reception area, followed by another and then another, until six women were sprawled on the floor, all talking at once, but making little sense.

"Put me down!" "You can't do this." "I need my egg removed." "What's going on?" "We're perfect women, don't you know that?" "We are not allowed outside." "Why aren't you letting us watch the pretty lights?" "I want to go back and watch them." It was a veritable diatribe of misrelated comments, questions, and even orders.

Quickly, the women helped the six naked women to regain their feet, as they seemed unable to do it themselves. Henry and his group of volunteers appeared. Each took hold of one woman and despite their ravings, teleported them away. "Good work," Henry commented. "I'll stick around now and help coordinate."

"Boy, they are in horrible shape!" Kathy commented mostly to herself. "They are so helpless."

"No kidding!" Orenda added.

Christina, who could only stand by and watch the others, said, "Well, if they would only practice walking more, they could get by. They fed us from plates, like dogs. They kept us naked so that we could easily go to the bathroom by ourselves. So there is a reason for their appearance."

"Still awful," Kathy said. Christina couldn't argue against that. "But I see what you mean. We've just taken them out of their comfort zones."

"Right," Christina added. They took their seats to wait for the next batch to come. They arrived a minute later, followed by another six three minutes after that. There was no way to tell if these were from three different facilities or from just one facility.

By the time the thirtieth woman appeared, everyone was totally accustomed to the women and began just handling them without any real reactions. Christina kept an accurate count of the women being rescued, and Ruth Anne double-checked her counts. An hour passed before Christina's count numbered sixty. Not long after that, Glasya and her team appeared, bringing the last six of their women with them. After counting the women and watching them being teleported to St. Anne's, Christina logged in each member of that team. Her idea was to verify personally that every one of the rescuers returned safely.

In this case, Peaches had sustained an arm wound, and Enya was right there pouring some of her healing potions into Peaches mouth, even before Peaches could ask for a little help. "Got in the way of one of their wicked swords," Peaches explained once she'd downed three potions. "Hey, it's worked already. Bleeding has stopped."

"Of course it has. My potions work very well. Should not leave any noticeable scars I hope," Enya replied.

"Hey, I best get my healing potions out," Kathy suggested, opening a large bag after un-shrinking it.

A few minutes later, Rob's group appeared, bringing the last six of their rescued women with them. Gregor and Able needed some fast healing. Both had nasty wounds from a pair of demons. "Hey, I got it in the end!" Gregor commented, swilling down on one of Kathy's potions. "Thanks. I needed that. Tastes pretty good."

"I put spearmint in it," Kathy explained rather proud of her potions.

"Hey, cool idea. I never thought of that," Enya exclaimed. "We should get together sometime and exchange potion ideas."

"Let's!" Kathy replied enthusiastically.

Once more, Christina made her counts and logged in all the members of Rob's team. So far, she thought, so good. Everyone now waited for the last group to arrive. Minutes went by, and Lindsey began to grow a bit worried about Deiter.

Then, Pam appeared, holding onto a still wiggling woman, whom she carefully sat down on her feet. At once, one of Henry's women took hold of the confused woman and teleported her away. Then Ashley, Amanda, Jasper, Ahana, and Brad appeared, unloading five more women.

"That's the last of them," Brad exclaimed. "Got pretty hairy at the end there. The battle ended right up on top of us! We just got out!"

"Where's Deiter?" Lindsey asked. He hadn't followed the six yet.

"And Monica?" Enya put in.

"Monica yelled for us to hurry up and use the Gate. They were right behind us," Brad answered, turning around to look at the empty space where they'd arrived and moved off to the sides of the room.

Everyone held their breaths, waiting for the two suddenly to materialize in the reception area. Nothing. "Something's gone wrong! I just feel it!" Lindsey wailed, growing afraid that she'd lost Deiter. "I should have gone with him."

"He will be all right. Monica's with him," Crystal said as soothingly as she could.

"If they aren't back in a few minutes, I'll go look for them," Glasya promised though she really didn't want to go back into that chaotic mess! "Wars are very nasty things," she whispered to no one in particular.

More worried minutes passed, and Lindsey grew more and more frantic. Actually, everyone was growing uneasy about the missing two companions. Even Rob was about to take off with Glasya to help find them, when suddenly they all saw the strangest sight ever! Monica came sort of crawling along on her knees, dragging Deiter with her, his legs spread out to either side of hers, his body below hers, his arms hanging tightly around her waist, her long hair covering his face.

Deiter whispered faintly, "Monica, I think you can stop crawling now. We're back."

Monica slumped down on top of him, utterly exhausted. Gently, he rolled her off him, moving some of her hair off his face. Now everyone could see the two very bloody bodies. "Oh dear god! Deiter! You're wounded. Potions fast!" Lindsey gushed running over to him. Kathy was right behind her, opening a potion bottle as she ran.

"I'm sort of okay now. She saved me and the alu-demon too," Deiter tried to explain, as Enya came up to Monica, ready to pour a potion into her. Lindsey looked at his wound and noticed that it was substantially cured already, but insisted he down the potion.

"Where's she hurt at?" Enya asked, having rolled Monica over twice but didn't see any signs of a wound. Rob knelt beside her and lifted her up, just as Lindsey was doing for Deiter.

"I don't think she's hurt. Probably my blood and the alu-demon's. We were bleeding pretty badly there. Glass shards. Whole darn building collapsed on us," Deiter attempted to explain.

Rob finally said, "I think she is just exhausted. Used up too much mental energies getting them healed and back here. She'll be all right with some rest."

"Deiter, start at the beginning and tell me properly what happened to you two," Lindsey ordered her husband.

"Well, we were all running back from the last building. The others were carrying the last of the women who didn't turn into dust," he began to explain.

"Hey, so some of yours did that too?" Crystal interrupted him. "So did four of ours from each of the five buildings."

"Same with us," Ericka quickly put in. "They just turned into ashes when we carried them outside the domes."

"Yeh, Monica said that was because they were cloned too many times. They were abducted, she said, several millennia ago and continually cloned, year after year. Guess their DNA got too diffuse or something," Deiter tried to recall just what Monica had said. "Anyway, we were all running towards the platform and Gate," he continued explaining what had happened to them.

"Honestly, dear, she had to help the alu-demon. She was bleeding badly and wouldn't have survived if she had not gotten to her first. Besides, I was the one who knocked her out. If I hadn't left her lying there, she would not have gotten hurt in the first place. Don't ask me how she was able to pull the glass shards out of her or me, though," Deiter continued his explanation, rather enjoying all the attention of everyone else. "I thought we were both goners when that giant of a demon came up on us from behind her. I saw his fist coming down and just held onto her as she asked. Next thing I know, we are moving through this grey void. She was sort of crawling us along. I don't think she could get to her feet. Don't know why. Then we got here."

Rob poured one potion into Monica anyway. The knees of her jeans were shredded and her knees were a bit bloodied, but with no real damage. After that, he carried her off to their room, while everyone else headed to the dining room, where Nisha had a hearty meal waiting for them. Once there, everyone began exchanging stories about what they'd done.

They were nearly done eating when Rob ushered Monica into the dining room. He had cleaned her up and gotten her into fresh clothes. The brief rest she'd gotten helped her some but she was craving food and then a good night's sleep. When the two entered the dining room, spontaneously a round of clapping broke out, led by Deiter. Monica smiled weakly.

"Thanks. Rob said no one was seriously wounded. I rather over did it some. Have to eat and sleep, and I'll be fine too," she said softly, while Rob helped her into a chair. Promptly, he began to feed her the hot stew that Nisha had whipped up. After wolfing down quite a lot of the stew, Monica slowed down and asked, "So how many women made it back here?"

Christina answered. "Seventy-eight women. All doing as well as can be expected. I checked with St. Anne's, and they are being decontaminated now. Good going all of you."

Monica smiled. "Seventy-eight more lives saved. That's something. Gosh, I am so tired."

"Come on, dear. It's bedtime for you," Rob said gently, helping her up gracefully.

As they passed Lindsey, she whispered, "Monica, thank you for saving my Deiter. I won't forget it." Monica barely managed a smile; she was falling asleep on her feet. As they left, Glasya quietly left as well; this time without any flashy departure.

Later in their own room and after a bath and change of clothes, Deiter crawled in beside Lindsey. "You know this is really strange. Dominus just saved my life, and healed that alu-demon and me. Never in a million years would I have ever expected to say something remotely like this."

Lindsey yawned and replied, "People can change. I'm glad that you did a long time ago. Remember our first year at

Bradbury's?"

"Oh god! Don't remind me of that!" Deiter exclaimed. "Guess you are right. People can change. It's just that I never expected Dominus would."

"Me either, me either," she whispered, snuggling up close to him.

Chapter 28—Recoveries

The next morning, various ones rose and headed to the dining room for breakfast at seemingly random times. Deiter joined Pam and Tom, "Lindsey's hitting the shower. Morning you two early birds."

"Morning yourself. Looks like you've healed up well," Tom replied. "Nisha's got a super breakfast going. Wish we could hire her to come cook at Bradbury's." Deiter grinned and dove into the bacon, eggs, and pancakes with real maple syrup.

Pam sat back sipping on her tea. "You know, Deiter, Monica saved your life yesterday. Yet she's really Dominus. How very strange."

Deiter laughed. "You noticed that too. Strange indeed. Lindsey says that people can change. Guess he or she rather has. Never would have expected it, though."

"Me either," Pam admitted. "Public Enemy Number One to Public Hero Number One. How strange. Still, we do owe her now, Deiter."

"I know that I do and that makes it all the stranger to me, but I'll do right by her. I pay my debts," Deiter replied, helping himself to a second round. "Still growing," he answered Pam's frowning questioning look. She smiled.

Just then, Enya, carrying her infant, and Kathy walked in, talking about potion making. Kathy explained, "Enya and I are going to get together real soon and compare our recipes. Isn't that cool? She's got a better lab set up here than we do. I'm going to have to spend some more money on new equipment, I can see that."

"Good idea. I bet you can both benefit from it," Pam replied. "Well, I've got to get back to Bradbury's. I have a full load of classes to teach today. See you all later on."

During the early morning, one by one or two by two, the Rodents packed up, heading for their homes. Monica rose late, still recovering, but Lindsey stuck around to make sure that she was all right and to thank her again for saving the aludemon and Deiter. Then she too left. Deiter had left sometime before, getting back to his job.

"Going to feed me this morning, Robby dear?" Monica asked him, as he sat down beside his wife.

"If you want me to," he smiled back, knowing that she was teasing him.

"That was kind of nice and really needed last night. I wouldn't mind being pampered just this once, this morning," she replied. He did as she wished.

Once breakfast was done, Monica headed for St. Anne's to check on the many new patients, arriving there around ten in the morning. She found the seventy-eight women were being kept sedated, while they were being administered the cure for their Idiot Mind spells and detoxified. The team of doctors gave her encouraging news. None of the women was in particularly bad shape. They were all doing as well as could be expected, given what they'd been through. The lead doctor told her, "Come back in a week. Once more, we will be bringing in a dozen who will be handling the removal of their physical and mental traumas. Once that's done, you can work your magic on them like before."

"Excellent news. Okay, let me know when I can start then." Monica breathed a sigh of relief. The women would be salvaged as long as her ring still functioned. She returned home.

On April 1, she returned to St. Anne's to begin her healing work on the seventy-eight women. She found them all in their right minds, clear headed, trauma removed, but very scared and worried about being able even to live as they now were. Checking in with the staff, she discovered once more the administration staff had done their jobs as well, identifying six of the women who had been abducted from their places of employment and who were covered under their company's worker's compensation insurance package. Not unexpectedly, Monica was told that their proposed settlements ranged between thirty-five to forty-five million dollars. Four of the six rejected the settlement if they could be fully healed. Two had partly decided to accept the vast sum of money.

Monica decided to do these four first, since if the ring didn't work any longer, they could at least accept their monetary settlements. Once more, she cast numerous spells just to get her precious ring off its golden chain and onto the little toe of the first woman. As it slipped on, Monica held her breath, letting it out only when she saw the familiar flash of magic occur. Thank heavens it still works! She thought to herself and began chatting with the woman, explaining that she'd be fully healed and out of here in two days. The relief on the woman's face was intense.

Monica mentally estimated that she'd not be done with these women until the end of August, but she didn't really care about the time. Saving their lives was really all that did matter to her. After handling the first four, she turned her attention to the other two who had a choice to make.

Abigail Van Slythe was twenty-one with shoulder length, auburn hair. She lived here in St. Louis and had worked as an accountant for one of the more upscale diners. Like Christina, she believed that with so much money, she could help support various women's causes, such as the Battered Women's Facility. Michelle Lynn Holmes was a twenty year old orphan who had worked as a secretary for a large insurance company. Her wavy hair was black and shoulder length. As an orphan, she had led a rather rough life and had somehow managed to land the secretary's position. But with a forty-five million dollar settlement, she'd be wealthy and could do pretty much whatever she desired. Christina, of course, had already spoken at length with both women and had asked them to join her, living at the fancy estate. Michelle accepted at once. She had so few friends, and this was a prime opportunity for her.

Hence, Monica was unable to talk either woman out of their decisions to accept the settlements. Neither wanted to wait for the ninety-day period before signing. Hence, after they had someone sign for them, Monica and Christina insisted that they move into the rooms closest to Christina's. They also insisted that the pair practice walking, and Christina promised to make sure that they did just that.

With the six handled, Monica set to work on the remainder of the women, handling one every two days, like clockwork. The days passed uneventfully, though she did take

Sunday nights off as before, soaking in the tub and snuggling with Rob. Days drifted into weeks on into months. At last, the ring slipped off the last woman, who like all the others was ecstatically happy to be perfectly whole and healthy once more, her life salvaged. Monica watched her enthusiastically check herself out of St. Anne's. Watching her brought a smile to Monica's face.

Just then, she heard a voice appearing in her mind somehow. "Are you finished with the ring? Another has need of it when you are done."

Once again, she recognized the voice! Further, she knew that she had a choice to make and went with her own intuition. She thought, "Yes, that was the last of the victims. Thank you very much, Diancecht. Your ring gave two hundred thirty-five young women back their lives. For that, I and they are eternally grateful."

The voice replied, "I'm pleased with your work. Come by and visit me sometime." Monica watched the golden chain and ring vanish from around her neck. For a moment, she had an awful feeling in her stomach. Had she done the wrong thing? She'd not cured herself on the hundredth usage of the ring as he had told her, choosing instead to help the next of the many women. Now she had just said that she was finished with it.

She felt as though a door, which had been open for so long, had suddenly closed and probably even vanished from sight. Monica swallowed hard and thought to herself. *I'm not worthy of it yet. I've not made enough amends for all the damage that I've done to other people, not by a long shot.* While she wanted to sit down and spill out her rising, mixed up emotions, she knew that she dared not give into them. Instead, she focused and cast her Teleport spell, arriving in her reception area again.

"Hi Monica, welcome back. Got the last one done, I take it," Jill said cheerfully.

"Yes. All finished with the last one. I do need a break, that's for sure," Monica replied, heading down to her own bedroom suite. Rob was again off doing something in Colorado for the Department of Magical Misuse. For this, Monica was grateful. She didn't want to become all emotional in front of him, not just now.

She cast quite a number of spells to get undressed and then crawled on her knees into their private bathroom, where she cast even more spells, levitating and moving her body into her bathtub. Soon, she was soaking in a full tub of hot water, soothing and relieving her nervous stomach. Had she made the right decision? Just taking a bath by herself, she had again come face to face with her almost complete helplessness, if it wasn't for her spells. Christina and now Abigail and Michelle all had their own private lady's maids to help them with such things. They had given up so much of their own personal independence for money. She wondered if it was really worth it to them to be so helpless just to have those funds?

Something Ross Mac Fluide had once told Dominus came to mind. "It takes money to make money. If you don't start out with a substantial amount, it is quite difficult ever to amass true financial wealth." She knew that she'd followed that route, though regretting that she'd had to steal that hundred thousand dollars as seed money to get things started this lifetime, but she'd paid back every penny and with interest to that bank, though they had no idea where the money had come from. Monica realized that Christina, who had only barely earned enough money during the year to pay her living expenses and a bit of college, would have likely spent half of her lifetime building up that first seed money. Probably Abigail and Michelle were in the same situation. Now she could see the viewpoints of these three women, but still, the sacrifices that they were making and enduring each and every day were like mountains, particularly so since they were not witches.

"Knock. Knock," a woman's voice said, entering her suite. Monica recognized her immediately. Bad timing, but she couldn't do anything about it.

"Come on in, Glasya. I'm in the bathtub soaking. Just finished up the last of the women," she called out.

Shortly, she saw the gorgeous woman in a bright red dress appearing at the bathroom door. Her long nails matched her lips and gown today. "Yes, I know. That's why I chose now to drop by. I promised you some lessons on how to improve your looks and appearance, so here I am. It's good that you're in the tub. First, I'd like to do your hair for you. I've found this fabulous shampoo and conditioner, and I keep dropping by Earth to pick up some more of it every couple of months." She produced the plastic bottle. "You don't mind if I do your hair, do you?"

Monica smiled. "No, we five used to do each other's while we were in magic school. Sorry, I can't do yours."

Glasya laughed. "No need. I've already done it. See how my hair shines and is so full of body? Yours will too. I would recommend that you have your hair about another foot longer, though. It will be far more impressive if it lies down to your knees."

"But won't I keep sitting on it?"

"Oh just toss your head around. With this shampoo and conditioner, it will feel and act as if it was silk hair. I'll do it for you. If you don't like it, we can remove that extra length," Glasya suggested. As she began working, she broached the next item on her "beautification of Monica" list. Now with your unique and fabulous shape, Monica, your breasts really should be larger. I know. When you were he, you loved them super-really large, but that's too extreme. You don't want to call that kind of attention to yourself. Rather, you want to emphasize your unique curves. Let me alter them some and let you see the final look. If you don't like them, why, I'll reduce them for you, okay?"

Monica chuckled. "You sure know a lot about me. Yes, I will admit that when we graduated school, I struck a bargain with Crystal and Ericka. They would have really big knockers for my sake, and I would have nails like yours for theirs."

"How did that work out?" Glasya asked disarmingly.

"Good, until this happened to me. After that, since I couldn't live up to my part of the bargain, I insisted that they alter their bosoms to what they wanted to have, which is what they now have."

"Wise of you. That way they don't feel cheated. You want them big enough to attract some attention to your curves, balancing your hips, you see. You have nice hips so you should have them balanced with your bosom, especially with your streamlined body shape. Don't worry. I'll have you fixed up properly. Then, we really should change your lipstick. They have this new kind that softens them and makes your lips looks like they are dripping with moisture. Extremely erotic. And it doesn't rub off on cups and glasses. Stays on until you apply the remover. Just fabulous. Don't you like the way mine simply shine?"

"Well, yes. I was wondering if yours came from, well you know, from Hell."

Glasya laughed. "Heavens no, Monica. It comes from your world. Honestly, your world has more great products for us women to use to make ourselves look beautiful than any other, short of using magic to do it. We should go shopping later, and I'll show you where I buy all of mine. There is a Felix's in nearly every major city in your country here." She chatted away, before casting a fair number of Dry spells.

"Let me help you out of the tub and get you dried off, dear. That way you don't have to cast all those spells. Honestly, you might consider hiring a lady's maid as the others have." She lifted her out, sat her on a towel, and proceeded to dry her off, while slightly enlarging her breasts for her, making doubly sure that they were perky and not drooping. Then, she carefully dressed Monica, putting on her finest black seamed nylons, garter belt, and then panties. Next, she altered her white slip to fit her new bosom and then slipped her into her fanciest red satin gown, altering it as well. Finally, she laced up her black patent boots for her, before saying, "Now, let's get your hair brushed out a little. Watch how I use the brush. It helps add body to it so it doesn't lie droopingly flat."

"Okay, up you go. Have a look in your mirror, dear. See how the upper and lower proportions are now perfectly matched? And look how your hair shines. It looks doubly thick as it used to look," Glasya commented.

"Wow. I do see what you mean, Glasya. It's subtle. The proportions being balanced, I mean. I never considered that before, but it does make a noticeable difference! And I do like my hair this way." While it was a foot longer than she usually wore it, especially since she lost her arms, it did look good this long, balancing the shapely proportions of her body.

Next, she did Monica's makeup, using the new products that she had brought for her. Glasya made sure that the various labels were kept together so that Monica could have them to use as a reference when she went to purchase more of them. A half hour later, she had Monica look at herself.

"I do look fabulous, don't I?" she exclaimed, rather surprised at just how much prettier she did look.

"Yes, you certainly do look like a model. Crystal and Ericka will certainly take notice now. I find few women really know how to bring out the best in their features, you know. But then, most don't have anyone to give them proper guidance either, and some just don't take the time to look as good as they could. Anyway, the labels are all there, and you can get more and different shades at any Felix's as I said."

Just then, a Message scrolled across Glasya's eyes. "Sorry. I have to go. Some minor troubles. Before I do go, Monica, there is one additional suggestion that I would like to make for you. I know that this might be hard for you to face, but you should take a trip to Denver and check out your ex-wife, Nadia, and her best friend, Jolina. They are married to Barnaby and Bailey Hampton, a pair of identical twins, and they run a fabulous dance hall in Denver. You can't miss it. They hold dances every Friday, Saturday, and Sunday nights, though I would recommend that you go on a Friday night. They are what are called fetish queens in the fashion industry. With your unusual body form, you would look utterly smashing in one of their fetish outfits, utterly smashing. Rob probably will go nuts over you in one of their outfits. However, I know that you might not yet be up to seeing Nadia."

"But, but she's dead. I had her. . ." Monica faltered mid-sentence. She couldn't quite bring herself to say murdered. She'd forgotten about how as Dominus she'd tortured poor Nadia, and then hired a Death Stalker to kill her.

"Hardly. She is a real fighter. She escaped just as the home exploded. Lindsey took her in and got her and Jolina healed up. She's a children's book author now as well."

"So I didn't kill her?" Monica asked, hardly believing her.

"Nope. Hurt her, yes, but not killed her. If you feel up to facing her, you really ought to go see her and get her advice on a fetish look, perhaps just for the bedroom if nothing else. Not all women have enough guts to wear those outfits in public, but those that do certainly attract attention. I'm sure she doesn't know you were Dominus. But I have to run. I'll chat with you another time. Bye for now."

"Bye. And thanks, Glasya. I didn't expect a devil would be so kind."

"I'm not, except to my friends. You've earned my friendship, Monica. Bye." She walked out of her room. Jill verified that she vanished though, sending word to everyone that she was gone.

A while later, Monica walked out to join the others, who were answering the lunchtime gong of Nisha's. Crystal noticed her at once. "Monica, you look so much better. You look, well different. You hair is fabulous. What did you do to it? So lush, shiny, much thicker or something."

Ericka joined them, "No, she's really got a model's figure. You've done something to your shape, haven't you? Glasya's influence? You do look stunning." Monica smiled and joined them, but had to take extra care to toss her wavy, full bodied, shiny hair out of the way so that she didn't sit on it. She found that it slid easily to either side, far more readily than it always had before. She was pleased with her new appearance and even more pleased that Crystal and Ericka noticed the difference right away. Ericka added, teasing her, "Wait until Rob sees you!" Monica actually blushed slightly.

While they ate, all the women wanted to know how she'd gotten her hair looking so fabulous, and she told them about the special product that Glasya had used. "We can get it at Felix's, though I've never been to that store before," Monica explained.

"We all just *have* to try it too!" Ericka declared. "Ladies, I'm going to drop by there and get us all some. It will be 'do hair afternoon' around here, yes, even you too Enya."

Enya blushed, "But if I look that good, I'll be having lots more babies soon." Everyone chuckled along with her.

When all the women walked into the dining room at

suppertime, including Nisha, Jill, and Christina, the women's hair looked vastly better than before, very noticeably so. Even their husbands loved their new appearance, pleasing the rather large number of women. So much so, that Monica began thinking about perhaps finding a way to help ordinary women look their best and inexpensively so. Slowly, that idea began to germinate in the back of her mind.

That evening, Monica used her voice-activated laptop software to control her computer while surfing the Net, instead of casting her usual large number of spells. She realized that she had just made a concession by doing it the way that Christina, Abigail, and Michelle did. At once, she found this vastly easier and far more relaxing. Using spells had made surfing a royal pain, anything but fun. Reverting to voice-activation turned the experience back into one that was enjoyable once more. Monica smiled and decided always to do it this way from now on. She didn't have to prove that she could still operate her laptop with spells. There wasn't anything demeaning about using the voice-activated software, she discovered.

She looked up Nadia and their dance hall, even going so far as to display the map of how to find it. If the website was accurate, they drew nightly crowds of at least five thousand or more. Friday nights were fetish nights. Saturday nights were teen rock and roll nights, while Sunday nights were devoted to elegance and waltzes. She brought up an image of Nadia and Jolina. Her eyes watered as she saw those familiar faces. Nadia had blossomed even more than when she had been Dominus' wife. Now, she understood what Glasya had meant by the fetish look and swallowed hard. Still, she knew that she had to face Nadia and soon.

That night after she slipped beneath her covers, she began thinking about Nadia once more. Should I tell her that I was Dominus and apologize for all the wrongs that I did to her and Jolina? She probably hates me and rightly so. I thought I had murdered her! I feel so shitty about having so mistreated her and her friend. Do I dare tell her? What if I do and she tells the world? Many will come gunning for me? Will someone put another bullet through my head? Well, I should just tell her.

Face the music, Monica. You have to tell her, that is, if you are truly sorry about torturing her. But I am sorry. I can't take it back no matter how much I wish I really could. Funny how that goes. Once I do something, I can't undo it. No one can, short of a Full Wish spell. How do I ever make amends with her and Jolina? Monica had no answer for that and drifted into a restless sleep. *Has Glasya just brought all this up just to torment me?* That was her last conscious thought before sleep took her.

When she awoke, she at least had an answer to one of her questions. If Glasya had been a demon, then yes, she would have brought up Nadia just to torment her. Though Glasya had an evil streak in her, she would always follow the proper protocols, the proper manners, and rules of society. While struggling to sit up in her bed, she concluded: *No, whatever reason Glasya had in telling me about Nadia, it wasn't to torment me.* As she sat there, another thought struck her. Glasya had called her a friend. A friend would give her a hint or a nudge in what she thought was the right direction. Monica knew that she would have and even had done so in the past. She decided: *Yes, this is something that I really must face, really must do, if I am ever to make amends with my past actions. I owe it to Nadia, to Jolina. Now I must get dressed and get breakfast.*

While dining with everyone and chatting, Monica compared her dining experience with that of Christina, Abigail, and Michelle, who appeared to her eyes to be quite happy this morning. They seemed relaxed and not bothered by the fact that they were being fed by their lady's maids; rather, it appeared to be rather a normal thing. On the other hand, Monica was quietly casting a rather large number of spells to accomplish it. *Am I just being vain or stubborn about this? Am I trying to insist that I am not inhibited by my physical condition? Am I trying to prove something here?* Somehow, she felt she was close to some basic truth about herself, but just couldn't quite grasp it.

"Crystal, I'm off to visit some shops in Denver today. Maybe I can catch up with Rob for dinner," Monica let her friend know where she was headed. Even though the demon situation had apparently been resolved, the five still followed their own guidelines, letting one of the five know where they were going when they left the estate. In her room, she cast her protection spells on herself and checked her appearance in her mirror. Satisfied with her appearance in her light red satin gown, she took a deep breath and cast her Teleport spell, arriving on the streets of Denver near the B & B Dance Hall's main entrance.

On either side of the quadruple set of fabulously carved, oaken doors stood giant announcement boards that listed the nights the dance hall was open and the venue. She noted that the admission fee was extremely inexpensive. She cast a spell to get one of the doors opened and stepped inside the entrance foyer. The inside was obviously magically altered space. Her eyes adjusted to the unexpected 5X expansion of the interior. She was standing on a plush red carpet, and she paused a moment taking in the royal ambiance radiating from the dance hall, left over from the last Sunday night's formal dance. On one side was an array of arrival teleport pads. On the other side were a number of ticket counters, but only one rather bored teenager was sitting behind them. She looked up and said pleasantly, "Can I help you?"

"Yes, I've an appointment to see Mrs. Nadia van Nye-Hampton."

"Sure thing. She's in her studio. Go down that hall. All the way down. Take the door at the very end." Then she flushed, "Oh, do you need any assistance?" She'd noted Monica's lack of arms and looked slightly embarrassed.

"No thank you. I can manage. Thanks." Walking on the soft push carpet was daunting, she quickly discovered as her toes wobbled more than normal. Perhaps I should have allowed her to steady me, Monica thought, but quickly banished it. No, this was something that she had to do, to face on her own, but it was a rather long unsteady walk. Reaching the door, she cast another couple of spells that roughly approximated a knock.

Then, she heard Nadia's voice call out, "Come on in; door's not locked." Memories of that voice swept through Monica's mind, temporarily disorienting her. Swallowing hard, with a nervous stomach, she cast a few more spells, opening the door. Carefully, she stepped inside, praying that this was the right thing to be doing! This was ten times harder to face than fighting demons!

Monica's eyes darted around the large room, trying to take it all in. She saw a rack of children's books near the door. One-half of the room held various graphic artist worktables with numerous illustrations in progress. Several completed ones were hanging on a whiteboard wall. She recognized Jolina sitting at one of the tables, drawing. Jolina looked at her and smiled, putting down her pens and rising. The other half of the room held bookshelves and a large computer station where Nadia was currently working. "Just a second while I save my work," Nadia called out, then momentarily rising as well. The two women smiled broadly and moved towards Monica, who had a fleeting notion that she should flee for her life. Somehow her feet didn't move, though.

Nadia looked fabulous, just as fetish as she remembered her. Today, she wore a light blue latex gown with a blue and white striped outer corset. Her black hose and six-inch oxford style heels were striking in comparison, but Monica could see that her gown didn't have any walking slit to speak of, forcing her to take tiny steps while her hips swayed back and forth rather seductively. Her blonde hair was both shiny and wavy, falling to the middle of her back. Jolina's outfit was quite similar, but done in light green. Her hair was just as blonde, and both women had luscious red lips. Monica realized that they must be wearing the same brand of new lipstick that she was, thanks to Glasya's gift.

"Wow, this is a pleasure and honor to meet you, Mrs. Monica Black-Finch," Nadia's sweet voice called out as she slowly approached her. "We've heard so much about you on the MAG news, you know. It's just fabulous what you've done for all those poor abducted women. Please, over here." She pointed out a refreshments table where the aroma of freshly ground and brewed coffee filtered into Monica's nose. She also saw a tiny refrigerator there with small cans of Coke visible through its glass door. A teapot was also present on a small hotplate. Monica allowed the two women to reach her before moving.

Their faces smiling, Nadia reached Monica and gave her a welcoming hug, followed by Jolina. "Come, sit. Coffee? Tea? Coke? Our mini-bar so to speak. This is our workshop. Please, have a seat. Where's your assistant?"

"Assistant?" Monica asked, slightly confused. "It's just me." She realized that Nadia and Jolina expected to see her accompanied by a personal assistant or lady's maid. "No, I just use spells. Tea would be fine. I've rather had too much coffee this morning." Monica tossed her head about, allowing her now slippery, silky hair to slip to her front and then sat down across from the two women. "You both look quite stunning."

"Thanks," Nadia replied. "And you are not how we pictured you. Your hair, lipstick? Are you using Felix's products too?" Monica nodded. "Cool! They are simply the best. Straw?" she asked, sliding a cup of tea over to her. She nodded and Nadia inserted one. Monica noticed that she too had rather long nails, painted an off-red.

"So did you really fully heal nearly two hundred fifty women?" Jolina asked curiously. "What was that Abyss place like? Were they really breeding our women to make more demons somehow? How is that even possible?"

"Dear, that's a lot of questions for our esteemed guest," Nadia cautioned her best friend. "But really Monica, we are keen to hear, that is if you don't mind telling us. You know how distorted the news is. We've heard bits and pieces from some of the Rodents. Really, we are keen to hear all about it. Oh," she stopped short. "Forgive us. We should let you ask what you've come to see us about first. Sorry. We do get a little carried away. After all, it's not every day that someone as famous as you are comes to see us."

Monica laughed. "Well, okay. I can tell you some of it, but mind you, it's positively horrid—what they did to the young women." She felt a sudden release of pressure. This, she could talk about and maybe break the ice or was it that she was putting off the real reason for this visit? She put that thought out of her mind and began relating some of what had happened during the past couple of years. An hour later she finished up.

"Wow, demons and devils!" exclaimed Nadia. "We never even knew they existed, did we, Jolina?"

"Nah, just fairy tales to scare children," Jolina added. "Guess we're wrong. Nadia, please don't put them into any of your stories because I surely don't want to draw them!"

"Don't worry, I certainly won't do that. Gosh, Monica, we've kept you telling us all that for an hour. Our manners have gone out the door! Please, what can we do for you?" Nadia said, somewhat embarrassed that they'd not let Monica tell her even why she'd paid them this surprise visit.

Her panic returned in a flash. It's now or never! I just have to do this! Monica cleared her throat. "Nadia, Jolina, I have an awful confession to make to the both of you. It's very bad. I don't know how else to say this to you both, but well, I'm really Dominus Malefic, er I was him, but a follower used a Cause Life spell on me, and I ended up with a twelve year old girl body. I just want you both to know that I'm truly sorry for what all I did to you both last lifetime. If I could undo it, I would, but I can't. I know you both hate me with a passion. Like thousands of others, you wanted me dead, want me dead now."

Both women had shocked looks on their faces, disbelief in their eyes. "You, you can't be him. We saw him being assassinated. It was on the news. Dominus is dead, quite dead, and buried," Nadia exclaimed. "You are a gorgeous young woman. Dominus wouldn't be healing all those women. What are you trying to pull on us?" she demanded to know.

"You wore a pink bikini when we were on my yacht in the Mediterranean off Cyprus. You found lipstick on my collar once when we were in Denver and knew then that I was cheating on you," Monica said quickly. Then, she added a few more very personal details that only Dominus would have known about both women.

"Really, I was him and was assassinated, just like everyone saw on the news. An old wizard follower dug up the coffin, but they had embalmed my body so he couldn't use a Clone spell on me. Instead, he reversed Cause Death, reincarnating me. Since I was just twelve, he sent me to the St. Louis School of Magic. Of course, I remembered everything, all my spells, everything, but I pretended to be a beginning witch. My four Red Hall roommates became my best friends, and we are still together, Crystal, Ericka, Enya, and Misty. I rather helped them excel during our school years, and I helped set them up with their magic stores once we graduated. I have changed. I know now I was an insane fool back then. I think I have uncovered the reason why I was that way too. I've been working hard to be a better person, and I just had to come to you two, who I have treated so terribly bad, and let you know that I really am sorry for the torture I put you both through. And it is okay if you still hate me for that," Monica explained.

Monica expected the two women to unleash a veritable mountain of vitriolic anger at her. Instead, Nadia looked at Jolina, and they both broke into a hearty laugh, totally confusing Monica. Nadia finally said, "We don't hate Dominus. Okay, we did at first, but good heavens not now! If that hadn't happened to us, we would never, ever have gotten to where we are today! Trying to kill us got us to Lindsey. She and her friends healed us. Her mother, Lena, saved us both. She convinced Jolina and me to follow our true dreams. With her encouragement, we did. Do you realize that today I'm a famous young children's book author, and Jolina here illustrates all these books? That rack by the door holds all the books that we've done."

"Besides that, via Lindsey, we met the two greatest men in the world, Barnaby and Bailey, our husbands. All four of us created and opened up this fantastic dance hall, which is also quite profitable besides giving teens and older folks very memorable evenings. We each have two lovely children of our own now. We owe absolutely everything, our dreams, our goals, our happiness, our wealth, our everything to Dominus. If he, er you, hadn't sent that man to kill us, we'd never ended up at Lindsey's place, and none of this would ever had come our way. We don't hate Dominus, er you, we actually owe him everything!"

"Ya," Jolina added, "trying to kill us totally changed our lives around, giving us everything our hearts ever desired! How can we hate him for that? Hardly, but yes we did so way back before everything changed for us."

Nadia then said, "Still, Monica, I just can't believe that you were Dominus. He was so utterly wicked, vicious, malicious, scheming, treacherous, and vile, and you are almost completely opposite of him. I just can't see you as being him. You would have had to really, really change somehow."

Jolina ventured, "Maybe it was being in our Red Hall, Nadia. Passions, you know."

Nadia grinned, recalling those bygone school days. "Ya. Passions for sure. Maybe passions did help her change, Jolina. We Red Hall gals are sure full of passions!"

Monica actually cracked a smile, recalling her recent school days and nights. "Yes, passions rule." She gave a little laugh as well.

"Say, who all knows your secret, Monica? This knowledge could be very dangerous for you."

"Governor Lindsey and my friends. No one else, except the Rodents. It is not something that I am proud of, obviously," Monica answered.

"Well, we should keep it between us then," Nadia declared. "Say, have you seen some of our books? Had a tour of the dance hall?" Monica said no, and Nadia just had to show her several. "You see, small children just love our books. They are best sellers. We have to produce at least three new ones each year, just to keep up with the demands from the publishers for more, especially around Christmas time."

After showing her some, Nadia asked, "So where is your assistant? Surely, you have someone to help you with things."

"Er, no. I've been using my spells, more or less," Monica admitted.

Nadia tossed her head back and laughed. "Ya, that is so just like him, Dominus, I mean, always to have to be the one in control of everything." Monica flushed and hoped that her hot cheeks were not too red.

"Come. Let's show you our dance hall. After that, the fellows will join us for lunch. They've taken the kids to the park to play this morning. You just have to meet Barnaby and Bailey." Without asking, Nadia slipped a steadying arm around Monica's waist as they walked the long hallway to the main dance hall entrance. With that bit of assistance, Monica was able to walk far more securely and had to walk slightly slower than normal because the two couldn't match her pace in their tall heels and tight dresses.

"Incredible! This place is huge," Monica gushed as she got her first good view of the actual dance hall with its oak floor.

"Right now, it's set up for the next fetish night on Friday night. We magically alter the whole ambiance and decor for each dance night. Show her, will you Jolina?" By flipping a switch the room turned into a teenage hangout with flashing strobe lights and then into a romantic royal palace-like setting and then into the striking fetish look.

"What an incredible use of magic you have here!" Monica exclaimed.

"Ya. Thanks to Barnaby and Bailey," Jolina praised their husbands. "They do all the work. We just provide decor suggestions mostly."

A male voice suddenly echoed in the spacious hall, "Dears, you do. . ."

Another voice finished the thought, "far more than that. So who is this charming. . ."

"young woman?" the first man finished the question.

"Barnaby, Bailey, we want you to meet Mrs. Monica Nicole Black-Finch," Nadia proudly announced. To Monica, she added, "That's my Barnaby on the right. They are very hard to tell apart even for us."

"Not the. . ." Barnaby said.

And Bailey finished, "Monica, the demon slayer and woman-healer. . ."

"that's been on all the news shows," Barnaby concluded.

"Yes, her! She's told us all about it, dear," Nadia playfully teased him. "And you missed it."

"Oh no!" Barnaby put on a faked crushed look, so humorously that Monica couldn't help but laugh.

Bailey took on a childish pleading tone, "Maybe she will tell us if we beg her, Barnaby."

Nadia ignored their playful antics. "So where's the kids? You didn't lose them, did you?"

Bailey laughed. "Hardly. No, they got hot dogs and

sodas at the park. Now they are taking their naps."

Barnaby finished up, "We rather pooped them out—on purpose so we could have a quiet lunch with you, dear."

"But now that's. . ." Bailey continued.

"Changed. Will you allow me to escort you to lunch?" Barnaby broke in.

"Perhaps, she will allow me instead of you, Barnaby. After all I'm better looking."

Monica roared. "But you look identical down to your ties." All five laughed. "Do you always finish each other's sentences?"

"No, I never finish. . ." Barnaby protested.

"his sentences. He finishes. . ." Bailey interrupted him.

"my sentences!" Barnaby concluded.

"Boys!" Nadia declared, her hands on her hips, as though she were dealing with two young mischievous boys.

Both men escorted Monica to their private dining room, each with an arm around her waist. "Men!" Jolina teased them.

Their dining room was quite nice, but not extravagant. Comfortable, Monica thought. They had roast duck catered in, though, since none of the four cared much for cooking. As the men opened the boxes and began serving, Barnaby asked where her assistant was, and again, she explained that she didn't have one. All four did watch her as she cast numerous spells just to dine. Nadia eventually whispered, "Really, you ought to get yourself an assistant. No one would expect you to have to cast all those spells just to eat."

Barnaby then suggested, "Say, why don't you and your husband come by for some dances. Check us out. Fetish Nights are Fridays and Sunday night is Romantic Night, formal gowns and all that. Doubt that you want to be here Saturday nights, though. Place is swamped with teens and their rock and roll bands. Come on; you'll love it."

"Yes, you just have too," Nadia insisted.

"But I can't really dance any more. Not in these boots," Monica attempted to explain another thing that she couldn't manage any longer.

"Sure you can. Just move your feet, and let Rob lead

you," Nadia continued to insist. "Look, come by on Thursday, and Jolina and I will take you shopping and get you dolled up for Fetish Night and for the formal dance as well. Just bring along Rob's measurements too. We insist. Besides, having the famous demon slayer witch visiting B & B's Dance Hall will be great for business."

Monica felt that she couldn't turn them down. Getting them a bit more business would be at least something that she could do for them. "Okay Thursday then," she agreed. After a bit more pleasant chat, Jolina insisted that she see their children. That done, Monica headed off to meet up with Rob and tell him about going to the dance hall on two nights.

On Thursday, Nadia and Jolina took her to the most expensive dressmaker's in Denver. The store specialized in both fetish outfits and formal ball gowns. The latter were often worn by women attending the Presidential Inaugural Balls. "Your form will be greatly enhanced by just the right corset," Nadia explained.

"But you can't breathe in them. The pressure is awful. I'm sorry I put you through that," Monica whispered.

"Well, that's only true if you try to cinch down way too much and all at once. No, a good one should feel snug but not impede your breathing. Trust us. You'll see," Nadia insisted. Before long, they had her wearing a snugly fitting one and attached her black nylons to them. After slipping her into a bright red latex, form fitting gown with the tiniest of walking slits, they fastened another outer corset over it. This one had matching stripes with a black background that matched her hair. Once they had her dolled up, Monica got a good look at herself in a full-length mirror.

"It's not so bad. But look at me. My shape—it's really striking."

"Curves, Monica. It displays your magnificent figure quite well." To the saleswoman, Nadia said, "We'll take this one. Now let's get something for Rob." Monica felt she had an idea of what he would like and got him a soft suede suit in a dark brown color, one that she would have loved to rub her hands over if she could. That handled, they went into the other section of the store.

"But I won't be able to go to the bathroom easily ," Monica whispered. "I don't think I can even get myself out of this."

"Like I said, you really do need to get yourself a personal assistant to help you look stunning. You certainly have the body for it. The passions that you are going to raise in Rob will be something to watch!"

The elegant formal ball gown with its flaring hoopskirt was done in shades of a light red. Rob's new tuxedo was a light blue, blending with her new gown rather well. "Now I know I can't get myself into or out of this one!" Monica whispered, adding, "I know; get myself a helper."

Nadia chuckled. "Rob should go positively nuts over you in this one. So romantic. All the ruffles. Looks gorgeous on you. Don't worry. Jolina and I will help you through this weekend's dances. After that, you are on your own."

When Rob joined the three women early Friday evening, stepping into the room dressed in his new dark brown, soft suede suit, his mouth dropped open, as his eyes took in Monica in her new fetish dress. His hands never let go of her all night long. Monica didn't really think that she was actually dancing, but did move her feet some. It didn't really matter though; they both had one of the most pleasurable evenings ever. Further, they saw nearly five thousand other young couples dressed to the hilt, some far more exotic than they were, but all thoroughly enjoying the night out. The dance hall even provided all manner of refreshments as well. Monica and Rob were quite impressed with the setup.

Barnaby and Bailey had them look at the teens on Saturday night. Here was a very different group, mostly the younger set, but some five thousand of them were cheering, dancing, and thoroughly enjoying the live band that was playing.

The Romantic Night was the icing on the cake, as far as Monica was concerned. There was nothing like this in St. Louis. Here was fun, wholesome, and romantic enjoyment and pleasure for a very wide range of people, from teens to even older retired couples. "We just have to have one of these dance halls in St. Louis!" Monica exclaimed full of passion. "Barnaby, how can I twist your arm to expand and open up one in St. Louis? I'll cover all the costs."

His eyes opened up, swallowing hard. "All the cost? You got it!"

Bailey explained, "We've been meaning to expand our operations, but just haven't figured out where. Let's do it!"

"Better yet, guys, there should be one of these in every major city in the US. After you get one going in St. Louis, I'll finance them elsewhere. This is just an incredibly good thing that you four have invented here. I want to help share this with everyone else," Monica declared.

Later when she was alone with Nadia, Nadia exclaimed, "You sure have changed! If you ever were him. You've really made their day! Plus, this gives the teens something to look forward to and everyone else too for that matter. Keeps romance going too. Thank you. This means everything to the guys."

"No! Thank you for helping to put this incredible dance hall here," Monica replied. She was beginning to see some tremendously valuable uses for her rather extensive wealth, at least the way she saw it. When the two headed home late Sunday night, Monica was convinced that she would have to consider hiring a lady's maid for herself or at least someone to assist her in dressing and undressing.

The next day, Monica met with her three newly wealthy friends to discuss everyone's finances and their philanthropic endeavors. Christina had finally decided that she wanted to help sponsor the numerous Food and Clothing Pantries for those in need and in response to natural disasters. Abigail wanted to aid the many Battered Women Shelters, while Michelle wanted to donate heavily to the Women's Educational Advancements organization. All three were delighted to hear that Monica was also going to begin sponsoring all the new fancy dance halls in the larger cities. The four spent several days working out sound financial arrangements in which a portion of their funds would be continually invested to generate more money, while the excess would be funneled into the various organizations and projects. Each of the four cross-checked the other's financial plans in depth, correcting small errors when found. When all four were finally in complete agreement, the women began the actual execution of their long desired plans and then held a small celebration.

"At last, I'm making a really big difference," Christina bubbled with enthusiasm. "We all are. Congratulations one and all!"

On September 15, Leslie Traub, head of the Missouri Department of Magical Misuse summoned Monica and Crystal to the FBI headquarters in downtown St. Louis for a ten o'clock meeting. "Wear your formal gowns, and you will want to bring everyone from your place. They will want to witness this small ceremony. I can't tell you anything else, just look your best."

"What's this all about?" Rob asked, helping Monica into her bright red satin gown.

"I've no idea. Some kind of ceremony, that's all that Leslie said," Monica answered, just as mystified as all her friends.

Crystal joined them, brushing out Monica's hair for her and pumping her for more information, which Monica didn't have to give. She wore her favorite light blue satin gown. She finally said, "I bet they are going to give us the key to St. Louis or something like that for our help with the demons." Her guess seemed likely to everyone.

When they arrived and entered the small auditorium, on the stage was Leslie and three older men, one of whom they recognized as Amos Slaughter, the head of the States Justice Department. He was now rather a famous figure, having served for four years as acting President of the United States after the fall of Dominus. Monica whispered, "Who are the two much older looking men?"

Enya whispered back, "Have you forgotten your first year History of Magic already? The one on the right of Amos is Arthur Doms; the one to his left is William Sturm. They were instrumental in building relations with the normals when the wizarding world went public. They are incredibly famous men. What are they doing here?"

Wearing a very nice suit, Henry Wilkens, the head of the St. Louis Department of Magical Misuse, whispered, "Monica, Crystal, you are to go up there on stage by Leslie. Use the side door there. The rest of you, have a seat with us." Monica saw Ari and Parry were already here, long with Oliver and a number of others who had fought against the demons. Plus, there were a lot of reporters too. What was going on?

Crystal instinctively put her right arm around Monica and headed to the door at the left side of the stage. Once they went inside the narrow hall, Monica whispered, "What's happening here?"

"Don't know. Guess we play along. Probably giving us the key to the city or something," she whispered back. Smiling, the two walked onto the stage. As they closed the distance to Leslie, who was also very smartly dressed, some flood lights turned on, greatly illuminating the stage.

Turning to face the two women, Leslie began speaking quite formally. "I am Leslie Traub, Missouri Department of Magical Misuse. We are coming to you live from the Conference Auditorium of the FBI here in St. Louis. This morning, it is with great pride and humbleness that I am being allowed to introduce these three men to you, though you may already know them. This is Amos Slaughter, Head of the States Justice Department, Order of Merlin, Knights of Truth. To his right, Arthur Doms, retired, Order of Merlin, Knights of Truth, and to his left, William Sturm, retired, Order of Merlin, Knights of Truth. At this time, I will turn the proceedings over to Amos." She sat down, but indicated that the two women continue to stand. Well, there weren't any more chairs.

Amos rose and looked out over the small crowd, though millions would be watching this on the news stations. "This morning is a very special one for the whole world, not just the Wizarding portion of that world." Monica noticed that all three men wore identical golden medallions around their necks and prominently displayed on their chests. She resolved to get a good look at them afterwards. Why was this morning special?

"Since the dawn of time, the wizarding world has sought out the best of the best to honor them for their achievements. These very few wizards and witches have demonstrated power, power beyond the normal. Yet, with that all that immense power they have shown wisdom, intelligence, compassion, and understanding for their fellow man, wielding that great power for the good, the betterment of mankind. Down through the ages, there has lived thousands upon thousands of wizards and witches. Yet, among them, but a handful can reach this highest standard of excellence, this pinnacle of power used to better all mankind—oh, so dreadfully few, I'm afraid to say."

"In my own lifetime, until this morning, I have only had one opportunity to honor such people, though my esteemed colleagues here beside me have done so four times. It is said that these are the best of the best, for these cherish truth above lies, wisdom above stupidity, generosity above avarice, bravery above cowardice, and a dedication to mankind above self. It is the highest possible honor for Arthur, William, and me to be here with you this morning to bestow this award, this title upon those who have displayed what is greatest among us all. And for William, who is now ninety-nine years young, this morning holds an even greater honor, for his is now the oldest person ever to have the honor of bestowing this highest of honors upon his fellow St. Louisians."

"Normally, if we are incredibly fortunate, we may make one such award in our lifetime. Not so this morning. Yes, we three are here to present the Order of Merlin, Knights of Truth award to two of the world's greatest witches, Mrs. Monica Nicole Black-Finch and Mrs. Crystal Holiday-Mac Pheerson." Monica nearly fainted! Crystal held on to her securely, though she too was shocked.

"These two brilliant witches have gone far beyond the call of duty and have in no large part played key roles in saving our entire world from being overrun and conquered by the demons from the Abyss. Twice, Crystal has invented new ways of detecting these vile creatures, and who doesn't know Monica's role. In fact, two hundred thirty-five mutilated and tortured women have had their lives fully restored by her. As a side note that some of you historians might be interested in, these two witches are from Red Hall. Yes, these are the first wizards or witches from Red Hall to have ever received this, the highest of honors."

"Mrs. Monica Nicole Black-Finch and Mrs. Crystal Holiday-Mac Pheerson—will you please come forth to receive your robe, certificate, and medallion?" He whispered to Crystal, "Please take Monica's robe and certificate for her." He formally shook Crystal's hand and gave Monica a hug, while handing the certificates to Crystal. They moved a few feet down the line and Arthur presented them their robes, again handing them to Crystal, shaking her hand. A bit further, and William rose and hung the heavy pure gold medallion around Monica's head and then around Crystal's. Following William's whisper, they stood to his left facing the bright lights and the small crowd.

As if somehow signaled, the audience erupted into a surprisingly loud round of cheering and applause. Monica sensed that Parry was using an Amplify spell just for the benefit of the cameras. Monica stood there with trembling knees. *I don't deserve this, not for what little I've done. God, do they know that they are giving it to me—I was Dominus after all! Please, don't let me faint!*

After the applause died down, the bright lights vanished. The cameras were turned off at last. Now, Monica recognized the world-famous newscaster, Hugo Whitefield. He'd been quietly reporting during the filming of this event. Amos said, "Congratulations, both of you. I'd best take these two back home now." He then helped the two proud wizards up. Monica could see that they were in rather failing health. The three vanish, leaving Leslie and the two women on stage.

Leslie said, "Let's go join the others. I know that they want to congratulate you as well. Then, Hugo Whitefield wants to interview you for his newscast. You don't have to do that, but he'll certainly be pressing you for the exclusive interview." The three made their way off-stage and were swarmed by their friends and their hearty welcome.

Hugo waited patiently for fifteen minutes before he interrupted them. "Excuse me, but we really do need to do this interview now. If you two Red Hall beauties will take a seat on the stage, I'll join you, and we'll get this done pronto." He flashed them his disarming smile, showing his overly white teeth. Since they were married, he decided against flirting with them, though he really wanted to do just that. Their husbands were beside them, keeping his libido in check.

"Come on; let's get this over with," Crystal whispered to Monica.

"I really don't want to do this," Monica whispered back. "You do all the talking, please!"

A few minutes later, seated on the stage with Hugo sitting between them, the bright lights flooded them once more. Typical of Hugo, he began, "Historic day, yes indeed. I am sitting here with two gorgeous Red Hall beauties who have just made history today, Order of Merlin, Knights of Truth, charming their way into these rare and most valuable awards."

Already the interview was off to a bad start. Monica's ire rose, but Crystal's more so. She said quite disarmingly and coyly, "Oh dear Hugo, I'm so sorry that you have it so wrong. I'm afraid that charming isn't one of our specialties. In case you hadn't noticed, and I can understand that, what with you being cooped up in your studio all the time, demons don't care a rat's ass about charm. Since you obviously are ill informed about the nature of the demons, I'll point out to you that they are mostly immune to magical spells, which tend to roll off them like water off a duck. Trying to charm a demon will get you dead in *very* short order. With the demons invading our world and abducting and mutilating women, forcing them into their breeding program to make more Cambion demons, I had to invent a way for us to identify a human from a Morphed demon who looks just like you. Twice, actually, since these demons are not fools, like some men that I know." She stared at him. "And they found a way to circumvent my first method of detection. Intelligence and inventiveness would be a more accurate assessment for our winning these awards. Next question," she barked, having completely taken control over the interview.

Hugo recovered and said, "Well, why don't you describe for our audience what life is like in the Abyss? Tell us about your experiences there, Monica? And many of our viewers are wondering why you didn't heal yourself?"

Monica fumed. She retorted, "I saw before me another

hundred-fifty normal young women whose lives were destroyed unless I could heal them. I chose to heal them, not myself. As for what is it like there?" She grinned mischievously and then said, "I always say that a picture is worth a thousand words, don't you?" She looked directly at him.

"Well of course, but," Hugo started to reply.

Monica cut him off. "So glad that you agree. Illusion: Abyss!" she barked. Magical energies flashed. His microphone dropped to the stage floor, which had apparently turned into the grey, dank, spongy ground of the Abyss. The three appeared to be inside one of the transparent domed structures. Through the dome, they could see the dismal landscape and specter grey bare trees, a horrid parody of Earth's trees, along with several terrible looking, giant demons. What so shocked Hugo was that he appeared to be one of the abducted women, though Monica had the three of them wearing a simple dress that covered their privates for the sake of those watching. Poor Hugo was screaming, wiggling, and wobbling wildly to keep his balance while tottering on his toes, just like the women had been, his non-existent arms flailing wildly, though they weren't there of course.

Crystal gasped for a moment and then began laughing so wildly that Monica too joined her, lost her focus, and the spell ended, as Hugo fell flat on the stage floor as the illusion ended. Monica said, "Hugo, that pretty much shows what it's like in the Abyss and an inkling of what those poor women endured. Not much fun, is it?"

Shaking visibly, his face as white as his teeth, he picked up his microphone and directed all subsequent questions to Crystal, ignoring Monica for the rest of the interview. He was fortunate in that his microphone didn't pick up the muffled laughing from those in the audience. Crystal had the final words though. "So let me ask this of everyone who sees this interview. We believe that most of the demons are gone, but there well could be a few stragglers left. If you come across any, please contact your local Department of Magical Misuse at once. Do not ever trust a demon. Thank you."

Hugo signed off and the floodlights went out. He said, "I thought that you two were Red Hall, you know, passionate, sexy women."

Crystal retorted, "You fool. Passionate doesn't equal sex. Try passionate about magic!"

Gregor shouted teasingly, "You tell 'em, dear." The gang roared. Hugo had an interview that he wouldn't soon forget. After receiving more congratulations from Oliver and his staff, the group returned home, where everyone wanted to see their medallions, certificates, and even the robes. Only after lunch was over did things get back to normal, and Monica finally had some time alone in her lab.

Not only did she feel that she'd not really done anything to deserve this highest award, though Crystal certainly did, she felt badly for another reason. Governor Lindsey and the other Rodents had truly earned theirs by capturing Dominus and the many Death Stalkers. She felt rather as if her having gotten it greatly lessened the same honor given to Lindsey and the Rodents. Sighing, she decided to give Lindsey a phone call. A Message was just too impersonal. Once more, she had to cast a number of spells to get her phone out and the number for Bradbury's dialed.

After getting the school's receptionist, she was finally connected to Governor Lindsey. "Hi, it's Monica. I wanted to talk to you."

This was as far as she got. Lindsey interrupted her. "Congratulations, Monica. What a wonderful award and validation for what you and Crystal have done for the whole world."

"But I really don't deserve this. I feel as if I'm somehow making less of yours and those of all the Rodents. I could see Crystal getting it. She's earned it, but not me, not really. I wanted you to know that I feel badly about getting it and making your award and all the others sort of tainted."

"Monica, you certainly aren't doing any such thing! Put what you've done in proper perspective. None of us Rodents even knew that demons and devils existed, let alone that the Abyss was a real place. You rescued all those poor women, and what you did to find a way around that awful misuse of the Incinerate spell—why, I don't know of any other wizard or witch who could have done it. Might I ask one personal question, though?"

"Sure."

"Why didn't the ring heal you? Surely, you didn't want to be like you are. We've been kind of curious about that," Lindsey asked, knowing Professor Pam had been hounding her to find out about that detail.

Monica sighed. "Maybe it's my karma. I was supposed to use it on myself with the one hundredth use, but when I got to that point, there were so many other normal women just waiting as patiently as they could to get healed that I couldn't bring myself to use it on me. Besides, I'm a witch, and those poor women aren't and were having a horrid time just trying to stay alive. I just couldn't use it on me. Of course, now the ring is gone. Diancecht needed it for some others, so I think it is just karma. I must pay for the awful harm that I did to others back then. Are you sure that you are not affronted by my having gotten this award, Lindsey?"

"I see. Yes, quite sure. I'm sorry, but I don't really know anything about karma and all that. Just remember one thing, Monica. They didn't give this to Dominus. They gave it to Monica, and Monica surely isn't following his example. You've earned your reward, Monica," Lindsey replied. She added, "I take it that a regular Ring of Regeneration doesn't work in your case."

"Right. I researched that detail thoroughly. It can't restore lost appendages that have been fully destroyed by fire or by being dissolved in acid. Okay then, I best not take up any more of your valuable time. I just wanted to let you and the Rodents know that I do feel badly about getting this award."

"I understand, Monica. By the way, I think your illusion with Hugo was superlatively done. Can't stand that man, personally," Lindsey added. Both chuckled and said goodbye.

Even after she hung up, Monica still felt as she had, that she really didn't deserve this most prestigious award, even though it was mostly symbolic, she thought. Well, what's done is done, she finally decided. Best move on and forget about it, since I can't undo it. Why do I feel so nauseous in the mornings now?

Suddenly, she realized that she was pregnant! "Oh!" A

completely different experience began for her, one that as Dominus, she had absolutely no idea of what was going to be involved or even happen. She was going to become a mother. "I'm not ready for this!" she exclaimed to her computer. It didn't answer back.

She thought of the three others who were still living here, namely Christina, Abigail, and Michelle. *I will have to be brave for their sakes. After all, I have my magic, and they don't. But maybe I should get me a lady's maid or maybe a personal assistant, one who has nanny experience too. Maybe it is because I don't believe in religion. Well, I don't. So maybe it isn't karma after all, just my bad luck. I kind of think that you have to believe in this stuff before it is real, like magic. Still, I don't want to be like this, mostly completely helpless. Then again, if Michelle Folquet can manage, so can I.* Once more, she thought of her beloved sister. Pangs of loss and regret swept over her. Michelle, she thought. "Oh! Hormones!" She laughed at her sudden emotional swings, heightened by her new "condition." *I wonder if it will be a boy or girl?*

Unexpected magical energies flashed. Monica looked up from her computer and saw the familiar form of Diancecht standing beside her. "I have come to bestow a gift from the gods upon you, Monica Nicole Black," his soft but piercing voice broke the otherwise stillness of her room, purposely not using her "true" or full name. "Use it as wisely as you have done my ring." Before Monica could respond, she felt a tingling sensation in her body and in her mind. Then she drifted into a deep sleep.

"Monica! Monica, wake up!" the startled voice of Crystal impinged upon her consciousness, rousing her. "What's happened to you?"

"Huh? Asleep, I think. Diancecht!" Suddenly, Monica remembered seeing the Physician of the Gods here in her room. That woke her fully. She was still in her gown, but was lying on her bed. Her boots had been removed. In a flash, she saw that she had her arms again and that her feet were normal, no longer fused. "Diancecht!" she exclaimed a second time.

"It's a miracle; that's what it is!" Crystal declared.

"Wait—Diancecht was here?" she asked finally putting it all together.

"I'm whole again!" Monica exclaimed. "Oh! Oh Crystal! I know how to cast the Regeneration spell! Diancecht has given me two incredible gifts! I don't think this whole demon mess is over. Oh, I'm pregnant too. I realized that just before Diancecht appeared here in my room. If it's a boy, I'm going to name him Diancecht!"

Chapter 29—Moving On

Moving on was precisely what General Franco Porti suggested to the small group who remained on Earth. The three succubuses, namely Gisella Harmoni, Bella Zaronetti, and Donatella Ratini, clearly agreed with him, once they received word from the Abyss of the massive downfall of Prince Graz'zt, and that Demogorgon and Orcus had invaded the prince's realm destroying much—particularly disturbing: the loss of the breeding centers and the DNA laboratory.

"What the heck am I to do now?" the lone remaining Dr. Menninger clone asked. "It's all been destroyed—millennia worth of work—gone—destroyed. All those painstakingly accumulated DNA samples—my work—gone!"

"Hey, take heart, doctor. Just be thankful that you were not killed with the rest of them," the general spoke up. "It was darn awful. Our forces were crushed. The question now is do we go back to the defeated prince or do we see if Orcus will have us?"

Bella said pointedly, "Heck, Orcus won't want us. We were Graz'zt's. He'll never trust us. If we're lucky, he'll send us off to the shit patrol. I'll be darned if I want to spend the rest of my life in the backwaters of the Abyss. There's no point in going back to our defeated prince. That's totally as pointless as trying to prostrate ourselves before Orcus."

"So what do we do?" Donatella asked.

Gisella, who had been silent up to this point in their gripe session, spoke up, "Look, Graz'zt was taken down because he had no idea what had become of this world. He saw it as it was well over two thousand years ago—a primitive world with bronze swords and the like. He didn't listen to us—probably didn't read our reports. These humans have evolved, rather significantly I might add. They have all manner of marvelous new inventions. Swords are wholly an anachronism in this world now. The only thing that has remained the same is its magic. Now that hasn't evolved in the slightest—well perhaps a spell here and there, like the Incinerate and Shrink

Wrap."

"So what? That's obvious, Gisella," Bella barked.

"So he completely misjudged their technology and weaponry. He expected his Cambions to be fighting with swords. I think the general here will back me up when I say swords are pathetic against all these new things, like guns and bombs," Gisella spelled it out.

"Aye," General Franco backed her up, "my Cambions should have been battling back with their own guns, tanks, artillery, guided missiles, and drones—ah, now drones would have been superlative! Why, with them, we could have bombed any target anywhere without risking a single one of my Cambions! Heck, with some of their modern weapons, we could have cut them down instead of being cut down. Jascat took one thousand of their large bullets before he succumbed. Even with their Skin of Stone spells, the wizards and witches couldn't hold out for a hundredth of that many shots, let alone the puny normal humans."

"He's precisely right," Gisella continued down her line of thinking. "We should have been acquiring their weapons for our own use, not kidnaping young normal women. Now the second thing that our defeated prince did wrong was to fail to know what the enemy leaders were planning. Not once did we have any idea that they had discovered a way to locate our incised pentagrams. Not once did we have any clue that they had somehow located all our breeding facilities around the world. Nor did we even have the slightest clue that they were planning coordinated raids on them."

General Franco spoke up, "She's right. We should have known about those things. If we had, we could have taken countermeasures and avoided the disasters. We spent all our manpower scouring the cities for appropriate young women for the breeding program, nothing else. Look where that got us—taken by total surprise and very nearly wiped out. Heck, we should have known about the attack planned by Orcus and Demogorgon too, for that matter. Graz'zt has paid dearly for that mistake. At least, we haven't."

"Talk, talk, talk," growled Donatella. "Piss over the pond. Dung in the fields. So what? Hindsight is perfect.

Everyone knows that. So what? Where does that get us now?"

Gisella grinned evilly, "Everywhere. We know what should have been done. But what's to prevent us from starting over and doing it properly? Eh? Nothing at all. We're here. We're powerful. Why can't we take over this world? Yes, us. We won't make the same stupid mistakes the prince did. We shall arm our soldiers with modern weapons. We will have top intelligence and so know what they are planning even as they make their plans. They won't make any move that we don't know about ahead of time."

"Yes, yes, yes. Sounds good but you are leaving out the *how*, Gisella. Just how do you propose that we do all this?" Bella barked sarcastically.

Gisella laughed and cut her down, "When you get as old as I am, Bella, you will have finally gotten some intelligence. We all ready possess what's needed to do all that, only we've not been able to use our skills, our powers. We figure out just who the key people actually are—say here in this country. We swap them out with some of us, use our own Morph spells to become them, and take their roles in the running of the country. We steal the weapons we need or even better get one of us Morphed into one of their leaders and have them to send them to us. So simple a child could have thought of it."

"Oh I like it, Gisella!" Donatella spoke up growing excited about the possibilities. "Instead of chasing around after pathetic human females, we can *become* their rulers and *dictate* what we want them to do! Oh I do like it!"

Dr. Menninger spoke up, "All well and good, but what am I supposed to do in all this?"

"Anything your little heart desires," Gisella replied. "Collect more DNA samples. Work on new experimental tortures that can't be undone. Heck, I don't know. Put your brain to work on that one. Sky's the limit, doctor. Incinerate that Monica woman's legs; turn her into a head and torso for all I care. Get into their electronic age. They do everything via electronics as I've seen. Cell phones that surf their Internet, take photos, make purchases, organize their days—shoot, these normals do everything with those tiny devices. Be inventive, doctor."

She went on, "The one thing that we have going for us is that their magic has not really evolved much at all for millennia. So we know what to expect from the wizards and witches and know how to combat that. It's the normal human's technology that we need to learn, steal, and use to bring this world to our knees."

"Well, if we Morph into one of their leaders, we are going to have to keep that person alive somewhere," Bella pointed out. "We can't go putting them into facilities like we did with the women. Not going to work."

Dr. Menninger spoke up, "We could put them in the human's facilities. That is, after I am done with them. They won't be able to communicate or cause any troubles for us, not like the egg producers did." He laughed wickedly. Gisella didn't like this insane man, but then Graz'zt had. Perhaps, he might yet be useful. Besides, he was their most powerful wizard, since Benedetta was gone.

"Say, what about seeing if Jonellith is still around?" Bella suggested. "She was able to effectively take out these wizards and witches. She was key to the abduction of Monica and Crystal. We could use some power like she possesses."

"But you can't really trust her," Donatella pointed out. "She has her own agenda. Besides, she has a craving for the hero man types. I agree she's powerful, but. . ."

"Point taken. Whenever we next communicate with the Abyss," Gisella decided, "I will see if she is still around and interested in coming to this world."

"The only flaw in your plan, Gisella, is that some of these top leaders are wizards and witches. How can we hope to impersonate them? They know zillions of spells that we don't," complained Bella. "I think we need a different plan."

"Hey, I never said this was going to be easy, Bella. Lots of them are just normal humans. We have to be picky about just who we replace. Unless you have a better idea," Gisella tossed it back into Bella's lap, knowing she didn't have an alternative.

"I can take over the Secretary of Defense or maybe the head of the Joint Chiefs of Staff," General Franco suggested. "Funnel some good new weapons our way and figure out how they were able to find our facilities."

"Okay then, I need a new, modern laboratory," Dr. Menninger spoke up. "You need me to invent a way to keep the men and women as restrained captives so you can replace them. This must be done before you can get on with your plans. Thus, my needs must come first," he declared. "I noticed that in the small town that we visited, Peoria, they have an advanced college of medicine. I should be able to fit my facilities in there nicely and not attract undo attention to us."

Gisella smiled coyly. *Now he's thinking again. Good sign.* She replied, "Excellent, Dr. Menninger."

Embolden by her agreement, he continued, "These humans have made some startling advances in genetics. They've sequenced the entire genetic makeup of humans. This may well open some vast new doors for us. Plus, I'm sure that some of these medical men will know just how the powers that be have been able to track our demons. So get me set up, and I'll soon have answers and solutions for you." Dr. Menninger played his hand fully, knowing that this was his best shot at furthering his reach on this world. If these chaotic demons would just play along with him for once, he'd be back in business on his own home world. He already knew much about the changes in science since he was last here, well over two centuries ago. He had not just been playing the demons' doctor this past year. Oh no. He'd read extensively and now knew just what needed to be done and what equipment he would need.

This is not to say that Dr. Menninger was ungrateful to the demons and their prince. Indeed no. Without them, he'd have been dead two centuries ago, though he also knew that he had to be a clone. Wisely, he'd never pressed the issue during his stay in the Abyss. Rather, he continued to focus on his own craven desires for perverted knowledge. Now armed with his own covert research knowledge and back on his home world, the world would once more learn of the genius of Dr. Menninger.

Yet because of the gigantic advancements the world had made since he was last here, he needed a bit more time to incorporate those into his own discoveries. Further, in secret while in Graz'zt's realm, he'd perfected his own non-magical methods for making clones. If he just had time to combine that knowledge with the recent genetic advances, he felt confident that finally he could create a race of super-men, among many other alterations that his diabolical mind had long conceived of. Plus, Gisella had just given him this golden opportunity, and he seized upon it.

He had one remaining problem that had to be solved: the demons. Unpredictable, chaotic, the demons seldom stuck to the "plan" at hand. Prince Graz'zt had been the exception to the rule, as far as he was concerned. He was the man in power, and he was driven by his own personal goals, sticking steadfastly to them for at least two centuries as far as Dr. Menninger knew. His minions seldom followed his orders, at least not completely. Turn a demon loose on this world, and it would soon forget its original mission, following its own notions of what ought to be done. This, Dr. Menninger believed, had led to the total failure of the Prince's Grand Plan, and this would likely interfere with his own new plans as well. He had to find a solution before he went much farther. Gisella was being very thoughtful and quite reasonable now, but he knew that wouldn't last for long.

"Hey look at this newscast!" Bella called out. She'd forgotten their discussion already and had turned on the motel's big screen. She'd just finished watching the ceremony honoring the two new Order of Merlin, Knights of Truth inductees, namely Crystal and Monica, and now the station was explaining Crystal's monumental discoveries.

"So you see, thanks to Crystal's discovery that anything coming to our world from the Abyss has an abnormally high particle decay that causes an infrared calcium spectral excitation line, our satellites are now scanning the world in the infrared, looking for that deep red line. Any demon arriving from the Abyss shows up instantly. Merely by overlaying the infrared image with a normal satellite image, we have the demon's precise location, down to within five feet. Pretty amazing. Our hats are off to this brilliant research work of Mrs. Crystal Holiday-Mac Pheerson." He talked further, but

Dr. Menninger had his missing piece of data!

"So that's how they found all of us!" Gisella barked angrily, frustrated because she had no way to deal with this fact of nature. "First, the detection of Gating energies and now this!"

"We're doomed," Bella added somberly. The general muttered a tirade of Abyss curses.

"Not so fast, not so fast," Dr. Menninger broke in, his mind racing down the path this tidbit of news had opened up. The demons turned to look at him.

"Well?" Gisella barked, annoyed that he stopped talking, leaving them in mystery.

"Well, it's only a temporary phenomenon. It's a matter of half-life, nothing more." Seeing the quizzical looks, he explained, "The decay process is fairly rapid. Within a fixed period, half of the particles decay. Another half decay in the next period, then another half in the following period. I do believe we here are now totally safe from this effect, since we've been on Earth for quite some time. We've flushed the material from our bodies and are no longer emitting in the infrared, but we do need to test this to be sure, just in case we still have measurable traces of Abyss contamination in our bodies. I have been working on an antidote." He brought out a small bottle of pills. "Take one a day, and I'm almost positive that you will not be detected by their infrared scanners." He handed one out to everyone and swallowed his first, defusing their reluctance to take a pill that he'd created.

That done, he continued, "Bella, you take your small group to downtown LA and hang out a while. Be prepared to make a fast exit if the demon hunters find you, but if my notions are correct, this new detection system of theirs will not be finding you, only the new arrivals from the Abyss. If they do not find you, then we know that we are safe, and I will work up a way to avoid this latest detection method."

"You want me to be your guinea pig?" she bellowed.

"If you are too chicken to try it, I will go myself," Dr. Menninger countered, putting her in her place.

He doled out more pills, and she took them. Grumbling, Bella agreed and took four of her close associates who had been on Earth with her for over a year and departed. Meantime, Dr. Menninger worked on his own Grand Plan, knowing Bella and her group would not be detected. Now he had a way to bring unlimited demons to Earth, keep them from being detected, and if his secret research project worked, a way to control the demon's actions, somewhat anyway. Part of it was simple. He knew that the hospitals used potions to flush the Abyss material from the rescued women's bodies. He could use similar potions on the new arrivals from the Abyss, only adding a second chemical to the mix, his secret invention.

After a week, Gisella was extremely worried that Bella and her group had gotten into serious trouble. Just minutes from launching an all-out search and rescue operation, Bella and her associates drove up to the motel. "Well, it's about time!" Gisella's worry morphed into intense anger with her fellow succubus.

Bella was all smiles. She wore a new, expensive designer gown, a half-million in fancy new jewelry, and drove up in a top of the line Jaguar car. One of her associates carried in a huge bag stuffed with "loot." "What a blast. Doctor, you are right again. No one detected us. We helped ourselves to a grand old time. Brought back more seed money for our venture. It is safe for us to wander the streets anywhere. We didn't encounter any resistance whatsoever," she gaily reported, confirming Dr. Menninger's theory. He merely smiled.

After Bella told them of her grand old time in LA, Dr. Menninger finally took control of the meeting. "Now then, it is time to begin executing my Grand Plan. Inexplicably, all the demons suddenly paid close attention to him, wholly unlike their basic nature! He noticed that his pill was now working as planned. Demon problem solved. "We need to purchase the new Lehman Medical Complex. Then, we need to purchase the specialized equipment that I need. After that, you may begin to take over key world personnel. I will keep their bodies alive in a sort of stasis at the new complex so that your Morph spells will continue to function at full effect. In the meantime, construct a list for me. We need to bring some powerful demons and wizards and witches here from the Abyss, but only ones that we can trust."

"Of course, Dr. Menninger," Gisella replied politely. "We will get on it today. Make up your list of equipment that you need. I feel so good now. We can't fail this time. No Graz'zt to muck things up for us."

Bella added, "She's right. We cannot fail this time. This world will soon belong to us and you, Dr. Menninger." The general smiled confidently. Renewed hope filled his mind. Quite why it should eluded him.

The End.

A Favor to Other Readers

How about helping other readers? Many readers rely on reviews to make the decision whether to buy a book. You can help them make their decision by leaving your opinions and viewpoint in a short review of the positive things of this book. Writing the review and expressing your opinion only takes a few minutes, and other readers will appreciate your efforts.

Click this link: Volume 7 Cross and Double-cross
scroll down to Customer Reviews; click on Write a Review, and enter your review. Thank you.

Author Information

Visit My Amazon.com Author Page
Vic Broquard Author Page

Follow My Blog
Vic Broquard's Blog

Follow Me on Social Media
Facebook
Google+
LinkedIn
YouTube

Other Books by Vic Broquard

Without Warning (fantasy)

The Trident Series: (fantasy)
     Volume 1 The Trident and the Book
     Volume 2 The Trident and the Scepter
     Volume 3 The Trident and the Resurrection

The Adventures of Elizabeth Stanton Series: (science fiction)
     Volume 1 The Evolution of the Path
     Volume 2 The Great Messiah
     Volume 3 Of Kings and Queens and Troubadours
     Volume 4 Chaos in the Aftermath
     Volume 5 Power Plays
     Volume 6 Age of Exploration
     Volume 7 Abducted
     Volume 8 The Emperor and Empress
     Volume 9 A Job Worth Doing
     Volume 10 Degradation
     Volume 11 The Second Crusade
     Volume 12 When Worlds Collide
     Volume 13 Dark Ages

The Lindsey Barron Series: (fantasy)
     Volume 1 The Rod of the Apocalypse
     Volume 2 The Board of Governors
     Volume 3 The Crown of Moses
     Volume 4 Dominus for President
     Volume 5 The National Health Care Program
     Volume 6 States Justice
     Volume 7 Cross and Double-cross

Zoran Chronicles Series: (fantasy)
     Volume 1 A Dragon in Our Town
     Volume 2 Dragons, Power, Courts, and War

Planet of the Orange-red Sun Series: (science fiction)
     Volume 1 When Kingdoms Fall

The Return of the Wizards: Twelve Companions – The Making of Wizards (fantasy)